Firestar

"*Firestar* is the answer to the prayers of anyone who ever watched Neil Armstrong take that step on the moon—a book in which interplanetary flight seems so close that you could reach out and touch it. *Firestar* is so plausible that I wondered if it wasn't really going on now."

—Maureen F. McHugh

"As Robert A. Heinlein did and all too few have done since, Michael Flynn writes about the near future as if he'd been there and was bringing back reports of what he'd seen. It's a near future I'd like to have, and it's a near future we can have if we reach out and take it. And Flynn remembers—when so many forget—that people come first, and that the future, like the present, is inhabited by human beings in all their splendid complexity, and reports with clear head and sympathetic heart on that, too. A splendid piece of work."

—Harry Turtledove

"Flynn has produced one of the better books of this budding subgenre. His plot is complex, but it stays on track. His large cast of characters, particularly industrialist Mariesa van Huyten, are generally well drawn; even the villains have depth. Flynn's detailed description of new space technologies is entirely believable, too.... Likely to please most fans of thoughtful hard SF."

—Publishers Weekly

FIRESTAR

Michael Flynn

TOR®

A Tom Doherty Associates Book
New York

FIRESTAR

Cover art by Vincent D. Fate

A Tor Book
Published by Tom Doherty Associates, Inc.
175 Fifth Avenue
New York, NY 10010

Tor books on the World Wide Web:
http://www.tor.com

Tor® is a registered trademark of Tom Doherty Associates, Inc.

ISBN: 0-812-53006-3
Library of Congress Catalog Number: 95-52692

First Edition: May 1996
First mass market edition: March 1997

Printed in the United States of America

0 9 8 7 6 5 4 3 2 1

For Joseph Francis Flynn, "Pere"

Acknowledgements

A lot of people put up with my pestering while I wrote this book, and they deserve my thanks for their information, advice, and patience. I may not have taken all of their advice, but that is my fault, not theirs. Some deserve special mention. Editor David Hartwell at Tor nurtured this manuscript, despite delays, and was especially understanding during the time when my mother died and I was unable to write. Marge Flynn, of course, put up with my asocial behavior during bouts of writing. Dr. Charles Sheffield was kind enough to read portions of the manuscript in progress and to comment on them. High Frontiers's Aleta Jackson, editor of *The Journal of Practical Applications in Space*, supplied information on SSTOs and other space technology, as did Drs. Arlan Andrews and Jerry Pournelle. Dr. Geoffrey Landis was especially helpful with lasers, asteroid orbits, and beamed microwave power. G. Harry Stine deserves credit for the fractional ballistic transportation network. Dr. Harry Turtledove supplied advice on military weaponry. Finally, thanks to ex-corporal Joseph Flynn, USMC, whose Iwo Jima squadmates provide the names for the "Red Hand" squad. I'm sure they will understand his literary promotion to lieutenant.

The Artemus Project is a registered trademark of the Lunar Resources Company. For more information about the Artemus Project, visit http://www.asi.org.

FIRESTAR

Part III: Shooting Star (AD 2007)

Prologue:

10 August 1972, Grand Teton National Park

Even years later, she would remember it as the day her life began.

She and Wayne had taken the boat out on Jackson Lake, and dropped the sails and drifted with the brightly twinkling waves. It was a clear day, a lustrous day. The sky was a deep, hungry blue with only a few, high cottonball clouds drifting through it. Across the lake, ragged peaks thrust into the skies, their flanks a patchwork of bare, gray rock and white, never-melting snow. The breeze, cool with the promise of autumn, raised a light chop on the water and whipped her long, fine hair into sudden streamers.

It was a bittersweet summer, the last one before college. The future then seemed chilly and uncertain, and his arm around her had lent her warmth and security. He was going to Yale, eventually into law; she, to Chicago. All the old anchors—of love, of family, of friends—were being cast loose. They had gazed out at the lake, the sky, the soaring mountains, and talked earnestly, as only the young can, about the world and the future and their plans for it, sensing that, like the melting snow high upon the Divide, their lives would run off in different directions now, empty into different oceans.

Wayne was square-built, with curled, ruddy-blond hair. The sort of boy who played gentleman's football, though he would not have lasted a minute in the proletarian version. He had the right family; he attended the right schools, where he achieved respectable grades; their families had summered together ever since boarding school. He was, altogether, the sort of boy that Mummy judged very suitable, and Mummy never missed a chance to throw them alone together.

"We'll see each other on breaks and vacations," she assured him. "Our families always come here to Jackson Hole."

"Promise?"

"Promise what?"

"That, no matter what, you and I will always meet here, each summer on August tenth."

She laughed. "Sure." Then she saw the anxiety in his face and put her own arm around his waist and hugged. "Sure," she said again. "Promise. August tenth." She gave him a quick kiss and snuggled against him.

"Chicago is so far, Riesey," he said. "You could have gone to Harvard. You were accepted there, too."

"And you a Yalie? That wouldn't be right. That would be like . . . like Capulets and Montagues." And there had been something about gaining admission based on legacy and Gramper's money that she hadn't quite liked. Chicago, at least, had not been *obliged* to take her in. "Besides," she added, "Chicago has a better business school. Even Gramper says so."

"Business?" She felt his surprise. "I'd assumed you'd be going into English lit."

It's not for you *to assume . . .* "Gramper won't live forever," she said. "When he dies, Van Huyten Industries will be mine." *It should have been Father's. Dear, dying, wasted Father. It should have been Father's, but Gramper is giving it to me.* Sometimes the thought terrified her. Sometimes she lay awake in the night wondering what she would ever do with it when she had it; praying that Gramper would live forever. At other times, she ached for the day. Not for Gramper's death, of course; but to seize the helm. To do something about the direction the country had been drifting in since those terrible gunshots had robbed it of its spirit. A business ought to be more than a machine for making money; it ought to be directed toward some goal.

Making money is my goal. Gramper had told her with that pirate's grin of his.

Wayne smiled at her and pulled her closer. "You don't have to *run* Van Huyten Industries," he said. "You just have to *own* it." His hand began to rub her back, between the halter string and the waistband of her bikini.

Who was he to decide for her? She gave him a jab with her elbow. A playful jab, but with just a little bit of force behind it, so that he oophed. He pulled her tight against him and tickled her, and she tickled him right back, and soon they had toppled off their seats onto the deck, laughing and giggling.

A sudden pause while they gazed in each other's eyes, then they kissed, deeply and eagerly.

When they parted, she rolled onto her stomach and stretched out flat. "Rub some oil on my back, would you, Wayne? I want to work on my tan." It was the work of an instant to unfasten her bikini top and toss it aside. It always started this way. They always pretended they were going to do something else.

She let herself relax under his ministry. His touch raised goose bumps and sent delicious shivers down her spine. Up along both sides, to the shoulders. A quick, gentle massage there; then down the central curve, dipping into the small of the back and cresting just at the edge of the bikini. His fingers paused there, teasingly, then repeated the cycle.

"Mmm," she said. "That feels good."

"Are you ready for me to do the front?"

It was not that he had never seen her. It wasn't even that they had not actually Done It yet. That was a formality awaiting only its proper time, though it was dreadfully unhip ever to admit to such a thing. It was simply assumed by all and sundry in their circle that they had, or that they would, and that was that.

No, what irritated her just the tiniest bit was that Wayne presumed so, too. As if it were not only natural, but expected that she would roll over and let him spread the suntan oil across her breasts. As if *he* were doing *her* the favor.

"Can anyone see us?"

"Not unless our parents are watching from the dock with binoculars." His voice was full of irony, and she did wonder if their parents were not doing exactly that, ready to pop the champagne and plan the wedding.

She rolled onto her back and he straddled her waist and dripped the oil on her breasts. She shivered, as she always did, at those first cold drops. "*Les Grands Tetons*," he said, as he had said the summer before when she had first allowed him to explore those peaks, on this very boat, on this very lake.

"*Mais non*," she said. "*Les petit tetons*."

She could never comprehend what sort of satisfaction he received by fondling her breasts. It did nothing for her, and sometimes he pressed or squeezed too hard. Perhaps if he were to take longer, work more slowly. But he always became aroused too quickly; he moved too fast, too rough. "Oh, baby," he would say. "Oh, baby." The words were always the same; the routine never varied.

Sooner than she was ready, he lay atop her, pressing her against the hardwood planking of the deck. One of these days he would ask for the bottoms to come off, too; or he would simply tug them off, presuming on her unspoken consent. She knew he wanted to; knew he ached to. And that day she would have to decide how much she really loved him; or, indeed, whether she loved him at all.

The boat bobbed under her back, gently rising and falling. The water slapped rhythmically against the hull. She did her best, for him and for herself. Legs spread, knees pulled up, she could sometimes achieve with him what she often achieved alone. Slowly, she felt herself grow ready, and she wanted to cry out, Oh, yes! She wanted to rip away the puritan cloth that separated them; and she might have just begun to reach down with eager fingers . . . when he finished, kissed her once more, and relaxed with a dreamy look upon his face, nearly crushing the breath out of her.

Absently, she ran her fingers through his curls, feeling the frustration like an itch that could not be scratched. Later, she promised herself. Later. He meant well. He was just clumsy and puppy-dog-eager, as boys his age generally were. He would probably make no worse a husband than many and a better one than most. He had breeding; he had not yet forced the issue. Ginny's boyfriend sometimes slapped her when she wouldn't Do It for him. Wayne had never raised a hand to her. Were it not for his cocky presumption about their future she might even regard him as highly as Mummy did.

"What are you thinking about, Riesey?" he said lazily, his hand gently stroking her along the flank from shoulder to waist.

"Oh, nothing."

Wayne raised himself up on his elbows, taking his weight off her, and looking puzzled and the tiniest bit hurt. The lake breeze raised bumps on her bare torso. Wayne said, "I'll show you 'nothing.'" He had just pulled her to him again when she saw over his shoulder a bright streak of light crossing the sky, as if God had struck a match across the heavens.

At first, her mind saw it as a jet contrail; but it moved far too fast and far too high for that. At the leading end, a ball of fire the size of a thumbtack vanished behind Ranger Peak. It clicked into place suddenly, and she gasped. Wayne, misunderstanding, tried to kiss her, but she pushed him away and pointed. "No. A shooting star! Look, Wayne, it's a shooting star!"

He leaned forward and placed a gentle kiss on her forehead. "Don't be silly, Riesey," he said. "It's daytime. You can't have shooting stars in the daytime."

So which of them had taken the senior-year astronomy course? Mariesa blinked and saw the dancing afterimage on her retinas. A purple line of fire across the sky. A meteor! She had actually seen a meteor with her own eyes! She wondered where it had hit ground. Perhaps she could buy a souvenir chunk. A few seconds earlier (or later?) in its orbit, and it might have struck those very peaks and . . .

Violet flame stretches from horizon to horizon, and the very air burns. Megatons of energy boil the seas, toss continents of earth into the sky, and . . .

She felt the brush of wings against her heart, like a newly conceived life quickening within her. In all the years since, she had not gazed at the sky without a shudder of dread. The world was living on borrowed time; and someday the loan would be called, with interest.

Looking into Wayne's broad face, she knew with certain sadness that she could never share her life with this smiling, well-intentioned slab of beef. It was not that he did not share her dreams. Dreams could not be shared; and everyone was entitled to his own. It was not even that he had laughed at her. No, the deciding factor was something so small that it was the biggest thing he had never done. He had not even bothered to turn his head and look.

She could remember that day, every detail of it. Sometimes, she could even remember the naive, young girl she had been and feel that first moment of certainty and purpose blossoming within her like a flower of flame. And she wondered, staring into the mirror at the woman she had become: How would her life have changed—how would the world's life have changed—had she let Wayne fuck her brains out on the boat on the lake on that day?

Part I

MARIESA'S KIDS
(AD 1999)

1.

Wake-up Call

The driveway at Witherspoon High School was unbearably brilliant with the melting snow. Broad patches of water winked like fallen stars against the black macadam; and a few hummocks of dirty snow lingered in the shadowed nooks and crannies of the school's facade. Everywhere else, slush fought the March sun. Mariesa van Huyten could hear the limousine's tires rolling through it, a sound halfway between a splash and a crunch. It was that oddly impatient time of year: not cold enough for winter; not warm enough for spring. It was the season when you sat at the window staring out at the desperate sunlight and just wanted to scream, Get on with it!

She took the folders from her briefcase and flipped through them once again, though by now she knew their contents nearly by heart. Her lawyers had gone over them with mine detectors and dowsing rods. John E. had personally dotted the i's and crossed the t's. They had developed contingency plans for each possibility; and contingency plans for the contingency plans. Still she wondered: What if there was something they had all overlooked? Some rabbit that the state or the union would pull out of their hats at the last minute. Something so obvious they hadn't seen it, and which would make them look like prize fools in front of the entire country.

She stuffed the folder back into the briefcase and closed it with a snap. She caught Laurence's brief glance in his rear-view mirror, and realized that she must have done that with the papers at least a dozen times during the ride over. *Why am I so nervous? It's a done deal. This visit is just a formality.* And she could have sent someone else. Egbo. Karr. Any of Mentor's top people. She need not have come personally.

There were a dozen or so teenagers lounging around the school entrance, chatting and laughing. Girls with their hair piled high and their makeup applied with a trowel. Boys with slicked-down hair parted in the middle. A lot of leather. A lot of black. Some of the kids were smoking, lounging insolently against the wall, butts dancing up and down in their lips as they talked. When the limousine stopped in front of the school, they all turned and stared at it, cow-eyed. One of the smokers flicked his butt at the car and it skidded off the right front fender in a shower of sparks. The others laughed, as if he had done something funny.

Laurence turned. "Ma'am, do you want me to walk in with you?" Laurence was two hundred pounds, none of it fat.

"No, thank you, Laurence," Mariesa told him. "I shan't be but a moment."

Laurence shook his head. "This is a middle-class neighborhood."

Mariesa could not tell if he was offering an explanation, an assurance, or a warning. "I won't be long," she said again.

When she opened the limousine's door and stepped out, the kids crowded close, trying to get a glimpse inside. The sight of the television, the telephone, the icebox set off a swirl of giggles and muttered comments. She heard one girl whisper, "Missy Rich Bitch," to a friend. When she saw that Mariesa had heard, she jutted her chin out as if daring her to make something of it.

The boy who had thrown the cigarette stood between her and the school door. He was dressed in a black leather jacket, but one without any silver studding or chains. Its very plainness showed its wearer had nothing to prove. He wore a pair of dark shades over his eyes, and his head was shaved along the sides and back. A pair of black crosses dangled from his ears. His arms and legs were grasshopper-long. He looked Mariesa up and down.

"You sure look fine, Mama." He grinned and showed teeth bound in wire. The other kids circled her, save three or four who, with a worried look back, drifted off toward the parking lot. Mariesa took a step forward and the boy moved to the left to block her. He was as tall as she was and carried more weight. "What's your hurry, Mama? We not good enough for you?"

"Hey, Chase," said one of the girls. "She's the rich bitch. Bet she don't even know how."

Chase smiled. "How about that? You ever . . . ?"

He stopped suddenly and backed away, looking past Mariesa.

"Ain't nothin' sadder," she heard Laurence's baritone say, "than a white boy pretending to be a homey. Kid, this is white-bread country. You don't even want to know what it's really like 'downtown.' "

Mariesa turned and saw that Laurence had stepped out of the limo, and all of the teenagers except Chase and two of the girls had vanished. Chase seemed fascinated by the edge of the shoulder holster that peaked from beneath the big man's chauffeur jacket. Laurence winked at her. "I'll mind the car, ma'am. Don't you fret. Chase and I, here, we're going to be real good friends."

The principal waited silently with hands folded upon his desk until the secretary had closed the office door; then he said, "Have a seat, Ms. van Huyten. I won't ask what I can do for you. Very little, I imagine." There was an edge of bitterness around his mouth, a sourness that thinned the lips into a line.

As she lowered herself into the visitor's chair, Mariesa glanced around the office. The diploma, laminated on wood, proclaimed to "all and sundry" that Robert C. Boucher had completed the requirements for a Doctor of Education. The bookshelves held volumes on administration and management, looseleaf binders crammed with district regulations and important memos. On the far end of one shelf, a handful of tattered history texts. Boucher's desk was littered with paper. Detention slips. Progress reports. There was a cube of plastic with a Boucher family portrait on each face. Each different, Mariesa noticed of the three poses she could see. A different family for every mood. One happy. One scowling. One... wearing Groucho glasses? Yes. Boucher, his wife and son, even the baby. She smiled briefly at a side of the man so unexpectedly revealed.

"Down to business, then," she said, extracting the documents from her briefcase (for the last time!) and passing them across the desk.

Boucher barely glanced at them. He read the title, flipped to the back page and checked the signatures. "These seem to be in order," he said. "Though how would I know if they were not? You're the one with all the high-price lawyers."

"The State of New Jersey and the NJEA had their own lawyers," she said.

He sighed. "Though not enough of them, it seems." He stared at the papers for a few moments longer, bending them back and forth along the folds. Then he tossed them to the desk. "So. What comes next?"

Mariesa sat up straighter and leaned slightly forward. "Mentor Academies, pursuant to Public Law Number—"

Boucher waved a hand. "Spare me the formal pronouncements. We are in your power. You know it; I know it. The district is now a subsidiary of your conglomerate. Congratulations."

"Not a subsidiary. We are simply contractors, hired to operate the district for the next five..."

"For as long as you can buy Trenton lawmakers."

The depth of his bitterness surprised her. "Mr. Boucher," she said earnestly, "I wish you could see this from the public's point of view. Or for that matter, from my own, as an employer. High-school graduates can no longer pass examinations that, a century ago, were given in eighth grade in rural one-room schools. My companies must, on the average, interview one hundred and twenty-seven applicants to find a single suitable candidate; and that is at entry level.''

Boucher shook his head. ''A school is more than job prep for big corporations.''

She had not come here to debate, but she leaned toward him, bending over the closed briefcase on her lap, willing him to understand this one point. ''Mr. Boucher, my time is valuable, but hear me on this. If young men and women are unable to function adequately in an entry-level job in a large corporation, where they are closely supervised and subject to on-the-job training and orientation, how on earth do you expect them to run a small dry cleaner's or deli? To vote intelligently? To compute their taxes? To sign contracts? To discuss issues of any real importance with one another? How *dare* you set them loose on their own?''

And more important, though she did not say so, you could not build the future with the rough timber the schools turned out today. She stood, briefcase clutched in her hand, barely able to contain the anger. It was not this man's fault. He could only work in the system, not on it. She tried to convince herself that he was trapped, too; as much a victim as any of the kids.

''Mentor's people will be here, and in the other schools, beginning next week. They will be taking inventory of the physical plant, observing classes, interviewing teachers until the semester's end, at which point, policy decisions for the strategic plan will be finalized. Your liaison during the transition will be Dr. Belinda Karr.''

Boucher dropped his eyes to the desk. ''Yes. I understand.''

Mariesa had reached the door and had her hand on the knob when Boucher spoke again. ''Ms. van Huyten?'' She turned and looked at him, and this time she saw neither bitterness nor defeat, but only an overwhelming sadness. ''Ms. van Huyten, all I ever wanted to do was teach children.''

Mariesa gathered her resolution about her and pulled the

door open. "You didn't do it very well, did you?" She closed the door behind her so he could be alone with himself.

In the car, Laurence asked how it went. Mariesa shook her head and rode back to Silverpond in silence.

Silverpond, the van Huyten family home, sat in the center of a hundred acres of satin lawn, atop the highest of a series of rolling embankments that were part nature and part artifice. The House of the Mound People, Mariesa had dubbed it, to Gramper's amusement and Mummy's annoyance. The land-scaping had been cleverly done, so that from the windows of the ground floor, all signs of driveways or stairs were hidden by the swells of the hummocks. In the bowl shaped by the last of them, at the bottom of the Great Mound, was a pond formed by a diversion channel from Runamuck Creek. In the late af-ternoon, the sunshine off the waters gave it a silvery appear-ance, almost like a mirror, its flat surface ruffled only by the breezes that wriggled through the sheltering banks and by the fish snapping at flies and mosquitos. Mariesa had allowed the outlet end, where the water flowed back toward the Run-amuck, to go to reeds and cattails. That, too, annoyed Mummy, who preferred a more manicured sort of perfection; but the ragged asymmetry it lent the landscape pleased Mar-iesa in some undefinable fashion. So did the bright wildflowers that littered the borders of the estate with their yellow and white and purple.

From the top floor of the house the view of the grounds was all different. From the dormer window of the Roost—her private office—she could see over the treetops, beyond the estate grounds. Mariesa set her Manhattan on the desk and leaned out through the open window, resting her waist upon the sill and bracing her arms against the sash like she used to do when she was a child, as if she were on the bridge of a tall ship, high above the deck and the rolling green waves. There was always a breeze up here, up where the birds hov-ered. It stirred the short-cropped hair she wore, and she thought fleetingly of the long tresses she had once sported and how they had snapped like a banner in the wind. Too much trouble. Washing, rinsing, styling. Too many precious minutes out of her day.

Around her, Wessex County struggled out of its winter coat. The land rippled and rolled toward the horizons, clipped off in the north by the line of the Watchungs and on the south edge of the estate by the low ridge called Skunktown Mountain. Dark brown squares in the western, rural part of the county announced the start of spring plowing. To the east, the village of Hamm's Corner, the busy line of Interstate 80 and, farther beyond that, nearly to the horizon, the dark smudge in the sky that marked the city of North Orange.

Hers, now.

With a pair of binoculars, she could pick out the buildings in the downtown area, maybe even locate Witherspoon itself. She thought for a moment of fetching the big pair she had bought for stargazing, but she changed her mind. Too much like the mistress in the castle gazing down on her domain. The Mistress of Silverpond.

She stared at the gray-black city. Not hers, not really. Only the price that the state had demanded for allowing Mentor to extend its chain of private schools into New Jersey. The bill had been depicted as a fresh, innovative idea for improving the public schools—dedicated legislators calling in expert consultants because Nothing Is Too Good for Our Kids—and if anyone had thought of it as an open admission of failure, no one, least of all Mariesa van Huyten, had been so rude as to mention it publicly.

She closed the window, muffling the sounds of the birds. Mentor had anticipated being forced to take over a public district. ("Privatize" it, the newspapers had brayed, though that was not quite the truth.) It would up their student head count by twenty-five percent, Belinda had noted, and, given success—or even the absence of outright failure—snowball into any number of further contracts. *The beginning of a ship is a plank.*

And what would Gramper have thought of her plan, she wondered? Disapproval? She conjured up the old man's image, thin and wiry, with the straggled gray Ho Chi Minh beard; thought of him pursing his lips and looking off high and to the right as he always did in serious thought.

No, she decided finally. Gramper had never disparaged dedication; and the only convictions he disapproved of were in a court of law. *I can't put a man down for believing in something, Riesey,* he had said one time. *Even something wrong. Even if I fight him every inch of the way. There are too many damned people out there who believe in nothing at all.* Not "too damned many . . ." Gramper had always spoken precisely.

Foolishness, she decided. He would have thought her project foolish. Gramper's own dedication had been to making money. It had defined his life as much as Project Prometheus defined hers. Mentor would never be a big moneymaker, and Prometheus itself was so blue-sky as to wholly redefine "speculative." In Gramper's eyes, that would have been enough to tarnish them.

A final look at North Orange before she turned away and went to her desk to review Prometheus's status. Events were beginning to move now. Track III was active—and soon enough they would begin testing and selecting the most promising students. Track IV kickoff was scheduled for next month. Two years of frantic activity lay ahead. A two-year window of opportunity, before the financial gales would blow and all the hatches were battened shut. Prometheus had to be in place by then; or else her forecasters had to be dead wrong.

The computer screen, a full, two-page spread, blanked for a moment as the search command went out over the fiber-optic link to her office. The system asked for a password and she said, "Firestar," slowly and distinctly for the built-in microphone. The sentry program matched her voiceprint against the access list and granted her admission.

A PERT chart appeared on the screen and Mariesa moused one of the nodes, opening a second window with a list of dossiers on potential pilots for Track IV. Chris and the selection team had already prioritized them, and Mariesa read through each evaluation carefully, making marginal notes of her own on each one. A dozen men and women to be tracked down and sounded out. How many would volunteer? Would any? The résumés were no help. Schooling and experience told you what a person had done, not what he would do. The confidential backgrounds were only marginally more help, and she sought enlightenment from the digitized photographs. "The eyes are the windows of the soul," Blake had said. One by one, she studied them, a succession of grinning, cocky men and women, trying to guess which she might count upon. Calhoun? Anderson? Krasnarov? Marachevsky? DuBois?

Afterward, she called up the action plan and examined the due dates for each of the activities. Track III in the schools; Track IV down on the archipelago; Track II, nearing completion . . . Windows proliferated on the screen as she called up subtracks. Everything on schedule, so far. Those activities that were delayed were off the critical path.

When she looked up finally and glanced out the window once more, she found the sky pitch black and North Orange a twinkling of distant lights. So late already? Ten-thirty by her watch. She rose and stretched, feeling the aching back muscles relax. She had been sitting for hours.

She did not need to do this, she knew. Work Group 22/1 would handle pilot recruitment without her oversight. *You always take too much on yourself,* Keith McReynolds had told her. *The conductor needn't play an instrument.*

Perhaps not, but she did need to know the score.

She returned to her vantage point by the window and gazed at the star-encrusted heavens. Her eye, by long practice, sought out the landmarks of the sky. The Dipper, the Pole Star, the Virgin. A ruby gleam in the eastern sky hovered over North Orange just below the Virgin. Mars, the War God. Not a good omen.

If you believed in omens.

Mentor held the district meeting in May, just after classes let out for the year; and Mariesa decided to attend, incognito. She had Leonard do her hair up differently and add a shoulder-length fall to her tresses, and she wore a cheap print frock and costume jewelry that her maid, Miss Whitmore, acquired at a discount store. Belinda recognized her, of course, but took the hint and said nothing.

Mentor had filled the main ballroom of the North Orange Sheraton with rows and columns of straight-backed, metal-framed chairs. The seats and splats were padded—in a horrible purple fabric—but the padding was light and the fabric was frayed and it was not a chair in which Mariesa desired to spend more of her life than was absolutely necessary. She took a seat near the back of the ballroom, so she could see more, and noticed a tall, broad-shouldered man across the aisle deliberately move his chair out of line before sitting down. Seeing her, he grinned. It was a wide grin that lit up his face.

"I know," he said, "It spoils the symmetry. But I never liked rows and columns. 'Rebellion in small things,' just so the world knows I haven't surrendered yet."

"Is it a war, then, between you and the world?"

He nodded gravely. "And the worst part is, the world always wins."

"Surely not," she said with amusement.

He patted the seat next to him. "Come on over and join me. Maybe we can get the Wave going, if we work at it." She took the seat he had indicated and moved it out of line as he had done. He chuckled, "That's the spirit," and held out a hand. "Barry Fast," he said, "I teach English lit at John Witherspoon."

Mariesa shook his hand. "Mary Gorley," she lied. "I'm new. And thank you."

He blinked and his brows knotted together. "Thank you?" he asked.

"For not saying 'language arts.'"

He laughed again. "Call me old-fashioned." Mariesa thought she had never heard a readier laugh. Harriet had introduced her to so many men over the years, but none of them knew quite how to laugh. "I hate faculty meetings," he said, still grinning. "And I especially hate district-wide faculty meetings. Most of all, I hate district-wide faculty meetings called on a Saturday. But . . ." And he sighed and shrugged elaborately. "What Mentor wants, Mentor gets. At least until everyone figures out where any bodies of major importance are buried."

Up behind the dais, two workmen unrolled the Mentor banner, a poster of "Earthrise over the Moon," and hung it on the wall. In white script lettering, the Van Huyten Industries motto twisted among the stars. *Dream your way ahead* . . . It was a motto she had always found inspiring, but Barry snorted when he saw it.

"Well, rah-rah-rah." He pointed to the banner. "I heard that van Huyten was a space nut. The papers call her the Moon Lady."

"Are you always so cynical?" she asked him.

He folded his arms and slouched in his chair. "Yeah, well, call it playing the odds. Five dollars says the Cynic is right more often than the Pollyanna. You're new. Teach long enough, and you'll grow armor, too." He waved an arm at the rows of chairs quickly filling up. "Listen to these clowns. . . ."

A hum of worried, defiant whispers ebbed and flowed around them. Teachers in small huddles along the walls and in the aisles. Teachers clumped in the back of the ballroom. Teachers leaning across each other in the seats. Teachers discussing the new world order.

"—we must have made the cut—"

"—the usual free-enterprise yap. Tighten the belts. No more sucking on the public teat—"

"—tamper with my seniority—"

"—whatever it takes to make a profit, and never mind the kids—"

"—corporate benefit package—"

"—cutting everyone's salary and working us longer hours—"

"—twelve-month year for the same old forty thou—"

"—I heard—"

"—they say—"

Mariesa wondered whether everyone caught up in mergers and acquisitions felt the same way. Tense, uncertain, but still trying to project confidence and self-assurance.

Barry said, "See what I mean? A flock of nervous birds. By the end of the day, we'll know the score—or as much of the score as Mentor is willing to reveal. Until then, pooling collective ignorance won't produce knowledge. I heard," he said, grinning in conscious self-mockery at adding to the fruitless conversation, "I heard that they plan to make us dress up. The whole gang up on the dais is wearing suits." He shook his head. "Rucksack, jeans, and corduroy jacket are more my speed. But . . . Go along, get along. We're in Rome now, and the Romans wear suits . . ."

The meeting began at eight-thirty on the dot, when Dr. Belinda Karr, senior principal of Mentor Academies, stood and gave a short "welcome aboard" address. Short, solidly built, mid-forties, and teetering on the brink of matronly, Belinda moved with the energy of a taut spring and spoke with clear precision. "Stick with me, Mary," Barry said, "and I'll show you the ropes. Figure out how Karr's mind works and you can figure out how to survive the new regime."

"Survival is your goal, then?" she asked in a faintly disapproving air.

"Survival is all. I made it through the sixties without being clubbed by cops or shot by strangers in black pajamas." He settled back in his seat. "I mean to survive this, too."

It was a long day. Mentor filled it with presentations on curriculum and pay scales and work rules and the upcoming summer training colloquia. In between were small group activities and workshops designed to highlight learning techniques. Even lunch was a working lunch. By four o'clock, when Belinda adjorned the meeting, everyone was tired. The teachers spilled out onto the mezzanine to stretch a bit before the dinner.

"They kept us all day," Barry grumbled. "Dinner is the least they can do." On the way out of the meeting room, Mariesa asked him whether he had discovered how Dr. Karr's mind worked.

Barry pursed his lips and looked thoughtful. He held up his forefinger. "Number one. Karr's into physical fitness. She practically *bounces* when she walks. Five dollars says her nickname will be Sports Karr before the new year starts. So, don't give up the jogging and the weekly workout at the Y. Number two. When the other corporate drones spoke, Karr listened as if what they said actually mattered.'' He grinned suddenly. "Maybe it did; maybe she's going to grade them on style and content. Anyhow she pays attention to small things. Number three. She started the meeting exactly on time; and she didn't tap or blow into the microphone first. Know why?'' Mariesa shook her head. "Because she *knew* that the microphone would work. So, precision and careful preparation will be the watchwords for the new regime.'' He stopped and looked over his shoulder at the dais as they headed for the mezzanine. The flow of teachers parted around them. "These people have very clear ideas what they want to do,'' Barry said. "And maybe that's better than the slaphappy ditziness I've come to know and love from District. But people who know what they want to do usually know what they want *me* to do, too.''

The swirl of teachers separated them when they reached the mezzanine. A strange man, she thought. He was attractive and clever and witty, and he would not be half so cynical about teaching if he did not still care about it very much. Barry Fast was not burnt out, not yet; but the match was lit.

Mariesa circulated among the teachers, engaging them in conversation, sounding out their opinions, getting their feedback on how the meeting had gone. She didn't take notes, but marked certain teachers and their comments.

"—in school all day, but they call it the Afterclass—"

"—like hourly workers. Instructors get paid overtime if they—"

"—but the building managers won't have any say in the teaching—"

"—institute of theirs shoving a standardized curriculum down our—"

"—Apprentice, Journeyman, Master, Principal—"

Mariesa joined a group of teachers by the railing, where the mezzanine overlooked the lobby. A faux waterfall—water dripping down a set of fiberglass rods—ran past suspended planters thick with green, fleshy leaves, to a penny-choked pool in the lobby. Beside the pool, a balding man in a tux played light pop tunes on a grand piano while hotel guests in overstuffed barrel chairs nursed their drinks and listened. The pianist sounded competent, but Mariesa thought him too well dressed to play Joel's "Piano Man" with any real conviction.

"Save the world?" She heard Barry's sardonic voice by her shoulder. "Now, that's a different sort of comment." She turned and the two of them locked eyes for a moment. Barry showed a friendly set of teeth and joined the group. He had two drinks, one in each hand.

Gwen Glendower, one of the teachers Mariesa had been talking with, shoved her glasses back up her nose. "Oh, hi, Barry. I thought I saw you earlier. Sitting near the back, as usual, ready for a quick getaway."

Barry laughed. "Be prepared. I used to be a Boy Scout. Hi, Gwen. And . . . Mary Gorley, right?"

"Who is the second drink for?" Gwen asked. "Or are you one of those two-fisted drinkers?"

"A middle-school teacher I know slightly. Shannon Morgenthaler, from John Dayton. Have you ever met her?" Gwen shook her head. "I thought I left her right here by the rail." He stood tiptoe and looked around the mezzanine, then shrugged and drank from the glass in his right hand.

"Barry," said Gwen, "where'd you get alcohol? Mentor only set up for soft drinks."

Barry shrugged. "Oh, the barman down in the lobby knows the difference between bourbon and soda. You would think that a corporation rich enough to buy a school district could spring for some real drinks." He turned to Mariesa. "Now, Mary, what's this about 'saving the world'?"

"Through education," Mariesa said.

"I would be happy just to save one kid," said a short, utterly bald man. He looked a little like a gnome with a beak nose, and gave the impression of constantly leaning forward. Bernie Paulson had introduced himself as a social studies teacher from Molly Pitcher, the high school on the other side of town from Witherspoon.

"Save enough of them," Barry agreed, "and you can wind up saving the world after all." Paulson smiled and nodded but said nothing. A young woman, early twenties, in a red, crew-neck sweater spoke up. Mariesa hadn't gotten her name.

"She mean's 'save the world' literally."

Mariesa thought the woman too young to give her comment the cynical twist she heard. It's the duty of the young to be enthusiastic. It was the older generation, the burnouts more interested in their pensions than in their students, who were supposed to sneer at world-saving.

Barry swirled the melting ice in his glass. "Really?" He looked once more at Mariesa. "From what?"

"From war, perhaps; or famine."

"Ah! The four horsemen . . ."

"It's a whole cavalry troop, I assure you. Pollution. A new retrovirus. A . . . rogue asteroid. Choose your own scenario." She cocked an eyebrow and Barry laughed and pointed a finger.

"You look like Spock when you do that. Your ears are even pointy."

Mariesa raised a hand and touched the tip of her ear, where it peeked through her fall. "It's a feature I get from my mother."

"So, schoolteachers are going to save us from the Apocalypse. . . ." Gwen Glendower leaned between Barry and Mariesa to set her now-empty glass on one of the small hotel tables nearby. "How?"

"Oh, it's simple," the bald man said mildly. "First, we duck into a nearby phone booth . . ."

"No," said Mariesa. "It's because you will touch a student. Someone. Somewhere. And she will mature into the scientist or the engineer or the doctor who finds the solution."

"Bread upon the waters," said Gwen.

"More like a trail of bread crumbs in the forest," said Barry. Mariesa looked at him.

"Meaning . . . ?"

Barry shrugged, remembering the drink in his left hand just in time to keep it from spilling. "Well, we can toss out seeds of knowledge and hope that one or two sprout. Or we can lay them down in a way that will lead the kids toward some goal."

"Education," said Bernie. "*E ducere* is Latin for 'to lead out.' "

The young woman in the sweater said, "That sounds more like indoctrination than education. Engineers, scientists, doctors . . . We need people who can feel more than people who can think. Who decides what the goals are supposed to be?"

"From now on," said Barry with a shake of the head, "it will be corporate managers."

"Is that worse than politicians and pressure groups?" asked Mariesa.

Barry shook his head. "The profit motive is as out of place in a schoolroom as a catcher's mitt on a surgeon. Education deals in intangibles, in things that never show up on an accountant's bottom line. Mentor will be lumped in there with steel and chemicals and—Lord knows what all is in the VHI corporate egg basket. Decisions will be made so far up the totem pole that they can't see children, only dollars. There will be constant pressure to cut budgets and do without necessary supplies."

Gwen cocked a smile. "Sure. Not like the cornucopia we were getting from the county freeholders."

Barry laughed, too. "I guess you're right. But corporate droids are control freaks. They won't tolerate free spirits."

Mariesa said, "But Dr. Karr explained that each school will be run by the teachers themselves—"

"By an elite group of teachers," said the young woman.

"—by the 'principal' teachers, like a law firm or an architectural partnership."

"Like any professional practice," agreed Gwen. "We call ourselves professionals; we should act like professionals. This takeover may be worthwhile if we can focus on *teaching* again."

"Believe it or not," said Barry, "I picked up a notion we

could use in the classroom from the role-play we did this morning.''

"What? The murder investigation?" said the woman in the sweater. "That exercise wasn't fair. We weren't told our briefing sheets were different.''

"What's fair?" asked Gwen. "We were told to solve the problem 'as a group.' ''

"Well, naturally, working in groups is better than working alone, but . . .''

"But not for the reasons you think, Dottie. Not for bonding or togetherness or because working alone is 'antisocial'; but because *you can't solve the problem unless you do*." Gwen paused and sipped her spring water. "The big lesson for me," she continued to the group at large, "was finding out that my own briefing sheet had a key piece of information; but I hadn't shared it with my team because I hadn't noticed it myself."

"Teamwork isn't easy," Barry agreed. "You need more than good intentions."

A nice aphorism, Mariesa thought. She would have to pass it on to Belinda. "How could you use that exercise in class?" she asked him. "Five minutes after the first period ended the answer would be all over school."

"It's not the answer that matters," Barry told her. "The point of the game was to learn how to work together and share information. It didn't have to be a murder-mystery role-play. You could take the same principle and apply it, say, to a reading-comprehension test in which each excerpt is a little bit different and you can't answer all the questions unless everyone shares their information. Or to a science test in which each student has data the others don't. It's just a matter of dispersing the vital information among five or so alternative versions."

Barry swirled the melting ice cubes around in his glass. "Not that it matters," he continued. "We won't be seeing any innovation. My brother works for a big corporation out in Seattle, and he tells me the most important thing is to follow procedures and don't stick your neck out. So, I imagine we'll have to follow Mentor's script from now on."

Dottie said, "There's too much emphasis on science in Mentor's 'script.' "

"That shouldn't be surprising," said Bernie. "Mariesa van Huyten is a space enthusiast. She even built an observatory on the roof of that mansion of hers."

Barry snapped his fingers. "That's right," he said, "I remember that now. I read about it in the papers, what? two, three years ago. Didn't she spot a comet or something?"

"An asteroid," said Mariesa quietly.

"Whatever. I didn't pay much attention at the time. It was just a local interest piece. 'Heiress's Hobby Puts Her Name in the Sky.' That sort of thing. Never thought she'd turn out to be my boss. Well, my boss's boss's boss, or whatever. I just hope she doesn't screw the school up worse than it already is. Benign neglect is what we ought to hope for."

"The science emphasis will put the girls at a disadvantage," Dottie insisted.

"Girls can't do math," said Barry with a smirk. "Is that it?"

She gave him a look. "It's a woman thing. You wouldn't understand."

"Actually," said Gwen, "it's a science thing."

The other woman turned on her. "But, don't you see? Science is a patriarchal activity. It breaks things apart, disconnects the whole. Woman-mind works differently. We're more connected, more intuitive."

Gwen smiled. "I teach chemistry."

The young woman colored slightly. "I meant in general. I want to be *real* in class and be a human being. And I want my students to know that they are free to be themselves and I'll listen to them. I want every one of them to have a chance to express himself or herself. Those are *my* priorities."

"I notice your priorities did not include your students' learning anything," said Gwen.

The young woman pressed her lips together. Her face matched her sweater now. "You just don't get it," she said, and turned away without another word.

Gwen shook her head. "I don't know what the world is

coming to. When I was a little girl, my teachers tried to discourage me from studying science. It wasn't 'ladylike.' Pure, two-hundred-proof male-chauvinist bull-puckey. Now I hear the same line from my sisters. What's the point of blazing a trail if no one follows you? Oh, Barry, by the way . . . you'll never guess who I saw here. Bob Boucher.''

Barry raised his eyebrows. ''Boucher's here? Hunh. I would have thought he'd be the first to get the boot. I heard van Huyten really shoved those papers down his throat; I would have loved to see that but I was teaching that period.'' He turned his head, scanning the mezzanine. ''Ah, there's Shannon,'' said Barry. ''Excuse me, Mary, I have a drink to deliver. Bernie . . . I'll see you at school, Gwen.'' He worked his way through the crowd toward a short, mousy woman near the railing. The two chatted for a moment, and Mariesa saw the woman open her purse and show Barry something inside. Then he handed her the drink he had been holding and they parted.

Mariesa turned to go and saw that Gwen Glendower was also watching Barry. Gwen laughed and said, ''He's really a thoughtful guy.''

''And quite clever,'' Mariesa said. ''We were talking earlier.''

Gwen pushed her glasses back up her nose. ''Were you? Barry and I have taught together at Witherspoon for the last five years. He's got the four best features a man can have.''

''He does? And what are they?''

Gwen craned her neck, trying to see where Barry had gone. ''He's smart, he's courteous, he doesn't try to push himself on you, and . . .'' She giggled and leaned close to Mariesa. ''. . . and he's got *great* buns.''

''He's not married, is he?'' Mariesa asked.

Gwen spared her a brief glance. ''No,'' she said, rubbing her left hand. ''Not yet.''

Mariesa bounded up the broad, flagstone steps at Silverpond, past Sykes, who, composed as always, stood patiently holding the door. The chandelier in the foyer tinkled from the breeze as she skipped through the open doorway. Sykes raised a discreet eyebrow at her appearance, but said nothing. He was a middle-aged man, but he had been in the family's employ in one capacity or another since his twenties. Portly, with a high forehead and a scalp smooth as an egg, he liked to cultivate what he imagined to be an English butler's imperturbability.

"We are rather cheerful this evening, miss," Sykes said as he closed the big walnut door behind her. The window in the door was fashioned from irregular segments of beveled, leaded glass, and the world outside, seen through them, was a dark and fragmented mosaic: a dozen ponds, large and small, sparkled in the panes. From different points in the foyer, different images would invert, though from chance or from a careful calculation of focal lengths, Mariesa had never managed to learn.

"We certainly are, Sykes." The foyer floor was laid with mosaic tiles in a clever brown-and-green geometric pattern. As a child, Mariesa had believed the pattern to be an intricate maze and she had spent hours trapped in the center of it, unable to discover the key. She placed her left foot on the first brown tile. A half-turn to the right, then ahead two tiles . . .

"Nearly all the teachers stayed on. Belinda had been so afraid we would start the semester shorthanded." Left, one step . . . "Perhaps professionalism means as much to them as job tenure and security."

"Perhaps," Sykes conceded. "But one does not lightly forgo a position in these days."

Mariesa paused. "No, I suppose not." The Christmas Recession seemed to drag on and on . . . A recovery would begin next month. Detweiler had forecast it, and the investment firm she retained was seldom wrong. It would be an anemic and short-lived recovery, gone almost before the public realized it was there; but enough of a swell that Prometheus could "surf" on it for two years. Anticipating the trough, VHI was already snapping up assets at bargain prices.

"Your mother has been asking for you, miss,"

"Has she." Back up one step . . . "Where is Harriet now, Sykes?"

"In the library, I believe. There will be guests for dinner."

Mariesa nodded. Another of Mummy's incessant efforts to expose her to the Right Sort of Man, in the hope that chemistry, lust, or sheer desperation would strike a spark. It would be one of Mummy's friends, she knew. One who just happened to have an out-of-state nephew or cousin visiting. A left turn on the mosaic and she would be trapped in a cul-de-sac. She stepped to the brown square on the right. "That's fine," she told Sykes.

"Shall I have Miss Whitmore lay out some clothing for you?"

"One does dress for dinner. The Tartucci, I think. I have yet to wear it." Another twist, a step ahead and . . .

"Mariesa, dear!"

. . . Trapped.

She had run out of brown tiles. Well, it was a silly game, anyway, and Lord only knew what Sykes thought of it. He hadn't been butler back then, Old Frederick had. Sykes had only been Father's driver; he had never watched her hopscotch around the foyer mosaic. Old Frederick had looked on with a tolerant smile, perhaps understanding, perhaps even longing to join her.

"Hello, Mummy," she said.

"What on earth are you doing? And why are you dressed in such tawdry clothing?"

Mariesa lifted the hem of the floral frock. "What, this old thing?" She pirouetted. "What do you think? It was a Blue Light Special at Kmart."

Her mother's glance dismissed the cheap clothing. "I have been searching for you high and low. Where have you been all day?"

"Playing Haroun al-Rashid," she declared with a flourish of her arm.

Harriet scowled. "I don't understand."

Mariesa laughed. She scampered to the staircase, and swung around the newel post with her arm, coming to *croisée devant* on the first step.

"I never understand anything you say or do," Harriet said.

2.

The Sky Turned Black and All the Stars Came Out

When the stranger sat down across the table from him, Ned DuBois took no notice other than to make a quick appraisal of the man's build and reach. Finding neither of immediate concern, he finished lifting his mug of dark beer and let the bittersweet liquid trickle down his throat.

Nancy's was a dive on the Galveston waterfront, ripe with the smells of cheap booze and human sweat, smoky with tobacco, noisy with roughnecks and merchant sailors and stevedores, thick-necked and stubble-chinned, swapping yarns and brags and warnings. They were a surly lot, dirty and spent from work that would kill most others, speaking a polyglot mixture of English and Spanish and Creole and Vietnamese and Tagalog and God alone knew what else. Galveston in High Summer.

Not that Nancy's was a bad place. It was no worse than a score of others along the waterfront. If you wanted a drink—and most did—you could get one there. If you wanted a woman—and most did—they were available in a wide price range. And if you wanted a fight, well that, too, could be easily arranged.

For three months, Ned DuBois had tried to blend in with them, despite his soft hands and small feet and his oddly compact way of moving. He was short and wiry, but he knew certain things about close-in fighting that were both surprising and useful. These he had taught to those who came to him for the learning, though the price was high and few came back for a second lesson. The others might sense that he was an alien particle in their midst, but they allowed him a grudging respect and a certain amount of space. Joe Nancy (do you want to make something of it?) hired him as a bouncer now and then, when Ned was sober and inclined to do it. In a mean mood, Ned could be indiscriminate in whom he bounced, which was not good for the trade. Mostly, just his sitting there, scowling into flat, warm beer, was enough to keep those who knew in line, and that didn't cost Joe Nancy anything.

Ned banged his empty mug on the table, half an announcement, half a challenge, and looked the stranger in the eye. The man was gaunt, with high cheekbones and a hint of color in his cheeks and brow. Dressed well, but not expensively enough to attract interest: a white coat over a dark shirt, a bola tie fastened in place by an ornamental outstretched hand with a fireball at its fingertips. His hair was sooty black and pulled back into a ponytail. Ned grunted. "You buying or selling?"

The stranger seemed to consider that. "Buying," he decided finally.

"Good. I'm tired of this bilge water. I'll have a double."

The stranger smiled and beckoned to Joe Nancy with a curious backhanded, three fingered wave. "A double bourbon for my friend, please," he said. No accent, but with that carefully controlled, formal phrasing that marked the educated foreigner.

"I hate to drink alone," Ned said to no one in particular.

The stranger flicked him a glance and added, "And a glass of cachaça for myself."

Ned waited in silence while Joe Nancy brought the drinks. He wasn't sure what cachaça was, only that it sounded out of the ordinary; but it did not surprise him that Nancy's had a bottle in stock. He gave the barman a look as the man set the drinks down—*who is this guy?*—but Joe Nancy only shrugged with his eyebrows.

"All right," Ned said when they were alone again. "It's your whistle. You blow it. You can start with how you knew I drank bourbon."

The stranger lifted his glass, "Your good health, Captain DuBois."

Ned paused with his glass half lifted. "That's an Air Force title," he said. "It doesn't mean squat on the waterfront."

"You were once a test pilot at Edwards."

"I was once a lot of things. Who are you?"

The stranger set his glass down untasted. "João Pessoa," he said. "I am the general manager of the Daedalus Corporation."

Ned saluted with his drink. "Well, I'm sure impressed."

"I was told I could find you here," Pessoa continued. "I was also told not to bother. I can see now what they meant."

Ned took in the narrow eyes, the thinned lips. *Snotty bastard.* "You think I'm drunk, don't you?" Pessoa made no reply, and Ned laughed. "Shows how much you know. Come back in a couple of hours and I'll show you drunk."

Pessoa tossed off his foreign tipple without a blink. He pushed his chair back. "There are other names on my list."

"Wait." Ned took a careful sip of his bourbon, felt the warming liquor comfort his throat. "You haven't told me why you were looking for me. You make the offer; I refuse; you go on to the next name. That's the way it's done."

"Is it?" Pessoa considered him expressionlessly for a moment. "Very well." He pulled his chair forward again. "We need pilots to flight-test a new airframe."

Ned waved the hand with the drink in it back and forth. "Test pilots are a dime a dozen," he said. "Why me? Why not hire Rockwell or General Dynamics? Or the government? They have plenty of jet jockeys. Is it a military plane?"

"No. This is purely a private venture. We need pilots with no—ah—complicating ties."

"Gotcha. Somebody at loose ends; somebody that nobody around here wants. Like me." He thought about it for a while. "You're Brazilian."

Pessoa inclined his head.

"Brazil makes damn fine midsize planes."

"Thank you."

"But you don't make the high-performance jobs. So why are you sniffing after a surpled NASA washout?"

The Brazilian cast a glance over the bourbon, the empty beer mugs. He locked eyes with Ned. "Can you still fly?"

Ned curled his mouth around a smile. "I can fly better drunk than most men can sober."

"Most men cannot fly at all," Pessoa pointed out.

"Which just goes to prove my point."

Pessoa leaned back in his chair and folded his hands under his lip as if in prayer. He held the pose for a moment, studying Ned. Ned gave him back a cold, steady look. Then Pessoa nodded. "I think I will trust you with something. Those who told me where to find you, they told me other things as well."

Ned laughed. "I'll just bet they did."

Pessoa bent forward again over the table. "Single Stage to Orbit," he said in a low voice.

A snappy, half-drunken reply expired in a sigh, and Ned's heart flipped over. Involuntarily, he raised his eyes to the battered, stained ceiling, though there was nothing there but a slowly rotating fan.

He had been up there once. Almost. Toward the end, when they all knew the program was being killed and the X-33 Prime would never fly. He had deviated from the mission profile, taken his bird up higher and higher, pushing the envelope until the sky turned black with stars. He remembered that aching moment, hanging there as the jets starved out and the wings failed to bite, just before inertial coupling put him into a flat spin and his craft took on the aerodynamics of a lead pipe. He could not remember fighting the controls, breaking the stall as the high desert reached up to swat him. That part he could not remember at all. Only that the sky turned black and all the stars came out.

"Sounds interesting," he allowed. He did not permit any of the hope to show in his voice. *Never show them how much you ache.* "It's not some kind of scam, is it?" He did not permit skepticism any more than hope. He played it as cool as any test pilot considering the chance of a lifetime. *Never flustered. Always in control.*

Pessoa took no offense. He smiled a self-deprecating, Latin smile. "I understand your caution," he said. "This is hardly the standard approach for such an offer, but we have no wish to draw attention at this stage of the project. Daedalus is an international staging corporation headquartered in Fortaleza, Ceará State, with research-and-development facilities in Natal and Recife and special test facilities in the Arquipélago de Fernando de Noronha. It is all very legitimate, I assure you, under Brazilian law."

But maybe not under U.S. law? Ned's hand gripping his bourbon glass was clenched tight. It took a conscious effort to loosen it. "Maybe," he said. His voice came out hoarse and he coughed to cover it. "Maybe you could show me around. Help me make up my mind."

Pessoa's face cracked into a thin, wary smile. "I think that can be arranged."

Ned smiled right back at him. *You put me in an SSTO, senhor, and you'll need a crowbar to get me out again.*

Pessoa wasted no time. Ned found himself booked the next day on a commercial flight from Galveston to Miami to Belem. First class, no less. In the airport, his bags checked through and a few minutes yet to boarding, he approached a bank of pay phones. Time for one call.

Yuppie business travelers monopolized the phones. Hunched, squeezing the handles against their ears with their shoulders to leave their hands free to flip through their Day Planners. Expandable briefcases sitting at their feet. The obsession to telephone in public. Pay phones, car phones, air phones. There ought to be a name for it. *Is it just to demonstrate self-importance?* he wondered. A status display. Like the way they flipped their laptops open at every opportunity, a cybernetic peacock's tail.

Ned stood close enough to one businessman to overhear him and waited, rubbing a quarter slowly with his thumb and forefinger. Finally, the man gave him an irritated look and brought his conversation to a close. "I'll call you back," Ned heard him say. Then he gathered his briefcase and hustled off. To another phone bank, no doubt. More messages; more instructions. *No wonder they have heart attacks,* thought Ned. *It's a wonder they don't drop like flies.* The trick, as Wally Schirra had always said, was to "maintain an even strain." The trick—maybe—was not to care about things too much.

Ned dropped his quarter in the phone and punched the area code for Houston, then the phone number. He waited for the operator to tell him how much to complete the call; then he dropped coins in one by one. A very sincere computer voice thanked him for using AT&T. There was a pause, then a ring. Another ring. *They're out,* he told himself. No one home. A third ring . . . and a child's voice answered.

"Hello?"

Ned's voice froze in his throat. He opened his mouth to say something and nothing came out. "Hello?" asked the voice again. "Who is this?"

Ned could hear the pulse in his ears. Loud, like a hammer. What could he say? Tell Mommy that I'm going away again and I don't know when I'll be back? What else was new? Betsy didn't care what he did anymore. It had gone past betrayal; it had gone past hate, into indifference. He was a stranger, and she was a stranger, and the fact that they shared one small thing was not enough.

In the end he hung up without speaking. He rooted in his pocket for another quarter and stood there stupidly at the phone with the coin in his hand until he remembered that there was no one else that he needed to call. He turned and relinquished the phone to the next yuppie in line.

Just as well, he thought. He hated long good-byes.

*   *   *

The last leg of the flight, from Recife to Fortaleza, was by Daedalus company jet. The pilot let him sit in the right-hand seat and jabbered at him in Portuguese the whole time. Ned understood not a word of it, but smiled and nodded at what seemed the right moments. The flight was surreal, because the pilot babbling in Portuguese bore unmistakably Japanese features and, whenever he spoke to control towers along the way, he switched to "airplane English." It was a crazy world.

They flew up along the coast, around the northern edge of the Great Escarpment. Rivers hurled themselves off the Highlands, cascading onto the narrow coastal plain. Past Maceió Point, the land opened up and the coastal towns below appeared less frequently. The pilot pointed vaguely toward the horizon and shot off a Gatling gun of a sentence in which Ned made out the single word "Amazonas." Ned agreed that, this being Brazil, the Amazon was undoubtedly somewhere nearby.

The pilot turned to him and smiled. "You fly?" He indicated the yoke in front of Ned.

Ned hesitated a moment, then nodded. "Sure." His hands gripped the yoke, testing its feel. He tried the foot pedals and the plane sashayed a bit across the sky. Ned grinned. It felt good, after such a long time. Nothing like a bit of abstinence to resurrect the thrill. He pulled back and the jet began to climb. *Take it up till the sky turns black.* No, this little sky limo would never do that. Still . . . The rush of the air over the fuselage sank into his skin; he felt the thrust of the jets at his back, the hum and vibration in his fingertips. He was wearing the ship, like a second skin, feeling its every mood, soaring through the air like Peter-fucking-Pan. There had been times in the past year, times so far down in the bottle he couldn't see the neck, when he had feared he would never sit here again.

When the pilot—his name badge read Jorje Minamoto—asked for the controls back, Ned took them through a barrel roll first, down close to the deck, twisting through the air like a corkscrew. That had been Yeager's signature maneuver back in the old days, when flying had meant breaking new barriers.

Minamoto looked startled at first, but he grinned wide as he took the yoke back and said, *"Muito bem feitas, senhor! Muito bem!"*

Ned shrugged with his hands. "Thanks, I guess. Uh, *gracias.*" Minamoto looked puzzled, and Ned gave up. Even if he could remember his high-school Spanish, it wouldn't do him any good here.

Shortly, Fortaleza da Nova Bragança swept below them. The port city was larger than Ned had expected—three-quarters of a million Brasilieros, the airport brochure claimed. The silt-heavy Paejú River bisected the city. Minamoto passed over the new harbor facilities at Mucuripe Point in the northeast, where beautiful, sleak *jangadas* plied the waters in the bay. Preparing for next month's regatta, Minamoto told him. Then he banked around to the airfield south of the city, providing Ned with a view of the *sertão*, the arid hinterlands south and west of the city and the source of the Paejú's sediment. Minamoto pointed out Daedalus's headquarters, a tall steel-and-glass structure that glittered in the tropical sunshine, just inland from the harbor. Ned stared out the windscreen as they buzzed past. He still had not gotten that part of the puzzle. Why was Brazil, of all countries, experimenting with SSTOs?

A company car took him from Pinto Martins airport to the Novatel Magna Fortaleza, facing Meireles Beach on President Kennedy Avenue. While he was signing the registration form, an arm draped itself around his shoulder and a bass voice thundered in his ear. "Ned DuBois, you old son of a bitch! How the hell are you?"

He turned from the registration desk and looked up into the grinning face of Forrest Calhoun. "Well, hey," he said, "if it isn't the second-best jet jockey in North America."

Forrest grinned. "That's what I thought when I saw you walk through the lobby. Good thing we're in *South* America. I was a-setting in the bar over yonder, enjoying myself one of these dago beers, and I thought to myself, Forrest, this here beer is too damn good to be drunk by one person."

"Why sure." Ned took the room key from the clerk and,

by long habit, hefted his flight bag to his shoulder. When you traveled light, you didn't need much more. Never take more baggage than you can handle. Good advice for life, in general. "Why sure, Forrest. If you need help holding your booze, I'll be glad to teach you what I know. And I know a *lot.*"

"I heard." Forrest guided him toward the bar with his arm. "C'mon, son. There's some folks over here I want you to meet." The big man was three years Ned's junior, but he always called him "son." Probably short for "son of a bitch." Come to think of it, Forrest called everyone "son." Yeager had done that, too, Ned remembered, back in the old days, and he wondered if Forrest thought of himself as the Black Yeager, only biding his time until some great, record-breaking accomplishment would plaster his name across the headlines.

"So. Is Brazil collecting NASA washouts, or something?"

Forrest's arm squeezed his neck just a little "Son, I never washed out of NASA. The program just grew a little too small for me."

"I suppose that's one way to look at cutbacks."

"You military johnnies, at least you had a trade to fall back on."

"Yeah." *At least until you nearly wreck a very expensive airplane.* Then they gave you a desk to fly, which was no damn fun at all, and you didn't even get to see the sun, let alone touch the stars. "Ex-military," he said. *Ex-a lot of things.* One more thing that Betsy could not understand. Why, when he was safely on the ground and had an assignment that brought him home on time each day, he had felt compelled to offer his resignation.

The others were waiting in the bar, seated around a low cocktail table already littered with dead soldiers. Forrest introduced everyone. Bobbi McFeeley had been a civilian test pilot for McDonnell-Douglas until the Christmas Recession put a lump of coal in her stocking. *McFeeley. What a name for a girl.* He could imagine the jokes. Too obvious and repeated too often. Ned eyed her small, compact body, boyish face, and short-cropped hair as they shook hands. Butch? He imagined he would find out, one way or the other, in the course of their training.

The other two pilots were Russians: Gregor Levkin and Mikhail Krasnarov. Levkin was moon-faced, with Oriental eyes and a dark complexion. Krasnarov was thin and bald, with a fringe of hair like a monk's tonsure, and a mustache that seemed to account for every hair missing from his skull.

Levkin smiled crookedly when they shook hands. "Odd, that we have finally joint Russian-American space program, but in Brazil."

Ned took an empty chair from the next table and pulled it into the group. He sat down and made motions to the bartender to bring a round. Forrest settled himself into the chair he had vacated earlier. "Friend Pessoa is supposed to meet us tomorrow morning. I think he's out rounding up more Russkies."

Ned took the long-neck bottle from the cocktail waitress and stuffed a dollar in the tip glass. The waitress looked impressed and Ned figured he must have overtipped, a lot. He'd have to learn the local currency. And enough of the local lingo to get by. He wondered how you said "Your place or mine?" in Portuguese. "Why Russians?" he said as he opened the bottle.

Krasnarov shrugged. "Better pilots," he suggested.

"And modest, too," said Forrest. "Don't flatter yourself, *gospodá*. It's only that more of your folks are at loose ends. And you work cheaper, too."

Levkin smiled, but Krasnarov bristled. "Perhaps in fighter planes we see who is better pilot," he suggested.

Forrest laughed. "Sorry; but 'homey don't play that.'"

Ned saw the puzzlement on the Russians' faces, but decided that explaining the remark would only confuse things more. "You guys think you're the best, don't you?" Ned did not direct the remark specifically to the Russians, but they both turned and looked at him. "Top of the pyramid, right?"

The two of them nodded. Krasnarov said, "Is none better."

"Good." Ned raised his glass, to the Russians, to Bobbi, to Forrest. "I've always wanted to work with the best. And

I'm sure the four of you will enjoy the experience every bit as much as I would have."

They woke him by banging on the door. "*Faltam cinco para as oito, senhor.*" Ned groaned and pulled the pillow down over his head. The banging continued.

"Go ahead. Vamoose!"

A hand shook him gently by the shoulder. "They say it is time for the mister to awaken."

Ned groaned and rolled over on his back. The waitress rubbed her hand across his chest in slow circles. The tips of her nails tickled. "He say it is almost eight of the clock," she said.

He opened his eyes and saw that she was propped up on her elbow beside him with the sheets draped around her hips. He admired the curve and swell of her body, the hint at the edge of the sheet. When she saw that his eyes were open she leaned over and kissed him gently on the mouth. Her breasts rubbed against him, and her hand glided down to his belly.

"I guess you're trying to get me up, too," he said to her.

"*Senhor?*"

"Never mind. It's probably not funny in Portuguese." The banging at the door resumed and he grabbed his head in both hands. There went the theory that alcohol was a cure for jet lag. "All right!" he shouted at the door. "I hear you!" The clock read eight in the morning, but his brain still insisted it was five. He had never realized how far *east* South America was. He had lost three hours from Galveston.

He reached out and encircled the waitress's waist, pulling her to him. She moved against him and they kissed again, more slowly this time. He could feel her delicious curves pressing into him. He knew that she had told him her name last night. They had traded a few perfunctory sentences and surely names had been among them. But, damn-all if he could remember it.

He disengaged and sat up in bed. The waitress rolled over on her back, ready if he was, but not angry or even disappointed if he was not. It was just a thing with her, he thought.

It was just something that you did, like brushing your teeth. Some people jogged. He slid out of bed and stood and stretched, arms clamped behind his head, his back arched. There was a mirror on the inside of the half-open bathroom door. In it, he could see the girl from the bar, watching.

Ned knew that he had the sort of body that women were interested in. Broad shoulders, narrow waist and hips, everything tight. He pretended not to notice her regard and flexed a few muscles here and there, just loosening up. "I'm going to take a shower," he announced. "Then we're all going out to Fernando de Noronha." He turned and faced her. "Daedalus is putting us into barracks out on the archipelago. Maybe I'll see you sometime when I get into town."

Maybe. Tomorrow was another day and there was room in it for another girl. It had always been that way. At Lompoc, at Edwards, at Canaveral. There was never any shortage of willing females, eager to let an astronaut practice docking maneuvers. Betsy had never understood that, that he had never sought it out, that it came to him, that it was thrown at him and you had to be some sort of statue not to take it when it was offered like that on a silver platter. Betsy always thought it was a flaw in his personality, something that, at first, she had thought she could change.

The waitress joined him in the shower. The curtain parted and she slipped in beside him. He let her soap him up and returned the favor, so the shower took twice as long. Yeah, he thought as the hot water cascaded over their linked bodies, running over their shoulders, arms, and backs. There were some who accepted you for what you were, who never questioned, and who never, ever tried to change you. Girls who only wanted the same thing you wanted: not to spend the night alone.

Even in the tropics, Ned thought as the commuter jet soared across the gray chop, *even in the tropics, the Atlantic looks cold.* There were plenty of white-sand beaches, stretching from the Caribbean to Rio, places where the cold never seeped in, where Latin *wahinis* sambaed or lambadaed under palm trees, wearing string bikinis instead of grass skirts. But once you were out of sight of shore, once you were over the ocean itself, the Atlantic reasserted itself. East of Cape São Roque there was nothing much that wasn't wet, and the archipelago of Fernando de Noronha lay six hundred kilometers out. Another time zone down the tubes.

"Whoo-ee," said Forrest Calhoun, leaning across Ned to stare out the window when the islands appeared on the horizon. "Look at that. Nothing but a lump of volcanic rock with a few ole pebbles tossed on the side. How are they ever going to put a spaceport down there?"

João Pessoa looked up from the folder he had spread out over his lap. "That is only the test facility. The spaceport—" He clammed up.

"The spaceport what?"

The general manager smiled. "Is a dream of *o ficção científica.*"

Forrest looked at Ned. "Did he say science fiction, son?"

Ned shrugged. "That's what it sounded like."

"Then you tell me . . ." And Forrest leaned close to Ned's ear and whispered. "Why build an SSTO if you ain't planning on a bit of regular flying somewheres down the road?" Forrest turned and sat back straight in his seat. He closed his eyes. "I ain't planning on playing Moses."

The Daedalus test field occupied most of the north end of the island. A complex of low, gunmetal gray buildings, half still under construction, lined the coast of St. Anthony's Bay. The roofs bristled with radar and communication pylons. The windows were small, black, and anonymous. At the right end of the cluster was a control tower. Another tower was visible at the far tip of the island, on the other side of a broad, tarmacked landing field. Beyond that, a smaller island, Ilha Rasa, rose above the rocking waves. Breakwaters jutted out into the bay itself, enclosing the waters into a harbor. A large crane and wharf was mounted on the northern jetty.

Ned stood on the tarmac with the other test pilots as the whine of the jet slowly died away. There were seven of them now, just like the original seven Mercury astronauts, but four Russians and three Americans; five men and two women. The breeze was fresh and warm.

Pessoa had told them that the island was rocky and semi-arid, supplied with food from the mainland. Farther south, to the left of where they stood, Ned could see a smallish peak rising along the middle coast. About three hundred feet, he guessed. There was a nature preserve on that side of the island, Pessoa said; but it had been closed to tourism for more than a year, because of damage to the ecosystem by well-meaning but too-eager tourists. Ned wondered at the juxtaposition of a marine national park and an aerospace testing facility, until he remembered the same held true on Cape Canaveral.

Two large buildings, each maybe two hundred feet tall, stood at the southern end of the field. *The hangars and support facilities*, he guessed as Pessoa guided them toward the main building. That's where they keep the bird.

Pessoa waved his arm in a broad gesture. "In the early days," he said, "the island was used as a penal colony. Her two thousand inhabitants live mostly in the two villages of Quixaba and Vila dos Remédias. Since the tourism was stopped, her main product is guano, though that too may be running out."

Forrest said, "No shit?" Ned laughed and Pessoa gave them both a sour look.

It was a tight little base, Ned decided. The staff numbered only a couple of hundred, and some of those were construction workers, who would be gone when the last of the buildings was finished. Daedalus was not wasting any money on the facilities—most everything was prefab—but they were not cutting corners, either, not where it counted; and that was a good sign. You didn't want to fly a bird designed by accountants.

Pessoa took them to the front offices, where they met Bonifácio de Magalhães, Daedalus's operations manager for Fernando Test Field, and Heitor Carneiro, his deputy. De Magalhães was a short, dapper, bantam cock of a man with slick, black hair and a Latin mustache, the sort of man you always imagined catching in the wrong bedrooms. Carneiro, standing cross-armed by the wall behind him, was taller, plumper in the face, but bald and sporting a bushier mustache. De Magalhães shook hands with them and called each of them by name, which proved to Ned he had done his homework. The man's office was austere and functional, the only out-of-place item being a samba drum in one corner.

Ned sat against the wooden credenza littered with books and papers that lined one wall. It was de Magalhães's bell. He could start ringing it anytime.

"Welcome to Fernando Test Field," de Magalhães said. "I am sure you must be tired after so long a trip, so I will be brief. Heitor will show you to your billets, where you may rest and acclimate yourselves. Tomorrow, Heitor will take you on a brief tour of our facilities. On Monday, we begin your technical briefings on the design concepts and Heitor will give you your assignments. Once you have become familiar with the design, you will begin training on the simulator. Our simulator—" and the man swelled visibly "—is state-of-the-art virtual reality. It will be like flying the real thing."

That remark told Ned the one thing about de Magalhães that he wanted to know. Whatever his skills at administration, and they must be considerable to have merited this assignment, the man was not a pilot.

The next day, Carneiro showed them around the site. Their quarters, first: private rooms with a housekeeping staff on call. Then the recreation facilities, the gymnasium and indoor track, the library, the mess hall, the much-acclaimed simulator, even the as-yet-incomplete Payload Processing Facility, one of the two large buildings at the south end of the field. Ned kept a grip on his patience. He knew that Carneiro, like a good showman, was saving the best act until last.

"The Support Hangar," Carneiro told them as they approached the last building, "covers two square kilometers of space. It contains one Payload Mating Station, where vehicles will receive prepared payloads, plus four maintenance bays.

Only the Phase II prototype is inside. Three Phase III vehicles are under construction and will be delivered soon. Watch your step as you pass through the door, please; and move to your left at the top of the stairs.''

After the walk through the tropical brightness, it took a moment for Ned's eyes to adjust to the dim interior of the hangar. Blue and red guide lights lined the ladders and walkways. White light leaked from an office on a catwalk high above them. A dark shape slowly emerged from the gloom. Ned touched his lips with a quick movement of his tongue. The orientation had been interesting; the facilities, satisfactory; but the payoff was the bird.

Carneiro hit a wall switch and a bank of floods bathed the ship in light. *Showoff...* But Ned sucked in his breath; and he noticed that the others beside him—even Forrest, who was never impressed with anything—gasped at the sight.

The vehicle was a truncated cone, slightly oblate, with a carbon-carbon heat shield on one side. Two hundred feet tall and sixty feet in diameter. Graceful, smooth, gleaming silver, except for the scorch marks on the lower edge. Beautiful in a way that lovers of lesser beauty could never appreciate. It stood—*it crouched*—on five hydraulic legs spaced around the circumference. Ned whistled when he saw that. Vertical takeoff and landing, just like the comic-book spaceships of old; except that this bird had no flaring fins. Pessoa had not told him that.

Ned's gaze traveled toward the nose, caressing the sweet, aerodynamic curve of the hull. The aeroshell, extending from just below the nose cone to just above the wells for the maneuvering flap, was a skin of titanium aluminide, to withstand reentry temperatures. The catwalk clanged under their tread as they slowly circled the ship.

"What sort of engines?" one of the Russians asked, leaning over the railing and staring down into the work pit. A new arrival, Valery something or other; and what a godawful name for a guy. "I cannot see the nozzles from here."

"Aerospike." It was a new voice, and Ned looked up to spot a squat man in a white lab coat standing outside the lighted office on the open-grille metal catwalk above them. He had broad features, half Indio, half Negro. He stood with his arms crossed and studied them. João Pessoa was with him.

Carneiro nodded. "This is Luis Mendoza, our chief project engineer. I will let him explain. . . ." Carneiro's voice hooked a small question mark on the end of the sentence, like he was not too sure that Mendoza would.

Ned did not know what the engineer was looking for or if he found it, but finally the man grunted and pointed toward the base of the ship. "Truncated aerospike. Reduces operating pressures." His accent was liquid, guttural—different from the barmaid's or from Pessoa's.

Ned waited for more details. When the silence lengthened, he said, "Reduced to what?"

"Fifty-five dynes/cm². " A pause; then, grudgingly, "Extends system lifetime."

A man of few words, thought Ned. The Space Shuttle Main Engine operated at 225 dynes/cm². If Mendoza spoke sooth, it meant a lot less wear and tear on these engines.

Krasnarov spoke up. "What does she burn?"

"Liquid oxygen and slush hydrogen," said Mendoza.

Yekaterina, Valery's wife, looked up sharply. "Slush? Is using standard pumping and cryogenics, no?" Mendoza nodded and did not elaborate.

Bobbi said, "Why an aerospike? Don't you lose efficiency that way?"

A shrug more elegant than words. After a glance at Mendoza, Carneiro spoke up. "We have used high-strength ceramics and ion-implantation manufacturing to reduce the corrosion and heat dissipation that NASA's old aerospike design suffered."

"What's the payload ratio?" Forrest asked.

Mendoza gave him a long, calculating look. "Design is three percent," he said at last. Three percent of gross liftoff weight was pretty fair, Ned thought, but not spectacular. Most of any rocket's power went into lifting its own fuel and oxidizer.

Forrest scratched his chin. "That's design, son. What's actual?"

Mendoza turned and said something to Pessoa, who said something right back. It was not Portuguese. Mendoza turned abruptly and entered the office behind him. The door slammed. Pessoa glanced at Carneiro, then shrugged, smiling uncertainly.

"Dr. Mendoza said that actual performance is what *you* are to tell *him*, through flight-test data."

Forrest leaned close to Ned's ear. "Friendly cuss, wasn't he?"

"Not everybody's as mean and ornery as you are, Forrest."

"Know what I think? I think the reason Luis doesn't smile is because that'd show how his teeth were filed down to points."

"He should be an accountant, then, not an engineer." Ned wasn't sure about Mendoza, either. Unfriendly, or simply taciturn? He only knew that when the man had looked at the ship it had been with the eyes of a lover.

Pessoa descended the stairs to join them. "What do you think of our beauty, my friends? Has Heitor explained everything to you?"

"Everything," said Forrest Calhoun, "except what you're really up to."

"Ah." Pessoa exchanged a look with Carneiro, who shrugged. Pessoa nodded, then addressed the group. "This project is under the most strict secrecy," he warned them. "It is known to the project team within Daedalus, and to a wider group within the parent corporation, selected officials of the Brazilian government, and a small group of sympathizers in North America. . . ."

Forrest chuckled. "Hell, son, why not just take out an ad?" Pessoa was not amused.

"We do not expect to maintain secrecy indefinitely, but we wish to retain our advantage for as long as possible. As Heitor may have already told you, this craft has been built with off-the-shelf technology. Some details of the plug nozzles, some of the microavionics, and so forth, are proprietary, but nothing would be difficult for any of our competitors to duplicate. Our objective is reliable and inexpensive access to Low Earth Orbit. Disposable spacecraft are costly. Imagine what an airline flight would cost if, after each flight, the entire plane—or even just its engines—were then thrown into the ocean!''

Levkin chuckled. ''I have done that; but not on purpose. . . .''

''We have designed and built the Plank for Class-A recovery,'' Pessoa continued. ''Everything is reusable. Everything is modular. Turnaround on the ground will be greatly reduced, in time and manpower. We expect to drop the cost to airline operating regimes: less than a third of an ounce of fine gold per kilo, compared to the Shuttle's fifteen-to thirty-troy-ounce range. In fact, we propose to have the Plank certificated, like an ordinary aircraft.''

Forrest cocked his head. ''Why gold, son?''

Pessoa looked uncomfortable and shrugged. ''Daedalus's parent corporation prefers to do its accounting in gold. It, ah, simplifies international currency exchanges.''

Bobbi spoke up. ''Will we be paid in gold, too?'' The Russians said nothing, but their attitude expressed their interest. Pessoa shrugged again.

''Yes. In drafts based on the daily Zurich fix and convertible to whichever local currency is most convenient. Most likely, to Brazilian *reals*.''

''Why not in dollars?'' asked Ned. Not that it mattered to him. They were working in Brazil, after all; and the dollar had long ago assumed its natural value as a small piece of finely printed paper. Ned never had gotten used to the new bills with the off-centered portraits. It looked like play money to him. Still, the salary Pessoa had quoted in Galveston had been in dollars.

Now Pessoa really looked uncomfortable. He shifted his stance slightly. ''You may take your pay in dollars, if you wish. Or in rubles. Perhaps some of you wish to send money home, yes?''

But Pessoa would not take dollars on a bet. Why? High finance was way out of his league, Ned decided. As long as his paycheck didn't bounce and there were plenty of women to spend it on, he didn't care if he was paid in gold dust or coconut juice. But he wondered what Pessoa, or Daedalus, or the mysterious parent corporation knew. Maybe it was time to stuff the mattresses again?

Ned hung back while Pessoa led them out into the sunshine. One last look. The Plank squatted there as thickset and laconic as Mendoza.

There was something funny going on. Low cost regime. The comparison with airlines. Pessoa had mentioned certificates of airworthiness. That was not a government talking. Standard, off-the-shelf technology. Building three prototypes just for flight test. That was a standard docking collar fixed to the bird's nose. And, unless he was sore mistaken, those fittings on the upper and lower fuselage meant it was refuelable in orbit. Whoever was behind this project was already thinking in terms of docking and maneuvering and extended operations.

Most of the energy needed for space travel was to get off the earth and into orbit. Once there, you were halfway to any-where in the solar system. He followed the others out of the building and looked up into the moist, tropic sky. Two hun-dred miles, straight up. Space was closer than Rio. Closer than Galveston. Closer than Betsy.

3.

"Dream Your Way Ahead"

Barry Fast drove slowly down the narrow, two-lane black-top, searching for driveways hidden by the thick, summer foliage, late for a meeting with his new bosses. Old Coppice Lane was bordered on both sides by bright yellow forsythia bushes and dense stands of sycamores and maples, interrupted here and there by clusters of orange tiger lilies. The plants grew on raised berms on either side, so that the road seemed to wend its way along a shallow trench.

Barry's Escort banged through another rough spot, and he prayed the shocks would hold up. Old Coppice Lane was surprisingly potholed, considering the gentry that lived off of it.

Through gaps in the foliage, Barry caught glimpses of vast, rolling estates. Large houses in elegant settings. Victorian houses. Modern houses. Rambling houses of nameless architecture. Driveways that vanished behind hillock or copse on their way to even more remote dwellings. Once, he spotted a distant horse and rider in graceful midleap over a deadfall.

Amazing, how the local Rich and Famous, heirs to long-vanished textile mills and ironworks, managed to live in isolation only a brick-toss from the barbecues and ranch houses of the Unknown and Just Getting By. The subdivisions lapped around the edges of the estates like barbarians encircling the palaces of Rome with their rude encampments. Barry grunted to himself as he negotiated another crack in the pavement. Maybe they thought that by keeping the road in disrepair they could discourage casual bourgeois sightseers.

That was the stoplight up ahead where Old Coppice crossed the state road. He slammed on his brakes and his car skidded to a stop. Damn! He must have come too far. How could you get lost on a two-lane road with no turnoffs? Well, Karr had warned him that the driveway was hard to spot. Barry put the Escort into reverse and listened to the gears grind and clunk into place. The old crate needed work, no doubt about it; and someday, when he had the cash to spare, he would get it done, no fooling.

He backed the car around and retraced his route more slowly, watching for the promised driveway. *Why does the Boss Lady want to see me?* he wondered again. She didn't know him from Paddy's pig. If he knew why he had been invited, he could prepare, lay out his arguments or excuses or thanks. But to go in blank . . . Mentor business, of course. But why at the van Huyten mansion? Karr ran Mentor; van Huyten only owned it. He ran his hands around the rim of the steering wheel, tapped it with his fingers. *This lady can buy and sell you,* he told himself. *She can blow more on a single party than you make in an entire year.*

There it was! He hit the brakes again and turned hard left onto a dirt driveway set between two towering black oaks. There was nothing more than a small placard on the gate announcing "518." And if you did not look for it, you would never know it was there.

The driveway passed through a massive wrought-iron gate hidden by the trees, and meandered through a grove of white birch over a slight rise and across a broad dell covered with pink and violet wildflowers. Where the ground rose again at the rear of the property, well out of sight of the road, a large building perched atop an artificial hill. The building was vaguely Colonial in appearance, with a cupola and rows of jalousie-shuttered windows. At the base of the hill a flock of brown-and-green geese floated and honked on a wide pond. Flagstoned stairs led from the parking apron and basement garage entrance to an arched doorway. There were a half-dozen cars parked there. None of them made his Escort look good, and two of them made it look positively ramshackle. Around the mansion, the wild grasses surrendered themselves to manicured perfection. *Field* became *lawn,* clipped to precise length, garnished with elegantly shaped trees and shrubs. Barry shook his head. It had cost him a hundred a month for the biweekly lawn service, back when he could afford the luxury of not mowing his own grass. He could not imagine what it cost to maintain so many acres in putting-green condition.

Or to sculpt a small mountain to set your house upon.

The rich are different from you and me, Fitzgerald was supposed to have said to Hemingway.

Yes, Hemingway had drawled, they have more money.

Sure. And the only difference between a firecracker and an artillery shell was more powder. How big did a fortune have to be before it became self-sustaining, immune even to wastrel heirs? Where even the annual interest was wealth beyond his imaginings. At what point did a difference in degree *become* a difference in kind?

Don't let it get to you, he warned himself. *The only thing money does is it insulates you from reality.*

He looked again at the sprawling building, the leaded-glass windows, the statuary and shrubbery, and shook his head. *And that's one hell of a lot of insulation.*

A butler showed him to a long, comfortable sunroom set with cushioned wicker chairs. The ceiling and one wall were paneled in glass, providing a view of the woodlands that backed the estate at the base of Skunktown Mountain. In the distance, the afternoon sunshine highlighted a doe and two fawns grazing warily just by the edge of the trees.

Several people were seated around a low glass coffee table at the far end of the room. They looked up when he entered, and Belinda Karr separated herself from the group and strode over to greet him. Barry sent a sincere smile in her direction. He wondered how long the meeting would take and whether Shannon would wait for him as she had promised.

The best-laid plans . . . Robbie Burns had sure pegged that right, Barry thought. The same went for the best-planned lays. All of Shannon's careful arrangements, torpedoed by one unexpected phone call. Barry smiled as if he were glad to be here.

"Mr. Fast," she said. "I'm so glad you could come." She took his hand and squeezed briefly but firmly. "Let's go meet the others." She conducted him back to the table, where a sideboard had been set with a coffee and tea service. Barry recognized the two Institute Fellows that Mentor had brought in to facilitate the transition and run the summer training seminars.

"Dr. Wu," he said, extending a hand across the table. "At least when I don't have my homework at tomorrow's session, you'll know why. . . ." Benford Wu had a classic Oriental face, heightened by long, black mustaches; yet he spoke with a flat, General American accent. His family had lived in the Willamette Valley of Oregon for more than a hundred years. Barry nodded to the other Institute Fellow, a Nigerian named Onwuka Egbo. "Sorry I'm late," he said. "Hi, Wanda." Wanda Szyzmanski, a slim blonde, taught algebra at Witherspoon. He recognized the bald man, Bernie Paulson, and the new teacher with the elf ears, Mary Gorley. The dark, chubby woman, then, had to be Mariesa van Huyten.

But it was the tall woman from the hotel who rose and extended her hand at Karr's introduction. Barry stiffened. "You," he said.

Van Huyten nodded. "Me," she agreed. She was wearing a navy skirt and a simple white blouse under an unbuttoned suede vest. A plainer outfit than the printed frock and costume jewelry she had sported at the district meeting, it was of a distinctly better cut.

Barry took the offered hand. "Well, I guess I know why I'm here," he said flatly.

"Really?" Van Huyten resumed her seat and draped one

arm over the back of her chair. "Why do you suppose?" Barry suddenly realized, seeing her sitting that way, how young she was. Rather early in life to have made the mark she had made; though her short, tawny hair was accented with streaks of premature gray and her eyes had small lines at the corners.

"It's obvious, isn't it?" he said. "I shot my mouth off pretty good at the hotel, and right to your face, too. So let's get this over with. Ream me out or fire me or do whatever it is you have in mind. But let me just say that it was pretty damned sneaky the way you tricked me."

"Was it?" Van Huyten seemed amused. "How else do you suppose I might hear people shoot their mouths off?"

"Eh?"

"Mr. Fast, people in my position seldom have a problem hearing what people think we want to hear. 'Kissing up,' I believe it is called. I dislike having others decide what *I* want to hear. I want good advice and good ideas, Mr. Fast, whatever the source and however unpleasant. And that is why you are here. Please be seated."

"It is." With a nervous smile, Barry lowered himself into the offered seat. That put him across the table from van Huyten. Good advice and good ideas? Even his wildest scenarios had not included that.

"You may already know your colleagues: Marie DePardo, Wanda Szyzmanski, and Bernard Paulson. Like you, they are teachers who said things at the orientation meeting that I found interesting. Dr. Karr and the Institute Fellows have been observing you during the last school quarter and at the summer training seminars, and they concur."

Well, goody for them. Barry looked at the other teachers and they looked at him. He saw his own what-am-I-doing-here look reflected in their eyes. Wu reached for the service. "Coffee or tea? Sweet roll?"

Barry took a cup of black. The cups and saucers were fine china, the sort that in middle-class homes might be hidden away to await special events. Everyday china to the van Huytens. He took a sip and found the taste fresh and clear, with very little bitterness. Made with a fresh filter, he decided, and in a clean pot; the beans, roasted no more than five hours before grinding. No beverage in the country was served more often than Bad Coffee; it was refreshing to drink a well-made cup. He took another sip. "Jamaica Blue Mountain?" he asked. Living in Seattle had taught him to recognize most of the common varieties.

Van Huyten raised an eyebrow. "A special blend. But Jamaican, to be sure." She sank back in her chair with her hands clasped under her chin and her elbows propped on the arms. She looked to her left. "Belinda? This is your show."

Barry sat back and cradled his cup in his hand. Special blend. Yeah. Try buying this down at the A&P. You were rich enough, you could buy anything, even a school district. Maybe not the teachers, though. He put a cooperative look on his face. He would get through this somehow or other.

Belinda Karr looked at them one by one, engaging their attention. "I have asked you here this afternoon to discuss Mentor Institute and its role within Mentor Academies. Ah, thank you, Benford." She accepted a cup of coffee, tasted it, and nodded. "This is fine. Now, I understand"—with the briefest glace at Barry—"there was some concern whether Mentor would be open to innovation. Let me assure you that innovation is as necessary in education as it is in other industries. Onwuka?" At Karr's signal, Egbo handed each of them a packet containing a booklet, a slickly produced brochure, and a variety of papers and forms. Barry set his cup down on the table and took them, aware of van Huyten's silent regard. *If this is Karr's show, why is* she *kibbitzing?* He flipped through a page or two of the brochure. Beautifully staged photographs of teachers and children in a variety of classroom settings, from "traditional" to "under the trees." The children all looked impossibly eager; the teachers, improbably dedicated. A teaser line in brush letters asked, *Which Way Works?*

That was an easy one: (d) all the above. (Or—more likely these days—(e) none.) It depended on the teacher, on the students, on the subject or circumstances. Scanning the ad copy, he was surprised to find that that was the very answer Mentor gave. Funny. He had had them pegged as Back-to-the-Basics enthusiasts. According to Shannon, the elementary schools were going to be using the old McGuffey's Readers, and if you went "back" much further than that, you'd be poking reeds in mud trays. He closed the brochure.

"My impression from the orientation meeting," he said to Karr, "was that this institute of yours dictated the courses and materials for the schools."

Karr exchanged a brief glance with van Huyten. "Not dictate, exactly; but since all our graduates bear the Mentor name, we require a certain amount of product uniformity—"

"Students are not 'product,' " he interrupted. *Let's see if van Huyten really wants to hear unpleasant advice.* Barry would go along with a lot of shit, but he had drawn a few lines in the sand, here and there.

"No, of course not," Karr said smoothly, as if she had handled the objection countless times before. "The students are our *customers*, not our product." She plucked one of the booklets from the table in front of her. "This is our 'product catalog,' ladies and gentlemen. We produce and deliver courses of instruction, both individually and packaged into diploma programs." She flipped it open. "The courses come in several 'models,' geared toward different student backgrounds or toward different 'production processes'—that is, different instructional methods."

Customers, products, models, production processes . . . Barry grinned. "I suppose the textbooks are our 'tooling'?"

Karr closed the catalog and tossed it back on the table. "Along with other instructional aids. And the tests and examinations are your 'inspection gauges' . . ."

"I was joking. . . ."

Van Huyten interrupted, giving Karr what Barry took to be an impatient glance. "I realize that many of you, perhaps most of you, may dislike Belinda's manufacturing analogies. I should like you to be informed by them, as well. Any process can produce defective products and shoddy workmanship. Education is no exception. Learn to recognize and deal with them, as any machinist or engineer would."

Barry held his peace. According to his brother Raymond,

the engineers where he worked dealt with defects mainly through Denial.

Karr waited a moment longer to be sure van Huyten had finished before she resumed. "Institute fellows are tasked with curriculum R&D for all of Mentor's self-governing academies, including those public schools we have contracted to operate. Mentor and the State of New Jersey impose some mandatory requirements, but they are confined primarily to learning objectives." A sardonic glance at Barry. "Call them the 'functional specifications,' if you like. That is, we care *what* you accomplish, not *how* you accomplish it. Each of our practices is free to adapt to the needs of its own student-customers." She leaned a little forward over the table. "Think of the Institute as Mentor's nervous system, networking information from practice to practice. When one of our masters proposes a new method, Institute Fellows study its effectiveness, determine the reasons for its success—or its failure!—and develop and facilitate training seminars to disseminate the information to other practices, so that other teachers may learn how, and under what circumstances, the same method may work for them."

"Which is not as easy as it sounds," Egbo added smoothly in a deep, rolling voice modulated by strange accents. "Too much so-called innovation in our field has come from fast-talking salesmen shilling unvalidated materials with catchy, feel-good labels at sales meetings thinly disguised as 'seminars.' We at the Institute must validate methods with statistical rigor."

Barry nodded. "I see. And what has that to do with me?" He glanced at the other teachers. "With us?"

Karr raised her eyebrows. "Why, isn't it obvious? We would like to invite you to join the Institute staff."

Barry sat back in his chair. "Join the Institute?" He turned to van Huyten. "After all I've said?"

"There is an application form with your packets."

Barry glanced at the folder, then back at van Huyten. "I've heard a lot from you people this summer that I like," he admitted, "but I've also heard a lot that bothers me. The education-manufacturing comparison . . . Maybe there are some useful insights here. I'll have to think about it. But you can carry it too far. I don't want education at Witherspoon to become something 'manufactured' by some impersonal, corporate teaching machine.''

Van Huyten nodded. "Then, who better to have on staff?"

"Who better . . . ?"

"To guard against that possibility."

Barry cocked his head to the side and considered the woman. "I'll say this, lady. You've got guts."

"I want Fellows who can innovate," van Huyten said bluntly. "You do not want education 'mechanized.' How can you better achieve your goal than by helping me achieve mine?"

Barry shook his head in genuine admiration. He reached out and picked up his coffee cup again. "Is this what they call a win-win situation? You scratch my back, I'll scratch yours?"

"Is there something so terribly wrong with that concept? Or have you never suffered an inaccessible itch?"

Barry laughed at the sudden, incongruous image of van Huyten and himself, hunkered down like two chimps, scratching and grooming one another. He raised his coffee cup to his lips and studied the woman over the rim as he sipped. Too much skin and bone, he thought; not unattractive, but not as well upholstered as Shannon.

"Will the position require relocation?" DePardo asked with a nervous sideways glance at Barry. "Where is the Institute located?"

Karr placed her cup back on its saucer. "The Institute is wherever its Fellows are," she said. "They usually meet on-line, on VHI's network. Sometimes they teleconference, but there are occasional face meetings, too. We hold an annual technical conference; and each region usually includes a handful of Fellows who gather socially as well as professionally."

Wanda Szyzmanski waved a hand. "Wait. You mean this is in addition to our regular teaching job?"

Karr nodded. "We lighten the teaching load for Institute Fellows, but we still expect them to keep a foot in the classroom. Surely, you prefer that curriculum development be in the hands of working teachers, rather than academics?"

"Of course, but . . ."

Barry pointed to Karr's lapel. "Is that the Institute's pin the four of you are wearing?"

Karr's hand went to her jacket lapel and she stared down at the brooch fastened there, as if astonished to find it. It was a gold pin in the shape of a fireball streaming from an outstretched hand. A small, red gemstone accented the fireball. Karr, van Huyten, and the others exchanged glances. Then van Huyten shook her head. "No, Mr. Fast. The pin is for members of a special task force that includes personnel from several VHI divisions."

And a pretty damned important task force, too, if it includes the Boss Lady. Barry sat back, leaning on one arm of the chair, and rubbed his chin with his hand. The hand-and-fireball logo meant something big. He could tell by the way the four had looked at each other before replying and by the fact that it was van Huyten who had answered for them. Whatever it was, it was bigger than the North Orange school district; bigger than Mentor itself. It involved VHI at its top levels. Barry had no idea what the logo signified, but it was something to keep filed away in the back of his mind. Whatever else the takeover had done, it had opened up opportunities not normally available to lowly school teachers.

Szyzmanski shook her head. "I don't think this Institute deal is for me. I mean, I do like trying out new ways to teach the subject, but the rest of it—the development of the materials and putting on seminars for other teachers, in addition to teaching my own courses—well, I don't know if I want to do that."

Karr nodded. "I understand. Though, we hope you will still contribute ideas." She turned to the other woman. "Ms. DePardo?"

The dark woman smiled. "Are you kidding, Dr. Karr? It's a job to die for. Why, I used to do that sort of thing every day when I was in the training department at IBM. We'd put together all sorts of seminars for the managers and engineers.

Write the training manuals. Prepare slide shows. Booklets. And all on a deadline, too.''

Karr nodded again. ''Thank you, Ms. DePardo. I think you will be a definite asset to the Institute. Gentlemen?''

Bernie Paulson simply bobbed his head. ''Surely,'' he said gently.

Barry grinned at her before she could ask. ''Count me in, too. I like a challenge.'' One thing Raymond had taught him, before he had vanished into gray-suited anonymity in the corporate ranks. Barry, he had said, never, ever turn down an offer. Because if you do, they'll never, ever make you another.

It was sundown when the meeting ended and they left the mansion. Barry twisted the ignition key and pressed the gas pedal to the floor. The motor growled and turned over, but the engine would not catch. The battery wasn't dead—the whole car shook when he cranked it over, like a teased animal straining at its leash—but if he kept at it, the charge would drain and then he would really be stuck. He switched the key off and smacked the dashboard with his right hand; then he slumped in his seat.

Van Huyten had stood at the front door to bid her guests good-bye. Now, as the last car departed, she descended the steps to the parking apron and stood by Barry's Escort. ''Are you having trouble?'' she asked.

No, this is the way it always starts. He didn't say that, but he thought it rather loudly. And, hell, it was near enough true. ''There's something wrong with the fuel pump or the distributor. It's an intermittent fault and the shop hasn't been able to trace it yet. It'll start okay if I let it sit for a while.''

''Oh.'' Van Huyten looked puzzled. Well, she had probably never had to contend with a balky machine. She had probably never had to stretch a car out beyond its warranty, patching and replacing as she went, trying to squeeze just another fifty thousand out of it and then maybe another twenty, because it wasn't worth jack cheese as a trade-in anymore and who had the down payment for a new one anyway? The Escort was a good car, as good as any of the imports in its price range; but not even Ford had intended them to be driven as long as this one. "Would you care to wait inside?" she asked.

No. I'd rather sit out here in the dark. "Sure. Thanks." He climbed out. The sun was on the crest of the hills. The first few stars were blooming in a sky already a deep, somber blue. "I hate to impose, though."

Van Huyten hugged herself. "It's growing chilly. Come inside. I'll have Sykes call Laurence Sprague and have him send a man over to see what he can do."

"You don't have to go to all that trouble, Ms. van Huyten. It'll start again if it just sits for a while."

"It's no trouble," she assured him. "And you may call me Mariesa."

Oh, gee. Can I? Barry grunted. No trouble, at all. *She* wasn't going to fix his car. She wasn't even going to send someone to fix his car. She wasn't even going to *call* someone to send someone to fix his car. She would tell Sykes; and Sykes would call Sprague; and this Sprague fellow would pull some poor bastard of a mechanic away from his dinner table to come out to the country and futz with a ten-year-old Escort. Is that what it meant to be rich? That you never had to give a second thought to that sort of thing?

He got out of his car and locked it (silly habit . . . who'd steal it here? who'd steal it anywhere?), and they climbed the flagstone steps to the front door. "Why don't you join me in my eyrie while we wait?" she said. "I was planning a bit of stargazing tonight."

Barry hesitated the barest moment. "Sure," he said, and followed her inside. He'd be a great fool to turn down an invitation like that.

Belinda Karr was waiting in the mosaic-tiled entry hall with two glasses of sherry in her hands. When she saw Barry she raised her eyebrows. "Barry, what's wrong?"

He made a face. "Car trouble," he said. He saw that van Huyten had gone off to locate Sykes. "Mariesa is going to have someone come over and fix it." Van Huyten's given name sounded odd on his tongue, as if he had taken liberties. "Meanwhile," he finished with a nod of his head toward the ceiling, "I've been invited to an astronomy session."

"Have you?" Karr looked momentarily at the glasses in her hands. "Would you care for some wine?" she said, offering one. Barry accepted the glass but did not drink from it immediately. After a moment, Karr said, "Didn't you mention another engagement earlier?"

If Shannon was still waiting in the motel room . . . "Do you think Mariesa would mind if I used her phone?"

Karr pointed to a set on a small table near the elevator doors. "I am sure it would be all right."

Barry went to the phone and set his glass on the table. He punched the numbers from memory and listened to the warble at the other end. Looking around, he noticed Karr sipping her sherry alone in the vestibule, staring out the darkened windows in the door. Barry picked up his own glass and swallowed half its contents. It was a warm, mellow sherry; just the right thing. He set the sherry down again just as a voice answered the rings. "Room 310," he said softly into the mouthpiece. There were more rings, then another voice.

"Hello?" Shannon. Eyes closed, Barry could picture her lying nude on the motel bed with the phone resting on her stomach. Deliciously flushed. Ready. Damn.

A short woman in shoulder-length brown hair. Stubby nose, small breasts, plain mousy features. Not someone he would normally look at twice. Shannon had never been more than a hi-how-are-you, good-to-see-you casual acquaintance, but Barry never questioned good fortune—especially when it landed, quite literally, in his lap.

Which it had done, quite literally, at the Tri-State Conference in Philadelphia three years ago. Barry could still remember every detail of that first encounter. The sports decor in the hotel lounge. The buzz of the patrons competing with ESPN on the wide-screen TV. The sticky leather feel of the booth. The stale, salty taste of the complimentary popcorn. The stupefyingly dull chatter of the Pennsylvania teacher he shared the booth with. North Orange was maybe not such a big city, but his Keystone Kompanion came from a town where the Welcome To and Please Come Back signs were hung on the same post. It was a welcome diversion when Shannon slid into the booth beside him. And an even more welcome diversion when she began running her stockinged foot up and down his leg. Barry almost spilled his drink, but the Pennsylvania teacher either had no idea what was going on under the table in front of him, or he was the Mother of All Poker Players.

Barry had gone to Shannon's room afterward, where her enthusiasm in bed had more than compensated for her unremarkable looks. They missed most of the rest of the convention—another plus. Since then, they had continued a casual though regular liaison. In public, they always kept their conversations professional. They never touched. It would not have been prudent, and even Shannon's dim-bulb husband might have wondered. Barry barely noticed her looks anymore. That was just packaging. He knew the woman inside, now.

"Shannon. It's Barry. Look, I didn't have a chance to call earlier. The meeting just ended—you won't believe what it was about—but now my car won't start. . . . Yes, like that time at Sandy Hook . . . I know that's twice we've had to. . . . Uh-huh, but we shouldn't have set this up for the same day as the meeting. . . ."

"I can't always pick the day . . ." she said. Half rebuke, half complaint, but at least she wasn't angry. Sometimes, her anger frightened him; the more so for its rarity.

Barry saw van Huyten returning and said hurriedly, "Look, I have to go now. I'll make it up to you. Promise. What about Saturday?"

"No. John and I are taking the girls to the zoo. I'll call you. Think about me tonight, in bed," she said. "I'll be thinking of you."

He cradled the phone just as van Huyten and Karr approached. He hated it when Shannon mentioned her girls. It reminded him of another part of her life, an alien part he never shared. It reminded him that she *had* another life.

"But I said you could stay the night," he heard van Huyten say and, for a weird moment, Barry thought she had addressed him. Then, he realized that his hostess was speaking to Karr, who shook her head.

"I've thought it over, Mariesa. You know what your mother . . ."

"My houseguests are my own affair."

"As you wish. But in any event, if Keith and John E. are flying in tonight, it would be better if I were at the hotel to greet them. We can breakfast the agenda before we come out in the morning."

Van Huyten's frown made a small wrinkle above her nose. "If that is the way you feel . . ."

"It would be more sensible." Karr nodded to Barry. "Barry," she said, extending her hand, "it has been good seeing you again. I look forward to working with you, both at Witherspoon and at the Institute."

Barry made a smile. "I'm sure it will be a rewarding experience."

"I will see you out," Mariesa said. "I shan't bother Sykes." The two women walked out toward the vestibule. Barry saw them stand by the door and exchange a few sentences in low whispers. Then Mariesa opened the door and they stepped outside together. A short time later, Barry heard a car start. The sound of the motor Dopplered out, was masked for a moment by one of the hummocks, then reappeared, a more distant hum. After it had disappeared entirely, van Huyten reentered the house, an empty wineglass in her hand, and stood in the foyer. Absently, she ran a finger around the rim and placed it between her lips.

Barry cupped his hand and coughed into it. Van Huyten blinked and shook off her distraction. "Mr. Fast," she said. "Please excuse me. I was studying the evening sky. It promises to be a fine night for observing." She joined Barry by the elevator door, placing the wineglass next to Barry's on the telephone table. "Sykes will take care of these," she said, opening the accordion cage to the elevator. Barry followed her inside.

It was an old-fashioned elevator. The grille was a Victorian filigree of polished brass, the struts bursting at their tops into sprays of gilt metallic flowers. There was even a control handle inside the cage, though a more familiar button panel had been set into the wall beside it. Barry wondered if the elevator had been salvaged from an older building.

The panel had seven buttons, three of them labeled B1, B2, and B3, so there was more to the building than met the eye. He wondered what was in the subterranean floors. Storage? Money vaults? He imagined Mariesa van Huyten wallowing naked in her money like Scrooge McDuck.

Van Huyten pressed the button marked "O" and the cage hummed and began to rise. Barry thought that he should say something polite; but what did you say to someone with her kind of wealth? Read any good books lately? Nice weather we're having? How about those Mets?

Van Huyten saved him the trouble. "Tell me, Mr. Fast— may I call you Barry?—have the summer training seminars gone well?"

"Well enough," he said. "It was a lot to absorb. You're asking for a big change in the way most of us have conducted our classes."

"I am sure you will manage. As a principal teacher, you will—"

"Need to show leadership to the others." He smiled. "See? I paid attention." He paused and then, because he felt something more was required, he said, "The idea of coordinating subject matter across disciplines is interesting. . . ."

"Only interesting?"

"Well . . ."

"Come, now, Barry. I asked for your honest opinions."

And Mao had asked for a thousand flowers to bloom . . . *What the hell.* "If Mentor gets rid of the Mickey Mouse we've always had to put up with, I'll be happy. All the teachers will. But . . . cross-discipline lesson plans, morning assemblies, the 'afterclass,' computers for the kids. They are all good ideas, but five dollars says they won't work."

Mariesa looked at him. "Why?"

"Because there are no easy fixes. You're raising false hopes. In the polls . . . Some of the parents think you're going to wave a magic wand and everything will be like it was when they went to school, when the toughest discipline problem was chewing gum in class. I don't know that life will ever be that simple again.''

''I do not know that it ever was.''

The cage hissed to a stop, and van Huyten pulled the handle to open the gate. Barry felt the knot of frustration in his belly. ''It's not like it used to be,'' he said, following her out into a small vestibule lined with astronomical photographs. A galaxy of stars, planets, comets. ''Not like when you or I went to school.'' Briefly, he wondered what schools Mariesa had attended. Not the Seattle public schools, that was for sure. *This lady has never been a teacher, yet she thinks she can reform education.* Of course, to be fair, Dr. Karr and the others *were* teachers. . . . ''The kids today . . . I don't know. It may be too late. They don't *care* about anything. If you try to punish them by taking something away, they just stop wanting it. Their salute isn't the peace-and-love gesture, but the shrug. Their battle cry is 'Who cares?' Street-smart and cynical, the best of them don't care and the worst go wilding and kill for fun. They play for long odds.''

''Yes. They have no dreams.''

Dream your way ahead . . . Right. ''They have a hell of a lot less than that,'' he told her bluntly. Could someone as rich as her even imagine that?

''No, Barry. Without a dream, how can you ever know what you lack?'' She looked away for a moment, stared at a glossy photograph of stars. ''We are in danger of losing an entire generation of children,'' she said. ''An entire generation. There will be some big winners—for some, those long odds will pay off—but there will be bigger losers. They are 'dropping down the ladder rung by rung.' ''

''Kipling,'' Barry said. To her look of surprise, he responded, ''I am an English teacher, after all.''

''Yes, Kipling. He knew this generation. Do you know how the lines go?

      '' *'We have done with Hope and Honor, we are lost to Love and Truth.*

We are dropping down the ladder rung by rung:
And the measure of our torment is the measure of our
  youth.
God help us, for we knew the worst too young!' "

"Tell me, Barry, if that is not today's youth."

Barry nodded. "It does sound as if he had gotten it right."

"So what do you propose we do? Other than tell one another what losers they are."

This time, it was Barry who turned and looked into the photographs. White diamonds scattered on black velvet. Hazel
discs. Discs banded in brown and white. A blue-green disc with
a faerie ring encircling it. Swirling sheets of colored mist en-
shrouding sparkling stars. To his right, a starfield with no distinguishing features except that, directly in the center of it, one of
the stars was smeared. Give the woman her due, at least her concern was genuine. And who knew, there might even be some
agreement on a few of the methods. Barry was suddenly glad he
had accepted the Institute job. The struggle might be futile, but
it ought to be waged. "I don't know," he said as he turned away
from his scrutiny of the pictures. "Keep on trying, I guess. At
least your people seem open to new ideas. The politicians . . .
New ideas always make someone nervous; and those are the
ones who write the letters and attend the board meetings. I'm
not sure that any of Mentor's gimmicks can work on the cynical
kids we have to teach nowadays; but I do know that if we don't
try at all, we're bound to fail."

She nodded slowly. "An honest appraisal." She looked him
in the eye. "Promise me that you will always give me honest
appraisals."

Barry tried to look unconcerned. "Sure." His hands began
to tremble and he stuffed them into his pockets. The impact
of his Institute position was beginning to sink in. Van Huyten
did not just *own* Mentor; she took a personal interest in its
doings. Well, who said that rich people could not have social
concerns? Barry did not believe private schools were the answer; he wanted to make the public schools work. Was contract management the inspired compromise, or the chimera that

combined the worst features of both? Either way, it looked like one of the perks of his new job would be hobnobbing with the richest woman in North America, and that was nothing to turn your nose up at. What would Mama Fast say if she could see her little boy now?

Barry followed van Huyten into the observatory, a large, circular room with a high domed ceiling. He saw a telescope cradled in a large horseshoe mount. Cameras, computers, and other equipment lined the walls. Barry whistled softy as van Huyten strode purposefully from panel to panel, slapping switches and buttons. There was a great, echoing thunk as a relay tripped, and Barry looked up in time to see the dome above them part. Cool air fell into the room and a slice of the night sky was revealed.

Behind the observer's chair hung a photograph of a large, banded planet—Jupiter, he thought. From the edge, a great splash of brightness spewed forth like a fountain. Jupiter was a large planet, he remembered, the largest in the solar system. That plume must be awesome. He straightened up and saw van Huyten watching him with a strange intensity in her eyes.

"Impressive," he said. "I remember it was on TV a few years ago."

"That was Comet Shoemaker-Levy 9," she said, "when it struck Jupiter in July 1994."

Barry looked at the photo again. It was signed in the lower right corner. *Mariesa, best wishes, from "Glo" and the gang at JPL.* "That must have been some hit. Imagine if it had struck the Earth, instead."

Mariesa stiffened for a moment. Then she said, with studied calm, "If that concerns you, here is another comet that might interest you."

She led him to another photograph farther along the wall. "Do you see the bright spot in the upper left?" she said as he joined her. "The one with the arrow pointing toward it? That is Comet Swift-Tuttle. It is outbound now and it will not be back for a hundred and thirty-four years; but some astronomers think that when it swings around the sun again, it has a chance—perhaps one in ten thousand—of hitting us."

Barry raised his head. "Us?"

"The Earth. In 2126."

He grinned. "I'll make plans to be out of town that day."

"We all should," she said with a tight smile. Then turning away abruptly, she strode to the observer's chair. "This is not the best location for a telescope," she said as she pulled on a cardigan sweater that had been hanging by the telescope. "There is a bit of glow from New York over the horizon, but the western sky is acceptable. There are no large cities between here and the Pennsylvania border."

"Why didn't you build your observatory out in Montana or someplace where it's dark at night?"

Van Huyten looked surprised. "This is where I live. I can come upstairs whenever I am in the mood. This is just a hobby; I am not a serious astronomer."

Barry looked around at the equipment. "It looks pretty serious to me. Didn't you once discover an asteroid, or something?"

Van Huyten shrugged. "You were looking at the photograph in the vestibule. The streak in the center was 2278 Gramper."

"Gramper?"

"I named it after my grandfather." Van Huyten dropped into the padded swivel seat at the eyepiece of the telescope and fiddled with the controls. A computer screen lit up and Barry felt the floor shift slightly. When he looked down he saw that the center of the room was on a revolving plate. Something hummed and the inclination of the telescope altered slightly inside the horseshoe mount. The numbers scrolling by on the computer screen kept time to the direction and tilt of the telescope. "Gramper was a great influence on me."

And your father was not. The public record had been quiet on Pieter van Huyten. Old Willem had had enough clout, especially in those days, to keep things out of the papers; but enough hints and innuendos had surfaced that Barry could guess at heavy alcohol dependency, at the very least. He supposed that having a roaring old pirate like Willem for a father could be overpowering. Safer to be the granddaughter of such a man, than the son.

Van Huyten pressed a button on her control panel. Then she turned her swivel seat around and faced him. "We were speaking of dreams a moment ago. Come here for a moment and I'll show you one." She rose and Barry took her place at the eyepiece. He remembered that van Huyten was a space nut, and that people who welcomed criticism on most things often drew the line where it touched them most deeply. *Show a little interest in space, Barry, and who knows how far you'll go?* "What am I supposed to do?"

"It is all targeted properly. Just look through it."

Barry leaned into the binocular eyepiece. The rubber shield was soft and cool around his eyes. What he saw looked as if Jackson Pollack had snapped a paintbrush at a black canvas. There was no order, no feature that stood out. Those pinpoints were vast balls of fire, he had read someplace, some of them bigger than the sun. That pale haze, there, with the faint hints of color within it . . . a cluster, or a galaxy, or something. Those were hundreds—or was it millions?—of suns, unimaginably distant. "It seems to go on forever," he said at last.

"Wait a moment, while I superimpose an image captured last week." Barry could hear her fussing about. There was a click like a camera shutter and suddenly the view doubled. *Two times infinity.* One of the views shifted until the dots all matched.

Not quite all, he noted. Some of them became short smudges. Recalling the photograph by the elevator door, he said, "Those are more asteroids? The smudges, I mean."

"Most of them," he heard her say. Suddenly, the stars faded from view, leaving only the asteroids behind. Startled, he looked up, out the crack in the ceiling, and Mariesa van Huyten smiled.

"Computer deenhancement," she said.

Barry gave a nervous laugh. "For an instant, I thought . . ."

"Yes, we would miss them, were they gone." She indicated the eyepiece. "That was the Main Belt you saw. 'The vermin of the skies.' Astronomers once hated them because they cluttered things up so. They appear as short lines on the computer composite because they have moved against the background stars between the two images. By measuring the displacement and knowing the declensions and right ascensions, one may . . . Ah, but, I shan't bore you with my hobby."

Thank you. He looked up, searching her face for clues. "Interesting," he said in as noncommittal a voice as he could manage.

"That is our future. Out there. That is the future for those children of ours, if they could but realize it. If you dream it, you can make it so."

"Well, for those with an interest in science, of course. I thought the space program was worthwhile, back when we could afford it."

"We cannot afford to not afford it. For the sake of the human race—" She stopped herself suddenly and crossed her arms over her chest against the night air. "I did not mean to preach."

But . . . thought Barry.

"But there are practical reasons for going. It is not all science and space pilots. All of us will benefit. Communications, manufacture, transportation. Space is full of resources, Barry. Vacuum, microgravity, temperature extremes. Light metals on the moon, heavy metals in the asteroids, volatiles from comet heads. There is unlimited solar power . . ."

"Solar power in space?"

"That's where they keep the sun."

Barry laughed, and van Huyten turned and looked up through the opened slot of the observatory roof. "No need to ruin desert environments," she continued, "with acres of solar panels. No need ever again to strip-mine the Earth or foul its air and water."

Careful. Don't step on her blue suede shoes. "It sounds like it might be worth trying—"

"Oh, it is, I assure you. Each of those asteroids you saw could supply the Earth with a year's or more worth of heavy metals. And there are tens of thousands of them out there."

"But it's beyond what we're capable of. I mean, how do

we get out there? The asteroids are awfully far away, and we can't even go to the moon anymore. . . ."

Van Huyten gave him an approving look. "Good for you. Most people seem unaware of that fact." She walked to a display case against the far wall, where she stood quietly for a moment. "But where the asteroids are concerned, the mountains come to Mohammed." She opened the glass door and removed a stone the size of her fist. "Here," she said. She brought it over and handed it to him. It was cold, smooth, and heavy, brown on the surface, though he could see from the cross section that the interior was black and the surface was melted crust that had refrozen.

Barry studied it, turning it over in his hand. "What is it?"

"A meteorite," van Huyten told him. "A piece of asteroid that fell to earth. The original was nearly a foot long and weighed twenty-two pounds. It punched a hole in the trunk of a young woman's car in Peekskill, New York, a couple of years ago. I bought a piece of it for my collection." She gestured toward the display cabinet.

He laughed suddenly. "Can you imagine that poor woman filling out her insurance papers? Hit by a meteorite in her driveway!"

"Not all the asteroids are out in the Main Belt, Barry. The Apollo-class asteroids actually crisscross the Earth's orbit. Some of them are so close we can rendezvous with them, using technology we already have. I am supporting one such venture. A one-way rendezvous with 1943 Anteros."

"It sounds . . . not as interesting as another moon landing."

She smiled. "Oh, I am supporting that, too. I think it is high time we went back. And stayed. After all, 'if we can send a man to the moon, why can't we send a man to the moon?' "

Barry handed her back the meteorite. Van Huyten took it and stroked it absently, as if it were a pet.

"You've got big plans," Barry said.

She looked up at the sky, where it was visible through the crack in the dome, and a peculiar look came over her face. "The beginning of a ship is a plank," she said.

It was only much later that Barry realized what that look had been, and it made no sense to him. If he hadn't known better, he would have said that Mariesa van Huyten, the Moon Lady herself, was terrified of the evening sky.

INTERLUDE:

Role Call

Styx Looked into the mirror at the face that she never thought of as Roberta Carson's. Pale and white—accentuated by the dim, colored bulbs that she used to light her room— her face was thin to the point of gauntness. The faux-starvation look, heightened by face powder and liner. She leaned closer toward the glass and puckered her lips, painting them with coal-black lipstick. Then she stood back, pressed her lips together for a moment, and admired the look. Spiderweb nylons. Heavy, black, steel-tipped, retro Docs on her feet. She flipped her long, straight, dark brown hair behind her shoulders and straightened the baggy, black, dropwaisted smock. Morticia, the other kids sometimes called her; or Elvira. Until she showed them what the heavy shoes were for.

On the wall, Gothic Shell, with that absolute *dream*, Alaryk Castlemayne, mushroom-faced, shocked hair, black-bagged eyes, something disinterred after three days in the ground, gazed out at her with a look so sensitive, so soulful, that you knew that he knew things and they made him oh, so dreadfully sad. A *Little Knowledge*, that was their latest album; even better than *Empty Inside*.

"Roberta?" Her mother's whiny voice pierced her ears like an icicle. "It's almost time for the school bus."

Two quick, dancing leaps carried her to her bedroom door. She cracked it open and peeked out at the hallway. Beth was nowhere in sight. "I'll be right out, 'Mother.' " Mother never let Styx call her Beth.

"Don't be late."

Pegged. Beth was in the bathroom with her makeup (as if it mattered to the other women in data processing how she looked). Styx closed the door quietly and turned the lock. It was not as though her mother were on the fast track to anywhere except a cold and lonely old age. Punch in, punch the keyboard, punch out. That wasn't life, it was survival; though she gave her mother credit for that much. You did what you had to do. (*Just do it!*) But why did she have to prattle on so about fancied promotions or where she stood in her pay grade or the silly, meaningless politics in a silly, meaningless office?

It took only a moment to pull open the bottom drawer of her dresser and reach under the wadded-up clothing for a bottle. Clear, water-white glass, shaped to fit the grip of a hand; clear, water-white liquid inside sloshing near the bottom. Only a few swigs left. Styx unscrewed the cap and put the long, hard neck to her lips and tilted her head back. The icy vodka filled her mouth. She swirled it around (*a piquant bouquet with just a touch of sass . . .*) and swallowed.

And the liquor hit her with an electric shock. She shuddered, sucked in her breath, and blew it out again. She ran her forefinger around the inside of the neck of the bottle, pulled it out, and sucked on it. Then she screwed the cap back on, tight, and shoved it back under the clothing. She did not bother closing the drawer.

She relocked the bedroom door behind her just as Beth emerged from the bathroom, fussing in her purse, like she always did, as if she had forgotten something. Styx halted to let her go by. It was always a dance in the mornings when they both had to be somewhere. The hallways were narrow, and narrowed further by the boxes stacked against the walls. The whole bungalow was cramped with packing cartons never unpacked and a jumble of furniture shoved together or dismantled and stacked. It was like living in the back of a U-Haul. Once, a long time ago, when she had been a child—when she had still been Roberta—they had lived in a larger house. Then, something had happened. She was not sure what, except that it had involved a lot of shouting late at night when she was supposed to be asleep, and that one day they had had to sell the house and move here without Daddy, where the swoosh of traffic on the highway outside never stopped and had become, in fact, almost as natural a sound as the wind rushing through trees. They just scraped by each month, choosing which bills to pay or sending in less than the minimum, but Beth would never consider selling off the old furniture. Someday, they'd move back again into a larger house. Someday, real soon.

"Oh, Roberta, look at you. On the first day of school, too!"

"It's just another day." Not true, because it marked her annual loss of freedom, when a bunch of old lizards would can-opener her head and stuff it full of useless facts. She saw no reason to celebrate.

"Your lipstick is smeared already. You don't care how you look, do you?"

"No, I guess not." Two sharp blasts of a horn announced the arrival of the school bus. Maybe she could time it better tomorrow. Avoid Beth entirely. "Gotta go." She kissed the air near Beth's head.

"They say school will be different this year," Beth called after her. "Some new people are running it."

Styx paused at the door and turned around. The bus driver could see she was coming. She was entitled to one more toot before the bus could leave without her. "It's mostly the same teachers as last year," she told her mother. "And mostly the same kids. So I expect it will be mostly the same shit."

Slam. Bang. Thank you, ma'am. She skipped out the door and off the porch. On the school bus, through the already grimy windows, she could see the geeky freshmen staring at her. And Jimmy Poole, the Ultimate Dweeb, grinning and probably saving the seat beside him just for her. *Oh God*, she prayed to an entity she was sure did not exist, *let there be more than one empty seat left*.

Chase lounged with his back against the brick wall of the school building, watching the buses pull in. He was checking out the scene. Sniffing out the situation. It was important to know who was in school and who was not. Sometimes there were guys who owed him money, though that was usually later in the year. On the first day, he liked to let the fresh-babies know who was in charge.

Bus Seven pulled up and disgorged its usual gang of losers from Eastport. White trash from "the Locks" along the old canal route, with the look of failure already in their eyes. Knee-grows bused from Molly Pitcher, looking tough as broken glass in their shades and leathers, but outnumbered here and knowing it. And mega-twerp Jimmy Poole, Chase stuck his foot out and the fat, little nerd went sprawling. The other kids parted and flowed around him, not looking at Jimmy and certainly not looking at Chase; except the freshies, of course, who didn't know any better, yet. Chase gave them a curled lip that sent them scuttling for the doors.

Jimmy picked himself up. The knee of his trousers was torn where he had body-surfed on the pavement, and the palm of his right hand was scraped and bloody. "Why'd you do that, Chase?" he asked with the whine that twisted Chase's backbone five different ways. Chase stood away from the wall and Jimmy took two quick steps backward, colliding with another loser.

"Because it's what I do, stupid."

Poole scurried into the school, his head bent down and his raw hand tucked under his left armpit. Chase shoved his way into the incoming flow of students and fell into step beside Morticia, the Mushroom Girl.

"Good morning, Ro-ber-ta." He knew Styx hated being called that. He leaned close to her ear and whispered, "You know, I've always wanted to fuck with a corpse." Then he twisted away with a laugh before she could do anything. Chase was not afraid of anything, but he had a healthy respect for Styx's boots.

Leilah Frazetti touched heads with her girlfriend as they walked toward the school. "Did you see Chase try to put the moves on Styx?"

Tanuja Pandya shook her head. "I did not know you could slime a vampire."

Leilah giggled. Tani had such a way of talking. Half the time she made no sense, and half the time the sense only came to Leilah hours later, which would make her laugh, apparently at nothing, which would make her father frown and her mother look worried. Which was cool.

"I wonder what school will be like this year . . . ?" Tani's voice sounded curious and even excited, which was not cool; but the Asian students tended to be that way. A little nerdy, though not like that creep Jimmy Poole and his propeller-headed friends. That was one of the reasons Leilah let Tani hang around. Serious and studious, doughy-faced, bulby-nosed, dark-skinned (but tan, not, God help her, black!), and with that silly fabric spot pasted to her forehead, Tanuja Pandya made Leilah seem even prettier and cooler than she already was.

"Why should it be any different this year?" Leilah asked. "It's just school." Which was to say, not very important. Leilah came to show off her clothing and her hair, and because her father would just *kill* her if she did not. Daddy always gave her the most *marvelous* outfits, though he wouldn't let her wear her best jewelry to school because the kids from Pitcher might steal it. Leilah craned her neck to see what the other girls were wearing.

Just inside the doorway the stream of students knotted into eddies around the bulletin boards, where computer printouts listed everyone's homeroom. As usual, the taller students stood closer to the board than the shorter ones, who had to hop up and down to see. Leilah pressed her way to the front only to find that the Fs were listed farther to the left. So she slowly squeezed through the crowd. One of the boys, she didn't see who, rubbed her on the behind as she pushed past. She twisted her head, but none of the boys nearby were looking at her. Except, two were grinning. Okay, so it *might* have been accidental, the way they were pushed together like this; and one of the grinning boys was a genuine *hunk*.

When she finally located her homeroom assignment—it was dorky *Mizz* Porter, barf!—she turned around and found herself face-to-face with one of the boys from Pitcher.

She didn't know his name. She didn't know any of the Pitcher kids, and didn't want to. This one was taller than she was, but skinny. He wore shades, like so many of them did—it was some sort of statement—and a brimless, leather hat. His T-shirt read "X" in big, red, paintbrush strokes. He grinned down at her and his teeth were yellow-white against his coal black skin. The kind that Daddy called "deep purple."

"Yo, mama," he said. "What's yo' hurry?" And he pressed up against her, pinning her between his body and the bulletin boards. His two friends, flanking her on either side, each leaned an arm against the bulletin board, blocking the other students and blocking her escape, and pretended to read from the homeroom lists.

"Let me out, please. I have to get to my room."

"Yeah, me, too," he said in a who-cares voice, and pressed harder against her. Leilah found it hard to breathe. The boy had a smell to him, musty and tangy and not at all the way white people smelled. She looked left, right, left again, darting her eyes because if she turned her head away he might be insulted and hit her. Daddy said how people from Eastport would start fights for no good reason at all—even the white ones, who were no better than they deserved to be.

"Let me out," she said, "or I'll . . ."

"You'll what?"

"Coming through. 'Scuse me." A disturbance in the crowd, as another ni—boy, as dark as the first but shorter and broader, pushed his way to the front. He seemed to look straight into her eyes. Then he took his sunglasses off and said, "Move over, girl. I can't read through your head." There was a confusing tangle of bodies and suddenly an opening right in front of her! Leilah darted out into the open space of the lobby, where Tani was waiting.

She stopped by her friend's side, feeling irrationally safe, and took a deep breath. She shot a look back over her shoulder, but the boy who had accosted her was gone already. Tani looked at her. "What is wrong, Leilah?" she asked.

"Nothing," Leilah said. "One of the Pitcher boys came on to me; but I shot him down." Her heart was pounding. She could still feel his body pressed against her. She smoothed her sweater, straightened her jeans, but the *feel* stayed with her.

That was twice within five minutes that boys had put moves on her. Leilah tossed her hair back over her shoulder. At least the Pitcher boy had been direct. No furtive palm against her ass. There was no mistaking what he wanted. They all wanted white girls, because their own kind were so ugly. She thought he would be rough, the ultimate male animal. It would be a different kind of experience with someone like that. Not that she would! Greg was awkward and self-centered; but they looked *so* good together and Daddy hadn't caught them yet. She could just imagine what Daddy would say if he caught her with a Pitcher boy.

"Hey, bro, why you buttin' in?" Azim Thomas—Jo-jo and Zipper by his side as always—laid his hand on the brother's shoulder as he followed him down the hall. But he dropped it quickly when the other turned and Azim saw who it was.

"What you want, Matchstick?" Leland Hobart generally minded his own business, but Hobie didn't take shit from no one, black or white. Azim had seen him one time grab an iron poker from some white-ass out to bust nappy-heads—and bend it in half with just his hands. Azim had been deeply impressed, though not half so much as whitey, who proved that ice people could run just as fast as a brother if properly motivated. So Azim didn't want to provoke Hobie; but he couldn't back down in front of his skillets, either. Hobie came from the Dayton Parkway neighborhood, not from Eastport.

His father had a job. Shit, he *had* a father. But he also had to know how it was, didn't he?

"I was talking to a girl, man; and you let her get away."

Hobie gave him a look. He had a wide face and deep black eyes and he never let anything show there. Azim never knew what he was thinking. Azim never knew if he *was* thinking. He didn't hang with anyone in particular, except sometimes the other jocks, and if he had thoughts, he kept them mostly to himself. "I didn't see no girl."

"You kidding? She was standing right in front of you. You got between us."

"I never see no white girls," said Hobie, who then turned and walked away without a backward look.

"That Hobie," said Zipper, standing by Azim's right side. "He be bad."

"That Hobie," said Azim, now that Hobie was out of ear-shot. "He be dumb."

Zipper and Jo-jo laughed, and Azim was reasonably sure they would not repeat his remark to Hobie. He wondered where the white girl had gotten to. She had been one fine piece. Of course, all white girls looked like something from under a rock: pale, colorless skin like fish bellies, empty of sun, empty of color. Sometimes it was hard even to touch them. Like touching something dead. But they were built like any other bitch, had all the same equipment; and he could plug in there as well as anywhere. She'd say no, and say she didn't want it; but white girls all wanted a taste of chocolate, because they knew it had to be better than the thin, watery stuffing they got from their white-dick Ken dolls.

Meat slouched at his desk, sticking his feet well under the seat of the lame-o in front of him. With his two forefingers he drummed against his desktop, supplying the cymbal sounds with his mouth. On the backbeat, he kicked the chair leg in front with his right foot. He imagined himself onstage, doing a concert at the Meadowlands. Big screen. Larger than life, projected up there in living color. Smoke. Strobes. All the gimmicks. That would be for his roadies to handle. That was just show. It was the music that really mattered. And the words.

The crowd would be moshing. Jerking and banging into each other. He'd have his group with him. Their faces were a little hazy, partly with the imagined smoke effects, partly because he wasn't sure if Jerry, Buck, and Angel would really stick it out. He'd be stripped to the waist, his chest oiled. He'd have a Gibson axe and Gorilla speakers, amped to the max. He'd cover some classics. Metallica. Megadeth. Then he'd lay his own stuff on them. *You see him stand/A shadow in the sun* . . . Man, that would be something. They'd go wild. They'd mosh. Then, maybe hours later, they'd sit up straight in bed and go "Hunh?" And then maybe the next morning, they'd go "Yeah!"

"Yo, Meat!" Angel. Anthony—Tony—d'Angelo sat in the desk next to his. Meat looked at him.

"Whassat?"

Angel jerked his head to the front of the classroom, where their homeroom teacher sat. "Roll call, dimwit."

The homeroom teacher, Mr. Fast, looked at him. "Morris Tucker," he said with the air of having already said it several times already. Meat heard the snicker from Angel and the whispered "maw-reese" but he didn't pay it any mind. Instead he gave Mr. Fast his best blank look, as if he had never heard of the name.

"You talking to me?" The rest of the class rustled with repressed laughter. At Fast, or at him; it didn't matter. *(And nothing else matters . . .)* When Fast said nothing, Meat twisted in his seat and looked behind him. "Morris? Hey, Morris? Any you kids see Morris?"

The laughter bubbled to the surface now. Even some of the geeky Hindoos were smiling. Fast shrugged. "Meat," he said and waited.

The class fell silent. Meat could feel their eyes turn to him. The moment seemed to linger, like the silence between the end of a song and its sudden coda. Slowly, he straightened in his seat. "Yeah. Here," he said.

"Ssst," Angel hissed. "You gotta stand up."

"What?" Meat looked at him.

"You've gotta stand up and repeat your name."

"Why?"

"New rule."

"Rule?"

"That company that's running the school now. They got new rules."

He turned and faced the teacher. "Is that true, Mr. Fast?"

Fast smiled. "It's so hard waking up in the morning, isn't it? Yes, Mr. Tucker. There are new rules, for all of us."

The way he said it made it sound like he didn't care for some of the new rules himself. But, still . . . *Mr.* Tucker? He stood beside his desk and shook his shaggy, uncombed, shoulder-length black hair. He clicked his heels and saluted. "Meat! Sir! *Raw* Meat!"

The class tittered. Fast nodded and pressed a key on the computer on his desk. That was new. The teachers had computers now. Meat took his seat again. Did they have computers for the students, too? Maybe there'd be computer games, with power gloves and turbo graphics and all.

"A *test?* On the first day of *school?* Ms. Bosworth, that isn't *fair!*" Jenny Ribbon stood beside her desk (stupid rule, that you had to stand to speak!) and looked at the other kids. They looked just as surprised and distressed as she felt. Except for Cheng-I Yeh, who looked curious, and Karen Chong, who looked smug.

"You are right, Miss Ribbon. It is not fair. Nevertheless, it will be given."

"But we haven't *studied*. No one *told* us we would have to study." A pop test? On the first day? How would this affect her GPA? She had been on the honor roll for four semesters so far, and meant to make it four more times. This test could ruin *every*thing.

Ms. Bosworth raised both her hands, palms up, then laid them on her desk. "I have seen the test," she said. "You could not have studied for it." Ms. Bosworth seemed puzzled, too. Though how that could be, Jenny did not know. She was the teacher. Jenny sat down slowly.

"This is Mentor's Benchmark Test. They give it at the beginning of each year and again at the end of the sen—ah, graduate year. It covers . . . well, general knowledge, I suppose. We don't expect you to answer all of the questions; some of them are college-level. You will be evaluated not only on how well you answer questions, but on *which* questions you attempt to answer. Please notice . . ." And Jenny saw her eyes drop to the desk, so she knew the teacher was reading off of a card. "Please notice that I said 'evaluated,' not 'graded.'" (Jenny heard the breath hissing out of two dozen bodies. It was like those practice tests the state used to give for the HSPT. You had to take it but it didn't count. Good! Because it was not *fair* to spring it on them like this.) "These evaluations will be used to determine grade and level placement in your classes. During the next two weeks, while a panel of master teachers examines the tests, there will be no academic classes—"

Some of the kids—that bonehead Chase, for one—let out a cheer, which Ms. Bosworth waited out. "Instead—" And she waited a moment longer for quiet. "Instead, there will be intensive one-on-one interviews with counselors from the Mentor Institute to discuss your background and interests . . ." (Groans, and Jenny hoped that awful Mr. Snyder would not be her counselor this year.) ". . . and a series of 'survival' classes on a variety of topics, such as writing business letters, balancing your checkbook, how to do a job interview, home repair, cooking, and so on. Some of the classes will run for the entire two weeks, others may run only one single period. After the test is completed today, you will be given a list of optional classes from which you can choose. Some classes are required by Mentor . . . although not by the state."

Something in the way that Ms. Bosworth said that, the way she raised her eyes from the prompt card on her desk, made Jenny think she had added it as her own comment. Jenny frowned. Something was going on here, something involving the teachers, that she did not quite get. It was obvious that they did not all like the new situation, even though so many of them had complained last year about class loads, pay scales, the school board, and everything else that she thought they would have welcomed any change at all. There had been something in the papers over the summer about the union, the school district, and Mentor, but she had not understood what it was all about.

This year will *be different.* How different, or in which ways, she did not know. How would grading be affected? Or class standing? She and Karen Chong and Tanuja Pandya were neck and neck for class valedictorian. If the criteria were going to be different from now on, she should be told. It wasn't *fair* to keep them in the dark.

A four-hour test? Even with the promised breaks, that was a long time sitting down. Jimmy Poole passed the pencil back and forth from hand to hand. The school nurse had put a bandage on his hand, but the scab there hurt everytime he flexed it. Why did Chase have to pick on him all the time? He had never done anything to Chase. Never. Yet, the ((b*st*rd)) always singled him out. And the other kids laughed, too. Maybe just happy that Chase hadn't picked on them; but they laughed, so that made them the enemy, too.

A four-hour test. He would show them. There were none of them could do as well as he did on tests. He had an IQ in the genius range, though no one seemed to care about that. He was smarter than most of the teachers, too. They didn't like the idea of a kid being smarter than they. He bounced a little in his seat as he waited for Mr. Fast to hand out the exams. The metalhead in the seat behind him swatted him in the back of the head. "Sit still, you little creep."

He would show them all. He had read books over the summer. He bet that Meat and his pals had never opened a single one, except maybe a comic book, with those women superheroes with the big ((br**sts)) and ((*sses)). He had seen Angel once with one of those magazines that had pictures of naked women. Angel had seen him looking and opened the magazine to the centerfold and held it right up in front of

Jimmy's face. You could see everything, even the gross parts. Jimmy had asked Angel who the interview was with, showing sangfroid. See also, equanimity, composure, poise. Antonyms: discomposure, perturbation. Oh, he was ready for this test. No one else was, but he was.

Sometimes Jimmy thought he was not the same as the other kids, that he was a mutant of some sort, the first of a new, superior species destined to replace Homo sapiens. He could read minds, a little, sometimes. Maybe that was his mutant power. He thought that someday—when the time was right—his father would take him aside and tell him everything. Once or twice he had seemed about to do so, had asked Jimmy if he had a few minutes when they could talk—but he always backed out at the last minute. But Jimmy already knew how important it was to keep his powers secret, so if Dad was waiting until he was old enough . . .

Meat swatted him on the back of the head again. "Pass the tests, moron."

Jimmy saw that Mr. Fast had placed a stack of exam books on his desk. He blushed, knowing that everyone was looking at him and thinking about him. Meat should not complain about daydreaming, because he had been doing the same thing a few minutes ago, and probably not about anything really important like Jimmy.

Crowbait Jimmy and his band were charged with inciting a riot at a concert in St. Louis, MO. Find St. Louis on the map. How far is it from North Orange? In which direction?

Meat stuck the pencil in his mouth and began licking the eraser with his tongue. He remembered hearing about that business with Crowbait. It had been on MTV. St. Louis . . . didn't they make beer there? The map was no help. Nothing was labeled. There were outlines of squares and funny shapes. And dots. At the bottom of the map was a circle with arrows marked N, E, S, W. Those must be directions. So, if he knew which two dots were North Orange and St. Louis, he would know which direction to go. But, how far . . . ? There was no way to measure the distance that he could see. Unless the bar with the numbers on it had something to do with distance. He scowled and made a face at the paper. Who cared where St. Louis was, anyway?

He went on to the next question.

Explain why you were unable to answer the previous question.

Meat laughed. That one, he could handle.

Your car gets 23 miles per gallon. You want to take your date to the shore, a round trip of 50 miles. If you work after school at the supermarket and make $5.00/hr., how many hours do you have to work to buy enough gas for your date?

Chase read the question twice to make sure he understood. It was a stupid question. You wanted to buy enough gas that you would run out at some secluded spot. He snickered. Besides, if he couldn't goose more than 23 mpg out of an engine, he'd never show his face down at the garage again. Smartass test. They didn't even give you the formula, so how could you solve it? He started to write a wisecrack, changed his mind and erased it. The eraser smudged the paper. After thinking about it a little more, he grinned again and wrote, "Quit dorky supermarket. Go work at gas station. Get gas for free."

There. You didn't even need to know any math to solve that one . . .

"Many hands make light the work." "Too many cooks spoil the broth." Explain what each proverb means. Explain why both are true.

Jenny shook her head. She peered closer at the paper. They *couldn't* both be true. Having lots of help either made things easier or messed things up. So there had to be a trick. Except, what was it? What kind of test was this, anyway?

When the astronauts went to the moon, they brought back moon rocks. What were the rocks made of?

Azim stared at the question. What did it mean? Rocks were rocks. They weren't *made* of anything; they just *were*.

It was like most white tests. Full of questions to which he

knew no answers; which, for all he did know, *had* no answers. It was designed to embarrass sun people and make them feel inferior. Just like busing them to this white-assed school. *(You're too dumb to learn anything unless we mix you in with white kids.)* Azim toyed with his pencil and let his eyes drift left and right. Did anyone else know the answer? He couldn't see, and he wouldn't trust any answer he could lift off of Jo-jo's sheet, nohow; 'cause Jo-jo, he was dumber than a stone.

It was all brothers and sisters in this classroom. Just like being back at Molly Pitcher. Even the new homeroom teacher was a brother. It was just like whitey to bus them all halfway across the city only to cram them into a ghetto homeroom.

The room decorations were mostly African. That was a Zulu shield and an assegai on the wall. And an Ashante mask. He recognized them from a rap video. But why was there a picture of a doctor giving a blood transfusion? Or bags of sugar stacked up on pallets? Stupid. The picture on the front wall above the blackboard drew his attention again. Astronauts walking toward the camera, smiling and waving, five of them. Grinning white-bread pasty faces. One man, in the lead, waved his Buck Rogers helmet over his head. Two others were grinning at each other, like maybe they were queer for each other; and what the hell, what did they do up there in space when they didn't have a woman along? The fifth astronaut was in the rear, a little in the shadows, his face not clearly visible, gloved hand half-raised more in a salute than a wave. Azim shook his head. He had noticed a lot of that space-cadet shit around the school.

He turned the page of his test book and saw a photograph. A dingy alley, filled with trash cans, two of them tipped over, a broken bottle in a smelly puddle of water (he knew it was smelly; he'd whiffed too many of them). Gang signs spray-painted on the brick walls. To one side a man (a boy?) squatted down against the wall, head hunkered down.

What the hell?

Describe what has happened in this picture. How does the person in the picture feel? How did he get there? Where is he going?

Where he going? Shit, he ain't going nowhere. Azim could see that clear as day, just like he could smell the urine and hear the drip-drip-drip of the water. He knew that there were rats, too, rooting in the overturned garbage. And the boy, maybe his gang got beat, or his homeskillet was shot. He be in the alley 'cause there no other place for him to be. There was a window high up on one wall and a ratty curtain pulled a little to one side. Was there a girl up there? Maybe his squeeze? And maybe she blood in another gang, like Fatima. So he just hangs out maybe hoping she'll come to the window.

Azim clutched the pencil in his fist and began to write. I'll tell them, he thought. I'll make them look. Make them see. Whitey think this just a picture and a . . . essay? I'll make them hear it and smell it and maybe even taste it so they gag.

Write a poem about something that interests you. Explain what makes it a poem. How good is it? Why do you think so?

Jimmy Poole stared at the question in dismay. Write a poem? Write a *poem?*

If you drop two objects at the same time from the same height, which will hit the ground first: the heavier or the lighter of the two? How do you know?

Leland Hobart bent over his desk. His right arm was curled around the test paper, which sat nearly sideways, so he could write with his left. They never made it easy for lefties. With his pencil he made dots on the page. Tap, tap, tap. The heavier would hit first, wouldn't it? If it was heavier, it would fall faster. Or was that too obvious? Sometimes the teachers liked to trick you. He beat a tattoo with his pencil. *How do you know?* That was the hard part. You could guess on the first part. Fifty-fifty. You could flip a coin. Hell, why not? He reached into his pocket and pulled out a coin. Two coins, a quarter and a dime. He scowled at them a moment, an idea nudging him in the back of the head. The quarter was heavier, right? He looked sideways from the corners of his eyes. Left and right. No one was watching. So he placed them on his desk and slowly nudged them both toward the edge so they would fall at the same time from the same height.

The coins toppled over and hit the floor with a rattle that made the other kids look up. The quarter rolled up the aisle, where he saw Jo-jo snatch it and put it in his own pocket. No matter. Hobie had seen both coins hit the floor at the same time. Then he noticed that the homeroom teacher was watching him. Flushing, he hunched over his test booklet and wrote his answer. *Neither. They both hit at the same time.* Now he had to explain his answer. By dropping two coins off his desk? He wondered if that had been cheating in some way.

The hell with it, then. He wrote, ''I know it's true because I saw it myself,'' and described what he had done with the coins. Maybe that wasn't very scientific, but he felt oddly *sure* of his answer. If that was cheating, they could hang him. ''Feathers, leaves, balloons and stuff are different,'' he added, ''but I don't know why.'' Then he licked his thumb and turned the page. For a moment, he stared into space without seeing the question written there. Why *did* leaves and feathers fall different?

What if the bird will not sing?

Styx studied the question, read it over again; but it read the same way the second time, too. *What if the bird will not sing?* What kind of question was that? Styx picked her pencil up and hovered it over the blank space. *Who cares?* She started to write that, stopped herself, and erased it. She thought about a bird sitting on a branch, silent. Why? Why did birds sing in the first place? And if they didn't, how could you make them? Maybe it was a biology question. She didn't know biology. She had a headache from her morning ''mouthwash.'' Styx pinched the bridge of her nose and rubbed it. *They don't expect us to answer all the questions, anyway.* She thought about the silent bird for a long time while she listened to the sounds of pencils tapping and feet shuffling. In the end, she left the answer blank.

4.

A Meeting of the Pantheon

Christiaan van Huyten III, who hung in gray-bearded, frock-coated splendor in the parlor at Silverpond, had begun naming his companies after mythological characters shortly after he took control of the family holdings during the crisis of 1873—Vulcan Iron and Steel Works, Thor Foundries, the now-defunct Apollo Rail Road—and ever since then, with only a handful of exceptions, new acquisitions had been "deified." Asklepios Pharmaceutical Laboratories, Heimdall Communications, Demeter Agricultural Consortium, Hermes Trading Corporation, Antaeus Realty, little Mentor Academies . . . even Project Prometheus, the unacknowledged bastard. Perhaps it was inevitable that the presidents called themselves "the Pantheon."

The presidents who lined the broad mahogany table ranged in age from cocky, twenty-something entrepreneurs to a single, crusty, mossbacked septuagenarian. They were bright with expectation; they were dour with experience. They were capable and ambitious; and they were satisfied and content. Some Mariesa had inherited from Gramper, some she had bought with their companies. Only a few were her own choices. Facing her at the far end of the table, at the vanishing point of two lines of perspective, sat Belinda Karr.

VHI was an odd sort of holding company; more of a federation than a single entity. Some of the companies were VHI-owned outright. In others, VHI owned a controlling interest. In still others, a dominant though minority ownership. Complicating the matter further, ownership was sometimes vested in VHI itself, sometimes in the Van Huyten Family Trust, sometimes in the personal portfolios of Mariesa or her cousins. Old Christiaan had organized it so, modeling it explicitly on the Federal Union. Sometimes Mariesa thought it resembled the Holy Roman Empire more than the United States, with fealty and vassalage counted in stock blocks rather than in oaths and fiefs.

Four times a years she gathered sundry presidents off to management retreats for briefings, training, and networking. Sometimes there were conflicts to settle. Sometimes the gods quarreled.

Mariesa folded her hands under her chin and studied the man who leaned forward on two beefy arms, glaring across the table at his accuser. Aggressively short-sleeved and open-necked among his suspendered and suited peers, Bennett Longworth was an anomaly, a fossil. "The Old Bull" had run Vulcan since a time "the memory of mankind runneth not to the contrary." He was a fixture on Olympus. It was said that when God built the world, Bennett had poured the steel. He not only knew where the bodies were buried; he had by damn helped bury most of them himself. He and old Willem van Huyten, with pick and shovel and a few well-timed proxies. Bennett was very nearly bulletproof, and he knew it.

Very nearly. And he knew that, too.

Mariesa studied his eyes and saw a mixture of hostility and defensiveness. This meeting could go very badly if she was not careful. The other division presidents fiddled with their papers, or conducted private, whispered conversations, or they watched the confrontation with unfeigned interest. Could the

Rich Girl take out the Old Bull? There was a pool of some
sort among the senior staff; and not all of them, Mariesa knew,
were betting on her. Some of them, jealous of their divisional
autonomy, secretly supported Bennett, like barons ganging up
on the monarch. She knew their names; some of them. Keith
McReynolds, her Chief Financial Officer, was a comforting,
fusty presence by her side. Keith she could count on. Keith
knew the price of everything, but he knew the value, too.

"Well, Bennett?" Mariesa said when she had judged the
silence had gone long enough. "Have you any answer to
João's complaint?" There was something mythological about
that, too; that it was Daedalus that faced the Bull in the laby-
rinth of corporate politics.

Longworth's face was flushed, the liver spots less visible.
He ran a hand through the unruly wisps of hair that danced
on his scalp and brushed them momentarily flat. Then he
propped both his elbows on the tabletop and balled his hands
together like a supplicant praying grace, though neither his
eyes nor his voice mirrored piety.

"We followed procedures," he said. The badger in his den.
The Immovable Object. Feeling safe because he had Gone by
the Book, yet defensive, because things had not worked out.

Safety was an illusion, Mariesa knew. A horrible illusion.
She could not allow anyone to feel safe. "You followed procedures," she repeated.

Longworth thrust out his chin. "My works manager did. I
don't oversee every decision at every works in the Vulcan
group."

"Of course not," said Mariesa, "but what we say and do
as executives sets the tone for our managements. The heat in
question was rolled at the Huntingdon Works, was it not?"

"Number 40922A." Longworth's eyes barely flickered to
his notes. "Poured and rolled there, both. Half the billets were
through the mill stands before Leffert got the lab analysis
back. So, yes, he knew the heat was off-spec. Nitrogen was
high, and copper. But what could he do by then? The chem-
istries were only off by a few points, so the Material Review
Board and the metallurgist signed a waiver."

"Daedalus did not sign any waiver," said João Pessoa through unsmiling teeth. "As the customer, that was our prerogative."

Longworth looked at him. "Leffert figured you could cut him a little slack, João. We all work for the same boss." There was a quiet edge to his voice. Pessoa had not been a "team player." A capital offense in Longworth's world.

Which could be useful. It might give her the handle she needed. Mariesa looked to her left and caught the attention of a fiftyish, sandy-haired man in a brush cut who sat toward the far end of the table. "Steve?"

"Yes, ma'am?"

"Suppose I were to request that Thor's machine-tool operation ship out-of-round mill rolls to the Huntingdon Works?"

Steve Matthias cocked his head and looked thoughtful. He glanced at Longworth, then back at Mariesa. "Thor does not ship off-spec tools," he said. "Not even for the CEO."

Somebody—Mariesa did not see who—made a kissing noise. Matthias scowled but made no comment.

Mariesa could not read Steve Matthias. Careful, methodical, he produced consistently good results. His balance sheet ran ahead of the industry. But she was never entirely sure when he was being sincere and when he was kissing ass. Of one thing she was certain, and that was that Steve looked out for Steve; and as long as Mariesa was Queen of Olympus, that meant their interests converged.

"Not even if the rollers are only a few hundredths off spec? Bennett has already said that does not matter to him."

"You've made your point," Longworth growled. "Jesus. You give me out-of-round rollers and I'd cobble steel all over the mill."

"Have I? I wonder." Mariesa picked up a pencil from the table before her and turned it end over end in her hand. "If you will not tolerate deviations in what you buy, do not tolerate them in what you sell. You deliver what you promise to deliver. But where Daedalus is concerned, I must emphasize the importance of delivery to spec in no uncertain terms. We are all on the same team, Bennett; and you must not throw a bad pass to a teammate.'' There. Let him see his actions in the light of his own value system.

The look Longworth gave her, quickly suppressed, spoke volumes. *What do you know about what goes on down in a steel mill? What do you know what it takes to keep my furnaces and mills rolling?* Mariesa could hear him as clearly as if he had spoken. She had known for a long time that she would never have the cachet in Longworth's eyes that old Willem had had. He would never look at her the way he had looked at Gramper. Had she been a stranger, he would at least have given her standard respect, but it was hard to take instruction from someone you had once dandled on your knee.

João hunched forward over the table. ''A few points of copper,'' he said, ''can adversely affect the corrosion resistance of our airframes in the heavy salt-spray environment in which they operate.''

Officially, Daedalus built airframes: midsized commuter jets for the business market and short-range tactical fighters for the Brazilian Air Force. Unofficially, it built the Planks for Prometheus. That there was a secret interdivisional, aerospace research project under way was known to everyone present, but the precise nature of the project was closely held. Of the twenty-four in attendance, only six were members of the Prometheus team, and they did not display their pins at these meetings.

''Sure, João,'' said Longworth. ''Like I said, you've made your point.'' He looked at Mariesa, and Mariesa could tell that her remark about teamwork had struck home. ''But I don't want to hear anything next quarter about not making tonnage if I wind up with too many pourbacks because of Daedalus's specs.''

Keith, God bless him, spoke up. ''It is largely out of our hands, I'm afraid. There is a legal issue involved. Daedalus is chartered under Brazilian law, and imports must conform to MERCOSUR standards.''

Longworth grunted. ''Why don't you just buy Brazil?''

Recognizing the peace offering, Mariesa smiled. "I've leased it."

The others laughed. Heartily, because it broke the tension; but a little nervously, because they wondered if, just maybe, she might be able to swing the deal. Only Keith knew how close to the mark the joke had been. She had not "leased" Brazil, but her timely intervention in the currency markets had forestalled an attempt by the *keidenran* to do very nearly that.

Intervention . . . in return for certain concessions in Ceará State, and on the archipelago.

Long days only grew longer. It was some sort of positive-feedback cycle.

Dinner had been tedious. It was always the same. The barn-yard dance for precedence, the bragging conducted carefully in her hearing, the less than subtle innuendos of those who had come vice their presidents. Notice me! Notice me! And the closemouthed ones. Some had nothing to prove. Bennett. Steve. Belinda. But some kept their own counsel because they had their own plans and being noticed was not part of them.

Machiavelli had described two sorts of states, the Turkish and the Frankish. In the Turkish state, all power flowed from the Sultan and all offices were in his gift. In the Frankish state, each baron was a power in his own right, with liberties and privileges to be guarded—as John Lackland had discovered at Runnymede.

Were Machiavelli alive today, he would be a management consultant. And a damned good one, too. Mariesa's kingdom was a Frankish one.

A few moments, at least, were her own. Mariesa stood in the foyer outside the meeting room and stared out the great floor-to-ceiling windows that lined the north wall. Sugarloaf Conference Center perched atop a steep hill northwest of Philadelphia and, although the city had come out to lap around its base, the flanks of the hill were still shrouded by gold-tinged woods. They swept down the ravine to the half-hidden cobblestones of the Germantown Pike and gave the grounds a sylvan setting.

The gods used to gather on Olympus, Mariesa thought. Hilltops gave them a lofty view of things. Distant. Detached from the details that so often obscured thought. There was a touch of chill in the air beyond the double-paned window. Across the roadway, the greenery of the Morris Arboretum flourished in sheltered splendor, but on the hillside below the meeting center, topaz and rubies were ousting the emeralds from the foliage. The muffled wind blew gravel and small twigs against the glass. She did not feel godlike.

The reflection of Keith McReynolds appeared, ghostlike, in the window . . . a small figure that grew gradually larger as he crossed the room behind her. His white, curly hair; the dark, old-fashioned, horn-rimmed glasses; and that absurd red bow tie. Mariesa smiled. Everything about the public McReynolds was like that. Just a shade this side of a put-on; as if Keith were playing a role. As if God had been holding a Broadway tryout and hollered out, "Crusty, eccentric accountant!" and Keith had raised his hand and said, "Ooh, ooh! Me! Me!"

The private McReynolds was—not different, but perhaps deeper. Kindly, understanding. Infinitely patient. A sympathetic listener. At his age, as he had often told her, his ears were his most useful organ.

"A beautiful sight, autumn," he said without preamble when he reached her side. "I like the fall management retreat. I walked around the grounds this morning, and every inch of it was hot with color."

Mariesa turned and looked at him. "Hot?"

"The leaves are red and yellow, like flames."

She turned back to the view. "It disturbs me."

"What? The autumn colors?"

"It's a metaphor. Nature is most colorful when she is dying. The end of the millennium is coming."

Keith smiled gently. "Sooner or later," he said.

"Yes. What is the popular tag line? 'Not Quite Yet.' "

" 'If you can't decide, celebrate twice,' " Keith quoted. "Though, aside from a few preachers on late-night television and the fact that Manhattan might sink from all the people who plan to be in Times Square in December, it has been a low-key year. A year for reflection and taking stock.''

"No," said Mariesa, considering the autumn leaves once more. "It is not the Millennials. If a few thousand people climb hilltops come New Year's Eve and await the Rapture, it will not matter much. What bothers me more is the sense of winding down. There is a feeling at large in this country that we have already given everything our best shot and we are now living in the 'epilogue of history.' "

"Fin de siècle," Keith said. "The same mood prevailed a hundred years ago among intellectuals in the arts, in philosophy, in literature. To the ordinary people, of course, it was just another year at the desk or stove or factory. Then, the sun comes up the next day, just as it always does, and people realize that it was not just the end of a century, but the beginning of one, as well."

Mariesa sighed. "I know, Keith. It is only that . . ."

"Are you having doubts again? I thought that was my job."

She laid a hand gently on his forearm. "About Prometheus? No. Just . . . everything else in the world."

"Oh," said McReynolds. "If that's all . . . ."

She laughed. "I know.

" 'Take care of your small corner of the world.
Its portion is as great to hold as all.' "

McReynolds dipped his head. "You remember. I'm flattered."

"I treasure your poems, Keith."

"Your grandfather thought them frivolous."

"Gramper was not a . . . sentimental man." She sighed and leaned close to Keith. "I never realized," she told him, "that saving the world would have so many petty details."

McReynolds patted her arm lightly. "You mustn't be too harsh with Bennett, you know."

"He is obstructing Prometheus. I cannot allow that, even for Bennett."

"He is not privy to all the facts."

"He should have retired years ago."

"About some things your grandfather was very sentimental."

She sighed. "I know. He gave Bennett his word. Uncle Ben, I used to call him when Gramper brought him to Silverpond. He had all his hair then. I thought he was nice. That is why I found it so hard to slap him down today."

"He does have his good points. Give him a task to do, give him a goal to achieve and, by God! he will 'pile Ossa upon Pelion' to reach it."

"Yes. And he will cut corners, too."

Keith made a flip-flop motion with his hand. "His was a can-do, get-the-job-done generation. So different from the committee-minded, process-oriented managers that seem to be the norm these days. I've always felt a little awed."

She turned and looked at him. "You? Awed by Bennett?"

"No, not Bennett himself; but he and his generation fought fascism across the face of the entire world and won, hands-down; and then they came home and transformed the world. My generation fought to a draw on one little peninsula in Asia."

"While *my* generation tried not to fight at all. Keith, I never thought of you as warlike."

He smiled. "No one does. Korea is a forgotten war. That was why Governor Dukakis looked so absurd in that campaign commercial, riding around in a tank. Damn it all, the man was a veteran! He fought. Only he picked the wrong war."

"Have I picked the right one?"

Keith shrugged. "It is not exactly a war, is it?"

"I think it is. A global war. Against stupidity, against foolish complacency. You know what is at stake."

"Perhaps if everyone knew . . . if Bennett and the others knew . . ."

She shook her head. "We have been over that, Keith. 'Three may keep a secret if two of them are dead.' And how many do we have on board Prometheus already? No, it is difficult enough to find enthusiasts who are both discreet and practical-minded. You know where the economy is headed. Our window of opportunity is short. I cannot waste time convincing the skeptical or battling the hostile or wrangling with the government over Chapter 35.''

''Not to mention 'the reason beneath the reasons.' ''

Mariesa froze for a moment, then turned and scanned the otherwise empty meeting room. ''Do you know,'' she said, ''that entire months sometimes go by when I do not think about why I started the project?'' She checked her wristwatch and saw it was five minutes to six. ''It is almost time for Prometheus to meet. We had best join the others.'' She turned away from the window, but McReynolds continued to gaze out.

''It's not even true, you know.''

She turned and looked at him and he pointed to the motley that swathed the hillside below them. ''It's not death,'' he said. ''Only diastole. It is change, not death, that brings color. Stasis is monochrome. The green of summer or the white of winter; both of them frozen in their own way. Both of them *suspended,* waiting. Systole comes in the spring. There is color then, too.''

She quoted from another of his poems. '' 'Nature's heart is slow / But beats.' ''

He smiled modestly. ''Nature isn't like art, Mariesa. There are no happy endings, no sad endings. No endings, at all. Only change; and getting on with things.''

Mariesa smiled at him. ''Are you telling me to get on with things?''

McReynolds shrugged and turned away from the window. ''Me? I'm just the bean counter. I sit at the right hand of majesty and whisper unpleasantries about budgets and incomes.''

Mariesa offered him her elbow and he slipped his hand in it. ''You're a dear, Keith. Without you, I should do nothing all day but mope and despair.''

''I somehow doubt that.''

''Promise you will always advise me.''

McReynolds looked suddenly solemn. ''For as nearly 'always' as I am able.''

*   *   *

They met in a small room in one of the other buildings that dotted the grounds. At one time, it had been a mansion, and this, the living room. Now it was used by the conference center for business meetings. A large, ornate fireplace graced one wall, a reminder of the old, robber-baron era. Everything was painted an uninspired "institutional white." Mariesa studied the agenda while the others settled in.

João Pessoa poured bourbon into a glass from a crystal decanter. He set the decanter back in its rack and held the amber-filled glass up to the light, studying it with a squint. "Why do North Americans drink this?" he asked.

"They don't," said Will Gregorson. "Only Kentuckians do, from a warped sense of duty." He wore headphones, which he held pressed to his right ear with one hand. In his left hand, he held something that looked like a Sony Walkman. He pointed the antenna this way and that, listening with an intent frown.

"I prefer a Martini, myself," said Keith McReynolds. "Very dry." He surveyed the rack on the sideboard with disfavor. "Though, I suppose a port would be acceptable. A sherry for you, Mariesa?"

Mariesa nodded. "And for Belinda when she arrives."

Will took his headphones off. "The place is clean," he announced. He was a large man, with thick, black curly hair that wrapped itself around his face and peeked from the open top of his plaid sports shirt. "Werewolf" Gregorson had nurtured his avionics firm from nothing more than a few bright ideas and a workbench in his garage to a major player in the aerospace game before Van Huyten Industries had plucked it up. Expecting the golden kiss-off, he had instead been promoted to head up VHI's electronics research and development.

"The places are always clean," Correy Wilcox complained. "I don't know why we bother." At forty-five, the vice-president of Demeter was second in age only to McReynolds of those present. He already had his drink of choice, a lemon-lime soda, resting on a coaster on the table in front of him.

Mariesa looked at him. "Because the day we stop checking

is the day we become vulnerable. Maybe no one is listening. Maybe no one will ever think of listening. But we will not stop taking precautions."

Belinda Karr entered the room and closed the door behind her. "Sorry to be late," she said, taking her seat. "Glenn wanted to talk and talk." McReynolds handed her a glass of wine. "Thank you."

Mariesa waited until they were all seated before holding up her glass. "The Goal," she said.

"The Goal," they responded, lifting their own beverages in salute.

After a moment's contemplation, Mariesa set her sherry aside. "Well, the children are all in bed now. Do you have your agendas? Good. Keith, will you see that John E. and the others who could not be here receive copies of the minutes?"

Keith had flipped open a laptop computer. He nodded without looking up.

"Very well. The first item is a late addition not on your lists regarding our flight-test program down in the archipelago. João, would you like to share with the others the news you gave me earlier today?"

Pessoa sat stiffly in his chair with his hands pressed flat against each other, as if praying. "Brasilia has asked that we add a Brazilian pilot to the cadre in training; and they have suggested in very strong language that he be designated the prime."

There was a chorus of groans around the room. Wilcox looked at Mariesa. "I thought we had an understanding with their government."

Pessoa said, "There is an issue of national pride."

"Politics," said Wilcox, as if discovering something unpleasant in his glass. "The elevation of politics over engineering is what wrecked *Challenger*."

Pessoa looked at him. "Do not discount pride," he said carefully. "Especially in Latin America. Someday it may be very important for our program's success that Brasilieros feel they contributed more to it than the rental of some real estate."

"Participation is the key to cooperation," Gregorson

agreed. "But Daedalus is largely Brazilian-staffed, isn't it? And the ground crews . . ."

"*Senhor*, who manned the ground crew when John Glenn made his flight?"

Gregorson looked at him and cocked his head. He ran his stubby fingers through his beard. "Point taken," he said.

Mariesa held up a hand to still them. "João, does it affect the critical path?"

Pessoa shook his head. "No, *Dona* Mariesa. The man they have suggested is good. In fact," and he grinned ruefully, "he already works for Daedalus. He had been, ah, 'top gun' in Brazil's air force before joining us as a test pilot. I told the minister I would accept the man into the program and that I would strongly consider Brazilian sensitivities in selecting the prime pilot, but that Captain da Silva must earn the berth by his performance in training and simulation."

"And Governor Gomes accepted that?"

"Yes. I told him that to bestow the honor as a political plum would dishonor Brazil, since it would imply that a Brasiliero could obtain it in no other way."

McReynolds lifted his port. "Well done, sir."

Pessoa nodded to Mariesa. "Always the Goal," he said.

"Always the Goal," said Mariesa. She knew that João would allow no incompetents into the program, no matter what the political pressure. No presidential brothers-in-law. But they should have anticipated this issue; placed less of a premium on astronaut or cosmonaut training when selecting cadre. After all, no one had simulator hours, let alone flight experience, in a Plank. Shuttles and Burans handled differently. In fact, Brazil's Captain da Silva might have an advantage over Calhoun, Krasnarov, and the others. Less to unlearn. And they might be glad indeed to have a Brazilian pilot handy if Washington chose to enforce Chapter 35. She checked the first item off her list.

"Next item. We have already heard Correy's update on hydroponics development during the regular management committee meeting." She looked at Wilcox. "I take it Hyacinth will mature in time?"

"You put people in orbit, Mariesa, and I'll feed them." Wilcox smiled. "That is assuming that Brad doesn't slash the program."

Meaning that Brad Hardaway was still president of Demeter and still completely in the dark over Prometheus, while his vice-president of research consorted in private with the highest levels of the corporation.

Keith looked up from his keyboard. "I am sorry, Correy," he said, "but Brad's P&L is too good. Mariesa has no pretext to force him out. Besides which, most of Demeter's affairs are peripheral to this project."

"And if we did put you in his place," Mariesa said, "who is next in line for your R&D spot? Karen Bishop, whom I happen to know personally; and she would *not*, I repeat *not*, be a friend to Prometheus."

Wilcox made a face. "I'm too valuable where I am, right?"

Mariesa studied the way Wilcox slouched in his chair. Correy needed some raw meat. Being privy was not enough. The extra compensation was not enough. He needed some public form of recognition. *Have we not just been talking about pride?* she wondered. Perhaps they could spin some R&D functions off of a few companies and combine them. Put Correy in charge. A smaller pond, but the head fish. *Make a mental note to discuss this with Keith. See what he thinks.* "Do not bind the mouths of the kine that tread the grain." Correy Wilcox was concerned with the future of Correy Wilcox at least as much as he was with the future of Hyacinth, or even of Prometheus.

"Brad cannot cancel Hyacinth," Belinda pointed out. "There would be too much negative publicity if he cut the budget now. World hunger . . ."

"Don't be too sure," Wilcox told her. "Brad called me to his office the day before I flew up here." He looked at Mariesa. "I think he was pissed that you asked for me to come in his place. . . ."

Mariesa said, "I informed him that I asked for you because I wanted a detailed briefing on Hyacinth."

"Yeah? Well, that didn't make him not pissed. In fact, that

may be what got his dander up over Hyacinth. He called me to his office and started going over the project, You know, questioning the expenses and so forth. I gave him the song and dance about world hunger and the starving masses, like Belinda said. So, he starts in on how famines have nothing to do with food availability. He showed me the figures. It's politics and war, not food production, at the root of famines.''

Mariesa pursed her lips. ''You mean that as far as our official justification for Hyacinth goes, 'the emperor has no clothes'?''

Wilcox shrugged. ''The papers and the public will still buy it, but your own senior management at Demeter do not. Or will not, when Brad is through convincing them.''

Mariesa smiled sardonically. ''You may inform him that you have presented his arguments to me; but that I am a bleeding heart with no technical training, an eye for favorable public relations, and a spoiled, rich girl's whims.'' She made a note to talk with Hardaway. ''Next item?''

McReynolds coughed. ''That would be me. The Mir project. We are still negotiating with Energia and the other consortium members, but the agreement seems to be a done deal. I have already cleared the camouflage project—a cooperative venture on *Znamya II*, the orbital mirror—through State and Commerce. We may need to charter a subsidiary in Moscow or Baikonur and employ Russian and Kazakh staff there, but prospects appear very good. Russia wants to keep the launch complex and Kazakhstan wants the hard currency the lease brings in. So far, everyone stands to win.''

''Well,'' said Mariesa, ''once it is settled I shall pay a visit to the archipelago.''

''You are always welcome, *Dona* Mariesa,'' João said with a slight bow.

''Next item. The Anteros rendezvous mission is off. Congress cut the item and NASA played possum. The Japanese and Europeans were still willing, but all the preliminary plans had been based on American participation. It is too late to replan the mission.''

There were a few groans and Belinda muttered, ''Damn.''

Mariesa said, "The next potential rendezvous is not until 2009, when asteroid 1991JW reapproaches. Total delta-V for that mission will be only 5.9 kilometers per second, which actually makes it more accessible than Anteros would have been."

"We should have planned for that one from the beginning," said Keith, "even if it was a longer wait. The economy will be picking up by then."

"That is a moot point, now," Mariesa told him.

"What I find amusing," Correy said lazily, "is that the Japanese and Europeans could have pulled it off if NASA hadn't yanked the rug out from under them."

"Like with FREEDOM," said Belinda.

"Will, contact Dolores at Pegasus. I would like the two of you to spearhead our work for the 2009 probe. I will expect a preliminary action plan on my desk by the twentieth. No, João, let Pegasus Aerospace handle this one. I want Daedalus to keep a low profile." She scanned the rest of the agenda. "Chris tells me that the aerogel project has hit a snag; but that Argonaut is close to arranging a licensing deal to manufacture Bellcore's magnetic transistors. That is where he and John E. are this week. You will all have a full report when the deal is consummated." She checked the last item off the agenda. "All right, Belinda. The rest of this meeting is your show."

Belinda Karr leaned forward over the table and laced her fingers together. "We have just finished evaluating the Benchmark Tests for this year. The cross-correlations have been normed and scored, and the committee has delphied the 'special' questions from all of our practices, public and private. The results are mixed, as usual. Our private practices in the western states did well. Close to twenty-five percent of the students show potential, of which Prometheus may ultimately count on five to ten percent joining us."

"What about North Orange?" Mariesa had taken a personal interest in the district, since it lay so close to Silverpond.

Karr made a face. "Hard to say. We are starting from scratch there. The students in our private practices have gone through at least one year, sometimes four years, of our instructional methods, which snowballs the impact. But the North Orange group has been under public instruction up through last year, and most of the public school staff is still in place. Old habits are hard to break. In fact . . ." And she made another face. "I was forced to let go two teachers who were unable to benchmark properly."

Mariesa raised her eyebrows. "Belinda, that is not like you."

A sigh. "I know. I would have retained them 'in training,' but one insisted that it would be too humiliating, and the other could not understand why the test could not be multiple choice. I mean she literally could not understand. Each time I tried to explain that we were looking for skills and creativity and not for rote learning, she responded that 'multiple choice is easer to grade.' "

Pessoa laughed. "And she believed *that* to be the most important aspect of a test?"

Karr looked sad. "Not funny, João. Not funny at all. Mariesa, some of the students left the entire test blank. Some of them wrote obscene comments."

"Some of them will wonder," said the Werewolf, "why they never got anywhere in life."

"You cannot simply cast them aside," Belinda said to him, "like defective components. Some of the most hopeless cases may be the ones most worth saving. Edison was expelled from three high schools as a behavioral problem."

"We are not in this to save them," said Wilcox.

"Yes, we are," said Mariesa.

Wilcox looked at her and their gazes locked for a moment. Then Correy looked away. "I didn't mean that way." Correy was one of the four Steering Committee members who understood the threat from rogue asteroids.

McReynolds intervened. "Did any of the North Orange students appear promising, Belinda? We invested a great deal in the contract. We must see a return."

"Life is not all ROI," said Karr.

"Yes it is," said McReynolds, "though the return may not be in dollars."

"Especially not in dollars," said Wilcox with a laugh.

"Listen to some of these answers," Karr said. She placed a pair of reading glasses on her nose and consulted a sheet of paper. " 'Almost every animal is a preyed-upon animal. Therefore, this results in animals eating other animals; in other words, it is the habitat.' "

Gregorson rubbed a hand over his face. "Jesus, did that mean anything?" Wilcox laughed.

Karr looked up. "That was one student's explanation of the food chain. Would you like to hear about diffusion or atomic structure?"

"No, thank you," said Wilcox. "No wonder the poor kids are suckers for every scam that comes along." He wiggled his fingers in the air, like menacing tentacles. "Electromagnetic fields is gonna get you. Watch out for dat ole electric blanket." Gregorson snorted and looked away.

Pessoa said, "How likely is it that any of these children will mature into the sort of scientifically literate adults we will need later?"

Karr took a long breath. "From the senior class, almost nil. We won't have them long enough to make a difference in their lives. From the middle and elementary schools, it is too soon for an estimate. But we have a number of good prospects in this year's junior class and a few others in the lower classes. The Institute Fellow, Barry Fast—do you remember him, Mariesa?"

"Yes. He came to Silverpond that time. His car would not start." *A good-looking man with an air of confidence, and worry lines around his eyes.* "What about him?"

"He has a few ideas that may reach some of these students." Karr began passing the folders around. "I will want these back after the meeting for reasons of confidentiality." She paused and looked at the folder in her hand before handing it to Gregorson. "They could become total failures or they could become tomorrow's heroes. But they may not be the sort of heroes you have in mind."

Mariesa opened the folder she had been given and saw that it contained two dozen profile sheets, handwritten in Belinda's extroverted cursive. The file numbers in the upper right, she knew, were keyed to the actual test records. The student photos stapled to the upper left were as bad as student photos since the invention of the camera. On the first sheet, a cynical sneer set in a thin, black face. The next, a pasty-faced girl in black who looked as if she were staring out through her eyes from a million miles behind them. An Indian girl, a couple of Orientals, all of them looking serious and halfway normal, though perhaps a little desperate behind the eyes. Another girl who seemed to be all makeup, hair piled as high as the Washington Monument, a face produced by some parody of the lost-wax method: the makeup applied and the real girl melted off, leaving nothing behind but this shell. A pudgy-faced caricature with large, black-rimmed glasses and a vacant otherworldly look. Mariesa shook her head. And Belinda thought these were the cream of the crop.

So, don't judge a book by its cover. You knew what you were getting into with this school. Just your basic, late-nineties, blue-collar, suburban youth. After ten years of ''affective education,'' of keeping journals and sitting in consciousness-raising ''magic circles,'' of the New Math and the New Spelling, of ''educating the whole child,'' the wonder was that there was anything left to salvage. Next year Mentor would be opening private practices in Princeton and Morristown. Witherspoon and Pitcher were the price for being allowed to do so.

Being *allowed* to educate children . . .

''So tell us what you have, Belinda.''

''Well, there was one boy—his father is a Marine sergeant and his mother is a private nurse—he reinvented Galileo's experiment.''

The Werewolf cocked an eyebrow. ''He did, eh? Which one is he?''

''The fifth sheet. Hobart. And we picked up a nicely creative solution to the running-out-of-gas problem from a boy named Chase.''

Chase. Mariesa flipped through the sheets until she found him. An insolent-looking boy who contrived somehow to turn his class photo into a police mug shot. The look he gave the camera begged no excuses and dared the world to catch him. With a shock, Mariesa recognized him as the boy who had blocked her entrance to the Witherspoon school many months before. "What about the others?"

"We'll go through them one at a time, but . . ." Karr passed out another sheet of paper. "I'd like you to read one of the poems we received."

Mariesa looked at it and saw that it had been retyped from the original handwritten test paper. It was titled "Voice from the Scrapyard" by Roberta Carson.

> *We are the scrapped generation,*
> *Forgotten, despised, and forlorn.*
> *Our parents took pills not to have us;*
> *A third of us never got born.*
> *Don't ask why we're sullen or angry;*
> *You never could handle the truth.*
> *Just ask what you've done*
> *To your daughter or son.*
> *Just ask what you've done to your youth.*

Carson, thought Mariesa, looking at the haunted photograph on the profile sheet. Wednesday's child. There was an ocean of hurt in those lines.

"It is only a bit of doggerel, of course," said Karr. "The modern fashion in poetry eschews meter and rhyme—"

"Sure," said Gregorson, "it's easier that way. It's 'Madison Avenue poetry.' "

"—but it is quite interesting for the level of maturity of its author. Take the line 'You never could handle the truth.' Is it past tense or future? The two slightly different meanings give the line a sort of three-dimensionality, like the two views in a stereopticon. And in the last line, 'your youth' could mean either 'your offspring' or 'your own adolescence.' "

Wilcox grunted and dropped his sheet. "Wonderful. You found a budding poet. How does that help Prometheus?"

Mariesa reread the poem and stared again into the tunnel

eyes of Roberta Carson's photograph. *We are the scrapped generation . . .* "Dreams need any number of things," she told him. "They need dreamers, first of all; and they need doers, too. But they also need a voice."

Might this be the voice? Someday, perhaps. Healed of the hurt.

Later, after the meeting had ended, after the others had gone, after Keith had given her a kindly, avuncular kiss on the cheek and retired, Mariesa met Belinda by the jogging path that wound through the meeting grounds. It was a half-moon night sliding in and out behind somber clouds. The wind rustled the parachute leaves. Above, on the crest of the hill, the lights from the dormitory windows shone, muffled behind curtains. Belinda was dressed in a baggy gray warm-up suit and a sweatband around her forehead. She was bent over, doing stretches. Arms reaching out toward the right foot, then for the left. Long slow breaths. Mariesa watched her for a while in silence.

Belinda stood and noticed her. "Hi," she said after a pause.

Mariesa said, "You wanted to talk."

Belinda nodded. "There's a bench down this way." She set off at a light jog and Mariesa followed at a walking pace. When she caught up, Belinda was sitting on a wooden bench by the side of the path. Mariesa sat beside her.

"What is it?"

"It's about the kids."

"Of course it is."

"I don't like picking winners and losers."

"We do not pick losers."

Belinda cocked her head and gave her a curious look. "I could take that two ways, I guess. All right, we pick winners; or we try to. These are the kids—you, you, and you—that we are going to groom to take over the future. You have a role to play. We may not be quite sure yet what role that will be; but, by golly, we're going to push you toward it."

"Is it so terrible to encourage people to become successful?'' Mariesa asked. ''Or even to identify those with peculiar promise early on?''

Belinda sighed. ''There's a difference in our thinking, Riesey. You want to motivate and educate the kids to push our dream. I want to push the dream to motivate and educate them.''

''Is there a difference, 'Linda?''

''I use you; you use me. Between the subject and the object, which direction does the arrow point? We both have the same goal. Back into space; and do it right this time. Hell, Riesey, I've lived with this longer. I grew up reading Norton and Heinlein and Moore. You didn't. But I don't want the kids to become nothing more than pieces in this grand design of ours.''

''You and I are pieces in the design, too. And Keith and the others.''

''By assent. We all agreed, each and severally: 'Our lives, our fortunes and our sacred honor . . .' But not the kids. They haven't decided yet.'' Belinda turned her face up, white in the fleeting moonlight. ''Tell me, Riesey, are they even real to you? Or are they simply photographs on dossiers?''

Mariesa could not see Belinda's eyes in the dark, could not read her features. ''Real? Certainly they are real.''

''Always the Goal, Riesey?''

''Always the Goal.''

''Don't let that Goal eat you up.''

''I won't.''

''And don't let it eat up anyone else.''

''I won't.''

Belinda smiled. ''All right. I've said what I wanted to say. Give me a kiss and go to bed. I plan to jog around the grounds a couple times and worry about my kids.''

Mariesa kissed Belinda and squeezed her hand. ''I will see you in the morning, then, at the breakfast meeting.''

She watched Belinda's pale, gray shape blur into the night. Then she raised her face to the sky; imagined spinning worlds above her. Always the Goal; though not always the goals Belinda knew of. Get back into space, yes; but that was only a means, not an end. There were a score of threads to manage.

The SSTOs. The power-beam technology. The solar cells. The megawatt lasers. The orbital factories. And all the support and auxiliary that tied them together. Some of them vital in themselves; some of them only an excuse to develop others.

An entire world to save. Children and all, as she had reminded Correy earlier. A target world. Her shoulders hurt from carrying it. Sometimes, she ached to share it with more than the handful who knew. Sometimes, she felt so lonesome holding on to it that no one else in the world did seem quite real.

5.

Ezekiel 1:4

The cabin lurched hard to port, throwing Ned against his safety harness and knocking his breath out. *What the hell?* His eyes danced across the readouts even before he had straightened up. The deck canted at a sharp angle and the Plank settled into an erratic twisting motion. Vertigo crawled up his throat and . . . Dammit, no puking during landing maneuvers! Find out what went wrong and fix it!

Airspeed, increasing. Altitude, decreasing . . . Shit. *That* sumbitch was dropping *way* too fast. Why? Why? He glanced here, and there, and . . . There! A blinking red light announced that the Number Four engine had shut down and the computer was not compensating. Dandy, just dandy. Projected approach running below red line. Check the backup gauge, just in case. Positive downward velocity at zero altitude. Dropping from two miles up, terminal velocity would be very terminal, indeed. . . . He licked his lips with a quick touch of his tongue, but they stayed dry.

"Ground control," he said, "we have a problem."

"I see it, son." Forrest's slow drawl was a comfort in his earphones.

"It's getting worse," Ned reported. "No joy on the stabilizing engines. The computers are not compensating. Going to manual override." His hands lived a life of their own, dancing across the controls. Switches snapped, one by one. A detached part of him watched while his body, knowing what to do, made the right moves. "Number one, throttle down. Number two, throttle up. . . ." The ship could still land with two engines dark, *if* the computer could compensate. The swaying motion seemed to dampen slightly. Good. Good. Keep a light touch. Don't *over*-compensate. He teased the controls, playing them against the sway. First you have to steady the yaw. . . . "Oscillations damping out. Descent speed still increasing."

Get her up in the green. . . . "Firing all retros," he told Forrest. "Might slow me up some." Hey, let's be casual about the whole thing. He lifted the gang switch and the main engines let go. The Plank bucked as the ship strained toward the sky. Ned watched the altitude and airspeed readouts. The trick was to bring velocity and altitude to zero at the same time. It would do him damn little good to stop a hundred feet above the ground, and a whole hell of a lot less to stop a hundred feet below it.

A suboptimal solution, as they liked to say.

The sweat was pouring off him now. He could smell the stink of it. Should he reengage the computers? They hadn't compensated for the yaw triggered by the engine shutdown. A mechanical problem with the jets or a programming glitch? No time for experiment. He played on the throttles, gradually slowing his descent. He watched the altitude and airspeed gauges with one eye apiece, integrating them through his nerves, through his hands and feet, through the vibrations he could feel with his bones. Slowly, the cursor on the computer projection approached the green zone. Oh, yes, baby.

He had just about reached a respectable hover, one hundred and twenty feet above ground level, and ready to ease her in, when Number Two blew and the Plank tumbled like a bad punt. Sky followed ground followed sky across his viewscreen, the ground rushing up far too fast to meet him, like a big, black, volcanic fist.

But that's not fair! he thought. *I had everything back under control! It's not fair!*

"Fair," said Forrest Calhoun slowly, drawing out the syllable. "'Fair' is not in Mother Nature's vocabulary. Ned DuBois was my best friend, leastwise if he had a few dollars and I was thirsty." He held his beer mug high. "So let's turn down a glass in his honor. Bobbi. Comrades. They just don't make 'em like Ned anymore."

"Up yours," said Ned; but he drank his beer along with the rest of them, draining his glass and setting it, mouth down, on the mess table. The others mimicked him. The mess hall, otherwise empty, echoed with the thunks. "Damn," he said, "those VR helmets make you forget where you are, things seem so real." He thought again of those last few moments, with the computerized images on the viewscreens and the mock cabin spinning in its three-axis frame. The ground rushing up too fast to think. "You know what the biggest shock was? When the impact *didn't* come. Like when you're walking up a flight of stairs and you think there's one more step left and it isn't there? Jesus."

"It is the latest," said Forrest solemnly, "in simulator technology."

"*Da,*" said Levkin, the moon-faced Russian. "Is why Daedalus coverall pants are brown."

"So." Forrest turned and engulfed Ned's hand in his own. "Let me congratulate the newest member of the Walking Corpses Club. The computer says you punched a damn respectable hole in the landing field."

"I like to make a good impression," Ned told him.

Levkin grinned. "I drowned," he remembered. "Kersplunk! into San Antonio Bay." He gestured broadly, poking with his forefinger. "Then I hit Flotation Collar Disengage instead of Hatch Open." He wagged his left hand back and forth. "*Pospeshísh'—lyudei nasmeshísh'.*"

"Levkin sleeps with the fishes," said Forrest somberly.

Krasnarov frowned. "It will not have been so funny, Levkin, if it has happened in real flight."

"Oh, lighten up, son," boomed Forrest. "You and me, we'll join the club, too, before the training is over." His broad grin showed that he only half meant it, and no mistake which half. Krasnarov bristled, but Volkov put a hand on his arm. *"Nye serlítyes, továrishch. On—durák."*

"What I want to know," said Ned, "is when do we stop playing with the simulator and start flying? We've got three test birds now. What's Mendoza up to, down on the test stand?"

"Static engine ground tests," said Bobbi.

"And better we should auger in on a few training sims, first, good buddy. They don't have so many birds they can afford to waste 'em."

"Or pilots," said Krasnarov.

Forrest waved a hand. "Now, don't take me wrong on this, *tovarishch,* but you and I have a real low replacement cost compared to the hardware. Have you ever noticed that they call us 'test pilots,' never astronauts?"

Krasnarov scowled. "So . . . ?"

"So, you lose a 'test pilot,' you name a street after him and keep on flying. You lose an 'astronaut' and you shut down the program for a year or two. Pilots are a dime a dozen."

Volkov laughed and nodded toward the cafeteria serving line. "And here comes last month's kopek's worth."

Ned twisted in his seat, and saw Baltazar da Silva, the new Brazilian pilot, standing in the chow line. He saw them looking at him and waved. Nobody waved back, but Bobbi tipped a salute with her empty beer bottle. "He and Katya must have just finished their sims," Ned said.

"Nomenklatura," said Valery Volkov. "His father pulls strings."

Bobbi McFeeley shook her head. "Maybe he is in the program by special dispensation. I don't know. I wondered why there were no Brazilians in our cadre to begin with. But I've seen him fly, and I worked ground control for him in the simulator. He knows his way around a cockpit."

"He auger in yet?" asked Forrest with casual interest.

"No. He is damned good," added Bobbi.

"I just bet he is." His eyes narrowed and he studied the other man. "Have you taken him out on a test flight? He looks like the kind you'd like to fly."

Bobbi stood up and slapped herself on both hips. "Yep. Young and healthy, they don't give out as fast as some. You guys want another round? I'm buying."

Forrest watched her go. "Whoo-ee. She's a bobcat, all right." He nudged Ned with his elbow. "You have any of that yet?"

Ned shook his head. "I'm still studying the situation," he said.

"So. I thought she mentioned you there a moment ago."

Volkov sighed. "That woman looks as good going or coming."

Ned cocked an eye at the Russian. "You know how she looks coming?" he said; but Volkov didn't get it.

Levkin nudged his comrade. "Do not let Yekaterina hear you say such things."

"Tscha! Katyushka is in library; my heart is here." He sighed melodramatically.

Ned thought Volkov's wife a little on the muscular side, the kind of build that used to give Olympic judges drinking problems. All the right equipment and in all the right proportions but strong as spring steel. Take *her* out for a test flight, brother, you better expect some turbulence. She smiled more than all the other pilots put together, Levkin excepted. An invitation, or just being friendly? Ned was not sure what sort of understanding she and Valery had between them. Volkov flirted with half the women on the base; but that did not mean he was serious, or that he would tolerate his wife doing the same.

Ned thought fleetingly, irritatingly, of Betsy: never asking him where he had been, not even looking up from her paper when he came home late. How would he have felt had she started cheating, too? Jealous? Vindicated? Relieved? It was hard to tell now. What he had felt, what he would have felt, what he thought he should have felt . . . It was all jumbled into a knot somewhere in the center of him.

On her way back, Bobbi dropped off a bottle of Xingu at da Silva's table. Da Silva looked up, startled; then he flashed her a smile.

"Looky there, son," said Forrest, "and tell me she doesn't want him in the sack with her."

"He does have those dark, Latin good looks," Ned allowed.

"Brown," said Krasnarov. "From kissing politicians too much where they like to be kissed."

Forrest turned and looked at him as Bobbi resumed her seat. "Son, you can get a tan like that in lots of ways. Did you know that Brazil imported three and a half million slaves back in the old days? That's *seven times* what the good ol' US of A brought in."

Krasnarov gave him a look. "Well?"

Forrest spread his hands wide and smiled white. "Well, today forty percent of Brazilians admit to having African blood. And sixty percent are liars."

Weeks were swallowed easily by the monster, Routine. Simulator training; tech specs; hands-on disassembly and reassembly in the Prep Building; control center training—they would be doubling up in Mission Control and had to be ready to sit at any of the consoles. Ned was startled to realize he had been on the archipelago for several months and had not yet written Betsy to tell her where he was.

She probably thought he had fallen off the edge of the earth, if she thought of him at all.

Outside the base complex, he could visit the nature reserve, where the wardens treated him as if he were out to mug his mother—and probably with good reason. Bonny de Magalhães told them all that the reserve had still not recovered from the tourism of the previous decade. There you could see twenty-four different species of marine birds, two different kinds of marine tortoises, and, if you snuck into the water, sharks. Which might be the last thing you saw. From Mirante dos Golfinhos you could watch the dolphins sport in the bay. A few of the beaches that lined the island were open for swimming, but the surf was often rough and Bonny discouraged it on most days.

To Ned, one marine bird looked an awful lot like another. And after one scuba dive to the wreck of *Paquistão* under St. Anthony's Bay, he figured he had pretty much seen a shipwreck. Even the humvee races that Forrest organized between the complex and the Vila became routine after a while.

Ned kept up a brisk walk on the gymnasium treadmill, elbows held tight to his sides, torso twisting side to side, one foot planted before the other could be raised. The walking gait causes the rear end to wag, and Ned wished passingly that Bobbi or Yekaterina were working out, too. He grunted. If Katie Volkovna was starting to look good to him, maybe it was time for some quick R&R in Fortaleza. Check out one of the trainer jets; grab a little sky and pour it on. Work the kinks out. He had forgotten how much he had hated the training part. The constant workouts, the endless hours in the simulators. The study and the drill until you *dreamed* tech specs and drawings. He would rather be behind a stick, looking down at the clouds; but you didn't dare let up, even for a moment. There were eight competitors and only one prize.

Prime Pilot on an unproven design. Except for the short-lived X-33, there had never been anything like The Planks. It was hard to know where the edges were. The engineers said one thing; they talked about the design envelope; but engineers didn't know shit. It was all pencils and drawings and formulas; and they all said that it would do this or it wouldn't do that; but in the end some squarehead with hairy ears who didn't know any better would have to put iron between his legs and ride sky. Afterward the engineers would all nod to each other and say, Yep, that's just what she was designed to do.

Except sometimes they said, well, maybe that decimal place should have been over one.

There was something indefinable about taking a new iron into the sky, about being the first to push that particular envelope. Maybe it was the risk or the glory. Maybe it was the challenge of facing the nameless unknown and giving old No-Nose a kiss on the lips. Or maybe it was just sheer hell-raising bravado. It didn't matter. Maybe it was all of that, all balled together.

There would be many test flights. They would all get to fly her sooner or later. But it would only be the first time once. There would only be one pilot that all the others would have to say that they followed him up, that they took hold of the yoke only after someone else proved the sumbitch would fly at all.

He had never been able to explain that to Betsy, what it meant to be *número uno*, explain how much more *alive* he felt out there on the edge. She used to give him round-eyed looks when he left, as if she never expected him to come home; as if every time he left, he died.

Forrest emerged from the locker room. He had a towel wrapped around his waist and another thrown across his shoulder. His body gleamed with beads of water. *Jesus,* Ned thought, *that guy has a body.* He must have to scrape the women off with a putty knife.

Forrest watched him walk the treadmill for a while. Step, step, step. He shook his head. "You don't seem to be getting anywhere, son."

Ned looked at him.

"Don't get me wrong. I admire your persistence—just like a squirrel in a cage—but why not jog or run?"

Ned increased the pace. Step-step-step. "I'm power walking. Wogging."

"Good thing it's a ridiculous name, because you sure do look ridiculous doing it. I swear every part of you is moving a different direction. Me, I just spent an hour in the weight room." He flexed his shoulders.

"Carrying coals to Newcastle, were you?"

Forrest laughed. "Son, you're going to have to update your clichés. Not many folks could wrap their mind around that one anymore. How about 'pump oil to Arabia'?"

Ned turned the machine off and rode the treadmill to the back end, where he stepped easily onto the deck. He picked up his towel and slung it over his shoulder. He said, "How about 'inflate the ego of a test pilot'?"

Forrest put on a thoughtful look. "Not bad," he said after a moment, "but it lacks the common touch." He held the door to the locker rooms open and followed Ned inside. "What is it about folks like you and me?" he asked while Ned pulled his shower towel and soap from his locker.

Ned looked at him. "How do you mean?"

"Well, look at us. We have those class sessions on the technical specs, right? So where were you and I yesterday afternoon? And where are Bobbi and Levkin right now? Boning up on the drawings in the library, right? And the physical therapists, they've laid out a training regimen, right? So we pump a little iron on the side. Wog a few miles."

"You have something better in mind? Or did you discover some hot nightlife in the Vila?"

Forrest followed him into the shower room. "There's a fellow, Claudio, who has a bar down that way. Not much of a bar, maybe; but then this ain't much of an island."

Ned turned the water on, hard and hot, and the spray hit him like a bundle of knitting needles. A cloud of steam welled up in the shower stall. Through the rippled, frosted glass, he could see Forrest's silhouette drying itself. Muted black and oddly shaped, as if he had been painted by one of those "modern" artists Betsy had been so hot on. For a while he had tried to learn, to understand her hunger for the sort of culture she had not been born to, following behind her through Dallas and Houston galleries, trying not to look bored. Now here was one of those odd, cubist bodies in real life, all colors and masses with no real shape. He thought for a fleeting moment that he would have to tell Betsy about it. Then he remembered where he was and where she was and that there was a letter in his desk that he still had not finished.

He called over the hissing waters. "Do you want to hop over to the mainland next Friday and sample the nightlife in Fortaleza?"

The silhouette paused. "Now, that's a real attractive offer.

The gals down here, they aren't as fussy about certain things as back home.''

Ned thought of the waitress in the hotel while he soaped up. Maria? Whatever. Sex had been a natural thing with her, a recreation. Smooth and easy and no questions asked. Betsy had been no prude, yet it had always been a big deal with her, with a lot of preliminaries and a lot of talking. "Well," he said, "it's the Latin culture."

"I wonder if the nuns knew that when they made me study Latin."

Ned rinsed. The steamy water ran down over his face and body. If Forrest said anything more, he didn't hear it.

When he emerged from the showers, Ned was surprised to see that Forrest was still there, sitting with his back to Ned on the long, low bench that ran between the two rows of lockers. He sat nearly dressed with a distant look on his face, holding a single sock in his hand.

Ned stepped up behind him and snapped his towel against a locker door. It crashed like a car wreck. Forrest jerked and turned his head. "You son of a bitch, you near gave me a heart attack."

"She must really be something."

"Who?"

"Whoever you were dreaming about."

"Ah." Forrest cocked his head and pursed his lips. "Yeah, she sure enough is. Something, like you said."

Ned's own locker stood across from Forrest's. He threw his towel over the open door and pulled out his fresh underwear. "Well? What's her name. And does she have a sister?"

"Several sisters, actually. I've been thinking of calling her *Sojourner Truth*."

"What?" Ned turned to look at him. "What are you talking about?"

"Pull your shorts up, son. You look foolish and it'll scare the girls. I was talking about the Plank. The test pilot usually gets to name his ship. That's a tradition that goes back to the old X-1, *Glamorous Glennis*.

"Yeah, until Gus Grissom named his Gemini capsule *Mollie Brown*."

Forrest shook his head ruefully. "Ah, bureaucrats got no sense of humor."

"And, what makes you think that *you'll* be the one to—".

"Sojourner Truth used to lead the slaves to freedom. 'Follow the Drinking Gourd.' The Big Dipper. That was its African name. Aim for the Pole Star and keep on a-going. 'Left foot, right foot, traveling on . . .' Shit, Ned, my folks have been chasing stars a long time. Call it a family tradition." He cocked his head and scratched the stubble on his chin. "Maybe *Bessie Coleman* would be better. She was the first black pilot. Had to go to France to get her license, though . . ."

"Well, now, Forrest, come to that, I've been thinking over names myself."

"Have you?" Forrest considered that. "So. Everybody needs a hobby. I suppose da Silva is thinking he'll call her *Southern Cross*, and Krasnarov has *Red Star* or some other unregenerate commie name in mind. And the others, too. Well, if I weren't training with a gang of jet jockies who didn't each think that he was the hottest damn pilot who ever flew iron I would be sore disappointed." He paused a moment. "Tell me, old son, have you ever wondered what this program is all about? I mean: Why Daedalus? Why Brazil? Why a little slab of rock out in the middle of the Atlantic Ocean?"

"I suppose, 'why not?' is not an adequate answer."

Forrest smiled slightly. "Everything happens for a reason, Ned. Look, if Brazil wants to launch satellites, why not rent space on the Shuttle?"

"Because it's ten times more expensive . . . ?" Ned suggested sardonically.

"So why not rent space on an Ariane? The French launch cheap."

"National pride? How should I know? Maybe they want their own launch capability."

"Then why are they hiding out here in the ocean?" Forrest shook his head. "You've been studying the Plank specs and the configurations. Tell me you haven't. How do those specs read to you? Cheap?"

"Well, let's say inexpensive."

"What about turnaround?"

Ned tilted his head back and thought about it. "I'd say pretty rapid," he decided. "Everything is modularized. Pull it out, plug it in. You could be down and back up in, oh, less than a week."

"Yeah. That's about what I thought, too. Did you notice that the crew cabin is a module, too? Pull it out and what do you plug in?"

"Instrument packages? A cargo module? What difference does it make?" Ned couldn't see that it mattered. What mattered was flying.

"Put in an additional cargo bay, you can fly it by remote or by computer. So, why have manned flights at all? Why not just loft the satellites and pop them out? Fly it back with a fucking VR helmet on your head. Why the docking collar at the nose?"

"What are you getting at, Forrest?"

Forrest finally noticed the lone sock in his hand and he pulled it onto his foot. Then he shoved both his feet into a pair of worn sneakers. "I think this program is bigger than it looks. A lot bigger. I think it's more than Brazil getting into the satellite launch business. A cheap way to get people and materials into orbit? Quick turnaround, groundside? I think someone's planning some serious shit up there."

Ned's Fortaleza trip was aborted before it was even half-planned. The word came down from Bonifácio de Magalhães that a party of Daedalus executives was junketing in from the mainland on Friday and the astronauts were cordially invited to have dinner with them in the executive dining room; by which he meant, "Don't make any plans."

Lacking anything more exciting to do, Ned decided to watch the arrival from the widow's walk above the main administration building. When he stepped outside, the Atlantic wind slapped his face and filled his nose with the sharp odor of

brine. The door to the admin building smacked shut behind
him, Katyushka Volkovna, leaning on the railing on her forearms, turned at the sound. With her close-fitting shorts and
blouse and her short-cropped hair, she seemed oddly unruffled
by the sea breeze. "*Privyet*, Ned," she said, shouting over the
wind.

Ned joined her at the railing. The landing apron was clear,
but at the far south end, in "the Box," the Plank nestled in
its test stand. A dozen or so technicians swarmed around her.
Ned nodded in that direction. "What's Mendoza up to? A
crew from Pratt-Whitney flew in day before yesterday, and
Bonny told me they've slipped the schedule again."

Katya shrugged. "More tethered tests. Is what engineers do.
For them, Plank is something to test, not fly." Ned laughed,
and Katya added, "He is unhappy."

"Who, Mendoza? How can you tell?" The techs cleared
the test bay. A little orange-and-white electric truck carried
them back into the hangar. Ned pointed. "I guess they're
ready."

For a while nothing happened. Then a billowing cloud of
vapor grew beneath it. Engine precool. Running liquid hydrogen through the system to bring everything down to operating
temperatures. Then a flash as the engines ignited and the vapor
burned off. Flames barely visible in the bright tropic sunshine
burst from the engines. The ship rose in its cradle, straining
against the cables that bound it to the earth. A moment later,
the rumble reached them.

"I wish I could cut those bonds," Katya said, leaning closer
to him.

"Wait until I'm aboard," Ned told her. She laughed and
studied him with some amusement, their faces only inches
apart. Ned searched, hesitated; and Katya pulled back. Well,
he who hesitates is lost. Perhaps later; perhaps just before he
strapped himself into an untested Plank and the need to live
became overwhelming. And perhaps when he knew Katyushka
Volkovna well enough to read her signals.

"That is they." She pointed to the sky above the Plank: a

rapidly approaching speck in the air. "The *papakhas*," she said.

"The what?"

"The *papakhas*," she said again. "The 'big hats.' It is what we call the bosses in Rossiya. Big hats for swelled heads."

Ned grinned. "We say 'bigwigs,' But wigs have been out of fashion too long. I like your version better."

The Plank settled back into her test stand, but it seemed to Ned that the roar of the engines continued, like a distant hum. He wondered if Mendoza had scheduled the static test to coincide with the executives' arrival. It never hurt to put on a show for the fat cats, especially around budget time.

Katyushka sucked in her breath. *"Shto eto?"* she said, drawing Ned's attention back to the approaching airplane, which looked to be just above Boldró Beach on final approach. Ned squinted against the sun. Something looked wrong. The craft was losing airspeed far too quickly for a normal landing. If the control surfaces failed to bite, the airplane would drop from the sky. Ned looked up over his shoulder at the control tower, but the angle was bad and he could see nothing. Did the ATC know there was a problem? Floriana was in radio contact; she *had* to know!

Closer now. Twin fan-jets aft, but . . . no stabilizer between them! Ned's first thought was that the tail had been ripped off in some catastrophic failure, like that airliner in Japan, years ago. Yet, the craft's approach was on the beam, not what you would expect from a rudderless craft. It was steady. It was just . . . Too. Damn. Slow. Ned gripped the railing with both hands, willing the plane to pull up, gain speed. "Come on, you bastard!" he muttered. "Come on . . ."

The distant hum had grown. Not an afterecho of Mendoza's test, after all; but some noise produced by the approaching plane. The aircraft was large enough now for him to spot the details. Narrow, sweeping wings set far aft on the fuselage, and . . . Damn, the stabilizers were on the wingtips! And there were a pair of canards just behind the cabin. What kind of airchine was it? Ned squinted at the craft as it passed between him and the sun, slowing almost to a stop, which was

God-damned impossible. He reached out and grabbed Volkovna by the arm. "Look at that!" he said. "See those louvers on the wings? It's a damn hoverjet, Katie! There must be half a dozen turbo fans in there." Not exactly on the wings, he saw, but on a kind of running board that ran the length of the plane and blended into those graceful, faerie wings in the rear. Venturis for three giant fans—eight-footers by the look of them—became visible as the louvers opened fully. The air blasts stirred tornadoes from the dust on the landing field, and the air filled with the familiar buzz of propellers—there must have been more than a hundred blades on each! It sounded like the Mother of All Beehives. On amphetamines.

The door to the widow's walk slammed open and Forrest Calhoun braked himself to a halt at the railing, "Sweet Jesus," he said, watching the eighty-foot craft slow to hover and gradually descend to the apron below. "I think I'm in love." He shielded his face against the dust devils whipped up by the great rotors. "And, behold," he cried, "a whirlwind was come out from the north, a cloud enveloped with brightness, from the midst of which gleamed a form like unto electrum."

Ned exchanged a look with Volkovna, who shrugged. "Is Bible, I think."

Slowly, the craft moved sideways to the very center of the apron. Ned swatted Forrest on the arm. "Look at that, would you," he shouted over the noise. "Playing with the fans on either side, I bet."

Forrest turned a bland face on Ned and the Russian woman. "It goeth straight, in any direction, without turning," he said. Then he blinked and lost the blank-faced look. "Bet it's damn tricky, though, a 'chine that size."

"I'd like to try her," said Ned, thinking how much of his soul he would mortgage for the chance to sashay around in that beauty. "I've never seen anything bigger than Ospreys and Harriers pull that trick." Bold, black italics across the fuselage proclaimed *DACX-102, ELIJAH*. Forrest nodded his head toward it.

"Should have called her *Ezekiel,*" Forrest said as the great lift rotors wound down to silence.

*   *   *

It was, Ned thought, a most spectacular arrival. When the big hats emerged from *Elijah*, it was almost an anticlimax. João Pessoa and some of the Fortaleza staff, a Brazilian official in sunglasses and a civilian outfit that somehow looked military, two broad-chested men in rumpled suits, and a white-haired, dough-faced old geezer with a bright bow tie. . . . A motley crew, indeed. One tall, thin woman on Bow Tie's arm, Boss's secretary? Hell, maybe she could sneak him aboard *Elijah*, if he played his cards right. Turn on some of the old astronaut charm that women found so alluring.

For that matter, she might know something about the Plank program. Secretaries were privy to an awful lot of information, Ned had learned back in the old days. They had solved the FTL communication problem and if you wanted to know what was coming down in any company, the secretaries could tell you weeks before your own boss knew. If you were on friendly terms with the secretaries, that is.

Betsy hadn't understood that, either.

The tropic breeze caught the woman's scarf. She reached up and pulled it back and held it to her throat, locking glances with Ned as she did. Ned grinned down at her, a welcoming grin that said he was available if she wanted it. She smiled a crooked smile back that said she didn't care if he was or not. Then she turned and spoke to Bow Tie. Probably her sugar daddy, he decided as they passed from sight below the balcony: Those had been mighty expensive clothes on display. The gal was a bit on the bony side for him, but the old guy probably had to take it where he could get it. Or where he could buy it. At that age, no one came and threw it at you. Sure, he had given Maria some money after that night in the hotel in Fortaleza; but that was different. That was to show appreciation, to let her buy herself the gift that his schedule did not allow him the time to buy. It was not as if he had to pay for it.

"Maria," he said.

Forrest looked at him. "What's that?"

"Nothing. I just remembered something I'd thought I'd forgotten."

At the reception that preceded the dinner, Ned contrived to cut the secretary out of the herd. He located her in a small group that included Bow Tie, Pessoa, Bobbi McFeeley, and a few others. The secretary was listening intently to something that Bobbi was saying, sipping from time to time from a glass of sherry. Ned watched for a while, then slipped away to the bar.

The seminar room had been converted into a lounge by the simple expedient of removing all the chairs and desks, covering the flatscreen on the wall with the Daedalus banner, and setting up a free bar. The company logo featured a stylized set of wings against a solar disc. Every now and then Ned had to remind himself that it had been Icarus who had flown too close to the sun, not Daedalus. Daedalus had flown on to safety.

Though Icarus had been the true test pilot, pushing at the outside of the envelope, finding out just what his father's new design could do. As to which of the two had been the better pilot, it was, in Forrest's immortal phrase, a matter of 'a pinion.'

"A bourbon, Ellenis," he told the commissary woman who was doubling as bartender. "And a glass of sherry."

"Oho, you have your eye on someone, *senhor?*" The woman was young, perhaps nineteen. Young enough for Ned to feel his own age.

"I always have my eye on someone," he told her. "Sometimes, you." The girl giggled and looked down as she poured the drinks. When she handed him the glasses, she managed to brush his hand with hers. Ned grinned at her.

He stood off to one side where he could catch the secretary's eye and waited with both drinks in his hands until she finished her sherry. Then, just as she looked around for a waiter, Ned hoisted the sherry glass. The gesture caught her attention. She looked momentarily puzzled, then pleased, and broke off her conversation with the others to come to Ned's side.

"Captain DuBois, I believe," she said, accepting the glass with her left hand and extending her right. Ned placed her empty glass on a nearby table and shook her hand.

"Just Mr. DuBois, these days," he said.

"A courtesy title, then."

"Enjoying the party?"

"Yes, you meet such interesting people." She laid one hand lightly upon his forearm. "Such as yourself, Captain. I have been looking forward to meeting you—and the other test pilots—for some time."

Hot damn, a groupie! This was almost too easy. "What are you doing after the dinner, uh . . . ?"

"Mariesa," she said.

"Mariesa. That's a very nice name. Out of the ordinary."

"Yes. Quite." She smiled and her eyes seemed to twinkle with a secret amusement. "After the dinner? I'm afraid I have a number of meetings to attend to."

"Business meetings. They must be boring."

"Oh, they can be. So many details, you can lose sight of the goal."

"Look, there isn't much nightlife on the island, but there's a great ocean view from atop Morro do Pico. You can see the breakers glow at night. And there's a crazy spot just ten meters wide down in the nature reserve where it sometimes rains without a cloud in the sky. Then afterward maybe we can sneak aboard *Elijah*. Man, that bird must be something to see. I think I can find someone from the steno pool who could sub for you at your meeting."

Mariesa laughed. "It sounds . . . tempting; but I really don't think that . . ."

"Leave everything to me, honey. I . . . Oh, shit." He had seen Pessoa approaching.

João Pessoa smiled broadly as he joined them. "Ah, I see that you have already met," he said.

"Not formally," said Mariesa.

"So." Pessoa bowed minutely. "Allow me the pleasure,

then. *Senhor* Edward DuBois, of our pilot cadre, may I introduce dona Mariesa van Huyten, chairman of the board of Van Huyten Industries, parent company of Daedalus Aerospace. *Dona* Mariesa; *seu* Ned.''

Ned closed his eyes. ''I haven't made too much of an ass of myself, have I?''

''Not at all, *seu* Ned,'' said Mariesa. ''It was quite flattering, really, to have a good-looking man 'hit on' me without knowing who I was.'' She paused and gave Ned the once over. ''And if it is any consolation, I might almost wish I *were* a secretary.''

''Might,'' he said, with a grin returning to his teeth.

''Almost,'' she replied with a bright smile.

The briefing was held in the conference room early the next morning. Too early. Ned felt as if his head were packed in cotton. He always did that. He always drank too much, and he always ate too much; and now he would have to do penance in the gym, burning away those calories that he and Ellenis had not burned away last night. Forrest did not help things with a booming greeting that reverberated like a church bell in Ned's skull.

''Up early, are we, son?'' Forrest slapped him on the back. ''Say, you do look a might peaked, if I do say so. Morning, Bobbi. Comrade.'' He stood beside Ned and stared out the window that ran along the west wall of the conference room. ''Now, there's a sight I never tire of. Bird's-eye view of a bird.''

The conference room was situated on the top tier of the offices, labs, and workshops that lined the south wall of the Hangar building. Its window gave a panoramic view of the interior, where the Plank sat in its cradle. Ned watched the technicians swarming over her, checking her out after the latest test. Mendoza stood on the top-level catwalk, with his arms folded across his chest. Every now and then, he shoved a portaphone to his face, listened, then barked into it.

It might have been his Indio blood, or it might have been coincidence; but shortly, Mendoza turned and stared directly up at Ned. Ned waved, but the chief engineer only stood there. After a moment, Ned gave up and resumed his seat.

"Where are van Huyten and the other big hats?" he asked of no one in particular.

Forrest shrugged. He pulled out the seat next to Ned and dropped into it. "I hear, you approach her right, she gives tours of *Elijah*." Ned gave him a sharp glance, but Forrest was the picture of innocence. Krasnarov only shook his head.

"It is too fine a morning, Calhoun. So today I tolerate you."

"Why, that's real white of you."

"In Brazil . . ." It was Baltazar da Silva who spoke, and he stopped short when the others turned to look at him. "In Brazil," he said again after a moment, "we call our bosses 'whites.' Even if he is a *prêto*, we say he is '*meu branco*,' 'my white.' If a *prêto* has become wealthy, we say 'he used to be black.' So *branco* has to do with power and wealth, not with being white-skinned."

"Gee," said Forrest, to no one in particular. "I wonder how that came to be."

Da Silva leaned forward over the table. "The races of Brazil . . ." he said heatedly.

Bobbi interrupted him. "What do you call someone like Mendoza, Bat? Is he, um, *prêto* or *branco*?"

Da Silva sank back in his chair, holding his hands up, palms facing out. He held that pose for a moment, then laid his hands on the table and turned to Bobbi. "Neither," he said. "He is a *caboclo*, an Indio who has taken to Brazilian ways."

Forrest leaned close to Ned. "*Prêto, branco, caboclo, mestiço, mulato* . . . Good thing they ain't race-conscious down here," he stage-whispered. Ned saw that da Silva had heard.

"Don't bait him," Ned whispered back.

"What? Who?"

"Any of them. Krasnarov. Da Silva. I mean, we're all in this together, right?"

Forrest's face darkened and he turned away. "You go on thinking that, old son. You just go right on thinking that." Ned tugged on his sleeve.

"What is it?"

Forrest's eyes took in the others around the table. "Later," he said.

Ned thought that Bat wasn't such a bad sort. A little—aristocratic, maybe; a bantam cock of a man. And he was entirely too close to de Magalhães. Sure, they were both Brazilians—both "*cariocas*" even, whatever that meant—but it smacked too much of brown-nosing and favoritism. You didn't climb the pyramid through connections, you did it because you had what it took, between the ears and between the legs. "You know," he told Forrest privately, "we really aren't the best, only the most available. Only what Pessoa could get cheap."

"Van Huyten," said Forrest.

"What?"

"Van Huyten. It's the van Huyten woman behind all this; not Pessoa." He said that loudly enough that the others heard him.

Da Silva scowled. Bobbi gave him a curious look. Krasnarov shook his head. "What difference does it make who—?"

"A lot of difference, son," Forrest told him. "I couldn't see how Daedalus could take this thing too far. Not as far as those tech specs said it ought to be taken. But Van Huyten Industries? Man, that's a whole new ballgame. Do you know who that fellow was that was with her last night? Not McReynolds, but Gregorson, the one with all the hair."

"Yeah," said Bobbi. "They call him the Werewolf. Big time in electronics. Started from nothing and all that crap. His firm did the avionics for the—" She glanced at the Russians, shrugged. "For an airchine I used to flight-test."

Forrest grinned. "That's right, little lady. Werewolf Gregorson, himself. And Mariesa van Huyten, who has the faucet for one of the biggest and oldest family fortunes in America—not to mention a highly diversified holding company. And João Pessoa, who is maybe not such a big name in the US of A, but sure enough swings weight down in these parts. And last night our friends across the table—" He indicated Levkin, Krasnarov, and the Volkovs. "—were thick as thieves with that fellow from Energia."

"Vyachislav Rukavishnikov," said Levkin.

"Sure, that's easy for you to say." Forrest leaned back in his chair and spread his arms out, palms up in a great shrug. "VHI, with Werewolf and Daedalus; plus Energia . . . The engines are Pratt-Whitney. The landing gear are Ruger AG. How many others are backing this thing?"

"Enough," said Ned with sudden, quiet certainty, "to make it really happen."

Van Huyten and the big hats arrived shortly afterward. She sat at the head of the conference table, flanked on one side by Rukavishnikov and on the other by the governor of Ceará. Gregorson, McReynolds, and de Magalhães sat at the other end with Pessoa, who was technically the host. Mendoza stood in the corner with a look of infinite patience.

Introductions had been made, pleasantries exchanged; everyone had a mug of strong Brazilian coffee in front of them, except Rukavishnikov and Krasnarov, who—so heretical for this country!—drank outrageously sweetened tea. Rukavishnikov actually put a sugar cube between his teeth and drank his tea through it. Ned had never seen anyone do that before.

Van Huyten spoke with a smile like the cat had when all the feathers were floating in the air. "Because of its off-the-shelf design, state-of-the-art electronics—" A nod to the Werewolf. "—and rapid turnaround, unmanned Planks can lift satellites into Low Earth Orbit at less cost than disposable boosters. But the real payoff will come from the use of manned Planks to retrieve and service those same satellites, bringing them in for repair, upgrade, and maintenance. This will extend the useful satellite life and save millions of dollars for their owners. It will also allow less expensive satellites to be launched in the first place."

Ned listened politely while she talked. It was her hand, she could play it. But he didn't give a flying fig whether satellites did or didn't need triple-redundancy and gold-plated quality. Come to that, he didn't even care if van Huyten's program was profitable in the long run. Not that he wished her ill, but the flying itself was enough for him. Just the thought of soaring up and out, into the void, into the black soundlessness of space, gave him chills. Did you really need a reason beyond the going itself? What could be better than touching the sky ... except touching another world, maybe; and *that* was not in the cards. Not in his flying lifetime.

"By combining a low-cost regime," van Huyten said, "with a frequent and reliable schedule, we hope to attract enough customers from telecommunications companies, weather services, geological surveys, and so forth to maintain a lively launch and repair business. For complex tasks, we envision returning older satellites to Earth for refurbishing; but the routine maintenance and upgrade work must be done on-orbit. So, needing a 'repair shop' where our payload specialists and technicians can work shirtsleeve, we have recently—"

A little wheel in Ned's head went *click*. He could do simple arithmetic. Van Huyten plus Rukavishnikov equaled . . .

"Jesus," he said aloud. "You're going to rent Mir!"

He saw Krasnarov across the table suddenly stiffen and heard Forrest's low chuckle in his ear. Mir. The Russian space station. Occupied continuously for how long? Now sporadically, since the "Otrivátnia." The Russians had a "garage" in space with no money to refurbish, upgrade, and staff it; van Huyten had a lot of money and no garage. No wonder half the pilots were Russian. Everything had a price, and the price was not always money.

Van Huyten turned a tight smile on him. "That is correct, Captain DuBois." He could not tell if she was pleased that he had reasoned it out or frosted that he had stolen her thunder. Shit. Rule Number One: Don't piss off the boss. Turn on the old charm, fast. "Sorry to interrupt," he said, "it's just that my enthusiasm—"

"I quite understand." Van Huyten looked around the table and made an inclusive gesture with her hands. "I trust the rest of you are equally enthused."

Ned looked, too. Bobbi, the governor, most of them looked pleased as a horny man at a nymphomaniacs' convention; though Krasnarov's expression was oddly wooden, and Forrest had a thoughtful look on his face. And nothing at all might have been said to go by Mendoza's attitude. Yet, oddest of all were the reactions of Pessoa, McReynolds, and Gregorson. It was just a fleeting glance, exchanged among themselves, and Ned might have missed it if he hadn't turned his head when he did. Naturally, they could not have been surprised by van Huyten's announcement. They were on the inside, and near the top. And it wasn't surprise that he saw. Pessoa raised an eyebrow at Gregorson and Gregorson smiled like a patient cat and old Bow Tie's hand rose and fingered his lapel pin, an outstretched hand holding a ruby.

On the balcony again. At night. The stars gleamed against the skin of the hoverjet crouched below. The sea breeze blew moist and cool. A perfect place to bring a woman, Ned thought, if only there were a woman to bring and a little privacy beside. Girls there were in plenty on the base—there always were, they appeared by magic—but only a few women. And fewer still who could understand the beauty of the jumper that waited on the tarmac and the spacecraft that waited in the hangar and those lights that glittered—also waiting—overhead. Volkovna, surely; but Ned did not know how thoroughly married she might be. And Bobbi. Beneath her tomboy overalls, she must feel her heart beat faster, too.

And van Huyten. Mariesa, for at least a few self-deluded minutes. No beauty herself; but a lover of this sort of beauty. Ned had seen the way she had stroked *Elijah's* skin when she had disembarked. Could a shared love of *this*—Ned's mental arm swept out to embrace the machines, the sky, the stars—could it bridge the gap of money and class?

Dream on, Ned. Seducing your boss's boss? That was boss-squared. Boss-cubed, if you counted Bonny de Magalhães. And he didn't even feel a sexual attraction to the woman. It was just that he sensed they were . . . soulmates? He hated that word. Betsy had used it constantly, always in the negative. But, yes. Soulmates. They dreamed the same dreams, at least sometimes. He thought that, for Mariesa van Huyten, just being out there would be enough, too. And all the rest of it, the

Plank, the satellite maintenance program, the leasing of Mir, was just an excuse to get her out there.

I'll be your chauffeur, he thought. *Damn me, if I won't.*

The door opened softly behind him and for a weird, mystical moment he thought it was van Huyten herself come out to look at the stars.

"You must like it up here, son."

Ned did not turn around. "Hello, Forrest. What's wrong; you bored?"

"Naw. Just looking to chew a little fat. What did you think of our tame whirlwind down there?"

"I think she's the second most beautiful sight on the island. I wanted to fly her so bad my hands ached."

"Yeah, I noticed you left fingerprints in the seat arms when Ortega took us all up for a spin. But Benedicto was right. None of us are checked out on her. She's a chancy gal. Still in flight test, really. Still an X-plane. And noisier than a Baptist convention. I think they brought her out just to impress the governor and the Energia folks. It'll be a while before Benedicto sets her down on one of those center city airports he's dreaming of."

"Maybe," Ned allowed. "But the future has a way of arriving ahead of schedule. Quiet her down; prove her out; and, yeah, I can see those airliners floating up past downtown skyscrapers."

"No more runways," said Forrest. "No more airports miles and miles outside of town. No more landing patterns over the . . ." A sudden, hard look, instantly gone. "Over the less desirable neighborhoods."

"Well," said Ned, "I think Ortega would just as soon trade places with us."

Forrest nodded in the dark. "All van Huyten's boys have stars in their eyes. That McReynolds fellow—the CFO?—he told me she's an amateur astronomer, herself. Did you know that?"

"No. No, I didn't." Ned studied the constellations overhead. Familiar stars dropping away in the north. Strangers peeking over the edge of the southern horizon. No pole star down here, he thought, but that's Alpha Centauri just kissing the western horizon, the closest of them all. So. They both liked to look at the night sky; she just looked a little more closely, was all.

"So, Forrest," he said, "you want to tell me what's bugging you?"

"I augered in during a sim yesterday," the big man said in a brooding voice.

"I heard. Does that mean I have to teach you the secret handshake now for the Walking Corpses Club?" Forrest jerked his head and gave him a hard stare; and Ned sensed that humor was not the appropriate response. "Hell, Forrest, it was bound to happen sooner or later. You said so yourself. You lasted longer than any of us."

"Yeah. And someone didn't like that." He brought a fist down, hammerlike, on the rail. Ned frowned and touched his friend on the shoulder.

"What do you mean?"

Forrest didn't move but he made no attempt to brush Ned's hand off. "Ned, old son," he said after a moment's silence, "how bad do you want Prime Pilot?"

"So bad I can taste it."

"Yeah. Me, too. Same for everyone. Valery, he's in love with danger; while for Krasnarov, it's a matter of professional pride. Bobbi wants to prove girls can be pigheaded fools, just like boys. You . . ." Forrest grunted a soft laugh. "You always wanted to be Tom Corbett, Space Cadet. I remember that from back in Edwards."

"And what about you, Forrest?"

Forrest studied the jump jet where it crouched in the night. Slowly, he rubbed his two hands together. "Yeah. Well. Glory and honor, you know. The usual shit."

"Seems to me I remember something or other about being a role model."

Forrest snorted. "I was drunk. The day I become a role model for some poor kid in Bed-Stuy is the day this country's in real trouble."

"I can't argue with you there, Forrest."

Forrest chuckled. "But tell me, Ned," and his voice had turned serious again, "just what are you willing to do to get the Prime slot?"

"My best."

"And what if your best isn't good enough?"

"That's awful hard to imagine."

"Try."

Ned shrugged. "I'll wave good-bye when you take off."

"Thanks for the vote of confidence, old buddy; but someone doesn't like that notion. Ned, I augered in because someone boogered my sim."

It was like a punch in the gut. Ned sucked in his breath. "You think so?" Or was Forrest just sore because his streak had ended? Forrest Calhoun had never been the sort to make excuses, though.

Forrest smiled with half his mouth. "Naw. Maybe that paper clip got stuck in that relay box by accident."

"Damn. Does Bonny know?"

"Told him right off. Don't know what he can do about it, though, except boost security."

"You think it was pranking?"

Forrest shook his head. "Not over-the-top enough for a good prank."

Ned hesitated a long while before asking, "Do you think it was someone didn't care for the top-scoring pilot being black?"

Forrest's smile was without humor. "Son, I surely do hope so. Because where I grew up, I learned to deal with that. If that's what it was, and I find out who it was, he's gonna be walking mighty funny for a long time after. No, I'm afraid it could be worse than that."

"Worse how?" Another thought, more chilling, struck him. "Someone out to sabotage the program?"

A shake of the head. "Not a big enough hit for that. It's a whole lot worse."

Sometimes Forrest's cryptic ways irritated him. Ned snapped, "What the hell could be worse than sabotage?"

"Betrayal, Ned. Betrayal. I think one of us wants to be Prime Pilot in the worst possible way."

6.

Whatever Works

They called it the Afterclass.

Barry Fast hurried down the nearly empty hallway toward the building manager's office. It was 4:20 and school was still in session. Oh, the bitching and moaning there had been about that; and not just the teachers. Still, Barry had to admit that Mariesa had a point—unless it was Belinda's point. Most people pulling down forty-five a year—the *average* teacher's salary in New Jersey—worked an eight-hour day and more. And it wasn't as though the students were in class the whole time.

The Afterclass. Barry chuckled to himself. Chase Coughlin called it Universal Detention.

From three to five, everyone was in study halls, in gym classes, or in extracurriculars. Barry thought putting all of the gym classes at the end of the day was a good idea. It gave the kids a chance to wind down and blow off steam before they went home. And requiring that the day's assignments be turned in during the Afterclass study hall was one way of dealing with parents who didn't stay on their kid's case at home. Maybe not the best way, but Barry didn't know that there was a best way.

Last year, the kids had gotten out of school in midafternoon. That might have made sense back when one parent was always home; but in an age of single-parent and two-parents-working households it did not. Some of the kids, Barry knew, used to go up the street to the public library—kids like Jenny Ribbon and Cheng-I Yeh and Karen Chong. And Tani Pandya went straight to her dad's deli. But most of them had gone home to empty houses or just ran around North Orange. Sometimes they got into trouble. Chase Coughlin had been suspected of shoplifting, though the store had later dropped the charges; and Azim Thomas had actually been arrested for getting into a fight down around the Locks. Last year, Shannon had told him, a girl in the Dayton middle school hurt herself in the kitchen and her parents hadn't gotten home until after six. The doctors had fixed the girl up, but she had to go to a special school now.

Barry reached the building manager's office and waved to Samantha Ybarra, the assistant manager. She wore the Mentor uniform: a below-the-knee jumper that shaded from green at the hemline through blue and purple to black at the shoulders. It looked better than it sounded, partly because of the cut and style. On her breast was the Mentor logo, a broad, black M superimposed over a tall thin A sat atop an inverted red triangle. It had taken Barry awhile to figure it out, but the combination looked rather like a rocket ship with fins over a plume of flame.

It had taken him even longer to decode the shading of colors on the jumper . . . until he realized that the "rocket ship" badge was positioned on the edge of the black. . . .

Ad astra per haute couture.

Sam Ybarra smiled at him. "Good afternoon, Mr. Fast. The Man is waiting for you." Barry nodded politely. This had once been the principal's office, when Bob Boucher had been the principal. Now there were four principals, except they were called principal teachers and they had no administrative duties. They acted like the senior partners in a law firm, and their offices were in their classrooms. The building manager handled the administration.

"Hi, Grant," he said entering the office. "What's up?" Grantland deYoung was a thin, wiry man with long, blond hair tied up in a ponytail at the back. An earring stud accented his left ear. He wore green slacks and a black blazer with the Mentor badge sewn on the breast pocket.

DeYoung nodded to the woman sitting in the visitor's chair. "This is Mrs. Ribbon. Jenny's mother."

Barry smiled and held out his hand. "Hi. Pam, isn't it?" He knew damn well it was "Pam" because Pamela Ribbon came to the school more than all the other parents combined—or so it seemed to Barry—and always with the intention of wringing some advantage for her daughter out of the rules and regulations. Pamela Ribbon recognized only one capital crime: Coming in Second. Barry assumed that Ribbon-*père* felt the same way about Winning *über alles*, but he was usually tied up in some high-level corporate dogfight and seldom had time to visit the school.

Barry knew there was trouble when Pam did not accept his handshake. Instead she shoved a piece of paper at him. "I want to know," she said sternly, "why you are forcing the children to recite prayers in school."

Barry glanced at the paper and recognized it instantly. He frowned, his puzzlement deepening, and looked at Grantland deYoung, who gave him an "I've been through this already" look. "This isn't a prayer, Mrs. Ribbon. It's a pledge we recite each day at the Morning Assembly. . . ."

The Morning Assembly reviewed what would be done that day and recognized student accomplishments, not only in school, but also in community service and any other notable outside activities. Anyone who reached or passed a benchmark was recognized, not just those who came in first. Competition stirred achievement and self-esteem; but it was competition against a goal and not against other students.

"Read it out loud," Pamela Ribbon insisted.

Barry shrugged and exchanged another look with deYoung. He didn't have to read it anymore. It had been committed to memory. But he held the slip of paper up, anyway.

"*This day has been given to me fresh and clear. I can either use it or throw it away. I promise that I shall use this day to the fullest, realizing that it can never come back again. I realize that this is my life to use or to throw away.*'" He folded the paper and looked at Mrs. Ribbon.

"That sounds pretty prayerlike to me."

"It's the Marva Collins Pledge. She once ran a small private school in the Chicago ghetto . . ."

"I've been waiting for something like this ever since those right-wingers took over our school."

It probably wasn't the politic thing to do, but Barry laughed out loud. "Pamela," he said, "nobody 'took over' the school. The legislature let out a Request for Proposal, Mentor Academies bid on the proposal, and the Select Commission on Schools awarded the contract to Mentor. Mentor has five years to show tangible results to the commission to qualify for renewal. If Dr. Karr has any religion at all besides education, I haven't discovered it. And as for politics, right or left, she votes the Whatever Works ticket."

"And that rich woman out on her estate?" Mrs. Ribbon waved her arm, pointing. It was the wrong direction, but Barry didn't correct her.

"As far as I know," he said, "she practices a purely conventional Dutch Reformed."

Pam Ribbon exhaled. "I will instruct my daughter not to recite this prayer."

Barry thought about correcting her again, but saw that it would be futile. "Jenny must stand along with everyone else in the Assembly, but that is to show respect for the school and her fellow students. She does not have to recite the pledge. After all, that's what the pledge is all about."

Jenny's mother looked at him suspiciously. "What do you mean?"

"'This is my life to use or to throw away,'" he quoted.

Barry hated Saturday meetings. Saturdays, at least, should be his own, with time to pursue his hobbies. But the Institute

Fellows were going to meet face-to-face, and Barry was one of the faces. Most of their business they conducted on-line, but Onwuka Egbo had suggested that a monthly gathering would help cement the group.

That left early Saturday afternoon for his hobby. An all-too-short afternoon.

"Do you have to go?" Shannon asked as she pulled away from him. The sheets fell from her, revealing her soft, rounded flesh, and Barry stroked her lightly along the arm with his fingertips.

"Institute meeting," Barry said. "I have to be there."

The bedsprings squeaked and Shannon rolled out of the bed, leaving Barry's fingertips hovering in midcaress. She began gathering her scattered clothing, tucking it under her arms. Barry stayed in bed and watched. "Where is this meeting?" she asked when she straightened up. The clothes in her arms draped her imperfectly.

"At Silverpond," he said.

Shannon paused before turning toward the bathroom. "You're out there a lot, these days."

"It's where the Institute meets."

"Why can't they meet at your house?"

Barry sat up in the bed, pulling the sheet up to his waist. "What difference does it make?"

"Suppose you tell me."

Barry sighed. "Mariesa has taken a personal interest in the school."

Shannon walked into the bathroom and left the connecting door open. Barry heard the water start. First, a gushing as it ran into the tub; then a hiss as the shower turned on. "Why such a personal interest," Shannon called over the sound of the shower, "in one teachers' task force at one school in one 'industry' "—Barry heard the twist she gave *that* word—"among the hundreds that she owns?"

And that was a very good question, one that Barry himself had pondered with no answer. The lady had steel mills and pharmaceutical labs and Lord knew what to worry over and eat her time. Yet, he had never seen her distracted at a meeting. "I don't know," he said. "I think she really is serious about improving education."

He heard the shower curtain thrown back with a hard swipe. "Don't tell me you buy into that teachers-have-failed-us crap!"

Just the tiniest bit of irritation nudged him. "No. And I don't think she has, either."

There was a moment's pause, then Shannon appeared in the bathroom doorway. Behind her, the water hissed unheeded in the stall. She looked . . . erotic in her very ordinariness. She gave him a funny look. "Why do you say that?"

"If she did, would she have kept as many of us on as she has?"

"Compared to replacing the entire staffs of two high schools, three middle schools, and a dozen elementary schools all in a few months? Maybe." Shannon turned about and stepped out of Barry's sight. Soon, he heard sounds that meant she was in the shower. He sighed and pushed himself out of bed. His own clothes were hung across the chair at the writing desk.

Cocking his head, he listened to the shower and imagined Shannon with the water streaming off her, skin gleaming, the soapsuds draping her body; and sighed. *I must be getting old,* he thought, pulling on his socks. Time was, he would have been in there with Shannon—soapin' and gropin'.

Barry did a neck roll, loosening stiffened muscles, and looked slowly around the room. The padded bucket chair by the lamp had unequal springs and a low back clad in a fabric of shopworn orange. The mattress on the bed sagged in the middle; the sheets were faded. The wallpaper in the motel room was a patternless tan turning slowly to gray. A water stain darkened one corner near the ceiling. *What a dump,* he thought. *Why do we even come here?*

But he knew the answer to that: because none of her friends ever came over this way; because there was less chance of discovery. The Sheraton, or even the Ramada over by the highway, were too exposed, too open to notice. They came here because there were few other places they could go. They came to a place where the desk clerk knew them by name, without ever knowing their names.

They had used an empty house, once. Barry had gotten the key from the realtor on the pretext of being an interested buyer. A large, upper-middle-class home set back from a shady avenue off of Dayton Parkway. There had been a fish-pond in the back and a child's swing set. He and Shannon had spread a blanket over the wall-to-wall carpeting and made love for an entire Saturday afternoon in front of the cold, clean fireplace, between times discussing the latest movie or the book she was reading or how she would decorate the house if it were hers. Barry had, at least in a part of his mind, imagined that it *was* their home; that they had just bought it, that they were about to move in. Maybe some of that fantasy had soaked through his skin into Shannon, because she had never repeated the experiment, no matter what houses went up for sale. He looked back on that afternoon now as something of a high point in their relationship, though the only thing he had to show for it was junk mail from every realtor in town.

Barry finished dressing and rummaged in the battered old army knapsack that he affected as part of his middle-class bohemian teacher image. He selected a book and settled himself into the battered chair to wait for Shannon. The chair legs were uneven and it wobbled when he shifted his weight.

Shannon emerged from the bathroom already dressed. She leaned over the arm of the chair, draping her left arm around his neck. Almost by reflex, Barry placed his own right hand on her buttock. Her skin was deliciously clean-smelling. Her kiss tasted of mint.

She removed his arm from around her and stepped to the mirrored dresser. "What's van Huyten like?" she asked. "In person, I mean."

Barry looked at her, but Shannon was adjusting her blouse in the mirror and he could not see her expression. "Oh, friendly, I guess, but in a down-your-nose way." A glib analysis, and unfair. Barry sensed an intensity in Mariesa van Huyten, the eagerness of a Thoroughbred waiting the opening gun. And underneath: stainless steel; a determination that had kept her at the top in what was still largely a man's sphere. "I don't know her that well," he added.

"Good."

He chuckled. "Don't worry, Shannon. She's not about to invite me to stay for breakfast."

Shannon's fingers froze on her buttons. "I didn't mean that," she said in a voice that told Barry she had.

Say the wrong thing, and Shannon could fly out of his life as mysteriously as she had flown into it. He didn't know how that would feel, only that he would feel it. "Come on, Shannon," he said lightly. "Someone that rich wouldn't look twice at someone like me." He wondered, *Should I get up and try to soothe her, or is this one of the times I should just lie doggo?* He never probed, never questioned their relationship. He had never asked why she had slid into the lounge booth with him that day three years ago, almost as if the reason were so fragile that exposure would burst it.

"I'm not worried about *her* looking at *you.*"

Well, well. The green-eyed monster. Shannon's eyes *were* green; but just now they seemed emerald. Barry felt the tiniest twinge of irritation. Married, Shannon had poor grounds to hold *him* to any standard of faithfulness. "Why should I look at her when I can look at you?"

That must have been the right thing to say, because Shannon relented. "I just don't want to lose you to money."

Barry shook his head. "Money can't buy me. Money can't buy . . . what we have together." He had almost said money can't buy love, but that was a line he had never crossed. Whether from some deep-seated reservations of his own or from some cockeyed respect for John Morgenthaler and his daughters, he did not know. But sometimes, late at night, on those nights he and Shannon did not have together, he ached to share those hidden and inaccessible parts of her life. He ached to have all of her and not just this one part. Perhaps that *was* love. Or perhaps it was only envy.

Shannon straightened her bow and brushed at the blouse to

smooth the wrinkles. "Did you remember to get all those things on the list?"

"Your groceries? Sure. I put them in your car." Shannon needed something to explain her absences. Several bags of groceries that Barry had bought earlier nicely accounted for the time Shannon had spent away from home, in case John ever turned into the kind of man who questioned his wife's absences.

Shannon checked herself in the mirror one last time before turning to leave. Barry wondered how she explained that inner glow she had when she went home to John. Didn't it cry out, "Hey, I've just had sex with my lover"? Maybe it faded by the time she got home, or maybe John thought it meant "Hey, I've just had a bang-up time shopping." Or maybe he just never noticed it at all.

When the door had closed behind Shannon, Barry settled himself back into the chair to wait a decent interval, so they would not be seen leaving together. The faint odor of Shannon lingered in the air; the mint of her toothpaste in his mouth; the softness of her flesh in his fingertips. This was always the worst part: waiting alone in the room.

Relationships assumed a life of their own, independent of the lovers devoured by them, and they lived or died in their own time. You could no more control them than you could control the seasons. Shannon would never leave John; and in his more rational moments Barry was just as happy to have his Shannon without the complications. But sometimes you looked ahead as far as you could see and you couldn't see anything. No closure, no fulfillment, no dénouement. He and Shannon would just go on and on; and when they reached their forties—their fifties—they would still be looking for out-of-the-way motels.

There was more than one way for things to end. Sometimes they just kept going, and going, and going; fading gradually into nothing, the way pop songs did. No cannons, no crashing cymbals, no final chorus. Just something fine and wonderful and spontaneous clouding into something ordinary and routine.

*   *   *

Sykes gave Barry a curious look when he opened the door. "Mr. Fast," he said with just the right blend of greeting and surprise. "I am afraid the meeting has been canceled."

Barry stood on the porch of Silverpond and stared at the butler. "Canceled? Why?" After that long drive out from North Orange . . . "Why wasn't I told?" he demanded.

Sykes managed to shrug without moving. It wasn't his problem and there was no point in complaining to him. "Both Mr. Egbo and Ms. dePardo were forced to cancel by unexpected circumstances earlier this afternoon. I informed the others, but when I attempted to reach you, there was no answer and I was forced to leave a message on your answering machine."

The way Sykes said that, it sounded almost unclean. Well, tough noogies, Sykes. Answering machines were all the middle class could afford for butlers. "I'm sorry," Barry said. "I haven't been home all afternoon." He wondered if telling Sykes where he *had* been would be the way to crack through that cultivated, butler imperturbability.

The phone rang. "One moment, sir," Sykes said. He backed away from the door and Barry took a step inside. Barry was fascinated by the bizarre windowpane in the front door and never missed a chance to study it. He wondered if the architect had had some secret code where, if you knew the distance at which each image inverted and matched it up to the appropriate panel, you could spell out a message. Silly, really. But he liked playing silly games, sometimes.

"Oh, miss. Dr. Andrews is on the line."

Barry turned around in time to see Mariesa pause at the foyer entrance. "I'll take the call in the Roost. Give me a minute . . . Barry? Oh, dear." A pause. "You never received the message, did you?"

"Sykes just told me. No bother. I'll be going now."

"To drive all this way only to drive back? I'll not hear of it. Sykes, have Mrs. Pontavecchio set for three at dinner."

"Very good, miss."

"And show Mr. Fast to the library. I will take the call here, instead." She took the phone from Sykes and covered the mouthpiece. "I shan't be a moment," she said to Barry.

"This way, please," said Sykes.

Barry wanted to tell him he already knew the way, but, hell, you followed the rules, right? Behind him he heard Mariesa talking. "Arlan? Yes, sorry to be so long. NORAD? No, the test will be restricted to 'Indian Country.' Recife and Fortaleza ATCs will handle everything else, and Governor Gomes will handle the ATCs. . . . Check with João just to make sure and then pass the word, unofficially, to the general."

Barry did not hear the rest. Sykes bowed him into the library and then, without a word, turned and left. "Well, yes," Barry said to the empty doorway, "I would like a drink, thank you. Bourbon-and-water. Early Times, if you have it—and I know you do." So much for hospitality. He jammed his hands in his pockets and walked idly around the room.

So, Barry, a little private dinner tonight? Just you and her. Well, and her mother, too. He'd eaten at Silverpond before, but usually a working lunch for Institute meetings.

Sykes reappeared in the doorway with a silver serving tray in his hand and, perched upon it, a bourbon-and-water. And without being asked. Barry smiled and accepted the drink. Touché.

Mariesa joined him in the library a few minutes later, followed shortly by Sykes with the inevitable Manhattan. "I've told Mrs. Pontavecchio to move dinner up to seven. She was quite put out about it, but I know she will cope."

"You didn't have to go to such a bother."

"It was no bother. We do not often entertain at Silverpond, so it will be pleasant to have someone else to talk with." She led him to the back alcove of the library, where two high-backed leather chairs did not quite face each other. Barry waited until she had settled herself in the left-hand chair before taking the other for himself.

"Your mother . . . ?" he said.

"She does not take the cocktail hour; but she will be joining us for dinner." Mariesa pressed her lips together briefly. "She will be dressing, I'm afraid. We normally do, for dinner; but I thought, under the circumstances, less formality was in order."

Which only showed, Barry thought, what different worlds they lived in. Mariesa had changed to a black and white "cocktail" dress, with the hand-and-fireball brooch pinned above her right breast. Not too elaborate—he had already noticed that Mariesa preferred the simple and spare—but it was not the sort of outfit Barry would have called "not dressing" for dinner.

He knew what the "circumstances" were, too. Barry hadn't brought his tux with him, so let's not embarrass the poor peasant.

"Did you finish the book I lent you?" Mariesa asked.

The Practical Applications of Space. Barry sipped his bourbon-and-water and placed the glass down upon the coaster on the lamp table. "Yes," he said, carefully. "It was interesting. I hadn't realized there was so much potential."

Mariesa leaned forward in her chair, turning toward him. "People know that rocks were returned from the moon, but they never stop to wonder how the ores assayed out."

"Lunar mining. Asteroid mining. The minerals are there, I suppose; but I wonder if you and your friends aren't a tiny bit overoptimistic. I mean, maybe someday in the future . . ."

"We shall take things a step at a time," Mariesa tucked her chin out, "as we should have done initially. It was a mistake to go to the moon so early."

"Eh?" Barry retrieved his drink and took another sip. The liquor warmed him. He and Shannon never drank together. She could not go home to John and the kids with the smell of liquor on her breath. Yet, Barry enjoyed his drinks. "What do you mean?"

"MISS. Man In Space Soonest. That was what they called the Mercury program initially. To show up the Russians. . . . Oh, I'd rather not bore you."

Barry waved his drink side to side. "No, go on." He settled back in the chair.

"Well, once upon a time, we had a space program: the X-planes." Mariesa leaned so far forward she rested her arms on her knees. "And there were real rocket pilots, men like Joe Walker and Bob White and Scott Crossfield. Men you have never heard of. They flew their planes up to the edge of space, and a little beyond—some of them even earned astronaut wings. The X-15 with the Big Engine had boost and altitude that matched the Mercury-Redstone suborbitals. It might have been our first true spaceship, had we not been sidetracked."

While she talked, Barry found himself studying her, the way she sat, the way she spoke. The way her eyes looked when she laughed or frowned. Her movements betrayed her finishing-school upbringing. They were smooth, economical, precise. And her conversation seemed to come at ideas from unexpected directions, apt to turn Barry's preconceptions on their head. He had never heard anyone refer to America's space program as a diversion from a space program. In that quality of unexpectedness, she was much like Shannon.

"What happened?" he asked. Odd. He realized that, thanks to Shannon's jealousy, he was thinking of Mariesa van Huyten as a woman. Not Mariesa van Huyten, Wealthy Buyer of School Districts; but simply Mariesa, plain, elegant, young, intense, convinced.

"The program was canceled. It did not have the glamour of riding atop towers of flame. The X-20, the Dyna-Soar, was never built. No one cared about space pilots when they could watch human cannonballs instead." Mariesa scowled into her Manhattan and set it aside half-finished. "Understand, I do not dispute the bravery or the piloting skills of the astronauts. Armstrong was in the X-program himself. But the race to the moon, in a very real sense, distracted us from going into space. Like the man who leapt across the chasm and back and never set out to build a bridge. We could have had the National Aerospace Plane thirty years ago."

Barry folded his hands under his chin. "I remember the old Disney cartoons when I was a kid. There was supposed to be a space station."

Mariesa looked away for a moment, retrieved her drink. "Yes. There was."

"And will there be?"

Mariesa blinked. "Be what?"

"A space station." He pointed to the brooch. "That pin

you and some of the others wear. A VHI project, you told me once. I'll bet you the price of tonight's meal that it's tied in with space somehow.''

Mariesa ran a finger across the jewelry. ''I suppose the pins were not a very good idea.''

''Are you a subcontractor on Space Station Alpha? The future on that doesn't look good, politically.''

''No, not with an administration that borders on Luddite. Perhaps, the coming election . . .'' Mariesa swirled the drink in her glass for a moment; then she sat up straight. ''Tell me, Barry. If it was your project what would you do?''

''Me? I don't know enough to have an opinion.''

A smile. ''That would not stop certain other people. But seriously, I am interested.'' She placed her drink aside, sank back in her chair, and folded her hands under her chin. ''I have just appointed you space czar. What shall we do?''

Barry hesitated. ''Well, do you mean the Alpha project, or just in general?''

''In general.''

''Is it all right if I parrot back some of that book you lent me?''

''Only if the parrot has conviction.''

''Hmm. Well, I would start with satellites, then.''

''Really? Why? Satellites are not very glamorous.''

''Did you want glamour or a space program?''

''Go on . . .''

''The satellite program not only 'spent money here on Earth,' but *made* money here on Earth.''

''Most people,'' said Mariesa, ''do not realize that the space program was a moneymaker.''

''Myself included,'' said Barry, adding with a touch of caution, ''that is, if the articles you gave me were accurate.''

''They were. How many citrus crops were saved by weather satellites? How many lives by new fire-retardant materials? The computer technology alone . . . But, no. You are the czar, not I.''

Barry accepted that. The data would be easy enough to verify; and most important, they felt right, once you thought about it. "People hardly consider satellites as part of the 'space program' anymore," he continued. "They're just *there*. Weather satellites. Resource monitoring. Mapping. Navigational tracking. Emergency locators. Wasn't there an incident a few years ago where the Russians helped us locate a downed airplane with their navigational satellites?"

"There was."

"What I'm trying to say is that if you want to sell space to the public, that is the place to start. Close to home, with something immediately and obviously useful." Barry spread his hands. "So, there you have it. Build a cheap spaceship, like that Delta Clipper that was in the news a while back. Then go on a step at a time. Don't snow the public with dreams of Asteroid El Dorado."

"The Delta Clipper was canceled," Mariesa pointed out, "and the astronauts that had been selected for the program were laid off. How do you propose I convince the government to refund it?"

She wants us to go back to the moon, he thought. *And I think she even wants to go herself*. How's that for the whim of the spoiled rich! I want the moon, so I'll nudge the whole country back into space to do it. The ultimate in jet-setting.

"Round up some of those astronauts," he said, perhaps a little harshly. "You can probably find loose government change in one departmental pocket or another. But, Mariesa . . . ." He leaned toward her and actually wagged a finger. Feeling his oats or feeling his liquor (and in the morning, feeling stupid?). "Mariesa, if you believe in this as deeply as you say, you should be willing to put up your own money, not just the taxpayers' money. Do it yourself."

Mariesa and he stared at each other and the moment dragged on. He had just realized how gray her eyes were when it hit him. "Oh, God," he said, sagging back into the chair. "You *are* doing it, aren't you? You're planning your own private space program."

Sykes came to the doorway and announced dinner. Mariesa rose and, a moment or two later, Barry did, too. Mariesa offered her arm. "You are an interesting man, Barry Fast. I think we made an excellent choice naming you to the Institute.''

Barry smiled numbly and thanked her. *The hand-and-fireball . . . that must be the project logo. A private space program? How long has it been going on? How big is it? She can't be doing it herself; even VHI isn't that big. Who else is in on it? Other companies? Government agencies?* He couldn't imagine the president lending support, though the vice-president had some techie leanings. But the government had numerous nooks and crannies; and the left hand did not always know what pocket the right hand was picking.

Maybe even other governments . . . *''The moon belongs to everyone, the best things in life are free . . .''* He felt as if a hand had clutched him around the gut.

Barry sat on Mrs. van Huyten's right, facing Mariesa across the width of a long, dark table polished so bright you could comb your hair by it. A pearl white tablecloth draped the table diagonally, set off by dark, contrasting candles set in silver holders of dazzling simplicity. A single willow branch painted in spare strokes graced the rim of the bone-china place settings. The glassware rang like bells and caught the light in tiny rainbows. This was ambience and service you would expect at the finest restaurant; ''eatin' in'' to the van Huytens.

Armando, the underbutler, brought out the first course and set a bowl of clear soup on the plate before him. Tasting the soup, Barry found it quite good, which surprised him. He was used to heartier fare.

''So, Mr. Fast,'' said Harriet. ''You are a schoolteacher, I understand.''

''That's right,'' he said. ''Fifteen years. Here, and in Seattle before that.''

''I see. And your family . . . What did you say your father does?''

''Mother!''

Harriet turned to Mariesa. ''I was only asking after his family.''

''I know what you . . .''

''It's all right, Mariesa,'' Barry said. He laid a smile on

Harriet. "My father was a fisherman. He owned two boats that he used to fish the Sound."

"Why, how very useful!"

"Mother?" This time Mariesa's voice was low with warning.

"It was hard work," Barry went on. "It didn't pay well, but he made enough to put my brother and me through college." You didn't have to tell them how, after the War, Raymond Senior had given up his own dreams of college for a young wife and a newborn child. How brother Ray had been the first in the family ever to matriculate. You didn't have to tell them that hard work made for hard men; or that someone who stood against gale-force winds wouldn't bend for much else, either. And you damn well didn't have to tell them how strong a man's hugs could be when he hauled on nets for a living.

"You said 'was.' Is he retired now?" Harriet asked. Mariesa sucked in her breath and Barry could see her knuckles stand out where she gripped her soupspoon.

He shook his head. "One day he took *Billie G.* too far up toward the Straits of Juan de Fuca and a sudden storm broke him up against the rocks on Whidbey Island. He—" Barry stopped, surprised at the force of the sudden memory. "He always wanted a burial at sea." He finished, bending low again over his soup.

"Oh," he heard Harriet say. "I am so dreadfully sorry." And he heard that she meant it, too. But sorry about his father's death years ago or sorry to have brought up an awkward topic of conversation at dinner? Across the table he noticed Mariesa's look of concern. *She knew. She knew that about Dad.* Just how thorough a background check did they do on Institute candidates?

"I lost my father early, too," Mariesa said in hard tones. "Like yours, he died doing the thing he loved best."

"Mariesa!" This time it was Harriet who warned.

Armando took the bowl from Barry and they all three fell silent while the table was cleared for the second course. Barry let his eyes dance from mother to daughter and back. There were as many tangled lines around this gleaming, wooden table as there had been around the wobbly old Formica one at home. Perhaps more; perhaps more hurtful. In Seattle, it had been loud shouts and fists hitting tabletops; here, dead, icy silences. There was a lot to be said for shouting. Like a storm wind, at least it cleared the air.

"It was nice out today," he said after a moment. A safe topic. You could not quarrel about the weather.

Oh, couldn't you just! Harriet sniffed. "Too much sun is bad for you. Because of that ozone business."

"Oh, Mother." Mariesa's voice was light, but had an edge to it. "You know there is nothing to that. I have explained before. UV radiation measurements at ground level have been decreasing for years."

Barry said, "I didn't know that."

Harriet stuck by her guns. "Everyone in my circle says it is so."

Barry could almost see the words jam up in Mariesa's throat like cars at a toll booth. "Well," she said at last, exacting a token of each word, "that's fine."

The salad was a plate of May King lettuce mixed with arugula and mache and accented with an odd-tasting but not unpleasant dressing of moist crumbs. "The soup was excellent," Barry ventured, hoping that the family cook, at least, was a safe topic.

"Thank you," Mariesa said graciously. "I will tell Mrs. Pontavecchio you said so." Harriet said nothing, but smiled slightly.

Barry was happy to have found a topic on which the two agreed. "My favorite soup is seafood chowder," he added. "Which I guess you might expect for a fisherman's son. My mother used to make it up thick with what Dad brought home. There's a restaurant down in Perth Amboy that makes a really good bowl, though not quite as good as Mom's."

Both van Huytens said, "Really?" But Mariesa's "really" indicated genuine interest, while Harriet's meant she would *never* patronize the sort of restaurant that Barry could afford. Funny. He had always thought of Mariesa as snooty, perhaps because of her precise way of speaking; but set her next to Harriet's polite but condescending attitude and she was downright, slap-your-back chummy.

When Armando set the main course on the table, Barry saw that it was a baked fish, seasoned with a bread-crumb topping. He looked at Mariesa, who flushed.

"You don't mind roughy, do you?"

"Why should I . . . ?"

"Your father? The menu had already been selected before we knew you would be dining with us."

"No." He looked at the fish again. "No, I don't mind." There was a time when he had sworn he would never eat a fish again. The steady diet of seafood in his youth . . . And again, later, when he could not swallow anything from the sea that had swallowed his father. But that had passed long ago; and if he did not love the sea the way his father had, he no longer hated it. Only, the sea had left so much unfinished.

"Kent Chatworth is in town," said Harriet to Mariesa. "I ran into Dorothy at the club. He was asking about you."

"Was he?" Mariesa said with studied lack of interest.

"What shall I tell Dorothy?"

A small, exasperated sound . . . "Tell her that her son is a boor who never had an interesting thought in his life, and he has more hands than a bridge tournament." She looked at Barry. "Mummy is constantly trying to fix me up with men."

"Men whom you never find suitable," her mother said with a tart voice.

"That is hardly my fault."

"Is it not?"

There was a moment of strained silence. Then Mariesa laughed. "Mummy, you know Kent. All he can talk about is his fox hunting and his racing stable. He bores *you*."

If it was an attempt to make peace, Barry thought it fell flat. He felt like an intruder. Was every meal as uncomfortable as this one? He stole a glance at Sykes, who stood with a placid, unreadable face by the wine bucket, watching over Armando like a mother hen. There was no hint of reaction on the man's face. Barry began to realize why reticence and poise were sine qua non for butlers.

Harriet sniffed. "Well, he is more suitable than some you have brought home."

Mariesa colored and her lips became white. "I will not hear you insult my guests, or impute motives to my inviting them." She turned suddenly on Barry. "Barry," she said. "That restaurant you mentioned, on the waterfront . . . ?"

"The Armory?"

"Is that its name? Yes, I would be delighted to dine there. Would Saturday be suitable?"

A piece of fish tumbled off Barry's fork. Carefully, he laid the fork aside and picked up his napkin and dabbed his lips. The richest woman on the continent had just asked him for a date.

Well, not "asked," exactly. When he thought he had his voice in control, he answered, sparing only the briefest glance at Harriet. "Um, yes. I suppose." His lips twitched. "Proper attire is required, but not formal wear."

Mariesa smiled. "I can manage."

Harriet looked at Barry. "I was not referring to you, Mr. Fast."

Like hell you weren't. Barry smiled and said, "I did not suppose you had," and Harriet gave him an uncertain look.

The rest of the dinner was full of awkward silences and secret communications to which Barry was not privy.

INTERLUDE:

School Daze (I)

The ashes weighed less. Tani adjusted the glasses on her nose and studied the reading on the balance. She recorded the number in her lab notebook like you were supposed to and compared it to the weight of the original wood chip. Yes, definitely less.

Ms. Glendower went from table to table, checking everyone's results. She made the metalhead correct his. "Meat" must have read the scale wrong. Tani checked her own results a third time, just to be sure.

"For crying out loud," muttered Jimmy Poole, her lab partner. Jimmy was smart, but Tani would not just take his word for things, which seemed to irritate him.

Earlier, they had weighed and burned a sample of sulfur—and did that stink! Fire and brimstone, Ms. Glendower had told them; and brimstone had once been "burn-stone" because the soft, sulfur rocks caught fire so easily. The ash in that case had also weighed less.

"All right, class," Ms. Glendower said, returning to the

front of the room. "Can anyone tell me why the wood and the sulfur both weighed less after burning?"

The kids looked at each other, then looked at Ms. Glendower. The teacher waited and the silence stretched on. Finally, Jenny Ribbon said, "Well, we burned up some of it . . . ?"

Tani heard the curlicue of the question mark at the end of the response. She waited for Ms. Glendower to tell them whether the answer was right, but the teacher only nodded and wrote what Jenny had said on the blackboard. "Are there any other ideas?"

"Was Jenny right?" asked Tony D'Angelo.

"What do you think?"

Jimmy Poole muttered under his breath, loud enough for Tani to hear him. "He's a moron. What does it matter what he thinks?"

"Uh," Tony looked around for help and decided that agreement was the safest response. "Sure. It sounds good to me." His lab partner, Morris Tucker, agreed.

"Some of it went up in smoke," he said. He and Tony looked at each other; Tucker wiggled his eyebrows and pantomimed a sucking motion with his lips and fingers.

"I bet I know what he smokes," said Jimmy Poole.

Several of the other kids, sensing a bandwagon, chimed in. "Yeah." "The flame uses up some of the wood." "And the sulfur, too." "That's what fires does." Tani was about to add her own agreement, but kept quiet when Jimmy Poole muttered "stupid phlogiston theory" under his breath. Tani leaned close to him.

"Why *does* the weight go down?"

Jimmy looked superior. "Because some of the material combines with the oxygen in the air and becomes a gas. Carbon dioxide for the wood; sulfur dioxide for the sulfur."

"Oh." Tani thought that over for a moment. "Then Meat was right?"

Jimmy turned red at the throat. "No way. He's banged his head so much his brain's broken up inside like peanut brittle."

"But you both said it goes up in smoke."

"Are there any other ideas, class? Yes, Leland?"

"Uh." The football player struggled to his feet. He looked at Ms. Glendower, then at the other students, then at his own feet. "Uh." There was a giggle, quickly suppressed.

"Did you have a question, Mr. Hobart?"

"Well, uh, is it true?"

"Is what true?"

They called Leland Hobart the Doorman, because as the conference's best offensive lineman he "opened doors" for Greg Prescott and the other backs to run through. The Doorman looked briefly around the room. His eyes looked so round—like those of a bunny rabbit that Tani had once inadvertently cornered by the garage at home, hunting for an escape and finding none, freezing into immobility. Imagine comparing the Doorman to a bunny rabbit! Tani ducked her head, lest he see her grin and misunderstand.

"That things weigh less after you burn them."

This time the snort—it came from Meat—was definitely audible. Hobart looked at the metalhead. "You want, I can lift you off the ground by that ponytail of yours."

"Please, class." Ms. Glendower clapped her hands sharply. "Mr. Hobart, explain your question. You saw what your weights were. I checked them."

"Wood and sulfur."

"Meaning . . . ?"

"Uh, what if you burned other stuff? Does *everything* lose weight when you burn it?"

Ms. Glendower regarded him for a moment. Then she turned and wrote on the board: *Do all things lose weight when burned, or only some things?* Cheng-I called out, "What things gain weight?" and Ms. Glendower wrote that, too. Leland, seeing that no one was watching him anymore, quietly resumed his seat.

"Who's teaching this class, anyway?" muttered Jimmy. "The students?"

Tani decided the best tactic was to ignore him. Jimmy was smart, but not about everything. You could be smart without being a pain in the neck. And even smart people could do stupid things. (Those pills in her purse, they weren't illegal; they weren't even prescription. Anybody could buy them. She just needed them sometimes to stay awake in the morning. That was all. Just to stay awake.)

Ms. Glendower did the next demonstration herself. Cheng-I and the Doorman weighed a pad of steel wool, and Ms. Glendower called on Tani to verify the scale reading. Then she donned a set of goggles and heated the pad until it was glowing red hot. Some of the kids oohed and aahed over the way the steel glowed and sparkled, not quite catching fire. Ms. Glendower looked like an alien in goggle and mitts, the flames searing the asbestos pad on which the steel wool lay. Finally, she had Tony transfer the burnt steel to the scales using a tongs.

It weighed more than before.

Meat grinned. "Hey, heavy metal!" And the class laughed.

Ms. Glendower cut through the chatter. "Why?"

"It didn't actually burn, did it?" asked Jenny. "There were no flames."

"But why does it weigh *more* now?" said Cheng-I thoughtfully.

"Mr. Hobart, what do you think?" Ms. Glendower picked out the football player over the heads of the others. The Doorman only shook his head. He had an odd look on his face, almost as if he were afraid. Almost as if he were waiting on the line for the snap.

"For your Afterclass," Ms. Glendower said when they had resumed their seats, "tell me why you think the wood and sulfur weighed less, but the steel wool weighed more. Please do not look it up in the library. I want you to act as if no one has ever discovered the reason. What are your ideas? Hand the assignment in to your homeroom teacher before you leave today and we will discuss them tomorrow."

Tani noted the assignment in the little notebook she kept for that purpose. Open-ended questions like this sometimes scared her. No right or wrong answers, just "What do you think?" What did it matter what she thought? Maybe in literature, because that was more "Did you like it?" But science was different. Opinions didn't matter.

"I don't have to look it up," Jimmy Poole told her as he hoisted his backpack to his shoulder. "I already know the answer." He smiled and tossed his head slightly.

He wants me to ask him what it is, but I won't. Tani knew that someone had to be Jimmy's lab partner, but it was going to be a long semester. "Too bad," she said, not knowing why she said it, except that Jimmy was really bugging her.

Jimmy looked puzzled. "Why?"

"Because if you already know the answer, you won't learn how to find it."

She didn't know why she said that, either; and when she thought about it later, it didn't even make sense.

Jenny Ribbon locked her door and stood with her back leaning against it. She had homework to do. There was always homework to do. And when it wasn't homework, she could make notes or outlines; or practice her ballet, because there would be a recital later in the month. Or maybe go out to the pool and swim a few laps, because there was a meet coming up. Or . . .

There was always something to do. There was always a competition.

Stick it out until graduation. Another year. Without the diploma, there were no jobs that would not drive her herbies. She backed away from the door, to the window. Second floor, tree limbs out of reach, no escape that way. Graduation was an eon away. She would never see it. The moon shone through the barren, snow-crusted branches and bathed Mr. Rumples-the-Bear in a pond of milky light on the bedspread. Run off far away, where they'd never find her. Maybe pills. Maybe gas. Somewhere where she would not feel the pressure, PRESSURE, PRESSURE.

The moon was kissing the horizon, riding above the crest of the hills. It looked so big and so close, as if it were just beyond the gap in the Watchungs, only a short run away. It looked as if the Grey Horse Pike led straight to it, like a boarding ramp.

Azim threw the ball at Zipper and it bounced right through Stork's hands. Zipper grabbed it, twisted, and jumped, and the shot sailed nice as you please through the chain-draped hoop. Nothing but air. "Way to go, skillet." Azim slapped him a high-five. Jo-jo took the ball on the rebound and handed it to Wash. "Twenty to sixteen," he told the other boy. Azim faded back to cover Stork as the other threesome brought the ball in.

The basketball court was a pool of light under the streetlamp. A white-ass nightmare rec center. Black macadam, paved over the site of a demolished crack house, painted with chipped and faded lines. It was hemmed in on two sides by dull, red-brick apartment buildings and surrounded by a chainlink fence. There were two openings in the fence: a gate on the New Berwick Avenue side, and a flap cut open with bolt cutters on the back side into the alleyway. Trust whitey to build a playground with no escape route.

Wild grass and dandelions pushed up through the swollen and cracked macadam. The fences were rusted and bent; the hinges frozen with the gate half-open. Shahazz the Mound had a hard time squeezing through. There was debris around the fences and at the base of the walls. Scrap lumber, an old tire, a patio chair with broken straps and bent legs that Old Lemmy sat in while the others played. The walls of the two apartment buildings were scrawled with artwork, warnings, announcements. Near the street a sign was sprayed that this was Lord turf.

More like a wreck center.

Old Lemmy, all of twenty-eight and missing an eye, so he was hopeless at the hoops but could still see damn good and looked *bad* when he wore that eyepatch and downright *evil* when he didn't, he suddenly gave a whistle and the game braked to a stop. The ball caromed off the backboard from Jo-jo's hopelessly hotdog shot and bounced away into an unlit corner of the playground.

Still as statues, they watched the old Chrysler roll slowly down New Berwick Avenue, past stores locked and bolted, metal shields, chain-link shutters drawn down tight over doors and windows, charlie owners gone 'burb for the night.

Dead eyes scanned him from the windows of the car. Dreadlocked and bearded. Azim's heart thudded. He felt his knees grow rubbery. Maybe this was it. Maybe the Nation was making its move. A lot of the Nation were into drugs and they usually packed sweepers. Shoot-n-spray though the chain-link and they all had it; but nobody moved. They all gave the same dead look back. All of them, Nation and Lords, and the NO-men, too, they were all born dead, and the only thing 'tween the borning and the dying was the waiting. Azim saw Zipper breathing hard and clenching and unclenching his fingers.

Don't do nothing stupid, Zipper. We be fish in a barrel here. Get seven Lords wasted and all for nothing. He could see the back of Zipper's head, the hair shaved from nape to crown and a star-V—The Lords of Victory—cut into the stubble by the clippers.

Here, around the old Eastport canal locks, was "the Lordship." The Lords of Victory ruled. Downtown North Orange, past Queenie, was NO-man Land. West was the Island Nation. Dominicans, Jamaicans, Trinidaddies. Foreigners. Black, but not American Black, looking down their noses at "de nahteeves." The gangs were a thin layer oozing like grease under the neighborhoods, making life a slippery thing, so that no one went out at night. And during the day the gooks and charlies looked crosswise at the black skins in the suits, who shrank just a little bit and hated the gangs for it worse than any *rabbiblanco,* safe—for the while—in his cozy white enclave, could imagine.

The Chrysler screeched suddenly and laid rubber. The Nation shot down to the corner and hung a sharp right at the fork there, going right through the red light. Someone in a blue Buick honked at them. Be just like Nation to shoot you for that.

"Look at them," Azim said, "cruising our 'hood just like they owned it."

"We fix 'em sometime, you bet," said Jo-jo. "Drive 'em out so far, they never get back in."

Stork said, "Those be damn stupid niggers, stopping under the streetlamp like that. We had my nine here, we take them out."

"Yeah," said Azim. "Then what? Those two, they bait."

Zipper shifted his gaze to Azim. "So what?" Zipper rubbed his hand across the stubble at the back of his head. "This for the Nation," he said. "Give them a bull's-eye."

Trapped inside the fence? No way you could win a fight like that. And winning was what Azim wanted most of anything. Zipper didn't understand winning. He had never been where winning was an option. That made him a good man to have by your side in a fight, but not so good for planning the fight.

"Because," Azim said, because he had to explain in terms Zipper would understand, "that takes out two of them and seven of us, which don't do the Lords no good."

"One Lord be worth five Nation and three NO-men," Jo-jo piped up.

"Yeah," said Azim, "so we don't let ourselves be wasted 'less we can take more of them with us."

Zipper shook his head. "Man, you always think deep." A compliment or a complaint? Azim did not ask. Zipper ran to the fence and jumped, hooking into it like a cat on a screen. His fingers curled around the links, his sneaker tips shoved in and found purchase. He shouted obscenities at the vanished car.

"And nearer fast and nearer does the *Nation* whirlwind come," chanted Azim, playing on the poem they'd had to memorize about two old gangs, the Romans and the Tuscans, when the Tuscans tried to burn down the Romans' 'hood and take their women, Jo-jo grinned like a skull and joined in. Surprisingly, so did the others, who went to Pitcher. Though the same company was running both schools, so it was not too much a surprise.

"And plainly and more plainly now through the gloom appears

> Far to the left and far to the right.
> In broken gleams of dark-blue light.
> The long array of helmets bright
> The long array of spears.''

Old Lemmy sat back in his guard's chair and stared at them as if they had gone crazy. *What the fuck?* his mouth said.

Azim laughed and he and Jo-jo traded slaps and mock punches. Those Old Romans had been tough dudes. Only one way into their 'hood, across a bridge, and no time to cut it down unless someone stood at the other end and held off the whole other gang with nothing but a fucking blade. Fucking balls to stand there and fight *while they chopped the bridge down behind you.*

Zipper dropped from the fence and in two swift steps he was standing in the half-open gate.

> "Then out spoke brave Horatius, the Captain of the Gate,
> 'To every man upon this earth death cometh soon or late.
> And how can man die better than facing fearful odds
> For the ashes of his fathers and the temples of his gods.' ''

He turned and gave a fierce look at the others in the play-ground. Azim traded a glance with Jo-jo. In the poem, there had been three dudes holding the bridge, so he and Jo-jo stepped up beside Zipper. Azim was surprised Zipper knew the poem. During the recital—which had run through both the English and history classes, so both Mrs. Szyzmanski and Mr. Boucher had talked about it, but in different ways—during the recital, Zipper had stayed zipped, like he always did in the white man's schools. Now Azim knew that the lines had some-how reached the bro. Fucking balls to stand there and fight *while they closed the rusted playground gate behind you.*

Zipper grinned and his hand brushed the V that had been shaved into the nap at the back of his skull. He said to Azim in a voice so cold that Azim's heart turned to ice and even

Jo-jo, who never caught half of what went on around him, sucked in his breath:

> "*And how can we die better than facing fearful odds*
> *For the ashes of our homies and for our fucking*
> *'hood?*"

Styx hit the bottle.

Sometimes, when the words wouldn't come, that was the way she would do it. She lifted the vodka bottle high and the last dregs trickled down her throat. *Need more*, she thought, stroking the thin, empty neck. Beth gone so much, it wasn't hard to sneak it in the house. And it wasn't hard to buy it, either. Just slip the money to a grown-up going in the store and he slips you the bottle coming out. And if he didn't, there were ways to take care of that, too.

She settled her journal more firmly on her lap and rubbed her cheek absently where Beth had slapped her. *I hate her*, she wrote. *I hate her. I'll get pregnant, then see what The Bitch says.* She shook her head and it hurt. No good. She was whining. She crossed it out with savage scratches, then drummed the pen against the open journal. She stared out the window at the three-o'clock night, just in time to see an old car with three black kids in it cut through a red light on the state road. It wasn't fair. They got to go everywhere, while she was a prisoner in her own home. Beth had even had bars installed on her windows. To keep out burglars, she had said, but Styx knew the real reason. She glanced at the tattered, gilt-engraved invitation propped on her dresser. *No, of course you cannot go. You have nothing to wear that wouldn't embarrass you.* From Mariesa van Huyten, of all people.

Try to stop me, Mother. If you or Missy Rich-bitch doesn't like it, tough. Take me as you find me. Missy Rich-bitch invited *me*, not you; and she's gotta have enough brains to know I'm no damned debbie-taunt with a sequined gown.

She hunkered over her journal and began to write:

> *Take me as you find me, or don't take me at all.*
> *'Cause I need you a damn sight less than I*
> *need to scrape and crawl . . .*

The words came more easily now, lubricated by the spirits. She hoped they would read as good in the morning. Sometimes in the morning, when she read what she had written, it was gibberish, and she ripped the offending pages from her journal. You weren't supposed to do that, she knew. You were supposed to leave everything as you wrote it. That was what Miss Kress had said back in grade school, when she had still been Roberta and Miss Kress first told her she had a talent. But that was a long time ago, in another school, in another town, in another house, when she had been another girl.

7.

First You Lace Your Bootstraps Up Real Tight . . .

"You did not receive a single RSVP," Harriet pointed out. "You don't even know if anyone is coming."

Mariesa sat at her dresser, holding a string of pearls before her throat. She could see Harriet in the big oval mirror, framed in the doorway, her face the usual mixture of bewilderment and disapproval. "They are only children," she told her mother. "And no one ever taught them proper manners."

"Not our sort of people, at all."

Middle-class kids, working-class kids, kids from the wrong side of the tracks. The Locks, wasn't that what they called that area? Parents who ran delis, who drove delivery trucks, who punched time clocks. Broken homes with single parents. Tract housing. Public housing. An old cottage of tarpaper and shingle. One student, according to Research, was almost surely a gang member. No, not our sort, at all.

Mariesa looked at the pearls she was considering. Was she overdressing? Sykes had brought out his formal evening wear and was looking especially butlerish tonight. It might be all too intimidating. Perhaps she should have saved those clothes from Kmart, after all.

"I don't know why you are having these children over tonight," Harriet persisted. "Joyce Allerton is in town and she has brought that cousin of hers. You remember Nelson. They are having a dinner party tonight at Three Birches."

"Then, you can go, Mummy. This is for the school." *And Nelson is an absolute cretin.* The Allerton fortune would never survive his stewardship.

"Public school," said Harriet, with a freight train of baggage in her tone.

"Quasi-public. I run it now." Mariesa decided to wear the pearls anyway. It would be foolish to dress down when the party was in a mansion. Be yourself. Kids hated phonies. "Have the chaperones arrived yet?"

"Sykes asked me to tell you that a Mr. Egbo has arrived. He is waiting downstairs in the library."

"Very well. The others will be here soon. The principals have agreed to act as chaperones at tonight's reception. Ask Sykes to offer them drinks, if he has not already done so. When the children arrive, we shall serve soft drinks only. The caterers have everything ready, have they not?"

Harriet shook her head. "I don't know why you go to all this bother."

"I have plans, Mummy."

Harriet came into the room and stood behind her. "Oh, Riesey, you are always so *busy*. Just like your grandfather." She took the ends of the pearl string from Mariesa and fastened them behind her neck. Then she laid her hands gently on Mariesa's shoulders and rubbed them softly. They locked eyes in the mirror and Mariesa saw how much alike they looked. She had always thought of herself as cast in Gramper's image, but there was not really much of him in her face, aside from the nose. The cheekbones, the eyes, the shape of the chin—even the little points at the tips of her ears—were all her mother's. The Gorley side.

That is me, she thought, gazing at her mother's reflection. She reached up and patted one of the hands stroking her shoulders. *That is me twenty-five years farther along.* A little rounder; a little softer in the features. But only on the outside. Inside, she was all van Huyten; hard as diamond; growing harder by the year.

The library was a large, dark-paneled room lined with bookshelves and furnished with high, comfortable chairs. A man's room, it had always reminded her of Gramper, not least through the lingering scents of ancient pipe tobaccos, absorbed somehow by the walls and released slowly back into the air.

The principals were waiting for her. Robert Boucher had taken a book from the stacks and was leafing through its pages. He looked up as Mariesa entered. Gwen Glendower sat in the window niche overlooking the rear grounds. Marie DePardo and Bernie Paulson, from Pitcher, were huddled in conversation. Onwuka Egbo, the odd man out, both by skin color and by being new, sat in the far corner in a large, wing-backed chair, an untouched drink beside him on the end table. He watched the others without seeming to watch them. She did not see Barry or Belinda; but then Belinda was chronically late.

"Good evening," Mariesa said as she entered. "It was so good of you to come."

Egbo smiled white as he rose and extended his hand. "When have I ever turned down your invitations, Ms. van Huyten?" His voice was basso; it commanded attention. Mariesa saw how his statement, implying prior visits, implying familiarity, caught the others' interest.

"Please, all of you, call me Mariesa," she told them. "I thought we might spend a little time before the affair begins to become better acquainted with one another." She looked around. "Where is Barry?"

Glendower indicated the side alcove, out of sight of the doorway, where a scowling Barry Fast stood beside the big floor globe with a drink clenched in his fist. "Ah, there you are. It is good to see you again, Barry." Mariesa extended a hand.

He transferred his drink to his left hand. "Did I have a

choice?'' he asked as he clasped her hand. His touch was cold and wet.

Why, how rude! Mariesa smiled and maintained decorum. ''Of course you did,'' she murmured so only he could hear. Turning to the others, she greeted them in turn and exchanged pleasantries about the weather, the grounds, the building. Barry remained taciturn and did not participate in the chat. Instead, he remained in the alcove, scowling out the side window at the birch grove and spinning the globe idly with his free hand. In the wrong direction, Mariesa noted. Sunrise over the Pacific.

Sykes appeared in the doorway with a perfect Manhattan balanced on his tray, and Mariesa took it. ''Thank you, Sykes.'' The butler bowed and left. ''How have matters fared at your schools?'' Mariesa asked the group. ''Has the new year started off smoothly?''

Barry spoke from his self-imposed exile. ''You can't imagine how different everything is now.'' He smiled and continued to play idly with the globe, alternately spinning and stopping it.

Mariesa looked for sarcasm, but saw only his pleasant, open smile. An odd fellow, she thought. Always a smile on his lips, but always an edge to the smile. Yet, he was not an unpleasant sort; and quite decorative, as well. Their dinner outing had been quite enjoyable. She had never been to a restaurant where she was not known. ''We did not expect that matters would change overnight,'' Mariesa assured him. ''Belinda plans to introduce Mentor procedures gradually.''

''I'm excited by the changes in the science curriculum,'' Gwen said after a glance at Barry. ''I've had a few informal sessions with the science masters at both schools. The first year may be a little uneven, but the summer seminars did help.''

''I don't know if the children are ready for it,'' Boucher said in a judicious tone.

Paulson shook his head and held up a finger, as if to admonish. ''History ought to be more than chronicles of wars and presidents, Bob,'' he said. ''Science and technology are part of history, too.''

''And of English,'' DePardo interjected. '' 'How Flowers Changed the World.' I hadn't known scientists could *write*.''

''No, that's not what I meant,'' said Boucher. ''I have no problem with the interdisciplinary strategy. I meant the science curriculum itself. I know—'' With a glance toward Glendower. ''I know I'm not qualified to comment on the content; but as far as teaching methods go, the children are accustomed to a . . . well, to a different mode of pedagogy.'' He laughed and shook his head. ''God, I have always hated that jargon! But I really do think many of the brighter students will be frustrated at the slower pace.''

''I have always found,'' said Egbo reflectively, ''that I learn a thing more thoroughly when I learn it 'hands on.' For me, maths and abstractions are more easily grasped when I have some concrete example in front of me.''

''Onwuka is right,'' Gwen said. '' 'Talk and chalk' sucks all the excitement out of science. It may be a fine way of covering a lot of facts in a short time, but . . .''

''Is that the trade-off we have to make?'' Boucher wondered. ''To learn a few things thoroughly or many things superficially?''

''No,'' said Gwen emphatically. ''It's what I've always tried to tell you, Bob. Science is no more a collection of facts than a house is a pile of bricks. We need to teach the *process* of science.'' Boucher shrugged, conceding the point.

''I think,'' said Egbo, ''that many of the difficulties will disappear as we begin to get students who have been taught in the same fashion in the earlier grades.''

''Yes, but what of the kids we have now?'' said Boucher. ''We owe them something more than to be a 'transition' class.''

Yes, thought Mariesa. Boucher was right about that. In the change from old to new, some would always fall in the crack. That was too bad. Still, not to make the transition was no answer. ''Robert,'' she said, ''I was looking forward to meeting your wife. Vivian, isn't it?''

Boucher grimaced. "She was feeling under the weather, I'm afraid . . . that bug that's going around." He smiled a bit and looked around the group. "It appears that none of us have escorts."

Glendower laughed. "Barry, most of all."

Fast drank down the rest of his cocktail and turned away. He gave the globe a shove with his free hand, setting it spinning. Mariesa looked at Glendower.

"Is something wrong?" Mariesa asked.

"Barry's old heap finally died on him. He had to bum a ride with me tonight."

Paulson chuckled. "Oh, that's what you meant. He doesn't have an Escort."

Fast glared at him. "It doesn't sound so funny if you have to round up the cash to fix it."

"Oh, I was laughing in sympathy, believe me. I owned a car once that used to quit cold on me while I was driving. The engine would shut off, just like that." He snapped his fingers. "It was a faulty computer chip."

"Ah, technology!" said Boucher.

Glendower said, "Go back a hundred years, Bob, and you'll find people who bought horses that hadn't been properly harness-broken."

"What sort of globe is this?" asked Fast. He had stopped the spinning and his finger was tracing shapes on the surface. "It's been drawn on with a marker."

She pretended not to hear him. "Onwuka," she said, turning to the Nigerian, "how is your homeroom group progressing?"

Egbo swirled the ice in his glass and pursed his lips thoughtfully. "Much too early to say, Mariesa. Much too early. It is difficult to prepare them for the future when some of them . . ." And Egbo's face clouded momentarily. "Some of them do not expect to live long enough for the future to matter. Still . . ." He visibly recalled himself, shifted his position. "Still, you must deal with people as they are, not as you wish they were. There are some who show promise."

"Has Thomas given you any trouble, yet?" asked Boucher.

"He was always the big troublemaker among the black boys."

Egbo shook his head. "Not yet. Nor do I believe he is the one to watch most closely."

"He's the ringleader," said Boucher.

And he would be here tonight, Mariesa recalled. Belinda had seen some sort of promise in the boy, something that had peeked through the tests and the interviews; and in such matters she trusted 'Linda implicitly.

Sykes reappeared in the doorway. "Ma'am? Mr. Sprague has arrived from the school with your guests."

"We shall be out directly," she said to Sykes. "Show them into the ballroom, if you please. Ladies, gentlemen, shall we?"

"An odd assortment you've invited," Boucher said, putting his drink down. "Some parents have been calling the school to complain because their own children were not included."

"You ought to forward those calls to Grant," said Barry. "None of the principals should be handling that sort of crap anymore."

"Nor should Mr. deYoung," said Mariesa. "It was not the school that issued the invitations. I can hardly entertain all of the children. These students were chosen by lot." That was not entirely a lie. Belinda's lists were most carefully selected; but chance always had a great deal to do with who washed up on them.

She led the way to the doorway and stood there while the others filed out past her. Boucher fussed a bit with his jacket, lingering. "Ms. van Huyten . . ." he said when they were alone. "I haven't said how grateful I am that you kept me on. As a teacher, I mean. I expected . . . Well . . ."

"You expected to be fired."

A moment's silence. "Yes."

"You were not a very good administrator."

The man pulled back, his face unreadable. "You are frank."

"Each of us has our own skills. Those were not yours. You told me once that all you ever wanted was to teach children. You have your second chance, now."

Boucher turned to go and Mariesa stopped him with a hand

lightly on his arm. "Bob," she said more gently, "do you know what decided me?"

He shook his head.

"That you kept your history texts, even after all those years."

"That was it?" He looked away from her. "A small thing for your career to hinge on."

"That, and the Groucho glasses."

Boucher gave her a startled look, then a low chuckle. "I will remember that."

After he left, Mariesa paused a moment in the doorway. She thought she could see several of the fault lines in the Witherspoon practice. Between Boucher and Fast; between Boucher and Glendower; between Egbo and the other three. Boucher had been brought down; Egbo brought in; Fast and Glendower raised up. New roles brought with them a thousand small frictions and adjustments. A new practice was much like becoming married.

She was about to leave the room when she heard Fast's voice from the alcove. "I never much liked him when he was the principal." She looked around the corner and saw that he was still toying with the globe.

"No? He is still a principal."

"A courtesy. Not even first among equals. A provisional principal."

"All of you are provisional for now. Until Dr. Karr has observed you for a year."

"Except Dr. Egbo."

"He is a known quantity. Dr. Karr thought it best that Witherspoon have one principal experienced in our methods and our goals."

"And to keep an eye on the rest of us."

She did not deny it. "The others are waiting."

"Wait. You haven't told me what these circles are all over the globe." He pointed to the black rings she had drawn so many years ago, in that first, terrifying flush of enthusiasm. Rings in the Caribbean, in Hudson Bay, the Sea of Japan, the Aral Sea. Big rings, little rings, until the globe had looked like a pond in a rainstorm and she had lain awake staring at the night sky in a cold sweat. One meteor a week struck the upper atmosphere with the power of a Hiroshima bomb. And those were the little ones, the ones that did not get through. Daddy had been quite put out, and even Gramper had scowled in displeasure. She had tried to explain. She had thought that Gramper of all people would listen; but he had only scolded her on respect for property. That was when she had learned that no one would listen; that no one would ever listen; and if you wanted something done, you would have to keep your own counsel and do it yourself.

"It was part of a project I did when I was in college," she told Fast, and the big, curly haired man nodded. After a moment, he realized no further details were forthcoming and said, "I see," even though he clearly did not. He set his empty glass down on the sideboard for Sykes to clear and followed the others out of the room.

Mariesa lingered a moment, studying the old globe. She pushed it gently—in the proper direction—and looked down, as if from a space station, as obsolete, dismantled countries spun past. The setting sun, streaming through the west window, created sunrises and sunsets on its surface. She had forgotten about the globe, forgotten how curious it must look to others. She had gotten used to its being there.

The ballroom was filled with clumps of awkward children clutching plastic cups of punch in their hands. They were a disparate assembly, solemn and skittish and shy and swaggering. The freshmen and sophomores huddled in self-defensive circles, not yet comfortable enough in their surroundings to speak too loudly, as if the austere portraits frowning haughtily from the walls could overhear them. They seemed overawed by the size of the room, the crystal chandeliers, the mirrored walls and gilt borders. The juniors and seniors tried to play it cool, like they saw this sort of thing every day. The room buzzed with the low susurrus of their whispers.

All of Belinda's "special guests" were here. All save the Carson girl—perversely, the one Mariesa had been most interested in meeting. Mariesa wandered among the students, greeting them, surprising them by knowing their names.

The conventionally bright students, Jenny Ribbon, Cheng-I Yeh, Tanuja Pandya, and the others. Smiling and polite and observant; responding with carefully rehearsed pleasantries, looking for the advantage, looking for the edge . . .

. . . and Azim Thomas, dangling a scantily clad girl on his arm and gold chains around his throat; answering insolently from behind an impenetrable pair of sunglasses . . .

. . . and Leilah Frazetti, trailing a handsome young man behind her and oohing and aahing over how beautiful everything in the house was . . .

. . . and James Poole, by some measures the brightest of them all, a statue in the corner until addressed; then unleashing a torrent of chatter in equal measures nervous fright and raw ego . . .

. . . and Leland Hobart, barely responding at all . . .

. . . and Chase Coughlin, lounging against the far wall with an acquisitive look on his face. Moving the valuable and delicate pieces to the vaults had not been cynicism, merely prudence; but it was best not to put temptation in one's path. Mariesa noticed how Chase carefully avoided watching her approach.

"Are you enjoying yourself, Mr. Coughlin?" she asked when she approached him.

The boy shrugged. "It's a bore. Isn't there any music?"

"I have engaged a 'DJ,' who should be arriving shortly." Chase rolled his eyes.

"Meanwhile, there are refreshments in the loggia to the rear."

"You mean that table full of food and drink? Gee. I would never have guessed."

Her lips kept a tight rein on her temper. "If you need anything else," she said evenly, "you need merely ask Sykes."

"Voice-activated . . . What'll they think of next?"

How did you reach someone like that? How did you break through the indifference that he had built around himself? Or did you even bother? Perhaps Belinda had made an error including this boy on her list.

When Chase shifted his stance, Mariesa noticed a bruise on his left cheek. "Have you hurt yourself?" she asked, extending a hand toward him. Chase twisted quickly away.

"No."

"What is that on your cheek?"

"Nothing."

"But . . ."

"Nothing that is any of your business, lady. I got in a fight, okay?"

"Fighting does not solve problems."

"Is this a party or a lecture? Fighting sure solved slavery, didn't it?" Chase laid a smirk on her: *Surprise, surprise. I learned something once in school.*

"No, Mr. Coughlin. Fighting ended the problem, it did not solve it."

"Whatever. I guess I'm stupid."

Mariesa thought that behind the hostility and the "cool" there was only a confused teenager trying to grow up; that perhaps he had his back to the wall in more ways than one.

From the corner of her eye, she saw Sykes step into the ballroom and stand by the entrance, looking imperturbable with his white-gloved hands folded in front of him. He looked good in tails—and knew it!—but so seldom had the opportunity to wear them. When he caught Mariesa's glance, he nodded once. "Excuse me," she told Chase. "I must see Sykes for a moment."

She caught up with Sykes at the front door. Belinda Karr had arrived at last, and with the Carson girl in tow. Black, long-sleeved blouse; black ankle-length skirt. Heavy, black shoes. Black eye makeup and lipstick. Black holes for eyes.

She must dress that way all the time, Mariesa thought. So drab! She would be positively pretty if she were to dress in a more flattering fashion. "Roberta!" she said aloud. "You came, after all."

Belinda slipped out of her coat and handed it to Sykes, who folded it across his arm. Sykes bowed by inches and left to hang the coat away. "I found her at the school parking lot," Belinda said. "She arrived too late for Laurence's van."

Mariesa looked at the girl. "Roberta, why didn't your mother bring you straight here? Didn't she know the way?" A horrible thought: had her mother simply dropped the girl at the school and left? Hadn't she noticed that the others were already gone?

"My name isn't Roberta. It's Styx."

"She walked," said Belinda.

Mariesa looked at the shorter woman. "What? She walked? From the Locks?"

"Boy, you pick up on things real quick, don't you?" said Styx.

Mariesa turned a hard gaze on her. "Have I done something to offend you?"

Styx shrugged. "Oh, hell, no. It's not your fault. I'm just pissed, is all."

And so you are trying to shock me, Mariesa thought.

"Her mother did not want her to come," Belinda explained. "So, she sneaked out of her house and walked to the school."

"It took me longer than I thought."

"Oh, dear," said Mariesa. "Your mother must be frantic by now. She will be calling here soon, looking for you."

The girl's smile was one of perverse satisfaction. "Don't hold your breath, lady."

"Then I shall have Sykes call and inform her. Meanwhile, the other children are in the ballroom . . ."

"Children?" said Styx. "Oh, happy, happy. Joy, joy."

When she had gone, Belinda shook her head. "High-school juniors do not think of themselves as children."

Young men and women, then? Mariesa thought not. At least, not yet. They were still colts, still awkward and unsure. Not ready to run; but, oh, eager to. "Did you smell her breath on the way over?"

Belinda nodded. "Yes. She is a very angry young girl."

"Why did her mother not want her to come?"

"From what was said—or not said—in the car, I suspect it is her wardrobe."

Mariesa raised an eyebrow. "Her wardrobe. Really. Granted, it is not very attractive, but I thought snobbery was the province of the wealthy." She looked at Belinda. "Tell me, 'Linda, why did you—"

"Speaking of wardrobe, that is a very nice dress you have on. I like the cut. It suits you."

"Do you think so?" Mariesa turned so that Belinda could see the back and sides. "I found it at a small shop in Florence. Quite out of the way. The woman calls herself a seamstress, not even a designer; but I found her clothing so fresh that I just had to have it."

"The color becomes you."

"'Linda, if you want one like it, I'll buy one for you. Just tell me why you stopped by the school tonight. It's not on the way from your hotel; and you knew Laurence's people were picking the children up."

Belinda looked through the archway toward the ballroom. "Call it a hunch, Riesey. Call it a hunch."

Once the music began, the children loosened up. A few began to dance; and the whispering chatter grew as it competed with the music. Mariesa had asked the DJ to keep the volume low, but it still seemed more than was necessary to get the point across. Classical musicians had understood the power of contrast. *Piano* versus *fortissimo*. Rock had forgotten, if it had ever known.

Mariesa drifted onto the loggia, where the caterer had set up the buffet. An ice carving—a swan poised at the moment of flight—dominated the center table. Young men and women in white uniforms stood impassively ready to serve. The chef de cuisine, wearing the distinctive high toque of his school, nodded to Mariesa as she passed by. The football player, Hobart, surrounded by an admiring cluster of smaller children, was talking to Onwuka. Good. She crossed Hobart off her mental list. She and Belinda and Onwuka had planned to draw out the special "Prometheus" students this evening. How did the old expression go? "Find out where their heads are at." And they had been doing so throughout the evening.

No one had spoken with Roberta yet. In fact, none of the chaperones had seen Roberta since shortly after her arrival. Off by herself somewhere on the grounds. Well, she was a poet, if only in the egg, and poets needed solitude; but they needed inspiration, too, and Mariesa intended to supply some.

Perhaps it was disproportionate to spend so much personal time on this one age cohort—there were many years ahead for Prometheus, many more classes would enter and graduate; and there was no possibility that she would be intimate with all of them—yet, good beginnings made for good endings. They had settled on North Orange for the bellwether project because its proximity to Silverpond facilitated Mariesa's oversight. Belinda could not neglect the day-to-day operation of Mentor for this one group of practices.

Behind the tables, French doors opened onto the verandah and attached patio. Several of the children had found their way into the ornamental garden beyond and were walking among the lighted hedgerows and flower beds, some of them alone, some of them hand in hand. One couple sat on the edge of the fountain, under the statue of Hyacinth, heads bent together in whispers. The lights in the water basin illuminated the streamers behind them. The garden hedgerows provided plenty of seclusion for young folks, and they could always claim, in the darkness, to have gotten lost. Perhaps "Styx" was among them.

Harriet, attired in her gardening clothes, reclined in the chaise on the patio, pretending to read a book, but watching the children who wandered among the larkspur, sweet alyssum, and fading roses. So, she had not gone to the Allerton party, after all. Mariesa smiled to herself. Even Harriet found Joyce's affairs tedious and, deprived of the chance to throw Mariesa into Nelson's lap, she had preferred the noisier event at home. *Children bring out the mother in her.*

Mariesa saw Barry Fast on the far side of the fountain, hands jammed in his pockets, watching the sky. The gentle scents enveloped her as she crossed the court toward the fountain. Her shoes crunched on the gravel walk. The young couples saw her coming and scampered back toward the house.

"Nice night," Barry said as she came alongside. "Not too warm; not too cold."

"Like Little Bear's porridge. Have you seen Styx?"

"The Carson girl?" He indicated a gap in the hedgerow. "She went down that way. Alone, don't worry. But you'll never find *her* in the dark." Barry's teeth were white in the moonlight. "I'm going to make the rounds in a little while. Make sure there's no hanky-panky going on."

"Thank you."

"Hey, what's a chaperone for, if not to bust up the fun and games?" He looked up at the cloudless sky again. "It's an awesome sight, don't you think? So full of stars. It makes me think of navigators. Phoenicians, Vikings, Polynesians, Portuguese."

"On nights like this, you think you can see forever."

He turned his head. "Oh, yes. The telescope." She nodded but said nothing. After a moment, he said, "Why?"

"Why what?"

"The astronomy. It seems . . . eccentric."

"Everyone should have a hobby. Why not one that makes you look up instead of down?"

"Look, I'm sorry I acted like such an ass in the library," he said. "I was upset over the car. Money problems." He looked at her, looked away. "Someone like you wouldn't understand."

"I have had money problems, too."

"Not this kind. Not not having enough."

She could hear frustration and bitterness in his laugh. "Barry, it's not my fault that I'm rich."

A chuckle escaped him and he turned his cockeyed smile on her. "Well, actually, the way I heard it, it is."

His grin was infectious. She had to return it. "Oh, well . . ."

"What did you do, double the fortune you inherited?"

More like tripled . . . "I suppose I could have squandered my inheritance, or buried it in a field. It was just that . . ."

"Just that what?"

One of the waiters drifted by with a tray of hors d'oeuvres. Mariesa selected a Viennese frank in a pastry shell and a slice of Gruyère. Barry took three or four franks and held them in a paper napkin. "If I told you I needed the money," she said when the man had gone, "you would think I was crazy."

"Maybe not," he admitted. "But it would be a stretch."

"Barry, *you* are wealthier than ninety-three percent of the people on this planet. Why not relax and enjoy your riches?"

"Eh? Oh. I guess I am. I never thought of it that way. But I've got expenses, too. I just squeak by each month paying the bills. The mortgage, utilities. You don't want to hear the list. All on a teacher's salary. I need more money to do the things I want to do."

She nodded. "There are things that I want to do, too."

"And you need more money to do them. . . . Go back to the moon? I guess you would need some extra cash, at that." A smile, almost a condescending smile. But he looked up at the moon when he said it. "How do you propose we get there?"

"It is very simple, really. First, you lace your bootstraps up real tight; then you lift, hard."

He laughed. "That might work at that." Then, more soberly. "If only it would work for our students, too."

"One effort might resolve the other," she said, then held her tongue before she said too much.

But, to Mariesa's relief, he saw the connection run only in the one direction. "What? Going back to the moon might somehow inspire these kids?" He waved an arm around the garden. "I wouldn't count on it. Reruns don't attract the same enthusiasm. I was just a kid when they landed on the moon; only in high school when they stopped. But even then, the tenses were all wrong. It was something that had *already happened;* not something I grew up anticipating. It was boring. *Scripted.* I've seen only one launch in person . . ." He stopped abruptly.

"Really? Which one?" But then she sensed the tension in him.

He shook his head. ". . . in the bleachers, with the other schoolteachers. They didn't follow the script that time. I . . . swore I'd never watch another." He turned away from her.

"Give them dreams, you said, when I was here last summer. But dreams can turn into nightmares."

She laid a hand lightly on his arm, and he turned and faced her. "Barry, you bury your dead and keep on moving. There is so much we can do in space. . . ."

"Navigation, communication, solar power . . . Yes, you've told me. It sounds . . . promising."

"But far out, right?"

"Just a little," he said with a weak smile.

"The most outlandish visions look timid in retrospect. There was a mayor in Ohio who, when told about the telephone, fearlessly predicted a day when every city would have one. And IBM's Tom Watson once forecast the world needing five entire computers. . . ."

That coaxed a laugh from him. "I get your point."

"What would the Wrights have said had you told them that billions of dollars would be invested in airplanes, aerodromes, and personnel *just fifty years after that first flight?* They would have thought you mad. Show people the *real* future and their first reaction is, 'That's impossible!' Yet, when the future finally arrives, that selfsame chorus sings out, 'We knew it all along.' "

"I look up and see romance; you look up and see . . . utilization."

" 'Farewell, Romance, the Cave-men said . . .' "

Barry chuckled. " 'With bone well-carved He went away.' "

"Yes, 'they don't make 'em like they used to.' Just do not be so sure that there is no romance in the coming age."

"The success of air travel doesn't imply the success of space travel," Barry pointed out reasonably. "The costs are different. Besides, if there was money to be made in space, companies would be scheming to get up there." He stopped suddenly and gave her a sharp look. "Oho! It's not just the glamour, is it?"

She was not sure why she suddenly found it so important that Barry understand. But, sooner or later, you had to preach to those who did not know the hymns by heart. "Come by

Silverpond some evening," she said suddenly, "and we'll talk some more."

He pursed his lips and nodded. "All right, maybe I will. If I can find new wheels. By the way, you'll be glad to know it wasn't the fuel-pump relay that your man fixed that time. It was the . . . Never mind, it would have been one thing or another. That heap was on its last legs."

"Talk to Laurence. He may have a car available."

He stiffened suddenly and his face lost its smile. "I don't accept hand-me-downs," he said. "Or charity."

"I was not offering charity," she said. "Nor, I assure you, will Laurence. But he trades his cars in every few years to keep his fleet up to date, so you may be able to purchase a late-model car from him at a considerable bargain."

"Oh. Sorry. I just don't like begging favors."

She saw the stubborn pride behind the eyes. "Don't apologize. There are too many people who like it all too well. People who know better how to spend my money than I do." She laid her hand lightly on his arm. "Let me treasure one who does not."

The evening was winding to a close. Most of the younger children were gone already. Laurence and his drivers had been taking them back to the school in shifts. Some parents, anxious to gawk at the mansion, had come themselves to pick up their child. Mariesa stood by the door and bade each of them farewell. When Bob Boucher left, he shook her hand and said, "Thank you for a most intriguing evening, Mariesa. Bernie Paulson and I fell to talking and we came up with a few ideas for next year's history curriculum."

And he spent the next ten minutes telling her about it with his overcoat half-on.

"That sounds fascinating, Bob. I look forward to your task group's report." It was funny, she thought, watching him go, how a man can turn around. When she had first met him, Boucher had been a defeated, hopeless man. But a coal in a brazier may appear dead, until you blow it back into life. Perhaps Mentor had proven less than he had feared; or more than he had hoped.

When Mariesa returned to the ballroom, the DJ was playing one last song and a few of the young couples were slow dancing in the center of the dim-lit ballroom. She saw Belinda, Gwen, and Barry standing by the fireplace. Barry stood hip-shot, leaning against the fireplace with an intent demeanor, not simply watching the children, but studying them, while the two women chatted across him. Mariesa approached them. "You look rather thoughtful, Barry."

Barry tugged at his chin. "I was thinking of something Onwuka said earlier. That you work with people the way they are, not the way you wish they were. We work with today's kids, but we use yesterday's techniques." His gesture took in the dancers, the bystanders, the children in the garden and beyond, across the state and country. "They aren't idealists like our generation; or 'good scouts' like our parents. They're risk-takers. You can't reach them the same way. Even when they do the same things we did when we were young, it's for a different reason. When they drop acid, they're not looking for the Tao; they're looking to kiss death in the face, and slip it some tongue."

Barry's comments sometimes bordered so on the flippant that Mariesa wondered if the chance to crack a witty remark might color some of what he had to say.

"I don't think it's quite fair," said Gwen, "to label an entire generation."

Barry laughed. "Sure, Jenny Ribbon, over there, she wouldn't risk her lunch money on tomorrow's sunrise. But I meant 'in general,' 'on the average,' or however you want to say it. Every generation has the same mix of kids. The wild ones, the studious ones, the bashful and the brazen. But the proportion seems to change from time to time. These kids, they take chances; push themselves to the edge. Hell, Azim Thomas takes a chance every day he wakes up. Chase . . . even Leilah Frazetti."

"How is she a 'risk-taker'?" Mariesa asked.

"What, are we playing Name That Risk?" asked Gwen.

Barry pointed toward Leilah and her date on the dance floor. "Look at them. That's not dancing; it's necking vertically. They're so close, he should be using a condom."

"That's not funny. Unprotected, you could become pregnant or contract a venereal disease, or worse . . . Oh."

"You see? Pushing the edge. Just different edges, is all. I've been thinking about this ever since I read through your guest list and figured out why you had invited who you had."

Mariesa exchanged a glance with Belinda. "Why is that?"

"The edges," he said.

"What?"

"You've got all the edges here. The smartest, the brightest, the most daring, the most desperate, the wildest, the . . . extremes, in nearly every direction."

Mariesa could not help but wonder how much of that was appearance and how much reality. Leilah behaved like a roundheel, but was she really? And Jimmy Poole, huddled alone with himself, watching the others from the corner, was so stereotypical that it almost seemed a role he had created for himself, a cloak he wore; as Azim and Chase wore "tough guy" and Leilah "easy girl" and Hobart "jock." And the others . . . "bookworms," "Asian grinds" . . . Only Styx seemed to defy easy stereotyping. Did that mean she was a more complex person, or only that Mariesa did not know the type?

She wondered, not for the first time, whether Prometheus could sprout from such unlikely seeds. It need not, she reminded herself. These children were not on the critical path. There would be other classes, other schools. These children were the long shots, the wild cards. The transition class.

"So, I was thinking," Barry said. "We should make use of their risk-taking, somehow. By making risk central to their learning."

"Do your homework or we'll hang you?" said Gwen.

Barry threw back his head and laughed. He looked quite attractive when he did. Past his shoulder, Mariesa noticed Harriet watching them from the loggia. She ignored her mother's frown. "Oh, Lord, no," said Barry. "Never be direct when you're dealing with teenagers. They can spot a head game a mile away. I can still remember some of my own teachers slapping a coat of 'social concern' paint over the same old, tired lessons. Phonies and cop-outs. But I can remember others who found that center without any transparent artifice. Do you know what marks a successful teacher?''

Mariesa shook her head and glanced at Belinda, who waited with an interested look to hear what Barry said.

''When your students are old men and women and they still talk about you.''

''Exactly so,'' said Belinda quietly. The loggia was empty now, Mariesa noticed; Harriet was gone. Probably, she had taken the back way up to her rooms.

''Unless you want them to risk their lives and safety,'' Belinda said, ''the riskiest thing I know of is starting a business. More than ninety percent fail in the first few years. I know Mentor almost did. Then the school officials barred us from the state science fair because we had won three years in a row and they wanted 'to give other schools a chance.' After that, we had more applications than we could handle.''

''That is what brought Belinda to my attention,'' Mariesa said.

''Barred because you won too often?'' Barry chuckled. ''It gives a whole new meaning to 'the thrill of victory,' doesn't it?''

''I hope Witherspoon can look forward to that,'' Gwen said. ''We always place last in the region.''

Barry cocked his head. ''That's not a bad idea, Belinda.''

''What isn't? The science fair?''

''No. Let them learn by taking risks. We let them set up little businesses. . . . They have to raise the capital—that will be the tough part—''

''Not necessarily,'' said Mariesa. ''But go on.''

''Hmm. Right. Raise the capital. Plan production. Maybe hire workers. Sell the product.''

''You are talking about Junior Achievement projects,'' said Belinda. ''There's nothing new about that.''

''More than that. We integrate it into the curriculum; make

it interdisciplinary, like we've already done with some materials. They'll have to keep accounts, prepare proposals, plans, advertising. So we blend in economics, math, English composition, art—who knows what else? History, maybe? I haven't thought this through yet.''

"Post it on the Institute bulletin board on-line," Belinda said, "and we will discuss it."

If Barry planned to say anything more, Mariesa did not hear; for at that moment, Styx ran through the ballroom, shoving little Jimmy Poole aside, barging against the dancers on the floor. "Hey!" said Prescott. Azim shoved a finger in the air after the departing girl. Mariesa heard the bang of feet on stairs. Sykes, standing by the archway, looked confused. Chase lounged against one of the pillars that lined the loggia, one cheek burning red and a smirk on his face.

Mariesa quickly excused herself and went in pursuit of the girl.

The Roost was dark. Only the starlight and a sliver of moon shining through the dormer window lifted the gloom and gave shape to the shadows. One shadow was a girl-shaped nebula spread across the starry panoply outside, black against black, but a face like a crescent moon.

Mariesa stood by the light switch, her hand near the toggle, but not moving it. She heard the rustle of papers. "Styx? Is that you?"

The shadow did not answer. Mariesa flicked the light on and saw the girl shield red-rimmed eyes with her arm. She sat cross-legged on the window seat. The raised left hand gripped a pencil. On her lap Mariesa recognized the pad from her desk. The coal-black lipstick was smeared.

"Dr. Karr is looking for you. It's time to go."

"Who cares," she said.

"I'm sure that whatever Chase said to you, he did not mean it."

"Who cares," she said again. "Chase is a null. A void. What he says doesn't matter. Not to me; not to anyone. Not even to him."

"I am sure . . ."

"You're not 'sure' of anything," she cried. "You don't understand anything." Styx lowered her arm. Mariesa saw that she had been crying.

"I was young once, too," Mariesa said.

"Young and rich and a long time ago. Things are different now." She turned her face again to the stars outside. "Would you mind turning the light out? I liked sitting here in the dark and staring at the sky."

Mariesa smiled. "So do I."

Styx looked at her and shook her head a little. Her eyes flickered like stars, catching stray light from the moon outside. "I know. I peeked in the next room."

Mariesa turned the lights out and crossed the room to sit beside the girl, navigating easily around the unseen furniture. "I like it, too. This is one of my favorite places."

Silence; then Styx said. "I can't see anything like this at my house, not usually, not this well. There's a highway; and a shopping center on the other side. It makes the sky so bright that the black turns gray and all but a few of the stars are washed away. This is better. You can almost see how deep and black the world is. Sometimes I feel . . ." Styx hunched in upon herself. "You can tell the sky anything. It won't talk back."

"It does," said Mariesa. "I've heard it." Mariesa pointed. "That one there, the bright one with the reddish tinge. That's Mars. It was at perigee—that's its closest approach to Earth—a few years back."

"This is different. This isn't dry and cold and heartless, like science. It's a . . . feeling I get. That it's the same sky everywhere. That the same stars shine for everyone, even if they're far away. It's like a connection. Like if there was someone you haven't seen for a long time, but you're close to them because we all look up at the same sky."

Almost, Mariesa told her that different stars looked down on the Southern Hemisphere; but she knew that Styx had been talking about something else and not the real stars in the real sky. "Speaking in tongues," she said.

"What? What's that?"

"The sky talks to us, but we each hear it in our own language. Mystery, adventure, romance . . . even utilization. To some, perhaps, endless despair. To others, endless hope."

"Do they . . ." Styx would not look at her. She looked down at her own hands, white, twisting in the dark. "Do they ever tell us what to do?"

Carefully, Mariesa did not laugh. "No. The stars are destiny, not fate. You tighten your belt and you do what you have to do."

After a while, Styx turned and looked at her in the dark, her face a moonlit oval. "I guess you do understand, after all," she said. "A few things, at least."

From *The Collected Poems of Roberta Carson:*

"The Early Years"
IN LIFE'S LABOR-YNTH
by Styx

In life's labor-ynth
We package our past.
Stack it and store it
And try to ignore it.
In barrel and box
Bolted and binned
Days packed away
Awaiting the light
Gathering dust.
Shall we peek within?
Maybe we may.
Maybe we might.
Maybe we must.

                    October, in the Rich Lady's house

8.

Messenger Boy (I)

Ned DuBois watched from the window of his quarters while Krasnarov and Levkin jogged past underneath. The early-morning sun cast them in pale shadows. Levkin had always seemed a little soft to him, not as much on his game physically as the others. He lagged behind Krasnarov on the cinder track. Tiring, or just pacing himself on his longer-legged companion?

"Handicapping the field, I see," said Forrest Calhoun. Ned turned away from the window and studied his friend, who lounged in the doorway. Forrest grinned and came into the room and flopped himself into the sofa. The pilot quarters were spartan cinder-block construction, but as well-furnished as any hotel room Ned had graced, and he had graced a lot of them. Furniture was utilitarian. Each room had a painting or a photograph of a legendary airplane or rocket. "Who do you like in the first?" Forrest asked.

Ned sat against the windowsill. "Me." Forrest snorted.

"How about place and show, then?"

"Krasnarov's in the running; so are you and Bat. Levkin's a scratch."

"What about the others?"

Ned shrugged. "In the running, but not favored."

"Yeah?" Forrest pursed his lips. "That's about how I read it. With a few minor differences."

Ned grunted. "I'll bet, a few minor differences. What pried you loose from the simulator?"

Forrest looked bland. "I was talking to Sergio in Ground Test. Scuttlebutt is that Mendoza is releasing the Plank for preflight."

Ned felt the shiver run through him. He stayed braced against the window. "About fucking time," he said calmly. "What about the schedule?"

Forrest shrugged. "Nobody tells me. Apparently some sort of word came down from On High. Bonny is on the horn to João just about every day. Maybe they slip the schedule; or maybe they skip the unmanned tests and go straight to manned flight." He looked thoughtful. "They missed a bet, though; not pegging the first launch to New Year's. A lot of symbolism gone to waste."

"Screw symbolism." Ned turned and looked out the window again. Levkin and Krasnarov were stick figures at the far end of the track. "As long as the ship is ready."

"As long as *we* are, good buddy," said Forrest. "As long as *we* are."

That night, Ned took Floriana to *O Mirante* on Alameda do Boldró, where the air-traffic warden had maybe a glass too many *caipirinhas* and grew all over Ned like a fungus. When Ned asked her what she wanted for dessert, she showed him in unmistakable terms; and what the hell, Ned always did go for sweets.

They staggered out to Boldró Beach, which at that time of the morning was deserted. Ned kept his arm around Floriana's waist and she kept hers around his. Between them, they managed to approximate one upright person. The sand was still warm and so fine it ran between his toes and his sandals like dry water.

The moon was half-full and gave the beach its only light. Floriana was tall and thin, dressed in a wraparound, ankle length skirt and a light cotton blouse that buttoned up the front. Her clothing billowed in the night breeze. Her face was a pale oval framed by black hair invisible in the night. Ned kissed her hungrily and she kissed him back, probing him while he groped under her fluttering blouse.

Floriana announced her intention of taking a swim and Ned pointed out that she hadn't brought her bum-bum. But, hell, a Brazilian bathing suit left you more naked than going bare-assed. Native slang called it "dental floss." So when Flori untied her skirt and let it fall to the sand, Ned did the only polite thing possible and followed suit.

The water was tropical warm, rocked by waves more gentle than those that crashed on Atalaia Beach or Caracas Point on the other side of the island. They stayed in the shallow water and splashed each other and played catch-me-if-you-can, which of course you always could. When they finally embraced and wrapped their limbs around one another, they let the surf lift them like some strange, entwined wood drift and carry them toward the shore.

They nestled in the soft, warm sand. Ned lay atop her, taking his weight on his elbows, watching as her breathing quickened. Her eyes were closed and her head tilted slightly back, with a faraway look on her face as she rode the waves that crested inside her.

Ned could see the Plank rising in his mind's eye. Fire spurting from it as it strained toward the sky, pushing into the heavens. A peculiar perspective. He saw the scene from within and without at the same time. His hands were on the controls, holding the stick steady and he pressed the buttons and acceleration pushed him steadily into the soft cushions of his couch.

Until everything was spent, and the ship ruptured in an unexpected failure mode and spilled its contents into the waiting void.

*   *   *

Afterward, the moon was setting and they hunted for their clothing in the growing dark. The rocking waves had carried them away from the point where they had entered the water. Ned searched with a growing sense of urgency; Floriana, with patient exasperation. After a few minutes, she gave up and declared she would return when the sun came up and the light was better. Then, after a final kiss, she walked away nude and left him there.

Ned watched her go. Water droplets gleamed on her skin like pearls in the moonlight, and patches of pure, white sand clung to her ribs and buttocks and calves, giving her an odd, motley appearance, as if she were wearing a clown's suit. It was one-thirty in the morning and her apartment was close by the beach. (Everything on the island was close to a beach!) So it was unlikely she would put on much of a show for anyone. Still, the casual attitude of some Brazilians often managed to surprise even him.

Ned was a more persistent searcher—and not nearly so casual about strolling through town—and a few additional minutes and a more systematic search pattern finally led him to his shorts and T-shirt. The sandals he finally gave up on.

He decided to walk back to the complex instead of driving drunk. There wasn't much traffic on the island's only major road, but he was not about to compromise his chances for making the cut by demonstrating abysmally poor judgment. Who knew how many naked women were out walking the nighttime highways? It could distract a man at just the wrong moment.

It was only about three klicks as the crow flies from Boldró Beach to the complex around St. Anthony's Bay. But no crow ever had to pick its way in the moonless dark along stretches of slippery, fine, white sand, or climb over rocky outcroppings in its bare feet. It was three-thirty before he found his way around to the quay and climbed the stairs that led to the boardwalk that lined the harbor behind the residence building.

As he slipped between the residence and the training facility, he nearly collided with another figure, dressed all in black, that emerged from the shadows. The moon was down completely and Ned sensed the other as much by its nearness and mass as by his inadequate vision.

The other figure leapt away with an astonishing grace and swiftness, and Ned had nearly convinced himself that he had seen nothing when he was struck in the ribs by a numbing kick. Training shoved surprise offstage. Ned turned and blocked by instinct the likely follow-up move. He took the leg on his forearms and lifted, sending his attacker sprawling against the paving.

A gasp of surprise, then nothing. Ned took two quick steps backward and one to the left and waited in a crouch for the next assault.

None came, and he thought he heard, through the murmuring surf behind him, the patter of catlike feet. After a few more moments of waiting, he relaxed. He searched by feel around the area and found two things. One was a small flashpen stuck between two slats on the boardwalk, as if it had been dropped and then stepped on. The other was the door to the training center, which was slightly ajar. Ned pulled it closed and heard the latch catch. When he tried the handle, it was locked.

The whole experience was mildly hallucinatory. A silent, unreal ballet conducted in the night with an invisible opponent. In the morning, Ned managed to convince himself it had been a cachaça-induced dream. One too many concoctions of lime, sugar, crushed ice, and cane alcohol. His head pounded like the Erie, Pennsylvania, foundry his father had worked in.

The big bruise on his ribs on the left side? He might have slipped and fallen scrabbling over the rocks while negotiating the beaches last night.

That afternoon, Bat augered in during a purely routine sim. He zigged when he should have zagged, and put the simulated Plank into the simulated bay just by the simulated wreckage of the *Ana Maria*. Bat's anger was not simulated. He swore later that it must have been a malf. He'd made all the right moves, he said; but the computer dumped him into the bay anyhow. Bonny put a couple of techs to work running diagnostics and the equipment came through clean. Bat complained that if the fault was a transient, twenty-four hours was too long to wait to run the diagnostics. Everyone else felt it was sour grapes, and the snooty *carioca* had gotten some well-deserved comeuppance. Only Levkin was sympathetic, because he finally had some company with him "under the bay."

Ned was thoughtful.

The rain outside hammered at the corrugated roof of O Amigo de Verdade. In the corner, perched on a high stool, Gisela Peixoto plucked resolutely at an acoustical guitar to no memorable effect. Her brother, Claudio, leaned his large, beefy arms on the bar top and chatted amiably with a group of locals. Every now and then someone said something that must have been funny, because they all burst out laughing.

"Friends," said Forrest Calhoun as he studied his cards, "we are nothing but Pavlov's dogs."

Ned DuBois eyed his cards with distaste. Only an idiot would try to fill an inside straight; and only a worse idiot would have dealt him one. He dropped two cards, picked up his bottle of Xingu, and tilted the neck into his mouth. "Does that mean," he said, putting the beer down, "that we're all sons of bitches?"

Bobbi McFeeley said, "I'll take one. And quit the flapjawing. Poker is serious business." Forrest flipped her a card. Her face remained expressionless as she pondered her new hand.

"None for me, *spasebo*," said Gregor Levkin. He grinned, looked at his hand, and grinned again.

Forrest looked at him. "Son, are you *sure* you've never played this game before?"

Levkin shook his head. "In the Rodina we have no such game."

Forrest grunted. "That's what the fox told the hens. Ned, old son, are you going to pick up those cards; or are you afraid they'll bite you?"

Ned sighed and picked up his two draw cards. *Ouch.* Before, he had nothing in his hand; now he had a pair of sevens, which would beat a den of Cub Scouts or your old grandmother, though he was not sure about the grandmother. Still, he had seen a few pots tonight picked up by high cards; and if you don't bet you can't win. "Five," he said, pushing a chip to the center. After their first game last summer—in which Forrest had bet in *reals*, Levkin in rubles, and Bobbie in gold dust—they had agreed that all poker would be conducted in American dollars.

The others covered him, which was not good news.

"No, what I meant is all this simulator training." Forrest folded his cards and laid them facedown. "Your five and five back. It's all supposed to condition us, like Pavlov's dogs; familiarize us with every possible sight, sound, smell, and vibration, together with the proper response; so when I take the bird up, there won't be nothing comes as surprise."

Ned did not look up from his cards. "If you take the bird up, that would be the surprise."

Forrest sounded hurt. "You don't think I'm the best qualified, son?"

Ned drained the last of his beer. *What the hell* . . . "Your five and five again." Sometimes if you had nothing, you had to act like you had it all. "No, Forrest, I think Mike will kill you long before the launch date is set."

Levkin sputtered. "*Da*," he said. "Mikhail Alexandrovich is—how do you say it?—pissed off?"

"Yeah," said Bobbi. "That's how you say it." She folded her hand and threw it in.

Forrest put on a look of aggrieved innocence. "Hell, Ned, all I did was bang on the simulator cabin a little."

"With a trash barrel, Forrest. Full of empty cans and bottles. I was riding console and now Mike thinks I was in on it. And, speaking of being 'in' . . . Levkin, are you in?"

"*Da, da.* I observe . . . no, I *see* you."

"Well," Forrest pointed out reasonably, "it's not like he never augered in before. We all have, time to time, even me." He pushed another chip into the pot. "I'll see your cards, too, son." He turned in his chair and caught Claudio's attention. He made the three-fingered Boy Scout sign and waved it horizontally a foot above the table. *"Tragam-nos quatro Antárctica, por favor."*

Ned knew that Forrest kept a wall chart of the Walking Corpses Club. A skull-and-crossbones went next to a name each time a simulation went bad. None of the others thought it was funny anymore and Ned had long stopped checking to see who was ahead.

Forrest leaned back and the wooden chair creaked. "You know what really bothered me?" he said reflectively. "You know how we're all wired up in there, with the heart rate and the breathing and the temperature wand up the old wazoo? So, here I dumped a load of scrap metal on Krasnarov's head and, that sumbitch, not a single one of those readouts so much as blipped."

Levkin shook his head. "Mishka has blood like Siberian winter."

"You ever do that to me, Calhoun," said Bobbi, "and you are dog meat."

"Pair of sevens," Ned announced. Forrest whistled.

"You got guts, son." He took his own hand where he had laid it and tossed it in with Bobbi's. "That beats me." Levkin smiled and shrugged. He turned his hand over and it was a pair of fives.

Ned stared. "I'll be damned."

"No question on that, son; but at least you'll be flush when you are." He pushed the pot toward Ned. "What's wrong, Bobbi?"

The former MacDac test pilot looked disgusted. "I *folded* with better cards than that!"

The door to the cabaret swung open and the wind blew the rain inside. Cards fluttered from the table; and the regulars clustered at the bar shouted something that Ned guessed would translate as, "Shut the fucking door!" The newcomer complied, then stood there with the rainwater draining off his yellow rubber slicker into a pool on the wood floor. He saw the poker players and approached the table, shedding his head gear.

"Heitor Carneiro," said Forrest, "you son-of-a-gun! Set

your ass on a chair and your money on the table, so's you and I can keep the game going after these other folks tap out.'' Quite a statement, thought Ned, for someone who had just lost a pot; but that was Forrest for you. Even when he lost, he came on you like a winner. Forrest said, aside to the others, ''I like playing poker with Heitor because he loses more than the rest of you put together.''

Heitor was unamused. ''I will win everything back, sometime. *Jeito.* On the *jogo de bicho*.'' *Jogo de bicho* was the Brazilian equivalent of the numbers racket. The *banqueiros* who ran it were small-time mafia and often used the money to finance the samba clubs that competed at Carnival.

''Son, you must *like* losing money. Otherwise you wouldn't do it so much.''

''Seu Ned,'' Carneiro said, extending an envelope wrapped in waterproof plastic. ''This has come for you from Fortaleza.'' Big red letters were stamped across the front in English: EXPEDITE.

Ned hesitated a moment before taking it. A hundred possibilities flashed through his mind. *Something happened to Betsy. Or to Lizzie.* He had written them both, finally. The letters had taken weeks to compose, and not entirely because he had to be careful of what he revealed of the project. So far, he had heard nothing in response. What if something had happened to his little girl while he was thousands of miles away?

He split open the waterproofing with his pocketknife and pulled the envelope out. He tore that open and pulled out a single sheet of paper. Forrest and the others watched while he read the memo. Then he read it again. He felt as if he had been punched in the stomach.

''Daedalus is sending me back to the U.S.,'' he said. ''To do a briefing for VHI higher-ups.'' He handed the letter to Forrest. ''They want me to pull together all our suggestions from the simulator runs and make a dog-and-pony show on how to improve the Phase IV crew module.''

Forrest whistled. ''Asking the troops for our opinions? What sort of generals have we got here?''

''Tell 'em they can move the manual overrides about two

inches to the left," said Bobbi. "They work fine in sims, but I think under acceleration they'd be just a tad too far a reach."

Ned waved her off. "Jeez, not now. Let me get organized first." He took the memo back from Forrest and reread it. "I've got two months to get this shit together. Mendoza's supposed to assign a tech to help."

Forrest pulled the scattered cards together and squared the deck. Levkin handed him the cards that had blown to the floor. Forrest cut the deck in two and riffled the cards; then he handed the deck to Bobbi. "Tomorrow's soon enough to get started, right?"

Ned folded the letter and stuck it in his shirt pocket. "Yeah. What's the game, Bobbi?"

"Stud."

Ned traded looks with Forrest. "You're sitting at the right table for that," he said, flexing his pectorals. Bobbi rolled her eyes and gave the deck to Levkin to cut. The letter in Ned's pocket felt like it weighed a pound and a half, and it was all he could do to keep his hand from patting it. *They don't give these "consolation" assignments to the jocks they've picked to fly.* The console jobs, the OEM visits, baby-sitting the journalists . . . He looked across the table at his friend. Forrest was looking uncharacteristically thoughtful. *Bonne chance, mon ami*, he thought. *This means I'm out of the running.* And that had to mean—no brag, just fact—that Bobbi and Levkin and the Volkovs were out, too. So, either Forrest, Mike, or Bat would get the nod. The American, the Russian, and the Brazilian. And wasn't *that* just a little too neat for coincidence!

He could see in Forrest's studied nonchalance that he knew, too. So did the others. They all knew how to read the signs. By tomorrow the rest of the pilots would know, too. Forrest avoided meeting Ned's eyes. *Oh, sure, I'll fly her eventually.* Maybe even the second or third flight. But not the first. He would not be Prime Pilot. He would be . . . a messenger boy.

His whole life—at the Academy, at flight school, at Edwards—he had always looked back at those he had left behind, at those who hadn't made the cut. Now here he was on the wrong end of the cut, watching others as they moved on. It was an odd feeling, a new feeling, and one he did not care for. He wanted to cry and he wanted to throw punches, and who in hell could he ever explain it to? Betsy? She was not here; and she could not possibly understand if she were.

"Deal the cards!" he growled.

Bobbi looked at him. Then she began flicking the cards at them. Forrest had a jack showing and took a peek at his hole card. "You know, I envy you, son," he said.

Ned was tired of Forrest's constant jokes, too. "Do you?" he said. But you never let them see it hurt. You took your lumps and moved on, dammit.

Forrest kicked back while Claudio set four more bottles of beer on the table. In the corner, Gisela began playing a samba. One of her strings was slightly out of tune. He could spill his guts to Gisela. She wouldn't understand, either. She only had a little English, and that related to transactions between men and women. But it wouldn't matter to her that he was prime or not. They were all *bandeirantes dos stellas* to her, and she bedded them all with equal fervor—except Bobbi and Katya; and hell, maybe them as well. Ned caught her eye and made a gesture and she winked and nodded. Claudio pretended not to notice; but he added it to Ned's tab.

"Why, sure, I envy you," Forrest drawled. "Here the rest of us are languishing in the tropics and maybe only get to the beaches every third day or so; but *you* get to spend an entire month in New Jersey."

"In winter," he added.

Mikhail Alexandrovich Krasnarov ran with precision. Ned watched from the sidelines as he made circuit after circuit around the indoor track. Legs pumping; arms like drive rods. Never any faster, never any slower. His lungs were bellows, sucking oxidizer in, expelling waste gas. They had all gotten nicknames—from each other, from the staff. Columbine, Angel, Cowboy . . .

Krasnarov was Senhor Machine.

Finally—perhaps when some predetermined number of laps was tallied—Krasnarov stopped. Just like that. He didn't slow down. He didn't jog to a halt. He simply stopped, as if he had been turned off. He put his hands on his hips and did a few relaxing stretches, his only concession to human weakness; then, flinging a towel across his shoulders, he strode over to where Ned waited. Krasnarov's T-shirt was black with sweat. His face, arms, and legs were beaded. He wiped his face with the towel. "What is it, Ned?" he asked.

Request for input.

"I'm preparing my New Jersey briefing, Mike, and I'd like to clarify a few items on the list you gave me."

Krasnarov nodded and hunkered down on his heels. He stretched both arms out to the side and flexed his fists open and closed. "Such as?"

Accepted. Program running.

"Well, dropping Forrest Calhoun from the program is not the sort of thing New Jersey was looking for. I won't pass along something like that."

Krasnarov did not quite smile. "I understand. He is your friend."

For a lot of years. Somehow it was harder to watch a friend move on than a stranger. "I know he can be a little hard to take, sometimes. But, it's his way."

Krasnarov rose from his crouch. "The man is a buffoon!" he snapped. *Data outside normal range. Please reenter.* "Every statement is a joke to him. He brags constantly." Krasnarov clenched a fist. "This enterprise—" Krasnarov paused at the very brink of emotion, and pulled back. "We are engaged in a serious and worthwhile endeavor, Ned," he continued more evenly. "Not only is it the ultimate test of man against machine, not only does it bring Russian and American together, but it may mean the future of humanity. Your friend is not serious enough for the role."

"Come on, Mike. Heroes aren't all steely eyed, jut-jawed, and celibate, staring out at far horizons. That sort of 'nobility' is for posers, not doers. Forrest has always had to assert himself, to prove himself. Because of his . . . circumstances."

"Because of his skin. *Da*, I understand. Your American race problem."

"He always had to show that he was twice as good just to get half as far."

"Calhoun is what you call an 'uppity nigger,' right? No, listen to me, Ned. He is good. Perhaps not so good as I . . . but good. I have watched him in the simulator; flown with him in the training jets. I salute his skills. Among us—among those who fly the new planes—that should be enough, *da?*" Krasnarov leaned close to Ned and pitched his voice low. "Tell him, he need prove nothing more to me."

"All I'm asking is that you cut him some slack. Roll with his gibes. Better yet, rib him back."

"Rib?" *Parameter undefined.*

"Give him what he gives you. Like I do; like Bobbi does. Hell, Mike, half the fun for him is trying to break through that iron-man facade of yours."

Krasnarov was silent for a while. *Computing . . . Computing . . .* Then he nodded. "We should all make allowances for imperfections."

Ned clapped him on the shoulder. Krasnarov looked at the hand. "That's the spirit," Ned told him. "Now, let's go over these other suggestions of yours."

They clarified the other matters quickly. When they had finished and Ned thought he had all he needed to write his report, they parted. On the way out, Ned remembered something Mikhail Alexandrovich had said. The Plank program was the ultimate test of man versus machine.

But if Krasnarov wound up as Prime Pilot, how could anyone tell who won?

9.

Slumming

The flagstone steps leading to the front door at Silverpond were a little too deep and a little too short to take two at a time; but Barry felt, with the odd lightness of exuberance, that he ought to at least try. The ever-vigilant Sykes opened the door before Barry could even knock and regarded him with that studied neutrality he always wore. They exchanged a few greetings and Barry waited in the foyer while Sykes left to tell Mariesa he had come.

The foyer was spare and elegant, high-ceilinged, with a crystal chandelier dangling above. Vases sat in columned niches on the two walls—real flowers, natch. You were rich, you had real flowers, even in November. The walls were dressed in light, comfortable earth tones. The one odd note in the decor was the floor tiling. Everything else was laid out in severe, Colonial-style symmetry; but the tiles were all a-jumble, as if the mason had simply dropped them in place at random. Barry studied the pattern curiously, as he had on his previous visits, trying to puzzle out the rationale.

A voice from the direction of the atrium—"Who is it,

Sykes?''—and, a moment later, Harriet Gorley van Huyten entered, clad in slippers and a flowing housecoat of Chinese red. Her nails matched her robe; her coiffure was perfectly arranged. Harriet owned most of Mariesa's features, save the nose and the height, but a more weathered version and with a weariness that Mariesa had yet to show. She stopped at the entrance, and the ghost of a smile passed across her visage. "Oh, Mr. Fast—'Barry.' Is there a meeting this afternoon?"

Barry reached to take the hand she had not offered, forcing her to respond. Harriet always observed the forms, however little she regarded their content. *You know damn well there isn't*, he telepathed. *But let's play Let's Pretend.* "I'm taking Mariesa on a ride through the country. Then, we're having dinner at a little restaurant I know in Metuchen."

"I see. Another restaurant 'outing,' is it? Is it to be a diner or a deli this week? I understand that the food served in such places can often be interesting."

Barry could hear the verbal bullet ricochet off the rocks, like in an old Western. "No," he said. "As a matter of fact, it's a *cordon bleu* restaurant. The chef is Paris-trained, and they only do two seatings an evening." *And it costs a bundle, Barry. Let's not forget that. Way more than you can afford.*

"Really." It was fruitless to try to impress Harriet. And it wasn't the quality of the restaurants that concerned her, anyway. "Tell me, 'Barry' . . ." she said, rolling the words down on him like rocks off a mountainside. "I hold nothing against you personally . . ."

Much.

". . . but do you believe it proper to be squiring my daughter about?"

"It was her initiative," Barry pointed out.

"Yes, I suppose she has her reasons; and I suppose you must do as your employer bids. But it is unseemly for an employee to see his employer socially."

Ka-zinng! That bullet was a little too close to the mark; the ricochet scattered rock dust into his face. He looked down the hallway Sykes had taken. When was the cavalry going to show up? Lay down a covering fire. "Actually, Belinda Karr is my employer . . ."

An ephemeral pursing of the lips. "Belinda . . . Yes. Well, you certainly would not be escorting *her.*" Harriet was lost momentarily in foreign thoughts. "However," she continued, "the same principle applies. My daughter employs Dr. Karr, who employs you."

Barry had thought nothing could make him feel close to Karr, with her tight little technocrat's view of education; but Harriet van Huyten could achieve the impossible. If the Dragon Lady had found something to dislike in Belinda Karr, the senior principal must have her good points, after all. "Mariesa can call these trips off any time she wants," he told her. *So why doesn't she?* It had started as a lark, an impulse on her part; but it was well on its way to becoming a routine.

Harriet gave a small sigh and said, "Yes, I suppose she could." *And ought to,* said the curves at the corners of her mouth. Odd, that Harriet and he seemed to harbor the same question—why?—but for different reasons. Harriet turned away; but paused and, after a moment's hesitation, spoke as if to the foyer at large. "Do try to show her a relaxing evening, 'Barry.' She is working herself entirely too hard." She did not quite turn around, but glanced at him over her shoulder. "Business affairs have consumed her these past few years, the more so within the past nine months. Yet, I cannot persuade her to accompany me to our clubs or to social affairs. I fear sometimes for her health." The gaze was unguarded and genuine, if fleeting—asking for his help—and reminded him that he was, after all, talking to a mother about her daughter.

"I try to show her a good time," he said. Harriet gave him a best-of-a-bad-deal glance and departed. Barry watched her thoughtfully. Even opponents can have a goal or two in common.

I suppose she has her reasons, Harriet had said. Yes, but what? The first time, it might have been nothing more than to "zing" her mother; but this would mark their fourth "outing" together, and Harriet was zinged, but good. Zinged, zanged, and ready for hosing down. Barry studied the intricate brown-

and-green tiles of the foyer floor, tracing them out with the toe of his shoe. Outings . . . Barry would not call them dates, even in his own mind. Perhaps they were only excuses to leave the stifling walls of this mansion. "Go slumming." Isn't that what the rich used to say? Experience the vicarious thrills of life in the slow lane. Maybe next time, he ought to try something really déclassé; take Mariesa down into the belly of the bourgeois beast, down into the proletarian peritoneum. A bar and grill? The all-night diner on Maple Grove? What was it Monty Python used to say? *Now for something completely different* . . .

A foil to fence with her mother; an excuse to escape. It didn't matter to him. Either way, Barry would go along with the gag as long as Mariesa was willing. Whatever worked. Mariesa was an interesting person to be with and, away from the mansion and the servants, you could almost forget she was rich. Her concern for education was genuine, even if her solutions tended toward the utopian. And get her talking about space . . . Barry grinned to himself and shook his head. Enthusiasm could be contagious. Yet, she could converse equally well on his home grounds: literature and the arts, where her taste in music ran to early classical and in authors, to the likes of Austen, Kipling, and Chesterton.

"I am ready, Barry." Mariesa van Huyten, pulling a pair of black leather gloves over her hands, entered the foyer. She wore a midlength cashmere coat and patterned scarf and, on her head, a matching cloche cap. "Where shall we be dining this week?"

Barry dipped his head. "Did you know the tiles on the floor form a maze?"

Surprise, then delight, brightened her eyes. The gray twinkled like ice in the sun. "Do they?" She laughed and slipped one gloved hand into the crook of his arm.

"Yes." Barry pointed with his foot. "You enter the maze here . . . and you come out . . . there."

Astonishment replaced surprise, and he could feel the tightening of her fingers. "The green tiles!"

"I'm surprised you never noticed."

Her gaze fixed on the tiles, she whispered "The green tiles" again, with an intensity that Barry could not fathom.

November became December and Barry could almost begin to think of Mariesa and him as "an item." Of course, it did not exactly make the society pages, but that was just as well. Barry liked to keep his life segmented. There was no point in making it more complicated than it was already. If Mariesa Gorley van Huyten needed a willing pair of ears, he was perfectly happy to provide them. If nothing further came of it, so what? Something might, and if it did, he would accept that, too.

Barry pulled off the exit ramp from the nearly gridlocked Grey Horse Pike and into the parking lot at the Berwick Plaza shopping mall. Small flakes, not quite hefty enough to be called snow, flew in irregular gusts across the windshield. The forecast was for a light dusting, but forecasters didn't know beans. Yesterday, they had forecast clear weather for today. The lot was jammed, the holiday shopping season being in full frenzy; and parking vultures cruised slowly up and down the lanes, waiting for package-laden shoppers to emerge from the mall and vacate a stall. Barry negotiated his Lincoln through the crowded aisles and headed for the far end of the lot.

"This will be quite the walk," said Mariesa, turning to look behind at the mall entrance. She wore a navy blue parka with furred collar and hood and a pair of contrasting slacks.

"Not really," Barry told her. "That's where we're headed." He pointed to a long, low building standing alone in a corner of the lot. Bowl-a-Rama. God help him, the place was called Bowl-a-Rama, an echo of the Fifties, when everything was "Something-a-Rama" or "This-and-that City." It had probably been there long before the mall was built.

"Bowling?" Mariesa said with some amusement.

Barry grinned. "Bowling. You roll a big heavy ball down a wooden alley and try to knock over as many pins as you can."

"My ancestors *were* Dutch," she said dryly. "Now I know why you asked that I wear slacks today."

"You said you liked sports. None of the local teams are in

town this weekend and it's too cold for tennis or golf.''

"You do not know my cousin, Brittany. She is quite intense on her golf.''

He gave her a quick look. "I didn't know you had cousins.'' He studied the chill, December landscape. "But anyone who'd go golfing in this weather is nuts.''

"Oh. Then you *do* know my cousin Brittany.'' He looked at her again and laughed. "Her game is said to be rather good,'' Mariesa admitted, adding cryptically, "All of her games.''

"Hmm. Everyone should learn a trade. How does 'Cousin Brittany' do with the windmill? You've got to time your shot just right to get it through without those blades blocking you.''

"Whatever are you talking about?''

"You're serious, aren't you? Tell you what. Come spring, if we're still on speaking terms, I'll take you to a course I'll bet your cousin has *never* golfed. It's got a windmill and even a loop-the-loop.''

He helped her from the car and escorted her toward the bowling alley. *Talk about slumming.* The December wind made her shiver and she pressed close against him. Barry hesitated, then decided to take the chance.

"Besides,'' he said, "you look good in slacks.''

She made no direct answer, but she didn't pull away from him, either.

Inside, out of the cold, Bowl-a-Rama was filled with the familiar rumble of balls, the explosive clatter of pins, the dry smell of sawdust. It was a big alley. Twenty lanes lined each side of a central island. The island held the snack bar, pro shop, and shoe rental and other conveniences. Barry paid a deposit and signed for the shoes. Rented shoes? Had Mariesa's feet ever slipped into footwear that a hundred others had worn before her? Yet, she had made no comment. Noblesse oblige? What the hell. Maybe this was so far out of her ordinary experience as to qualify as "exotic.''

On their first few outings, he had treated Mariesa to day trips and some very nice restaurants. You couldn't fault places like Michael Anthony's or the Renaissance Experience. You could easily pay twice as much for meals half as good. Still, even at the high end of his price range, he couldn't compete with Mariesa's usual circuit. Was he being a little too aggressively proletarian in showing her the low end? *You're middle class now, Barry. You left the Seattle wharves a long time ago.* Why on earth this impulse? Just to flip the bird in Harriet's face?

Yet, what was so terribly wrong about knocking down some pins, or hoisting a couple of cold ones at the bar and grill with your friends and neighbors?

Barry scanned the lanes, looking for the one they had been assigned, and the smile froze on his teeth as he saw, ten yards to their left, Shannon Morgenthaler stride briskly toward the foul line on number 32. John Morgenthaler, at the scorekeeper's table, peered down the lane toward the pins. The two girls perched in the plastic bucket seats behind him swung their legs in and out, looking bored. Barry turned quickly away. Jesus H. Christ . . . What did he do now?

"Maybe this *was* a bad idea," he said to Mariesa. "Why don't we just go on over to the restaurant now? It's called the Gamecock. They serve all five kinds of South Carolina barbecue." South Carolina was all the rage lately; you couldn't find Cajun to save your life.

Mariesa studied the balls on the rack and hefted a few experimentally. "As long as we are here, Barry, we may as well play. These other people seem to be enjoying themselves."

Then it was too late. "Barry!" He heard John Morgenthaler's jovial voice, turned, and saw the man bouncing toward him with that big, perfect salesman's smile plastered across his face. Barry forced conviviality into his voice and clasped the man's soft, moist hand. "Hey, John. Fancy meeting you here."

"Ah, Shannon saw you standing up here looking lost. Shannon and me, we're taking the girls out. Course, they'd *die* to be seen with their parents. But the bowling is the price they have to pay before we unleash them on an unsuspecting mall. Who's your date?"

Date? Barry felt his throat close up. Sounds could not force themselves through. "Ah . . . Not a date, exactly . . ."

Mariesa stepped smoothly forward. "Mary," she said. "Mary Gorley."

John's paw engulfed hers. "Pleased to meet you, Mary. Say, why don't you two join us at our lane? Make it a foursome."

Over John's shoulder, Barry could see Shannon watching them with still eyes. "Uh, won't the girls . . . ?"

"Nah. All their friends are over at the mall anyway. I swear, that's all kids want to do these days."

"It is the new village green," said Mariesa.

John Morgenthaler blinked. "What? Hey, you know, I never looked at it that way before." He nudged Barry. "That's a real bright gal you've got yourself, Barry. Better not let her slip her leash. Come on, Mary. I'll introduce you to my better half."

They let him get a few paces ahead. Mariesa whispered, "Slip my leash?"

"It's just his way of talking. He's not a bad guy, really."

"He is . . . astonishing."

"He'll try to sell you a car before the night is through."

Mariesa said, "I can deal with it. I am a 'real bright gal,' after all."

John peeled off two twenties from his roll and gave one to each daughter. "Go meet your friends, you two. We'll rendezvous at five by the fountain, the one with the kids' statue. Synchronize your watches, everyone." The Morgenthalers made a show of matching their timepieces. A family custom of some sort; Barry had seen it before. No two had the same time. That was another part of the custom. "Plus or minus five minutes," John announced. "Close enough for horseshoes and hand grenades."

He clapped his hands as Mandy and Jill scampered off. "Oh-kay, time for some serious pin-knocking. Shannon, this is Barry's date, Mary. Hey. Barry and Mary. It's got a ring to it."

Barry closed his eyes. *Please don't take it to the next step.*

"Barry marry Mary has a 'ring' to it, too." It was just the sort of joke John would find uproarious.

Shannon pumped Mariesa's hand. "Mary . . . ?"

"Gorley."

"Of course." Shannon bobbed her head and, with a moment's sly glance at Barry, said, "You work for Mentor, don't you?" And there went Barry's hope that Shannon hadn't recognized Mariesa.

Mariesa nodded. "In administration."

Shannon's smile would have sent a diabetic into a coma. "That must be how you met Barry." Then she turned her green eyes on him. "Barry, it's been too long."

And did that mean the three weeks since they'd been to the Knight's Castle Motel west of town, or . . . "Since the cookout at Noreen and Bob's last September," he remembered.

"Yes, why didn't you bring Mary to that. There must have been a dozen or so Mentor teachers there." To Mariesa: "You should have heard the moaning and groaning about the Mc-Guffey Readers."

"We weren't . . . uh, going out . . . at the time." Barry forced the words through his teeth.

Mariesa said, "The *New* McGuffey Readers. What was the problem?"

Shannon batted a hand. "Oh, the vocabulary and readings are much too advanced for the grade level. The very first lesson in the 'fifth eclectic reader' had words like 'articulate,' 'modulation,' and 'affected.' "

"I see. And you teach . . . ?"

"Seventh grade, at Dayton."

"And a book that was used a hundred years ago in the fifth grade is too advanced for today's seventh graders?"

John had been at work changing the scoresheet. He brushed the eraser rubble from the page and said, "You're up first, Shannon."

"In a moment, John."

Barry said, "We don't need to talk shop today."

"No, Barry, we do," said Shannon in a voice at once both sharp and syrupy. "How often do we get to talk to someone from 'administration'?'' She turned back to Mariesa. "The first reading was about the king of Prussia," she said. "The king of Prussia! How is that relevant to children today?"

Mariesa looked thoughtful. "Perhaps it lends a 'fairy tale' air," she told Shannon. "Kings, Days of Old . . . You would have to ask the textbook committee; but as I recall the review, that particular passage was not 'about' Frederick the Great, but the benefits of elocution in reading. The king was unable to read a petition because of an eye problem, so . . ."

"So he asked a couple of pages to read it aloud," Shannon finished. "They blew it, and he asked the gardener's kid, who did such a good job that the king granted the petition. End of story." Shannon made an exasperated sound.

"But that is only the surface of the parable. You must focus on the essence. The two pages demonstrated common errors made in reading aloud, while the gardener's child demonstrated proper techniques, as a consequence of which everyone involved, from the king to the woman who wrote the petition, benefited."

"As you said," said Shannon. "It does have a fairy-tale air."

"One dramatizes for the sake of the lesson," Mariesa said. "Such points are more easily absorbed through story than through lecture. 'Show, don't tell' is Dr. Karr's motto, in reading as in science. I might also point out that, the gardener's child being a young girl, the student learns that neither gender nor class is relevant to reading skills; and that, since the two young pages learned from the experience to later become successful, there are no 'losers' in the reading game. And as a further benefit, the children glimpse another time and place, which they may recollect in later history classes."

"Shannon," said John with poorly concealed impatience, "you're holding up the game."

Shannon hefted her ball, spared Mariesa a thoughtful look, and strode to the foul line. John shook his head. "I apologize, Mary. She's always spouting on about books and things and forgetting what she's supposed to be doing."

Mariesa shook her head. "Oh, my." She said it with a

straight face, and Barry had to cover his mouth to keep from laughing.

"You know it, doll. Hey! Strike!" He grinned and made an X on the scorecard. "Man, she threw that ball like she was mad at the whole world. You're up, Barry."

Barry stepped to the foul line and Shannon gave him a Mona Lisa smile as they passed. Not the whole world, Barry saw; just a small corner of it. Barry managed an eight-ten split and barely converted with his second ball.

After John rolled a strike, Mariesa threw her first ball. Her approach was awkward and she put too much English on the ball, which curved round the Brooklyn side and clipped three pins off the back corner. Shannon made a *tsk* sound. "She doesn't have much of a form, does she, Barry?" John chuckled and nudged Barry in the ribs with his elbow. "Oho, I get it now. She didn't seem the bowling type to me; but now you get to teach her."

When Barry hesitated, Shannon said, "Yes, Barry, show her the right way to grip the balls."

Hard, thought Barry, *and then you twist.* Barry approached Mariesa just as her ball came back down the runway. She straightened from the rack, with her ball held chest-high in both hands. "Yes, Barry?"

He nodded toward the table where the Morgenthalers sat. "I'm supposed to show you how to bowl properly."

"Very well. What shall I do."

"Umm. I'll have to put my arms around you. That's why John is sitting back there grinning like an idiot." He lifted his arms and hesitated.

Mariesa cocked an eyebrow. "The prospect cannot be too repulsive, Barry. Golf pros have corrected my swing without any demonstrable ill effect." She replaced the ball on the rack, turned and faced the pins, and waited. Barry wiped his hands on his pants and stepped close behind her. He put his right hand on hers, his left on her waist. She fit comfortably against him.

"Your foot on the mark? Good. Step off on the right foot and start swinging the ball back. Four strides. You don't have the arm strength for three. The trick is to release the ball at the bottom of the swing right at the foul line. Ready?'' They stepped forward together as if they were dancing the tango, and Barry was uncomfortably aware of her body moving next to his.

She asked him to take her through the approach twice more. Then she tried it on her own while Barry watched. She almost seemed to dance down the runway, her arms and legs moving with fluid grace. When she returned, Barry said ''Ballet?'' and she smiled.

Her second ball picked up five pins, leaving only two standing. She returned to the seats looking inordinately pleased with herself. When Shannon stood for her next frame, she leaned close to Barry and murmured, ''How did her form feel to you?'' Barry knew then it was going to be a long game. They would bowl three rounds, and John would probably come up with the bright idea that they should all eat dinner together at the food court in the mall; and there was absolutely no way out of it that he could see.

Driving Mariesa back to Silverpond in the dark, Barry said, ''I guess this will be our last outing.'' Perversely, the snow had picked up in intensity and the gusts, glaring white in prematurely reflected headlight beams, gave him the impression of being boxed inside a small room. The windshield wipers slapped intermittently back and forth. He wished the snow would either stop entirely or else quicken, so he could turn the wipers on full.

Mariesa seemed astonished. ''Why do you say that?''

He hesitated while the car *thadump*ed rhythmically over the seams in the paving. Was it possible that she had sensed nothing of the byplay between Shannon and him? ''Well, the food court was not what I had in mind. . . .''

''It was charming, though the souvlaki was perhaps not up to the standards of Diana's. And Berwick Plaza was a fascinating combination of a village green and a medieval market fair. Merchants offering wares for sale; entertainers in the courtyard . . . I am not at all sure why so many of my class seem to sneer at them.''

Barry focused on his driving. Even late, even in the snow, the Grey Horse was crowded with traffic. And it gave him a reason not to look Mariesa in the eyes. "Shannon seemed a little, um . . ."

"Assertive? She has strong opinions. Assertive women do not bother me. Better that she have a mind of her own than that she need to borrow her husband's."

Barry grinned at her joke. "Oh, John's okay. He's just not an intellectual."

"Shannon can hardly be satisfied with a man like that. Sooner or later, she will seek out more stimulating companionship."

Barry swallowed. Perhaps she had sensed something, after all. Though *intellectual* stimulation was not what had brought Shannon to him. "That would be . . . uh, too bad."

"Every choice brings good and bad in its wake." Her voice was wistful and she fell silent for a moment. Then, with a distant air of changing the subject, she said, "Harriet is planning a party for New Year's Eve—the end of the millennium, you know—and she has invited all sorts of people that I find distressingly boring. So I have invited a few guests of my own. I do wish you would come. Belinda will be there; and Onwuka."

So join the line of pawns in the chess game between Mariesa and her mother. Harriet was undoubtedly rounding up a herd of Eligible Bachelors on the other side. But, hell, it was better than spending New Year's Eve alone. Shannon had the best of both worlds. The excitement of an affair; the stability of a family. There were no Fast family customs. There was no Fast family. Just Ray, three thousand miles distant. Although they spoke often by phone, they had not seen each other in years.

He would probably have to rent a tux for Harriet's bash. He couldn't imagine the elder van Huyten running a casual affair. "Sure, I'll come."

"Excellent. I shall have an invitation sent to you promptly."

Barry relaxed behind the wheel and pulled briskly around a red Camaro that was inexplicably obeying the speed limit. He had come through the evening better than he had feared; better than he'd had a right to expect once Shannon had spotted him. "Isn't it a little early for an end-of-the-millennium party?" he asked.

Dryly. "Yes, by about a year. But there is no convincing Harriet. There is something about all those digits rolling over. My own party shall be planned for next year or perhaps a few—"

She stopped speaking suddenly and Barry looked at her and saw the worry had returned to her face. *Outing's over. The brain is back on the job.* "Perhaps a few years later? Why?" he asked her.

"Perhaps, there are other millennia, that begin at other times."

INTERLUDE:

School Daze (II)

Chase shoved his hands in his jeans pockets and stomped into the building manager's office. He bumped the door open with his hip and shoulder, and it swung wide and banged against the stop. In front of the desk, he hooked the leg of the visitor's chair with one foot and pulled it to him. Then he flopped into it, throwing his left leg over one of the arms. He gave the building manager his best vacant stare. No fear.

Grantland deYoung sat back in his chair with his hands clasped behind his head and returned Chase's stare. Finally, he spoke.

"Don't know why you're here, do you, Mr. Coughlin?"

Chase tried to look unconcerned. Most likely he was in trouble over something, except he didn't know what. The knot in his stomach was a fist. So far, he hadn't had any run-ins with the new owners—everyone was keeping a low profile, even that knee-grow troublemaker, Azim, because no one knew how the new discipline code worked.

One thing for sure, a man wearing a ponytail wasn't going to be hassling him about haircuts. DeYoung looked like he had never found his way out of the sixties. Peace and love, man. Groovy. Grown-ups had their heads so far up in the clouds that their feet never touched the fucking ground. Thought they had a lock on Truth and Virtue. Sit-ins. Love-ins. Save the whales. Make love, not war? So, you go kiss Saddam and see if that stops the tanks.

Life was a game; and there were winners and there were losers. Too bad, but that was how it was. Sometimes it was bad luck because the deck was usually stacked, and sometimes you just didn't have it; but losers were losers either way. You could cry over them if you wanted to, but that didn't make them not losers. That was reality. That was the great, big, ugly, death-stinking reality. "The sound of hooves knocking at your door." He smiled at deYoung and waited for the man to speak.

The building manager pursed his lips, then kicked himself upright. He picked a folder off his desk and held it out to Chase. "Two things," he said. "First, I've been asked by the principals to offer you a cadet instructorship in auto maintenance for next semester."

Chase hesitated with his hand half-outstretched. He looked at deYoung, then at the folder, then at deYoung again. Chase shook his head. He took the folder and opened it and stared at the papers inside. *An Offer of Employment (Part Time).* He looked back at deYoung. "You're offering me a job?"

"Not me. I only employ building staff. This offer comes from the principals. I am only acting in their behalf as a favor. You seem to have an aptitude for car repair. You work part-time at Patel's Transmission and Service Station, I think."

"Yeah. Mostly, I pump gas; but they let me rebuild trannies or do tune-ups and stuff. Hatma checks me out, because it's his license that's on the line; but I do good work."

"I'm sure you do. Mr. Snyder has already spoken to Mr. Patel."

"So, what's this 'cadet' sh—stuff?"

DeYoung crossed his arms over his chest and sat cocked in his chair. "Mentor has a policy of employing students whenever we can—in building maintenance, office work, or even as instructors, if they have what it takes. Cadet instructors work under the supervision of a master teacher—yours will be Mr. Snyder, the shop master—who will help you prepare lesson plans and conduct classes. Mr. Snyder will be responsible for grading and maintaining decorum in the classroom and will evaluate your performance.''

"It sounds like a lot of work. I never planned on being no teacher.''

"Certainly not of English,'' deYoung said with a fleeting smile. "As for the work, we don't expect you to donate your time. You will be paid.''

Chase straightened in his chair. "How much?''

"Minimum wage, less the usual taxes and Social Security. You may be paid in gold equivalent, drafts on our Zurich account, if you like. If Mr. Snyder finds your work acceptable, you may receive raises for each semester afterward you elect to continue, as well as an appropriate grade in Industrial Arts.''

Shit. I come home with an A in anything, it'll give the old lady a heart attack.

"The principals would like your decision by Monday, so you might like to talk this over with your parents.''

Oh, golly gee whiz, can I? "I'll let you know,'' he said. New Jersey law said you could ditch school when you turned sixteen, and you could sign yourself out, no matter what your parents said, when you turned eighteen. He'd been planning to skip next year and take the GED instead. Except now the school was paying him to come. He wondered if Mentor knew his plans and was bribing him not to drop out. They couldn't be that clever, could they? "What's the other thing?''

The Man smiled. "I thought since you liked machines, you'd be interested in our new security system. Do you know how picture phones work?''

"Nah. I guess they got a little TV camera inside, and a tiny little picture tube. So what?''

"So, TV signals can't go over nonoptic phone lines in real time. Too much bandwidth. What they do is they digitize the signal. Every few microseconds, a processor compares the current image to the previous image and then it encodes and transmits only those pixels that have changed since the previous packet. The picture on the other end comes out a little bit jerky, but what the hell, right?'' DeYoung smiled cheerfully.

Chase scowled. "What has that got to do with the school? You got picture phones here or something?"

"In a way. The security cameras we installed over the summer work the same way. Instead of taking continuous pictures, they capture an IR image only if something moves around the school grounds. The image is enhanced and stored on CD-ROM. That way, Security doesn't need to view twenty-four hours of videotape. Even at fast forward, that's boring."

Chase rolled his eyes up high. "Well," he said, "I feel very happy for you."

DeYoung spread his hands. "It's a high-tech world."

When he left deYoung's office, Chase took a detour before heading back to his study hall. He walked to the front entrance and stepped outside into a blustery winter day. The sun shone brightly in a cold, cloudless sky. Volcano dust, the news said. Second or third year in a row, now. Chase did not have a jacket, so he ignored the chill. He stepped out onto the sidewalk and turned and looked back at the pale gray bricks of the wall left of the entrance. Someone had spray-painted the wall last night in flat black. Nothing clever. No slogans. No message. No art. Just a spaghetti jumble of black paint.

He thought about taking a smoke. He was already outside, so he was already in violation, so why not? Last year there might have been a dozen or more kids hanging around outside. Not anymore. He was alone. And those special cameras would already have him pegged. He looked at the eaves and overhangs and the window frames, trying to figure where the cameras would be placed. Spy cameras. Like a fucking police state.

Let it ride. He had plenty of time to spot the cameras, then figure out how to game them.

He hugged himself against a sudden gust of wind. Time to get back in. Someone might see him out here shivering. He took one last look at the spray paint and felt the knot in his stomach unwind. At least now he knew why he had been called down to the office.

* * *

There was something about the damn photo gallery that kept drawing Azim back to it, even after the other kids had left. He lingered in Mr. Egbo's homeroom, studying the prints. It wasn't that the pictures made no sense—half the crap that whitey shoveled out in school made no sense—it was that Brother Egbo made no effort to explain them. It was as if they were a puzzle waiting to be solved. A shoe. A bag of sugar. A traffic light. It annoyed Azim that he could make no sense of it; as if the inability to do so were a comment on him, somehow. That Egbo was laughing at him.

A shoe. An ordinary, black, wingtip, white man's shoe. With laces.

Shee-it.

The picture that bugged him the most was that of the astronauts. It seemed out of place. There were people in some of the other pictures—the woman receiving the blood transfusion; the doctor sewing up the heart—but this was a picture *of* people. The others were pictures of things, in which people sometimes appeared.

He could see through the window that the buses were late. Snow choked the driveway. Plowed one way in, one way out. A few odd flakes still drifted down from the dishwater sky. Thicket Street at the end of the driveway was at a standstill as cars inched slowly past. Buses weren't coming anytime soon.

He scowled at the astronauts. Six pasty-white ice people grinning like skulls at the camera; but that one dude in the back, cast in shadow, helmet crooked under one arm, the other raised in solemn greeting . . .

A shoe. A bag of sugar. A traffic light. Blood. A heart sewn up. Buck Rogers. Find the clue. Find the secret. If there was one. Maybe Egbo had put these pictures together for no reason at all but to drive Azim crazy.

"Interested in shoes, Mr. Thomas?" Egbo's voice was distinctive, unmistakable. A deep voice that swelled with African accents.

Azim grunted and stepped aside. He went to the window

and rested his arms on the sill and his head on his arms. The snow outside was already turning from blinding white to sooty gray from the traffic. He could see the other kids huddled around the bus stops. Stupid to wait outside. "All God's chilluns got shoes," said Egbo. Azim turned and looked at him.

"Who cares?"

Egbo grinned and spread his hands. " 'God's chilluns,' I suppose. Did you know that shoes were once made by hand? Each one, individually sewn on a hand last. That made them very expensive, so they were made in very few sizes and without making them left and right."

"So what?"

"So try playing basketball when your sneakers don't fit your feet."

Azim scuffed his sneakers on the floor. "Ain't interested in that . . . stuff. Manufacturing. Business. That be for ice people."

"Is it?" Egbo shut his computer down and gathered his lesson books together. Then he leaned back in his chair. "Do you know what my name means, Mr. Thomas? Egbo? I am an Efik man, from Old Calabar. The old city-states of the Oil River—Ibani, Warri, New Calabar, Brass, and the market towns of Old Calabar—were thriving centers of trade long before the Europeans came. They were ruled by merchant's associations, and great trading houses like Pepples of Ibani, which became famous even in Europe. They assured fair commerce and high profits—and punished Europeans who did not play by the rules. Egbo—the word means 'leopard'—was the association that ruled in Old Calabar. Old ties of kinship broke down in the merchant towns. Clan mixed with clan, tribe with tribe. It mattered less who you were born than what you made of yourself. Anyone could join Egbo who could pay the membership fee. In your history class, Mr. Boucher will teach you about the Hanse, the Hanseatic League. You may tell him of Egbo, for they were cut of the same cloth. Capitalism and commerce are the work of all men, Mr. Thomas, and not only of the white ones."

Azim kept his face like stone. He had never known that

about Africa. It was all just warriors, wearing feathers and fur and shaking spears. Living in grass huts. He hadn't known there were cities and merchants and shit like that. Shit, the Lords talked all the time about Mother Africa, and the preacher where his mama dragged him every Sunday, too; but here was a real live African in their homeroom, and they hardly ever asked him about it. "So what's all that got to do with shoes?" he asked finally.

Egbo turned and studied the photograph. "The most difficult of all the steps in shoemaking is building the upper on a last. Until that step was mechanized, shoes remained expensive and poor people could not afford them. Men often shared a single pair. Finally, someone invented a mechanical lasting machine, and shoes became cheap and plentiful. So, I say 'all God's chilluns' have him to thank that they have shoes on their feet."

"Who was it?" Azim asked, bored because the buses were late and interested because he was bored.

Egbo frowned. "I don't seem to recall," he said slowly. Then he looked out the window. "The buses will not arrive for quite some time, it appears. Would you do me a favor, Mr. Thomas, and check in the library for me? I am sure there is a book on shoemaking in there. Mrs. Flynn will help you find it, if you ask. Check the index for 'last, automatic' or something similar, and see if it names the inventor."

So, what the hell. There wasn't anything else to do.

The inventor was named Jan Matzelinger, and he was a black man.

And wasn't that some kind of kick in the head? Who ever heard of a black man inventing things?

As the school year dragged on, Azim discovered who had done the worlds' first open-heart surgery, who had discovered how to store plasma safely for transfusions, who had invented the automated traffic signal. And the vacuum pan for refining sugar. And the drip-cup lubricator. And the railroad telegraph. And . . . He began to wonder if there might not be other possibilities in life, even for a black man.

He even learned the name of the astronaut in the shadow in the photograph. Not Ronald McNair or Guion Bluford, both black men and one a martyr, but another man, named Forrest Calhoun. "You haven't heard of him yet," Egbo promised him, "but you will someday, soon."

Before long he began to call Mr. Egbo "Leopard." It was their private joke.

10.

Sales Call

Mariesa's office was large, but simple and furnished in dark woods. Masculine, some said. *Too masculine* was the unspoken subtext. Sprays of bright flowers, clipped daily from the corporate greenhouses, lightened the effect only a little. The north wall was a window facing the woods that draped the lower ridge of First Watchung Mountain. Hard-edged paintings graced the other walls: rockets launching in a flower of flame; space stations floating in the void above the Earth; fabulous planetscapes. The paintings were finely detailed, almost photographic, almost as if the utterly fantastic subject matter required that extra dose of realism. People, if portrayed at all, were small dots or suited figures dangling at the ends of umbilicals. Mariesa found the paintings inspiring. Others found them disturbing, or even the slightest bit wacky.

Mariesa had just finished the reports on the Tokyo deal, when Keith McReynolds brought her Prometheus's cost projections for the next fiscal quarter. Late by nearly two weeks. It was not like Keith. The CFO delivered the hard copy personally, laid it on her desk, and walked to the windows that looked out toward the Watchungs. He stood there, staring at the winter desolation while she read the executive summary.

When she finished, she closed the folder and laid it carefully on the symmetric stack of finished items destined for the shredder. Then she folded her hands into a ball and leaned back in her chair. The chair squeaked, pulling Keith away from his contemplation.

"Nineteen percent over budget," she said.

Keith nodded. "Mendoza has expanded the test program again. It's the additional testing, not the original forecast that accounts for most of the variance."

I am not questioning your forecasts, Keith; and if Dr. Mendoza believes additional testing is in order, I do not begrudge it. But there are procedures to be followed. João ought to have submitted a Request for Variance or a Capital Allocation Request." She picked up the budget report again and batted it once against the palm of her left hand. "I suppose a test flight before the end of the calendar year is now out of the question." She could hear the frustration in her own voice. Keith shook his head and Mariesa sighed. "The symbolism would have been appropriate for the dawn of a new age."

"The Steering Committee made a deliberate decision to avoid 'symbolism,' " Keith reminded her; and Mariesa waved an impatient hand.

"I know. I know. Still, it rankles."

"João wants to slip the schedule to April," he added.

"April! That rankles more. Time is running out. Demand has started rising again—and prices with them—but we have only until August of ought-one to have our infrastructure in place."

Keith studied the wall calendar, a computer-controlled liquid crystal that displayed a running twelve-month interval. December 6 blinked slowly, announcing today's date. He traced the numbers with his fingertip. "Mondays are always rotten," he said. "Bad news always waits on Monday." A silence, which he broke finally. "Do you think there will be a war? In ought-one?"

Mariesa dropped the report back onto the "Destroy" pile,

where it fell askew. "There is always a war. Recessions spawn them the way stagnant ponds spawn mosquitoes. Ought-one, ought-two . . . Even Detweiler will not be too precise. Whether our government sees fit to use a war as a means to break the recession will depend upon next year's elections. Jim Champion is not the sort of man who would do so."

"Yet, you'll not take sides . . . ?"

"I do not wish to draw media attention—which would surely be the case were I to take a public stand against the current administration. No, Keith, it is best to keep our own counsel and hope for the best."

Keith nodded toward the stack of reports. "Meanwhile, what should I tell Daedalus?"

"Tell João that we are anxious to see more progress and more effective cost control; but do not belabor the issue. We named Daedalus as Prime on this project for good reasons—legal, as well as technological—and he is still the man in the field. I will not second-guess him from this far behind the frontlines."

After Keith had gone, Mariesa rubbed her face with her hands, feeling the weariness sweep over her. A four-month slip? Who was it who said that no battle plan survives contact with the enemy? Some general, with plans an order of magnitude less convoluted than her own. She spoke up, enunciating clearly. "Computer. Calendar." The border on the wall calendar glowed a pale yellow and she said, "Prometheus. Key dates. Display." A score of dates over the next twelve months turned red, an even half dozen blinking, starting with Friday, December 31, the original test flight date. "Memorandum. Nine-nine, one-two, three-one. Play."

A pleasant, sexless contralto spoke softly from the speaker on her terminal. "Cross-reference to Plank thread update, log on nine-nine, one-two, ought-three, indicates low probability of meeting this projection. Beta equals dot-one-zero."

"End query." Mariesa slumped in her chair. So. The GANTT expert program has already integrated Keith's data into the timeline. There would be no launch this year. Very well. Mankind had waited thirty years to reclaim the planets. Another four months was nothing. Still, she could feel the anxiety building below her ribs. What if, when the crucial moment came, they were still four months short of completion? A low-probability node, as Detweiler would say. In all likelihood, Prometheus would be complete long before it would be called upon to perform. But "low" was not "zero"; and it was all up to her. "You shall know neither the day, nor the hour." She rubbed a hand against the pain in her stomach. If there was to be no test launch on New Year's Eve, she had no excuse for evading Harriet's party. A lesser disappointment, but still keenly felt. "Computer. Calendar," she said again. "Barry. Key dates. Display."

The upcoming Friday was highlighted, which slackened the knot within her, a little. She looked forward to these fortnightly excursions with Barry. They were delightfully refreshing, an entre into a calmer and less complicated world than the one in which she normally moved. She could leave behind all the baggage that her family, her business, or her convictions entailed. People asking favors, people pushing agendas, people scolding her—or dragging over incidents best forgotten. Mummy especially, who had a way of bringing things up without even mentioning them.

And the excursions were often enchanting in themselves and Barry, an attentive and congenial host. He had driven her through the autumn splendor between the Watchungs and Schooley's Mountain, where you could see nothing for miles but gold and red leaves carpeting the ground, mountain ridge rolling behind mountain ridge, the Kittatinny a line of rust on the horizon, with the great notch of the Water Gap where the rocks and trees tumbled down to meet the Delaware. Two weeks ago, they had driven down to the great, double-turreted lighthouse at Sandy Hook, and climbed the spiral staircase to the top of the north tower, and he had explained in the fierce November sea wind that blew up there how the double light had guided ships into Lower New York Bay. It was the sort of thing that a fisherman's son would know. Line the two of them up, the taller above the shorter, he had said, and you had a pilot channel through the treacherous shoals and shallows.

Second star to the right and straight on to morning. There were other lighthouses, for other pilots.

Mummy disapproved of their biweekly jaunts, of course; but then Mummy disapproved of a great many things. It was decidedly annoying, given Harriet's goal of grandchildren, that the only man Mariesa had found even remotely interesting she judged "entirely unsuitable." *I do not plan on wedding him, Mummy. He is simply a friend.* Barry could discuss issues with her without oozing the condescension so many males of her class did; and he was not afraid either to challenge her arguments or to be convinced by them. The men that Mummy pressed on her fell short on too many grounds: on the issues, on their patronization—and even on their taste in restaurants, where they preferred exclusiveness to flavor.

And Barry had solved the riddle of the maze! That should count for something. No one else had even seen that there was a maze. But . . . the green tiles . . . ? When he had pointed that out, it had seemed to her as if the entire floor had shifted suddenly under her feet and she had very nearly lost her balance. To think that, for all those years since childhood, she had fixed on the wrong image; fixed on it for so long, that she had been unable to see any other pattern.

Saving the world cost a great deal of money, a great deal more than Mariesa could freely dispose of. It would be better, she thought, if she could fund everything herself. That way, you never had to explain anything. You never had to plead or cajole or convince. You just went ahead and did it. You did not have to come, hat in hand, to beg funding from people who lacked the vision. Who lacked *any* vision. Sometimes she wondered if saving them was worth the price; or even if they could be saved.

The VHI auditorium that Wednesday was full of money. Old money, new money; risk capital and family fortunes. Comfortable money nestled in the wallets of satisfied men and women; eager money burning holes in impatient pockets. Mariesa surveyed the audience from the dais, where she sat with Keith and the officers of Argonaut Research. Dim, pasty-white, glow-in-the-dark faces; dusky faces nearly invisible in the lowered auditorium lighting. Some studied their prospectuses with narrowed, calculating eyes. Some had rolled theirs up and batted their open palms with them while they listened. She wondered how much of that money would walk when the presentation was finished and how much of it would stay.

Christiaan van Huyten changed slides and displayed a schematic diagram on the wall-sized screen behind him: a sandwich of gold film between two layers of magnetic material. The light pointer danced around the drawing as he explained the aftereffects of electric current on electron spin. Mariesa saw a few heads in the audience cock in interest. As for the rest, eyes glazed over. *Keep this part short, cousin*, she thought. *Just enough to show feasibility*. The real hook was not Johnson's theory, nor the successful lab trials at Bellcore; but the potential returns to be had.

As a rule, the van Huytens were more concerned with having money than with making money. As long as Mariesa kept their dividends coming, her cousins would not second-guess how she ran VHI. Chris, a few years older than Mariesa, was the exception. He had majored in engineering and law at MIT and had been in place as president of Argonaut even before Mariesa had become chairman of the parent corporation. He was innovative—he had modeled his "Forward Looking Group" after Bell Labs' pioneer trend-watching department—and he had a keen eye for the dollar, smart enough to know that "cutting costs" was not the same as "spending less." He was the only relative Mariesa had invited into the Prometheus circle because, if there was one thing that might cause the rest of the family to vote their shares *en bloc* against her, it was the thought of their monthly allowances being shot off into space.

Among the faces in the audience Mariesa could number both friends and foes. That was the way it always was. Some came to these affairs because they were interested and saw a chance for their money to earn dividends. Some believed in what she was trying to do and would invest even on long odds. Still others were simply curious. But there were always those who had other agendas. The competition. Wilson, for one, played his own game. And Forsythe's lab would love to graze on the same funds that Chris was angling for. There were others in the audience, she knew, shilling for Bell or MacDac or the Skunk Works, feigning interest only to discover what the Argonauts were up to. And others still who would block anything she tried to do. They were not the competition, but the opposition, and their battle cry was "Never!" Next to them, competitors were allies.

One face in the back row of seats was thrust forward, listening intently to everything Chris said; and a nagging familiarity trapped her gaze. She knew that face, but from where? Kauai? Ventimiglia? Manhattan? There had been a trade show in Bruxelles . . . No.

When it clicked, she sucked in her breath, sharply enough that Chris glanced momentarily in her direction before resuming his presentation.

"Keith," she whispered behind her hand. "Back row, center. Do you see him?"

A pause. then, "Yes. Phil Albright. What is he doing here?"

Mariesa shook her head. "It is not to buy stock."

Phil Albright, the country's premier Luddite. She had not seen him earlier. Perhaps he had arrived late, after the lights had been turned down. Albright noticed Mariesa's regard and his lips parted slowly in a lazy smile. He nodded a greeting.

Mariesa nodded back. *Show me your teeth*, she thought. *Sharks have teeth.*

Albright had started his career in a volunteer consumer-interest group, the kind that sent idealistic kids door-to-door asking for donations. Hard work and a willingness to tackle unwelcome tasks were useful in any profession; in a volunteer organization, they were the royal road to power. Albright had worked his way to leadership of his organization, not because he had staged a "coup," as some bitter ex-associates had charged, but simply because the others were willing to "let Phil do it" once too often. Now, as chief coordinator of the People's Crusades, Albright took only a modest salary . . . plus a cut of all those donations his army of followers collected. Somehow (the funds were not open to audit and were moved around under a variety of interlocked nonprofit shells), he had parlayed his public-spiritedness into the second-largest financial empire in the advocacy industry.

An ambitious man, Albright would have risen to the top in any organization. Mariesa approved of ambition, mostly.

After the formal presentation, Christiaan invited interested parties to socialize in the reception hall outside the auditorium and discuss details of the investment with the officers of Argonaut. The hall was a large, comfortable room, adorned in pale woods and lit with indirect lighting. It bordered on deco without ever quite falling over the edge. From the outer lobby drifted the muted sounds of light piano music. Waiters circulated with drinks and hors d'oeuvres. A few investors—mostly the older crowd, but including a number of the younger, go-go entrepreneurs—stood outside on the flagstoned verandah waving cigars and cigarettes in the air as they spoke. Mariesa drifted among the chattering focus groups looking for Albright.

Chris waved to her as she made her way through the press. "Mariesa," he said, "I was just explaining to Britterige, here, that he has an opportunity to get in on the ground floor of something that has all the potential of the transistor or the microchip."

Britterige worked his lips. His skin sagged at the jowls and under the eyes. "I'm afraid the long-term potential holds little interest for me these days," he said. "Whatever this gizmo of yours grows into, Christiaan, I shan't see the fruits of it."

"Then your heirs may."

Britterige made a face. "My heirs are worthless ne'er-do-wells. They lived too comfortably off their daddy for too long. They have become leeches. Ah, they'll clean my bones when I am gone." He turned his rheumy eyes on Mariesa, eyes watery from too many cigarettes given up years too late. "Mark my words, young lady. Make your children work for what they get. Give 'em everything they want, and they'll end up wanting everything."

"I have no children, Mr. Britterige. But when I do, I shall take your advice."

"Good for you, girl. Jaspar, you pay attention." He slapped a younger man lightly on the shoulder. "This electric flapdoodle is right up your alley. Mariesa, thank you for a lovely evening." Britterige worked his way toward the exit.

"Electric," said Jaspar Moore. "When I was a boy, I played with an electrical set. Made buzzers and lights and all sorts of useful things, don't y'know. But magnets? Those were for tricks."

Christiaan nodded. "Everyone thought so. Johnson was the only physicist left at Bellcore doing basic research in magnetism. The others were all being assigned to computers and software and other, more trendy research. The situation at Bell Labs and at IBM was not much different. Even Argonaut," he admitted, "had no magnetic-research projects."

"A bird in the hand," said Portia Wentworth. "I will place my investments where I can see more immediate returns. One must be practical. You may never learn how to produce these magnetic switches in useful quantities. Then, what of my money? I would do as well entrusting it to a savings and loan."

Everyone laughed. Christiaan nodded, "Yes, immediate gratification does have its rewards."

More laughter. And a frown from Portia. But Chris had agreed with her, and with such a congenial air that she could hardly take offense. *I like to hold up verbal mirrors,* he had told Mariesa one time. *It is much more pleasant than disagreement.*

Mariesa finally located Albright standing beside the *dai* bonsai, Hosukawa's *Lifted Up.* Albright was shorter than she had expected—shorter than herself, although she was tall for a woman. Dark-complexioned, with prominent eyebrows, he always reminded her of Rod Serling on the old "Twilight Zone" show, a resemblance heightened by his well-known, gravelly voice. Albright's evening clothes fit him well, and he wore them with style. She would not have expected a man-of-the-people like Albright to own a set of proper evening clothes. But, then, one heard stories. . . .

"Ms. van Huyten," he said as she approached. "I've looked forward to meeting you." His teeth were even and white. He smiled perfectly. Mariesa took his hand. His grip was firm and dry.

"Have you?" she said. "I have not seen you at previous investors' meetings. Do you have interests in my companies?"

"A great deal of interest, but usually I send someone from my staff to monitor. I'll have to say, you put on quite a show. Cocktails. Hors d'oeuvres. The pianist in the lobby is very good."

"Thank you. I am asking people to entrust their money to me, to risk it on a speculation. They know there is a chance they may never see it returned. The very least I can do is entertain them."

Albright nodded to the sculpture. "I always thought bonsai were supposed to be small. This one is, what? Almost four feet."

Mariesa contemplated the graceful, soaring limbs and taut foliage. The clever shape carried the eye ever upward on a twisting journey. " 'Bonsai' refers to the art of sculpting trees; not to the size. Quite fascinating to watch a master caretaker at work pruning and wiring and potting; though results may be a trifle slow in showing. *Mame* bonsai, the smallest class, may be the size of your fingertip; but *dai* bonsai may be up to four feet tall. They are rare, however. Above a certain height, they are considered too tall to be 'good,' and reflect poorly on their caretaker's competence."

Albright nodded again. A small smile played across his lips. "Yes, rather like corporations."

Mariesa looked at him. "There is a size appropriate to every task. Bonsai recognizes four classes; and even Nature provides both shrubs and sequoias. I am feeling a little warm in here, Mr. Albright. Would you mind walking with me on the veran-dah outside?"

Albright offered her his arm. "I would be delighted."

They crossed the reception hall to the French doors. Keith and John E. Redman, her top lawyer, were engaged in earnest conversation with a few interested investors. She nodded to them in passing. Keith raised his eyebrows but said nothing. Albright opened the door for her and she stepped out into the night.

The smokers had abandoned the verandah to the evening breezes. The wind drove dead leaves across the flagstones with the sound of a thousand scurrying feet. Watchung Mountain, darkening in the sunset, loomed behind the skeletal woods that surrounded the campus. Patches of snow dotted the ground among the trees, remnants of last week's snowfall. Denuded, the trees all looked alike. Birch, maple, oak . . . winter had robbed them of their individuality. The occasional furtive evergreens seemed like interlopers. Mariesa reached up and pulled the neck of her jacket together.

"Colder than you thought?" asked Albright.

"A bit," she admitted. She thought for a moment of going back inside, but the air out here was so fresh and clean she decided to endure the chill. "I thought it was no longer correct for a gentleman to hold the door for the lady."

Albright shrugged. "What is correct is to treat people decently. Sometimes that means holding doors. Sometimes it means not holding doors, if the person doesn't like it."

"Considerate enough, but how do you know?"

"In my case," he answered with some amusement, "trial and error."

Mariesa smiled in return and began to promenade. Albright paced her. "I understand your family was prominent in Baltimore society," she said. Certainly, his manners reflected well on his upbringing, irrespective of his public persona.

"My father owned a factory. Is that prominent enough?" Mariesa detected an edge in his voice but was not sure at whom the cut was aimed.

"I only meant . . ."

"I know what you meant."

So much for idle chitchat. Mariesa came to the point. "Why

the personal visit, Mr. Albright? Are you not afraid to be seen consorting with 'the enemy'? Or have you decided to buy a few shares in our next venture?''

Albright laughed and rubbed the side of his nose with his index finger. ''No, there are more important places to invest than in—what were they?''

''Spin transistors. Johnson magswitches.''

''Magnetic switches, yes.'' He shook his head. ''Gadgets and gizmos. Why not invest in the environment or in fighting homelessness, Ms. van Huyten?''

''Tell me the specific project and show me the prospectus. You cannot 'invest' in a generality.''

Albright's face lost its smile at the word *prospectus*. ''Some returns can't be measured in dollars.''

''Why, Mr. Albright,'' she said, stopping and touching him briefly at the elbow. ''I believe we may have something in common, after all.''

Albright looked uncertain, then shook his head again. ''I doubt it.''

''Perhaps more than you suppose.'' She resumed her walk. ''I do fight homelessness.''

''Really.'' He looked surprised. ''How?''

''I create jobs.''

''Jobs for some,'' he said after a moment's hesitation.

''One does what one can.'' They had reached the west end of the verandah, where the floodlights along the building's roof created columns of light across the facade of the building and teased the rolling fields out of the·night. Albright found a rattan patio chair and sat on it while Mariesa studied the night sky.

''You're fueling the American penchant for technomania,'' he said, ''when we should be concentrating on improving the quality of our own lives.''

''Is there a difference?''

''A big difference. But I would not expect someone like you to understand. You're in love with technology. I'm in love with the earth.''

''Keith was right. You are a believer.''

"We have to do what is *right* for the people of this planet."

"Oh, I quite agree. We are both of us moralists at heart."

"How do your magnetic transistors help the planet?" Albright flipped his hand toward the French doors, toward the auditorium. Inside, she could see Keith and the others laughing at something John E. had said. *It is too cold out here,* she thought. *We should have stayed inside.*

"Who can say?" she replied. "At the time of its invention, who could have predicted how fundamentally the electronic transistor would change our lives? All I know for certain is that seeds like this *do* sprout; and often in unlikely directions."

"Exactly my point," he said. "Unlikely, and perhaps unlikable." He stood up and jammed his hands in his pants pockets. "My people will be looking into these switches of yours. I'm not opposed to them in principle, understand; but their manufacture probably involves toxics of some sort. The public will want assurance that when you start making them, you won't be poisoning the environment."

"Mr. Albright, if you have come here to provoke an argument with me, you shall not have one. The issue of 'toxics' is ground that has been raked over again and again. Certainly, one ought to take precautions, but every environmental panic since the mercury-in-the-tuna-fish affair in the seventies has proven to be either an exaggeration or made of whole cloth. The facts are there for anyone to examine. You shall not change my mind; nor I yours."

Albright nodded. "It's not important that the possibility be true," he said, "as long as it elevates our awareness. But you're right. I didn't come here for that." He joined her at the railing and leaned on it, gazing into the growing dusk. She noted, with some amusement, that while she gazed at the stars, he gazed at the trees.

"Then, why did you come here?" she asked.

Albright took a deep breath and let it out, sending a puff of steam in the night air. "Curiosity," he said. "On another issue entirely. Otherwise I would have sent a staffer." He hesitated again. "What do you know about a secret space project somewhere in Latin America?"

Mariesa felt the question as a blow; but hesitation could be read as acknowledgment. "In which country?" she asked with a show of interest.

"How many Latin American countries have secret space programs?" he asked with heavy sarcasm.

"I know of no Latin American nation," she said carefully, "that is conducting such a program. I only wish some of them were."

"Hm, you would. There have been rumors. Say, from Ecuador?"

Maintaining her composure, she turned and they began walking back toward the doors. Albright was smart, and he was connected; but he had not quite grasped that governments need not lead the way. "And so, naturally, you thought of me. Mr. Albright, if I did know something about mysterious goings-on in Ecuador, why would I tell you? So you could stop it? Or because you have asked me so politely?"

Albright bit his lip and looked uncomfortable. He rubbed his nose again. "Sorry. It's just that I'm . . . curious, that's all. And I tend to be a rather direct sort of man."

"Curiosity is what makes us human; and you have piqued mine. I fully intend to look into this matter." This time, Mariesa held the door for him.

"If you do learn something," he said just before stepping inside, "I would be interested, too."

When she followed him, the reception hall felt like an oven. Keith and John E. were still there, laughing. The others had gone. Mariesa wondered what sort of jokes lawyers and accountants told each other.

She walked Albright to the main door, past the indoor reflecting pool with its arcing statue, and the horseshoe desk where the night sergeant watched his monitors. One of the monitors showed the Giants game at the Meadowlands, but Mariesa affected not to notice. She extended her hand to the activist. "It has been interesting talking with you, Mr. Albright. Do come again."

He gave her a secret smile. "Oh, I will," he said. "I will."

*   *   *

Once Albright was gone, Mariesa took the others to her office for a council of war. VHI's corporate headquarters was a long, rectangular building. The central core, cruciform in shape, was open from the ground floor to the skylighted ceiling three stories above, with the offices grouped in the four sectors between the arms. At the far end of each arm, the outside walls were glass, so that during the day sunlight bathed the entire interior. Catwalks ran around the edges of the cross and around the outside perimeter of the building; two catwalks on each level crossed the central atrium above the fountain.

It was a short walk from the ground-floor reception hall to the private elevator in the atrium, but no one spoke. Their footsteps echoed in the nearly empty building. The day shift had gone home, but when Mariesa looked up through the hanging plants and trees, she could see that several of the offices facing the core still blazed with light.

It could be an eerie building at night. Some found it uncomfortable: too large, and too empty to be so large, its geometry impersonal. Sounds had a way of wriggling from sector to sector, amplified by the open core and focused by the corridors that interlaced the office blocks. You could get lost among rows of identical offices. Even during the day, managers and associates had been known to walk into the wrong office, thinking it their own, only to find they were in the wrong sector.

But if you accepted the building on its own terms, it had its charms. Not simply the atrium and the fountain, but the unexpected food served in the restaurant, the impromptu art exhibits staged in the core, the way that some employees had discovered that twice around the catwalks was a jogger's mile. In a way, the three-thousand-plus individuals who worked in the building had created a small village. It was the people, not the steel and glass, that dictated whether the structure was impersonal or not.

Take away the gravity (and the fountain), Belinda had once said, and it might be a space habitat.

Practice makes perfect, Mariesa had told her.

*   *   *

Zhou Hui, Mariesa's personal secretary, was still at her desk when Mariesa emerged from the elevator with Keith and the others. Charlie Jim Folkes sat on one corner of the desk chatting with her while she locked folders away and shut down her computers. Hui came in under five feet, even if you counted the hair, which was combed high on top and hung down past her shoulders. She was fine-featured, doll-like, and looked frail enough to snap in two. If you wanted to be Jesuitical about it, you could say that Hui's very appearance was a lie; but it was sometimes convenient to have a bodyguard who did not look like one.

"Ms. Zhou," Mariesa told her as the others filed into her office, "we shall be meeting for a short while. Have the rest of the staff gone home?"

"Yes, miss," said Hui.

"They've gone, anyway," said Charlie Jim with a broad smile.

"Charlie, I shall be ready to leave within the hour."

Folkes was a stocky man with a broad, dark face and jet black hair that he wore in two braids. He checked his watch. "I'll have the bird on the roof warmed up *ahcheba*."

Mariesa said, "*Yokoke.*" Charlie liked to pepper his speech with Chah'ta time particles. It was a game her pilot liked to play. *Ahcheba* meant "in a while," one of several future terms he used. Every now and then he came up with a new one Mariesa hadn't learned.

Hui closed the door on them, and Mariesa and the others gathered around a low, circular coffee table by the north window. Redman settled back in the club chair, and the soft leather creaked. "How much does Albright actually know?" he asked in his soft Virginia-horse-country accent. The chief lawyer was only a few years older than Mariesa herself. Yet, he was already gray along the temples. He sported a salt-and-pepper goatee and gaudy suspenders. His hair in the back curled over the collar of his shirt.

Mariesa shook her head. "He may only have heard rumors. The sort of thing that slips from spouse to neighbor to the clerk at the convenience store. He has the name of the country wrong; but, 'an ounce of prevention,' you know.''

McReynolds folded his hands together. "We could not hope to keep such a project secret indefinitely.''

"I know, Keith; but we are not yet ready for publicity.''

Chris van Huyten said, "What I want to know is whether he is serious about blocking development of the magnetic switches. If he makes magswitches into one of his 'crusades,' we could be in serious trouble.''

John E. answered with eyes half-lidded. He liked to give that sleepy approach, as if he were only paying half attention. "He can try.''

"Fine,'' said Chris. "And another innovation gets tripled in costs by lawyers' fees. No offense, John E. The spin coupling effect improves when size is reduced. Do you know how *small* we can build personal computers if we learn how to mass produce spin transistors?'' It was a rhetorical question. They all knew. Dick Tracy wristwatch computers. Desktop Crays.

"What can he do?'' asked Mariesa.

Redman held up fingers. "He can tie us up in permits. Especially EPA permits. No one in this government likes to be seen as 'antienvironment' or 'anticonsumer.' ''

"We need a couple hundred permits already,'' Chris said. "Even if the paperwork goes through without a hitch, that is still a big cost.''

"Secondly,'' said Redman, "he can stage demonstrations. That is even more effective than working through his friends in the bureaucracy. With enough money, you can *buy* the necessary permits. If you have to, you can buy the necessary *bureaucrats*. But the media will simply reprint the news releases that the Peoples' Crusades gives them.''

Chris sighed. "Where is investigative journalism when you really need it?'' he asked of no one in particular.

"What's in a name?'' said Redman. " 'Peoples' Crusades to Save the World' has a nice ring to it. Much nicer than say, 'Van Huyten Industries.' You don't find many politicians bragging about their support for a big, bad Special Interest.''

"It seems to me,'' said Chris, "that the original Crusaders

had special interests of their own, and dressed those up with pious rhetoric, too."

"Perhaps Mariesa should rename the corporation and call it People United to Make Useful Things."

"People United to Create Jobs," said Chris.

"Please," said Mariesa. "This is no joking matter. We must preempt Albright before he can cause us trouble."

"I wasn't joking," said Chris.

"John E., do we having anyone in Albright's organization?"

Redman cocked one eye. "Do you mean a spy? A mole?"

"A whistleblower," said Chris van Huyten. "That's what they would call their man in our ranks."

Keith looked up. "And they very likely have one." There was a moment's silence as they all looked at each other. Then Keith added uncomfortably, "No one too high in Prometheus, or Albright would have had more pointed questions to ask."

"No one at the Brazilian end, either," said Mariesa, "or he would have known location. . . ."

John E. shook his head. "He may know. He may only have wanted to rattle you. And from the looks of things, he succeeded." He pulled a legal pad from his briefcase and positioned it on his knee. From his jacket pocket, he extracted a fountain pen, removed the cap with his lips, and began to write. Mariesa watched him silently. Chris squirmed a little in his seat, frowned, and crossed his arms.

After a moment or two, Redman removed the cap from his mouth and held up the pad to the light. "As I see it, we have several tasks. First: How much does Albright know about Prometheus? Second: How does he know it? Third . . ."

"Don't you have one and two reversed?" asked Keith.

Redman studied him for a moment. "No. *What* he knows may help us discover *how* he learned it. Third: What does he intend to do with the knowledge?" He studied his list again, as if assuring himself that he had actually read what he had written. Then he went on. "Under item one, we should find out whether any VHI employees with ties to Prometheus are members of the Peoples' Crusades or any of its unofficial subsidiaries.''

"Given a normal distribution of political opinions," said Chris, "and the size of our employee population, there are bound to be a few."

The lawyer looked at him. "Do you always talk like that?"

"If we can identify who they are," said Mariesa, "they may be able to tell us what is happening in the Crusades."

Redman turned to her. "Mariesa, if any of our people joined the PC *voluntarily,* they are probably the source of the leak."

Mariesa nodded slowly. "Yes, perhaps we can do a cross sort. Is there any way we can get our hands on the PC membership list?"

"Not legally," said Keith. "And inquiring into the political beliefs of our employees could be counterproductive. Isn't that right, John?"

Redman nodded. "That was how Nader got his start. The $425,000 settlement from General Motors on his invasion-of-privacy suit provided the seed capital for his organization."

Mariesa gave them a steady look. After a moment, she agreed. "Nothing illegal. The last thing we need is a public scandal. That would bring out the investigative reporters."

"There are better reasons than that," Keith McReynolds said.

There was a moment of awkward silence. Redman coughed and said, "As your lawyer, I could not advise anything illegal, although the Crusades may *sell* their mailing list to selected buyers. We might investigate that." After jotting another brief note, he continued. "I spoke earlier of *voluntary* Crusaders. We could always work it the other way."

"Do you mean that we should plant a spy in their ranks? VHI does not have the manpower to waste on that sort of thing."

Redman made a note. "Point taken. But I will ask Chisolm in Security. She may have a few ideas."

McReynolds shook his head, glanced at Mariesa, and said nothing. "Sauce for the goose, Keith," she said softly. To

Redman she said, "Chisolm could add two and two from the questions we want answered."

"Chisolm should be told, anyway," said Chris. "She will need to know eventually, when she provides security for Prometheus's domestic operations."

"Luanda Chisolm," said Mariesa, "does not care one fig for the space enterprise."

"So what?" Chris responded. "I don't ask my security people to love R&D."

"It's not the same," said Mariesa. "The space enterprise . . ."

"It is the same, coz. We have got to stop mystifying space. Romance doesn't work as collateral. We have to show business leaders that there are real opportunities up there—real*istic* opportunities. We are not a bunch of starry-eyed Trekkies."

Keith coughed. "Actually, I am. A Trekker, I mean."

Chris rolled his eyes. "Wonderful. Let's go to the bank wearing propeller beanies. The loan officers will stuff money in our pockets."

"Pointed ears, you mean," said Keith.

Chris sighed and slouched in his chair. After a moment he looked at McReynolds. "It was a helluva show, wasn't it?"

Mariesa looked at Redman, and he dipped his head slightly. Mariesa settled back in her chair. What needed to get done would get done.

"Albright looks smaller in person than he does on television," Mariesa said as she and McReynolds rode the elevator to the roof.

"Everyone does," Keith said. "It's the frame around the television screen. Things always look bigger when they are framed."

"What surprises me the most about him is that he really believes what he says." Why should it surprise her, she wondered, that an opponent could be sincere. "An honorable enemy" is what Gramper would have said. *Every man should believe in something. . . .*

McReynolds gazed carefully into her eyes before answering.

"The problem with a True Believer is not that he fails to see the other side's point of view, but that he fails to see that there even is another point of view."

She laughed lightly and laid her hand on McReynold's arm. "And you, Keith? Do you see all the other points of view?"

He stiffened just a little bit. "I believe that it is only fair to hear what others have to say. The world is not all black and white."

The elevator doors opened to a glass-enclosed waiting lounge. Outside, on the roof, the helicopter waited on the bull's-eye with its rotors slowly chopping the air. "Tell me, Keith," she said, watching the copter, "is it more important to be fair than to be right?" When she heard no answer she turned and looked at him.

"I believe in what we are doing," McReynolds said. "My mind is not so open that all my brains run out."

"Sometimes," she said, "we must resort to tactics that, in other circumstances, we would shun."

"Like planting spies and buying politicians?" he said.

"If we did not buy them, others would. They come with their strings already attached."

"You sound like Willem, now."

"Do I?"

"Always the Goal?" said Keith.

She searched his face for any sign of irony, any hint of cynicism. *I depend on you, Keith. Do not let me down.*

But, oddly, all she could see in his eyes was sympathy.

11.

Not Just the End of the Century

Walking into Harriet's party was like walking into a butlers' convention. All the men wore dark tuxedo jackets, with white shirts starched enough to stop a small-caliber bullet. Only their cummerbunds made any concession to color and diversity, coming in a variety of hues and patterns, from flat black to Stewart Hunting tartan. A handful of older men were more formally attired—Barry had been startled to learn that the tuxedo was regarded as a "casual" alternative to white-tie-and-tails; but then Barry had grown up in a milieu where "formal" meant "wipe the mud off your boots before you come in." Here and there, a few of the younger guests sported more daring attire: open-necked, Los Angeles-style laid-back mellow, or the neck-to-shoes, jacketless black that had been all the rage among desperately hip Manhattanites for the last few years. One man wore finely tooled cowboy boots and a bola tie with a large turquoise-and-silver clasp. But then, one made allowances for Texas oilmen. . . .

The women were a different matter altogether. They were decked in every color of the spectrum from far infrared to deep ultraviolet, in every conceivable fabric from silk to chiffon. Even including burlap...? Lord, what some people will wear.... Perhaps men's clothing inclined to the plain and the black-and-white in order to form an unobtrusive background against which the women could display themselves. Slits and hems, necklines and décolletage, variously concealed or revealed shoulders, cleavage, backs and legs, and even the odd midriff or two; sometimes through a scrim of gauze, sometimes wrapped provocatively or augmented with appliqués or jewelry, sometimes openly on display. There were five bosoms more-or-less laid out for inspection, two of which ought not to have been. Barry thought there was a fine line separating haute couture from stand-up comedy.

Harriet's guests were a diverse mixture of family, society, business, and entertainment. Barry recognized a major box-office draw, an up-and-coming starlet, and a newsreader for one of the five networks. There was a scattering of olive, tan, and black faces, too, which surprised Barry; but then at the altitude where Harriet and her friends moved, the only color that mattered was green. Most amazing of all was Harriet herself, who actually looked stunning and who even managed to be reasonably charming when Barry presented himself at the door. In the colonnaded patio area behind the ballroom, a string quartet played gentle, complex music. Barry could not help but compare the gathering to the noisier one Mariesa had hosted for the kids earlier in the year.

Mariesa herself, dressed in an off-the-shoulder, black-and-white sheath highlighted by a corsage at her breast and with her short-clipped hair held in place by a golden circlet, looked somewhat like a high-tech flapper. She stood at the center of a solar system of young men. Newton's Theory of Romantic Gravity: large masses of money tended to attract one another. Barry moved into the outer circle, imagining that he was an asteroid among the gas giants. He made a mental note to tell Mariesa later. He suspected the imagery would amuse her. Mariesa noticed him and waved him into the inner circle.

"Barry," she said, clasping his hand and kissing the air just beside his cheek. "I am delighted you could come."

Barry considered and discarded several flip answers and said, "It was good of you to invite me."

One of Mariesa's admirers, a man several years Barry's junior, spoke up, "That is an off-the-rack tuxedo, isn't it, Barry?"

Barry looked into a pair of blue, heavy-lidded eyes and a large, rather fleshy nose. The man was making a perceptible attempt to look down at Barry from a position several inches too low to carry it off. "Yes," Barry said. He planned to leave it at that, but Mariesa spoke up.

"It was terrible, Kent," she said, laying her hand on his arm.

The short man cocked his head. "What was?"

"Barry had to replace his own tux at the last minute," Mariesa said with a straight face.

Barry could not remember whether Kent was the "cretin," the "boor," or the "groper," decided he didn't like him either way, and said, "Turpentine absolutely destroys the fabric. Thank you, Sykes." The butler had come quietly to his side with a bourbon-and-water on his salver.

"Not at all, Mr. Fast," said Sykes. "I personally insured a stock of Early Times." Kent looked curiously at Sykes, at the drink, at Barry.

"Turpentine," said Kent.

"It was impossible to remove, Mr. Chatworth," Sykes contributed with a shake of his head. When Barry stole a glance at Sykes, God help him, the man *winked*.

"The hip boots were a total loss, too," Barry continued, "though I can always rebraid the lariat."

"Oh, my, yes," said Mariesa.

"Excuse me, miss," said Sykes, who bowed and walked rapidly toward the pantry. Barry hoped he would make it before he cracked up and blew his image.

Kent, now clearly baffled and uncertain of Barry's status, nodded. "I see." A few of the other men around Mariesa were smiling; others had the same pained look of concentration Kent wore. "One does what one can to cope."

"Foxes," said Barry, suddenly remembering the context in

which Kent Chatworth's name had come up. At that, the man brightened.

"Why, yes, I am Master of Chatworth Chase. Do you follow the hounds, too?"

Barry decided that betting on greyhounds out west didn't count and said, "No, deep-sea fishing is more my style. Pitting your strength against the best the ocean throws at you. I fought many a battle from the decks of my father's boats." Sure, they were fishing boats, and he had trolled with nets, but . . .

"I understand marlin are particularly difficult to play," Kent said earnestly.

Barry nodded. "You have to keep an eye out for that sword-bill of theirs. A marlin attacked our boat one time. Can you imagine? Leapt right up out of the water and went for the pilot."

"Really! What happened?" Two of the other men in Mariesa's circle made hurried excuses and rushed off, covering their mouths. Barry shook his head sadly.

"Why, I picked up a harpoon and dueled with the creature to distract him. Fortunately, I had studied fencing." Barry pantomimed *lunge in quarte*. "Never thought I would use it under such conditions, though. No foils on either tip. One false move and . . . shish kebab. Finally, I beat through the marlin's parry and scored a touch. That proved enough for the creature." He shook his head once more as if at the memory and downed the rest of his drink.

When Kent had moved off and he and Mariesa were alone for a moment, she whispered to him. "Barry, that was simply terrible!"

He returned her grin. "You started it."

"I did not know you were a fencer."

"Epées and sabers. I coached the high-school team back in Seattle and managed to stay one lesson ahead of my students."

"I have asked several of my personal guests to gather in the Roost later to welcome in the new year. I would be delighted if you could join us."

When the alternative was to spend the evening with Harriet

and her circle? "Well, gee," said Barry with exaggerated caution, "I'll have to think about it."

The young woman standing beside the buffet table in the loggia was as tall as Mariesa and bore the same long, thin nose. Everything else about her was different. A chunkier build. A rounder jaw. Her eyes were hazel; her dark brunette hair fell to shoulder length. A fine, even tan—Barry made an uncollectible bet with himself that it was absolutely uniform—maintained even in December. He knew before she spoke that she must be Cousin Brittany.

Brittany van Huyten-Armitage, to be exact.

"Barry Fast," she said with a cock of the head and a thoughtful look after he had introduced himself. Her voice was husky, lower-pitched than Mariesa's. "I believe Riesey has mentioned you." Brittany was younger, but looked older. The tan had dried her skin, aged her, given her that young-old look that amateur athletes often bore.

"Really?" Sykes had replenished Barry's drink. Barry lifted it to his lips and took a sip of the cold, sharp liquid. "Nothing good, I hope," he said with a quick grin.

Brittany studied him. "Hmmm, yes. I can see what she meant." Whatever *that* meant. More seriously, she added, "Riesey needs the respite from her work. She takes entirely too much on herself. She really ought to relax and employ a professional manager."

"That's what Harriet said. Maybe she just enjoys the give-and-take of business the same way you enjoy . . . golf, isn't it?"

Brittany nodded. "Yes, Grandfather's influence, I suppose. She was closer to the Old Man than the rest of us; and I suppose that a family member really ought to be at the helm. Except for my brother, Chris, none of us take an active hand in our holdings—too many cooks, by far! Still, with Riesey, one must be careful that her flights of fancy do not affect her judgment."

"Flights of fancy?"

"Surely, she has bent your ear with tales of wealth in space?"

"She has mentioned it a time or two."

"Or three," said Brittany with a smile.

"Or three," Barry agreed. But, as they chatted, he found himself arguing Mariesa's case for her. Because he believed in it? Because he believed in her? or simply because it was pleasant chatting with Brittany Armitage?

He went looking for Mariesa afterward. Mariesa had told him to mingle, but Barry found little in common with the men and women around him. Brittany had been pleasant enough, and she kept invading his personal space and brushing up against him. She was either very friendly or she was coming on to him, information that Barry filed away in the back of his mind.

He found Mariesa deep in conversation with an older man, nearly as tall as Barry but with snow-white curls and a jowly, red-lined face. He was trim and his face was tight with the evidence of past face-lifts. The fellow clenched a whiskey glass in his right hand and poked a finger at Mariesa as he spoke. With every thrust, the liquor threatened to slosh out and splash her, but the man either did not notice or did not care. Obviously the sort who confused aggressiveness with certainty. Barry drifted to Mariesa's side. If the man did splash Mariesa, would he have the nerve to retaliate? It would be a waste of good liquor.

". . . even dangerous to our interests," the man told Mariesa in a hoarse, gravelly voice.

"Oh, tosh, Cyrus. New technologies present new opportunities." Mariesa sounded calm, but Barry could see the flush of red along her neck, just behind her ear.

"Yes, but for whom? How many canal and barge companies became successful railroads? How many railroads fly airliners today?"

"For pity's sake, Cyrus. You cannot be advocating a return to canal-boating!"

"Don't talk nonsense, young woman. I said no such thing. But neither do I see a reason why I ought to endanger the future well-being of my nephews and their children or of my associates. Why sow, if others reap?"

"Join the reapers," Barry said. The older man looked at him, as if seeing him for the first time.

"Sir, this is a private conversation!" Then he looked at Barry again, as if reconsidering the "sir."

"Barry is a friend of mine," said Mariesa. She turned and said, "Cyrus is comfortable with the status quo. He is afraid that, if circumstances were to change too much, it would disturb the existing order."

"I am not 'afraid,' young lady," Cyrus said. "And I do not need to listen to a woman tell me that I am. I look after my own interests, that is all; and the policies you advocate in Washington and elsewhere work against those interests!"

Barry smiled. "King Knut." Cyrus looked at him.

"I beg your pardon?"

"King Knut, the Danish king of England, issued a royal edict that the ocean tides not come in and wash the beaches away. But the tides came in anyway. In some versions of the fable, he even mans a broom and tries to sweep the tide back."

Cyrus colored. "I fail to see your point."

"Why, only that 'looking after your interests' may not be as simple as it appears. When those railroads you mentioned ignored the possibilities of air transport—"

"Do you have any notion of the amount of capital that was sunk into trackage and equipment, and into trained labor?"

He shrugged. "There are times when you may have to leave your luggage behind. Where are those railroads now? Bankrupt, or on government welfare, most of them. So where did their interests really lie?"

"Welfare? Now, see here . . . !"

"If a business fails to compete, it ought to go under, and not go on the government dole. Isn't that what free enterprise is all about?"

"Free enterprise!" Cyrus snorted. "You sound like a conservative, or even a libertarian."

Barry laughed. He had always considered himself a moderate lefty. Mariesa said, "Cyrus, the future comes whether

we will it or no; no matter how many wield the push brooms."
To Barry, she added lightly, "Cyrus is 'conservative' only in
that he wants everything to remain as it is. He finds Freeman
and Hayek as threatening as Marx."

"I accepted this invitation out of friendship for Harriet,"
Cyrus informed them, "in the expectation that it would be a
pleasant social gathering. I did not expect a radical harangue."

He started to turn away, when Mariesa said sharply, "It was
you who brought the subject up."

Cyrus turned back and stared at her. "Yes," he said, quietly. "For your own best interests." He tapped his temple with
a forefinger. " *'Verbum sat sapienti.'* "

"What a jerk," Barry said when he was gone. It was nice
to know that rich people had their share of jerks. But Mariesa
looked worried and thoughtful. "What is it?" he asked.

She shook her head. "Cyrus Attwood has a great many
important and influential friends who think as he does. 'A
word to the wise is sufficient.' Barry, that sounded like a warning."

"A warning." Barry sought out the curly white hair among
the throng of guests and spotted Attwood chatting amiably
with a group of older men. Attwood took a swallow from his
drink and said something that caused the others to laugh.
"Against what?" asked Barry.

Mariesa shook her head again, watching Attwood. "It's
ironic when you think about it. A man who fears the future,
and would 'sweep it back' if he could, has flown all this way
to celebrate the new millennium."

Three floors above the party, the sounds of laughter and conversation were muted. The group that gathered in Mariesa's
"Roost" was a smaller one and quieter. Belinda and Onwuka
were there; and the accountant, McReynolds. A pair of amateur astronomers that Mariesa knew and who had been in
town; a few other close, personal friends.

"Well, Barry," said Belinda when he settled into the group,
"what have you been up to lately?"

Something about Belinda's eyes told him that she knew

quite well what he had been up to and that a part of her approved and a part of her did not. Well, tough, if she thought it was "inappropriate." He hadn't gone asking for it; it had been thrust at him and, if he had not exactly spurned the offer, who in his right mind would? "I went bowling a couple of weeks ago," he said. Mariesa, standing by the dormer window and looking out at the western night sky, turned and spared him a brief smile.

"Actually, Barry has been lending me a sympathetic ear these past few months."

"Really." Belinda raised an eyebrow. "Keith," she told the accountant, "isn't that your job?"

The older man smiled benevolently. "There are more ways than one to listen," he said.

". . . but how could you just *lose* it, Curt?" one of the astronomers asked, a young man named Tom Kalvan, who had an observatory in the High Sierra and was, like Mariesa, heir to a family fortune.

"Blessed if I know," said the other, a lawyer with a "backyard" setup somewhere in Montana. Barry had forgotten where. There had been too many introductions. "Maybe if I had the sort of equipment you have . . ."

"What have you lost?" Mariesa asked.

"An asteroid," said Curt.

"How do you lose an asteroid?" Barry asked of no one in particular.

"Curtis is part of the pro-am asteroid tracking community," Keith McReynolds explained. "Skywatch. He is supposed to report the positions of his 'adoptees' to the Astronomical Union every so often."

"There are far too many asteroids for the professionals to keep track of," Tom added, "so they depend on amateurs—people like Mariesa, Curt, and myself—to keep their databases informed."

Curt shrugged. "Now I'm going to have to start the search process all over again. I'll try somewhere else along its track. Could have been a software glitch."

"Was it an Apollo asteroid?" Mariesa asked, leaning toward him.

"No," Curt told her. "Main Belt."

"Easy to lose it against the background," Tom said with some sympathy. Barry thought he heard an undertone of *"I'd never lose it."*

The elevator doors chimed and a moment later Sykes entered, bearing a tray of drinks and noisemakers. Several of those gathered in the Roost praised Sykes as a lifesaver. "Thank God," said a woman named Tracy whom Mariesa had gone to college with, "dehydration was beginning to set in."

"It is nearly midnight, miss," Sykes informed Mariesa. She nodded.

"I have been tracking Jupiter," she said, pointing to a bright spot hovering above the black shadow of the mountain ridge. "It shall touch the crest of First Watchung Mountain at precisely midnight." Sykes glanced out the window and gave a noncommittal acknowledgement before leaving.

Mariesa laughed. "Poor Sykes! I believe he does not entirely trust the relationship between time and the heavens."

"Five minutes," said Tracy after a glance at her watch. "I heard on the television that the phone lines to the National Observatory were jammed and their computer overloaded. I believe everyone in the country tried to call in and get the exact time, so they could set their watches."

Barry remembered Shannon and her family and their synchronize-your-watches game. He wondered if tonight, for the first time, all the Morgenthalers were in the same time zone. He thought of them sitting in their living room watching the ball come down over Times Square on their television. He stared into his glass and then gulped down half the contents in one swallow. He barely felt it hit. *I've drunk too much. They'll have to pack me in a cab to send me home.* His fingers and toes tingled and he could feel the maudlin mood creeping over him as it did so often when he'd had too many.

He noticed that, while the others watched the clock on the

wall, Mariesa remained at her post in the window, watching Jupiter. She was watching a ball drop, too; only a bigger and more distant ball than the one they showed on TV. Barry admired the set of her calves. Another effect of the liquor. He began to imagine what it would be like to be with Mariesa.

Finally, everyone began counting together. Then it was all a bedlam of "Happy New Year!"'s and people hugging one another and kissing and blowing on their noisemakers. Barry could hear the faint roar from downstairs, too. He quickly slugged back the rest of his drink, just in time to be hugged by Tracy, who also planted a Very Serious kiss on him. Over her shoulder, Barry saw Belinda do the same with Mariesa, and McReynolds exchange an *abrazzo* with Tom Kalvin. Then—*change your partners, do-si-do*—and it was Mariesa offering an embrace and a kiss and, hell, he'd have to be a damn fool to turn it down. If Mariesa was startled at the intensity of the kiss, she made no sign; and she gave back as good as she got.

When they had settled down, Mariesa addressed the group. She raised her wineglass. "Gentlemen! Ladies! To the new millennium!" Barry's glass was already emptied, but he went along anyhow, because it was the spirit of the moment that mattered. Still, he and one or two others answered with the stand-up routine some of the comics had been playing with during the year: "Not! Quite! Yet!"

Mariesa grinned at the sally. "The millennium is like the day," she told them. "It may begin at midnight, but the dawn is yet to come."

"Always the Goal," said Belinda quietly while the others chatted, tipping her glass toward Mariesa. McReynolds, standing nearby, lifted his in salute.

Barry had overheard. "What goal is that?" he asked.

The three of them looked at one another. Belinda said, "To inspire the children."

Barry nodded and tipped his glass back to catch the last few drops of bourbon. "Hell, I can drink to that." But he couldn't help thinking that he had been given only part of the answer.

12.

Messenger Boy (II)

Far below the curve of the airliner's wing, Ned could see the white line of breakers smashing into the Florida coastline. It all looked very regular, very predictable; no hint of the chaos that, viewed up close, would dominate the senses: the crash of the unruly surf; the smack of brine on the lips and tongue; the winking of the sunlight off the chop. Ned sighed and his left hand groped for the button that made the seat recline. He hated flying when he wasn't in the cockpit. He hated giving up control to someone else. That was the drawback of flying commercial.

"That is sure a gorgeous sight," said the man in the aisle seat, leaning partway across Ned to stare out the window.

One of the drawbacks.

Ned smiled briefly and closed his eyes, hoping his seatmate would take the hint.

Subtlety was wasted.

"Sure will feel good to get back to the good ole USA," the man said. A middle-aged man with a large nose, prominent glasses, and a Mephistophelian beard. A laptop was open on the tray table in front of him. A businessman, Ned judged. "How long were you in Brazil?" the man asked.

Ned was not in the mood for conversation, but there was no point in being rude. "Eight months." It hadn't seemed that long. The days were full and they went past like telephone poles from a train window. Time enough to write two letters. Not time enough for an answer.

"Eight months?" The businessman hummed and shook his head. "That's too long away from the little woman, for me. I try never to book clients for more than a two-week stretch."

There was no way out, Ned decided. The bearded man blocked his way to the aisle, and the window seat was not by an emergency exit. Trapped. Two aisles ahead on the left a woman in a blue business suit read a paperback. Her hair was dark and cut in a bob, and both seats next to her were empty. There was no justice in the world.

They were beginning the descent into Miami when Ned realized something that should have been obvious. He would be making his pitch on ergonomics and cabin layout to the managers of Daedalus's parent company, including Mariesa van Huyten, who, if memory served, had stars in her eyes. What was to stop him from making a pitch for one more change in the cabin layout: namely, that it was right and proper to lay Ned DuBois out in the pilot's seat?

Not directly, of course. You never begged; and he didn't even "know" that he was out of the running. But it was a chance to let himself look good in front of people whose opinions mattered. Even if João decided on Bat for Prime Pilot—and Ned figured one *carioca* looked out for another—that wouldn't matter if van Huyten herself took a shine to him.

"That's the spirit," the businessman next to him said. "That's the kind of smile coming home should get."

The man waiting at the end of the jetway was as short as Ned, but with a dark, brooding appearance. His brows were thick and grew close together. He was dressed in dark suit pants and polished shoes and wore a navy blue windbreaker jacket. "Ned DuBois?" he asked as Ned stepped into the gate area.

"Yeah." Ned shifted the duffel bag on his shoulder and stepped to the side, out of the flow of passengers. He hated the huggers and greeters who stopped right in the gateway and embraced each and every relative all the way down to Great-Aunt Mabel. "You the driver?"

"Welcome to Newark, Mr. DuBois." The man reached for the duffel bag but Ned kept his grip.

"No trouble," he said. "Which way is baggage claim? I've got one more suitcase."

"Follow me." The dark man led the way to the concourse and into the turbulent flow of people. The people came in all shapes, sizes, and degrees of urgency. Most of them walked briskly and purposefully; a few strolled. One man ran with his suit bag flapping against his legs and back. A woman shepherded an unruly flock of children. Ned followed the driver onto the slidewalk. "Walk left; stand right," the sign read, but no one paid it any attention. Walkers bulled their way through clumps of standees. Ah, Metro New York, where no one knew the meaning of the word "rude."

The driver stood with one hand on the rail. Ned lined up behind him. Other travelers pushed past them, striding in seven-league boots toward the baggage claim. Ned wondered what their hurry was. It was not as if their luggage would be there waiting. The voices of gate agents clashed on the loudspeakers, announcing the boarding of two different flights. Ned grinned and shook his head. "Sci-fi," he said. The driver turned his head.

"What?"

"The airport. It's sci-fi." Ned waved a hand around the concourse. "Moving sidewalks. Airliners carrying hundreds of passengers through the stratosphere. People lugging computers in shoulder bags. Look there . . ." He pointed to an ATM with three people lined up waiting. "You can get money from your account almost anywhere in the country with just a little ol' plastic card. We're all living in a science-fiction book, and we don't even know it."

The driver laughed. "Yeah, I guess we are. But you live in the next chapter."

"How so?"

"Well, you're with the space project, right?"

Ned looked at him. Would a driver have need-to-know? De Magalhães had drummed into them the Plank's confidential nature. There were competitors, legal issues. Not even all VHI personnel were privy, he'd been told. Still, they would not have sent someone outside the project to meet him, would they?

"Why do you ask?" he said.

"Hey, you were a blackbird, weren't you? And NASA had you tabbed for the X-33 project before it was canceled. 'The last of the astronauts.' " He smiled and nudged Ned with his elbow. "And you weren't down in Brazil just to enjoy the beaches, were you? So, how's it going?"

Ned didn't bother to correct him. "It has its ups and downs," he said.

The driver chuckled. "Ups and downs. Hey, that's pretty good. Has anyone gone up, yet? Or are they still ground-testing?"

And that was the last issue he wanted to be reminded of. The end of the walkway was approaching and Ned hefted his duffel bag and hung it over his shoulder. There had been men like this at Edwards and Canaveral, too. It wasn't just the lollipops. There were men who didn't have it, men who would never have it, but who wanted to talk like they did. So they hung out and they bought you drinks and they wanted you to tell them what it was like. Enthusiasts bugged him. They let too much show. "It was a long flight," he told the man. "I'm tired."

"Sure. Sure. Didn't mean to bother you."

Ned stepped off the walkway and followed the swarm of people to the escalator leading down to the baggage carousels. People were backed up there. The arrivals from all the gates on the concourse funneled down to this one narrow passage. The joys of planning. He wondered if architects ever flew commercial. The stairway beside the escalator was empty, so he swung over and hopped down, taking it two steps at a time, reaching the bottom before he would ever have set foot on the escalator. There was a lot to be said for low tech, too.

The area at the base of the stairs was cordoned off by a line of men and women holding signs. For a moment, Ned fantasized that he was a game animal driven by beaters into a line of hunters. Then, he thought it might be a protest demonstration. But it proved to be a line of limo drivers waiting for their charges, so he had been right the first time. The signs all bore the names of people, companies, or limo services. A large black man stepped forward.

"Mr. DuBois? I'm Laurence Sprague. Ms. van Huyten sent me. I'm to drive you to the North Orange Radisson."

"What?" Ned saw that the sign read SPRAGUE LIVERY and DuBois had been printed in marker pen in the blank space. Sprague himself was easily two hundred pounds and well muscled. He wore a dark gray suit and a livery cap. "But, I was met at the gate," Ned said. He looked around for the small, heavy-browed man he had followed down the concourse, but they had gotten separated at the escalator and now he saw no trace of him.

Sprague frowned. "Livery drivers must wait in this area," he said. "Airport regulations."

"No, I mean that someone *did* meet me at the gate. He knew my name."

The scowl deepened. "I think Ms. van Huyten will want to speak to you personally."

The estate lay an hour's drive past North Orange, in Berwick Township. The head babe's personal palace, Ned thought as he studied the building atop the terraced hill. A Bell helicopter settled onto the lawn just behind the building and two figures emerged. They paused, one holding a hat clamped to his head, and watched the approaching limo for a moment. Then they hurried up to the building and vanished into a rectangle of light as a door opened for them.

The front door opened even before Sprague had brought the limo to a complete stop, and several people descended the steps to the parking apron. Ned waited for them, but they walked right past him, all but one man who paused and gauged Ned. The other man topped him by a good couple of inches and sported a head of curly, off-blond hair. As the other cars started and pulled away, the man waved to them absently. "I don't know who you are, mister," he told Ned, "but you're the first messenger ever to cut an Institute meeting short."

Something about the other man irritated Ned. Whether it was the grin or the attitude behind it, he did not know. "The name's Ned," he said.

"Barry." The other man stuck out a hand and, after a moment, Ned took it. "I'm one of the Mentor Institute Fellows. First time Mariesa ever took a phone call during a meeting; and her mind was half a world away afterward. As soon as Sykes told her your car was coming up the drive, we were out of there."

"This way, Captain DuBois," said Sprague, who was halfway up the stairs.

Barry waved to the chauffeur. "Hi, Laurence," he said.

"Mr. Fast, I didn't see you there. How is the Lincoln driving?"

Barry made a circle of his thumb and forefinger. "Like a charm." Then he looked at Ned. "Captain, eh? Well, well. And I bet I can guess captain of what, too."

Ned followed Sprague up the stairs. When he heard Fast open his car door, he turned. "Hey, Barry." And he made a circle of his thumb and forefinger. Fast, surprised, smiled and nodded back before he shut the door of a maroon Town Car. Ned whistled as he climbed the rest of the stairs. He saw no reason to explain that in Brazil the gesture meant "you're an asshole."

A butler ushered Ned to a small, close room, then slid the doors shut as he bowed out. A morning room? A drawing room? Must be great to have so many rooms each one had a special purpose. There were three people waiting. From their rumpled appearance, Ned guessed that two of them had come in on the helicopter. He recognized van Huyten, seated at a wooden secretary beneath the window at the far end of the room, and the old man with the bow tie who had come down with her on the jump jet. The third man standing beside the secretary was introduced as John E. Redman, a lawyer. Van Huyten folded her hands as if praying.

"Now tell us, Captain. What happened at the airport?"

Ned stood at ease, though he felt anything but, and locked his eyes on to a point just above van Huyten's forehead. He had been called up by superior officers often enough to know the drill. Answer the questions, and don't volunteer. As succinctly as he could, Ned described the man who had met him at the gate and the questions he had asked. Ned did not think he had done anything wrong, but sometimes just the association was enough to put a career on hold. Not guilty of anything, exactly; but not entirely trusted, either. Ned realized, even as he recited his experience, that he might be arguing for more than his place as Prime Pilot, now. Before this was over he might be glad enough simply to remain in the program.

"I didn't tell him anything of value," Ned concluded. "I was not feeling communicative after the flight, and I had doubts about the fellow's need to know." *Fellow* . . . "And that reminds me. When I was coming in, the driver called me 'captain' and some guy named Barry, who was just leaving, said he could guess at captain of what."

The other two looked at van Huyten. She smiled and shook her head. "Barry is entirely too good a guesser."

"You shall have to bring him all the way in," said McReynolds, "or shut him all the way out."

"Who is 'Barry'?" asked Redman.

"That is not important now, John E." She looked at Ned, forcing him to return her gaze directly. He looked into her eyes, trying to find some shred of hope. But gray eyes are the coldest eyes, the color of northern winters, the color of the seas off the Newfoundland coast. "You are certain you told him nothing."

Before Ned could answer, the lawyer spoke up. "Of course he didn't. When the Air Force puts a man in the blackbird program, they sew buttons to his lip. Keeping them closed becomes as automatic as keeping your fly closed." Ned's hand made an involuntary movement toward his pants flap. Van Huyten noticed and bit a smile from her lips. Ned flushed.

"But that does not mean," Redman continued in his soft drawl, "that your stranger learned nothing."

"But I didn't say anything," Ned insisted.

"Exactly. It was *how* you said nothing that told him what he wanted. If you knew nothing at all about an SSTO project, if the fellow's comments had come to you without context, what would you have said?"

Ned opened his mouth; closed it again. "I would have asked him what the hell he was talking about," he said at last.

Redman nodded, as if he had scored a debating point. He turned to van Huyten. "Whoever X was, he was only looking for confirmation of something he already knew—or believed he knew. Captain DuBois's lack of reaction was no doubt sufficient to that purpose."

"Look, I'm sorry it happened; but I was tired and I thought he was the driver. . . ."

Van Huyten raised her hands, palm out. "Do not blame yourself, Ned. It could have happened to any of us."

"May I remind everyone," Redman said, "what 'X' did know. . . ." He held up his fingers and counted the points. "One, he recognized Captain DuBois. Two, he knew something of the captain's background. Three, he was waiting for the inbound *Miami* flight. Four, he knew Ned had connected in Miami from Brazil." Redman stared at his fifth finger, as if disturbed there was not a fifth point to tally.

"He did *not* know about the archipelago base," said McReynolds. "Otherwise he would have used the information to prove to Captain DuBois that he was truly 'in the know.'"

Redman nodded. "Very likely."

"And he did not know the status of the program," said Mariesa, "since that is what he tried to learn from Ned."

This time Redman shook his head. "You never show all your cards. The purpose of the encounter may simply have been to let us know that he already knew some things. He may have been using our captain as a sort of messenger boy."

Ned winced and turned away. He stuffed his hands in his pockets. Messenger boy.

McReynolds said, "Does this sound familiar, Mariesa?"

"Show him the photograph, John E."

The lawyer opened a drawer in the secretary and extracted a folder, from which he pulled an eight-by-ten glossy. He handed it to Ned. "Do you recognize the man in that picture?"

It was a shot of several people standing about in a reception hall. A party of some sort. Ned studied the faces. That was the fusty accountant in the background, surrounded by a circle of listeners; but he did not think that Redman had meant him. Ned looked more closely at one man, half turned away from the camera. "There," he said. "That's him." He handed the photograph back to the lawyer.

"I knew it," said van Huyten. "Phil Albright, again."

"This man?" said Redman, pointing to one of the foreground figures.

Ned shook his head. "No. The one in back, over his left shoulder." He touched the figure he meant. "That one."

Surprise crossed their features. Redman arched his eyebrows. "Not Albright?" Redman showed the others the individual Ned had indicated. "Who is that? Do either of you know?" he asked.

Mariesa shook her head. McReynolds took the picture from Redman and studied it. Then he handed it to Mariesa. "That," he announced, "is Anthony Pocchio, confidential assistant to Gene Wilson."

"Wilson!" said van Huyten. She turned and looked out the window into the night. "Wilson," she said again. Ned saw a tight-lipped smile on her face.

Ned leaned on the railing of the catwalk that ran around the outside of the observatory dome and watched the helicopter depart. The lights swept a circle across the lawn as the craft rotated. Then it rose and disappeared rapidly into the night. The blinkers were quickly lost amid the stars. "I could have gone with them," he said.

"Nonsense," said van Huyten. "The helicopter would be too crowded. And it is too late in the evening to drive back to the Radisson."

Ned did not point out that Sprague was driving back in that

direction anyway. "What about the hotel room?" he asked. "It was guaranteed for late arrival. They charge you if you don't cancel before six o'clock." He looked at van Huyten and she looked at him. Then he said, "Oh."

"Rest assured, Captain, that our guest rooms are every bit as comfortable as those at the hotel."

"Well, yes . . ." He could not figure out why van Huyten had been so insistent that he stay at the mansion. Silverpond, she had called it. Unless she really was an astronaut groupie, like the babes at Cocoa Beach; or the sweet young things that used to show up at Edwards back in the storybook days. They'd pop up out of nowhere, the old hands used to say, right there in the middle of the high desert, like they'd been hibernating under the soil. You couldn't explain it. You turned around and there they were. The high-performance jets, or the men that flew them, attracted them like bright, searing flames drew moths. Often with the same results.

But you needed the recklessness of youth to hunt astro-scalps like that. Van Huyten was Ned's age. If she played the game, it was hunger, not fascination. He continued to lean on the railing, waiting for her to make a move. It could not hurt to snuggle in the sack with the CEO; unless, of course, she was the sort who bent over backward to avoid showing favoritism afterward.

When the helicopter had vanished, van Huyten turned to him and said, "So, Captain, how are affairs on Fernando?"

"We think we have consensus among the pilots regarding the cabin layout. . . ."

She laid her hand on his arm. "No, save that for your presentation tomorrow. I meant, in general. How do the astronauts feel about the program? Are they satisfied with the safety precautions? With the pace?"

"Well enough. I think any one of us can fly the craft blindfolded, now. The trick is not to lose the fine edge we've got through overtraining."

She looked at him. "Can one be overtrained?"

"Sure. When it goes past preparation to marking time." He shrugged. It was not something you talked about. "You've got to feel it," he said. "You've got to smell it and taste it. Otherwise, it isn't real."

She tugged at her shawl and wrapped it more tightly around her shoulders. "No," she said. "I don't suppose it is. It's all pages in a book. Pictures and paintings and stories and columns of figures and calculations." She looked at him. "What does it feel like, Ned? What does it smell and taste like?"

To fly where people had only been hurtled before . . . He hesitated before he spoke. "You know about the stunt I pulled with the X-33?"

She nodded. "It was why we picked you. I wanted people who *wanted* to go. In one way or another, all of you have that urge. You, Calhoun, Krasnarov . . . each of you has a notation in your dossier that drew our interest."

"And you?" he asked.

She studied the sky. "With me, it's different. There are things to do up there. Important things." She clenched her hands around the rail—cold metal in the winter night. "There is so much that needs doing," she said, "that I don't know if I can do it all. So many bits and pieces to fit together; so much to be timed just right. Then there are nights like tonight when you think it might all unravel on you. Sometimes 'impatient' is too tame a word. I want everything *done* more than I want the doing. But . . ." And she stood away from the rail and hugged herself, tucking her hands under her arms to warm them. "But I shall not build this house upon the sand. Every rung must be in place if we are to climb successfully."

It was odd, Ned thought, how two people could have the same goal yet have such different reasons for seeking it. For himself, the journey was enough; for her, what mattered was journey's end. She was pulled, he was driven.

A shooting star crossed the heavens and Ned sensed the woman beside him stiffen. "Cold?" he said.

"No. Yes. Maybe we should go back inside."

Ned shucked his leather pilot's jacket and draped it over her shoulders. "On such a fine, clear night as this? Wouldn't you rather gaze at the stars?"

Van Huyten indicated the observatory dome behind them. "That's why I have that."

Ned shook his head. "It's different when you do it with someone, out in the open, where the stars can see you, too. I still haven't taken you out to Sancho Bay to see the phantom rain."

She regarded him for a moment, and then she laughed. "Do you think you are that good?"

"Well . . . Of course, I may be biased." He hesitated a moment, then added, "I would seriously value your independent assessment."

In for a penny, in for a pound. As the silence lengthened without reply, he wondered if he had blundered badly. But when she spoke there was a current of amusement in her voice. "Does that line work very often, Ned?"

He gave her the honest reply. "About half the time."

She laughed. "If I were to render an 'assessment' . . . it would not mean anything beyond that."

"It never does."

Fair was fair. If she wanted to use him to achieve some sort of vicarious cockpit experience; he would use her to achieve his own goals. The hammer used the carpenter, when all was said and done.

13.

Between the Lines

There it is," said Styx. "That's the place."

Beth slowed the old Chevy and gawked at the mixture of Colonial, Gothic, and modern buildings that lined the left side of Nassau Street. On the stairs and in the airyways between the buildings, students, bundled against the March winds, bounced on the balls of their feet as they stood chatting in small, self-warming huddles. "There? Are you sure?" The car behind them began to honk, and Beth pulled ahead to the traffic light.

"Of course I'm sure, Mother! You went right past it!" She waved the letter in her mother's face and Beth batted it away.

"Don't do that when I'm driving!"

Styx seized her anger and pulled it back inside her heart. The New York oldies station on the radio faded in and out with the distance, warbling forgotten songs by forgotten singers. Grating to the ears; but Mother would not change it. Styx turned and faced straight ahead out the windshield, making sure to bounce in the seat. The right side of the road was lined with small retail shops, chic boutiques, college hangouts.

Weekend shoppers, come to gape at the hip college town. Styx stared through them. Beth was a real bitch. Someday, she would get her own car, and she wouldn't have to depend on *her* to take her anywhere.

The street ahead of them forked into a Y and, when the light finally changed, Beth dithered, opting for the right-hand branch at the last possible minute. The car behind them honked again, then took the left fork. "Idiot," said Beth.

"Yeah," said Styx, exploiting the ambiguity to comment aloud.

A short distance down the road stood a marble monument fifty feet high. General Washington led troops to battle, while another officer with hairbrushes on his shoulders lay dying heroically of his wounds. Styx stared at the giant Revolutionary figures as Beth looped the car past the monument and back out onto Stockton Street. Bet it wasn't so heroic when it was happening. Bet that dying general—Mercer, the inscription read—I'll bet he screamed like a stuck pig when the bayonets went in.

Back at the Y-intersection, they were caught again by the light. "There," Styx said, pointing to the corner. "Did you see *that?*"

"That" was a large sign with a big red arrow: PARKING, NEW JERSEY STATE POETRY SYMPOSIUM. The signs pointed off Nassau Street to University Place. When the light changed, Beth turned and followed the arrows into a parking lot, where young men in bright orange vests directed them to an empty slot. "There aren't many cars," Beth said doubtfully as she nosed into the space.

"Well, I guess it's not a football game, is it."

Beth looked at her for a beat before pushing the shift handle into park. "Are you getting out?"

But Styx was out of the car before the sentence was out of Beth's mouth. She slammed the door behind her and stalked to the curb. It was a long drive from North Orange to Princeton, and not only in miles. The wind blew in sharp gusts, tugging at the scarf around her neck, bringing tears of cold to her eyes while she waited for a break in the traffic. Blair Hall, across the street, was a gray-stone castle, with two narrow, crenellated towers flanking a great arched doorway. It was like a palace gate, thought Styx. Like a palace; and she was a peasant.

Beth came around the car and joined her. Styx held her arms straight at her side. "Mother, you're not coming to this, are you?"

Beth put an arm around her shoulder. "You're my little girl," she said, shaking her gently. "Of course I'm going to be there. It will be so *exciting* to see you up there. You know . . ." Styx shrugged out of the embrace, and Beth looked away for a moment. "I used to write poems, too, when I was in school."

"Mother, it's just me and four other high-school students from around the state." She held the letter rolled up in her fist. She must have opened the invitation and read it fifty times since it had come in the mail. *New Jersey State Poetry Symposium . . . Enrolled high-school student . . . Magazine or journal publication . . . Young Poets Panel . . .* She thought she might have to show the letter to someone to get into the building. She thought she might keep the letter forever. And the chapbook that had appeared so mysteriously in the mail with her poem in it. *GeneraXions,* Emmett Alexix, ed. And there was *her* poem, "In Life's Labor-ynth," attributed to Styx and not to dorky Roberta. She could remember writing the poem, but she could not remember sending it out; nor could she remember where she had heard of *generaXions*.

"We're going to talk about why we write poetry," she told Beth grudgingly, "and then we're each going to read one of our own works." God! She sounded so pretentious! *Our works . . .* Imagine trying to talk about the words that were inside you—about the secret pools where the words came from—and your *mother* is sitting out there listening!

Grown-ups didn't want to hear how teenagers felt, anyway. They said they did, but they didn't. Not the real feelings, not the flames smoldering behind the Ray-Bans that would fry you where you stood if they ever leaked out around the edges of the eyeballs. Grown-ups were so consumed with themselves, you were lucky if they even noticed you were around; and luckier still if they didn't; and luckiest of all if you weren't.

God, she needed a drink! She was shaking, and not entirely from the cold. But if she drank, she might not remember *this* day and that would be unbearable.

When the light at the corner changed, she and Beth slipped between the stopped cars and followed the signs to the quadrangle behind Blair. Massive metal and stone sculptures were scattered around the grounds—as if a giant child had dropped her playthings. The buildings really were ivy-covered, Styx saw, or they would be when the spring came. The bare, brown lacework of ivy runners looked deliciously odd where it gripped the sides of the more modern structures. It didn't seem right, somehow. Ivy-covered steel-and-glass?

There were not many students up and about on a Saturday morning. Styx watched them scurry from building to building, spending as little time in the bitter wind as they could. They were not much older than she was, yet they seemed a lifetime more sophisticated. Not "boys" and "girls," not high school; but "young men" and "young women." When they laughed, as did two young men passing her, the laughter seemed more knowing, more worldly. Styx jammed her hands into her jacket pockets and tucked her chin down.

It wasn't fair, what wealth could buy you. Freedom and independence. New vistas for the mind. Laughter, most of all.

It was possible, just possible, that she would go to Wessex Community College when she graduated. It didn't cost much and the entrance requirements were mostly that you were breathing and had a body temperature of 98.7°F—though you might even get a waiver on the body temp. But it would be like being in high school forever, surrounded by mouthbreathers and GEDs. *And best of all, Roberta, dear, you can live at home and commute to school.* It bordered on fantasy that she would ever go to a real college, like Rutgers; and far beyond the border to imagine attending a place like Princeton.

A trickle of people flowed toward a building at the far end of the quadrangle. The signs pointed that way, too; so Styx headed toward it at a brisk pace without waiting for Beth to catch up. Styx noticed that the building on the south side of the quadrangle was named Witherspoon Hall. Now there was good karma! She picked up her pace, held her head up, willed herself to look as if she belonged here, as if she were alone and had no connection with the woman trailing behind her.

But her mother caught up with her in a few brisk strides and walked beside her. "What poem do you plan to read?" she asked.

"I don't know," said Styx. "I haven't decided."

"Is it one I've heard?"

Styx gave her a look. Stupid question. "No, I don't think so." *Because how many of my poems have you* ever *heard?* She let that comment die unspoken, but Beth looked suddenly awkward, and Styx wondered if she had heard the thought anyway, with that odd clairvoyance mothers sometimes seemed to possess. The most important things were never spoken; you had to learn to hear them. You had to read between the lines.

Well, which poem *was* she going to read? She had brought several with her, stuffed into a large manila envelope. "Our All Night?" She could imagine the grown-up jaws dropping and maybe smashing on the floor if she read *that* little tongue-lick of erotic fantasy. But the feelings she had expressed in those lines were too private; she could never read them in front of strangers. And she could imagine Beth all the long way home going how embarrassed she was in front of *all* those *people.*

"I wish you would show me your poems more often, Roberta."

Maybe she would go over to the Exchange after the panel. The fanzines all said how that was where the alternative people in Princeton hung out. People like her, who listened to the groups the whores at MTV never played; who traded cassettes and song lyrics by mail; people who were real, and who *knew.*

But Beth, oh ghawd, would probably want to tag along.

It was not a big symposium; though packed into one wing of the hall it seemed larger than it was. The program she received at the registration table listed ten panels, running two at a time. The crowd was mostly Princeton students, equal parts preppy, serious, and hip; but there were a scattering of older people as well, some fusty and academic-looking, some looking like the sixties had never ended.

The Young Poets panel was scheduled for the first session. It was set up in a lecture hall, so the chairs were the kind with folded desks on the arms and they sat on a series of ascending tiers, with Styx and the rest of the panel on the lecture platform at the bottom. *Like ducks in a barrel*, she thought. She and the rest of the panel sat behind a long table facing a mostly college-age audience, leavened with high-schoolers; plus two mothers and a father; plus one old fart with a red bow tie who sat way up in the back.

The moderator was Emmett Alexix, the editor at *genera-Xions*. He dressed grunge, and *no* one dressed grunge anymore, so it was almost like he was Making a Comment. So, either he was Way Cool, or he was an asshole. Styx had never been on a panel before, and was not sure what was expected of her; but Emmett helped by briefing them on the kinds of questions he meant to ask and chatting with each of them. Emmett was cute, in a brooding sort of way. In his early twenties, skinny and hollow-eyed with life experience, he seemed to be perpetually leaning forward. He had the same sort of sensitive lips and eyes that Alaryk Castlemayne had, even without any makeup. If he unbound his ponytail and let his hair hang loose, he might almost look like a girl.

STYX LOWERS THE BOOM
from *The Collected Poems of Roberta Carson*

Your generation never grew up;
Ours has grown up all too soon.
Our generation scrabbles and grubs;
Yours abandoned the moon.
But please rest assured
We "know where it's at,"
And someday we'll do what we can

To pick up the pieces
And clean up the messes
While you go and play Peter Pan.

Your generation partied and rocked;
Ours has to take out the trash.
Our generation will somehow get by;
Yours will get high on your stash.
But please rest assured,
We mean to survive,
Not that you ever will care.
You'll do what you will;
You'll have your "Big Chill"
And you'll go to revivals of "Hair."

Oh, you'll always be young
And you'll always be fair
And you'll always be girls and boys;
And you'll never grow old
And you'll never grow cold
And you'll never let go of your toys.

You were the joy of your parents, you know.
They raised you with love and with care.
But when we were born
And it was our turn,
Then, damn you, you never were there.

Styx would not meet her mother's eyes when she had finished reading. The college students clapped; the other parents
looked rewardingly uncomfortable. The old man in the back
row nodded his head slowly. *Probably asleep*, Styx thought.
One of the other kids on the panel asked in a snooty tone why
Styx wrote in rhymes, because wasn't that like old-fashioned;
and Styx went how she used rhymes because it was more of
a challenge that way, and you wouldn't settle for free verse
just because it was *easier*, would you?
Mrraauu . . .

After the panel, some of the audience members came to the front of the room to talk with the panelists. Several of the college students clustered around Styx and went how much they liked her poem and asked her questions about how she had written it and why. She answered as best she could. She just *wrote* the things; she had never reflected on them, but she did not want to look stupid in front of college students. One young woman with long hair and round glasses asked if she had ever read Chesterton. Styx drew a blank, but smiled and went how she hadn't and the other girl went how she ought to. Styx didn't know if she meant to be helpful or stuck-up.

Emmett asked for a copy of the poem to put in his magazine, and then, like that was a cue that she really was Hip, they were all asking for copies. Styx hadn't thought to bring any, so Emmett offered to run some copies in the office down the hall and left, trailing a wake of wannabes, including other panelists, who were trying to press *their* poems into his hands; and that left Styx alone in the room with Beth.

Silence, while she gathered up her things. There was a distant tap-tap sound, which might have been the heating pipes, and the muffled sound of voices buzzing in the hallway outside the lecture hall. She could hear the writing arm rattle against the desk as Beth squeezed out of it. *They liked me. They actually liked me.* She hadn't realized until the relief set in how afraid she'd been.

Hugging the manila envelope to her, she started up the tiers to the door, but Beth met her in the aisle and grabbed her by the sleeve before she could run off. "Roberta . . ." Beth hesitated a long moment, as if afraid to speak. "Your poem . . . That last line was aimed at me, wasn't it?"

Styx pried her sleeve from Beth's fingers. "Of course not, Mother," still not looking her directly in the eye. "It was just a poem."

"Because, I've always *tried* to be there for you; but with the job and the commute and everything, I—" Beth turned away and was silent. "I know you come home to an empty house. It wasn't what I wanted. Somehow, I always thought it would be like when I was young; that you and I would experience everything I remembered between Mom and me. Fresh-baked cookies and Band-Aids on the knee and you rushing home from school bursting to tell me everything you had learned that day . . . But none of it worked out the way I thought it would. I didn't live my mother's life; and I can't give you what she gave me.''

''You mean, like a father?''

Beth stiffened. ''Don't be so quick to judge. Things were different on the commune where Mark and I met. We were young and silly and had egos as wide as Wyoming. We believed in sharing and free love and the Revolution and never growing older than thirty. I would have given you a father, I tried to. Oh, hell, *Mark* tried to.''

''I could hear the shouting. Did you think I couldn't hear the shouting?'' Styx clenched her fists and asked the question she never asked. ''What went wrong?''

''He still believed in free love,'' Beth said with a wisp of venom, ''even after we were married.'' She looked right through Styx as if she wasn't there. ''Growing up is when you discover that the world changes you more than you change the world.''

''Love is never free,'' said Styx. ''You always have to pay.''

Outside the lecture hall, Styx nearly collided with the old man in the bow tie. She smiled a little-girl smile at him and said, ''Excuse me,'' which translated as: *Move, you old fart. You're standing in the way.*

''Not at all, miss. I was waiting for a friend.'' A glance away to scan the passing crowd; a sudden glance back. ''Oh! You were one of the panelists in there, weren't you? Yes, the Girl in Black. You gave a nice reading. I'm glad your poem was not aimed at me.''

''Uh, thanks.'' So was this guy a professor, or what? ''Why do you say that?'' Beth, standing beside her, watched the old man suspiciously.

The old man smiled. ''My generation never 'partied and rocked.' Mostly, we 'jitterbugged and did as we were told.'

There were the Beats, of course; but even when we had rebels, they didn't have a cause.'' He smiled, as if at some sort of joke; but Styx hadn't understood half of what he said. Alzheimer's, probably.

"Keith! There you are!" A woman emerged from the crowd. Mariesa van Huyten, dressed preppy-style, in a sweater and skirt. Styx gasped and tugged on Beth's sleeve. "Mother! Mother! It's *her*!"

"Why, Styx!" said the Rich Lady with a bright smile as she approached them. "What a pleasant surprise." She extended her hand and Styx took it.

Beth said, "How do you know my daughter? Are you one of the teachers?"

Styx cringed. "No, Mother. It's Miss van Huyten. She *owns* the school." *And she has a lovely house and she can sit in the dark and listen to a weeping child in the attic of her home.*

"Oh?" Then, "Oh!" Beth hesitated a moment before shaking hands and gave the other woman a careful study. "What are you doing here?"

She's rich, Styx thought. *She can be anywhere she wants.*

"The Van Huyten Family Trust is one of the symposium's sponsors," van Huyten said. "But I really came to hear Keith. Oh, excuse my manners. This is Keith McReynolds, a sterling poet; but in his spare time he is chief financial officer for VHI. Keith, these are Roberta 'Styx' Carson and her mother, Mrs. Annabeth Carson." The old man beamed an Orville Reddenbacher smile and shook hands with each of them.

Emmett had returned with copies of her poem. "Here you go, Styx. Here's your original back and some extra copies I made. I added a copyright at the bottom. People snapped them up as fast as I could run them off."

McReynolds said, "Did you give a copy to the committee for the symposium chapbook?"

Emmett nodded. "Of course I did." He squinted at the other man's stick-on name badge, then at the man's face. "*You're* Keith McReynolds?" he said. "Did you write 'The Seasons'?"

McReynolds nodded. "Yes, though I think every poet writes at least one poem on that theme."

"Oh, man," said Emmett, shaking his head. "I had no idea you were so old . . . Well, gotta go. Styx, keep the lines open." He gave her a quick squeeze on the upper arm. "Drop by the *generaXions* office when you have the chance."

Styx rolled her eyes in Beth's direction. Like fat chance Beth would let her train into the city, let alone hang in the Village.

Emmett understood. He leaned close to her ear. "It's easier to get forgiveness," he whispered, "than permission."

"Is that your poem, Styx?" asked van Huyten. "May I read it?"

"Her name is Roberta," said Beth. "We have to be getting back north. We just came down so Roberta could be on her panel." Beth ran a hand through Styx's hair. "You had fun, didn't you, sweetie?"

"Mother, the symposium isn't over yet. . . ."

"But, aren't you done now? I thought you said you were only on this one panel."

"Mother . . ." *Did you bring me down here just to put me on display? Did you ever think I might be interested in what these other people had to say?* "Just one more panel? Please?"

Beth sighed and relented. She always sighed and relented. "Oh, all right."

"Would you like to sit with us?" van Huyten asked. "Keith and I had planned to attend the epic and ballad session. Paul Zimmer will recite 'Logan.'"

What she wanted to go to was the Exchange, but not with Mother tagging along. "Well, I guess so . . ." Van Huyten had listened quietly and sympathetically that night. She knew how to use her ears, and not only her tongue.

Beth hesitated, and van Huyten looked at her. "If the poetry does not interest you, Mrs. Carson, there are some very fine shops in Palmer Square, across the street. When the symposium is finished, we could meet, and I will take you both to dinner at Lahiere's."

Beth hesitated. "It's such a long drive. . . ."

"Please, Mother? I really wanted to attend the whole symposium."

Beth seemed to deflate. "All right, Roberta. If that's what you really want."

The restaurant was fancier than any that Styx had ever seen. Bun-and-runs were the usual Carson dining-out experience. A couple times a year they managed a Sizzler or a Denny's. But she had never been anywhere where the tables had cloths instead of mats, anywhere where the waiter knew you by name. (Tommy Patel over at McDonald's didn't count.) The waiter not only greeted the Rich Lady by name, but showed her to "her" table and asked if she wanted to see the special menu. Styx had never known there were such things as special menus, or that the world was divided into those who were shown them and those who were not.

Van Huyten ordered for the four of them, which was just as well because Styx had never worked very hard in Mrs. Bonerz's French class. The food was delicious and the Rich Lady and the Old Geek told a lot of entertaining stories. Mc-Reynolds recited some of his own poetry for them. Styx found it cloying and sentimental, but she did not say so. *Nice* was the word that best described poems, sentiments, and McReynolds alike. He was a cloud; there was no *edge* to him. The old man radiated *nice* the way honeysuckle radiated its gagging fragrance. Next to him, Mr. Rogers was "gangsta."

During dinner, they discussed the symposium, the three of them trading observations and opinions and Beth silently playing with her . . . *"poo-lay sauce Ro-sham-bow."* At first, Styx felt awkward when the Rich Lady asked for her opinion, because she often did not have one and, when she did, did not want it ridiculed or dismissed. So, she tried to guess what it was van Huyten wanted her to say. But it really did not matter. The Rich Lady listened closely to Styx's answers; nodding sometimes, disagreeing at others, but even when disagreeing treating her opinions with respect.

Styx had not thought she would enjoy the dinner, but she

did. The food was delicious and the conversation—for the first time around any dinner table she could remember—interesting. At one point she and the Old Geezer engaged in a bit of improvisation—"dueling stanzas," he called it—on the respective merits of youth and age; until finally they had both been reduced to helpless laughter. As poetry, it left a lot to be desired, but the experience itself was exhilarating. Who would ever have believed that an old man like that could be so *real?*

"Styx," said the Rich Lady, "in your poem, when you wrote 'Yours abandoned the moon,' what did you mean, exactly?"

Styx looked down at her plate—also a poo-lay, which just meant chicken, but sounded so much more sophisticated in French. "It wasn't what I *meant*, Miss van Huyten. It's what I *felt*."

Van Huyten nodded almost to herself. "It is something about which I have also felt strongly." A self-mocking grin. "They do not call me the Moon Lady down in Washington for nothing." She lifted a forkful of her fish and asked, as if as an afterthought, "Do you think we ought to go back?"

"It's not that," said Styx, "it's—"

"It was a waste of time and money," said Beth, placing her own fork firmly down on the table. "There are too many problems here on Earth."

Styx looked at her mother. "Maybe it *would* be a good idea," she said. To Ms. van Huyten: "But I guess it really wouldn't make much difference one way or another. I used it because it seemed like the right image for the ultimate spoiled child, which is what most of that generation is, no offense. To 'promise the moon' means you would do anything. So here their parents actually *deliver* on the promise and they just turn their noses up at it."

Van Huyten lifted her water glass and looked at Styx with her head slightly cocked. "Some of us have not abandoned it."

"It's a silly notion," said Beth.

"Well, maybe it isn't," said Styx a little more firmly than she had meant to. Beth did that to her sometimes.

"It is a subject that deserves its own epic," said McReynolds suddenly. They looked at him and he blinked, as if surprised he had spoken out. "Poetry has gone all lyric these days, and is poorer for it. And I say that even though I write lyric poetry myself. Feelings are all very well; but story should have a place, too."

"Story *with* feeling," said Styx. "Like that poem, 'Logan,' that we listened to."

"Exactly so," said van Huyten.

"The epic was the mainstay of poetry for ages," McReynolds continued. "But where are our new epics? 'We are met upon the gravesite / Of a million murdered children . . .' It gave me shivers, listening to Paul read that. Especially when he reached that last line . . ."

" 'Who are *we* to mourn for Logan?' " The three of them recited the line together. Styx felt the electric thrill of the line run through her again. The perfect ending line to that tragic story. Beth stared into her plate.

"Well," said McReynolds, "does not Apollo 13 deserve an epic? There was drama and heroism enough there, I'll tell you. And Aurora 7 . . . Those long hours when they could not locate Scott Carpenter, and Walter Cronkite nearly wept on television, thinking the man had died. And Cernan barely making it back inside the capsule after his spacewalk; or Armstrong fighting unconsciousness to bring his spinning Gemini-Agena back into control."

"And the actual moon landing itself," added van Huyten. "Armstrong nearly ran out of fuel hunting for a level spot to set down on."

"Well, yes," McReynolds said. "The whole grand drama, from beginning to—" He stopped, looked uncomfortable. ". . . end."

"Have you ever attempted it, Keith?"

The old man shook his head. He pushed his dinner plate a little away from him and a waiter swooped down and carried it off. "No," he said. "I know my limitations. I dabble at the art."

Van Huyten turned to Styx. "Perhaps it is a task for a younger heart," she said.

Styx felt a tingle in her stomach. The thought of writing such a poem . . . to move people the way Zimmer had moved them . . . Some in the audience had cried. "I don't know if I can, yet," she said.

"Oh, I'm sure you have the talent for it. It may only need maturing."

" 'You want youth for something fresh,' " McReynolds recited, " 'but age to give it savor.' "

"If you want background material," said van Huyten, "I could send it. Or you could come visit at Silverpond . . . and watch the stars again up in the Roost."

"Roberta has schoolwork," said Beth. Styx turned a look of frustration on her. Everything nice that ever tried to happen to her, *she* got in the way and made it stop.

"Mariesa," said McReynolds suddenly, "could she not apply to the Muses School?"

"The Muses School?" asked Styx, looking from one to the other. "What is that?"

Van Huyten answered. "Every summer, Mentor Academies gives scholarships to its most promising art students. They gather—Where is it this year, Keith?"

"In Denver, I believe. Somewhere in Colorado. Belinda will know."

"They gather for intensive workshops and classes. For some, there are even university scholarships on graduation. I see no reason why North Orange students cannot be considered. They are Mentor students, too. Keith, remind me to speak of this to Dr. Karr at the next board meeting."

There was a crack in the door to the box that was her life. Styx could see it, see the light shining through from the open world outside. She could not trust herself to speak, even to say yes; so she nodded dumbly. The waiter came and described the dessert menu, but Styx had no idea what she ordered.

*   *   *

"I thought she was nice," said Styx.

"She was rude and arrogant," Beth said, hands gripped tight around the steering wheel, eyes squinting against the headlights of the oncoming cars. "Like all rich people. And now we have to drive home in the dark." The Turnpike here had widened to eight lanes in either direction. A flood of traffic flowing north and south. People constantly seeking to be somewhere they were not. By staying in the right-hand lane, Beth had managed to get them stuck on the outer roadway with all the semis. They roared past the old Chevy, rocking it with their slipstreams.

At least she listened. Ms. van Huyten had. *Respect*, Styx thought. *She treated me with respect*. Not like *someone else* she could think of. "Well, I thought she was nice," she said again.

"I didn't like being . . ."

Sudden silence. Styx turned and stared at her mother's hard features. Beth's face strobed in and out of shadow as they passed under the harsh lamps that lined the highway. An odd effect: the bleached, halogen lighting made Beth's eyes sparkle, as if they were wet.

"You didn't like what?" *You never like anything. It's always a complaint or a put-down or an order or a . . .*

"I didn't like the way you were kissing up to her."

"I was *not!* I don't kiss up to anyone!"

"Rich people like her put this country where it is today. They had a free ride for a lot of years, and now we're paying the price for it. So, exc-u-u-se me if I don't get all ga-ga because she sprang for a meal at a fancy restaurant."

Styx folded her arms and slouched in her seat as far down as the shoulder harness allowed. Trust Beth, trust *her* to kick over the slats of maybe the best day of her life, a day when people had actually taken her seriously, and bring the whole thing crashing down like a building demolition. "Well, hey," she said after another silent mile had gone by. "Look at the positive side. If I kiss up to the richest lady in North America, it's just possible she may kiss me back."

*   *   *

The limousine rolled down the narrow, two-lane blacktop, its headlamps scything light out of the rural night. Mariesa van Huyten sat in the rear with her hands folded on her lap, and watched the countryside roll past the tinted side window. Dim shapes, muted further by the opaque glass. The ghosts of landscapes. The limo was a local service, hired for the day; the driver, a stranger. The stereo played a Vivaldi quartet, *pianissimo*. The glass bottles in the bar tinkled like Chinese wind chimes from the vibration of the road. *Poor Styx,* she thought. The girl had been in her shell so long it almost hurt to pry her out.

"Still no idea why Steve asked for this meeting?"

"What?" She turned to Keith, who sat facing backward in the jump seat. He had unbuttoned his overcoat in the car's warm interior. One hand had draped across the seat back; the other, across his knee. He had been silent since the car had left Princeton.

"Steve Matthias," he said. "You haven't learned why he asked us to come over?"

"Oh, sorry. I was thinking about Styx. Steve, yes." Deliberately, she turned her mind from the black-garbed girl with the eyes as deep as craters. "He had scheduled a seminar for his senior staff at the Forrestal Conference Center . . ."

"Concerning Thor's Baldrige Award application."

"Is it? I haven't been following that thread." Somehow, anything not connected with Prometheus seemed less than real to her these days. "When Steve learned that we were to be in Princeton today, he E-mailed me on VHINet and invited us over. I suppose he wants to brief me personally on Thor's affairs."

Keith grunted. "Or to give himself a little personal exposure."

Mariesa laughed. "I do not mind self-promotion, Keith, provided the job gets done. The Werewolf is no shrinking violet, either. Nor is Correy Wilcox. It is only when it is decoupled from accomplishment that self-promotion becomes tiresome."

McReynolds reached up and pressed a button on the ceiling

console. The soundproof divider slid up, shutting off the driver's compartment. The driver glanced in the rearview mirror before returning his attention to the road ahead. "About the Carson girl," Keith said.

Mariesa regarded him carefully. "What about her?"

"I liked her."

She nodded slowly before answering. "Styx can be charming when she is not lashing out. At the symposium, for once, she could be herself, with no constraints."

"No constraint but her mother."

"Well, yes. I have had some experience with that, myself."

McReynolds smiled without mirth. "Harriet is an acquired taste. What drives Mrs. Carson?"

"Bitterness, I gather. Have you read Chisolm's reports? There was a nasty divorce when Styx was a child. Mrs. Carson kept the house in the settlement, but was forced to move out because she never received any support payments. Styx has very little memory of her father, except as a shadowy figure who is now gone. We talked once when she was at Silverpond. She has an idealized memory of him quite at odds with her mother's."

"Ah. No wonder they clash. Is there anything we can do to help them?"

Mariesa had been waiting for the question. It was as much in Keith's nature to want to help as it was in Correy's or Steve's nature to look out for number one. Both impulses, rightly channeled, could accomplish much; but neither could be allowed free rein. "Help them in what way?" she asked cautiously. "Styx will surely receive a scholarship to the Muses School." Not that the fix was in. Mariesa did not believe in unearned rewards. More importantly, neither did Belinda, who made the final decision. But she had a sure confidence in Styx's ability.

Keith grimaced. "Did you see her eyes when we mentioned the program? It made me ashamed of the charade we were playing."

"Charade?"

"Don't play one on me, Mariesa," Keith spoke with unwonted asperity. "I helped set it up, remember? The symposium . . . How long have you waited to be able to use my avocation as a Prometheus asset?"

"Did you say anything to the girl that you did not believe? Did I? Then I fail to see the charade."

" 'Why, Styx!' " quoted McReynolds. " 'What a pleasant surprise.' "

"One presents one's case by the most effective means possible. A direct approach may be counterproductive. And it *was* a pleasant surprise. She might not have come; her mother might not have brought her."

"Mariesa, I don't believe . . ."

"Keith," she said sharply. "If I had made a direct offer of help to Roberta, what would have been the result?"

"I . . . don't know."

"You most certainly do. You did not reach your position— under my grandfather's tutelage, I might add—without being able to read people."

McReynolds sighed and looked past her out the rear window of the limo. "She would have declined."

"Declined? You mean she would have run away from it as fast as she could."

"Too good to be true," said Keith softly.

"Yes. She would be suspicious of any good fortune handed to her. Nothing in her life has prepared her for that."

"So you simply 'arrange' for the good fortune."

"It is the difference between finding a million dollars and having someone try to give it to you. You may rightly wonder in the latter case what the catch is. And that is why . . ." She leaned forward and laid an admonishing hand on Keith's knee. "And that is why she must never learn that I sent Emmett Alexix that poem she left behind at Silverpond. She would think that it was my influence and not her talent that caused its publication."

"She does not know Emmett well enough, yet."

"Keith, listen to me. At this stage in her life, nothing must allow her to question her talent. It is too fragile a blossom yet."

"Can we help her in some other way? Financially? Doesn't her mother work for a subsidiary of ours?"

"For Croesus Financial Services, their data-processing division."

"Well, then . . ."

"Well, then, what, Keith? Should I arrange a promotion for her? So they can afford a better house? So that horrid burden of debt can be lifted? And what of all the other Mentor children? And the children Mentor does not reach yet? Styx is by no means in the worst straits."

"One child at a time," said Keith. "Isn't that Belinda's motto?"

She looked away from him, out the tinted window. The Forrestal Center was visible now, just off the approaching junction with Route 1. Modern, functional buildings, bathed in light. The parking lot was full and banks of windows glowed with activity. Matthias's was not the only seminar under way this evening. She chose her words carefully in answering Keith, shaping them with her tongue, and not enjoying the taste.

"I can't tamper with her life, Keith. If we assure her comfort, what happens to her poetry? Is it not the very confinement of her circumstances, that yearning of hers to break free, that is the wellspring of her talent?"

"Perhaps," McReynolds allowed. "But it's a bit disingenuous to claim you are not tampering with her life. Is finding a poet so vital to the program?"

"Keith, you were on the working group that identified that need."

"Not a need; just something that might prove beneficial. You're giving it too much priority."

Along with five dozen other priorities, a thousand objectives; plans within plans. The need for security battling with the need for open communication. Political maneuvers in Brazil and Russia. The upcoming elections. April Fool, next spring's test flight. For just a moment, the weight of it made her dizzy and she reached out to grip the cushioned armrest on the door. "I don't know," she answered. The problem with tinted windows was that you could not see the stars. None of them were bright enough to show through. She pushed the button on the armrest and the window rolled down, admitting a rush of frigid night air; and the dizziness passed.

"There are other promising poets among the Prometheus students, are there not?" said Keith.

"There are seven, enrolled in or graduated from other Mentor practices. You have the list."

"Then why Roberta Carson, in particular?"

"You are a poet, Keith. You tell me."

"No, Mariesa. I want to hear it from you."

The wind from the open window battered her face. It tousled her hair. She felt as if she were flying forward at great speed. "The human race is trapped in a box," she told him. "We need to break free of it if we are to have a future. If we are even to be safe. None of the others can understand those feelings half so well as Styx."

"I see." McReynold's voice was hard, almost to the point of contempt.

"Do you, Keith? Do you see that we cannot *let* her out of her box, that she must break free herself?"

"Can the Goal possibly be that important?"

Mariesa stroked the brooch that adorned her blouse. "You know it is, Keith. You know it is."

McReynolds shook his head. "Sometimes I wonder."

Steve Matthias greeted them in the lobby of the Forrestal Conference Center. He was all smiles and handshakes and small talk as he led them to a meeting room he had reserved for his own use during the seminar. "The consultants have my managers squirreled away in breakout rooms. They'll be slaving on their workships until ten o'clock, at the least."

"Shouldn't you be with them?" Mariesa asked. The room had been turned into a home-away-from-home. A laptop and a portable printer sat on the table with a stack of folders nearby. A modem and a fax machine had been routed through a splitter into the phone line. A half-dozen disposable coffee cups were scattered about like chess pieces in an end game. Matthias closed the door.

"No. I felt this was more important. Have a seat." The table was ringed by red upholstered bucket chairs on wheeled spider legs. He waited until Mariesa and Keith had seated themselves, then he resumed his own seat.

Mariesa smiled at the equipment cluttering the table. "You certainly have moved in, haven't you?"

Matthias spread his hands to encompass the equipment. "Thor does not run itself," he said.

Mariesa sometimes wondered if a well-managed company might not do just that. But no, there was always the unexpected. There were always decisions that could never be automatic, that could never be delegated. "Well, Steve, what can we do for you?" What was that turn of phrase Ned had used that time he had stayed at Silverpond? *It's your deck. Start dealing.*

Matthias leaned his elbows on the chair arms and balled his hands under his chin. He was silent for a moment, and Mariesa began to sense a certain amount of tension in his attitude: the stiffness of his interlocked fingers, the tightness in the corners of his eyes. Then he took a long breath and let it out. "Prometheus," he said.

Now it was Mariesa's turn to be silent. She exchanged a glance with McReynolds, who shook his head slightly but offered no advice. She barely changed posture in her chair as she said, "What about Prometheus, Steve?"

The president of Thor nodded. "Yes, you want to know if I know more than just a name." He reached out and picked up one of the empty coffee cups and rolled it slowly back and forth between his palms as he spoke. "You are running a pocket space program out VHI's back door. I don't know how big it is or what its ultimate goal is. All I know is that I want a piece of it."

Matthias was no fool. If she played dumb, it would only anger him, and to no good purpose. She had not kept him out of Prometheus so much as she had never invited him in. "It is a confidential project, Steve. Closely held."

"And I can appreciate that. I have told no one about my guesses."

"How did you learn of it?"

"It was no one thing," said Matthias. "And nothing that came out of the project itself. Your security so far has been very good."

Though not good enough, Mariesa thought. Phil Albright knew something; and Gene Wilson, of course. Even the U.S. government must have some inkling of what lay beneath the cover stories. "Go on," she said.

"Everybody in the pantheon knows that there is a top-secret aerospace project going on, but everybody buys the story that it is a high-performance/high-altitude recce plane to replace the old SR-71. I did, too. But I was in military intelligence in the service. I wasn't career, but I learned enough of the methodology to be able to pull scattered clues together. I learned to read between the lines. For example, the newspapers announce that Werewolf Electronics plans to lease time on Mir. Ostensibly, the Russians will loft a very-thin-film crystallography experiment and a payload specialist to orbit, which gets NASA's shorts in an uproar."

"Energia offered better rates than NASA."

Matthias smiled, as if to show he appreciated a well-laid cover. After all, the best cover story was one that got you into a little bit of trouble, with maybe a few trips to the Washington Woodshed for a Buy-American scolding. Then they wouldn't look for anything deeper. Administration policy was to support the Russian Republic, Mariesa had argued, so why shouldn't an American company make a little money for itself while doing so, at no risk to the taxpayer? The Senate subcommittee had bought it, with a little help behind the arras from the general. Hadn't NASA itself considered an actual merger of the Russian and American space-station projects during the prior administration?

"Or another: Mike Gravestone, a design engineer at my precision-bearing plant, gets an order from Daedalus for a whole shitload of magnetic bearings; but he can't juggle the parameters to do a proper costing because Daedalus won't specify the performance regime. When I was at Northrup, we used to buy mag bearings like those on NASA contracts.'' He held up a hand. ''I know, I know. They have other applications besides in hard vacuum. But it was a host of little things like that. Tidbits picked up here and there. Take them one at a time and they don't add up to anything. But taken one thing at a time, nothing ever adds up. So, I started putting them together and evaluated what we used to call a capability. Consilience— 'rope' logic. No single thread can support the conclusion; but wrap them all together and you can get a pretty strong cable.''

Matthias could probably go on at length demonstrating how sharp he was. ''You would like to join the Steering Committee,'' she said. Was there an unspoken threat? What if she did not invite him? The trouble was that Steve *was* sharp; otherwise they would not be having this meeting. But she still had doubts about his commitment to anything beyond the surface of his own skin.

''I'll bet I could name half the members of the committee. I know who I would pick if I were running the show.''

''You do.'' Mariesa leaned to one side and challenged him. ''Tell me.'' In his early fifties, Steve cut his hair unfashionably short; and he dyed the gray parts. Mariesa had known so many like him in college. Brainy and ambitious, with ego diameters exceeding skull diameters by an order of magnitude.

''Werewolf Gregorson and João Pessoa, of course. Pegasus may be in on it, but you've got to keep the big show offshore because of Chapter 35. And Heinz Ruger in the European office. Bennett, because you'll need his steel; and Jimmy Undershot, for the plastics. The head bean counter, because you can hide everything except the dollars.'' McReynolds inclined his head in gracious acknowledgement. ''Probably the head shyster, too, so you can break laws the right way. And me, of course. You missed on that one.'' Matthias's smile took some of the edge off the remark. Mariesa wondered what he would say when he discovered that four of his middle managers were already playing supporting roles in Prometheus. ''You have to be interfacing with the research labs, so I would guess your cousin is in. Then you'd need a few highly placed people in the government. There is probably a survivors' network, a 'support group,' for veterans of SDI, Freedom, NASP, and the X-33 running through half a dozen agencies and national laboratories. Throw in a few collaborators in Brazil and . . . Russia, right? . . . and there you have it.''

And there, indeed, he had it. Bennett and Jimmy were not on the Steering Committee. They did not have the vision. And there were others Steve had overlooked. Correy was not an obvious choice; and Wallace was in only because Wallace dreamed of dying on the moon, not because Odysseus Travel and Cruise Lines contributed to the project. As for Belinda and Mentor, Matthias did not realize even yet how deep and how far forward Mariesa's plans were laid. Steve had picked names from a sense of practicality—who had the glass and steel and so forth. Mariesa had picked them for their dedication, mostly. ''Very well, Steve. I shall present the matter to the remainder of the Steering Committee for their concurrence, but I do not see any insuperable obstacle to your joining us.''

Matthias sighed. He set the cup he had been rolling between his palms back upon the table. ''But you don't really trust me. You don't know where I'm coming from. Ah, never mind.'' He rolled his chair away from the table and rose, turning his back to them. He took a step toward the dry-erase board and stood there a moment, contemplating the scribbled figures: due dates, shipments, schedules. The he thrust his hands in his pockets and faced them. ''Am I moonstruck? No. Not like Keith, here, or Will. Do I think there is profit to be made by going into space? Maybe, some; probably most of it from dirtside spin-off. But if it starts raining soup, I want to have a damn big bucket in my hands. The risks are large and the payoff uncertain, but I've managed Thor for seven years now the careful, precise way—and done well, no one can fault my management!—but, damn all, Mariesa, sometimes a man needs to prove that he can risk something important on a dream.''

''Even if you don't share the dream?''

Matthias raised his eyebrows and shoulders. ''Maybe especially if I don't share it. Maybe I can see things your rose-colored glasses would filter out. Maybe your project needs a splash of realism in the face. Have you piecemealed the project and farmed out the pieces to working groups to PERT and write up procedures? Jesus, the documentation alone would be a tremendous project. Did you challenge your assumptions with a devil's advocate?'' He removed his hands from his pockets and placed them on the tabletop, leaning forward over his straining arms. "I want a piece of this; and I think you need me on board.''

"You have certainly found a novel selling pitch, Steve," Mariesa said. And who knew? Maybe he was right and she did need a doubting Thomas on the Steering Committee. Maybe she should have approached him earlier. They did have working groups, scores of them, within the corporation and as outside contractors, but maybe Steve could spot something they had missed.

Matthias stood upright, then turned and approached the large outside window. He turned aside one of the vertical slats that blocked the night outside. "Did I ever tell you why I left my first company?" Mariesa, puzzled at the change of topics, shook her head, forgetting that he was facing the window. But he must have seen her reflection in the blackened glass, or else he did not wait for her answer.

"I was corporate QA director. Everyone else on the CEO's staff was a vice-president, but you know how that goes. Quality is always one rung down the hierarchy. I had my QEs and techs analyzing the scrap and the downtime and the field complaints, looking for trends and significant concentrations." He turned from the window. "Pareto's Law. There are always a few problems that account for most of the headaches. I took the list to Kelly, the manufacturing VP, and do you know what he said to me?"

Mariesa said, "Tell me."

"He said, 'Steve, I intend to be the next president of this company. If these problems get solved, Johnson looks good to the Board and they keep him on until retirement. If that happens, Steve, then when I *do* become president, your ass is fired.' "

"And what did you do?"

"I quit. Period. It took me six months to find another position as good, but I didn't regret one minute of it."

Mariesa studied the challenge on Steve's face, not understanding it exactly, but knowing that there was something angry inside the man. To sacrifice his self-interest like that—she could check on the story, she had sources—was out of character for him. "Very well," she said, not taking her eyes off him, but hearing Keith's surprised breath. "You are 'in.' "

Later, in the helicopter, beating back to the north, McReynolds said, "There was a man who knows what side of his bread is buttered."

"He ought to," Mariesa answered. "He buttered it himself."

14.

Tropical Sunrise

It was Krasnarov. Mikhail Krasnarov, Dniepropetrovsk's favorite son; the lean, mean flying machine with the monk's hair-do and the Genghis Khan mustaches; picked by an American company to fly their Brazilian craft in its first test. And the only salve for his erstwhile colleague-competitors was that he wouldn't actually fly the sumbitch at all. . . .

At least, that was how Forrest Calhoun saw it, and Ned was inclined to see things the same way. Why, it wasn't as if he had lost out in competition for a genuine flight test. You couldn't even say exactly that Mike would be an aviator on this go-round. All he would do was sit at the simulator panel, wearing his gloves and VR helmet and conn the ever-loving, sweet, smooth-sailing bitch of a sky-hopper by ree-mote control.

It was just another goddamned training sim!

Senhor Machine would sit at a machine and run the machine. Oh, there was fine irony all around; and it meant that when the time came to pick a *real* pilot to conn the *real* flight, when it came time to put the iron between the legs and eat sky, why maybe they would be looking for entirely different qualities, like *cojones* the size of watermelons. Maybe being a machine, having oil for blood and current for thought, was all right *when the job was to run a remote*. But when the pedal hit the metal and it was your ass hanging out over the edge of the envelope, pushing it out and pulling it back just before it could sour, then you needed balls, not ball bearings.

The very idea—that nothing was final yet—was enough for Ned, and he walked large steps the night before the test launch, talking and drinking and drinking and driving, and driving and . . . up and down that miserable excuse for a road that was all they could fit on that miserable excuse for an island in the middle of a miserable excuse for an ocean. Why, he out-Forrested Forrest that night! And he must have out-Nedded Ned DuBois himself—which was damn hard to do—because when he left Claudio's after the talking and drinking, he didn't leave alone. And he and Bobbi McFeeley made their way atop Moro Pico and lay out on the blanket and watched the stars sparkle in the waters of St. Anthony's Bay.

Bobbi had a boyish body, flushed hot and red with burning alcohol; but a supple, hard body, and she knew how to pilot it. Oh Lord, did she know how to pilot it! She'd logged many an hour in the ole cockpit; behind the stick, and could bank and turn and pitch and yaw with precision and control. She was a laugher, Ned discovered. She laughed when he caressed her, she laughed when he went in, and laughed when she came. Not put-down laughs, not laughing *at* you, but happy laughs because, by damn, she was happy! Because, when push came to shove—and, Sweet Jesus, did push come to shove—it was herself she saw in that command chair riding a pillar of fire into the sky, not Senhor Machine. So maybe it was the liquor doing the laughing, but maybe it was the test pilot, just so shit-out, old-fashioned, Normal Rockwell happy at the way things had turned out that she had to ball the nearest stud because there wasn't anything else in the whole world that could come close to expressing just how happy she was. And wasn't it God's own justice that when she felt that way, Mrs.

DuBois's own little boy, Ned, was standing right there, ready, willing, and able.

So, Ned spent the night pushing the outside of the envelope, pushing it out and pulling it back in. Or maybe it was the other way around. But he achieved a communion with Bobbi that he had never achieved before, not with Gisela, not with Maria, not even with Betsy; and certainly not with a hundred or more of those lollipops that blossomed by magic in every bar and honky-tonk from Edwards to Cocoa Beach. Because only Bobbi knew what it meant to lay your hide on the line.

In the morning, when the sun smashed into them as only a sudden tropic dawn could, Ned and Bobbi dressed in total silence. The sun had baked all the alcohol from Ned's brain, leaving behind only a sharp, salt residue that itched the inside of his skull for hours.

He settled himself behind the wheel of the company humvee, one of the all-purpose vehicles that Daedalus kept at the training center for staff use, and waited while Bobbi zipped up the front of her coverall. When she finished, she tugged at the sleeves and crotch, then vaulted smooth-as-you-please over the humvee's door into the passenger's seat, where she cocked her boonie hat forward over her face and propped her feet on the dashboard, crossed at the ankles, as if she planned to nap on the drive back.

Ned shoved the gearshift into reverse and backed the vehicle into a turn. Then he took it down the steep, rocky track to sea level. Bobbi swayed with the bouncing and Ned admired the swaying. Damn! That had been worth the wait. He felt himself tingle. The evening had used him up; but it was morning now.

"It ain't gonna happen again," Bobbi said through her cap.

Ned spared a glance at her as he conned the humvee onto the level road, and jerked the lever hard when he shifted gears. Wham, whirr, thank you, sir. He gave her a lazy grin, wasted, with her hat covering her face like that. "As good as it was, it's worth thinking about."

Bobbi was silent for a moment. "Well, shit, don't you say the sweetest things? Why, you'll turn my li'l head."

The hell with it, then. Ned hated that was-it-good-for-you-too? crap anyway. People always lied about it, so you never really knew for sure. It had been good for *him*. That was all that mattered.

He tooled down the road, fast but not ripping it. Bouncing the humvee bounced his head and, as fragile as that swollen protuberance was this morning, was not to be undertaken lightly. He wondered how the others had celebrated. Gisela had been playing guitar, as usual, and a few of the clerks and technicians liked to hang out there after work, too, soaking up a little of that *potent astronaut presence*. And who would have believed that this barren piece of rock in the middle of a barren ocean, where you had to go a couple hundred miles just to reach nowhere, that this guano-shrouded hunk of pumice would grow its own bumper crop of eager lollipops? If the others had spent the night alone, it had been from choice.

As for Iron Mike . . . he had no doubt spent the evening interfacing.

"Once more," he said when the test-site buildings hove into view around the curve of Biboca Beach. "It'll happen once more." Bobbi lifted her boonie cap and gave him the eye.

"Yeah? And when'll that be?" Her voice implied a low temperature in a warm place.

Ned kept his own eye on the road. "When you come back, safe."

Bobbi's mouth quirked a little bit at the corner. Then she settled back and lowered her cap again. "Twice more," she said through the fabric.

Synchronicity, they called it. Two events unconnected by causal links, yet happening, significantly, at the same time. Fiction shunned it, but life ran on it. When Ned reached the astronauts' quarters, he found that a letter from Betsy had finally arrived in that morning's mail.

He pulled the envelope out of his mail slot and studied the familiar address. Ricardo, behind the front desk, asked, "Good news, *senhor*?" Ned slapped his left hand with the envelope and then shoved it back in the slot for later.

"Yeah. Great news."

He headed for the lounge, but stopped in the doorway. Krasnarov stood silhouetted against the backdrop of windows that overlooked the landing field, watching the tractor-tug guide the Plank from the Vehicle Prep Building to the launch pad. Forrest Calhoun stood a little behind and to the side. Krasnarov spoke in a whisper, but somehow the geometry of the window bay projected his voice to Ned. "But they will not let me fly it. . . ." Forrest said something low that Ned could not hear. He put an arm on the smaller man's shoulder and squeezed. Krasnarov's fingers tightened around the window frame and his arms trembled.

Ned backed out of the room without speaking. This was a day for miracles, all right. He'd gotten the best lay of his life *and* a letter from Betsy. *And* he'd seen Senhor Machine and the Cowboy do a fair imitation of sorrow and solace. Four miracles. Who said they came in threes?

Not until he was in his room did he remember that he had left Betsy's letter in his mail slot. But he was half undressed for his shower and there were a hundred launch details on his personal to-do list, so he figured to snatch it later on his way to the cafeteria.

Mariesa van Huyten lifted the last of the papers on the clipboard just as the jet began its descent to Fernando de Noronha. She looked up when the whine of the engines changed pitch and the cabin tilted forward. So soon? It seemed as if they had just left Fortaleza. She glanced out the side window of the executive jet and saw nothing but ocean. Engine trouble? Small, white lights, like flashbulbs, marked the chopping waves. She certainly hoped there was an island down there! A glance across the aisle at Steve and Belinda confirmed that. He was pointing to something off the starboard side and she was nodding. Neither of them seemed the slightest bit alarmed. Mariesa carefully straightened the papers on the clipboard, closed the cover, and placed it in the pocket of the seat in front of her. She settled back in the seat and gripped both armrests. It was funny—though she was not laughing—that the Moon Lady was afraid of flying.

* * *

When the jet's engines finally wound down to silence, Mariesa unbuckled her seatbelt and retrieved her clipboard. She lined up in the aisle behind Belinda and waited while Jorje Minamoto, the pilot, unsealed the door and lowered the built-in steps. She was tall enough that she had to bow her neck to avoid hitting her head on the ceiling. The clipboard with the test plan checklist was tucked under her arm.

"This is the big day," Steve Matthias said behind her.

"*A* big day." This test was just one more step. Not the first; not the last. The first steps had been taken long ago. She had arranged them the way a gardener arranged the seeds and cuttings in an ornamental garden: so they would bloom and beautify at the right times.

Then, why did she tremble?

With the door opened, the whine of the hydrogen compressor, muffled until now, filled the air like a banshee's wail. It was an eerie sound, half the screech of machinery, half the voice of a distant chorus. The high-pitched shriek of lox played counterpoint to it. Ninety Kelvin, not too far from nothing at all. At the top of the steps, Mariesa shaded her eyes and stared across the tarmac at the spaceship poised in the morning sunlight. The sunside of the craft gleamed a golden color. Hoarfrost coated the couplings where the fuel was being pumped in. *Fins*, she thought. *It really ought to have had fins.*

McReynolds and Gregorson met her at the bottom of the steps. They had flown down earlier with Wallace Coyle. Mariesa greeted them and they shook hands all around. The Werewolf wore the biggest grin Mariesa had ever seen, as if his face had been frozen at the moment of pure joy and anticipation. Keith twitched an eyebrow when he saw Steve Matthias among the passengers. He glanced at Mariesa, but said nothing.

"Are the others here?" Mariesa asked. Keith shook his head.

"Neither Heinz nor Vyachislav could come; but they will be watching by remote. Correy, too." McReynolds shrugged as if it did not matter and rubbed his chest with his fingertips.

"Let's get out of this wind. De Magalhães has refreshments and a briefing set up inside the main control building."

"Will," said Mariesa, as they started in that direction. "Are you sure the remote cannot be intercepted? The general and some of our other advisors will be watching, too; at the Pegasus test field near Phoenix. Dolores and John E. are hosting them."

Gregorson rumbled before he spoke. "The signal is protected by an RSA trapdoor encryption scheme, with dongles on both ends. It cannot be broken."

"As far as you know," said Steve Matthias, who had come up behind them.

The Werewolf gave him a what-the-hell-are-you-doing-here look. "True," he said, "but I know a *lot*."

The president of Daedalus huddled with his site manager and the chief engineer at the entrance to the main building. De Magalhães waved his hands in small, controlled movements when he spoke. The Indio engineer listened silently. They looked up when Mariesa and the others approached. "Is everything all right?" Mariesa asked them.

Pessoa exchanged glances with his site manager and engineer before answering. "There were some delays this morning, and we are behind schedule; but it is nothing serious. The test will proceed as planned."

"Yes," said de Magalhães. "A few telemetry problems. Nothing to do with the craft itself."

"Famous last words," Mariesa heard Steve mutter. She turned and leaned close to him.

"These people have been living with this project for months," she whispered. "Years, in some cases."

"All the more reason," he whispered back, "that they could overlook something."

Steve was right. Familiarity could breed carelessness; you started to see what you expected to see, not what was there. "João," she said. "Be extra careful on this test. I don't want anything to go wrong."

Pessoa nodded. The chief engineer simply looked at her, and Mariesa wondered if she had insulted him, somehow, by questioning his readiness. What did "extra" careful mean, anyway? "It will be done, Dona Mariesa," said de Magalhães. He waved to the engineer with his clipboard and the two of them turned and strode off toward the waiting ship, where the ground crew watched meters and checked fittings and did whatever it was that ground crews did.

Pessoa opened the door for them. "This way, Miss van Huyten. We have a briefing scheduled for you and your staff in the ready room."

Mariesa glanced upward toward the second-story balcony, but there was no one there.

No, she thought, they all had more important things to do today than watch the *touristas* arrive. She recalled Ned DuBois grinning down from the walkway that time she had come to the island. A glance at the briefing sheet reminded her that Ned was working the weather desk today. A bare-bones staff meant everyone had to do most everything.

Ned had a certain animal charm about him. The two times they had met, he had tried to hit on her; yet she had felt oddly *safe* standing with him on the observatory catwalk and wearing his flight jacket. It had been a long time since she had dallied with a man—a very long time, when she stopped to count the passage of it; and there had been a moment, standing on the platform, watching the stars and shivering in the night wind, when she had entertained the thought of accepting his offer. Oh, Mummy would have been mortified!

Discretion won, of course. Discretion always won. The man was an employee; and socially quite impossible as an escort. Ned DuBois on her social circuit would be like emery paste in a piston engine. Sometimes, at night, she regretted her decision to put first things first; but not often, and the ache was quickly rubbed away. There was too much at stake to risk it all on a schoolgirl infatuation with a walking bag of testosterone.

And then some times, some very rare times, she wondered if there might not be other treasures at stake, risked in other games, where she lost because she did not play.

* * *

Ned DuBois handled the briefing. He was dressed in a sharply creased pair of brown Daedalus coveralls. The Prometheus hand-and-fireball logo graced his left shoulder patch. His name was stitched across his left breast, the Daedalus emblem on his right. He winked at Mariesa when he strode to the front of the room, and Mariesa smiled back at him. It was impossible not to smile when Ned was in his charming mode. He shook hands with everyone.

When Steve asked Ned if he was flying the ship today, Ned's smile grew distant. "They're saving me for the real thing," he said.

They took their seats: Steve, on her left; Keith, on her right. João sat at the far end of the row; and Werewolf and the others took the second row. Mariesa opened her clipboard portfolio to the first page of the test protocols. A glance at her watch showed that everything was on time, until she remembered that she had not yet reset it. They *were* behind schedule. The accumulation of a host of minor delays. Well, better that they fall behind a little bit than to rush things. She flipped to the last page and checked the timing. As long as the delay was not too long. An American spy satellite was due to peak above the horizon at 8:07 local time.

Ned stood on a small platform with a pointer in his hand and explained, with a series of slides, what would happen today. The Plank had been configured with a standard crew module, but today's flight would be by remote. (Mariesa noticed a peculiar satisfaction draw across Ned's lips at that.) The flight would be a simple test-of-concept. The Plank would take off vertically, hover in place, translate sideways a few hundred meters, then land, also vertically.

Steve, who really should have kept silent, asked a question. "Didn't I see all this on TV a few years ago?"

DuBois tapped his pointer against his left palm. João turned to see who had spoken. This question had been answered long ago; but then, Steve was new to the team. "Ah, Steve," he said, as if that explained everything. João had not been happy about Matthias wriggling his way onto the Steering Committee.

"I can explain it, Joe," said the astronaut. He looked straight at Steve and said, with slow and measured words. "The VTOL concept was proofed by the DC-X tests. That happened in '93, '94. They used a one-third-scale model. They were halfway through development when the project was killed. The funding was appropriated, but the bureaucracy sat on the money and wouldn't release it. Our test is on a different design. It is a full scale, man-rated vehicle. You never assume that what worked in model test will work the same way in scale-up. Does that explain the purpose?"

Steve's face had gotten redder and redder while DuBois spoke. But, if he felt insulted by the astronaut's tone, he did not show it when he responded. "Thank you for clearing that up, Ned. As a new team member, I am not up to speed on all the background." He hesitated, then added with a grin, "All I know is what I read in the papers."

"Not your fault. Not even the media's fault. There are damn few reporters who know enough about aerospace to report on it accurately." He grinned. "Tell you what, Steve. After the briefing, I'll take you over to the canteen, buy you a beer, and explain why you should never let liberals, who don't want to 'spend money in outer space,' and conservatives, who don't want to spend money at all, get together with NASA bureaucrats, who don't want anyone trespassing on their turf."

Steve matched Ned, grin for grin. "Best offer I've had since landing," he responded. "I'll save any other questions for then, too. Don't want to waste time plowing ground the rest of you have been over already." Steve crossed his arms over his chest and settled back into his seat. He listened to the rest of the briefing in silence.

Mariesa did not want to be a pest, but it made no sense to come so far and not inspect the vessel personally. She knew nothing of cabling or piping or mechanics, of course; but she could at least admire it as a work of art. Ned took her out to the ready line along with Steve and a few others. This was Wallace Coyle's first sight of it up close and personal. He must have whistled, because Mariesa saw him purse his lips; but between the singing of the cryogenic fuel and the foam of the ear protection they wore, she could not hear him.

A half-dozen technicians serviced the Plank, a fraction of the swarm of attendants the Shuttle required. They ignored Mariesa while they went down their checklists. Maybe they didn't know who she was—the hard hat she wore was anonymous company orange—or maybe they knew and didn't care.

The Plank really was a thing of beauty, Mariesa decided. Sleek, austere, functional. She towered two hundred feet above them, gleaming in the midafternoon sunlight. Flared as a lifting body for cross-range capability, she seemed to be climbing even while sitting on the tarmac. *Maybe I should have put in for an NEA grant*, she thought. Surely this qualified as art.

Steve clapped his hand to his head to keep his hard hat from falling off while he looked up toward the nose. Walter reached a hand out to touch it; but they were standing outside the black-and-yellow line painted on the tarmac that marked forbidden territory, well out of reach. Suddenly reminded of the scene in *2001*, when the ape-men had jabbered and hopped around the monolith, Mariesa laughed. Between the noise and the distraction of the Plank, no one noticed, which was just as well.

Krasnarov and Volkov came around the gantry deep in conversation. Krasnarov paused and ran his hand down one of the landing legs, as if fondling his mistress, which, for all Mariesa knew, he was. According to his psych profile, Mikhail Krasnarov was a cold fish; yet his diamondlike concentration made him the ideal remote pilot, able to conn a ship, even in the distractions of the mission control room.

The two Russians saw them and Krasnarov pulled his hand quickly from the strut, as if his mistress's husband had come home unexpectedly. The screech of the compressors cut off at that moment and the technicians leapt to decouple the hosing: the oxygen near the base and the hydrogen up near the nose.

Steve stepped forward with hand outstretched. "You must be the pilot, Krasnarov." He spoke loudly to be heard through the hearing protection. Krasnarov, a puzzled smile, took the hand.

"The virtual pilot," said Ned with a grin, and Krasnarov gave him a guarded look.

So that's it, Mariesa thought.

"It is an adventure for the spirit," the Russian said. "So let a 'spirit' be the pilot." He touched the strut once more. "I have named her *Nesterov* after the first man to fly a loop-the-loop."

"Hey," said Ned. "That's the spirit. There will be plenty of manned test flights down the road. Cross-range testing. Low-and high-altitude throttling. All sorts of edges to this envelope."

The trucks were pulling away from *Nesterov.* "We should return to the control room," Mariesa said. "The launch is already three hours behind schedule."

"Da," said Krasnarov. "No more delays."

But there was one more delay.

Watching from the observation deck that overlooked mission control, Mariesa saw Bobbi McFeeley take off her headset and put it down on the console. "Telemetry's out again," she announced. The digital clock above the wall screen in the front of mission control froze at *T 00:20:17.* On the screen, a digitally enhanced image of the waiting spacecraft wafted steam from a vent high up on its side. *Now what?* she wondered.

A chorus of groans rippled across the room. Pessoa struck his palm with his fist, and glanced briefly her way. Then he turned and beckoned his operation chief with a curt, two-fingered wave. Pessoa and de Magalhães bent their heads together, but before they came to a resolution, the door to the telepresence chamber opened and Krasnarov emerged, unfastening his VR helmet. "I have lost contact with my controls," he announced.

"We know. We are sending a man out to check," the operations chief told him.

"No," said Krasnarov. "I will go. Volkov is at downrange observation. Have him meet me there." He tapped the helmet.

"I will know when downlink is restored, without need for translation to and from your technician."

Pessoa made a face, then swatted the back of his hand. "Yes. It will be faster. Go. Go."

Krasnarov hustled off with his helmet tucked under his arm. Steve leaned over to Mariesa. "Another delay?"

She sat rigid as a pole, holding herself so tight she practically trembled. "I like things to work the first time," she said.

"But it's better if they work right."

She had to will every muscle to relax, one by one. "Yes. Of course. That's the important thing."

"Don't worry. You've got good people here. They know what they're doing. They won't let you down."

"Do you know how to pray, Steve?"

"Only in Hebrew."

"That will do. That will do. You handle the Old Testament, Steve; I'll handle the New."

"Too bad we don't have a few Muslims here."

"Some of the ground crew come from Surinam. And there are probably a few Hindus among them, too. And Jose-Luis Tanaka, monitoring the fuel systems, is Buddhist."

"So, then all we need is a Taoist and a couple of Mormons and this launch is a done deal."

Mariesa laughed.

The minutes dragged by in silence. Mariesa noticed McReynolds nervously rubbing his chest with one hand while his other drummed on the armrest. Coyle kept sucking on his lower lip. Past Coyle, Belinda Karr sat expressionlessly.

Bobbi McFeeley suddenly gave a signal. "I've got telemetry!" she said. "Mike's on his way back."

"About time," said Ned DuBois from his console. "Goddamn weather's still holding; but we're losing daylight." He looked up and over the top of his console to where Pessoa stood with his hands clasped behind his back. Pessoa bit his lower lip.

"Resume the countdown," he said.

"Mike isn't back, yet," McFeeley pointed out. Pessoa checked his watch.

"He has time."

There were only a half-dozen people seated at the consoles, but then communications and computer technology had come a long way since Mercury-Apollo days. Even the Shuttles used outdated 1960s technology. The digital clock began clicking down again. On one of the TV screens Mariesa saw a humvee race away from the ship toward mission control.

When the clock reached *T 00:10:13*, Krasnarov broke into the room, his VR helmet already strapped back into place. He looked, thought Mariesa, like the monster in that movie, *The Fly*. How could Krasnarov see with that thing over his head? There must be a control of some sort that allowed him to switch between normal and virtual viewing.

Pessoa held the count until Krasnarov was plugged into the system. "Is everything all right, pilot?"

Krasnarov's voice over the speaker was clear. "Everything is A-OK," said the Russian. A-OK. Space flight might not be all that old, but it had evolved its own traditions already.

"Telemetry?" asked Pessoa.

"Go," said McFeeley.

"Go," said the disembodied Krasnarov.

"Fuel?"

"Go."

"Onboard computers?"

"Go," said the black astronaut, Calhoun.

"Weather?"

"Go," said Ned.

"Pilot communications?"

"*Poost vyezyot. Syeychás!*" the blond Russian astronaut at the communications panel said. "Go!" Levkin looked at her in surprise. " '*Vyezyot*'?"

Mariesa stood abruptly and headed for the door that led from the observation gallery to the viewing platform outside. The wide-screen monitor on the wall was not enough. This was something she had to see with her own eyes.

"Downrange? Downrange?"

"What? Oh, *da. Da.* Go," said Volkov's voice over the speaker.

Outside, gathering dusk had shrouded the field. The ship was a monument bathed in floodlights. The others had followed her out onto the balcony and lined up along the rail. Below, Mariesa saw a score of staff people gathered outside: commissary, maintenance, administration. No one wanted to stay indoors. "It's still light enough, isn't it?" said Wallace Coyle. A round, cheerful man, he had been more responsible than anyone else on the Steering Committee for the birth of Prometheus. *Forget the lobbying,* he had told her. *You'll never turn this administration around.* Now he stayed happily in the background, unable to contribute anything but his enthusiasm and concepts gleaned from thirty years of reading science-fiction and popular-science magazines.

"Yes," said Mariesa, "but they should have been landed already."

"Hey, Cheops's Law, remember? Nothing gets done on time." He leaned forward on the railing. "Imagine what it will look like when there are dozens of these ships, climbing and dropping."

Mariesa nodded silent assent. Taking things and people up; doing what needed to be done up there. Wallace was a science-fiction buff. It was the means, not the end that enthralled him. Yet, ironically enough, he was also one of the few in Prometheus that Mariesa had taken into her full confidence. One of the few who understood how vulnerable the Earth was. Behind her, she could hear the countdown through the open doorway. Ten seconds.

She held her breath as a flash of light ignited under *Nesterov.* Was it supposed to happen that way? The light blossomed into a ball of flame that spread its orange light across the field. And with it, racing behind a fraction of a second, a sound like a body punch. The entire field lit up. Tropical sunrise, thought Mariesa, like in that Kipling poem.

> *On the road to Mandalay*
> *Where the flyin' fishes play*
> *An' the dawn comes up like thunder outer China 'crost*
> *the Bay.*

Bright clouds billowed from the base of the craft. The windows behind her hummed and the railing vibrated with the sound. Slowly *Nesterov* climbed on a column of flame and the noise rose to a great bone-shaking, subsonic roar, as if God Himself had hollered defiance.

"It's beautiful," said Mariesa.

"Behold," said Wallace Coyle as he watched the vessel rise, "the Lord preceded them in the daytime as a column of cloud; and at night, as a column of fire."

Nesterov reached a height of several hundred feet and stopped. It hung there "way up in the middle of the air" while the wind of its exhaust swirled across the landing field. And then, oh, so slowly, so majestically, it slid sideways. Small bright puffs of gas from side ports guided it. From inside the building she heard Pessoa say, "Now bring her to a halt," and Volkovna relayed the message in Russian, because who wanted to risk a misunderstanding between a Brazilian and a Russian jabbering to each other in English?

Outside, high up in the dusky sky, the floating titan slowed to a halt. It hovered there, flames pouring from its engines. "Now the hard part," Keith whispered on her right.

Hard? The damn thing had floated in the sky! It had danced in the air!

A shout from inside the control room brought her around. Footsteps rang and Ned DuBois came out onto the catwalk. The cord of his headset dangled on his chest; and he paused and took one deep breath. "We lost telemetry again," he said. "The VR controls are blind."

Her heart froze. "The automatic landing sequence?"

"No response." DuBois pushed past them to the rail, where he stood with his fists wrapped tight around the metal. "We're going to lose her," he said. "Oh, God! We're going to lose her."

Wallace said, "Damn," and banged his fist on the rail.

Steve Matthias simply folded his arms and watched impassively from a position a few steps behind the others lining the rail.

Nesterov hovered a few moments longer, then began a slow

descent. Mariesa held her breath. Every second was a lifetime; but the ship slid smoothly down a pole of invisible fire. When the fire touched the ground, it became a flaring pedestal that bloomed underneath the ship like a cushioning pillow of light.

Ned sucked in his breath. "I'll be damned," he said softly. Then, more loudly, "I will be God-damned." He shook his fist at the distant craft. "Krasnarov, you son of a bitch! You son. Of. A. Bitch!"

Steve Matthias unfolded his arms and stepped closer. "What's going on?" he asked.

DuBois whirled around and stabbed an arm toward the gently landing Plank. "He's on board! That sneaking whore of a Russian! He took it up himself."

Keith McReynolds blinked in confusion. "Then . . . who is in the VR relay booth?"

"Volkov," said DuBois, "or I'll wear my guts for garters."

Mariesa stared at the craft until the ball of light beneath it winked out and the darkness of night returned. A *man* had sneaked aboard that thing, that untested, untried experimental craft, and bet his *life* against it. It might have exploded; it might have smashed into rubble on the pavement. And Krasnarov had *lied* his way aboard.

"Why?" asked Steve.

"That bastard!" said DuBois.

"Yes, why?" Mariesa's voice was calm and steady. It was a request for information, not Steven's bewildered question.

"Why?" drawled a new voice. "Because ole Mikey must have realized the telemetry was unreliable." Calhoun, the black astronaut, leaned against the doorway. "He was feeling mighty punk about not testing it himself; and I can't say I blamed him. Hell, it's how I would've felt in his place. They are fit to be tied in there. Levkin is cussing in that heathen tongue of his; and Bobbi is crying. So's Katyushka, but I think she must have been in on it. On comm? Sure, she had to be. And she said something during the ten-second hold that clued Levkin in."

"What did you mean," asked Mariesa, "about the telemetry?"

"He surely figured João would launch the bird, come hell or high water, once the ship was on-line again. With you here, there was a lot of pressure for things to go off on schedule; and he was way behind. So, Senhor Machine, he must've added two and two and asked himself what would happen if he lost VR contact during the flight. Lose the Plank, for sure, because the automatics use the same telemetry. The onboard computer would never hear the abort order. Oh, nobody would blame *him*, but no way would he get another flight. We all know how that works, don't we? Failure is an orphan, right?"

"He may not get another flight, anyway," said Mariesa icily.

"Ma'am . . ." Calhoun stood erect. He was a short man, like most of the astronauts, yet he seemed tall. "Lady, that Russian cowboy just saved your spaceship. João should've scrubbed the launch the second time the telemetry scrambled. I know that. *You* know that. Hell, even he knows that. You should see him in there . . ." He turned to Steve Matthias. "You asked why Mike climbed into that airchine? I'll tell you why. *Because that is what he does.*"

"Give the bastard credit for one thing," DuBois said.

"What is that?" asked Mariesa.

"Son of a bitch followed the flight profile to the letter."

Calhoun laughed a great booming laugh. "Course he did, son. He's a professional."

DuBois shoved his hands in his pockets. He aimed a desultory kick at the railing strut. "So. You know what I'm going to do when he climbs out of that thing?"

Calhoun gave him a cock-eyed smile. "No, what's that?"

"First, I'm going to punch his face for stealing the first flight."

"And then?"

"Then I'm going to kiss that hairy-nosed bastard right on the lips. Because he is fucking beautiful."

Calhoun laughed. "Yeah. He's *número uno*, now, ain't he, Ned? Not you, not me, not any of the others can ever change that."

The two pilots laughed and disappeared back inside mission

control. Steve shook his head. "I don't get it. They treat it like a big joke."

"No," said Mariesa. "How could you get it? How could I? Their daily job is to risk their lives. Some of them wind up as heroes; and some wind up as holes in the high desert. The odds of survival are better in combat. They seat themselves behind the controls of a new design and they take it up a little higher, or they turn it a little tighter, or they push it a little faster, *just to see if it falls apart around them.* Steve, some of those experimental planes have crashed on takeoff. Could you live with that fear? I could not. So I will not question too closely the sort of defenses they have built for themselves."

"Then, you'll let it go? There won't be an investigation?"

Mariesa looked up at the sky shrouded now with stars. "There is a great deal to answer for. Krasnarov. Mendoza. Will Gregorson—the telemetry was his system. João, for proceeding with the launch. Even I will have to answer, to God, if there is no one else. Had I not been here watching, I am sure that João would have postponed the test. And now we must all consider how our plans will change." She pointed to the sky.

Steve followed her outstretched finger to a dim star drifting slowly toward the northern horizon. "That's a spysat, Steve. A reconnaissance satellite. The launch has delayed too long, and that beautiful ball of flame we saw is photographed, digitized and on its way to Washington by now."

"Well, what does . . . ?"

"Whom the gods notice," said Mariesa van Huyten, "they destroy."

INTERLUDE:

What I Did on My Summer Vacation

Azim did not know what sort of reaction he would get from Zipper and Jo-jo, so he didn't tell them; but they found out anyway.

"What you mean you got a job?" asked Zipper. He tossed a rock into the canal and watched the ripples in the scum. The old canal still held water along the stretch through North Orange, between the Morris Lock and the Number 13 Lock. Someone had the notion once of building a park along the towpath and adjoining land. Someone stupid. Man cut down the weeds, fixed the locks, filled the canal bed with water, but there wasn't no one crazy enough to come to Eastport to picnic, so now it was just a place for the homies to hang out. The water had gone bad and the weeds had grown back and the locks were coated with graffiti. A rank, fetid smell permeated the area. A perfect place to be when you didn't have to be no place.

"It's what I said, Zip. Leopard got me a job for the summer."

"Yeah, doing what?"

The chirruping of the cicadas swelled momentarily, as if every bug along the towpath had decided to shout together. Why did they do that sometimes? Azim wondered. Was it the heat? "Freight docks down by Christopher Shipping. Pay five-fifty an hour."

"Working for the white man," said Zipper.

"My boss, he be a brother."

"Then, *his* boss be white. Higher up you go, the whiter they get."

"Yeah," said Azim. "But it pays, so what do I care?"

"Stork, he makes five-fifty a *day,* but none of it clinks. It's all green."

Azim waved a hand at the canal water. "So's that. You want to drink it?"

"Stork gots him a fine car and a dozen bitches who ball him anytime he want."

"Now who be working for the white man?"

Zipper scowled and pushed Azim in the chest. "Stork work for himself."

Azim pushed him back. "Every snort he sell make the ice people high. They love it, we sniff our brains out. Where you think shit comes from? Or don't you listen none to—"

"To Jessie Jackoff? Brother Fairycon? Man, they ain't *down* here. They on TV. So what do they know?"

"Stork be dead before he twenty. The product don't get him, the Nation will."

"We all be dead. So why not live? Moving boxes around, that's stupid."

Jo-jo had been prodding with a branch at an old trunk tire, half submerged in the water. When he lifted it up, it was coated with the green scum, and streamers like collard greens hung off it, dripping water. The branch broke and the tire fell into the water, splashing them all. Azim and Zipper cussed him good.

Maybe it *was* stupid, Azim thought. Maybe it was a sad-ass way to spend the summer, and old Mr. Simpson was the saddest ass of all. Old man had shown him what to do. It wasn't hard. You took pallets off the truck with a handcart;

you checked everything against the bill of . . . of lading. It was mostly lifting and pulling, except adding up the numbers, which was the hard part. "I promised Leopard," he said.

"Leopard. Shit," said Zipper.

"Hey," said Azim, hoping to smooth things over with the Zipman. "There's s'posed to be a meteor shower tonight. You wanta grab some bitches and we can come out here and watch?"

But Zipper only stared at him. "Man, I don't know you no more." He turned and started to walk away. Jo-jo began bouncing on the balls of his feet.

"Azim," said Jo-jo in an agitated voice, "why you and Zipper fight?" Jo-jo had not understood the argument, Azim realized. Jo-jo did not understand much of anything. Sometimes, Azim thought the boy should be in a different school, with different kinds of teachers, except nobody really cared enough. And maybe nobody even saw it. Just another dumb nigger; maybe a little dumber than most. Azim felt a sudden rush of tenderness and grabbed Jo-jo around the shoulders and squeezed.

"Hey!" Jo-jo laughed and swatted Azim. "You queer, or something?" He placed both hands flat on Azim's chest and gave a playful shove. Up above, on the road on the other side of the canal, Azim heard a car horn honk and Zipper's curse. "Fucking gooks!"

Azim and Jo-jo hung around the locks a while longer, but it wasn't much fun without Zipper, and the warm, putrid odor of the water began to bother Azim; so after a while they headed back to the Eastport tracts, across the plank that someone had laid across the crawling water, and up the steep embankment to the state road. A fat woman pushed a shopping cart half-full of groceries along the side of the road. When she saw Azim and Jo-jo, she shook her fist.

"You kids stay out of there," she shouted. "Or I'll call the police on you!"

"Yeah, right, Mama," he said, flipping her the bird. Jo-jo laughed and said, "Yeah, right."

The woman said, "Don't you go sassing me, boy." But

Azim was already ignoring her. She could call, but the pigs never came. Too busy protecting white folks on the west side; too busy eating donuts where they don't get shot at. Wasn't nobody going to take care of things on *this* side of town, 'less you took care of them yourself.

He dropped Jo-jo off at his house: a clapboard bungalow with a yard that made the canal look well kept. Most of a car sat on blocks along the curb. The rotty in the yard barked at them and strained at his chain. Azim made sure Jo-jo got into his house okay. He waited until he saw a light go on; then he walked down to the corner and turned left onto Clay Street.

The houses along Clay were duplexes, about sixty/forty kept up to falling apart. Rotted porch boards, sagging roofs, plywood for windows. "You're never too poor to tidy up," his mama always sniffed. But half the fallen-down houses were empty; nobody in them, poor or not. The landlords had walked away and now the city owned them; and the city wouldn't sell 'em and the city wouldn't rent 'em and the city wouldn't tear 'em down. City was a worse landlord than any tight-assed, down-your-nose ice man, for all that the mayor was a brother. Brother lite. The man had too much cream in his coffee to suit Azim.

People on Clay Street moved out of his way. The little kids ducked; and even the grown-ups stepped aside. The mamas on their front stoops watched him as he walked by. He could feel their eyes on his back after he passed. Yeah, they knew he was bad. They knew he was a Lord. You didn't see people move aside for Lloyd Simpson, Mr. Loading Dock Supervisor. Mr. Simpson had treated Azim to lunch at the East Side Diner and all you heard was "Hey, Lloyd" and "How's it going, man" all the way down the street. No fear; no respect.

But what else was there, you grew up in Eastport? You joined a gang because you joined a gang. Even the white trash near the locks had a gang—fucking skinheads. And the Koreans and Vietnamese on the other side of Old Cornwall Road. It was what it was. You were a member, or you were nothing. Like his mama. Like his dad, whoever that had been.

The light was on in the living room. Mama always left the

light on. Then . . . Yeah, there she was, fast asleep in the chair with the TV glowing, still wearing her uniform. Maid in the Shade Cleaning Service. Shit. Spend your life cleaning up after ice people, and even after dots and gooks and, worst of all, toms. Azim went into the kitchen and made himself a sandwich by the light of the open refrigerator. He held it in one hand, took a bite; then, a can of soda in the other hand, he headed for his room.

In the hallway, he stopped, as he always did, by the portrait photo mama got at Sears so long ago. The whole family was there, all his brothers and sisters, surrounding Mama with grins, dressed up and shiny. Had it been a cleaner world back then? Azim didn't remember. He was the little one, on Mama's lap. He didn't know shit back then. But Bob, so serious standing there with one hand on Mama's shoulder, he was a tech sergeant in the Air Force now; and Titania had taken data processing at the trade school and moved to Boston; and Justin was an artist in the East Village. None of that mattered. They had escaped, and Azim didn't blame them that they hardly ever came back. Someday Azim would leave Eastport, too.

A car drove slowly down Clay Street, its stereo thumping out a rhythm that made the windows buzz. Shouts and the sound of a bottle thrown from the car smashing on the paving stones. Yeah, Azim told the smiles in the photographs, it's because people like you left that only people like that are left.

The other two smiles, Kindy and Hassan, only a little bigger than the baby—Hassan was holding Mama's skirt so he wouldn't fall—they would never leave Eastport. They would stay long after everyone else was gone, inseparably side by side, four blocks north and two blocks west and six feet down.

"The job is really quite tedious," the face on the other side of the desk explained. "You will have to learn both C plus plus and Pascal and check hundreds of lines of game code for grammar and protocol errors." The face looked uncertain. "I was led to believe you would be older."

"When do I start?" asked Jimmy Poole.

* * *

Baba smiled and nearly bowed as he counted out the woman's change. The woman, of course, counted it again before, satisfied that the *dot-head* hadn't cheated her, she hefted her grocery bags and left. The door chimed after her.

"But it's a good job, Baba," Tani said from the stockroom, once the woman had left and they were alone again in the store. THE store. Pandya's In-and-Out. Baba's pride and joy. A sign that the American Dream still worked, if *you* worked. And worked. Tani found the carton her father had asked for and pulled it from the shelf. It was heavy and she set it down quickly on the floor and pushed it out into the store proper with her foot.

Her father shook his head. "I need you here."

"Only sometimes. In the evenings." During the day, people did their regular shopping at the supermarkets. It was for the emergency runs, when they were short one little item, or to pick up some odds and ends, or, during the school year, for the kids just to hang out, that they came to the convenience store, where they could complain about the prices and never mind that part of what they paid for was the convenience itself: the long hours and the short stock levels of a hundred items that you ran out of and didn't feel like driving all the way down Maple Grove Avenue to a supermarket the size of a convention center. "You can give Meat and some of the other kids more hours."

" 'Meat.' " Baba shook his head in perplexity. "The Tucker boy does cleanup and stocking. I do not want him behind the register."

"Oh, Baba, he's honest . . ."

"Then he should *look* honest."

Tani pushed the shipping carton to the center aisle, vegetable canned goods. "That's not the real reason you want me."

Her father leaned his arms across the counter and looked down the aisle at her. "What is the real reason, child?"

"It's you would have to *pay* Meat and the others. Me, you get to work for free."

"Family members," Baba explained again. "You are part

of the ownership." He said that so proudly, as if owning a convenience store in a strip mall on a corner of North Orange were as grand an accomplishment as Shah Jahan building the Taj Mahal. Though, come to think of it, that had been a tomb, too. "After I pay my suppliers, and the rent, and the gas and electric, and the government takes most of what is left . . . on that remnant, must I support my family." Baba spread his hands, "I cannot afford too many expenses. Perhaps later, when the business grows . . ."

He still believed that when Tani was older, she would want to take over the store; that the great Pandya's In-and-Out would pass onward from generation to generation. But Tani knew she would go positively mad behind the counter, her mind whirling and whirling and finding no purchase on any matter weighty enough to engage it. "The job with Mentor Institute pays a salary," she said, "for helping to write training materials. I could give you the money I earn. Then you could pay Meat to work longer hours."

"The Tucker boy is a good worker," Baba admitted, "but he is never here on time."

Tani signed. She could see no way out. It was as if her father had locked the doors of the store so that she could not escape. "The Mentor job is during the day," she said. "They asked me and Jenny Ribbon and Karen Chong. It's only a twenty-hour week. So . . ." She fumbled at her belt for the slitter and pulled it from its holster. A flick of the thumb and the blade emerged. "So," she said, "what I could do is I could work during the day for Mentor and then come here in the evening for the rush times." It was a razor. It would slice through skin and flesh and veins as easily as through tape and cardboard and string.

Baba looked at her sadly. "But then you will have no time for play."

Tani slit the carton open and began pulling cans out and stacking them on the shelf. "I never have had the time for that."

* * *

"A good poet," shrieked Howie Karp, perched behind Styx on the side tube of the raft, "can compose a poem on demand at any time."

The raft fell into a hole in the river—how can a liquid have a hole in it? but it did, it did!—and drenched Styx with icy water. Icy water in the summertime? Oh, she was in a different world, all right. No doubt about it. "I know that I will never miss," she shouted over the crashing rapids, "Another river quite like this."

Moira Thomas, straddling the tube on the other side of the raft, whooped as the rubber vessel bucked and arched. A small girl, she looked lost in her huge orange life vest. "It was a dark and stormy river . . ." she said. Moira was at the Muses School studying the novel. Like most of the others, she attended a private Mentor practice. They didn't look down on Styx because she came from a public school. Not exactly. Not twice.

They rounded a bend in the river and the water settled down to a gentle boil. The guide put the raft into a sharp turn and for a while they floated backward with the tired current. "That's what we just came through," he announced.

There were oohs and aahs from the other kids. Sheer walls bare of vegetation choked the river. The spray boiled and leaped forth from the narrow cleft like water from a sprung pipe. High up in the air beyond, the ghostly peaks of the Continental Divide hovered like a distant mirage. Today, they seemed sketchy as if the artist had abandoned the drawing undone. A trick of the atmosphere. At other times, the peaks stood forth clear and massive, every detail precise, as if, under cover of the night, they had marched forth and camped in the back of the lodge where the Muses School met.

Styx contemplated the vision in silence. Oohing and aahing was for Western geeks. But, oh, the sight tugged at her throat. Nothing you could see from North Orange was worth the seeing quite like this. There was an image niggling in the back of her mind. Massive ghosts. Floating mountains. But the image would not come clear. She wished there were a way to snag some vodka. Sometimes, when an image was embedded in her mind like that, like a fossil in the dusty rocks, the acid wash of the vodka could dissolve the imprisoning matrix and free it.

"It was the best of streams; it was the worst of streams," said Nellie Hatch.

"I can't believe we came through that," said Howie, falling out of the literary mode. Unless he was pastiching some science-fiction story. Genre stories often began scenes with lines of dialogue. Howie was into sci-fi. Half the kids at the school were. Captain Planet stuff.

"Oh, that's only the Devil's Cauldron," their guide said. "That's nothing."

"Nothing to you." "Yeah, you do this every day." "Sure, you've even been out in space. . . ."

Out in space . . . Tanned, squint-eyed, clad in beat-up old sneakers and a baseball cap that read *STS Atlantis*, Jerry Godlaw still walked with the limp he had gotten on that Shuttle's famous last flight. Now he sat in the back of a rubber raft and ferried kids and tenderfeet down a stretch of mountain river. Styx wondered what went through the man's mind when at night he looked up through a crystalline sky at a realm from which he was forever barred. "On the Beach," she had named the poem, as yet uncomposed. How could she hope to capture such an emotion, when she had never even been outside Wessex County before? Would she feel the same way if she were barred from returning to this magical land two miles up in the sky?

No, she decided. It was a lovely place. The deer and elk and the Dall sheep and the bald eagles . . . the soaring peaks and the clouds so close you could touch them . . . and the men and women who lived here, so different form the mewling masses in the concrete and asphalt world she had left . . . She would miss it, but it would not break her heart to leave. Because . . .

The river entered a lazy stretch, meandering through tall cattails and meadow grasses. Styx lay back on the tube, nearly in Howie's lap, and basked in the searing high-altitude sun. Her jeans and T-shirt, soaked by the waters of the high-up

Colorado River, clung to her in a cold embrace. Here was another mystery: how could you be both hot and cold at the same time? Howie said to her, "Lean back just a little bit farther."

Right in his lap. Yeah. The little weenie wanted some action. Someone had stuffed his head with fantasies of summer romances and he had fixated on Styx as the object of his ephemeral desire. (That was a good image, too, she thought. An object of ephemeral desire.) He hadn't touched her. Styx thought he was afraid of her. All the Western kids were—a "chog" from Jersey—as if they expected her to grow fangs. But Howie was constantly trying to convince *her* to touch *him*. She would sooner have touched what blorped out of a stuck drainpipe.

"You wouldn't like it, Howie," she said up to his face. "I got teeth. And I bite."

His grin became fixed and he shifted his paddle to a more defensive position. Styx ignored him and watched the lone hawk hovering and circling in the sky far above. The windhover . . . This summer she had been exposed to a great many things, and the best of them were the poets of whom she had never heard. She still was not sure but that a poem in English ought to rhyme. What made a poem was pattern in the sounds of words, not the delicacy of the emotions expressed. A poem could be bawdy and robust as easily as fragile and beautiful. But perhaps a rhyme and a thumping meter were not the only ways.

"Lift your paddles," Godlaw ordered. "And we'll stroke out into midcurrent."

Styx did a sit-up and repositioned herself on the raft. It was a little like riding a horse, actually. A long, oval, rubber horse, with five kids on each side and the supplies in the flat part between. Styx was in the front position on the right, as much because the others did not want her behind them as because Styx was *always* in the front. She saw that the raft had turned wide around a bend in the river and was approaching the shore. They pulled on their paddles against the sluggish water and Styx noticed that the current had picked up a little when they reached the center of the stream. Up ahead, twin buttes rose shear from the alpine meadow. The river headed toward the narrow gap between them.

Nellie Hatch, the lead paddle on the left side, raised her blade from the water and cocked her head. "What is that roaring sound?" she said.

"Yes, sir," said Jerry Godlaw, turning the rudder, keeping them centered in the current. "The Devil's Cauldron, that was nothing."

After they had emerged from the rapids—it was a damned waterfall, Styx insisted—the consensus was that he was right. A camera crew had been set up on a ledge on the cliffside and had taken their picture as they came through the flume, hanging right to the ropes, paddles lifted on high. If they clicked the shutter at just the right moment, Styx thought in that instant of pure weightlessness when she lost her grip on the raft, they would catch her in midair, paddle flying loose, arching forward like a dolphin. She did not even have time to shriek and then she was in the water ahead of the raft, swirling and bouncing with the lunatic stream.

The water was numbing cold, but after the first, intense shock of immersion, she felt it not at all. Her life vest kept her afloat, but the rapids bounced her around like a cork. One whorl brought her hard against a rock, but in the cold she felt nothing. Coming around, she saw the frightened faces of nine kids, themselves clinging for dear life to the ropes, staring at her in terror. *What do they know?* thought Styx. *They would never have organized this outing if there were any* real *danger*.

For assurance, she sought out Jerry's eyes when chance and the current brought her around again. He was watching her and watching the current and watching his other charges, but watching her most of all. It was only after glimpsing Jerry's intense concentration that Styx began to worry. His concern worried her more than the others' panic, because they didn't know what was going on and he did. *Stay calm. Watch where the water takes you. Use your hands and feet. Panic is the enemy, not the river.* They would not have given a briefing on what to do if the occasional tourist did not get tossed from the raft.

The rapids emptied into a pool as the river opened up past the buttes. The groping hands of the river ceased to fondle her and she drifted in the steady current. The raft, paddles lifting and pulling like a Roman galley at ramming speed, closed the distance rapidly. Styx could imagine Jerry, sitting in the guide's seat at the rear of the raft, beating on the great drum and cracking the whip over the sweating slaves.

Which is why, when they closed on her, she was laughing and said, "What kept you?"

Jerry wrapped her warm in blankets from the raft's locker. When they stopped for lunch on a small sand-spit of an island—snacking on gorp, which tasted as good as it sounded, and on rattlesnake meat, which Styx relished just so she could tell the others back at Witherspoon that she had eaten it—he took her aside and with one hand on her shoulder said, very seriously, "Now you know what it feels like."

She asked him what he meant, but he just smiled and shook his head and walked away to join the others. His limp seemed more pronounced than before.

While they were coming down the rapids, Jerry's smile had been frozen on his face, his lips pulled back with a terrible determination. This was the world he had chosen, not as good as the one from which his injury had barred him, but one with its own challenges to overcome. He warmed himself by the bonfire that the rafting company kept on the island for the dozen or so rafts that made the trip each day. And—all of a sudden—Styx knew that what Jerry missed most of all being stranded on the Earth was the danger. That electric moment when you knew you had it to do. Was that stupy, or what? Someday, she promised herself, she would challenge a river where the commercial traffic was not quite so heavy, one which was not quite so domestic as this one. Just to feel that lightning run through her again.

The distant hawk screeched in the sky and plummeted toward the earth. Below, something small and furry died.

She would not miss this world because there were other worlds, as different from this as this was from the Locks. Worlds of prairies, of bayous, of gull-shrieking bays. The sun-drenched palms of lotus land; the cathedral forests of the great Cascades. She would see them all. She would be damned if she let them put her back in her box. She would see all the world there was.

And other worlds, too, if Mariesa van Huyten could be believed.

Chase took the gauge block from its plush-lined case and set it in the fixture, lining it up carefully against the stop pins. When he was satisfied, he pressed the READ button and the digital display lit up: 2.305. There was a fourth decimal place, too, but it kept changing. Ed had told him to ignore it when it did that. We can't machine things that finely anyway on this jig, the old man had said. Let the precision shop worry about the more exotic decimal places.

Chase wrote the result in the calibration log book, then he selected a second gauge block to check the other end of the measurement range. It wasn't a whole lot different from working down at Patel's transmission shop. Machines demanded careful measurement. If you didn't do things right, they cut you no slack. Yet, when everything worked, when two parts you had machined fit together perfectly the first try, there was no feeling like it.

So when he had seen the posting for a machinist's apprentice on the school's Summer Job board, Chase had gone the same day to deYoung's office and filled out the card; and Dad had been sober and signed his permission. Only after cashing his first paycheck did Chase realize that it was more than Dad brought home. Not sure how the old man would react to that— it could be jealousy; it could be he'd wheedle to get *him* a job there, too—Chase had kept only enough to cover what he wanted to do and slipped the rest to Mom and hoped she would hide it well enough that Dad would not find it. Whatever else Mom might spend it on, it would not gurgle out the neck of a bottle.

The jig was nearly complete, now. Chase ran a feeler gauge between two surfaces. It needed only a few other parts mated. Chase knew he could do it. Ed had taught him to read drawings; but it hadn't been hard. The blue lines had leapt from the page straight into his mind. He could finish the jig, but Ed had said to wait until he got back. *So what do I do now? Steal a smoke?*

"Hey, son, is Ed Hamilton around?"

Chase turned to see who had come into the machinists' cage. Only authorized personnel were supposed to do that, but the man who was peering at the half-finished part in the machine seemed the sort who would authorize himself. "He went over to the parts crib," Chase said, wiping his hands on a rag. "He'll be back in a while. You shouldn't touch that."

The man straightened and looked at him. A short man, hazel-eyed, with light hair cut off short. He leaned an elbow against the machine. "Who are you?" he asked.

"I'm Mr. Hamilton's assistant."

"Are you?" The man seemed amused, which irritated Chase. "My part's not done," he added, jerking his thumb at the machine.

Your part. Right. "You from Daedalus? The shop order says Daedalus Aircraft in Brazil." The guy didn't talk like a spic, but you never could tell.

"Yeah, I'm from Daedalus; and I'm supposed to do a little source inspection while I'm here." He picked up the router sheets and flipped through them. "This insect is supposed to have a centerless grind and another eighth taken off the small diameter."

"What else did you teach her?"

"Hmm?" The stranger hung the router back on the hook and turned to Chase. "Teach who?"

"Your grandmother, after you taught her to suck eggs."

The man laughed. "You're feisty, son."

"Don't call me 'son' when I'm not."

"Everyone is someone's son."

"Yeah, like everyone has an asshole. Doesn't mean I gotta like it."

The other man raised his eyebrows. "I like your style, kid." He wiped his hand on his pants leg and stuck it out. "Name's Ned DuBois, but you can call me 'sir.' "

Chase snorted, but shook the proffered hand. "Chase Coughlin," he said. "The part'll be done by three, as soon as we get the jig finished and mounted." Chase pointed over his shoulder to the tooling assembly area.

"So, why isn't it finished?"

"Because Ed told me to wait for him to get back."

DuBois nodded. "I get it. You're summer help, not a regular machinist."

"Maybe I am, but I could put that jig together blindfolded. Sir."

"Is that so? Tell you what, kid. You put that puppy together—never mind the blindfold, we'll chalk the brag up to incipient Calhoun-itis—and if Ed gives it his okay when he gets back, I'll buy you both dinner when the shift ends. Him for being a good teacher, you for having enough brains to listen. Me, because I'm hungry and on an expense account."

"And if he doesn't okay it?"

"Why, then, you get to take the jig apart and put it back together right while Ed watches and tells you what a moron you are."

Chase looked at the man for a moment, then he stuffed the rag back into his back pocket. "Watch," he said.

DuBois leaned against the wire cage that cordoned off the machine shop. "Oh, I'll watch, never fear. It's my life we're talking about."

Chase had picked up a dowel pin. He paused before inserting it and looked at DuBois. "Daedalus must have some damned strict quality control. That's what I call enforcement."

DuBois grinned. "It's not that, son—Sorry, it's a habit of speech I picked up from a friend of mine."

"You have a friend?"

"I pay him." DuBois shook his head. "Hazard pay, at that. But, look, Chase—was that right? 'Chase'? Do you know what happens when you are all finished miking clearances to the nearest thousandth, and checking finishes to microinches, and calipering all those diameters?"

"No, what?"

"Why, I get to put on a big, fat glove and try to grab ahold of it in one snatch; and if I can't do that, then you have just made one fancy paperweight."

"Well, then," said Chase, shoving the dowel pin home, "I sure hope you haven't been drinking when you grab for it."

DuBois laughed. "Chase, if the day ever comes when I have to snatch that handle for real, I'll be spinning and yawing so bad that a bottle of Kentucky sippin' whiskey would probably make a damn fine simulation."

Chase rummaged in the fittings drawer for a hex bolt and stuck it in the business end of a driver. He pulled the trigger and the bolt whirred home, tight. He checked the tightness with a torque wrench. "You're a pilot," he said. "What do you fly?"

DuBois gave him a lazy grin. "Anything with wings and a few things without."

"You're a test pilot." This time DuBois just nodded. Chase said, "Cool," and bent again over the jig.

"You don't sound too impressed, kid."

"Should I be?"

DuBois laughed. "I don't know about you, but I sure am. You play your cards right, kid, and someday you may get to grab at handles with a big, awkward glove on your hand."

"Well," said Chase as he put his tools down and wiped his hands again on the rag in his back pocket. "I can hardly wait."

"Kid," said DuBois, "I'll buy you that dinner anyway. And I hope someday they tell you what the hell it is you've helped build."

Hobie shifted his feet and waited for Dr. Venable to notice him; but the principal researcher continued to scratch away at the notebook in front of him. Once, he picked up a computer printout and studied it, ran a finger down a column of figures and copied one into the book. This could go on a long time, thought Hobie, and accomplish nothing. So he coughed.

Dr. Venable sighed and raised his head. "What is it, boy?"

Dr. Venable was not deliberately offensive. It was just something that came to him naturally. He spent so much of his life inside his own head that he had no clue how to connect to anything outside it. When Dr. Venable spoke, his words were rude and blunt, as if he resented the activity and spent as little time as possible choosing his words. At least, that was how Dr. Hughes had explained things, and Dr. Hughes was an all-right guy. Hobie had learned to put up with it once he saw that everyone else in the lab, from assistant researcher to the lowliest gopher, came in for the same sort of absentminded abuse.

"It's the mass spec, sir," Hobie said. The job at Argonaut Labs paid pretty good, and it was the first time he had ever seen scientists up close. They were pretty much like other people. They talked about their girlfriends or boyfriends, about fashions and sports—Hobie could join in on that! But sometimes the chatter at the cafeteria table ran off the sidelines and out of the stadium and the scribbling on the napkins would start and the jargon that sounded awfully like English until you actually tried to understand it.

"What about the mass spec?" said Venable impatiently.

"It's out of calibration, sir. Has been for a while."

Venable turned in his swivel chair and pulled the glasses off his nose. "It is? And how do you know that, boy?"

Hobie felt the words jam up in his throat. He was going to start stammering again. He knew it. He took a long, slow breath and let it out. "I . . . I was ch—checking the calibration stickers, sir, like Dr. Hughes told me, be—because the lab certs are up for renewal and . . . and . . ."

"And what? Spit it out. I don't have all day."

"And . . ." The words were freezing in his gut, forming a great ice ball. He was going to look stupid again. Dr. V was smarter than any man Hobie had ever met, but he made no allowances for anyone else. Mom would wait patiently for him to finish what he had to say. So would Dad and Greg and the Coach. But not this old coot, more anxious to get back to his long thoughts than to hear what the lab assistant had to say.

"And the sticker on the mass spec is a year and a half out of date." The words came out in a rush, as if they had popped a cork out of his throat.

"It is? Why have you come to me? Have you told the lab manager?"

"Yessir."

"You cannot assume the equipment is giving false readings simply because the sticker is out of date. The two statements are not logically equivalent."

"No, sir, but Dr. Hughes had me check the machine. He showed me how to run the standard and watched while I did it. Then he calculated the ... the bias. It was five percent high." It had been fun running the standard. For a moment, Hobie could pretend that he was a scientist himself, thinking long thoughts and discovering new things. And then, like a flashbulb inside his head, he *had* seen something, so clear that it appalled him.

"Has he called the calibration service?"

"Yes, sir. They'll be coming by tomorrow. Meanwhile, I hung the red out-of-service tag on the machine."

Venable beamed—the programming said you smiled at this point, and too bad he did not have a better issue grin in stock—and said, "Good boy," and turned and bent again over his notebook.

Good boy? What was he, a dog? Hobie coughed again and Venable laid his pen down with an audible smack. "Now what?" The irritation shoved aside any show of manners. Hobie took a step backward. But that was the wrong thing to do when the defensive tackle lunged at you, so it was the wrong thing to do now. There was nothing for it but to dig in and block.

"Well, we don't know when the machine started to fumble the ball ..."

"Fumble the ball ..." Venable sounded puzzled, as if he did not recognize the phrase.

"Give bad numbers. It was working right a year and a half ago. This morning it wasn't. So—so—" He gulped and plunged ahead. "So you can't depend on any of the mass spec readings for the last eighteen months. They might be wrong."

"Or they might be right. The instrument could have malfunctioned only this morning."

"Yes, sir, it could have." Hobie knew he was right. He *knew* he was right. "But my mama she always told me never put nothing in my mouth 'less I knew where it'd been."

"Wise advice, I am sure."

"Well, it seems to me, Dr. Venable, that if you publish that paper you're writing, you'd be putting numbers in your mouth without you know where they've been. If you know what I mean. Sir." That was as close to insubordination as Hobie cared to come, because it *was* a good job and it *did* pay good. So let's see if the old man is a *real* scientist, like Mr. Egbo had explained.

Dr. Venable picked up the stack of computer printouts and shook them under Hobie's nose. "Do you know what you are telling me, boy?" he asked in a harsh voice. "You are a lab assistant, summer help, and you are telling the head of the laboratory that he must repeat his researches for the past year! Boy, you have a lot of nerve."

Nerve, you have to have, to work the offensive line. If Dr. Venable meant that as a slur, Hobie took it as a compliment. "Once you publish the paper, Doctor, all the other scientists, they'll try to pick it apart, like defensive tackles. Those numbers are your linesmen, Doctor. And you gotta be sure you can depend on them."

Venable cocked his head and squinted one eye. He thought for a moment longer. Then, he sighed. "I suppose you are correct, boy. But, a year and a half of work to repeat . . ."

"No, sir, you might not have to."

"Eh? But you said . . ."

"I know, sir. But I gave this a lot of thought while I was standing outside your office. Because I sure know I wouldn't like repeating a year at school. Anyway, I thought of the retains."

"The retains . . ." Venable leaned back in his swivel chair and crossed his arms.

"Each time we run a test, we seal the remainder of the sample and label it and put it in the vault." That was part of Hobie's job. Dr. Hughes had explained how important record-keeping was to a scientist. And of course, to lab-accreditation boards and the EPA and others. "We can extract a—" What was the word? Al-something. Hobie did not want to look stupid, not now, when he had Dr. Venable almost convinced. "Aliquot. We can extract aliquots from the retains and run new tests. If they agree with the logged numbers, we'll know that the instrument was still good on that day."

Venable pursed his lips. "A couple hundred samples, at least. That's a lot of work you want me to authorize, boy. And none of it is in the budget."

"It might not be so bad, Doctor." Now, before he lost his nerve entirely. "We can retest a few retains from nine months ago. If they come out the same, we don't need to test anything earlier, because we'll know the calibration was still good. Then we'll test some from four or five months back, then from two months, and so on. See, that way we'll hit from two sides and pin down when the problem started. You only have to rerun the experiments from the time when the machine was actually fumbling."

"Do I? What of the other researchers? Have you told them the good news?"

"No, sir. I figured if you said it was the right way to go, the others would go along."

A smile cracked Venable's face for a moment. "They had better," he said. He turned back to the notebook, picked up his pen . . . and stared at the numbers written there. Then he sighed and tossed the pen back down again. "Discuss this with Dr. Hughes," he said. "Set up the protocols and bring them to me for approval." He looked at Hobie for a moment. "And put yourself down as the researcher. It's a simple matter, but I think you've earned that. Just follow Dr. Hughes's advice on the sampling. He knows his business, when he's not panting after Dr. Bechtel."

"Yes, sir. I'll do that." Hobie began to back out of the office. Me? *Me?* He had gone in wondering if he would still have a job when he came back out. But Dad had always said you can't stop a man who knows he's right and keeps on coming.

"Oh, one thing, boy."

"What's that, Dr. Venable?" It was all Hobie could do to keep the grin from his face. But the boss might think he was happy about the research being screwed up.

"Test last week's retains first. We might just be luckier than we deserve to be."

Later, as he passed the open door to Venable's office, Hobie noticed the old man staring at the window with a grimace on his face. "The things I do for that woman," he said, which had nothing to do with the problem they had been discussing, so Hobie decided not to bother him again if he was upset by something at home.

Part II

Morning Star
(AD 2000)

1.

The Notice of the Gods

When the shoe finally did drop, it took her by surprise, for all that she had been anticipating it. Hui had standing orders never to interrupt overseas calls for anything but an emergency, so Mariesa knew there was trouble the moment the intercom buzzed. She excused herself to her caller and said aloud, "What is it, Hui?" making it very clear that "it" had better be very important, indeed. There were only twenty-four hours in a day and, once frittered away—Gramper's phrase—they could never be recycled. *You can spend money,* he had once told her, *because you can always make more. But* time *you spend like a miser.*

That was why the single clock in the room, on the wall facing the desk, was a Disney product, and featured Scrooge McDuck on its face.

Zhou Hui appeared on the CRT inset in her desktop. "You have a visitor, miss," she said. "He claims to be from the Office of Commercial Space Transportation."

Mariesa closed her eyes a moment and rubbed her forehead. "Show me."

A splitscreen opened with a view of the reception area. The government man was about five-nine; young, but already running to the unobtrusive flab of those whose work involves desks and long lunches. His auburn hair was cut in the Beverly Hills style now popular inside the Beltway. Suspenders of incredibly outré design; a pastel shirt with no pockets, monogrammed in, of all places, his lower left abdomen. All very chi-chi these days. The fellow stood with his hands clasped behind his back and bounced on the balls of his feet. The impatient sort.

"Very well, Hui," she said. "You know the drill."

Mariesa switched back to the waiting call; and Hui's face was replaced by a stock photograph of Mount Fujiyama overlaid with digital readouts of times and file numbers. The Tokyo line was still voice and data only, which was just as well. It was six in the morning over there and Arthur Kondo must look awful. "I apologize for the interruption, Arthur," she said. "Please continue."

"Yes. As I said, the Japanese have elevated the Stall to an art form," Kondo told her. "In some ways, you have to admire their virtuosity. Our one big advantage is they've never dealt with an American negotiation team composed entirely of nisei. They keep waiting for us to mention it and we don't and it drives them nuts."

"Do they know that Bill and Jenny understand Japanese?"

"We haven't let on, but I think they suspect."

"What is your action plan for today's meeting? Piper is anxious to—"

This time the interruption came from the doorway. The government man stepped boldly into her office, followed closely by Hui. The first thing Mariesa did was to hit the security button with her foot. The second thing was to shake her head ever so slightly at her secretary, who stood ready behind the intruder. There was no physical threat, and you never played your hole card until all the chips were on the table.

The third thing she did, before the man could no more than open his mouth, was to stand and speak sharply to Zhou Hui. "Miss Zhou! How dare you admit this person without my leave!"

"I'm sorry, Ms. van Huyten," Hui said in her best little-girl voice. "He barged right past me." Hui had certain effects on male hormones, and was not above making use of that fact from time to time. Let the fellow feel guilty for getting an innocent worker bee in trouble.

"Building Security will be here shortly, Miss Zhou," she said frostily. "Meanwhile," she turned to the government man, "I am discussing confidential matters."

He stepped toward the desk. "Vincent Michaelson. OCST."

Mariesa ignored the outstretched hand. "So you say. Miss Zhou, has his identification checked out?"

"Not yet, ma'am."

"So. You may wait outside, Mr. Michaelson, until your bona fides have been verified. I have only your word for it that you represent the Washington government; and I will not discuss matters with someone whose identity I cannot verify. Miss Zhou! Does Mr. Michaelson have an appointment? I do not recall so from my calendar."

"No, ma'am."

Mariesa shook her head. "See if you can find him a spot on tomorrow's schedule, once his identification is confirmed." Hui nodded and used her throat mike, *sotto voce*.

"Tomorrow?" said Michaelson. "I didn't come all the way up here to get the brush-off."

"The lack of planning on your part does not constitute an obligation on mine."

Hui held a hand to one ear of her headset and listened. "You have no openings tomorrow, miss," she said. "Unless someone cancels at the last minute."

"You may return tomorrow, if you wish, Mr. Michaelson, and 'fly standby.' " She dropped her eyes to her phone. "Meanwhile, because of your interruption, I am tempted to charge the additional cost of this phone call against the government. Or would you prefer to wait for Building Security?" She paused and looked at Michaelson, who hesitated a moment longer, then allowed Hui to lead him out.

When the door closed, Mariesa spoke aloud to activate the relay to Hui's headset. "Hui, when he presses the issue, we will 'grudgingly' slip him into my dinner slot tonight at seven-thirty. Make the reservations at Red's, and have Charlie Jim stand by on the helipad from eighteen-hundred hours. Oh. And if Security is out there by now, ask why it took them over one minute and thirty seconds to respond to my summons. End memo.''

Mariesa resumed her seat and put Tokyo back on the speakerphone. ''I apologize, Arthur, for the *second* interruption. Please continue.'' She leaned back in her chair while Kondo resumed his briefing, but her mind refused to stay on the subject, and his words buzzed in her ears without registering. When he finished, Mariesa focused long enough to thank him, grateful that the entire conversation had been downloaded for later review.

Afterward, she sat in her high-backed, contour chair with her hands folded under her chin, and pondered the situation. Granted, the government would have stumbled onto Prometheus sooner or later, but she had been hoping for later—after the elections. The economic forecasts promised a change of Administration in November—with the new watch likely to be friendlier. Of course, the incumbent was no more to blame for the state of the economy than Bush or Clinton had been; but sacral kingship was an old North European tradition. When the harvest went bad, you put the king in a wicker basket and set him on fire. Not very effective—and you used up a lot of kings that way—but it was preferable to the god-king traditions of some other cultures.

The Steering Committee had brainstormed Government Disclosure scenarios years ago and had revisited them after ''April Fool.'' The contingency plans were as up-to-date as conscientious planners could make them; but there was no way to select the appropriate contingency until she knew what message Michaelson bore. To shut her down? To co-opt her? To demand a piece of the action? Maybe no one could actually ''sweep back the sea,'' as Barry had pointed out at the New Year's party; but the U.S. Government could purchase a great many brooms—on credit.

It was useless to speculate. The president had no firm convictions of his own, and the range of possible responses depended on who had gotten his ear first. Then cross-multiply his coterie of advisors with the permanent bureaucracy, which often ran its own agendas. Prometheus had made best guesses and assigned delphic probabilities to each scenario; but if you tried to prepare for every possibility, you wound up prepared for none.

If only Keith or John E. were here. On matters such as these, their advice and support would be invaluable—John for his legal acumen; Keith for . . . just for being Keith. But they were both tied up in tax court down in Washington. The half dozen Prometheans in Legal and Regulatory Affairs here at headquarters were mostly in middle-and lower-echelon positions. They would happily provide factual background, but they would be terrified if called upon for grand strategy.

Mariesa tapped a special function key on the inlaid desk keyboard and called up E-mail. She typed, "The gods have noticed," merged the Prometheus address macro, and sent it on its way. The message would appear in a red priority window on screens from Erfurt to Los Angeles, and all of them—Correy, Will, Dolores, Heinz, João, Wallace, Steve—would understand.

Because if you were a member of the Pantheon, you could read that two ways.

The Hoboken/Weehawken waterfront had undergone a renaissance during the eighties. Old buildings and warehouses had been torn down or renovated. Condominiums and hot new restaurants had moved in; and ferries now joined Weehawken and Manhattan. Growth had slowed somewhat during the stagnant nineties, but there was still a very definite quality-of-life gradient drawing people out of their West Side apartments onto the Jersey side of the river.

Red's sat on a pier jutting into the Hudson River; and the plate-glass windows lining the east wall provided a panorama of the Manhattan skyline, from the garland of light marking the George Washington Bridge in the north to the twin slabs of the World Trade Center in the south. The *U.S.S. Intrepid*

Air and Naval Museum was moored just upriver. Opposite the restaurant, the Empire State Building thrust above the skyline and, beyond that, the Chrysler Building, still the grandest, if no longer the tallest, of the midtown skyscrapers. The buildings of Midtown Manhattan were bathed in a pure, dusty rose by the setting sun, and looked unnaturally clean and orderly. Their lower reaches were shrouded in mutual shadows. *Already night on the city streets / but daylight in the towers. . . .* Another of Keith's poems.

The maitre d' showed them to a table facing the skyline, and they settled in with their preprandial drinks—she, her usual Manhattan; he, a Perrier. Mariesa said, "I hope you don't mind meeting like this; but it was the only time when I could squeeze you in. You did arrive unannounced." Zhou Hui and Charlie Jim Folkes, co-opted for the evening, had taken another table a discreet distance away.

"Not at all," Michaelson said. "I understand." He looked around the restaurant. "I'm surprised, though. I expected something fancier."

The waiter brought menus and handed them first to Mariesa, then to Michaelson. "A friend of mine brought me here a few months ago," she said. "It is unpretentious, but charming; and the food is excellent. I recommend the tenderloins of beef and the Bailey's mousse for dessert."

They studied the menus in silence for a few minutes before Michaelson set his aside and said, "Washington sent me to make a few inquiries."

Mariesa laid her own menu down. *To business, then.* "I thought Washington was dead," she said in a bantering tone.

The government man chuckled. "That's a good one. I'll have to remember that."

"Mr. Michaelson, a city cannot 'send' anyone. You were sent here by a person." She arched an inquiring eyebrow.

"Ah. I am not at liberty to divulge that." The regret she heard in his voice was a flattering imitation of the real thing. They both knew how the game was played. You never said, but you always knew. The White House Chief of Staff was the "power behind the throne." OCST reported to the Secretary of Transportation, but the Secretary was a nonentity and would not erect a highway sign without permission from his political master.

"So. And what is it that your principal wishes to know?"

Michaelson leaned forward. "We have intelligence in hand that you are running a private space program. We find that disturbing."

Mariesa nodded. "I have intelligence that you are *not* running a public space program. I find *that* disturbing."

He gave her a political smile, one that admired the cleverness of her riposte. "I am afraid the country has different priorities," he said. "You may wish differently. Perhaps even I may wish differently. That's not the point. The point is that you never obtained the necessary clearances and licenses. We know it's true. We have satellite photos, as well as other intelligence—of exports, of movements of matériel and talent. It all converges on the equatorial coast of Brazil."

Mariesa's hand tightened on the stem of her glass while she listened to the man with the professional smile. "Now that you mention it," she said carefully, "I believe that a Brazilian firm in which we hold interests is pursuing an aerospace venture with private financing and the cooperation of the Brazilian government. I do not see what 'clearances' are needed."

"Under the provisions of 49 United States Code, Chapter 35—"

"The so-called Commercial Space Launch Act."

"You've heard of it, then? Judging by your actions, I had supposed you hadn't. Under the provisions of the Act, you must apply for a license, obtain approval *for each mission* from the Secretary of Transportation, and allow OCST agents to witness and verify each launch and payload. Paragraph 2605(a)(2) states that no U.S. citizen shall launch a launch vehicle or operate a launch site outside the United States unless authorized by a license issued under Chapter 35."

Mariesa lifted her Manhattan to her lips and set it down without sipping. Try to imagine commercial aviation ever flourishing under a law such as that! "I was not aware that a Brazilian company needed your permission to engage in business in Brazil.'' She paused and added, ''Paragraph 2605(a)(3)(B)(i).''

Michaelson laughed and gave the table a slap with his free hand. ''You're very good. Did you know that?'' He set his mineral water on the table, and leaned back as the waiter set his meal down before him, a Cobb salad plate, splendidly displayed. Mariesa had selected the baked cod.

Michaelson continued after the waiter had gone. ''Under the act, a foreign company operating on foreign soil *still* requires a license and mission approval from the United States Government when an American citizen or corporation holds a controlling interest in that company.''

''Mr. Michaelson, my lawyers tell me that the provision does not apply if the foreign government—in this case, Brazil—exercises the customary oversight for safe and proper operations of a spaceport.''

''Launch site,'' he corrected her.

''You have your paradigm; I have mine.''

He shrugged, dismissing the point without conceding it. ''Ms. van Huyten, the Brazilian *government* needs our permission to wipe its . . . to wipe its nose.'' He poked his salad with a fork as if probing for hidden treasure. ''Need I mention such issues as national security?'' he said offhandedly. ''Exporting of sensitive technology . . . ?''

''For all of which we have government export licenses,'' she replied. Of course, you could dot every *i* and cross every *t* and the government could still come down on you with an arbitrary reversal. It depended on what they wanted and how badly they wanted it. The law was a tool; and, like any tool, could be used to hinder or facilitate, depending on who wielded it.

Michaelson sighed and chewed on his salad for a few moments. ''The country already has a launch service—NASA. The government sees no need for another. The Industrial Policy Board believes that there are more attractive investments, with better chances of return.''

It was too much for Mariesa. She laughed and reached a hand across the table toward him. ''Mr. Michaelson, am I to believe that your principal is motivated by fear for my companies' profits?'' His returning grin was equally crooked. She laid her fish fork aside and leaned back in her chair. ''Tell me. Do you know why 'radio' was at first called 'wireless'?''

He seemed puzzled at the change in subject. ''No . . .''

''It stood for, 'wireless telephone' or 'wireless telegraph,' those being the communications paradigms of the era. The new invention was expected to provide supplemental 'narrowcasting' for regions where it was impractical to string telephone or telegraph wires. When 'broadcasting' was proposed, the experts could imagine only one reason why large numbers of people would want to listen to the same thing at the same time: Sunday sermons; and demand for that was insufficient to provide a viable market. Thank God, we had no Industrial Policy Board back then.'' *Industrial planning* was, in Mariesa's opinion, a code word for rewarding cooperative businesses and those with the right connections.

She studied his polite-but-patient face and wondered why she bothered making the case. They would not have sent someone open-minded on this mission. Michaelson was either a true believer or a mercenary. But that thought reminded her of the curious mix on her own Steering Committee, and she twisted uncomfortably in her seat. ''As cost-to-orbit drops,'' she continued, ''previously marginal activities will become profitable, and the market will grow. There will be enough for everyone.'' Michaelson was not here to debate, but she would play the game to its close.

''The government will not use your services.''

''Perhaps not at first, but . . .''

''Nor will government contractors use it; not if they plan to remain government contractors. If necessary, we can impose regulatory restraints and licensing fees. Those don't require awakening Congress. The Secretary believes that the satellite launch business needs stricter regulation. To protect the public.''

She smiled thinly and settled back in her chair. *To protect established interests, you mean.* ''I see. The number of permits that would have to be filed would create a stack of paperwork tall enough that we could *climb* to the moon before anyone ever 'bent tin.' " She waited for the "or else." Threats meant nothing unless another course of action was offered.

Michaelson set his mineral water on the table. "Just between you and me, Ms. van Huyten, we do not believe it is wise for a Third World country like Brazil to be in space."

She toyed for a moment with her cod. It was growing cold as they talked. A waste of fine food. "You refuse to understand. It is not Brazil's space program; it is Daedalus's. The Brazilian government is simply contributing facilities and infrastructure support. In exchange, Daedalus employs a substantial number of people in an otherwise economically depressed area."

"Why not employ 'a substantial number of people' here in the US of A? We have economically depressed areas, too. You own an American aerospace company . . . ?"

"Pegasus." Michaelson surely knew that. He would have done his homework.

"Right." *As if she had passed a quiz.* Mariesa reminded herself that this was just a messenger boy, and he had yet to deliver his message. "Why not develop this program of yours through Pegasus?" he continued, spreading his hands in a plea. "Why the secrecy? The development of space capabilities is hideously expensive. You could have applied for government funding, under Chapter 84, the Space Commercialization Act. Pegasus has facilities in several states, which would attract congressional support; and Washington has more cash to hand out than Brasilia."

"When it is 'funny money' either way, Mr. Michaelson, I do not see that it matters who has more. Tell me, have you ever heard of Samuel Langley?"

Michaelson shook his head. "No."

"His story is instructive. In the summer of 1903, with a fifty-thousand-dollar grant from the Smithsonian and another twenty thousand from the U.S. Army, he and a large staff of aides tried to develop a heavier-than-air flying machine. It was, if you will, the first government-funded aerospace program; and was suitably ridiculed by the *New York Times*, which wondered then, as now, why the money could not be spent 'here on earth.' In those days, seventy thousand dollars was a great deal of money. However, by the end of the year, for less than a thousand dollars, a privately financed venture succeeded at Kitty Hawk, North Carolina. So you see, while the venture may be expensive, it need not, absent the government, be hideously so.'' She took a sip of the wine she had ordered with her meal.

''As for basing the venture here,'' she continued, as if by afterthought, ''I would rather not see the effort strangled or turned into pork, or second-guessed by politicians and bureaucrats. Some of our potential competitors wield a great deal more influence in Washington than we; and are in a position to buy laws that would protect them against upstarts like Daedalus or Pegasus.''

''Something that might be worth keeping in mind,'' said Michaelson. He leaned forward over the table. ''I suppose we could play 'Dueling Lawyers,' but why help the legal eagles get rich? Look at the situation from our point of view, Ms. van Huyten. Why should we go out of our way to help a political opponent?''

''What do you know of my politics, Mr. Michaelson? I have made no public statements regarding the election. Nor have I contributed to either campaign.''

''In times like these, Ms. van Huyten, whoever is not with us is against us. The country is at a crossroads; and we need to decide what sort of America our children will live in.''

''Oh, on that we quite agree.''

''We need a president who can bring us together, not divide us the way Champion would. Our platform does not ignore the poor; but we don't bash the rich, either. The campaign accepts contributions from people in all walks of life.''

She kept her voice neutral. ''I believe I understand.''

Michaelson smiled and resumed the attack on his salad. ''I was sure you would.''

The VHI corporate boardroom was a mixture of high-tech and traditional. Fax machines and laser printers sat on floor-to-ceiling bookshelves surrounded by printed reference books on law, finance, and quality control. Heads-down computer screens were inlaid at a comfortable angle into the dark, rich wood of the board table. Keyboards sat on sliding racks underneath. Twelve videoconference monitors, half of them now occupied by scowling Second-Prometheans, bracketed the wide, brass-accoutred double doors. On one of the screens, Vincent Michaelson ate his Cobb salad from the night before.

Incongruously still and dark among the brightly flickering television images, the Pieter Lastman portrait of Henryk van Huyten hung above the doorway opposite the chairman's seat. It had hung in that same position in three successive boardrooms, ever since old Christiaan III had salvaged it from the smoking ruins of the original family mansion in the upper Hudson Valley. *To remind us how many generations are watching our stewardship,* Gramper had told her once with that great booming laugh of his.

Henryk had been the first of the family to rise to prominence. The son of a ship's captain, he had sailed with Piet Heyn when Heyn captured the Spanish Treasure Fleet off Matanzas; and, later, he had developed close ties with the ''Seventeen Gentlemen'' of the VOC. Family legend held that it was old Henryk who had loaned Pieter Minuit the sixty guilders the governor had needed to swing a certain real-estate deal in the New World.

The boardroom was silent while Mariesa and the others watched the videotape of her meeting with Michaelson. Keith stood with his back to the group, staring out the window at the flowers that surrounded the grounds. It was a bright morning, but Mariesa had gotten little sleep since the night before. John E. Redman slouched in his high-backed, leather swivel chair across the board table from her. No one else was physically present, but Steve Matthias, Belinda Karr, and Dolores Pitchlynn were telepresent, as were Heinz Ruger from Erfurt and João Pessoa and the Werewolf from Fortaleza.

Mariesa glanced at Keith and saw his disapproving scowl. She fingered the camera brooch she had worn last night and which she had brought with her to the meeting along with the tape from Zhou's recorder. *What's fair?* she wanted to ask him. *They have a sky full of satellites and thousands of spooks and agents.* Was it ethical for a government to spy on its citizens—and on a friendly power—but not for the citizens to spy on the government?

"*. . . don't bash the rich, either. The campaign accepts contributions from people in all walks of life.*"

She stopped the recording. "Well?" she asked. "Did he ask for a bribe, or did he not?"

"Sounded like one to me," said Gregorson. There was no doubt in his mind. Gregorson saw things in black and white. "I've dealt with enough procurement officers to know a solicitation when I hear one."

Keith pursed his lips. "It's chock full of deniability."

"You're talking like a lawyer, Keith," said Redman. McReynolds looked at him.

"And I wish you would, John E. Whatever happened to 'the preponderance of the evidence'?"

"We are not in a court," the lawyer reminded him. "Investigators only need 'probable cause.' "

"Keith," said Mariesa, "I was there. There was a definite threat in Michaelson's words."

McReynolds shook his head. "I listened to the tape, too, and I heard only a Washington flunky doing his job."

"Perhaps I do not know the English well enough," said Ruger over the European link, "but your president is looking for the contributions. Is that not legal?"

"They repealed the Hatch Act," Redman told him. "Now they're seeing how far they can push the new limits. Michaelson did not actually solicit a 'contribution.' "

"No," said Mariesa, "but the intent was clear. If I come out for the president and drop a hefty piece of change in the purse, all the difficulties in the way of Prometheus will melt away."

"Always the Goal, Mariesa," said Keith McReynolds.

She turned and looked at him. "What do you mean, Keith?"

"If the Goal matters that much, why not do it? Toss a few

million in the pot—you can launder it so you don't violate the PAC laws—make a few speeches. Then, Prometheus has a blank check and a green light.''

''No, Keith, I won't do it that way.''

''Why not? You get one opponent off our back and they can run interference against Wilson and against the Peoples' Crusades.''

''No, Keith. I am not saying that Michaelson's boss cannot be bought; but I am not sure that he will stay bought. If the wind shifts, he will tack with it. And there are other forces inside the government. It is a fiction that the president wields absolute control, even in the executive branch. He can issue directives, but they will not always be followed two or three levels down. It is ludicrous to suppose that his appointees would stand up to Phil Albright and his media cheerleaders, even if he orders it. They would 'leak' all over the nightly news before anyone had gone home for the day.''

''In other words,'' said Gregorson, ''in exchange for everything, he offered nothing.''

Mariesa slapped the tabletop with her two palms. Keith and John E. looked at her in surprise. She rose and paced the conference room. ''It still makes me angry,'' she said. ''To be threatened by one's own government.''

''Where were you in the sixties?'' drawled John E.

She turned on him. ''What shall be our response?'' she asked.

''Maybe it is time,'' said Dolores's image, ''for Prometheus to go public. Bring some of it to Pegasus. If we bring some jobs into the USA, we'll gain some allies in Congress.''

To Pegasus. Meaning, to Dolores. João Pessoa's eyes flickered left, looking at his own videoconference monitors. He opened his mouth, as if to say something, then closed it into a thin line. He had been silent for most of the meeting. Mariesa wondered if he still smarted over his April Fool blunders and was unwilling to remind everyone by drawing attention to himself. ''We are not ready yet,'' he said finally. ''The Plank has tested well so far. The remote link has been repaired and Krasnarov and the others have flown it successfully. We will be ready for manned cross-range tests in another month. But the design could still have hidden flaws. That is what flight test is supposed to uncover. If it were opened to the media prematurely, those flaws would be reported as failures, not as normal development work.''

''João is right,'' said the Werewolf. ''Remember the early phases of Mercury? The press went crazy—*our rockets always blow up*. They had no idea that it was normal for flight testing a new bird. And it never seemed to occur to them that there were failed Soviet launches of which they never heard.''

Mariesa looked at the screens. ''You think there may be a failure during the test series, Will?''

''Mariesa,'' said Gregorson somberly, ''it is almost a guarantee. We should keep it in the bag a while longer yet.''

''The 'bag,' '' said Keith, ''is beginning to look an awful lot like a colander. If there is a test failure, and the program has been kept secret, the media may pounce even harder.''

''All right,'' said Mariesa, ''this is what we'll do. . . .''

Keith said, ''Shouldn't we wait for the full Steering Committee to meet?''

Mariesa brushed her hair back. A group of more than five people could not decide when to eat lunch, let alone set an effective course of action. ''Notify them, Keith. We will meet here on . . .'' She tapped a few keys on the keyboard under the table and called up her calendar on the screen. She cleared a day and copied Zhou Hui on the changes. ''On Wednesday. Everyone is to clear their calendar for that day. Those who can, should be here in person; otherwise be telepresent. John E., what is it?''

''Court date.''

''Send Alan. Call in sick. Get a postponement. Do what you have to do. Meanwhile . . .'' She keyed off and returned the tray under the table. ''Meanwhile, this is what we'll do. Dolores, talk to your contacts inside the Beltway. See what you can learn from the aerospace community; but don't let your questions reveal more than their answers. Will, contact the general and find out what his government contacts have heard. Keith, whom do you know in Wilson's organization?''

"Norton, their CFO. We've met at a number of conferences."

"Good. See what you can find out through those channels. We may have common interest. Meanwhile, we shall have to awaken Heimdall."

"Bring Gene Forney in?" asked Greg. "Might as well bring everyone in."

"I want *The American Argus* to begin a series of articles *educating* the public to the realities of flight-testing. Let them know that people die testing experimental planes."

"Won't that turn them off?" asked Keith.

"Only the old and cautious. I think the younger audience is ready to look at bravery and heroism as something beside a subject for mockery."

"Then make a movie," said John E. "Who reads newspapers anymore?"

"No time," said Mariesa. "The test program will become public too soon. *The Argus* will have to do. Cliff downloads to two hundred thousand terminals and has hardcopies in every hotel and vending machine in the country. Meanwhile, I shall meet with Jim Champion and sound out his views."

There was silence in the room. Then John E. said in his slow drawl, "I thought we were staying neutral in the election."

"That was before the incumbent chose sides in *my* contest."

"We don't know that Champion will be favorable . . ."

"No, but at least he may be neutral. Privatization is one of his planks. We don't want government support, only a lack of government opposition."

"Meanwhile . . ." John E. Redman leaned across the conference table and hit the EJECT button. The VCR hummed and the cassette emerged into his outstretched hand. ". . . there are a few things we can do with this."

Chris delivered the quarterly technical progress report on Prometheus two weeks later. He was not smiling when he did. Mariesa read the report while drinking her afternoon tea in her office. She sat by the north window in one of the low, leather chairs and, between sips, studied the charts and graphs. She ignored the columns of figures, checking only a few numbers at random to assure herself that there were no gross errors in the charts. She paid more attention to the assumptions behind each hypothetical scenario. No matter how well plotted and analyzed, the numbers were only as good as those assumptions. The value of the dollar, the trade balance. The expected reaction of the administration, the coming election. Projected revenues versus operating expenses. Projections, estimates, forecasts.

She closed the report and Christiaan, who had been pretending to study the space art with which Mariesa decorated her office, turned and looked at her. "Well?" she asked, dropping the report to the coffee table. She knew Chris as well as she knew anyone. Since childhood. And Uncle Chris—Christiaan, Sr.—had tried as hard as anyone in the family to draw Father away from the booze and the pills. There was no reason for Chris to have flown all the way from Phoenix to deliver the FLG report personally, unless he had simply wanted to take tea with her, or unless he had something else to tell her. And he had not touched his tea.

Chris nodded toward the red-covered booklet. "The problem with the Forward Looking Group is that they are optimists. Even their lower bound forecasts may be a little rose-colored."

"So . . . ?"

He joined her in the nook by the window and stood looking out at the flank of Watchung Mountain. "So, I formed another group to evaluate the same suite of scenarios with the same data we've been getting from the test flights down in the archipelago. The two groups worked in parallel. Neither knew of the other's effort."

"Really?"

"Yes. I've called the new team the Murphy Looking Group." Mariesa laughed and Chris said, "It was Steve Matthias's idea."

"I remember he said something of the sort," Mariesa said. "A devil's advocate, he called it."

"I was unsure of Steve, at first," Christiaan admitted. "I thought he wanted to ride aboard the bandwagon without playing any of the instruments. But he has been pulling his own weight on the working groups and technical committees he's joined."

"He is methodical. It's his way." Mariesa recovered her tea from the coffee table and relaxed with her elbows on the arms of the padded chair and with the teacup in one hand hovering over the saucer held in the other. "I take it the Murphy version of the report is not yet ready. Is that good news or bad?"

Chris shoved his hands in his pockets. "That depends on your definitions, doesn't it?" When he looked out the window, his back was to Mariesa.

"Then, it is bad news. Chris, do you know something you are not telling me?" The teacup clacked onto its saucer, spilling some of its contents.

Chris shook his head. "No. I don't *know* anything. It's all projections. Scenarios with delphic probabilities. Have you spoken to João lately?"

"Last week. They are halfway through the maneuvering tests. All three Planks are in dock now for retrofitting based on the feedback from the pilots and from the technical staff. You had better not tell me that João is withholding information!" Her confidence in João's judgment had dropped after April Fool and had not yet recovered. Perhaps Steve was right. Perhaps you needed the realists *more* than the enthusiasts.

"No," Chris assured her. "Nothing like that. It's just that Murphy sees a wider range of performance profiles than FLG did. And that range overlaps the mass-fraction critical point."

This time she most definitely spilled the tea. Chris turned, startled, and took a step forward. Mariesa waved him off as she put her cup and saucer aside and dabbed at her skirt with her napkin. "No, no, don't bother. I'm all right. It's nothing. Chris! If we come in under the critical point, the Plank cannot achieve orbit with a profitable payload and return!"

Chris nodded. "I know. It's a matter of achieving the expected engine efficiency with the aerospike. The data so far falls below the expected mean and, while one expects to fall below average half the time, five times in a row becomes suspicious.''

"The design was supposed to be robust! Why was this not brought up before we froze the design approach?''

"Easy, Riesey. It is only a low-probability scenario. It delphied out to around five percent. The bulk of the projections fall comfortably above the critical point. Earlier feasibility studies concentrated on the maximum likelihood scenarios. Murphy . . . checks the long odds.''

"What do we do?''

"I spoke with João yesterday," he told her, "before I flew out. He's set up a cross-functional contingency team just in case. Mendoza is in charge. But no one will know anything for sure until we begin the high-altitude tests and we see what the engines can really put out.''

"That will be too late. We will have to go public for the altitude tests.'' Mariesa could not remain seated. She stood abruptly and crossed the room in a few quick strides to stand before the long mirror on the south wall. In it, she could see the window and Chris watching her. She smoothed her skirt and saw a brown stain down the front. Bother! She clenched her fists by her side. João and Governor Gomes had kept everything quiet by testing over the Atlantic out of the regular traffic lanes; but the altitude tests would take them up to sub-orbital and over other sovereignties, and that required public notification. "Chris, I cannot go public only to have the design end in failure. We would look like fools.''

"That sort of thing happens all the time in development testing," Chris pointed out. "Even promising designs do punk out, you know.''

"But investor confidence would not survive. Not for something like this. The public and the media are accustomed to scripted performances. They expect that, when something goes before the cameras, it will work perfectly.''

Chris shrugged, as if to say there was nothing to be done about that. "Look at the positive side," he said. "Everything may work out. That's still the maximum likelihood, after all.''

Mariesa shook her head. "No. Never copper Murphy's bet." She raised her voice. "Hui."

"Yes, miss?" Zhou Hui's voice from the speaker was soft but clear.

"Cancel all my appointments for today and tomorrow and reschedule. Find Keith and John E. and have them come to my office, now. Then call the executives on the Plank Technical Development list and arrange a teleconference for eight o'clock, eastern. No excuses, unless they cannot access a secure terminal. Tell João to include his tech people, Mendoza especially."

"Understood. Shall I repeat?"

"No. Tell them it is priority one. Out."

Chris was grinning. "You don't waste time, do you?"

"Never. Chris, what are our options? Quick list."

"Well . . . Murphy has not completed its analysis. . . ."

"I cannot wait for Murphy. What do you have so far?"

Chris pulled his hands from his pockets and began ticking off on his fingers. "One: We can further lightweight the structure. Replace metals with ceramics or composites. Honeycomb the solid pieces. Or use solid smoke, if we can perfect the production problems down in our Houston lab. That would mean massive design changes on the next series of Planks and probably two years' delay. We pretty much minded all we could on downweighting during the initial phase. But if it is a marginal situation, some marginal reductions may be all we need. DuBois—the pilot on Mendoza's task force—said that he would fly a cardboard box to orbit, but he had serious doubts about reentry in that case."

A fleeting, involuntary smile . . . "Yes, that sounds like Ned. What else?" She began to pace back and forth across the office while she listened to Chris.

"Two: When spin transistors become available, much of the electronics will shrink by an order of magnitude."

"Too long and no milestone projections yet. Electronics is not the major weight driver. What else?"

"Three: Trade payload for fuel. The Plank needs five hundred and forty-four megs of fuel to carry an eleven-meg payload to LEO on an easterly insertion. It's a non-linear response, so we needn't trade kilo for kilo."

"No. What is the point of reaching orbit cheaply if we cannot take enough cargo when we do? FLG estimated that the Plank had a payload capacity of three percent of its gross liftoff weight. If the engine efficiencies do not come up to expectations and it wipes out that margin, we have no service to sell. What else?"

Chris glanced at his fingers. "Um, four: More efficient engine designs. Better specific impulse."

"Horizon?"

"Six months to one year, with no guarantee."

"And a developmental engine instead of a proven design. What else?"

"Look, Riesey, Murphy's report will be ready next week. I don't remember everything Bryce told me during the briefing."

"*What else?*"

He looked at her and shrugged. "Off-load the fuel, or most of it. Use booster guns. Laser launch."

"Someday. But we cannot even see the dust cloud on the horizon. I want to see this started in my own lifetime. What else?"

Chris had stopped counting. "Take half the fuel load and refuel on-orbit for the return trip."

"Cryogenic refueling in orbit has never been attempted before."

"There is a first time for everything."

"Where do the heavy-lift tankers fall on our PERT chart?"

Chris grimaced and did not answer her. "Go with the old Black Horse concept. Take off without oxidizer—fuel only— and suck air until rendezvous with a tanker at upper atmosphere."

"Black Horse was a winged vessel, horizontal takeoff and landing. The Plank could not perform such a rendezvous. We would be redesigning from scratch."

"Settle for suborbital capability. With fractional orbit transport, we can deliver cargo anywhere on Earth in a half an hour.''

''I did not get into this to compete with Federal Express. I know we are counting on Earth-to-Earth services to carry us through the first decade until the markets adjust to the idea of inexpensive access to space. But if that is *all* we can offer, the project is a bust in the long term. What else?''

''Fall back to concept B. Ferry the Plank on the Lifter and release it upstairs. Two stages, but both manned and everything would still be reusable.''

''But the economics would be marginal. The cost of the spaceship is the financial driver. The price projections for a Plank fall between one-and-a-half to three million troy ounces. Double that or more by adding the development costs of the Lifter and we may be unable to underbid Ariane. And that is if the Lifter can be developed at all, starting this late. The first Lifters would not reach flight test for another three years, even with fast-tracking and concurrent engineering. You've seen the economic projections. Our window of opportunity— is starting to close.'' Her pacing had carried her back to the window. Chris reached out and seized her wrist.

''Calm down, Riesey. You are working yourself up.''

She tugged her arm from his grip. ''How long before Michaelson learns of my meeting with Champion? Inexpensive access to orbit . . . I was so *sure*! I threw it in his face. Now you tell me 'the emperor has no clothes'?''

''Only that the hemline may be short,'' Chris said cooly. ''If the Plank *is* a blind alley, we need to know that, so we can try another.''

She knew he meant it. She knew he was the one person in the family who did not laugh at her behind her back. Oh, Riesey is a crackerjack CEO, no question, but—you know— on some subjects, she is just ''crackers.'' Let them think her ''obsession'' was beginning to govern her business decisions and she could find her options seriously restricted, even if they could not force her out entirely. She sighed and ran her hand through her hair. ''I know, Chris. I know.''

''And it is not as though we overlooked the possibility . . .''

". . . Only that we thought we had a positive answer four years ago. That is why I gave the go-ahead to bring Plan A to development and . . . Oh. Shit!" Chris raised his eyebrows at the vulgarity, but she did not care. Bad cases required bad words. "There is no point to running on about it. Can you at least have Murphy's draft by tomorrow's meeting?"

"I'll have Silver fax me a copy."

"E-mail. Encrypted." Chris nodded and started toward the door. Halfway there, he turned.

"It will work out all right, Riesey. You'll see."

"It is the pilots that worry me," she said softly. "You've never met them, have you? I'm afraid that Krasnarov or Ned DuBois or one of the others would go for orbit anyway. He— or she—will 'push the outside of the envelope,' as they say, because not one of them could bear coming so close and not going all the way. They might not abort to suborbital until it was too late and find themselves with not enough fuel to land safely."

"Or worse," said Chris. "Remember what almost happened to Scott Carpenter? Your friend DuBois could reach orbit and be unable to come back down at all."

When Chris had gone, Mariesa went to her desk and sat there for several minutes. There were a dozen reports or more awaiting her attention. The Japanese project. Preliminary figures on the upcoming quarterlies. The status of the Cleveland lawsuit. Items with no connection to Prometheus, and therefore of no importance. She forced herself to pick up the first one; opened it and stared blankly at the cover sheet.

Everyone had come in with positive reports four years ago. They could reach a three-percent mass fraction, perhaps even exceed it. The future had seemed a very sure thing back then. Had it been so sure because she had wanted it so badly? She saw that the papers in her hand were shaking as if they had come alive, and she pressed them flat on the desk with her palms.

It was only a marginal possibility, Chris had said. It had always been there; only maybe the margin was a little worse than they had thought. They had dismissed it from their planning and now it had returned to haunt them.

Maybe she should call Barry. He was a good listener and she needed someone she could spill her doubts and fears on. Barry had already guessed enough that she could tell him the rest; or as much of the rest as she had told the others. She could attach him to Belinda's working group. Or make him a personal assistant. Or . . .

"Hui," she said, before she could change her mind. "Would you please contact Principal Fast at Witherspoon High School and patch him in here?"

Hui acknowledged and, feeling oddly calmer, Mariesa picked up the report again and began to read. She had finished the first page when Hui announced over the intercom, "Dr. Egbo reports that Mr. Fast has already left the building."

"Oh. Very well, thank you, Hui. Out." She leaned back in her chair, a high-backed, comfortable affair of leather and wood. Her hand on her lap felt the damp spot left by the tea. Really, she ought to change. Keith and John E. would be here any moment. The dark spot must look awful. She felt it again with her fingertips. It was in just the wrong place, too.

"Hui, I am going to freshen up. When Keith and John E. arrive, have them wait until I am ready for them." It seemed odd sometimes, talking to the air like that; but the pickups were keyed to her voiceprint and the link was direct to Zhou's headset, unless she specified another access code.

The door to her private quarters was not exactly hidden, but was designed to blend into the paneling on the wall behind her desk. She entered, pulling off the jacket and skirt and draping them on a hanger for dry cleaning. The room contained a wardrobe, a shower, a day couch, and other comforts. A small apartment, really. Sometimes, when affairs kept her late, she would retire here and have Food Service send something up rather than chopper out to Silverpond.

She studied the clothing in her closet. Primarily business suits, of course. All of them in sensible, subdued colors. Two evening dresses for those occasions when she went to formal affairs directly from the office. She chose a light gray suit and then, on further reflection, a fresh blouse, as well. When she closed the wardrobe door, she faced herself in the full-length mirror. She looked tired. *Ah, Riesey, is the pressure getting to you?* There were bags under her eyes, and worry lines. She touched her hair with one hand. Had the gray spread? There was more gray there than she remembered. On men, a trace of gray at the temples was supposed to be distinguishing. Women were to look young until they died.

Perhaps if she wore a little more makeup or dyed her hair. . . . Mother said she did not look feminine enough. She used a little cosmetics, a concession that annoyed her; but men had no idea what a woman's natural face looked like and were likely to react negatively, without knowing why, were she to use none at all. She turned sideways. Her carriage was fine and her silhouette emphatically feminine. A different-style bra, a different cut of dress, and she could display herself to some advantage.

If she were the sort who displayed herself.

She hung her change of clothing on a butler hook and sat on the day couch. There was a telephone on the end table there, and she picked up the handset and punched Barry's home phone number. After three rings a voice answered.

"This is Barry Fast. I cannot come to the phone right now but if—"

Mariesa hung up without waiting for the rest of the message. She sighed and rubbed the bridge of her nose. Perhaps she should lie down. Just for a moment, just to relieve the tension. No, Keith and John E. would be waiting. There would be no rest and, tonight, little sleep.

If worry and loss of sleep could solve problems, Prometheus Station itself would be built and in orbit by now.

INTERLUDE:

Some Things That Can Happen to You When Someone Very
Important Takes an Interest in Your Life.

Department of Regulatory Affairs
Bacchus Winery and Distilled Spirits

Holly Bateson picked up the letter as if it were roadkill.
"What the devil is this all about?" she asked aloud. The rest
of her staff tucked in their shoulders and kept silent, which
did not matter, since the question had been rhetorical. "Get
me Clarkson at the ATF!" That was not rhetorical, and her
secretary had begun punching the numbers even before the
exclamation point twanged into the wall like a flung dagger.
Holly talked large and walked wide—she was a ranch gal from
the Wyoming boonies, after all, and you got nowhere fast by
taking small steps—but her people knew how to filter the excess punctuation and knew when she was dead serious.

"Clark!" she said when she had the Alcohol, Tobacco and
Firearms agent on the line. "What gives with this letter of
yours dated the twenty-ninth? Your clerical folks get your files
screwed up?"

"Holly, it's always a joy to hear from you." Clark's voice sounded wary, but maybe it was a bad connection. "Which letter was that?"

"You know damn well which letter, because you know damn well what goes down in your own office. What happened to the approval? I thought the label was a done deal?"

"Well, now, I don't think I ever said that. I said I didn't see any insurmountable problems. But the word came back from Washington and . . . they have better lawyers back East than we have at these dinky field offices."

"Oh, don't try to BS a BSer, Clark. The front office shoved some orders down your throat and you had to gag and swallow. Hell's bells, we've all had to do that a time or two. What I want to know is why? Which *i* did we forget to dot or which *t* did we forget to cross?"

"It's more than that, Holly. It's the whole label concept. Putting the ingredients on the label . . . the Bureau doesn't care much for false or misleading advertising. . . ."

"That list was true and accurate, and you know it!"

"Putting the ingredients on the label—especially all natural ingredients—you mislead people into thinking that wine and beer are nutritious."

"They are, Clark, in moderation. . . . Dammit, you've read the medical studies, I know you have. Besides, they put ingredients on colas and 'sugarcoated chocolate bombs.' They're *required* to. Tell me *those* are nutritious!"

"That's the FDA, not us . . ."

"And that does not explain why you rescinded your approvals of the other two labels. Dammit, you approved the 'Cherry Blossoms' label almost two years ago. It's in production! They tapped the first casks a month ago!"

Clark's voice took on a more severe tone. "Upon review by higher-ups," he said, "it was felt that the name 'Cherry Blossoms' was too enticing and created an impression that the contents were harmless."

Holly took the phone away from her ear and stared at it a moment. Then she resumed the conversation. "Clark, try to follow me on this. It's a label. Labels are advertising. They are *supposed* to entice.''

''It's Bureau policy not to encourage drinking.''

''They repealed Prohibition, Clark. Maybe they forgot to tell you.''

''This isn't prohibition, Holly, it's . . . Look, Holly, I'm really sorry. I signed off on those approvals myself; and if I had my druthers, there is a gang of racist gun runners operating out of Boise that I'd sooner be dealing with.'' He laughed, a little too suddenly. '' 'Cause they are sure enough easier to deal with than you.''

Holly thought for a moment, and tugged at her chin. ''Clark,'' she said at last, ''they try to shove something down your throat that you can't swallow, you can always upchuck.''

''What are you trying to say, Holly?''

''There's something in the woodpile that smells. And it smells political. Dealing with a bureaucracy is one thing. Dealing with one that changes its mind after the fact is another.''

''Hell, Holly.'' And Clark's voice was weary. ''We do that eight times before breakfast.''

Plant Manager's Office
Eire Forge, Thor Machine Tools Division

''What the hell?'' Sandy Hoover read the letter again. Surely, it could not have said what it appeared to say?

But it did.

A judgment against the company from the Postal Service for using Federal Express ''for non-urgent, first-class mail.'' A fine, plus damages? *The Postal Service?* They couldn't be serious, could they?

Yes, they could.

Vendor Quality Assurance Department
Aesklepios, Medical Device Division

Ike Feldman threw the audit report across the room and the pages went flying every which way. He knew he would have to collect the pages later and re-collate them, but nevertheless it gave him a feeling of immense, if futile, satisfaction. "Findings . . . I can live with," he complained to the rest of the room. "If there's a hole in our quality system, I want to know about it. But this . . ."

"Was that the GMP audit report, Ike?" asked Doris.

Ike stared at the fluttering pages. "Yeah."

"I guess they want some corrective actions."

"We had a death in the field," he said, and slumped into his chair. You always hated to hear that one. You always hated to hear that you had helped build something and that it had killed someone. But no one ever asked how many would die if you *didn't* build them. "The auditor went through the use-as-is dispositions on rejected components and traced one of them—a DCC-478—to the failed unit." He picked up the Inspection Report with the Material Review Board stamps on it. That was his signature on the bottom, bold as John Hancock's.

"Damn," said Doris. "That sounds bad."

"Oh, it'll sound worse on the TV news. There's only one little thing the audit report forgot to say. The DCC-478 defect was a cosmetic nonconformance, and the unit failed due to an undetectable flaw in the 223 crystal. Not even the same component."

"Wait a minute," said Jerry. "You mean the field failure wasn't related to the waiver?"

"No more than two people who get on the same bus."

"Didn't you tell the auditor."

Ike's temper boiled up again. "Of course I told the auditor! I did more than tell him; I showed him the damned Failure Analysis!"

"And?"

"And he left it out of his report! I tell you, I can deal with the nitpicking and the Mickey Mouse—and I admit sometimes an outsider can spot things that we've overlooked—but *this* is deliberate falsification by omission."

"Why'd he do it?"

Ike threw his arms out. "Who the hell knows? Maybe he has a quota to fill. He came in with an attitude. He told me,

'I know you're doing *something* wrong and it's my job to find out what it is.' "

"Even if he had to fabricate it?"

"He didn't fabricate anything, Doris. The audit report is the truth and nothing but the truth. It's just not the whole truth."

"So, have Norm hold a press conference."

"Sure, I can see it now. President of Giant Profit-Making Medical Industry Corporation Denies Responsibility for Beloved Mother's Death. That'll play on the six o'clock news. Then the cameras 'rebut' us with a sound-bite from the widower and his two kids." As if suffering a misfortune made you an expert in fault tree analysis. As if medical device companies stayed in business by killing their customers. He sighed.

"So, what are you going to do, Ike?"

Ike picked up the phone. "I think I'll call the American Argus Hot Line."

"Uh, shouldn't you clear that with higher up? It's cheaper to take the hit than fight it."

"Which makes it look as if we admit guilt." He paused a moment before dialing. Then he laughed. "'Cheaper to take the hit than fight it.' It's a helluva note, isn't it? Corporate greed means we don't argue the point."

Facilities Management Office
Shenandoah Works, Vulcan Steel

Pete Conroy made a steeple of his fingers and tucked them under his chin as he tilted back in his chair. He stared at his visitor a moment longer. "Run that by me again."

The EPA man showed infinite patience. "It's very simple, really. Our notice explained everything."

"Well, I'm just a simple country boy. It's why I asked y'all to come in and explain things personal." Actually, he had been hoping to make the EPA man see things, but so far . . . Well, try, try again. "Now, we were under a consent decree to cap our landfill and you-all wanted a plan on how we were going to line the site and cap it."

"Yes, so it will not leach into the water table."

Pete conceded the point with a wave of the hand. "Right. And our engineers worked with your lawyers for three years to come up with a cap-and-seal you would sign off on."

The EPA man did not react. He simply nodded. "That's right."

"And now you've turned it down!"

"That was by a different section within the department."

"And the reason you turned it down was . . . ?"

The EPA man brushed his lips and returned Pete's steady stare. "As the letter states, in the three years since you closed your landfill, marsh grasses have grown over the site and a family of muskrats has moved in."

Pete sighed. "Which means . . . ?"

"It is now classified as wetlands."

"So, I can't do anything to disturb it . . ."

"Correct."

Follow it through to the bitter end. "But . . . ?" he prompted the other.

"But, it remains a closed landfill site and we require an approved capping plan."

Only there was no end. They kept going around and around.

John Witherspoon High School
Mentor Academies, subcontractor

Leilah Frazetti liked nothing better than doing her hair. It was something she enjoyed and something she did well. All the other kids went how phat she looked. So, it was only natural, when the school announced the Marketplace project, that she thought about running a hair salon.

It was kind of complicated, because you had to raise money and buy your equipment and stuff. They said there was a law that she couldn't just use her stuff from home. And you had to rent the space on the athletic field from the school. (Though she didn't know why. Did stores have to rent their own places?) And on top of everything else, she had to figure rates and margins and what prices she should charge. Greg went how she didn't need a head for figures because her head already sat on the best figure in town. He tried to help, because he had taken accounting and bookkeeping, but she thought it might get in the way of their relationship, so she asked Billie Whistle, who was only a sophomore but was really good with numbers, if she would help and Billie went how she would but only for a share in the profits. They settled on 90-10 and Greg would audit the books. Billie ended up selling her accounting services to half the kids in the Marketplace.

When the first market day came, Hair de Leilah did pretty good. Three girls came into her tent and two more made appointments for the next market day. Leilah thought she did pretty good until Billie pointed out that three hairdos did not pay back the money already spent on the combs and stuff, not to mention the sterilizer jar and . . . She made Billie explain about "breakeven" over and over until finally she thought she understood.

But the thing that made the least sense of all was when the man from the city came and tried to make her stop. He went, you can't do that without a city license. And she went, why not? And he went, because of public health. And he goes how it's like *a thousand dollars* for a license.

All the barbers and beauticians had to have them or they couldn't do other people's hair. So Leilah wanted to know if it was okay if she did her friends' hair at home like they sometimes did when they had sleepovers and he said how that was okay, so Leilah asked what happened to the public-health questions, and the city guy got mad and said show respect, young girl. And Mr. deYoung, who happened to be walking past, said we did not need the government to protect us from a bad haircut, and public health was not the issue but collecting license fees was.

And wasn't this settled a year ago with the city clerk's office and the city guy, he goes how that was then and this is now and it's pay up or we shut you down and Leilah said . . .

" 'Pay up or we shut you down,' " she mimicked. "You sound just like my daddy when he's on the phone!"

The city inspector turned an annoyed face to her and said, "Yeah? Who's your 'daddy'?"

"Dominick Frazetti," said Leilah.

The inspector's face paled. "Dominick Frazetti?" Leilah nodded and the man carefully tore the citation he had been writing into quarters. "We'll make this a warning, then."

Sometimes Leilah did not want to know what her father did for a living. What the other kids said, it was all lies. But sometimes she found it useful to pretend it was true.

Later, she saw Mr. deYoung talking to a man and woman wearing headphones who had come out of a van parked at the end of the row where the tents were lined up and one of them made an OK sign with her finger and thumb. But Leilah had no idea what that was all about.

Post Operations Manager
Poseidon Shipping

Jimbo Henderson was grinning when he stepped into the port manager's office. "Karen told me we finally got the EPA reply. When can we start dredging?"

Larry Delgado shook his head. "We can't. They want us to pull a new set of sediment samples and send 'em down to their lab."

"A new set?" Jimbo scratched his head. "Why? What was wrong with the old set?"

"Nothing. It's just that the permit applications expired and we have to start the process all over again."

"What the hell? Larry, it's been three years we've been waiting for the dredging permit. The berths are silting up. If we don't start dredging soon, we won't be able to dock the big ships anymore."

The port manager shrugged. "The permit applications were good for three years."

"But it was the EPA that delayed things! We gave them the samples six months after we filed; and so did the other shippers who operate out of here. What have they been doing for the last two years and six months?"

"Two years and six months . . . and one day. It doesn't matter. It's their game and their rules. Karen's already started the refiling process. Tell your chemists to begin pulling the cores today."

Jimbo tossed his hard hat to the floor. "And wait another three years and hope they finish their analyses before the new permits expire? Hell, we had our own analyses done two weeks after we pulled the first set! Larry, if this port goes another three years without dredging, every shipper in the harbor'll have to shut down. They'll have to anchor the freighters and tankers out beyond the breakwaters and off-load everything onto lighters. Can you see unloading an oil tanker that way? If they were worried about spills in the bay . . ."

"They're worried about paperwork. And there's nothing you or me can do about it." The port manager's eye drifted toward his telephone. "Well, almost nothing."

Managing Editor, *The American Argus*
Heimdall Communications

Gene Forney studied the memos and arranged them on his desk, checking the dates on each one against the reporters' notes. An interesting pattern. A very interesting pattern. But why?

The phone rang and Gene answered it and his secretary told him it was the FCC. Five minutes later—after a one-sided discussion of broadcast license renewals and Fairness Doctrine regulations—he hung up. He pondered the phone call for a few moments; then he pulled a sheet off his memo pad, scrawled a few notes, and added it to the growing pattern on his desk.

The Observatory
Silverpond

Styx twisted from side to side on the little stool while she watched the Rich Lady aim the telescope. It was a warm night; the seasons had not yet changed. Through the slit in the roof an anonymous jumble of stars looked down. Now that she had her driver's license, Styx could come out here more often. Here, or anywhere. Away from the house. Tonight, the Rich Lady was hunting for a rock in the sky, an asteroid she had been tracking.

"Oh, damn!"

The Rich Lady hardly ever cussed, even when she was mad, so you knew she had to be royally ticked for even a "damn" to squeeze out.

"Is something the matter, Ms. van Huyten?" The Rich Lady never let anyone call her "Mariesa"—even other grown-ups—except a few old friends; and Styx did not see that it was worth making an issue of it. The Rich Lady let her hang out. Sometimes they spent time together, like now; sometimes Styx just sat alone in the Roost or outside on the walkway around the Observatory, just to think about things. Why jeopardize a sanctuary? Where would she go if she couldn't come here? Hang out with the dorky mall rats? Go cruising Queen Anne Boulevard and pick up guys? So, she "Ms. van Huytened" whenever she came to Silverpond, even though it sounded really herbie.

The Rich Lady (she *could* have her private names) sighed and pulled back from the eyepiece. "No. Yes. I am sorry, Styx, but I have been irritated all week. When there are more laws and regulations than any reasonable number of people can enforce, the enforcers must pick and choose which rules they will enforce and when—and against whom. And that makes enforcement essentially arbitrary and, ultimately, a political tool to force people into line."

"I don't understand . . ."

The Rich Lady shook her head. "No. It is my problem, not yours."

". . . But when someone tries to shove *me* into line, I shove right back."

Mariesa van Huyten smiled faintly. "Yes, I suppose you would. You and I are alike in that regard."

She was talking to herself, Styx realized. Something big, Styx decided. Something business.

The Rich Lady swiveled back toward the telescope. "Unfortunately, I have allowed my preoccupation to sabotage my relaxation. I must have done some calculations wrong. Either that, or there is a perturbation that I have failed to take into account." Didn't the Rich Lady *ever* use contractions? It made her sound prissy and uptight, and she really wasn't, not when you got her talking on a starry night. Could Mariesa van Huyten say, *Nuts. I been so hung up I can't hang out*, and still be Mariesa van Huyten? Maybe a simultaneous translation would help . . .

"Will the moon be up tonight?" she asked. It was more fun when they got to look at the moon—all those mountains and craters and shadows as sharp as ice. And Mars, too, though the detail was fuzzier, at least you could see it was a disc, a planet, a world.

The Rich Lady looked at the clock. "Yes, shortly. I shall get no more good viewing tonight."

That all depended on your interests. "Can we watch the moon come up from the catwalk? I like that."

"Everyone does." The Rich Lady smiled with a strange inward look, and Styx wondered briefly who she had shared nights on the catwalk with. *With whom she had shared nights on the catwalk* . . . (Was grammar contagious? Was it a disease?) It was weird to think of someone as old as van Huyten having guys over. Probably rich guys with long families, same as her. Thin-faced delicate men wearing blazers and dockers, waving their pinkies in the air as they sipped their tea and yapping on about the Riviera or wherever the hell rich people went on spring break.

Styx followed her out the small door behind the telescope and into the breezy night. Leaning on the rail by her side, Styx stole a glance at the Rich Lady and decided. She'd never go for guys like that; not this one. If she ever took a guy out on the catwalk, it was because they both would look up at the sky.

When the moon came up (Right on time, said Mariesa van Huyten with a glance at her watch, as if she had staged the whole thing), it was huge and orange and seemed to float just the other side of the city. Styx sucked in her breath. "That is a most excellent moon," she said. And then, because she just *had* to ask: "Why is it so big and red?"

"It's red because the light is refracted by the dust in the air. When we look toward the horizon, we look through the thickest slice of the atmosphere."

"Is that why it's so big? Because the air acts like a magnifying glass?"

The Rich Lady shook her head. "It is no bigger than it ever is. Nor any closer. Hold a dime up beside it and you will see. Its apparent size is only an illusion."

Styx watched the moon slowly rise and whiten—and shrink. The Rich Lady could say what she wanted about the size. It could even be true. But it was still a most excellent moon, and it *was* huge and very close tonight. And sometimes you needed every illusion you could get.

2.

The Cost of Counting Chickens

Ned was awakened by a muffled clanging and the sound of a ship's horn. He sat up in bed and rubbed his eyes. A strange room. He must have gone home with somebody yesterday. He yawned and stretched. The bedspace next to him was empty. The glowing hands of the dresser clock announced the small hours of the morning. About time to head down to Joe Nancy's. Distant voices and the chug-chug of a diesel motor drew him to the window of his room. He parted the curtain and peeked into the night.

The dark waters of St. Anthony's Bay splashed among the piers along the waterfront.

The illusion of memory. Wrong waterfront. Wrong dream. And he was alone in the room.

He craned his head as far to the right as he could and saw the hull of a freighter outlined against the starry sky. The derrick on the jetty was running out along its boom, and a crew of longshoremen scampered on its deck.

Quickly, Ned drew on a robe and hurried along the corridor to the common room in the main building. The windows there opened onto the landing field on one side and the harbor on the other. When he pulled the curtain open, he could see the cargo rising on its hoist: the by-now-familiar truncated cone.

"Is that Number Four being delivered?" asked a voice from over his shoulder. Ned turned and saw that Forrest had joined him. Forrest wore briefs and an air of dignity. Ned pulled his robe closed.

"Yeah," he said. "Number Four. That's got to be Mendoza out there on the gantry."

Forrest nodded wisely. "SSTO-X4," he said. "What do you plan to name her?"

Ned grunted. "Me?"

"You're the odds-on favorite to take her up first."

Ned hid his expression from Forrest. Yeah, the pilot to take up the fourth test ship.

"Mike named his after that war hero, *Nesterov*. And I named Number Two, *Bessie Coleman*, and Bat named Number Three, *Alberto Santos-Dumont*. So are you going to keep up the tradition, son?"

Ned grunted, refusing to be drawn into Forrest's game. The politics was obvious. One Russian, one American, and the sole Brazilian each got first crack at a new machine. *"Orville Wright* is a little too trite," he said finally.

Forrest pursed his lips. "Maybe so. But talk about taking a bird up when no one knew shit . . . That Orville, he was the original test pilot. What about *Lindbergh?*"

Ned shook his head. "Not my style. He was a showboat."

"I suppose *Wrong-way Corrigan* is out of the question. . . ."

Ned looked at him, but Forrest was the picture of innocence.

"I've got it, Ned. *Calbraith Rogers.*"

"Yeah? Who was he?" The crane had lifted the new Plank clear of the decks and swung its burden over the docks while the handlers held the guylines steady. Arturo Gusmão waited with the tractor and self-propelled sled. Men on the ground hollered and made hand signals to one another. Mendoza stood like a statue watching the entire process.

"First man to fly clear across the United States," Forrest said.

Ned continued watching the unloading. "I might consider that. He fly nonstop?"

Forrest laughed. "Hell, no. The sumbitch crashed fifteen times along the way. But I tell you something . . ." And Forrest clapped an arm on Ned's shoulder. ". . . that man never did know how to stop trying."

The downrange tower was the catbird seat. You always got first glimpse of the bird coming down. The others, back in the Pit, all they had was telemetry and radar and comm. From here, perched high atop the northern tip of the island in a glassed-in booth, you could hear the thunder in the sky.

The tower tech looked up from her panel at the sound, and Ned put down his clipboard and peered out the window toward the northeast. SSTO-X3 *Alberto Santos-Dumont* was only a speck among the clouds, but it grew even as Ned watched. He checked the tower clock. Right on the profile. Bat was nothing, if not punctual.

He pressed his face against the big, gimbal-mounted binoculars and watched the descent. Nose down, to simulate orbital reentry. "Flight, this is Downrange," said Ned. He spoke aloud for the pickups. "We have Bat on visual." You always lost your name when you worked mission control. You ceased to be Bonifácio and became Flight; you were no longer Katyushka, but Comm. Only the pilot kept his name. As was fitting.

"Copy, Downrange."

Da Silva was coming in fast. It always looked too fast. *Come on, you carioca. You've got to land on your ass, remember?* Bat did not have to remember, only the computer did; but you never could tell. Ned had watched the rotation maneuver twice from Downrange, five times from Flight Control, and once from inside the can itself. The worst part was waiting with your hand over the switches, just in case. Mendoza had told him that rotation was not the most dangerous part of the landing sequence; that in an actual orbital descent, peak dynamic pressure—"max Q"—would reach 260 psi, and acceleration would hit 1.2 g's, and if you got as far as attitude rotation, you were already past that. But Ned had said "worst," not "most dangerous." The pilots called the maneuver "the Swoop of Death." Unofficially, of course. A K-turn in the sky. Swoop down, then up; and then descend bottom-first.

"Commence rotation." De Magalhães's voice—Flight—came through clear on Ned's earphones. Tiny puffs of smoke blossomed on the vehicle's sides. The attitude-control engines. "Rotation maneuver initiated," said da Silva.

"Attitude engines firing," Ned announced just so they would know he hadn't fallen asleep. The instrument tech turned and grinned at him, and he grinned back at her. Telemetry was recording all of this faster and in more detail than any human eye or voice; but the chatter filled a need they all had. Yes, we are in charge of this. Yes, everything looks good. And come to think of it, only Ned was able to say yes, the damn things really are firing.

The approaching spaceship slewed sharply upward, as if Bat had suddenly changed his mind about landing. Ned switched frequency. "I can see your ass, Bat."

"Then you can kiss it, Ned. All engines idle. Bringing up One and Five."

Dull flame erupted on the base of the vessel. "Radar has you two hundred meters north by northwest of pad center," Ned reported.

"Commence translation," said Flight.

"Translation," Bat acknowledged. The side thrusters on the ship flared and Ned guided him until the ship was over the pad.

"Landing thrust," said Flight.

"Landing thrust," said Bat. The thruster flames brightened. As the ship descended, they grew into a pillar of fire.

"Six hundred meters; down at twenty."

"Landing gear deployed."

Ned swung the binoculars around as he tracked the craft in. Over the pad, now. Hydraulic legs popped from their sheaths and Ned confirmed the fact to Bat and to mission control. Like everything else—from the titanium-aluminide aeroshell and carbon-silicon carbide heat shield to the aluminum fuel tanks—the landing gear was off-the-shelf. Ruger AG had been making them for VTOL aircraft for decades. Daedalus had not quite ordered parts out of a catalog, but this was the next best thing. "A junkyard rocket," Forrest had called it. The bird was put together from proven components and subsystems.

Of course, so had been Frankenstein's monster.

"Everything nominal," announced Bat. "Down at zero."

Famous last words. Ned's fingers clenched the binoculars. It was a lot worse watching. Inside the craft, you were too busy to worry. Someday, it would be routine. After twenty or thirty launches, the fist in the gut will relax. That's when it will happen. Just to remind us.

A pillow of flame and smoke billowed under the craft, cushioning it. The ground effect. *Santos-Dumont* eased into it and disappeared.

"Contact," announced Bat. "Engine shutdown." Ned blew out his breath and glanced at his watch. One and a half minutes from acquisition to touchdown. Ned unshipped the binoculars as the cloud began to dissipate in the Atlantic breeze. Turning to the technician, he made the thumbs-up sign.

Yeah. All the components were proven . . . but the total system configuration was still the big question mark. Would all those parts and components mesh together, and would the whole accomplish its mission? That's why the pocket-calculator types had to hand it over to the jocks. Models and simulations could only take you so far. No one had ever landed an equation on the moon.

"File downloaded to Engineering?" he asked. She nodded. "Confirmed." A keyboard arpeggio, and a floppy shot from the slot on the console. Ned took it and slipped it into his shirt pocket. The floppy was only an archival copy. Mendoza would already be poring over the real-time figures on his own terminal, fairing them, extrapolating them.

The tech began shutting down the tower. *No more incoming flights expected today.* The thought made him smile. The tech handed him a second floppy, this one in a red cassette.

"On-line maintenance report," she said.

Ned slipped that in his pocket, too. The onboard computers kept a running check on all systems, noting and correcting anomalies and failures, switching to backups when needed, and providing a detailed maintenance list at the end of each flight. More off-the-shelf technology. Commercial airliners had had such capabilities for years.

He and the tech ran through the shutdown checklist, then locked up. Ned took the manlift—a continuous vertical conveyor belt with footrests and handholds—to the base of the tower and stepped out into the late-afternoon Brazilian sunshine. What time of year was it? Autumn? There were no seasons on Fernando de Noronha. An endless summer, sometimes wet, sometimes dry. Back home, October was creeping down from the north.

Mendoza would hold a technical debriefing in the morning. Once more they would stretch their database past the envelope, trying to guess where the curve would go as they pushed it higher and farther and faster. Flight-test data were messy, not like the neat, prim numbers in the textbooks that always marched along a smooth, predictable curve. Real data always wandered off to the side to pick flowers. The same pilot flying the same craft on the same mission profile did not always achieve the same results.

So it was a cloud of points, through which you could draw any number of smooth, textbook curves. That was all right when all the curves led to the same place. It was not so good when some led to orbit and some did not; when the "fuzziness in the data" was like a fog bank and you couldn't see two feet in front of your face. But each new test flight narrowed the range of projections. In the end, it would be one or the other. Like Forrest said, when you open the box, the cat's either dead or it bites you.

Ned rubbed a hand across his face. Life was more interesting on the margin, when you never quite knew which side of the line you were on. Sometimes, in a case like that, the right pilot could make the difference; grab the curve, goose it, make it go where it damn well ought. Up and out and the sky turns black.

But the Universe does not care.

He had forgotten who had said that. Some famous scientist. There were forces and stresses and weights and strengths of materials and it all added up to an answer; and it did not matter a rat's ass whether you liked that answer or not. *The Universe does not care.*

But Ned DuBois did. So it was only a question of which of them was more stubborn.

One measure of life on Fernando de Noronha was that running errands to Daedalus HQ in Fortaleza had become something to look forward to. A bit of proficiency flying, high above the empty, restless ocean, alone but for God and the disembodied voices of the ATC towers. A chance to be perfectly free, to roll and twist and soar; a time when he answered to nobody . . . except to God and the ATCs. If there was anything wrong with flying, it was that, in the end, you had to come down.

He ran into Forrest in the lobby of the Daedalus Building, the glass tower that loomed over Mucuripe Point. The lobby was an alien world of green marble flooring softened by planters and arrangements of large chrome tubes, as if a giant had smashed a pipe organ and scattered the pieces about. Forrest displayed his dental work. "*Bom dia*, Seu Ned," he said. "How're they hanging?"

"To the ground, Forrest. To the ground." He and Forrest exchanged grips. "You missed Bat's flight," Ned told him.

"Oh, me and João and the rest of the staff, we listened in on the command channel."

"Hanging out with the *brancos*, are you? Didn't you used to be black?"

Forrest chuckled. " 'Used to be black.' Yeah, these dagos have a funny way of talking. Sometimes, I think they never notice skin color at all. Other times, it's like they don't notice anything else. You come in to brief João on the flight?"

Ned hefted the pouch that hung from his right shoulder. "I'm the channel that can't be tapped or intercepted."

Forrest looked thoughtful. "Not unless you talk in your sleep." Then, more seriously, "How does it look?"

Ned did not have to ask what the other man meant. Now that the first flight was history, now that everyone had flown the Plank a few times, all of the astronauts were angling for the next prize assignment—the first orbital flight test. Even Levkin, who affected not to care. So wouldn't it be a kick in the crotch if it turned out there was no prize, after all? "Still in the twilight zone, Forrest," he said. "And we've gone about as high as we can without filing flight plans."

Forrest nodded. "Yeah, that's about what we decided up there." A jerk of the thumb over his shoulder. "We're going to go Phase IV."

Suborbital flights, Ned's heart told him. "What's all this 'we'?"

Forrest's perpetual grin showed signs of mortality. "You are looking at," he said, hooking thumbs into imaginary suspenders, "the newly appointed chief pilot."

Ned studied his friend's face and matched him smile for smile. *A consolation prize. It's what they did with Slayton back in the pioneer days, when the bureaucrats freaked out over his heart murmur. We won't let you fly, but we'll give you a fancy title. Only a bureaucrat would think that mattered.* "Mike Krasnarov must be thrilled, if you're his new boss. Hey, does this mean I have to salute you or something? Call you 'chief'?"

"Son, you can call me anything but late for chow." Forrest clapped him on the shoulder. "You want, I'll stick around till you brief the brass. Then we'll find ourselves a nice restaurant and maybe a couple of even nicer women. Then in the morning, I'll let you look at my afterburner while we fly back to the island."

"Forrest, the day hasn't dawned when I see your tailpipes."

"That's what I just said, isn't it? *Tomorrow*, we fly back. Tonight, we kick our heels up."

"Sounds good to me."

Silence. Ned looked at Forrest, and Forrest looked at Ned. "How much—" "Do you really think—" They both spoke at once, stopped, and looked at each other again.

Finally, Ned said, "They picked the suborbital crew, didn't they?" Silent, Forrest nodded, and Ned asked, "Who?"

Forrest sucked his lips. "It's confidential. They'll announce it next week."

"I promise I'll act real surprised. Tell me who it is." Though if it wasn't him, what did it matter?

"Two-man team," said Forrest at last. "They're going for a big show on this. Flight plan reads Fernando to St. Petersburg."

"Jesus! That's halfway around the world."

"Not quite, but near enough as makes no difference. The way João figured, taking off and landing was the hard part. So as long as we're going up, why not go somewhere else before we come down? So this way, Energia gets to show off, we check out turnaround at their test field, and the Boss Lady gets to demonstrate capabilities to slavering venture capitalists."

"Fractional ballistic orbit," said Ned. Yeah. The data allowed that. He could see the track in his mind's eye. Morocco, France, Germany, and Lithuania. And Russia, of course. Would they need overflight permission? It depended on altitude. Way back with Sputnik I, the Russians had established precedent by not asking permission.

"Yeah," said Forrest a little wistfully, "they'll touch the sky, but they'll come right back down." And the grapes were probably sour-tasting. Ned did not ask who "they" were. He'd been left behind, again. Brazil to Russia and back . . . Who else but the Bat-man and Senhor Machine?

"Do you ever worry when you fly the spacecraft?" asked the woman.

Drunk, Ned did not worry about a hell of a lot. In fact, the only thing that concerned him at the moment was getting the woman into the sack. The restaurant, April in Portugal, was just down President Kennedy Avenue from his hotel, so it wouldn't be too far to walk. The neon lights through the window behind her gave the woman an otherworldly glow, highlighting in reds and blues the coal black hair that swept across her shoulders. The highlights changed in brightness and intensity as the sign across the street marched through its routine.

"Who said anything about flying spacecraft?"

The woman shrugged. "Everyone in Fortaleza knows what happens on the archipelago. You and your friend, you used the terms of flying when you spoke. I am not stupid." She shook her hair back and stuck her chin forward.

Ned looked around the barroom, wondering where Forrest and his girl had gone. "It's not exactly secret," he said, "but it's not exactly public, either."

"Then, you *have* flown the spaceship."

He looked back and locked eyes with her. Johanna? Whatever. At least this one spoke English. "Yeah. Sure. A time or two." Why not? Sometimes they said yes.

"What is it like to fly such a craft? Are you not afraid?"

He swallowed the rest of his drink and wagged three fingers over the table as a signal. Then he turned and gazed out the plate-glass window at the sleeping port. A helicopter blinked like a firefly around the Daedalus landing field. *Are you not afraid?* What kind of damn fool question was that? "It's just a job," he said at last. "There's no time for fear."

"Not then; but later, perhaps? Afterward?"

No, afterward was for drinking and hell-raising and licking a lollipop or two. He turned and faced her. "There's always more training, more study. Flight profiles. Simulator runs. You don't have time for nonessentials."

She leaned forward over the table, giving Ned an aching view down the front of her blouse. He could see the whites of her eyes, see the hunger there, even in the dimly lit barroom. She wanted him; or she wanted something from him. Only fair, because he sure wanted something from her.

He gave her his devil-may-care grin. Mix in some of that stoic-in-the-face-of-death bravado with a little-boy bashful grin and women would hike their skirts up and stand in line. They all wanted some of that flyboy potency. A man would have to have a heart of stone to turn them down. "Sure, you could auger in, but you could cash out just crossing the street.

Hell, I'd be in more danger on the Schuykill Expressway, back home. If you ever thought about everything that could go wrong on the highway, you'd never take your car out of your driveway. Flying's no different, Betsy; just a different set of risks, is all."

She gave him an odd look.

"Is something wrong?" he asked.

"No, nothing."

The woman asked some more questions and Ned answered a few. Maybe not enough, and maybe not the answers she wanted to hear, because in the end she did not go to his room with him. He carried the ache down the street with him and made his way alone to his room, fumbled the key, and dropped it twice before he could let himself in. Inside, he dropped on his back onto the bed and stared up at the slowly twisting plaster ceiling. God, he always drank too much! He was going to be sick. . . . When he closed his eyes, he saw the woman's breasts when she had leaned over the table. He could imagine reaching out and caressing them, imagine the nipples stiffening under his fingertips. Oh, yes. Her tongue would have been sweet and agile in his mouth; her legs, lissome and strong around his waist. Oh, yes. From the room next door he heard the steady rhythm of bedsprings.

The ache was still with him when he rolled off the bed and dragged his sorry carcass to the writing table by the window. There was a cheap ballpoint pen and a portfolio with hotel stationery inside. He pulled out a sheet and wiped it smooth with his hand. Then he began writing.

How long had it been since he had slept in his own bed? Should he count it in months or in years? A succession of anonymous rooms. Hotels, barracks, dormitories. Sometimes he lived in them; sometimes he just slept in them. The tract homes of bored housewives, or the city apartments of starry-eyed working girls. In and out and gone. Never leaving behind anything permanent of himself.

Are you not afraid?

If the ship came apart on you, tens of thousands of feet in the air, you'd never even get a chance to fall. The wind velocity would strip you naked and tear your arms and legs from your body. Everything had a breaking point, a limit beyond which everything fell apart. People, airchines, marriages ... With a new design, who knew where those critical points would lie? At what radius of turn? At what angle of climb? Maybe if I push it a little bit more. Maybe ... now! Uncontrolled vibration. Dynamic coupling. Flat spin. Mind and hand working coldly, urgently. Try this. Try that. No joy. No joy.

Flying on the edge was the ultimate thrill, and it exacted the ultimate price. Damn that woman, anyway! Having asked the question, she could at least have helped him forget the answer.

He wrote for more than an hour, not even bothering to turn on the table lamp. A long letter, laying it all out, explaining himself to little Lizzie, wanting Betsy to understand at last. In the morning, though, when he reread what he had written in the night, he saw that it was drunken gibberish, so he tore it in quarters and dropped it in the trash can. Then he banged on the wall to wake up Forrest, because the sun was up and it was time to ride sky.

De Magalhães named Forrest Calhoun and Gregor Levkin to the backup crew, and Forrest managed to look surprised when he did. They trained with Bat and Mike; went through the same simulations, the same routines, until they had them down cold. Every possible permutation and combination of the transglobal flight was studied, analyzed, and rehearsed, until the responses became second nature, until the body could act without precious seconds lost in thought. "They do it that way," Forrest explained, "so that whatever kills us will be something new."

Ned pretended to laugh at Forrest's jokes. At the end of a good simulator run, he congratulated the crew and smiled his most sincere smile. He even bought Bat and the others drinks down at Claudio's from time to time. He threw himself into Mendoza's task force as if it were important. At night, though, he practiced the flight scenarios himself. Sometimes alone, sometimes with Bobbi or the Volkovs. They all had access to the simulator during the off hours. They all had dreamed of making the flight themselves.

Ned wrote three letters to Betsy and one to Lizzie and destroyed all four without mailing them. What could he tell them? That he had washed out again? That this time, he had not had what it took? Betsy would not understand. Betsy had never understood. Ned spent a lot of hours at Claudio's; and with Claudio's sister, where no explanations were needed.

Claudio's was never too lively; but at midafternoon it could make a cemetery look like a disco. Ned was the only one in the place beside Claudio and his sister. A perfect audience to spill his guts to, because Claudio never listened and Gisela had no English. What she did have was a ready smile, large brown eyes, and smooth, olive skin; and she never buttoned her blouse, tying the shirttails together across her midriff instead. Gisela knew how to please her men, whether in horizontal acrobatics or simply as a ready pair of ears. She took it all into herself, everything the man poured forth, with all of a village girl's unstudied enthusiasms. Sometimes, all a man wanted was to have his beer glass refilled, and she would do that, too, with the same delighted smile.

"I mean to take her up," Ned told Gisela. "The rocket ship. Me." He slapped his chest with the flat of his hand and made his left hand whoosh into the air. "Me," he said again. "Into orbit." And he would, too. These flights, they were only rehearsals, and Ned would get his dibs along with the other also-rans; but Phase V would come soon enough. By then, they would all know the ship, know how she handled. Krasnarov would still be prime pilot; he would still be Senhor Machine, the Iron Mike, who had taken the bird up when no one knew shit. But it was the orbital flight that mattered. Glenn had gotten more fame than Shepard; and it was Lindbergh that people remembered, not Read, not Alcock and Brown.

Gisela nodded her agreement. "You specimen," she said, which was as close to "space man" as she had ever gotten. Sometimes Ned did feel like a specimen. And a poorly preserved one, at that, the alcohol notwithstanding. *Homo intox-*

icatus. Notice, students, the complete replacement of blood plasma by ethanol. . . .

Ned smiled down Gisela's blouse. "You have a couple of nice specimens yourself." How did the old joke go? *You seen two, you seen them all.* It wasn't true, though; and Ned had seen enough to know. They came in a fascinating variety of shapes, all of them paradoxically perfect. Gisela's were full and round and soft. Betsy's had been smaller, flatter, harder. Betsy had a lean body; spare, but whip-strong. He could remember their first time, in that little motel off 277, near Sheppard Air Force Base. Things had looked more permanent then; the gypsy life, over. Ned had thought that he would finally settle down, and something about the waitress in that Wichita Falls steak house had stroked his fancy. Maybe it was the way she kicked the Texas two-step; maybe it was the brazen way she looked him over. Nothing shy about Betsy. Nothing undressing-under-the-nightie about a Texas cowgirl.

Shit. Sex had never been a problem; at least, not sex with each other. They had simply drifted apart over the years. The flyboy glamour wears off when you bring it home every night. And that C&W music had probably conditioned her from birth to expect betrayal. Perhaps, when it finally came, it came almost as a relief.

The door swung open, and Forrest Calhoun paused a moment in the doorway while his eyes grew accustomed to the dimness. When he came over to the table where Ned sat, his boots boomed on the plank flooring. He pulled a chair out, reversed it, and straddled it. A glance at Gisela sent the barmaid flying. "A little early for tying one on, son."

"I like to get a good head start." Ned reached the bottle, but Forrest's hand closed over his.

"What the hell you playing at, son?"

"None of your damned business."

"The hell it ain't. Someday, I may have to depend on your good judgment; and I'd like to think you had some." Forrest pried the bottle from Ned's grasp and set it just beyond his reach. "Seems to me this is what cost you the Air Force bars."

"Fuck you, you black bastard."

The pressure of Forrest's hand increased. "Only half-right there, Ned; because I sure as hell knew my father. A good man until they hung him." Forrest released his grip and Ned nursed his hand.

"And the horse you rode in on," Ned added.

"Stick to sheep, Ned. They're safer and they don't kick as much." The wooden chair creaked as Forrest settled into it. "It don't do no good to feel sorry for yourself."

"Sure. It's a rotten job, but someone's got to do it."

"Pay me enough and I'll do it," said Forrest. "You think you're the only one with problems? Someday, if I'm in a talkative mood, I'll tell you about my daddy and fun and games in rural Texas."

Ned shrugged. "Shit happens."

"Yeah, but you don't have to supply the raw material yourself."

"Well, that sounds real, fucking profound, Forrest; but what's it supposed to mean?"

Forrest pushed his chair back and stood up. He looked at the table, then at Ned; then he picked the bottle up and set it down hard right in front of Ned. "You figure it out." He turned to go.

At the door, he paused and turned. "Reason I came to look you up, old son, is there's been a change of plans. Bat's out. He slipped on the steps coming out of the simulator—a grease spot that wasn't cleaned up—broke his arm. Heitor is holding a safety meeting in . . ." He looked at his watch. ". . . about an hour. Try to be there." He pushed the door open and stepped into the bright November sun.

Ned called after him. "Forrest?"

Calhoun held the door half open, so that the distant sound of surf edged into the empty bar room. "What?"

"Who's replacing Bat?"

"I'm the backup."

Ned studied his friend for a long moment. Then he picked up the half-empty bottle. *What the hell was it a bottle of, anyway?* He found the cork and rammed it home with his palm; set it back upon the table. "Lucky for you it wasn't

Mike who slipped on the grease, then. They would have gone with Levkin in that case.''

"I guess they would have. Keep a Russian on the crew for a flight to St. Petersburg. What are you getting at, Ned?"

Ned said nothing. He just shook his head. Forrest pursed his lips. Finally, he nodded.

"Yeah. All right; but come to that, you've been spending a lot of evening hours in the simulator room yourself. Who knows how long that old grease was there before someone happened to step in it.''

"Could have been there for weeks," Ned agreed.

INTERLUDE:

News Break

Private Space Venture Results in Near Disaster

[*Your news organization name*] today confirmed rumors circulating in the Capital for the past several months of a near disaster involving a private, for-profit space venture. Operating secretly on a small island off the Brazilian coast, and in collusion with several foreign governments, an as-yet unnamed American company built and launched an experimental space capsule only to see it nearly crash on its first test last April. Reliable reports indicate that a human test subject was on board at the time. Despite this near-tragedy, testing has continued.

American authorities were not notified of the launch attempt.

The Office of Commercial Space Transportation has ordered an investigation to determine whether the American company violated any laws by operating in Brazil, beyond the reach of labor, safety, and environmental regulations; and whether any technology transfer or national security issues have been affected. According to informed sources within the OCST, the space vehicle can easily be turned to military ends. The Brazilian government has declined all comment.

"I don't like the lack of visuals," said the director. "This is TV, and you're giving me a talking head. Hell, even a shot of an OCST spokesperson would be *something*."

"This is all we get," the producer told him. "We run with it or we don't run it."

"What I don't get," said the on-air personality, "is if these rumors have been circulating since April, why is this the first time we've heard about them?"

The director and producer exchanged glances. Then the director shrugged. "What if we put a couple of crews on the street and get some reaction shots? C'mon. I need *something* on film."

Ed, here are the reaction shots we've filmed. What do you think?

". . . ~~Even if it does prove to be commercially feasible, which is far from proven,~~ too many launches a year could damage the fragile ozone layer . . ." [Edith Judd, spokesperson for Defend The Earth.]

". . . ~~It's an exciting idea, and more power to 'em.~~ I just don't see why they couldn't do it here in America . . ." ["Jessie," construction worker on 42nd Street renovation project.]

"For this country to build an affordable space transportation system, it's got to have some advanced technology. That's the bottom line no matter what they say about using existing technology." ["Bill," NASA spokesman.]

". . . They shouldn't launch those things until they know that they're perfectly safe . . ." ["Ruth," woman outside grocery on Eighth Avenue.]

*   *   *

"... It smacks of neo-colonialism. Another sellout of the people by the aristocracy to *norteamericano* business interests ..." [Arturo Genao-deLuna, spokesperson for the Latino Power Coalition.]

"This is great. It's really great. It's the best news all year." ["Patty," sci-fi fan at "Worldcon."] <ED, BE SURE TO USE THE VISUAL HERE; THE COSTUME IS PRICELESS.>

"We have subjected the possibility to intense scrutiny and have concluded that the margin for profit in any private space venture is too narrow to warrant serious investment. ~~We shall be watching developments closely, however.~~" [Ford Donnelson, Wall Street investment counselor.]

"I would not want to speculate on the 'unnamed company,' but since you ask, there is only one major industrialist in this country whose obsession with 'space travel' is no secret. ~~Wilson Enterprises agrees that our great nation needs an inexpensive booster to *supplement* NASA's Space Transportation System, but we feel that a *competing* system would be wasteful.~~" [Gene Wilson, CEO, Wilson Enterprises.] <SHORTEN THIS ONE UP, TOO, ED; WE AREN'T RUNNING FREE COMMERCIALS FOR WILSON.>

"This diverts badly needed resources into a hopeless venture while millions of Brazilians live in squalor. Remember, this same government is destroying the rain forest at unprecedented rates and endangering the world ecology." [Statement issued by the Rain Forest Defense Collective.]

~~"How do I feel? Proud to be a human being. The report said this was an international effort, right? Well, that's how it ought to be." ["Yussuf," waiting for train at Grand Central Station.]~~

"Of course, I am not happy to see the profit motive come in the way of space research; ~~but a new and inexpensive launch system may provide an incentive to NASA to improve its own~~

capabilites to meet the needs of the research community." [Daryll Blessing, space scientist, Columbia University.]

"It opens up a number of interesting possibilities; but it is much too early for serious investment. We shall await the conclusion of development testing." ["Jimmy" Caldero, *Bennett, Caldero & Ochs*, venture capitalists.]

"Geez, who cares about that moon stuff? What's important is getting this economy moving again. It's going on six years now." ["Connie," at lunch counter along 7th Ave.]

"As far as I'm concerned, it's just a stunt." [Unnamed Congressional staffer.]

"Hell, when do I book my ticket?" [A. Ray Plumber, at the Port Authority Bus Terminal.]

"I would rather not comment on such a fragmentary and uncertain report. It may be no more than a modest addition to the world's launch capacity. We could always use more communications and resource-monitoring satellites. There are a great many ramifications—for our environment, our economy, for resource usage and the like—that deserve serious scrutiny." [Phil Albright, The Peoples' Crusades.]

"Building boosters for Brazil is tantamount to giving ICBM capability to a Third World nation." [Ex-admiral Winslow Cathcart.]

Bill, we can't use all these reaction shots. Pull a bite or two from a couple of them—make sure they're "punchy"—and fill a two-minute window.

The managing editor tugged at his grizzled, salt-and-pepper beard. A relic of his younger days on small-town New England papers, it had graced his face and chin so long he would have felt naked without it. He read through the copy once more, then laid it on his desk. "This isn't the way the leak was worded, Joan," he pointed out. "That's why the copy desk bounced it to me. The leak was 'unofficial,' but it came with strict instructions to run it 'substantially as-written.' "

Joan dos Santos shrugged. "It left too many questions unanswered, Dan. Unnamed company. Reliable reports. Informed sources. When I don't name my sources, I want to know the reason. There is a difference between protecting sources and concealing them."

"If we play this the wrong way, we get bounced off the distribution list, like Heimdall Communications last year."

Dos Santos stood straighter. "Then maybe we become an investigative newspaper again and not a bulletin board for press releases and 'media opportunities.' "

Dan kicked back in his chair and swiveled to look out the window. Skyscraper walls lined the other side of the street. Anonymous windows, grimy with traffic, had begun to brighten with the coming evening. In the offices directly across from him, strangers laughed and chatted and did incomprehensible things. His next-door neighbors. Why didn't he know them? Physically, they were closer than the publisher's office upstairs. Sometimes, he thought it had been a mistake ever to have left New England. Small towns, with small vistas; but there had been a certain sense of community. Here, the vistas spread no farther than a few hundred feet to a wall of concrete and glass. And what did *that* do to your vision?

"What's your proposal?" he asked, but he already knew. Dos Santos lived in the Ironbound over in Newark, among the Portuguese immigrant community, and something was happening in Brazil, where they spoke Portuguese. It might be no more than a fizzled, poorly financed effort by wannabe space cadets; but it was a government leak that said so, and he had learned way back in the sixties how far he could trust the government. So, the only question was whether he was going to sign the chit authorizing the trip to Brazil or whether dos Santos would go on her own tick and hope for reimbursement later. It wasn't a tough call, and in his younger days he would never have hesitated. Money was tight since the "Christmas

Recession,'' but Joan had a reporter's nose. Who else was going to follow up? Television? ''Television journalist'' was an oxymoron. No, this would need the real thing. And if his own newspaper did not start rolling over rocks on its own just to see what crawled out, then it might as well roll over itself and be a branch of the U.S. Government Information Agency.

''Okay, Joan,'' he heard himself say, ''but don't fly first class and don't stay in the best hotels. Bring me the chit and I'll sign; but I want to see all the receipts afterwards.'' What the hell. If the suits upstairs called him on it, there were always slots on small, New England weeklies.

One of the men in the offices across the street—a stock-broker, a telecom whiz, a *macher*, who knew?—looked up from where he leaned smiling over a secretary's desk. Giving into a sudden, small-town, New England impulse, Dan bobbed his head in greeting.

But the other man was a New Yorker. He scowled and did not wave back.

Styx caught the item on Headline News. A space shot in Brazil. Sitting cross-legged on her bed with the channel-wand in her hand, she grinned at the screen. A picture of the Rich Lady. Rumors reported as fact, but Styx knew they were word up because it sounded like something the Rich Lady would do. *You tighten your belt and you do what you have to do.* ''Kool beans,'' she told the screen.

Poole came off the school bus Monday twitching like a dust bunny and bounced right up to Chase. ''Hey, didja hear it? Didja hear? On the news last night?'' He was bobbing on his toes like God was dribbling him in for a layup. ''Didja hear?''

Chase hated to appear as if he was out of the loop; but by the look of the other losers oozing off the bus, the buzz was buzzing, and he'd probably get it straighter from Jimmy Poole than from anyone else. Only if Poole laid on any of his I'm-so-superior shit, he would pound the herbie into the pavement. ''I hear lots of things,'' he finally decided to say.

''Van Huyten!'' said Poole. ''She's running her own space

program!'' said Poole. ''Down in South America,'' said Poole. ''It was all a secret, but the word leaked out,'' said Poole. ''Building a new kind of spaceship,'' said Poole.

It was like being hit with mallets. Poole couldn't just tell you something. He had to *TELL* you something. A lot of thoughts were turning around Chase's head. That test pilot he'd met during the summer. DuBois? And that handle he had helped machine. And DuBois saying, ''I hope someday they tell you what the hell it is you've helped build.''

''I bet you didn't know about it, did you, Chase?''

That goddamn superior smirk . . . ''Know about it, hell,'' he said, trading smirk for smirk, ''I helped build it.''

''Who gives a shit?'' said Zipper. ''Just honkers . . .''

''Spaceships!'' cried Jo-jo, tossing a stone high up in the air. He made takeoff noises with his mouth. The stone came down in the bushes near the canal and something—probably a rat—shot off through the rustling milkweed and Queen Anne's lace. Azim watched Jo-jo while Zipper talked.

''Just honkers going up in the air.''

It was more than that, Azim thought. Egbo had shown him. New inventions. Technology. Medicine. People lived now who would have died if there hadn't been no spaceships. And black men had gone, too. Maybe ice people kept too much of the pie for themselves; but that was no reason to stop baking pies. What was the point of getting a piece of the action if there was no action? Egbo had shown a space shuttle blast off on videotape and, man, that was *power*.

''Leopard say one of the astro-nauts down there be a brother,'' Azim said at last.

''Be a tom,'' Zipper replied.

Azim let it go. Maybe that Calhoun dude was a tom; maybe he wasn't. Only, what he had was balls, do what he did: sit on a couple hundred ton of explosives *while they lit a fire under you* . . . Man like that, he might do a lot of things; but he'd never shuffle.

''That space stuff, that got nothing to do with us,'' said Zipper.

Azim grunted his agreement. Yeah, they talk about going to other planets; but you live in Eastport, a lotta shit—ranch homes and two-car garages, college degrees and a steady job—that was another planet, too. And they didn't build no rocket ships to take you there.

Ned received two letters after the news broke, an upper and a downer.

> *Dear Captain DuBois, "Sir,"*
> *I don't know if you'll get this. I kind of hope you do. I'm sending it to this Daedalus company and I guess they'll pass it on. Maybe you don't remember me. I'm the kid who made the handle for you at Thor Machine Tools last summer. Chase. I saw Ms. van Huyten on TV the other day saying how you guys were going to fly halfway across the world, but I didn't hear your name when they said who the crew was going to be so I guess they must be saving you for something pretty phat which I figure it'll be the one where you actually go into space. I hope to see it on TV when you do and I hope you don't have to pull that handle I made for you. It's a real good handle but I'd rather you didn't have to use it.*
>
> *Chase Coughlin*

> *. . . could have been a bottle dream or just blowing smoke because you got to admit "assigned to a secret project" and "can't tell you where I'm living" sounds an awful lot like business as usual for Ned DuBois. The news reports back you up, though; so I guess you really couldn't tell me everything. Not that I don't appreciate the money you sent us, but I think you could have sent something more. There's a lot Lizzie needs at this point in her life. . . .*

No anger. No accusations. But reading Betsy's letter, Ned thought he would get frostbite on his fingers.

3.

Curtain Call

Everything packed, everything ready, everything poised on *go*. Mariesa walked Harriet to the door. Below, on the apron, Laurence shut the trunk lid with a final, satisfying chunk and walked around to the passenger door and waited. Maddeningly, Harriet paused in the doorway one last time. "I do wish you would come with me, Riesey," she said. "Everyone will be there. They say Prague is become quite the place to be in the summer."

Mariesa fought an urge to spin her mother around and push her down the stairs into the waiting limo. *Sykes, you take the legs and I will take the arms and . . .* A glance at the butler, patiently holding the door, showed no indication of psi leakage. "Business affairs, I am afraid." Mariesa made the excuses automatically. She could imagine nothing worse than a month in Central Europe with her mother. Lord alone knew how many obsolete archdukes and residual royalty Mummy would contrive to introduce her to. "I am sure you will have a grand time." Privately, Mariesa could see no reason why Harriet insisted on summering in foreign capitals. Paris or

Rome, one season; Prague or Budapest, the next. She always managed to take America with her wherever she went, like a small terrestrial dome on another planet.

Harriet reached out one white-gloved hand and touched Mariesa on the cheek. "You are working yourself positively to death, Mariesa. There are bags growing under your eyes. They are so unsightly on a woman."

They didn't look too good on men, either. . . . But for the concern in Harriet's thought Mariesa forgave her the packaging of them. "I'm sorry, Mummy. I will try to get more rest."

Harriet's glance was doubtful, but she did not press the issue. "Walk with me to the car, dear."

Mariesa obliged, if only to insure that her mother was actually placed in the car and sent on her way. Halfway down the steps to the parking apron, Harriet leaned for support on Mariesa's arm, and remarked in all casualness, "I do hope you do nothing foolish while I am away."

Which could mean anything; and if she failed to ask, she would receive the clarification anyway. "I try to avoid foolishness."

"In most things, dear," her mother said. "In business . . . I am no fool when it comes to business—I was senior trustee for the Gorley Trust for many years—but you, Mariesa, you have your grandfather's knack. However, when it comes to men . . ." She let the sentence linger for a moment. "When it comes to men, I think you will acknowledge that I am a bit more worldly."

"Yes. You showed such good judgment in your choice."

Harriet's fingers were suddenly talons, though her voice maintained the same level of sweet reason. "You never knew Piet when I knew him. You never knew him young and out from under his father's shadow. Willem destroyed him. He never meant to, and he never understood that he did; but he destroyed him, nonetheless. If it hurt you to see what your father had become, think how it hurt me to remember what he had been."

They had paused in their descent. Now Harriet urged them on. "And perhaps that does entitle me to judge. What point to mistakes, if we fail to learn from them?" Then, iron in the velvet voice: "I would rather you did not see your employees socially."

Laurence opened the limo door and held it while Mariesa helped Harriet inside. "You mean Barry," she said without inflection.

Harriet settled in her seat, smoothed her skirt, "Yes." Without looking at her. "I am sure he is a wonderful person and a credit to his people; but socially, he is quite unacceptable. You simply cannot be serious about him."

And was that a plea, an order, or an expression of disbelief? Mariesa controlled her smile. "I can make my own decisions, Mother."

Harriet nodded to herself. "Yes. Well. So can I. As I said, I am no fool in business matters." She pulled the door closed herself, yanking the handle from Laurence's surprised grasp. Mariesa and the driver exchanged glances. "She is anxious to be on her way," Mariesa said.

Laurence made no reply. As he turned away, Mariesa stopped him.

"Laurence? What is your opinion of Barry?"

The big man shook his head. "It's not my place to say, miss."

"I insist. You must have formed some impression of him from the times you've met."

Laurence chuckled softly. "Only a fool would stand between a mother and daughter, or between a woman and a man. And the last time I checked with Mother Sprague, her little boy was no fool."

So, Laurence had opinions, however loath he was to express them. "I see. Well, thank you anyway, Laurence." She turned her back on the car and started up the steps.

"Just one thing, miss."

She stopped and saw that he had paused by the driver's door. The limo stood between them like a barrier. "Yes, Laurence?"

"That time I sold him the Lincoln? Barry, he was no mechanic, but he sure did his homework. He knew what he wanted in a car and he wasn't satisfied until he got it.''

Mariesa nodded, unsure of what Laurence meant. She could imagine Harriet's response. *Bargaining is in their blood.* But setting a goal and pursuing it to the end was not a trait that Mariesa found unsuitable.

Mariesa watched the car down the driveway until it had disappeared behind the white birches that hid the entrance gate. Harriet meant well. She acted from love. If her words or actions often patronized, it was well to remember what she had survived. To remember *that* she had survived. Drunk, Father had not always been gentle; nor careful in what doors he barged through. Mother's demons might be gone, but her defenses still stood.

The news reached Mariesa like the first raindrops of a gathering storm. The first was Chris, who called at three to tell her that the networks had gotten wind of April Fool. Before Mariesa had even gotten to the television room to see for herself, Keith and John E. called, though they could add nothing to what Chris had already told her.

The all-news channel was deep into its cycle, presenting breathless information on the fall line of some Paris designer, and Mariesa stood impatiently with her arms folded, because she was too tense to sit down. While she waited, Steve Matthias and Correy Wilcox called to ask if she had seen it. Then the channel looped back through the national news, and the Plank story was number three. The facts were garbled, of course. Only a handful of business reporters understand their subject, and even fewer science reporters. Combine the two, and you had second-order naïveté. But the bones of the story were there. The newsreader delivered his script with a mix of concerned derision. A word emphasized here; a facial expression there. Mariesa doubted the man was even aware of his own body language. "Foolishness," he told the audience wordlessly, "but someone might have been hurt."

It was only a twenty-second bite. When it was finished, Mariesa sought out the sofa and lowered herself into it. She folded her hands under her lips and thought furiously. So . . .

OCTS has sprung a leak—accidently, or accidently-on-purpose? She had not responded to Michaelson or to the not-so-subtle harassment. Were they upping the ante?

Dolores called from Pegasus Field; then Wallace Coyle and Belinda.

The news leak had mentioned no names, but guessing would not be hard. Michaelson was naive if he thought he could wage a limited media war. He had played his only trump. The press had agendas of their own, and they would take the leak and worry at it like a dog with a bone.

How quickly the guessing would start, and how quickly it would converge on her, Mariesa discovered when the piece repeated on the half hour. McDonnell-Douglas, Wilson, Lockheed, and others were mentioned as possibilities for the "unnamed American company," but speculation already centered on "... well-known space advocate Mariesa van Huyten, chairman of sprawling Van Huyten Industries...." File tape from four years ago showed her testifying before the Space and Technology Committee. Prometheus had been only a collection of research projects then, their interfaces and potentials known only to a select handful. Mariesa barely recognized herself. Ah, how much younger she had been! Altogether too eager; altogether too naive.

She would have to hold a press conference, she decided, and soon, to quash the impression of a "near disaster." The media would call it "spin control," of course; as if everything was interpretation, everything was "spin," and there was no such thing as a fact. "Television. Off," she snapped, surprised at the sharpness she heard in her own voice. It must have affected her timbre too much, because the computer failed to recognize the command and she had to repeat it before the screen blanked.

There would be no point to denying the rumors. The Steering Committee had planned to break the news later in the year, anyway; but they had hoped to delay the announcement until after the fall elections. Template press releases had been prepared for various anticipated scenarios. Public Relations would need only a day or two to select and update the templates and fill in the details. So schedule the press briefing for, what? Friday? No. Friday evening was a media black hole. The news would vanish below the weekend event horizon. Make it Thursday. Chelsea's people could put in overtime setting things up.

The phone rang again, and it was the Werewolf calling with the news.

While Mariesa was still on the phone with Gregorson, a security detail coptered in and set up a perimeter guard around the estate. By the end of the first hour, Security had already stopped four curiosity seekers, two reporters, and a photographer. A second helicopter arrived shortly after and Chisolm herself supervised the erection of a guard shack by the main gate. For the first time since Mariesa could remember, the great wrought-iron gate at Coppice Lane was shut.

Rukavishnikov called all the way from St. Petersburg, where it was four in the morning. Someone had woken him up with a confused, fragmentary report. Mariesa assured him that the premature disclosure could be dealt with and that no change in the game plan was contemplated.

Then it was Chelsea Ford, her PR chief, wondering what the HELL was going on because her office was going BALLISTIC and the networks and wire services were all over her like a FREAKING FUNGUS. Mariesa realized that Sykes had been passing through only a fraction of the calls reaching Silverpond—unlisted number or no—and had been bouncing the rest to Ford's office.

Poor Chelsea. We should have briefed her long ago, no matter what the schedule said. It had been unconscionable to let her hang out there uninformed. A detail overlooked. (And how many more such details were there?) Apologies all around, and a meeting set for tomorrow (and points to Chelsea for being in the loop personally, even on a Sunday).

And then Cousin Britt was on the line.

"Riesey, darling, what on earth is this outrageous rumor on the networks?"

And then: "But, Riesey, it would be such a positive waste!"

And then: "I see. Mariesa, I am afraid I shall have to request a family conference."

The Roost was a refuge. It had always been her refuge. Mariesa curled up on the window seat and wrapped her arms around her knees. Inspiration was not all she had sought up here; often, it had been retreat. In the blackness outside, lights bobbed where Chisolm's people patrolled the grounds. Beyond the trees, traffic snarled the crossroads at Hamm's Corner. Reporters, camera crews, curiosity seekers . . . Headlight beams dueled like light sabers. From belowstairs drifted the muffled sound of the telephone ringing.

She felt as if she had been caught in a hailstorm, pummeled and bruised by a thousand interruptions and importunings. The Brazilian embassy called. A fax from Gene Wilson buzzed into the in-basket. Her E-mail repository filled and overflowed before the system defaulted to VHI headquarters. An "action news" helicopter buzzed the grounds, chased off by Chisolm's complaint to the FAA. In an odd sort of transference, the media frenzy had itself become the news and reporters were now interviewing other reporters over their attempts to cover the story.

And the worst was yet to come, Keith had warned her. The newspeople would go away when some new fascination came along to distract them. The government would go away in November, assuming the polls were right. The special interests, fearful of losing (or eager to grasp) a piece of the action, could be handled. But the nut cases would be showing up soon, and nut cases were forever. Not only opponents, not only the "man was not meant to" crowd of religious and environmental zealots, not only the budgetary bottom feeders who thought that every dime Mariesa spent was a dime *they* did not get; but the "friendly nuts," too. Space cadets. Nostradamians. Millennarians. People who had flown tourist class on UFOs. People looking for Signs.

Chisolm had agreed with Keith about the nut cases. There was someone out there *right now* who thought Mariesa was the Second Coming, and someone else who thought she was the Antichrist. Probably several someones. Possibly even the same someones.

The ringing of the extension phone on her desk jarred her. She unwound from her perch and walked to the desk, where she pressed the intercom button. Maybe Harriet had heard the news in Prague and was calling to upbraid her foolish daughter. "Yes, Sykes?"

"Mr. Fast is on the line, miss. Do you wish to speak with him?"

Sykes had fielded every call—from governments, corporations, media, strangers—passing them through or passing them off without a blink. Yet, for this one caller he felt he needed a ruling. Her hand twisted the phone cord into loops. "Yes, Sykes. I will speak with him."

Sykes transferred the call. "Barry," she said when the connection was made. Just that. Barry.

"Hi, Mariesa. Look, I can just imagine what today has been like for you. I've been watching the news. So I only called to say one thing: *Illegitimi non carborundum.*"

Don't let the bastards grind you down. She chuckled. "Thank you, Barry. I needed to hear that."

Barry's baritone laugh on the other end . . . "I'll be in touch." And then he hung up.

Mariesa cradled the phone and turned back to the window, hugging herself tight. A long day, and tomorrow would be longer. Planning the press conference with Keith and John E. and the others. And then her cousins in the afternoon. Cousin Britt, who had never to Mariesa's knowledge gazed at the sky with any thought other than to the weather, who had never imagined the potentials or the dangers that lurked there nor would believe them were she told . . . Now this golden-brown butterfly, whose life was circumscribed by her golf and her stable and her endless round of oh-so-discreet affairs, could circumscribe the life of everyone else on Earth. Mariesa could not allow that.

The phone downstairs jangled again. All day it had been ringing with calls—asking for instructions or clarifications or demanding explanations. Only Barry had called voicing nothing but support. For her program, or for her? She was not sure it mattered. She was not even sure there was a clear demarcation between them. Barry had called only to cheer her up. Throw that in the balance pan with all the rest.

Mariesa decided that an informal setting would be best for the family conference, so she arranged an afternoon tea at Silverpond. The front room was set in comfortable conversational groupings; finger sandwiches placed on the sideboard beside the large, silver samovar Albert van Huyten had brought back from Russia after the czar had fallen. If she could keep everything social, she might avoid the ugly necessity of counting proxies. "Between the two of us," she told Chris, who had arrived early to plot strategy, "we have close to a majority." She knew she was talking from nervousness and knew that Chris knew; and knew that Chris understood. Gramper had seen to it that Mariesa's shares constituted the largest single block. *A chairman must deal from a position of power.* But it was not a majority; and Gramper had seen to that, too. *Power must never be absolute, Riesey,* he had said in that half-twinkling, half-serious voice he sometimes used. *A chairman must learn to build bridges, not burn them.* Even with Chris's shares a sure thing, an actual vote could be crippling if the margin proved too narrow. And that depended on how many calls Brittany van Huyten-Armitage had made in the meantime and how persuasive she had been.

"If we convince two or three of the others, it should be enough. Norbert, I think. Maybe Pauline. What about your father, Chris?"

Christiaan van Huyten patted his blazer pocket. "I've got his proxy, just in case. He sends his regards. But let's hope it does not come to that. Family fights are always the ugliest." He studied the hors d'oeuvre tray on the sideboard. "Sis only wants assurances that you'll not squander her trust fund. Show her the facts. She can read a balance sheet as well as anyone."

Ah, but show her which facts? Mariesa rubbed the back of her left hand. One set of "facts" predicted the Plank would reach orbit and establish a profitable business. The other set showed the Plank could max out just under a useful mass fraction, and saddle her with the Mother of All White Elephants. Testing continued down on Fernando de Noronha; but Mendoza refused to commit himself.

And maybe—*would that not be an irony?*—maybe her critics would be proven right, after all?

"Perhaps not all the facts," she said. Chris looked at her sharply, then shrugged.

"No point in bothering her with what is still an open question," he agreed. Chris gathered a handful of assorted nuts from the tray and jiggled them a moment before popping them into his mouth. "Mariesa," he said, "who the devil is Barry Fast?"

An odd question to come out of nowhere like that. She noticed Chris's worried scowl. "An Institute Fellow from Witherspoon," she replied carefully. "I have been considering his recruitment into Prometheus. Why?"

"Ah, the Mentor thread . . ." Chris hesitated, then reached inside his blazer and pulled out an envelope. He batted his right hand with it. When he spoke, he did not look directly at her. "Before she left for Europe, your mother gave me her limited power of attorney."

She wasn't sure she had heard him properly. "She gave you what?"

He opened the envelope and removed a sheet of legal paper. "Special case only," he said. "I am instructed to exercise her proxy and vote her shares *against* your proposals, *if* you have continued to see this Fast fellow socially while she is away." He extended the hand with the paper in it. Mariesa could see the letterhead on the open flap. Harriet's lawyers.

Mariesa could not have lifted her arms had she willed it. She took an unsteady step backward and lowered herself onto a settee. She stared at her own hands clenched in her lap. Then she looked up at Chris. "But, I always vote her shares."

"And you may continue to do so, except for this one condition. Look, Riesey, I don't know who this Fast is and I don't want to know. Don't tell me anything; don't let me see anything. *As long as I don't know*, I won't have to exercise the proxy. This paper . . ." He wagged it like a rattle. "This paper can stop Prometheus cold."

"If you do what it says."

"I'd have to, Riesey. Professional ethics." His arm dropped to his side. "You can't suppose I'd *want* to."

He looked so distressed that Mariesa actually felt sorry for him. "I don't blame you, Chris. It's Harriet. She can be so difficult at times."

Chris refolded the power of attorney and tucked it back into his inside pocket. "Look, I can be the hear-no-evil, see-no-evil sort if I have to—I've had my own flings, before I met Marianne—but for God's sake, if you are seeing this man, be discreet. Don't force me to take notice of it."

"No, of course not. I . . . Chris, why you? Why did she pick you of all the cousins?"

He shrugged. "Because I am an officer of the corporation, I suppose. Or perhaps because of what Dad did for Uncle Piet when . . . Well, you know." He paused a moment before continuing. "I don't believe she knew that I was your ally."

"Or she did, and this is her own special cruelty."

Chris brushed his jacket where the letter lay. "It puts me in a rather awkward position." There was a muffled sound of car doors opening and closing and he glanced toward the windows. "The others are beginning to arrive."

Mariesa recalled the scene by the limo three days ago . . . *I am no fool in matters of business* . . . And now Mummy was warning that she would help to destroy the project if Mariesa did not stop seeing Barry. She did not even care what the project was; only that it was important to Mariesa.

And how very like her to leave town before delivering the ultimatum.

Chris would go out of his way not to notice things; but Harriet would not and Harriet would return in the fall. She reached a hand out toward Chris. "She has no right to dictate my social life."

"Perhaps not," Chris agreed. "But her shares were willed her for life. They do not become yours until she dies."

"But, what shall I do?"

Chris gave her a puzzled glance. "You'll have to pick one or the other before your mother returns. Fast or the Goal. I don't see an intractable dilemma."

Mariesa rose stiffly to her feet. "Always the Goal," she said in a whisper. The choice should not be difficult. Barry's friendship had come to mean a great deal; but it did not mean the whole world, not like Prometheus did. Just a small corner of it. Her fists were clenched so tight she could feel the nails digging into her palms.

He looks like Alfred E. Neuman, Mariesa thought, looking into the monitor where the *Nightline* host waited for his cue. She wondered how many other guests on the program had calmed themselves before the program with the same thought. She took a deep breath and looked at her notes. John E. had prepared them in large-point type so that she would have no problem taking them in at a glance. They had rehearsed all the questions and all the answers until Mariesa felt as if she were nothing more than a parrot.

She was participating from her own office. Gene Forney had sent a camera crew in with a cable feed so she would get no work done here tonight. Unless, as Keith had suggested, her work tonight would be her most important contribution yet to the program. Go light on the technical details, he had advised her, but cite a few, so the viewers will know you are well informed. Keep things practical. Emphasize the low-cost space access. This is just one more incremental step. Satellite repair and maintenance. Be sure to mention weather and resource-monitoring satellites. Communications and global positioning. When satellites can be retrieved and repaired at a reasonable cost, they don't need to be super-foolproof anymore and we can afford more of them.

Whatever you do, he had warned, don't mention Torch or FarTrip, or solar power satellites. Or asteroids.

Don't come across like a madwoman, she had said to him, and he hadn't disagreed. Some things people are not ready to listen to.

She took a deep breath and let it out. Keith and John E. sat across the room, just outside of camera range. So did Jack Barnes from Research, whose laptop connected to the Net and who could feed any unanticipated information onto her heads-down desk screen.

The light on the camera went green, and it was time to talk to the world.

The interview and the questions went by in a blur. She could remember them in flashes.

". . . patriotism; but because the island is almost directly on the equator. The Earth's rotation gives us an extra boost when we launch to the east."

"No, I am not disparaging the role of NASA. It is a fine research and development agency; but it is neither organized nor funded for routine operational chores. No one did a finer job than NASA did with the old X-planes; and I have every confidence that they will do as well with the X-planes of the future, once they have cast off extraneous burdens."

"I do not question the need for regulations. The players must know how the game is to be played; and government has a legitimate role in guarding against force and fraud on the playing field. However, each rule, no matter how useful, imposes some restriction on one's freedom to act. Given enough rules, action becomes impossible. And the lack of action has consequences, too. Meanwhile, others accept risks and move on. "I am reminded of something Oscar Wilde once said: 'We are all in the gutter, but some of us are looking at the stars.'"

"Of course, the Plank may fail. Any speculative venture carries with it an element of risk. Were it a sure thing, we would have more competitors than at present. . . . We know of only three others pursuing rival programs. . . . No, I am not at liberty to say who they are; and pooling our projects would not be optimal. I am sure their design approaches are different from ours, and who is to say which shall prove the best? Certainly, it is impossible to know this early in development. Only a bureaucrat would believe it possible to 'choose a winner' before the race has been run. . . . Unless the race is fixed.'' <laughter>

''Perhaps there ought to be several designs, for different purposes. The attempt to be all things for all people is what impaired the efficiency of the Shuttle.''

''Oh, yes, there are those who see this as a great opportunity. They want to hop up on the bandwagon and just 'hug it to death.' '' <laughter>

''. . . but it is not a space 'shot,' Mr. Koppel. It is a space 'flight.' The distinction is important. We want to shift the paradigm from 'artillery range' to 'airport.' We will 'fly ships.' We will not 'launch missiles.' And those ships will be certificated, like any other flying craft. Our landing fields—'spaceports' would not be an inappropriate term— will operate just as seaports and airports do. Routine and inexpensive access to orbit, and at a profit. That is our goal; not scientific research, and certainly not dramatic stunts or grandiose 'moon races.' ''

''You have a fairly large array of critics, Ms. van Huyten, who say it cannot be done.''

''Yes, while privately some of them work on their own ventures. We shall see. The proof is in the doing.''

4.

Without an Upward Look of Caution

The woman was thin, with fine features, almost like a model's. She wore a suit of bright purple and matching cartwheel hat that, contrasted against any other skin tone, would have looked too bold. She sat in one of the student seats across from Barry, answering his questions easily, as if she did job interviews every day.

"I'm sure you will be a fine addition to our faculty, Quinita," Barry said finally. "You come highly recommended."

The woman gave Barry a wry smile. "I am sure I do, Mr. Fast."

Barry gestured toward the folder on his desk. "Teacher of the Year Award. Governor's Citation."

"And out of a job."

"Your students signed a petition to your school board to keep you."

"Their parents did not. I did not give out enough As and Bs to suit them. And the other teachers resented that, too. They thought it made them look like easy graders."

"And were they?"

Quinita Bester considered him silently for a moment before speaking. "Mr. Fast, you don't make good basketball players by lowering the basket. We don't do these children a favor when we fail to hold them to a standard. My children understood that, even if their parents did not. They were supposed to be 'unteachable' and I had them doing Shakespeare, writing formal essays. I had them come to the front of the class and teach each other."

"I know that, Ms. Bester. It is Mentor's policy to hire teachers like yourself. If there are no further questions?" He stood and she stood and he reached across his desk to shake her hand. Hers was a light grip, more a hold than a shake. "Mr. deYoung will show you your new office and explain the company rules."

"Thank you." In the doorway, Quinita Bester squeezed past Shannon Morgenthaler, who entered Barry's homeroom with a stack of file folders cradled in her arms. Barry smiled at her. "Hi, Shannon. What brings you to this side of town?"

"You sounded like you believed what you were saying to her."

Barry gave her an easy grin. "I can sound any way I want. How about sexy?" He did not get a grin back from her, so he shrugged. All right, try official. "She is a damn fine teacher, and it *is* Mentor's policy. Too many of these 'award-winning teachers' lose their jobs, or leave the profession."

"Leaving only us second-raters?"

"I didn't say that."

"You sound like management." Shannon laid the folders on his desk. "It must be the company you keep." Barry let that one pass and, when she saw she would get no response, Shannon added, "Maybe the other school district had reasons for letting her go."

Barry decided not to argue the point. It was none of Shannon's business, anyway. "Maybe." He had seen the reports. *Too many Cs and Ds. Too strict. Makes demands beyond grade level.* He wondered if the principal who had sent those appraisals thought they would discourage Mentor. All over the country, there were teachers who managed Shakespeare in the ghetto and calculus in the barrio and who, after the publicity or the made-for-TV movie had played out, found themselves mysteriously at liberty. *Makes demands beyond grade level.* But the definition of "grade level" had been getting lower and lower.

He shook his head. It was interesting how a man's way of thinking could change in one year. He picked up one of the blue manila folders. "What do we have here?"

"Those are the records for the children who are moving from Dayton to Witherspoon this year."

Barry looked up in surprise. "You could have downloaded them into our files through VHINet."

She brushed the air with her hand. "I don't like computers."

"Well, me, either; but I'm finding a lot of things become easier when you get used to them."

Shannon selected one of the seats, folded the arm desk down and sat against it. "There are a lot of other things that are easier face-to-face." She glanced away for a moment. "That's if you are still interested in that sort of thing."

He paused a moment before answering. "Why wouldn't I be?"

She tossed her head and brushed the hair from her face. "Suppose you tell me. You seem awfully chummy with van Huyten these days. Dave saw you at Michael Anthony's with her just last week. You seemed to be enjoying yourself, he said. I suppose that was more Mentor business?"

Well, cut my throat and call me bastard. Barry shifted on his chair. But, damn it, why should he feel guilty? It was not as if Shannon had a claim on him. *Lord knows, I have no claim on her.* "She likes to dine out," he said. "If you ever met her mother you'd know why. I can show her all sorts of restaurants outside her usual orbit. And, yes, we do talk about Mentor issues." *And a lot of other things besides.* Sometimes they looked at the stars.

"How is she in the sack? Better than me?" The question

was light, but had an edge like a crosscut saw. Barry shook his head.

"I wouldn't know." *Though I wouldn't much mind finding out, either.* And, God, he hoped *that* did not show in his face.

But his flat and matter-of-fact response seemed to assure her. Shannon relaxed and a faint smile lifted her face. "Well, it's nice to know you haven't gotten into Mentor all the way."

Barry grinned nervously at the joke. This was not how they were supposed to work things. They were supposed to keep their privacy private. "How are you getting along with Wu?" he asked.

Shannon's face hardened. "You mean 'Emperor Wu'?" she said. "We butted heads all last year, and I don't think this coming year will be any better. You know he fired five of the staff, including Susie. And Susie had tenure."

"I hadn't heard. But you know as well as I do that Susie used her classroom for politics. . . ."

"Freedom of expression. I didn't agree with her politics, or that awful radio talk show she listened to; but that's not the point. Tenure is supposed to protect us from . . ."

"Mentor's tenure works differently. No teacher can be fired for what he or she says or does outside the classroom; but we are held strictly accountable for what we do inside the classroom, which is—"

"To teach basic skills and civic virtues," she singsonged. "Toe the party line, in other words."

Barry made a ball of his hands on the desk. "Look, Shannon, I'm a principal teacher now, so there are some things I . . ."

"Sure, you have to say what management tells you to say. I understand." She looked around the classroom, into the corners and recesses. "They probably have the place bugged."

"No, listen to me, Shannon. I haven't talked to Wu, but knowing Susie, I think it was less that she brought up politics in the classroom, but that she did it *instead* of teaching the kids. Each of us is responsible for what our students learn. We have an obligation to fulfill the promise we made the children when they registered in our school."

"You said that," said Shannon, "as if you had written the brochure yourself."

He felt his cheeks grow red. "Teaching kids is why we got into this game—"

Shannon stood and the chair honked as it slid on the linoleum tiles. "Don't you think I know that? It's the only thing I ever wanted to do. And not because I had to. I wasn't in the lower quartile of my class, like . . . Well, just say I had other options besides the School of Education. I'm doing this because I *want* to. I just don't like doing it for Van Huyten Industries, and I don't like the longer hours and the longer year, and I don't like the fact that my job security has been taken away from me."

"We all knew the new rules would kick in this year. We had all of last year to make other arrangements—"

"Like there were a lot of places to go."

"—and I chose to stay."

She did not say, *Sure, you're buddy-buddy with Mariesa van Huyten,* but Barry read it in the tightened lines of her face. The fact was that for Barry there *were* a lot of places he could go, if he played his cards right. Shannon smoothed her skirt. "I've got to get back to Dayton, or His Imperial Highness will think I'm goofing off." She slung her purse over her shoulder and took a step toward the door. "I told John I'd have to work late and do the shopping on the way home."

Barry hesitated only a moment before he said, "Have fun."

He knew the routine. When Shannon had gone, he paged through the folders one by one until he found the sticky note attached to the cover of one of them. A list of food and household items. It looked like John was out of deodorant, and Mandy and Jill were due for a macaroni-and-cheese casserole. The backyard floodlight must be out, too. By now, he thought, I should know the buying habits of the Morgenthaler household by heart. Inside the folder was a manila envelope with cash and a hand-scrawled message. *Keep the change.* It was Shannon's tag line. Sometimes she said it after their lovemaking.

There was a store of anger inside Shannon, like a head of

steam in a boiler, that Barry had never understood. He had seen it in her eyes and lips and in the flush on her cheeks and neck as she left. It bled off constantly in sniping and cutting remarks, but sometimes it swelled up from a dull glow to bright cherry red and she lashed out. Barry did not mind his occasional role of punching bag and heat sink. He could take it; he could absorb the scalding steam and shrug it off. Sometimes he wondered how she had relieved that stress in the years before they had met.

There had been times—after arguments with John or the girls, with Wu, sometimes even with Barry—when she had left him sore and exhausted in the bed. He touched his lips with his tongue. Other women had sometimes asked about the scars, and he had invented heroic lies to explain them; but there was no one else in his life just now to wonder at the wounds.

Unless all of Shannon's jealous dreams were fulfilled.

Mariesa was something of a stick, but she was a woman, and not an unattractive one, either, if your tastes ran that way. Why did Shannon always throw her in Barry's face? It would not be betrayal, he reminded himself. There cannot be betrayal without commitment; and if there were commitments anywhere, they lay between Shannon and John.

Barry straightened the stack of folders and put it to the side to give to Sam Ybarra later. There was still a ton of work to finish and it would not get any more done by daydreaming over Shannon. Or Mariesa.

He drummed his pen against his grade book and stared at the open page without seeing the names he had been writing. Mariesa in the sack . . . Now, there was something to contemplate. He could not imagine the woman displaying Shannon's ardor. He could not imagine Mariesa ever shutting down that mind of hers and losing herself in the pleasure. There would always be a part of her that watched and monitored everything. She would be precise, he thought. Scripted, everything planned out ahead of time, with the planning itself an erotic experience. And elegant, too; no cheap motel rooms. There would be satin sheets and soft lights. It would be romantic, rather than bawdy.

Barry linked his hands behind his head and grinned at nothing particular.

Hell, he could live with that.

Sykes showed Barry to the dayroom and returned shortly with a bourbon balanced on a silver tray. "I will tell Ms. van Huyten you have arrived." Barry accepted the drink with a salute. "Cheers," he said. But Sykes gave only a curt, butlerish bow before, tucking the tray under his arm, he left Barry alone. Barry took a seat by the coffee table and sipped his drink while he waited. The afternoon sun, filtered through the curtains, cast the room in a pale gold. A low, inlaid table of dark, rich wood. A silver tea service on the sideboard. Crystal and fine china in a corner display case. Dark-hued paintings of somber, Vandyked men wearing ruffled collars regarded Barry with penetrating eyes and acquisitive smiles.

"Hello, Barry." Mariesa stood in the doorway, one hand lightly touching the doorjamb. She was dressed in a bright blue-and-white outfit of a vaguely nautical cut. The blazer was double-breasted with gold buttons; the skirt, a flutter of white pleats. Everything in place, as always; everything tucked and folded and buttoned up. A striking appearance, save that her eyes were distant and her cheeks sunken; and the hand braced against the doorway did not quite hide the unsteadiness. Barry placed his drink on a coaster, stood, and pulled out a chair for her.

"You look tired," he said. "Sit down."

Mariesa sank into the chair. "Thank you," she said. "Affairs have been rather hectic lately. Keith says that I ought to clone myself." A brief smile. "Barry, about our outing tonight, I am afraid I must cancel. I should have called, but I have been so distracted that—"

"Hey, no problem, I understand." He pulled out the chair next to hers and turned it so he faced her. "You've practically been under siege here this last week."

"Here, and in the boardroom, and in the markets . . . People who want to damn me for defying God. People who want me to give them rides to the moon.'' She sighed. ''Some of my company presidents have upbraided me for 'diverting profits to a private hobbyhorse.' Others are upset because they were not included in the project. Bennett . . .'' She shook her head. ''Bennett was nearly in tears.'' She looked off to the side. ''I should have included Bennett,'' she said distantly. ''Not for his steel, but for his mettle.''

The lady was definitely out of town. Barry stood. ''I better be going. We'll reschedule for next week, okay?'' Mariesa made no reply. He nodded. ''I understand. You don't need one more hassle on top of everything else that's going on right now. I'll keep a low profile; and maybe later we can connect again, if it still matters to either of us.'' Barry waited a moment longer and took a step toward the door. If that's the way it was . . .

''There is more,'' she said as he reached the doorway. ''Harriet does not think I ought to see you. She believes it is improper to 'date' an employee.''

Surprise, surprise! He turned and gave her a steady look. ''And what do you think?''

''I think I dislike being threatened.'' She held a tight-jawed pose for a moment, but then it melted off and she would not look at him. ''But that does not mean the threats are unreal. We must weigh all the consequences of our choices in the balance.''

''I can see myself out,'' he said.

''No, wait,'' she said. ''Stay awhile.''

''Is it what you want?''

She gave him a wan smile. ''A majority of one.''

That gentle smile of hers . . . Suddenly, Barry wanted to reach out and hold her. His hands clenched hard at his sides. ''Two,'' he said, taking the other chair. She leaned her head back and rested it against the wooden palmette top and closed her eyes. Her hand sought his elbow and rested there.

''I saw your press conference yesterday,'' he said. ''You made a good case for your project.''

The hand squeezed his arm. "So did you, according to cousin Britt."

"Did I? When?"

"At Harriet's New Year's party."

He recalled the short, nut-brown woman, recalled sparring with her. "She was, ah, skeptical."

Another short-lived smile chased itself across her face. "Oh, yes. She is that. Though, I think we have reassured her, for now." She released his elbow and ran her hands slowly up and down the arm rails of the chair. "The criticisms that have hurt the most are from those who should have been allies, telling me that the single-stage concept cannot possibly work and that by investing in it so heavily I have diverted resources from more worthwhile ventures."

Barry said, "Meaning their own."

"In a few cases." She twisted her neck and rubbed it with her hand. She paused and gazed past him, over his shoulder. "Maybe they are right. Maybe they *do* know better."

"That doesn't sound like you." Normally, the woman radiated assurance; as if she were the only one in the world who had a roadmap of the future.

She took a deep breath, stifled a yawn. "I spent most of last night on-line, reviewing results with the flight test people. There are—" She stopped suddenly, and her eyes focused on him.

"—problems," he guessed. "And things don't look so good." She hesitated; shook her head.

"It is not as sure a thing as I had hoped," she admitted.

Barry grinned at her. "What ever is? If I only bet on sure things, I'd still be fishing Puget Sound." Though, remembering what precious little flotsam had been brought back from the *Billie G.*, not even that was very certain. If he hadn't gone off to college that same fall, he would have been in the boat, too. "Why turn aside from something you think worth doing just because someone else tells you you oughtn't do it? If you fail, it should be on your own terms; not because you let yourself be talked out of trying. Remember what Frost wrote?

" 'Have I not walked without an upward look
Of caution under stars that very well
Might not have missed me when they shot and fell?
It was a risk I had to take—and took.' "

She shivered. From a chill? From the Frost? She studied him for a long moment, and the corners of her mouth twitched. "That is better advice than you may realize. Never fear, Barry, I have every intention of pushing forward with the project."

"This program of yours . . . it's important."

She hesitated a beat before answering. "More important than you can imagine."

"I'll bet you call it Prometheus." She started, and he pointed to her brooch. "The hand-and-fireball . . . In Greek legend, Prometheus gave fire to humanity. Given your fondness for naming your companies after mythological figures . . ." He shrugged. "It was a straightforward deduction."

She shook her head. "It seems silly to keep you out of it," she said, "when you have already guessed so much."

"The benefits of a classical education," he said with a grin.

"Well, I shan't keep you out of it any longer."

That startled him. "Me?" he laughed. "What could I contribute to your space program? I'm a high-school English teacher, remember?"

"If engineering were all that mattered, we would be on Mars by now. It would resolve . . . It would resolve a number of difficulties if you were officially on board. What do you say?"

A flippant answer froze on his tongue. She wasn't joking. *Welcome to the inner circle, Barry.* His tongue felt suddenly dry and heavy. You spend a lifetime looking for the opportunities, and every now and then one gets plumped right down in your lap. *What should you say, Barry?*

Yes, of course. Never turn it down when it's offered.

But oughtn't there be a better reason for accepting than simply that it was offered?

There were any number of answers. Because it was a career opportunity. Because it was a personal opportunity. Because he liked her company and enjoyed their discussions. Because there was a ton of money involved and some of it might trickle his way. Because he could finally show Ray that a fisherman's son from the Seattle wharves could make it without pawning his soul for the passage. Because, just maybe, it was something worth doing? Barry was not sure himself which reason was true, or even if all of them were.

The gray eyes assessed him, judged him. There were no clues there. He stood up and took a few steps away. His pacing took him to the side table, where the tea service was set. Idly, he ran a finger along the spout of the silver kettle.

Because you had a vision on the road to Damascus. That was why. *Mariesa van Huyten has a window open on the future and you got a glimpse through it and now you want a closer look.* That was the truth, but still not the whole truth. It was *Mariesa* that drew him, more than her dream; and had the dream been of something else, he might still have been drawn as strongly into her orbit. And how on Earth did you explain *that?*

"If you think I could be an asset," he said finally, "I would be happy to be a part of it." His stomach plummeted like an elevator down an endless shaft.

"Excellent. I shall have a briefing set up with Keith; and materials prepared."

Sykes arrived in the day room with an apéritif for Mariesa. An amber liquid in a small, thin glass. He placed a coaster on the table and set the glass upon it, then he stood back a step. "Will that be all, miss?"

"Yes, Sykes. Thank you."

"Mrs. Pontavecchio has prepared a sideboard of breads and cold cuts. Shall I have her bring it here?"

"I shall ring for it, Sykes. Thank you."

The butler bowed from the shoulders. Straightening, he gave Barry a brief glance, then left. Barry watched him go. "No dinner tonight?" he asked.

"No, Mother is in Europe. I see no reason to trouble the staff solely on my account."

Aside from having your drink delivered and a sideboard

prepared. Well, it was all in the details anyhow, wasn't it? "Trouble" was always a matter of degree. "Just you and me," he said with a grin.

The comment earned him a wary look. "You and I and a dozen servants," she said, rubbing her neck muscles again. "I am sorry, Barry. As I said, it was a late evening yesterday; and there was a rather intense meeting with my cousins earlier this afternoon."

"Here, let me do that." Quickly, before he could reconsider, he crossed the room and stood behind her chair and began to knead the muscles at the base of her neck. Mariesa sighed and relaxed.

"Oh . . . That feels good."

Barry felt a twinge of guilt. Shannon had taught him massage; it felt wrong somehow to apply that knowledge to another woman. A new sort of unfaithfulness. Just the neck and shoulders, though. With Shannon, the massage covered a lot more ground. The back, the calves, the thighs . . . Scented oils.

She told him about the Plank. The test site on the archipelago. Mir and the cooperative venture with Energia. The Repair Shop in the Sky. Barry listened with only half an ear. The details were not important. McReynolds would fill in the details.

"You should take it easy," he said. "You are working yourself into a breakdown."

"I cannot. Affairs are at a critical juncture."

"You have competent people working for you, don't you? Trust them to do the job."

He felt the refusal in the tensing of her muscles. Oh, the lady was crazy, all right. When you were as rich and as powerful as she was, all you had to do was want something done. Others would handle the doing. Crazy lady—and he liked a vein of wackiness; but someone should teach her how to relax. *I wonder if that was why our dinner meetings came to be so important to her?*

Mariesa hunched forward. "Would you mind . . . ? Yes . . . The upper back around the shoulder blades . . . ?" Barry felt how hard the muscles there were under the jacket. Tension had turned them to steel. His thumbs pressed and worked them, felt them soften. "Oh . . ." Mariesa breathed slowly in and out for a moment or two. "Oh, much better. Wait. Let me remove my blazer."

She shrugged out of the garment without waiting for his answer. Barry hesitated a moment before he accepted the jacket and draped it over the back of another chair. He went back to work. Beneath the thin cloth of the blouse he could feel her flesh, the straps of her brassiere. "Is that better?" she asked him.

There was a thin line of sweat on his forehead. He would need a massage himself before the night was out. Were his manipulations affecting her? Some, maybe? There was more color in her cheek than he remembered. "Uh, yeah. Better."

Somewhere along the way, his movements changed from massage to caress. He was barely aware of the change and he wondered if she was. A touch is a touch. Study it scientifically and you can measure the pressure, the speed and direction, the duration, the location in an X-Y-Z coordinate frame; but what in all that can measure intimacy? Only . . . when it happened, you knew.

Prometheus the Fire Bringer. A little grandiose, he thought, for an improved satellite launch and repair enterprise. Hephaestus would have been more apropos. Well, what's in a name? There needn't be any significance beyond Mariesa's penchant for mythology. Just a handy demigod, is all.

Fire Bringer. Fire from the sky. *That's where they keep the sun. . . .*

His hands paused in their gentle motions. "There's more, isn't there?" he said. "This launch service is just the beginning. You're going to give fire to humanity, aren't you?" Sure. Not just fire; *the* Fire. The big one up there, that lights up the sky. He had read about the idea in one of the booklets she had loaned him. Orbiting mirrors. Sunlight microwaved to rectenna farms . . . Grandiose dreams for a world that had forgotten how to dream at all.

Mariesa did not answer, and Barry saw that she had fallen asleep in the chair. *They ought to leave her alone for a while and let her catch her breath.* Otherwise, she could . . .

Type A personalities. Workaholics. They dropped like flies. What happens to dreams when the dreamer dies?

He had no idea what his official project duties would be. Only one, that he assigned to himself. Keep this woman alive, somehow, before she killed herself.

He picked her up in his arms and cradled her. She was light, hardly a burden at all. Her legs dangled over his left arm and her skirt slid up. *Nice legs,* he thought. One of her shoes fell off and banged on the floor. She made a throaty sound and turned into him, but did not awaken. He carried her to the day couch by the window and laid her there, stretching her legs and arms straight and arranging a throw pillow under her head. He tugged the loafer off the left foot, then he went back and retrieved the other one and set them both by the side of the couch.

He walked a bit around the room, rubbing his right hand with his left. His fingertips tingled where they had touched her. It was just a rec room, he thought, like a thousand rec rooms in a thousand middle-class homes. The table was teak, or mahogany or something else he could never afford, inlaid with a quiet oceanside scene created by the clever use of different woods. The tea service was silver; the bric-a-brac, Belleck crystal or Dresden china. The paintings on the wall were originals, not prints; and one of them was a van Gogh. Everything about the room shrieked wealth; but underneath it all, it was still just a rec room.

And so underneath it all, you could find the same dreams, the same hurts. In that, the rich really were no different, after all; and money was only a means of achieving the dream, or soothing the hurt.

His circuit brought him back once more to the couch, and he stood there for a moment, watching her sleep, watching her breasts slowly rise and fall against the white of her blouse. He had touched her, stroked her body; and she had not objected. He had carried her in his arms. She was tired. That was one explanation. It was probably the only one. He turned suddenly away from the couch.

I can let myself out, he thought. *No need to bother Sykes.* He walked tiptoe toward the door.

"Barry," he heard her say, and he froze. Now the rebuke? But when he turned and looked, he saw that she had not awakened after all.

A month later, Mariesa invited him to watch the suborbital launch with her and a few others at Silverpond. Belinda and Keith and Chris van Huyten were all present. They sat on a semicircular sofa facing a large flatscreen in the "television room," but Mariesa saved a place beside her just for him. From time to time, amid the small talk, he traded glances with her and saw her secret smile. They shared a special friendship now. They both recognized that, even though neither had spoken about it. Somewhere along the line they had crossed a threshold and, even looking back, he was not quite sure when that had happened.

Barry knew it the moment Harriet entered the room. He saw it in Mariesa's suddenly stiffened face and the sardonic smile that flashed briefly on Belinda's lips. Mariesa exchanged a silent glance with Christiaan before turning around. "Good afternoon, Mummy," she said. "I think you know everyone here . . . ?"

Chris and Keith McReynolds stood, with Barry, half a second behind them. "Hello, Aunt Harriet," said Chris.

"Chris, how good to see you again. And Mr. McReynolds."

"How was Europe, Mrs. van Huyten?" asked Barry. "Mariesa told me you'd come back."

Harriet barely glanced at him before locking eyes with Mariesa. Mariesa said, "I have invited some of the Prometheus team to watch the suborbital flight with me. Would you care to join us?" She nodded to the flatscreen. One sector carried a test pattern, interrupted every now and then by a live shot of the control room or the launchpad while João and his staff tested the private feed. The other sectors carried commercial cablecasts.

"I was about to take the air in the garden," Harriet replied. "Space fails to interest me."

Barry sat down on the sofa, moving a little to the side. "Join us, please," he said. "We were just having some refreshments while we waited."

"I am sure everything will go well," Harriet said. She looked at Barry finally. "Mr. Fast. I trust your teaching goes well? I see Dr. Karr is here, too; so I imagine you will have a great deal to discuss." Harriet gave Mariesa another look and Mariesa's cheeks grew red.

Harriet left without waiting for an answer and Barry felt everyone in the room relax. Or was that only his imagination? Mariesa smiled apologetically at her guests, but remained quiet as the interrupted conversations resumed. Barry squeezed her hand and she squeezed back.

She had told him of Harriet's threat. And this was her way around it. She was not seeing Barry socially; not exactly. Barry was on the project now. There were chaperones present. And this was a business meeting.

Harriet had not been fooled. Barry had seen it in her eyes.

Mariesa was a successful executive. She managed one of the largest fortunes on the continent and had augmented it, largely through her own acumen. She was respected, consulted; deferred to everywhere save within the walls of her own home. Yet, here she sat, reduced to Jesuitical, schoolgirl games because her mother had taken a dislike to him. Outright defiance would be so much cleaner; so much more honest.

Sykes entered the room. "Security at the main gate has called, miss. There is a young woman there who wishes to speak to you."

"Oh? Who is it?" Not a casual tourist or busybody or Sykes would never have gotten the call; nor anyone on her short list, or Sykes would simply have announced them.

"She gave only the name 'Styx.'"

"Roberta? Why, yes! Send her up."

"The Carson girl?" said Barry. "What in the world is she doing here?"

Mariesa traded glances with Belinda. "Oh, Styx visits Silverpond sometimes, just to sit alone up in the Roost. Poets need their solitude."

Chris frowned. "Roberta Carson? Wasn't she one of the—" Mariesa's glance silenced him.

"One of the guests at our school party last year," Mariesa supplied.

Barry kept his thoughts to himself. Chris had not been at the reception, so how would he have known about Roberta? Belinda was a member of Prometheus. She was a sci-fi fan, like the other fellow he had met, Wallace Coyle. But could there be another reason besides? Did the children figure somehow in Prometheus's plans? How could they, as young as they were? Unless Prometheus had plans beyond the next few years . . .

Styx was dressed in her usual black. Midlength dress, heavy boots, a floppy black hat that came down on her forehead. When Sykes showed her into the drawing room, she seemed surprised to see others there. "Oh!" The briefest moment before hesitation gave way to brass. "You said I could come by here whenever I wanted." She stood with her arms behind her back, daring Mariesa to throw her out.

"I have invited some friends to watch the launch with me," Mariesa said. "Would you care to join us?"

Barry suppressed a grin. Mariesa had made that same offer, with considerably less sincerity, no more than a half hour ago.

They made a space for her in their circle and Styx settled between Belinda and Keith. She caught sight of Barry across the coffee table from her. "Mr. Fast? What are you doing here?"

There were a number of ways to answer that, but Barry only smiled at the girl. "Ms. van Huyten invited Dr. Karr and me to watch so we could discuss ways of incorporating the Prometheus Project into our curriculum." A safer answer than *Mariesa and I have something going*, and one that had the additional advantage of being true. The safest way to disguise a meeting as a business meeting was to *make* it a business meeting.

Because VHI was feeding the networks, João preceded the actual launch with some publicity footage that Chelsea Ford's people had prepared on Mikhail Krasnarov and Forrest Calhoun. It showed them in training, relaxing, speaking candidly to the audience. There was even stock tape of Dniepropetrovsk (courtesy of Energia) and of Shelbyville, Texas. Thumbnail sketches introduced the other members of the flight team. In one sympathetic scene, Baltazar da Silva, his arm in a sling, shook their hands and wished them well. It was all staged, of course.

Someday, the exposé writers would breathlessly reveal The Truth. How Ned DuBois drank too much and ran out on his wife and child. How Krasnarov and Calhoun hated each other. How Levkin had been cuckolded, and later suspected in the automobile accident in which his wife and her lover had died. How da Silva's family had cheated an Indian tribe in Amazonas of their land.

Yet, there was also truth in image. If heroes often had feet of clay, they were, at least, still heroes. How many other clay-footed humans could claim as much? Symbols had reality, too.

Ned DeBois and Bobbi McFeeley gave the commentary for the English-language feed. With split screens and computer graphics, they explained the flight plan and its purpose, introduced Rukavishnikov at the landing site, discussed soberly the many things that could go wrong. "There are no guarantees, folks," Bobbi told the audience. "Anybody who says so is a liar."

"The only guarantee," Ned contributed with a lazy grin, "is that the people who volunteer to fly these things are among the best there are. Their training, their reflexes, the practice and experience. We can't say they're ready for everything; but they're ready for an awful lot and flexible enough to think fast in a crisis."

"He has a high opinion of himself," Barry commented with a nod to the screen. DuBois struck him as a bit of a blowhard.

"He's entitled," Mariesa told him.

When the main engines ignited and the SSTO-X1 *Nesterov* climbed on a tower of flame, Belinda cried and Keith sucked in and held his breath. Mariesa watched more coldly and Barry saw that Chris was gnawing his lip. Yeah. Mariesa had told him about the questions they had on engine efficiency. The others might be overwhelmed by the sheer beauty of the drama, but it was the bottom line that mattered in the end. Without that, it was just another Saturday-afternoon matinee.

Quietly, so that no one else saw, Barry took Mariesa's right hand in his left and squeezed hard. She did not look at him, but squeezed back. He watched the ship disappear into the clouds with a peculiar mix of emotions. He was not a dreamer like Belinda or Keith, at least not of sci-fi dreams; nor was his eye with Chris's on the profits to be made. Those were not his dreams, either. But if not, what were?

As for Styx, he noticed at last, the girl's attention was not on the screen at all, but fixed squarely upon Mariesa, her large, dark eyes like twin bores: tunnels down which you might fall forever, or gun barrels cocked and waiting.

INTERLUDE:

Voices (I)

". . . what is the point of going from point A to point B faster and faster? We realize that the St. Petersburg flight was hyped as a great success, and we're not saying anything against the brave Russian and African-American pilots, but has anyone considered what hundreds of those flights a day might mean to the fragile ozone layer? We ought to be thinking about slowing down and taking things at a more natural pace."

"First it was supersonic airplanes that were going to destroy the ozone. Then it was chlorofluorocarbons. Now it is reusable spaceships. A hoped-for effect ever in search of a cause. Sometimes, I think their organization *wants* to believe in imminent catastrophe no less so than a Biblical literalist waving his Book of Revelations. After all, the new millennium *is* about to start."

"Well," said Phil Albright with a slight smile, "at least it's a *recyclable* spaceship. . . ."

*　　*　　*

Wilson picked up his phone on his secretary's signal. "Dave!" He made the greetings as hearty as he could, as if he and Dave were great friends long separated. "How are Wanda and the kids? . . . Oh . . . Sorry to hear that." Wilson made a note on his filecard: DIVORCED. "Look, the reason I'm calling—this is confidential, by the way. I'm just making a few informal inquiries—The reason I'm calling is what Riesey van Huyten said a while back about 'three other' companies working on private space programs. I was wondering if you hear anything from your old buddies at MacDac. Are they resurrecting the Clipper? Nothing, eh? Nothing happening, or you've heard nothing . . . ? I see." Which meant either they were sitting around over there with their thumbs up their collective ass—which he could not see Bill and Paul doing—or they were into something very hush-hush. "No," he replied to Dave's next question, "me neither; but I'm keeping my ear to the ground."

He cradled the phone and rocked back in his tall, leather-upholstered chair, swinging a bit from side to side. He still had a call in to Kenny, who had retired from the Skunk Works last year. Maybe Kenny had heard something from the Lockheed crowd, though Wilson doubted it. Usually there was *some* scuttlebutt floating around and if you knew who to probe, the skinny was usually straight; but all he had gotten so far was cricket chirps. That sort of silence might be more significant than wild rumors. He picked up the phone once more.

"Gloria? Get me Rick ten Boom down at 'The Boomer.' We need to re-think the PERT on his project."

"Well, I would say, John, that the successful landing gave the Reform Party quite a boost. I don't think anyone overlooked Chernomyrdin standing there on the reviewing platform, either. That sent a message about economic reform and the future of Russia's economy. And Energia had the shuttle—Plank, that is, turned around in three days and back to Brazil. A good advertisement for Russian technical expertise . . ."

DONNELLSON TO UNDERWRITE STOCK OFFERING
Daedalus Aerospace Launch Vehicles
"... because the funding, organization and engineering appear much better founded than was apparent from the first news leaks ..."

CHAMPION A CHAMPION
Popular Majority Over Both Opponents
Electoral Mandate to End the Recession
"... new mandate and a new millennium, and a new era of enterprise we all saw dawn earlier this month ..."

BRAZILIAN GOVERNMENT FILES PROTEST
Apology Demanded From Administration
Spokesman
"Brazil Does Not Need 'Permission' From the US"
"... Mr. Michaelson was asked to resign because of remarks he is alleged to have made during discussions with VHI officials. The source of the leak is not known. Meanwhile, investigations continue into alleged misappropriation of ..."

"Did you see him on TV, Zip? That Calhoun? Man, he looked bad."

"You watch too much TV, Azim. Too fucking much TV."

> **Breakout**
> by Roberta Carson
> from *Styx: In the Mud*
>
> It hardly counts who built the walls
> That hem you in,
> Or hold you down
> Beneath a roof of awful expectations.
> Your own hand or others', hell,
> The wall's as stout
> The roof's as firm
> Until you smash them through and into rubble.

I have seen the look when the walls come down,
(And felt it, too, in my own heart)
Eyes transfixed and lips apart
Amid the rubble
Of the past,
Alone, but looking up.

5.

Potshots

Hotel rooms tended to anonymity, but Ned had seen the inside of enough of them to become a connoisseur, and the North Orange Sheraton was acceptable, as the chains went. The bar was pleasant; the restaurant, adequate; and if the view from his room was a dismal one of shuttered storefronts and steel gratings, the appointments were comfortable—and you didn't *have* to look out the window.

Late on a Sunday night, the bar was quiet enough for a contemplative drink or two. An all-news channel played unheeded on a big-screen television. The colors were smeared, as if done by a child who could not stay between the lines. Only a half dozen patrons were present; business travelers, to judge by the rumpled suits and loosened ties. Driving rented cars out of strange airports at ungodly hours. A late check-in and a later dinner and the damn-it-to-hell alarm clock ringing at a morning hour that by rights should not even exist.

Floor-to-ceiling shelving behind the bar displayed an impressive range of liquor bottles against a mirror backing. A wheeled ladder hung from a runner in the ceiling. Ned made a bet with himself that the bottles on the top shelves represented Very Low Demand liquors and deliberately ordered one. Lozovacka, whatever the hell that was.

But the bartender surprised him by reaching under the bar and pulling out a bottle and setting up a brandy snifter. The impressive rack must only be for show. Well, having your employees scooting up and down a glass display case on a wheeled ladder would probably do wonders for your insurance premiums. The bottle had a different shape and label than the one on the rack, so Ned figured it was the "bar lozovacka." Probably not as good as the brand-name stuff. He backhanded the brandy snifter and something like magma poured down his throat. He put the glass down on the bar, hard. *Shit, that'll teach me.* He kept a composed face and nodded appreciatively. "Not bad," he allowed.

The bartender shrugged. "Me, give me a good Scotch double malt, any day. But management stocks that Balkan crap because Little Prishtina is just the other side of the river. The neighborhood what used to be Syria Town when all the Maronites lived there."

The last thing Ned wanted was a discourse on the changing neighborhoods of North Orange. "Is that a fact?" he said in a tone of voice that implied it to be an especially uninteresting one. But the bartender took no offense. He was a professional and Ned was a customer, right?

Ned pulled the folded itinerary from his inside jacket pocket and studied it for the umpteenth time in the dim light of the bar. Two days in freaking North Orange at one of VHI's schools. Toss around curriculum ideas with some Principal Fast and strut your heroic and righteous stuff for the kiddos. Somebody apparently thought that the Plank project would "enhance the learning experience." Then, the real reason for the trip: three days in Texas at one of Argonaut's research laboratories, to review options for downweighting the next generation of Planks. Mendoza would expect a trip report when he got back. Next to root canal, writing trip reports was Ned's favorite activity.

I'm a test pilot, dammit.

Usually. When he hadn't been drinking. *And up yours, Forrest Calhoun.*

Okay, so he was a test pilot *and* an engineer *and* an American citizen, so who else could they have sent to meet with Chris van Huyten? It wasn't as if they were shuffling him out of the way. Not exactly.

He folded the itinerary and tucked it back in his jacket pocket with the ticket folder. A tight schedule, with no slack time for sightseeing—not that there could be too damn many sights in North Orange. Meet with this Fast character Monday and Tuesday. Fly out to Houston Tuesday evening, and the first meting with Chris van Huyten and his staff was eight ay-em bright and early Wednesday morning. No slack, at all.

Except the flight back to Brazil wasn't booked until the following Monday, leaving him at loose ends for the weekend.

Argonaut was off the Gulf Freeway, near Johnson Space Center, just outside Clear Lake City. So the one loose fit in an otherwise tight itinerary was not more than spitting distance from home. Spitting distance. That should make it real easy for Betsy. *Up yours, Forrest Calhoun, Mr. Chief Pilot.* He circled his index finger around his glass. "Another one, friend," he told the bartender.

Big assumption here: that pale-green split-level on the cul-de-sac was still "home."

Shit. No wonder I drink. He lifted the glass. "Here's to friends," he told the bartender. The pinch-faced man sitting two stools to Ned's right glanced his way without interest. "Here's to friends who think they're clever."

"So?" the bartender said. "At least it means you got 'em."

"Yeah." He finished the brandy. "I guess I do." Clever or not.

At the other end of the bar, to Ned's left, a short, dark man with walrus mustaches nursed a mug of headless beer. He tipped his mug in Ned's direction. "The way I figure," he told Ned without preamble, "there are maybe two hundred and sixty million people in this country who don't know you from Adam's goat and couldn't care less. If you got a dozen friends, that's only forty-six parts per billion of friendship, which makes it barely detectable, even on the best instruments. A rare thing; and therefore, valuable.''

Ned snorted. "A real philosopher."

"Supply and demand," the man responded with a chuckle. "Friends are a trace element in the mixture. That's why you can always use another."

The all-news channel cycled through the sports trivia and entertainment trivia and then there was Mariesa van Huyten running a gantlet of reporters down the broad, granite steps of some official-looking building. Reporters shoved cameras and microphones at her, shouting questions. Protected by a wedge of attorneys and assistants, Mariesa smiled right past them.

The voice-over was too low for Ned to hear, but the thin man sitting to his right groaned and said, "Someone oughta straighten that broad out. She got money to spend, she should spend it down on Earth." The dark man at the end of the bar looked over but said nothing.

Where does he think she spends it? Ned waved his brandy snifter at the screen, where a flood in Louisiana had already replaced Mariesa. "What was that all about?"

The other man flipped the back of his hand. "Ah, the Moon Lady met with President Champion yesterday and he gave her a free hand with that space crap. To think I voted for the guy! 'This time elect a champion . . .' And, jeez, I fell for it, hook, line, and sinker."

"Hell, it's her money," Ned said. "What business is it of Champion's how she spends it?"

The man stuck his chin out. "I say it isn't in the national interest."

"Yeah? Well, too bad we didn't elect you president."

"We coulda done worse," the man told him.

Ned had his doubts, but he was not inclined to argue. It would have been lozovacka arguing with gin-and tonic, anyway. *Besides, it's my damn salary we're talking about.*

The two women in the back booth left together, which was too bad, because one of them really had it where it mattered. That reduced the pickings from slim to none and, at this time of night, the odds were unlikely to improve; so Ned paid his tab and slid off his barstool.

And collided with the dark man who had been sitting to his left.

"Sorry," the man said, holding Ned's arm to steady him. "My fault. I should watch where I'm going instead of watching those babes. Did you notice the one with the . . .? Hey . . ." He stooped down. "Y' dropped your plane tickets." He stood and handed the ticket folder to Ned.

"Thanks."

"De nada." The man hurried off after the two women, but Ned doubted he'd find any joy in that direction. Those women had been professionals—but the briefcase and travel voucher kind, not handbags and cosmetic cases. He grinned and started to stuff the ticket envelope back into his inside jacket pocket.

And there was already an envelope in his pocket.

He looked more closely at the one the man had handed him. Same airline logo, but without the seat and gate number the agent had scribbled on the cover in Miami. The guy must have dropped his own tickets, thought Ned, and he opened the folder to see if it contained an itinerary with a name on it.

The tickets read "Ned DuBois" and showed him booked from Houston to Fortaleza. The dates were right, too; but the routing was all wrong. Not Houston to Miami, but a more roundabout route. *Well, Ned, my lad. It looks like someone wants me to spend an eight-hour layover in Quito.*

That was when it clicked. The short, dark man with the eyebrows . . . Shave off the mustache (or maybe unglue it) and you'd have the phony limo driver at the Newark airport.

They had told him his name that evening, after he had picked the man out of a photograph. Anthony Pocchio. And he worked for Wilson Enterprises.

The next morning, a taxi dropped Ned off at Witherspoon. A one-story, light-colored brick building. The facade resembled that of a shopping mall, but Ned doubted any of the kids were fooled. Inside, two corridors branched off from a small, poster-laden vestibule. Left or straight? A kid with black, shoulder-length hair and a pair of earphones was shoving a broom across the floor and looking unreasonably happy about it. Ned motioned to him. "Hey, kid, which way is the principal's office?"

He had to ask twice before the boy unhooked his earphones and leaned on the broom handle with both hands. "Which one?"

"Which one what?"

"Which principal? We got four."

Four principals? "Um . . ." He dug inside his jacket pocket for the itinerary João had given him and shook it open. "Uh, Fast, it says here."

The kid pointed with his chin down the left-hand corridor. "That way. Fifth door on your left." He began sweeping the tiles again.

"Thanks." He half turned away and stopped. "Hey, kid."

Another pause, this one impatient. "What, 'man'?"

"You the janitor or something?"

The other shook his hair back over his shoulder. "Naw. I'm on detention. They make you work off the fine 'steada just couching."

"The fine?"

"Yeah, like a traffic ticket. I get paid, they subtract the fine, and I keep what's left."

"What if you dog it?"

"What if I *what*?"

"What if you don't do the work? Just 'shove broom' for a few hours . . ."

The kid snorted. "What, you think they don't check? Next time, I don't get a work order, and the fine comes outta my own allowance. Who needs that? Me, I don't mind the work. I'm saving up for the concert, anyways." A jerk of the thumb indicated a wall poster. MEAT WAGON: THE **RAW** CONCERT, 7:00, April 13, in the Witherspoon football stadium. Four youths with guitars slung over their shoulders like hoboes' bindlestiffs gave the camera the obligatory Sullen Looks. *Must be the annual talent show.*

"Never heard of them," Ned announced.

The conscript-janitor snorted. "They're seniors here. They play pretty good and the tickets aren't too much, considering."

"They *charge?*"

The kid gave the broom a shove and a thin line of dirt slid down the hall. He gave Ned The Look. "Word." (With that impatient sound halfway between a cough and a grunt that the backward-hatted crowd seemed to be using these days.) "They gotta pay Azim's security detail, and they gotta pay the poster people, and . . . They don't make it back on ticket sales, they're SOL. You know how it is. No free lunch."

The poster people . . . Peering more closely at the poster, Ned saw a logo printed at the bottom: *Chong & Yiu, Fine Designs.* "I see," said Ned, though he did not see at all. And the student-janitor evidently did not care, because he was already herding dust bunnies down the hallway. Ned shook his head and set off for Fast's office.

He found it without any difficulty. The "office" was also a classroom, but it was currently empty, except for a large curly haired man bent over a stack of papers. He looked up when Ned rapped on the doorpost. " 'Captain Ned,' " he said, rising and extending a hand. "Mariesa said you would be here today."

Ned pointed a finger at him. "I remember you. Silverpond, about a year ago. Barry, right?" It was beginning to look like Auld Acquaintance Week. First Pocchio, now Fast. Maybe he really ought to drop in on Betsy when he hit Houston.

They shook hands. "Tell you what," said Fast. "Let's go to the faculty lounge. They have grown-up chairs there. You did bring the Daedalus materials?"

Ned followed him down the hall. *No, I flew all the way up from Brazil without making sure I packed them.* A good swing of his briefcase would catch Fast right at the base of his skull, but would probably not be a good move, career-wise. Damn it, he might be nothing more than a messenger boy; but at least he was a competent one.

The faculty lounge was a small, narrow room with a sofa and a table and chairs. Against one wall were cabinets and sink, a coffeemaker, microwave, and a minirefrigerator. Like any break station in any factory or office. Fast stepped to the coffee machine while Ned pulled the folders from his brief-case. "Pull up a chair," Fast said, "and tell me what you like to drink."

"Bourbon," said Ned, "but I don't think you have any."

Fast grinned over his shoulder. "My kind of guy. We're going out to dinner later with Marie DePardo and Bernie Paulson; so we'll get our chance later. After dinner, we'll real-time on the Net with the other Institute fellows."

"Whatever turns you on." Ned pulled a chair out and strad-dled it. "Regular is fine. Black, no sugar."

"Hey, a real buckaroo." Fast poured two cups from the coffeepot and set the pot aside. "Mariesa may join us for dinner," he added.

Ned remembered a windy night on the observatory catwalk. A night black with stars, and a small, thin woman shivering against him. "Mariesa, eh? It's been a while since I've seen her." He could name-drop as well as anyone; and something about Fast rubbed him the wrong way.

"That's right," said Fast, cocking his head. "You must have met her, being one of the stars of Prometheus." He set the two cups on the table and took a seat facing Ned.

Ned cocked an eyebrow. "Prometheus?"

"Mariesa's space program."

He took a sip of the coffee. "Never knew it had a name. Didn't know it needed one. I just fly ships, is all." Sometimes, anyway. Some star he was.

"Well . . . the Plank program is only one phase of Prome-theus. There are several other programs involved. You know about Mir project, of course." A smile yielded no further de-tails.

Another flash of irritation. Now he knew what bugged him about Fast. The air of being privy. Of being in the know and hobnobbing with the suits, *and making sure you knew about it.* Ned nodded to the folders he had brought along. "And these files I brought up are another phase?"

"No, just a spinoff for Mentor. Our senior principal and a few others are involved in Prometheus because they're space junkies.'' Fast set his own coffee cup down and opened the folder again. He pulled the floppy from the built-in sleeve and looked at it, turning it one way and the other, as if he could read the damn thing if he'd only brought his bifocals. ''Dr. Karr and I thought we could use the Plank program to, ah . . . 'Enrich the curriculum' is what Belinda said.''

''Science class?''

''Whatever.'' Fast replaced the disk. ''We've been restructuring our curricula lately, making it more interdisciplinary.''

Ned shrugged. ''Your field, not mine. Sounds like school has changed since my day.''

'' 'If you always do what you have always done,' '' Fast said, '' 'you will always get what you have always gotten.' '' He laughed, ''Slogans . . .'' and shook his head. ''Mentor has subcontracted on three other districts this year, two in Massachusetts and one in Minnesota. We don't have a cure-all, understand. Some things have gotten better here in the last two years, some haven't; but then, North Orange wasn't a total basket case to begin with. It was stagnation more than decay. Some of the other districts around here . . .'' He shook his head. ''But Mentor doesn't bid on those.''

''Makes sense,'' said Ned. ''Triage. Some get better without any help. Some die no matter what you do. So—''

''Yeah, I know you've got to start somewhere, so it might as well be somewhere you have a chance of success. But no one deserves being written off.'' Fast stood and turned away from Ned, staring at the frosted-glass window at the far end of the narrow room. ''Two years ago, I was *this* close to burnout.'' Thumb and forefinger showed how close. ''I had a flip answer for everything. I could see the dark cloud around every silver lining. Mariesa—and Belinda—they showed me there was still cause for hope. You can't imagine what a prize that is. Hope. The least I can do is pay that debt forward and give it to someone else.''

''Sounds like you know the Boss Lady pretty well.''

Fast shrugged casually. ''Oh, she takes a personal interest in Mentor, and in the North Orange contract. We've had dinner a few times; gone to a show or two. She's an interesting person.''

''I know.'' Fast turned from the window and gave him a quizzical look. Ned grinned. Let him worry about what that meant. Still, if this *poser* had Mariesa's ear, it wouldn't hurt if he said nice things to her about Ned DuBois, Intrepid Space Ranger. He opened his copy of the folder and took out the inventory. "Let's go over what I brought, so we have our ducks in a row for tonight's meeting." *One hand washes another, Barry. I make you look good; you make me look good. We do this right, we'll both be handsome.*

It took a few hours to straighten out the details. Ned was amazed at how much he had to explain to the man. *And he's going to teach this to kids?* Well, no. Be fair. They were only trying to outline a curriculum at this point. And others would be involved. For lunch, Fast took him to a nearby Charlie Brown's along with two other principals, Gwen Glendower and Onwuko Egbo. They plied Ned with questions about the Plank, and discussed the arrangements for the meet-the-astronaut sessions the next day. Egbo was so black he made Forrest Calhoun look like an albino. "Nigerian?" Ned asked him. "Efik," Egbo replied.

Back at the school, he and Fast wrapped things up by mid-afternoon. Barry had a class to teach; so Ned stopped by the school office and asked the gal there to call him a cab. Stepping outside to wait, he noticed that a row of tents with signs and banners had been erected on the athletic field south of the building and a light crowd was beginning to gather. The first booth was set up on the parking lot. Two young men had their heads tucked under the hood of an old '93 Delta.

Ned grinned. It was the sort of thing he remembered from his own high-school days, when he and his friends used to fix junkers in his driveway. He could recall the tang of grease and motor oil and the slick feel of the hoses and wires. Stripped to the waist; the sun beating down on him, his biggest worry in the world whether the fan belt was tight. Life had seemed a real hassle then, a host of problems—girlfriends, grades, scrounging parts, getting into the Springs—enough problems to lap up against his chin even when he stood tiptoed, enough to drown him when the tides were wrong. And yet, looking back, they were a shallow pool compared to what he had faced since. *Of course, I was shorter then.* . . . His parents were the ones without the problems. They were the grown-ups; they were free.

And the grown-up looks back longingly on his carefree youth. Freedom always came at another time of life. Ah, who ever promised that life was fair, anyway?

Ned strolled over to the counter, half wishing he were not wearing a suit or toting a briefcase. The poster for Car-Aid (another Chong & Yiu job) announced tune-ups, minor repairs, and advice, but nothing that required heavy equipment or state licenses. Ads and coupons for Patel's Transmissions were stacked on the counter.

The "proprietor" looked up from under the hood. He was a tall, skinny youth, with his hair shaved on the sides and a New York Mets cap turned backward. Rags bulged in his grease-spattered jeans. "Hi." He did a double take and looked at Ned.

"Hey! Captain DuBois. 'Sir.' " He grinned and Ned suddenly placed him. Auld Acquaintance Week, indeed.

"Hi, Chase. What's up?" He held out a hand. Chase wiped his on a rag and came over to the counter to return the shake.

"They said there'd be an astronaut here tomorrow. I wondered if it'd be you."

"Yeah. Well, I had to come to the States on other business; so they decided to kill two birds with one stone." Ned gestured with his free hand at the row of tents. "What's going on?"

"This? They call it the Student Marketplace. It's a way to make a few bucks on school time, during the Afterclass. You set up a business, rent a booth, try to make sales. At first, only the other kids came around. Now we get parents and even folks from the neighborhood."

Chase offered to show Ned the rest of the Market. He told

his helper he'd be back in a few minutes and to holler if Ned's taxi showed up before then.

Some of the booths were little more than advertising drops. A baby-sitting consortium. "Payne in the Grass" lawn care. "Nerds R Us: We Have the Wonks You Want! Sign Up Now for Next Semester's Tutoring!" Other booths sold goods and services directly. Candy and refreshments from a short, chubby Indian girl. Handcrafted rings and pendants from "Jenny's Jewels." "Hair *de* Leilah." A martial-arts studio, an aerobics class, a comic-book and collector-card "stock exchange"—complete with price quotes handwritten on a marker board. Some of the booths carried flyers for the heavy-metal concert, and Ned was almost sorry he'd be back in Brazil by then. Though considering how loud kids played metal these days, he might get to hear it anyway.

Chong & Yiu featured paintings, some of them quite good, though their sideline of posters and decorated T-shirts seemed to generate more business. One painting featured a Plank roaring upward on a column of smoke and flame, and Ned paused to admire it. Probably taken off the TV broadcast, he thought. That's Forrest and Mike jumping *Nesterov* to Energia's test field southeast of St. Petersburg. *Damn, I wish it had been me in that can.*

"How much for this painting?" Ned asked the willowy Oriental girl with the paint-smeared smock. He didn't know if she was Chong or Yiu.

"That one is not for sale. It was done on commission for Ms. Van Huyten."

Ned raised an eyebrow. "Why am I not surprised? It's quite good." Not professional quality, but competently executed; and just enough shy of photographic exactness to make it work. "Why do you have it out if it's not for sale?"

The girl brushed a wisp of hair from her face. "As a sample of our work. And because I like to look at it."

Ned studied the painting some more. "Yeah." He glanced at his guide. "What do you think, Chase?"

The boy made a who-cares face. "It's okay, I guess." He

eyed the Plank casually. "Do you know if those handles were installed in this one?"

Ned wasn't sure if the retrofit had been complete in time for the launch, but he said, "Yeah, I'm sure they were."

"Phat," said Chase.

"Could you make a silkscreen of this," Ned asked the artist, "and do a T-shirt for me? No, wait. Make that eight T-shirts; six large, two medium. I'll give you a list of names to put on the back."

The Chinese girl said, "You are one of the pilots. I saw you on TV." Ned nodded and she said, "Then, there will be no charge for the shirts."

Ned shook his head and pulled out his wallet. "No, I'll pay. Fair's fair." He gave her his mail drop in Fortaleza and added extra for the shipping.

"We had a crew of city inspectors show up a few months ago," Chase told him as they headed back toward the parking lot. "Tried to close us down. Can you believe that crap?"

"So, what happened?"

Chase shrugged. "The building manager got it all on videotape." He pointed to a parking spot at the end of the row of tents. "There was a TV van from *The American Argus* parked over there, and they rodneyed the whole thing."

In the cab on the way back to the hotel, Ned reflected that Mariesa never left anything to chance. If that TV van was where it was, it was because she had known what was going to happen. He had heard some scuttlebutt at Daedalus about Commerce hassling the Pegasus people in Phoenix and about OSHA inspectors showing up at Werewolf. Nothing since the election, though, so Ned figured Mariesa had cut a deal of some sort. *Too high-level for me.*

And Mariesa never did anything without a purpose. And, sure, VHI had a lot of cauldrons bubbling besides the Plank project, but he had spoken with her often enough to know what was topmost in her mind these days. So if she was baby-sitting this Mentor situation, it had something more to do with . . . Prometheus, Fast had called it. Something more to do with Prometheus than a bit of curriculum enhancement.

But what?

And could it be that his visit here was at least as important to her plans as his visit to Argonaut later in the week?

When he returned the next day, Ned was supplied with a meeting room off the library; and, from time to time, individuals or small groups would come and meet with him. Rap sessions, they had been called when Ned had been young himself. Now "rapping" meant something else. Still, he enjoyed the discussions more than he would have enjoyed making speeches from a stage. He could be himself, a little.

It was an odd mixture of students. Older kids with suspicious eyes and chips on their shoulders. (*But coming to rap with the astronaut was voluntary. . . .*) Younger kids bused over from the middle schools, altogether more eager and bright-eyed. (*Though their chaperone, a mousy woman with dull hair, seemed withdrawn and never spoke a word to him.*) They asked a lot of questions—about the rockets, about flying, about the other "astronauts"—but the questions all boiled down to one: *What was it like to fly a rocket?* And Ned had no easy answer for them. He could tell them about the eager trembling just before he lit the torch. He could tell them about the pressed-into-your-seat power, or about hovering gently as a leaf. The sweet looping maneuver from cross-range attitude to landing attitude. (The Swoop of Death, but you never called it that aloud.) He could tell them that it felt like nothing else in the world.

And he could tell them that, if he were ever barred from doing it, his life would have no meaning. He could have told them that, but he did not. Yet, there was one young, gangly girl dressed in black who, it seemed to Ned, grasped the truth intuitively. She never asked a question, but sat in the back of a small group of girls and looked straight into him and nodded understanding—not at his answers, but at his silences. Only on the way out did she break silence, and that was only to ask, "Did you ever know Jerry Godlaw?"

"Briefly. Just before the *Atlantis* accident. X-33 guys didn't mix much with the Shuttle pilots. He was a quiet guy, studious. A real nature lover." He grinned. "Not at all like me."

"Oh, yes," she said. "Very much like you." But Ned had no inkling of what she meant.

The last group had come and gone and Ned was waiting for the car to take him to the airport. He was already deep into Argonaut's briefing papers when he sensed a presence in the doorway. He looked up and saw three black youths standing there, arms folded. One of them wore a half-vacant stare; another, one of unconcealed hate. The third, the skinny one in front, sported dark glasses, so he had no stare at all. They filled the doorway like a cork.

"Sorry, boys, the show's over. I have a plane to catch." He snapped the briefcase shut and stood up, but the cork did not pop.

"Got just one question," said the boy in front.

Ned shrugged. "Okay. I got just one answer left. Let's see if they match."

The lips flickered up at the corners for just a moment. "The other astronaut, that Forrest Calhoun. What kind of man he be?"

"Forrest? He's a stand-up guy."

"Like a stand-up comic? Like a clown?" The voice had an edge to it.

"No." And Ned gave his own voice an edge. "Because if there's ever a job that needs doing, he's the first to stand up." *Even if the job is to pull a bottle from a friend's hand.*

But, then, some jobs are more dangerous than others.

"Sure, let the nigger go first." That was the second youth, the one with the smoldering eyes. "Might be dangerous."

Ned laughed. "Dangerous? Why, hell, we plotted and schemed and elbowed each other just for the chance to be first. Mike Krasnarov even tricked his way onto what was supposed to be an unmanned flight." *And someone may have greased the step on the simulator, just to move ahead in the queue.* And possibly a few other incidents over the last year. Little things that tended to lower your proficiency rating, just a bit. That bothered him more than anything, more than the Death

Swoop, more than max Q, more than the fact that the ship might not ever make it all the way. It meant that there was one of them who could not be relied on, who might hang back when you needed a hand.

Or it might have been just what it seemed—careless maintenance—and everything else was only what he had poured from a bottle.

The leader stepped farther into the room, invaded Ned's space. "You saying he not a tom?"

Ned held his ground. "Forrest and me go back a long way. He is one of the finest men I know. He doesn't get in your face—he's too secure to bother—but he won't back down, either. You might want to try and make him, but you'll never try it twice."

A moment passed, then a grin split the young man's face and he stepped back. "Yeah. He sound bad. You taking a chance, letting a bad-ass nigger fly your ships."

"Which would you rather have, a 'boy' who does what he's told, or a 'man' who knows what to do?"

The skinny kid made an odd gesture with his hand. "Word up, man." Ned saw, over the youth's shoulder, that the burning eyes of the second boy were aimed no longer at Ned, but at the skinny kid.

They turned, uncorking the doorway. The skinny one turned back for a moment and removed his sunglasses. "Name's Azim," he said. He did not offer his hand. "Didn't see you ready to back down, neither," he observed.

Ned gave him a tiger's smile, the one he had worn at Nancy's, a lifetime ago, in Galveston harbor. "Hell, son, there were only three of you."

Betsy didn't say anything for the longest time after she answered the door and saw Ned standing there, as big as life. She braced one arm across the doorway and studied him. Finally, she said, "Well, well, well," stood upright, and turned back into the house.

Ned took that as an invitation—Did he need one? It was his house!—and followed her inside, admiring the sway of her hips. She wore a red-and-white checked shirt tucked into form-fitting cowgirl jeans; tan, pointy-toed shit-kickers on her feet. As slim and wiry as he remembered. She'd been keeping herself in trim, all right. For his sake? For her own? Or was there someone else? It was a creepy feeling. They had been married seven years, but he felt as if he were meeting a stranger.

She led him into the kitchen and he pulled out a metal-and-plastic chair from under the table. Same old furniture. Dishes were soaking in the sink. Betsy rummaged through the refrigerator and brought out a pair of Lone Stars and handed one to Ned. "So," she said, sinking into a chair across the table from him and setting her bottle down hard on the table, "what drags your sorry butt back into town?"

Ned twisted the cap off his bottle. "Business," he said. *You* . . . He tipped the bottle and let the ice-cold beer pour down his throat. "I was over in Argonaut's lab the last three days . . . You should see what they're working on there. Aerogels in commercial quantities. They add water to a silica gel–acetone solution. Then they draw off the acetone by . . . Well, the process is confidential, but the residue, the silicon aerogel, is so light they call it 'solid smoke.' Build a spaceship out of that and you could drop-kick the damn thing into orbit. Well, that's an exaggeration; but—"

"Ned?"

"What?"

"Try to imagine how little I care."

Ned grunted and took another swallow of brew. Betsy never had been too keen on the engineering side of things. Why was he babbling like this, anyway? He kept a tight grip on his Lone Star. Silence formed between them.

"Been a while," she said at last.

"I was hired onto a confidential project."

"I know, I watch the TV. Ned DuBois, Space Ranger. You could have written."

"I did."

"Sure. Every couple of months. Every season, a new letter. Leaves turning and the first snow and the first robin, and I wanted something more than a damn weathercock!"

"I'm no damn good at letters. You know that."

"Oh, I know it, all right. If it hadn't been for that Pess-owe fella calling me, I wouldn't have known if you were alive or dead."

"Would it have mattered to you?"

She looked away. "Jesus."

"I sent you money. I made sure the mortgage was paid."

"It wasn't enough."

"It was all I could afford."

She looked back at him, her eyes bright and knocking-around-in-honky-tonk cowgirl hard. "You still don't get it. *Money* wasn't 'enough.' Lizzie searched the house for days after you left, looking in closets and lifting up the bedspreads. I'll just let you guess who she was looking for."

Ned turned away, suddenly unable to speak. Out the kitchen window a group of boys played basketball in the cul-de-sac. The peculiar *boing* of dribbling and the shrieks of children filtered indistinctly through the thin walls. The cries sounded almost like the shearing of gulls over St. Anthony's Bay. No wonder he drank. You had to be sober to see how big a shit you were. "How is she?" he asked hoarsely.

"At a friend's house. She'll be coming home soon. Are you sure you want to be here when she does?"

He turned and looked at her. "What does that mean?"

"I don't want you stepping back into her life if it's just for one day."

"Jesus, any longer and she'll forget who I am."

"Well, I will keep that in mind."

Ned stared into his bottle, through it, beyond it. "I don't even remember what we argued about."

"I do."

He looked at her.

"Emma Loggerwood."

"Oh." Emma? A short, chubby cow of a woman. A neighborly smile some days in the driveway. Emma? He wouldn't look Betsy in the face. Emma had come over, upset over something and looking for Betsy, and had found Ned, instead. *It was right here, in the kitchen,* he realized. He could remember that much now, like a strobe flash of memory; but he honest-to-God could recall nothing else about it. Not why she had come over, not who made the first move, not even what she had felt like. It was all gone, down the drains at Joe Nancy's along with the argument and the walking out and everything else. Along with maybe his whole life.

"Strangers are one thing, Ned; but neighbors are something else. Strangers, I don't have to look them in the eye at the Kroger's, or chat over the back fence. Neighbors, I can't pretend they don't exist." Betsy twisted her cap off with a sudden jerk, like she was wringing a chicken's neck. The chilled air inside steamed out the open mouth. She made no move to drink from it.

"I'm sorry," he said.

"You're sorry." Betsy stared at him a moment, then shook her head. "Why the hell did you come back?"

What could he tell her about waking up in a Galveston bar with no clear memory of how he had gotten there, only knowing that somehow he had screwed the pooch for good and all. "I want to make things right," he said.

"It can't be done."

"Look," he said finally. "I want you with me. I want to be with you."

She upended her bottle and let the beer slide down her throat. "Took you two years to figure that out," she said, banging the bottle hard on the table. "Why?"

Because I think of you when I'm with other women. Try another angle, Ned. You'll never make salesman with a pitch like that. He reached inside his jacket and pulled out his plane tickets, the first set. The ones he didn't need anymore. He slapped them down on the table. Betsy looked at them but made no move to pick them up.

"They're in my name," he said, "but they're transferable. I bought a second set for Lizzie. I left the dates open, in case . . ."

"In case I didn't drop everything, quit my job, and rush right off with you?"

"Look, you can do whatever you want. I told you I want

to start over and do things right. I want to be a father and a husband. I want that more than anything I've ever wanted."

"More than flying?"

He cradled the now-empty beer bottle between his palms. "That's different," he said. "That's a different sort of need."

Betsy picked up the envelope at last and looked inside. "If I did come," she asked, "how many of your bimbos would I be sharing that island with?"

Three. No, four. "That's all behind me now."

"That's what you said seven years ago, at the Longhorn. Why should I believe you now?"

Ned turned and slapped his palm hard against the wall. "Because, damn it, when I'm with other women, I think of you!"

Betsy stared at him a moment. Then she burst out laughing. "Ned, you say the God-damnedest things to sweet-talk a gal." Betsy tipped her head back and swallowed half the bottle. When she put it down, she looked first at Ned, then at the tabletop, and grunted a short, sad laugh. "Hell, Ned, there's only one thing in the whole world you could have done worse than come back."

"What's that?"

"Not come back at all."

It was a crazy planet. From the sea-smashed, guano-pasted rocky islands of the Atlantic, to the gently rolling ridges of New Jersey to the scrub country around Houston to the towering indifference of the Andes. What the hell, he was a spaceman, right? So it was only fair that each time he stepped off his vessel he was on a different planet.

His plane from the States touched down at Quito airport a little after two and a little man with Indio features met him at the gate and escorted him to a smaller terminal where a Kaman Husky bearing the Wilson logo on its boom sat with its twin rotors scissoring in idle. His escort smiled him aboard and departed.

Inside the helicopter were nine seats, arranged in rows of two-and-one. A man in coveralls was just locking up the cargo compartment when Ned entered. He nodded, but showed no curiosity beyond that. A man in a khaki bush jacket sitting in the first row stood and extended his hand.

"Captain DuBois, right? Name's Richard ten Boom, project managing director. You can call me Rick." He gave a hand signal to the pilot, who nodded and did things with his hands and feet. The copter tilted forward and rose into the air. Hovering a few feet over the tarmac, he took them out the taxiway to the helipad.

Can't have him take her up right from the gate, it would give the ATC fits. Still, Ned thought it amusing that helicopters had to use the taxiways and runways, just like the jets and prop jobs. He settled himself in the seat across the aisle from ten Boom and buckled his harness. "And what project is that?" he asked with a smile.

Ten Boom smiled back. "You'll see. Relax and take a nap if you want, but I recommend the scenery along the way."

"Where are we going?"

Ten Boom pointed out the window toward the snowcapped peaks. "Up there."

Up there, indeed. The copter descended an hour later on a landing pad set in a broad alpine valley just below the peaks of the Andes and fronting on a narrow, high-walled pass. As the copter tilted and settled in, Ned saw a semicircle of low, utilitarian buildings and an oil pipeline stretching off toward the pass from a large, two-story shed. Rails paralleled the pipeline on both sides, and an electric car was parked at the pipehead, next to the shed.

The air was thin and blew cold when Ned stepped down. *Jesus, they should have told me to bring my jacket.* He hugged himself while ten Boom climbed down beside him.

"Invigorating, isn't it?" the man asked.

"Like a morgue."

Ten Boom laughed. "Yeah. The temperature in the sierra plateaus hardly ever gets above seventy-five Fahrenheit. At night, it drops to damn-near freezing."

Ned shook his head. Fernando de Noronha was just about due east of here. It might be wet, but it was mostly warm. He followed his host to the building at the center of the semicircle, which he took for the administration building. Why on earth had someone lured him here to see an oil pipeline?

Answer: It was not an oil pipeline.

He caught up with ten Boom and tapped him on the shoulder. "How many barrels a day do you pump out of here, Rick?"

Ten Boom paused on the steps and turned. He pointed toward the pipeline. They were close enough now that Ned could see it was a damn big pipe. Six feet in diameter. "This is an ideal location," he said. "High up and on the equator. You follow that out, straight as a Marine's crease, and past Antisana Peak is the Baeza pipehead, where they bring the oil in from the fields around Puerto Francisco de Orellana. From the air, or from the sky, this looks like a new section under construction."

Meaning that it was not.

"What the hell is it, then? And why did you bring me down here to see it?"

"It was Gene's idea," ten Boom told him. "He wants you to take a message back to VHI."

Ten Boom led him to a service car sitting on the rails that paralleled the pipeline, and they sped up the steep, rocky-sided pass. Smaller pipes ran out to armored sheds set a few hundred feet off. "We call it the Boomer," ten Boom said. "Sometimes, I think that was the only reason Gene picked me to head up the project, so if the name leaked out people would think it had to do with me." He paused and studied the track ahead, where a spur branched off to another of the armored sheds. "Like *Prometheus*," he added casually, "it could mean anything."

Well, it wasn't like the Plank launches weren't public knowledge now; but even Ned hadn't known about the broader program until that schoolteacher had told him. Prometheus. Whatever the hell that meant. The sled raced past groups of short, barrel-chested men in baggy field jackets checking levels and adjusting hydraulic jacks that supported the pipe. Andean Indians, ten Boom told him.

"We employ mostly locals for the rigging work. There are quite a few experienced riggers from the Napo fields. Folks from the coast sometimes have to wear oxygen masks up here—the air is so thin—and they look like they're walking around on some alien planet."

Ten Boom's pocket telephone beeped and he flipped it open. Ned wondered if the engineers who had designed cell phones had modeled them consciously after the communicators on the first "Star Trek" series. "Ten Boom here." The project manager listened, nodding. "Right," he said, and folded the telephone. "The 'pig' went down the line without a whistle," he said, as the car braked into a loop that dipped under the pipeline and slowed to a halt beside a bunker two hundred feet to the other side. From there, the return tracks led straight back down the valley. Ned was surprised to see how much higher they were from when they had started. The pipeline ended in a large shed where the pass dropped off toward the eastern jungles of the upper Amazon. "All systems are ready."

"Good," said Ned. "*Now* will you tell me what it is?"

They climbed off the car, and ten Boom stood with his hands braced on his hips and looked back down the pass along the length of the enormous pipeline. "It is," he said with the pride of a father, "the world's biggest pipe bomb."

"Actually," ten Boom explained when they had settled into the control room, "it's called a ram accelerator. Rams were developed in the early nineties to test diffusers for scramjet engines." A crew of five, wearing headsets and hard hats, sat before a bank of screens. They gave Ned and ten Boom barely a glance.

"Scramjets," said Ned softly. Every test pilot's dream. Hypersonic velocity. If you could keep the jet lit. No one had ever flown that fast in an air-breathing engine. As in any jet, the forward motion of a scram engine forced the air-fuel mix around the diffuser and compressed it against the cowling for ignition. But at Mach 5 . . . "Keeping the fuel mix lit in a hypersonic engine,'' he said, ''is like keeping a match lit in a speeding convertible.''

Ten Boom grinned. ''Too right. But tell me, Ned . . . what is the difference between air and fuel flowing between a diffuser and its cowling—and a diffuser-shaped projectile hurtling down a tube filled with fuel and air?''

Ned opened his mouth, closed it, opened it again. He looked at the big monitor over the control panel that showed the far end of the shed where it loomed over a sheer drop. ''Jesus H. Christ . . .''

''God's own shotgun.'' Ten Boom pointed to a display panel showing the entire length of the pipeline in schematic. Green lights winked at intervals. At the far left, the lights had turned amber. *At the breech end,* Ned thought. ''We fill the entire tube with a mix of methane, nitrogen, and oxygen. That burns at a cool enough temperature that the line doesn't rupture and explode.'' He grinned. ''If it did, this bunker may not be far enough away. We kick the projectile off at 2500 klicks per hour with compressed helium and throw a traveling plug down the line after it. The fuel compresses against the plug and ignites and the diffuser shoots down the barrel, accelerating all the way. When it hits transsonic speeds, the shock wave changes from vertical to oblique and you get a ball of plasma around the rear end of the projectile that pushes it faster than the explosive velocity of the gas.''

That was like a sailboat outracing the wind; but . . . Sure. The projectile carried its own ongoing explosion on its ass end. *Set my ass on fire, I'd go pretty fast myself.* Ned grinned as he imagined a six-foot-wide tapered shell roaring down the pipe with a ball of flame on its tail. Shit, you couldn't *fly* a sumbitch like that any more than you could ''fly'' an artillery shell.

''How fast does it come out the muzzle end?'' he asked ten Boom.

''Forty-four thousand kph.''

Speak English, dammit. Ned did the arithmetic. Forty-four thousand divided by one-point-six . . . Twenty-seven thousand miles per hour. *Damn* fast. That was a shade over seven miles per second.

Escape velocity.

"Jesus H. Christ," he said again. This time, it came out like a prayer. "You can put the damn things in orbit."

Ten Boom nodded. "It is a wonder what you can lift when you don't have to carry the oxidizer with you."

Liquid oxygen was the biggest fraction of the Plank's take-off weight. Nothing burned without oxygen, an element in short supply in Low Earth Orbit, so the Plank had to haul it along, compressed and at cryogenic temperatures, so it wouldn't take up so much volume. But . . .

An alarm buzzer went off and the first light on the schematic display went red. "She's off," said ten Boom, and he turned in his seat and hunched forward, watching the screens. Lights blinked red up the schematic, a large bullet traveling up a very long rifle barrel. "The air is thin up here," he said. "When the projectile exits the muzzle, it won't hit a brick wall of air, like it would at sea level. Just the same, we evacuate the terminal to stratospheric air density and ramp it up to ambient."

The sound came like a thunderclap. Even inside the bunker, Ned could feel it. The doors on the terminal flew open and . . . *You didn't really expect to* see *it, did you.* Just for an instant, maybe. A ferocious, tapered shape and a blossom of flame and . . . The downrange tracking camera kept it centered.

"I get the message," Ned said.

Ten Boom removed his hardhat and wiped his forehead. He looked at Ned. "Do you?"

"You can launch satellites a hell of a lot cheaper than we can with the Plank."

"Hmm. Those that can survive the brutal accelerations. Not people; nothing delicate. Wilson and van Huyten are competitors, but business is business. Gene thinks we can work a deal to our mutual advantage."

"A deal?" Ned asked, immediately suspicious. He was out of his depth in business dealings. Airplanes, rockets, the machines, yeah, he knew his way around as well as anyone who dealt with metal instead of equations. But where the money managers took over, he checked out.

Ten Boom took him by the elbow and guided him away from the crew at the monitor panel. ''When you pack for a trip, you don't cart along odds and ends you can buy at your destination.''

''So . . . ?''

''So the Antisana Ram can boom a pod into LEO with liquid oxygen in one compartment and liquid hydrogen in the other. Plus the usual cryogenic equipment and plumbing.''

Ned rubbed his hand across his cheek. ''Those are big shells, but they can't carry all that much fuel.''

''The way I heard it,'' ten Boom said evenly, ''you don't need that much more.''

They know about our fuel margins. There is *a leak on ''Fernado de.'' Shit. Bonifácio will be fit to be tied.* ''Our margin is admittedly tight, but I think we can haul enough fuel to get up and back.''

Ten Boom shrugged. ''Would you bet your life on it?''

Being brave does not require being a damn fool. ''We'll see how the tests run out. But, even if it turns out we can't lift enough with the existing design, no one has ever done cryogenic refueling in orbit.''

His host smiled and spread his hands. ''There's a first time for everything.''

''All right. Whether Daedalus accepts your offer is a matter for people who wear more expensive suits than me. But tell me this. What's in it for Wilson?''

''Range safety,'' called a heavily accented voice over the speaker.

''Blow her,'' said one of the men at the control panels.

On the downrange monitor, a ball of fire erupted in the sky. Ned whirled on ten Boom. ''You blew the bird,'' he said. ''Why?''

Ten Boom spread his hands. ''We've struck deals with Ecuador and Peru. We *thought we had a deal with Brazil, but there's been some foot-dragging lately, and Wilson has no leverage in Brasilia.''*

Aha. "And VHI does." Ten Boom said nothing. Ned dipped his head. "All right. I'll tell them. You'll have something in writing for me to take back? Good." He paused for a moment and cocked his head.

"Tell me, Rick. Am I supposed to overlook the fact that, since you've been unable to overfly Brazil, you've never actually inserted one of your projectiles into orbit?"

Ten Boom smiled again. "There's a first time for everything."

6.

Warning Call

Mariesa van Huyten slapped a palm down sharply on the table and, one by one, the voices and faces on the teleconference screens fell silent. Keith McReynolds and John E. Redman, who faced her across the broad, otherwise-empty conference table, shifted in their padded black leather seats, but said nothing. The faces on the teleconference screens looked likewise uncomfortable. Only Henryk van Huyten, frozen forever in colored oils above the main doorway, maintained his composure.

"I do not care about the equations, people," she said, biting off each word. "I did not major in orbital mechanics. I only want to know whether the proposal to use the ram and refuel in orbit will work. João!" Her words snapped like whips. "Your people have had two months to thrash out the details with Wilson's people. Is it feasible? A simple yes or no will suffice."

A barely perceptible delay on the monitor hinted at signals bounced off the twenty-four-hour satellite and down to Brazil and back. João Pessoa pursed his lips. "There are, of course, a number of problems that must be overcome—''

"I said, yes or no!" This time, the words slapped.

"Riesey," Chris said gently over the Santa Fe line.

They were all looking at her, some with curiosity, Keith and Belinda with concern, João with poorly concealed anger. Those who were telepresent gazed in odd directions, depending on where their monitors sat with respect to their video pickups. Mariesa noticed that she had crumpled the top sheet of her notepad into a ball, and she smoothed it out flat with her hand. "I am sorry," she said curtly and without a great deal of sorrow felt. "But we have an absolute deadline of August rolling down on us. Even if the recession does not hit the consumer markets until October, as some projections indicate, the financial juggler's balls will start dropping by then. I want Prometheus airtight before they hit the ground." And why did no one sense the urgency but herself?

"You cannot solve technical problems by sheer willpower," Keith pointed out.

Mariesa stared across the table. "Can you not?"

"Perhaps," Steve Matthias inserted smoothly over the New York link, "it would help if we simply listed the major issues first, without trying to resolve each one as it comes up. We keep getting bogged down in details that our staffs ought to handle." Steve smiled before a backdrop of Manhattan skyscrapers visible through his office window. Over his shoulder, Mariesa could see bustling activity in the newspaper building across the street.

"Very well, Steve," she said. "Let us prepare a list. Perhaps, tempers will cool."

Werewolf spoke from his Cleveland base in a voice heavy with skepticism. "You can start with the fact that no ram accelerator, including Wilson's Boomer, has ever orbited a payload."

Everyone's sanctum seemed to reflect its occupant. Steve's was orderly to the point of obsession, paper aligned neatly in baskets, to-do lists tacked to the wall beside his geometrically perfect desk. Werewolf's office, by contrast, looked like a clearance sale at the Wiz. . . . Through the windows of Dolores

Pitchlynn's sun-drenched Pegasus office a plain dotted with giant saguaro stretched toward the distant purple line of the Mogollon Plateau, a vista as flat and as arid as the older woman's personality, and with as much harsh beauty.

And what did Mariesa Gorley van Huyten's office say about its occupant? Was that why she preferred to videoconference from the more impersonal corporate boardroom?

"It should be easy enough to test," said Dolores. "And we ought to check it out before we go any further."

"Hold that thought, Dolores," Steve said genially. "We'll come back and revisit each line item once the list is complete and prioritized." A light blue background replaced his face on the New York screen, and the words CAN BOOMER REACH ORBIT? appeared in highlighted letters.

Mendoza grunted. "Access," he said. Then he added grudgingly, as if words were silver and he a pauper, "Can our orbits rendezvous with those accessible from the Andean site without excessive delta-V?" Mariesa saw Werewolf cock his head and type something on his own terminal. MUTUALLY COMPATIBLE ELECTRONICS: CHASER & TARGET appeared on the list under Mendoza's question. Steve had set up his screen as a bulletin board, allowing anyone on the conference to contribute. Clever. It defused the discussion by rendering it impersonal. Another gold star beside Steve's name. The chatter died away as each of the conferees realized what Steve had done and began posting their own thoughts.

Mariesa pressed the mute on her own console and said, "Computer. Phone line. Private. Pessoa. Select." She waited a beat and said, "João, can you hear me?"

"Yes, I can hear you." The Brazilian's voice was clipped, formal.

"You ought to conference one of your pilots into this. DuBois, I think. He worked on the ergonomics project and on the Plank upgrades. He might have some insights from the pilot's point of view. And he did see Wilson's ram up close."

"As you wish." The line went abruptly dead.

Keith spoke into the sudden, raw silence. "You really ought not to have scolded him in front of his peers."

She swiveled her chair so she faced him instead of the monitors in the far wall. "If João's skin is growing too thin, he ought to hand the reins over to someone who can take it."

"He has done yeoman's work," Keith replied softly. "This project would have tried an organization twice Daedalus's size."

"Your problem, Keith, is that you are too reasonable."

"We each have our cross to bear."

Sarcasm from Keith? "Sweet reason wins no victories," she said, tapping the table with her forefinger for emphasis. "The only thing that matters is failure, or success. If the Plank does not achieve its goals, we are doomed, and it will not matter that we feel good about each other when that day comes."

Keith cast his eyes down and his right hand, tucked inside his vest, squirmed, as if he had hidden a fox inside his clothes. "Actually, it may."

"Oh, yes, Keith. Then we can all hold hands on that day and say we tried our best and we shall receive good marks because we 'work and play well with others.' "

"There could be worse epitaphs in the Book of Life."

"Epitaphs?" John E. laughed. "Let's not be melodramatic. Granted, VHI would take some hits if Prometheus liquidates, but the corporation would survive."

Mariesa traded a look with Keith. John E. was not privy to the plans to counter asteroids, but Keith was, and Keith *knew* what was at stake; so why was he the weak sister here? "Perhaps you ought to run the figures again, Keith. The benefits against the *ultimate* costs." A not so subtle way of reminding him that the payoff from an asteroid strike was infinity, in both directions.

Keith stood suddenly and shook out his trouser legs. He picked up his portfolio and nodded to the bank of VC screens. "Steve seems to have the technical issues well in hand. I'm afraid my only contribution will be the price we are willing to pay Wilson for his service."

"Any price," Mariesa reminded him.

McReynolds hesitated and glanced a moment at Redman. "Even granting that," he continued testily, "it is poor bargaining practice to let Wilson know that. We may not need the insurance of refueling on orbit; so we ought to pro-rate our offer commensurate with the likelihood of the need. A ten-percent risk, I believe friend Mendoza said.''

''It used to be less than five,'' Mariesa pointed out. She flipped a hand at him. ''Go on. Crunch your numbers, Keith. It's what you are good at.''

McReynolds looked from her to John E. And back. Then he tucked his portfolio tightly under his arm and gave her a stiff nod. ''You'll see the preliminary workup in the morning. John E., we'll discuss the Wilson contract in the afternoon, if that is acceptable?''

The lawyer nodded and waited in silence until McReynolds had closed the door. ''Don't cut the mute button quite yet, Mariesa,'' he said. ''Keith was too polite to say so, but you are being a real bitch.''

His words stung and she felt herself grow icy-cold. ''Am I?''

''First class, gold-plated, true quill bitch. Standard and Poore's Triple-AAA rating. You owe Keith and João and a few of the others apologies; and you know it.'' Redman swung backward in his chair and favored her with a lazy grin. ''Mariesa, it isn't you.''

She did not return his grin. ''Who is it, then?''

He shook his head and his gaze became guarded. ''I don't know. But whoever it is, I wish she'd give me my old chairman back again. I kind of liked that gal.''

''Don't jolly me, John E. It's patronizing and I don't like it. I have been working toward this goal for most of my life and on this project for the last five years. Now everything is unraveling. People I trusted have shaded estimates, painted rosy scenarios, withheld information. . . . Mendoza *must* have known about the Plank's marginal capabilities. He *must* have. Why else would he have extended the ground-testing? And he told no one, unless it was de Magalhães and Pessoa. Had we known sooner, we could have—''

''Could have what? I am no technician, but I understand from Chris that our options were severely limited well before

Mendoza discovered any problems. You want straight talk?" He did not wait for an answer but rocked his chair forward so that he could rest his arms on the table. "As long as we are cataloging transgressions, Mariesa, let's talk about the leaks you set me to investigate."

"The leak to Albright," she said smoothly. But she saw the hesitation in Redman's eyes.

"There never was a leak to Albright. At least, not out of VHI. It seems that Albright picked up a secondhand rumor about Wilson's activities and jumped to the conclusion that it was you. That was why he sought you out at the Argonaut meeting last year."

"Oh! Then it was a false alarm all along? How can you be sure?"

"We have a sympathizer in Albright's headquarters now who passed some inside information along to us." Redman slouched in his chair and ran a finger across the keyboard under the table by his seat. "You did not formally charge me with investigating the leak to Wilson, who appeared to have rather more specific information on our operations than Albright did, but it seemed a logical extension of my task and I put it down to an oversight on your part."

Mariesa paused and the two of them stared at one another for a moment. Finally, Mariesa said, "You know?" Redman nodded, and she asked, "How long?"

"About a month," he replied, "and wondering what to do about it."

"Who else knows?"

He shrugged. "No one that I've told. Chisolm may know. She would not be chief of security if she could not put two and two together."

"Luanda knows. She was my conduit."

Redman nodded slowly. "I see." He was silent a moment longer. "We are risking billions on Prometheus; yet you revealed to a competitor—"

"I gave Wilson nothing proprietary, no company secrets. All I did was drop hints. He does not even know the hints came from me."

Redman shook his head. "We'll worry about the legalities later—and what the Trust will say, if they ever discover what you did. It's the motivation that puzzles me. Prometheus is your own creation. Your dream-child. As you said, you've been working on this project for five years. I know you must have had a reason, but I don't understand what it could be." He folded his arms and waited. Behind him, the digital calendar, a twin to the black obelisk in her office, blinked its array of approaching deadlines. Too many deadlines, approaching too quickly.

The pain began again in her stomach. Quietly, under the table, she pressed a hand flat against her abdomen. She glanced at the monitors, where Steve seemed to have things well in hand. They did not need her contributions; and they especially did not need her anxieties to cloud the discussion. She pulled the keyboard rack from under the board table and typed a memo to Steve Matthias, asking him to run the remainder of the session and report to her in the morning. Funny. Steve had joined the project only because of his personal ambitions, yet he was proving to be one of the more useful members. When he was involved, things got done. She logged off the net and pushed the keyboard into its recess as the videoconference screens went blank.

She stood from the table and walked to the north wall, where she could stare out at the bright afternoon sky. Skeletal trees, shagbark hickory and scarlet oak, lent the hillside a furry appearance. In the sky, billowing cumulus clouds sailed slowly and majestically toward the east. There was little snow left on the ground. This would be a warm year.

The clock was digital, so no ticking measured the beat of time. Redman waited with a lawyer's patience, ready to hear her out. To him, it was all lawyer's issues. How to navigate the tricky shoals of law and regulation. A crusade to keep the government from stifling the next rung up of enterprise. He had never lain awake at night soaking in a cold sweat. How much ought she reveal to him? Too much or not enough? Either could jeopardize his commitment. But sometimes it was best that the right hand not know what the left was doing.

Henryk van Huyten scowled down at her from his position above the door, but there was no clue in his gaze what course she should take. Gramper's ghost could not advise her; Gramper would never have taken this road. If he could tell her anything, it would be to cut her losses. But, damn it all, *she* was the chairman, not Christiaan III, not Henryk, not even Willem.

And quite possibly, Henryk, poised on the shore of a New World, with endless possibilities before him and no way to imagine, let alone measure, what might someday be—perhaps he would understand her situation more than any of the generations that fell between them. "This is all under the rose," she said turning to face him. "Privileged communication." Redman nodded.

She bought herself a little time to arrange her thoughts. "You know the goal of Prometheus, of course. . . . What lies beyond the satellite launch and repair business."

Redman nodded. "A solar power demonstration satellite of five hundred thousand watts; and beyond that, if things go well, a network of power satellites generating three hundred billion watts, twenty-four hours a day." He smiled. "Thirty years from knitting the first support structure to when the last of them goes on-line. If we eat right and exercise, you and I will get to see the end of it."

"It will cost a great deal," she said. "Eight hundred billion dollars."

"Risking billions in hope of trillions," he said, repeating the project's catchphrase. "I surely do wish you would get to the point."

"There are trillions enough for all. And it is important to humanity that *someone* succeeds. If not VHI, someone. The point is, John E., that there *must* be other players. VHI can build and operate perhaps two or three such stations. Beyond that . . ." She took a deep breath. "I wanted to coax Wilson into the game, by letting him know that there *was* a game. Nothing motivates like the thought that a rival may be stealing a march on you. . . ."

"It hardly seems wise to waken your rivals."

"John E., if you must have a financial reason for inciting competition, it is this. Competition will assure the bankers and the venture capitalists that the whole enterprise is worthwhile. One such project may be the foolish brainstorm of a deluded woman. The Moon Lady. Two or three or four such projects mean that hard-eyed analysts see a profit to be made."

He shook his head. "That won't do to slop the hogs, as we used to say down home. If a handful of orbital platforms is enough to recover our investment, what difference does it make whether other corporations build more of them or not?"

She turned and faced the window once more. "Those are my reasons, John E. It is not my fault if you do not accept them."

"The truth, but not the whole truth. Mariesa, I'm just an ol' country lawyer . . ."

Yes. The Virginia horse and hunt country. She was not the only one in the room capable of dissembling.

". . . but I can tell when a witness is being evasive." He stood and gripped his portfolio. "When you decide to be more forthcoming, you know where to find me."

She turned as he left and her hand, outstretched, fell to her side. Well, a few hurt feelings would be the least debit when this bill came due.

John E.'s problem was not that he lacked imagination, but that he lacked the right sort of imagination. He could envision the power satellites beaming power to an energy-hungry earth, but gigawatts were only numbers to him. He could not see those gigawatt laser beams focused and aimed, raw burning power, searing their targets, boiling them away, slicing them apart. He could not see that the power platforms were weapons platforms, too. It was something not only unthought, but unthinkable.

She had been thinking of them for nearly thirty years.

Cool air sweeping off the sides of the Maroon Bells carried a kiss of the glaciers to the balcony of the Aspen Conference Center, where Mariesa stood leaning on her arms on the rail. Springtime in the Rockies. Thin air, it was; light and fresh, almost as if it were newborn within the softening snows of the high country, slowly to make its way to sea level to die there as the damp, heavy, thick atmosphere of the coastal cities. It brushed her cheek with the scent of Parry primrose and fireweed. Corkbark fir and quaking aspen shivered on the mountain slopes around her. The trees and flowers gave notice that, if at this altitude it never entirely ceased being winter, it at least struggled constantly toward spring.

Zhou Hui sat in the wicker chair by the round, glass coffee table that furnished the balcony. Her open laptop gave forth a constant hum that rose and fell in pitch while she scrolled. Every now and then, it would scritch-scratch as it saved files to the backup disk.

"What does the remainder of my afternoon look like?" Mariesa asked her as she studied the distant peaks. There was a pass up there, through the Bells, and she wondered where it led.

"Some of the presidents will undoubtedly stop and pay their respects before leaving," Hui said. "I have allowed time for that. A pair of venture capitalists who are considering investing in Prometheus have arranged for an early dinner meeting. After that, you are free. Charlie Jim will be ready to fly us down to Denver, if you wish; but he prefers to wait until the morning, when the light will be better."

Mariesa nodded. "I will defer to the pilot's judgment on such matters." She turned away from the scenery. "Will anything on my morning agenda be affected by the later departure?"

Hui scrolled to the next screen. "We will pick up Mr. Pessoa and your cousin in Santa Fe and fly on to Los Angeles to meet with Mr. Wilson. Mr. Redman has E-mailed his preliminary report and expects that everything will go smoothly. The remainder of your affairs can be handled adequately en route."

In early times, the king's court was wherever the king was. Only later were there permanently sited "capitals" and "headquarters." Teleconferencing and telecommuting were recreating a sort of high-tech Middle Ages. In a way, VHI was headquartered wherever Mariesa happened to be. Perhaps these quarterly management retreats equated to those ceremonies where the barons renewed their oaths of fealty to their overlord.

As if on cue, Correy Wilcox stepped onto the balcony, dressed casually in tweed jacket and contrasting slacks. He set a compact suitcase on the redwood decking by his feet. ''The van will be coming in a few minutes,'' he said. ''Five of us are riding over to the airport together.''

Mariesa extended her hand. ''I trust it has been a productive retreat?'' Correy's was an extrovert's grip, always vigorous, always intense, but always a barrier, as if he were pushing you away even while he greeted you.

''Yes, very,'' he said. ''It's always interesting to learn what the other divisions are up to. Does Bennett *really* intend to retire?''

''So he says.''

Correy chuckled. ''A man who's put in as much as he has deserves a few years to relax and enjoy life. Oh. When you see Keith, tell him that I missed him and he should get well soon.''

''I will; but he has only gone in for some routine tests,'' she said. ''He will be glad to hear of the progress Hyacinth is making.''

The grin turned sheepish. ''Yeah. I wonder if anyone at the reception guessed what their bottled water was recycled from....'' In a more serious tone, he added, ''Speaking of Prometheus, though, what's with Piper and Brad? They sure don't think much of our project.''

There had been considerable comment on the SSTO program during the plenary session, not all of it favorable and some of it barbed and quite sarcastic. ''One cannot expect vision from everyone, not even from otherwise competent managers. So long as they manage their divisions effectively and provide Prometheus the necessary service and material, their opinions do not concern me.''

Correy dropped his voice a notch. ''Be careful they don't mistake tolerance for weakness. *I* think they're tworked because they weren't in on it. That's going to mark your management from now on. From now on, there will be those who were in on the secret, and those who weren't. And those who weren't are going to resent it. Like Steve."

"Steve is a member of the team," she pointed out.

"But he wasn't exactly *invited* to join, was he? He squeezed himself into a place at the table. Think he doesn't resent it that you never considered him? Now he seems to be everywhere. Coordinating. Facilitating. Never in charge, but always somehow running things. Second-guessing the rest of us. I think he's taking on too much authority."

She studied him carefully before replying. "He has proven an invaluable asset to our project."

"Oh, sure; but do you think it's wise to delegate so much to a man who lacks commitment to anything besides himself?" Correy held a defensive had up. "Yeah, yeah, I know what Werewolf and João say about me—especially when I'm not around. Of course, I look out for Number One. Who else is going to? The difference between me and them is that they don't admit it. My problem with Steve is not that he looks out for himself, but that I'm not sure he looks out for anything else. I *care* about this project of ours. Hell, I was one of the Original Four; and even though Hyacinth is not on the critical path, there are still things I know that the others aren't in on."

A not-so-subtle reminder there that only he, Wallace, and Keith shared her concern with comets and near-Earth asteroids. Only these three had not dismissed the notion when Mariesa had (cautiously) mentioned the possibility to them.

It was an odd triumvirate. She could not imagine *not* confiding everything in Keith; and Wallace, the long-time sci-fi buff, had actually broached the matter to her. If anyone was the father of Prometheus, if anyone had shown Mariesa a way out of her nightmare, it was Wallace—a man who, ironically, could play no further part in the project beyond ferrying the participants on Odysseus jets.

Correy was a man who neither welcomed confidences nor inspired them; yet when she had gingerly mentioned the thought that a comet or asteroid might someday strike the Earth, he had simply nodded and said in a serious, matter-of-fact voice, "Yes, I wonder why no one seems to be doing anything about it."

Yes, well, what could you do?

Get out of the way, for one.

Reach out and swat it aside, for another. There were not many on the project who understood the true significance of the hand-and-fireball logo—that was not, in fact, a hand *releasing* a fireball—nor the ultimate purpose of building gigawatt lasers in space.

It was not, however, a notion that she cared to hold up to public ridicule. Investors would bail out if they thought her mind unstable or obsessed; the Family Trust would unite to strip her of her offices. Reason had little to do with it. People joined shrieking campaigns against risks much slimmer . . . and blithely ignored others far greater. Even after the comet strike on Jupiter, the idea had been mocked and dismissed in the media.

"Steve doesn't have the same dedication," Correy said. "It's all power games and political maneuvers and —maybe— a chance to make his peers look bad."

"I think you do him a disservice," she suggested. And maybe Correy had stopped here on his way out to score points against Steve, and maybe he was truly concerned with Steve's role. He was, as he had reminded her, one of the midwives who had helped birth Prometheus.

Correy bent down and retrieved his suitcase. "Yeah, maybe I do. I hope so. He's a charming guy. Careful and intense and always ready to take on another responsibility. I can't fault him; but I can't trust him, either. Someday you may wake up and find out *he's* running the show and not you."

"I will take your concern under advisement."

"That's all I ask." He looked to his left. "Why, hello there, Belinda. Are you leaving, too?"

Belinda Karr appeared in the doorway that opened onto the balcony. "Oh, Correy, I thought you'd left already." She noticed Zhou Hui intent on her computer screen at the other end of the balcony. "I had hoped to catch you alone," she told

Mariesa. Hui looked up from her work and regarded Belinda impassively.

Mariesa would not quite look Belinda in the eye. "Affairs have reached a critical stage. Negotiations with Wilson, you know . . . I leave for Los Angeles tomorrow to sign the contracts. My calendar needs extra days."

Belinda glanced sideways at Correy. "You do promise to study the portfolios for this year's Promethean students?" she said at last.

"Yes, certainly, time permitting." It was not as simple as it had been in the early days. Mentor ran three times as many schools now. Even two years ago, after taking on the North Orange schools, the Steering Committee could review each year's crop of possibilities in a single meeting, and Mariesa had scrutinized each and every profile herself. She would never know any of the newer children as well as she had grown to know that first set from North Orange. She could say their names, each one of them, and see their photographs when she closed her eyes. Poole, Hobart, Frazetti, Coughlin, Ribbon, Thomas . . . and especially dear, troubled, blossoming Styx. *Yes, time permitting.* But time would never permit again.

Perhaps Belinda saw something in her eyes, because an expression much like disappointment washed across her features. Mariesa stepped closer to her and placed a hand on Belinda's forearm. "But that is why I have you, Belinda, dear. We are a team: Correy, you, I, the others. We each have a role to play. Yours is to nurture the next generation, so that the dream does not die with ours. In a way, you are their mother."

"And the children," Correy pointed out, "are not the critical path. Without João ships, without my life support, without Mariesa's *marketing*, there would be no point to what you are doing in the schools."

Belinda whirled and faced him. "No point to you, perhaps!"

Correy blinked and Mariesa swiftly responded. "And without what we are doing in the schools, Correy, there would be no point to the ships, the life support, or the marketing."

Correy knew when to back off. "I'm sorry. I didn't mean

to be dismissive, Belinda. I apologize. I just see things from Gaia Biotech's perspective; and you see them from Mentor Academies'. Our own roles always seem the biggest.''

"I understand. Mariesa? I'll be going now.''

"I will see you to the door. I shan't be a moment, Correy.'' Mariesa followed Belinda into the large suite that VHI had reserved for social functions during the management retreat. Empty cups and looted bowls of nuts and fruits from the fare-well reception were scattered on tables about the room. Correy had not apologized, nor had Belinda understood. It upset her when her own inner circle did not see eye to eye. It seemed wasteful. Friction. Waste heat. Everyone should see what needed doing and *just do it*.

And yet, it was that very diversity of thought that she often relied upon.

Belinda picked up a suit bag she had left sitting by the exit and slung it over her right shoulder. She waited for Mariesa with one hand touching the doorknob.

Mariesa halted one step short. "Well,'' she said.

"Well,'' said Belinda.

"Have a safe trip to Spokane.''

"I'm not going straight back. I'm stopping by Portland first, to visit Singley, Goerig and Wu.''

"Portland is a beautiful city. The 'Rose of the Northwest.' Tell Mariellen I said hello.''

"She keeps asking when I will let Ben Wu come back.''

"And when will you? You've kept him at Dayton Middle School for two years now.''

Belinda sagged. "I don't know, Riesey. I really don't. My top people are spread so thin, with the rate at which we've added new schools this year . . . I am afraid the quality of our instruction may suffer.''

Mariesa stepped forward and put an arm around the woman's shoulders. "You will not allow that to happen.'' Softly spoken, it was a statement of confidence; but it was an order, too.

"The best graduates are going into law or engineering or finance these days,'' Belinda said. "We cannot pay—no school, public or private, can pay salaries to compete. And so we get the bottom cut of the graduates—and those precious, precious few to whom children matter more than salary.''

"You will find a way." Mariesa hugged her gently. Belinda returned the embrace with her free arm, pulling Mariesa close with the tight, firm grip of the athlete. Mariesa tugged free. "I must see to Correy." Belinda turned quickly away, groping once more for the doorknob.

The two investors were waiting in the lobby when Mariesa entered. A black woman wearing a finely cut business suit rose from the high wing-back chair she had been occupying. Her companion, a short, thickset man with a tan complexion and laughter-creased eyes, turned away from the fish tank where he had been studying the darting gold, red, and yellow shapes.

"Mariesa van Huyten?" the man said. "I'm Jimmy Caldero; and this is my partner, Gloria Bennett."

Bennett had a rounded jaw and wore her hair short. Her smile, it seemed to Mariesa, had more than a hint of sadness to it. "We've heard a great deal about your SSTO program since you went public, Ms. Van Huyten," she said. "It sounds like exactly the sort of long-term investment that Bennett, Caldero and Ochs might be interested in. We'd like to hear more about it."

They exchanged handshakes. "This is Zhou Hui, my personal secretary," Mariesa told them. "She will join us for dinner and take notes, if that is acceptable." Hui, half a pace behind her, bowed. Her laptop hung in a padded case from her shoulder.

Caldero bowed in turn to Zhou Hui and said, *"Hau bu hau."* Hui dimpled and sang something back to him. Caldero grinned and led them toward the door. "I've taken the liberty of engaging a table at Roth's. It's a private restaurant. He does not advertise. Perhaps you know it."

"I know Thad Roth very well," Mariesa said, "and it has been far too long since I sampled his board." She understood Caldero's message: *We move in the same circles, you and I.* Though she had heard Caldero's name mentioned from time to time, socially and in business, she had never met him before. He was something of a recluse. Of Bennett, she had never heard, but Hui had run a D&B on the pair and on their investment firm and it seemed to be very well capitalized, with a reputation for shrewd and audacious investment strategies.

A black-and-silver Range Rover waited under the awning outside the conference center. In the shrubbery to the right of the entrance, a young man with a long, ragged beard sat draining a bottle wrapped in a brown paper bag. He wore a long, horridly stained overcoat and, as the four of them walked toward the car, he gave them a suspicious glare. Mariesa affected not to notice. It was terrible the way these people had been cast out on their own resources when what they needed was mental care or drug rehabilitation. Jim Champion had promised new programs, but so far nothing had passed the House.

The man noticed Mariesa's surreptitious glance and made eye contact with her. "Merry Christmas," he said with a curl to his lip. It had become something of a tag line since the Christmas Recession of a few years ago. The country had finally struggled out of it, though not so very far out, and now seemed determined to plunge right back in.

Caldero opened the left rear passenger door to the Rover, and Bennett said, "Jimmy will be doing the driving, I'm afraid. I hope neither of you frightens easily." Caldero laughed, and Mariesa wondered from the byplay whether the two were partners in more than their investments. Mariesa stepped aside to allow Hui to enter first, but as she did so, she smelled the most awful odor.

"Any you rich folks got a dollar?"

Turning, Mariesa found herself face-to-face with the man who had been squatting among the bushes. His breath stank like old fish and cheap wine and his clothing had been both home and bathroom, evidently for some time. He swayed slightly, and his red-veined eyes struggled to focus on her. Zhou Hui straightened without entering the car. Caldero stepped away from the driver's door. Bennett, on the other side of the car, frowned.

"No," Mariesa told the man. "I will not give you a dollar;

but if you will clean yourself up, I will give you a job." It was her standard reply to panhandlers and often helped separate the ones who could be helped from those who could not. Usually, they turned away when she said that and sought easier targets. A few had taken up her offer. Charlie Jim still worked for her. This man was different.

He grimaced horribly, and leaning forward, spewed his foul breath and spittle over her. "You arrogant bitch!" he shouted. The veins stood out on his neck, and his wine-reddened face darkened further.

Caldero cried, "Look out! He has a knife!"

Instantly, Hui stepped between them, swinging the padded laptop case in both hands. The knife went flying end over end and vanished into the grass. Caldero, in two catlike steps, positioned himself to the man's side and rear, where he stood balanced with his hands open and ready. The homeless man looked from one to the other, then gave Mariesa a bug-eyed grin over the top of Hui's head. "Hey," he said, holding weaponless hands up. "Hey-de-hey." A silly grin split his features and he skipped backward a few paces before he turned and leapt down the driveway.

"Drunk," said Bennett. "Or high."

Mariesa's knees felt like rubber, and she placed a hand on the roof of the Range Rover to steady herself. It seemed as if her perspective suddenly shifted and she was looking at the scene from a far, far distance. She could not draw a breath, only short, sharp gulps. Her legs began to give way; but then Gloria Bennett was beside her, supporting her. "It's all right," she said. "He's gone."

Caldero held the rear door open. "Here. Sit down before you faint." Mariesa lowered herself into the seat, sitting sideways with her feet still on the paving. The doorman had come running from the conference center along with two of the valet parkers. Caldero took them aside and spoke with them, pointing down the driveway, but when Mariesa looked in that direction, the man had already vanished. *A knife . . . Dear God . . .* her stomach muscles tightened. She felt as if she would throw up.

Bennett said again, "You'll be all right. Believe me, I know."

"Where's Hui?" Mariesa braced herself against the car's frame and rose shakily to her feet. The laptop case lay on the driveway, but Hui was nowhere to be seen. "Hui!" she called.

Caldero approached her. "The manager wants to know if you want the police called in."

"Yes, certainly. A man like that, violent and drunk, should not be running around loose."

Caldero shook his head. "He wasn't drunk. He moved too well."

"What do you mean?"

"No, he was not drunk." Zhou Hui had reappeared, and stood with her equipment once more hanging in place. A thin sheen of perspiration covered her forehead and beaded her upper lip, but her breathing was normal. "I followed him down the driveway. There was a brown pickup truck waiting for him by the state road. They left in the direction of the town."

Caldero ran a hand across his jaw. "He'll be long out of the county by the time the sheriff gets mobilized." He gave Zhou Hui a speculative look, which Hui returned.

Bennett said, "You took a terrible chance, following that man." But Caldero shook his head, still trading looks with Hui. "No. She didn't."

"We really ought to inform the authorities," Mariesa said.

Three high-pitched beeps interrupted them. It was a strange, alien sound that silenced them. Then it repeated, and Mariesa, recognizing the tones, suddenly laughed. Zhou Hui fumbled in her bag and pulled out the cellular phone and flipped it open. *Odd*, Mariesa thought, *how the familiar, coming unexpected, can seem so strange.*

"Yes?" said Hui into the handset. Then she fell silent. "Yes." She pressed the mute button and a second button and handed the phone to Mariesa. "He says it is 'a friend.' I have started the auto trace."

Mariesa nodded and accepted the phone. She hesitated a moment, then deactivated the mute. "Yes?"

"That was a warning." The voice was hoarse and gravelly. The faux-drunk who had just confronted them? No, it was a different voice. "And it could have been a gun, not a knife."

"A warning about what?" Mariesa saw Caldero cock his head, then glance quickly in all four directions. Hui sucked her lower lip between her teeth.

"You really need to rethink your priorities."

The line went dead. Mariesa pulled the phone away and checked the LED display above the call buttons. "The call was relayed across the Atlantic and Indian Ocean GEO satellites by way of the Senegal ground station," she said to no one in particular. "He was not on long enough to trace it further."

"No," said Caldero. "Of course not. It was probably black-coded to delay the trace, too. What did he warn you about, if you don't mind my asking?"

Mariesa studied the two investment capitalists and wondered if she was about to scare them off. Still, if they were going to risk their money, they ought to know. She folded the telephone shut and handed it back to Hui, who zipped it into its case. "I think someone does not want my SSTO program to succeed."

Caldero considered that. He nodded slowly and traded a thoughtful look with Bennett. Then he grinned. "It sounds like one hell of an opportunity."

The furnace room was a giant's barn. The walls rose two stories high with dingy, dirt-caked windows lining the clerestory. Everything was coated with a layer of fine ash. On the dirt floor, it was nearly ankle deep. An enormous electromagnet swung on chains from the overhead crane as the operator guided it from the double row of rail car gondolas heaped with scrap metal that lined the rail spur to a location over the open pot, where he released its quota of scrap in a crash that sounded like the devil had dropped all the pots and pans in hell. Mariesa turned to Bennett Longworth.

"Quite impressive," she said.

"Oh, the show hasn't even started yet. Watch." He stood

with his arms folded and his legs spread staring out the ash-grimed windows of the control room, looking down on the furnace like a lord from his castle wall. His retirement dinner was tonight. Tuxedoes and evening dress at the Exmoor Country Club by the lake—cocktails at six, yet here he stood in the furnace control room of Vulcan's Illini Works at three o'clock in the afternoon, dressed in hard hat and fireproof smock, watching one last heat be loaded. With the bright orange hard hat clapped fully on his head, Longworth looked a different man than he did in the boardroom or office. He seemed younger.

A cap slid over the enormous pot and clanged into place. "Screws locked in," the operator said. He pressed a button and the blare of Klaxons seeped through the soundproofing. A couple of car handlers on the floor quickly finished their work on the gondola and hurried from the building. "Electrodes down."

With a thump and a hum, three large cylinders descended from the ceiling and inserted themselves into openings in the furnace lid. There was a crunch and a sigh, barely audible in the control room. "Power," the operator announced, pressing a large, green button on his console. Then he grinned and said, "Popcorn time!"

The hum of dynamos rose and the lights dimmed. Bennett said, "I'll bet the lights flicker across half of Chi-town when we draw power off the grid."

Mariesa did not answer him because, out in the furnace room, man-made thunder and man-made lightning erupted. Thousands of volts of current ran through the scrap metal, heating it, melting it, causing it to writhe and churn within the pot. Pockets of steel bubbled and burst, sending sparks flying through the orifices and across the room in a steady rain of ash. Mariesa took a step back from the raw power she saw through the viewing windows, but Bennett remained staring at the cauldron and the melting steel struggling within it.

She noticed how Bennett hesitated before turning away from the viewport at last, taking his hard hat off and running a hand through the scant hair that survived there before he replaced it and tugged it down firmly into place. She wondered if she would ever find another president who so perfectly matched his fiefdom.

Finally, he did turn. "Well, let's get over to Ladle Metallugy and see how the experiment's going." He shook his head. "You know, nitrogen is always a problem with steel made from scrap and bushling. I mean, the melt sucks it right out of the air when you tap the furnace, but with scrap, you *start* with a high N, because the original pour took it up and now we're remelting it and taking up more. The idea that bacteria could . . ." He shook his head again.

"You can thank Correy Wilcox and Gaia Biotech. As I understand these matters, his biologists spliced a gene for nitrogen fixing into a 'sulfate-reducing' bacterium that thrives at high temperatures and then cultured the strain selectively for *very* high temperatures indeed. Under normal conditions, it is a spore, but sprinkle a packet into molten steel and . . ."

"And the nitrogen will be concentrated into the slag. Yeah, if it works." Bennett seemed happily indifferent to the possibility; or perhaps simply skeptical. At any rate, starting tomorrow, it would not be his problem.

"It is difficult to test the theory in the laboratory," she admitted. "Correy appreciates the loan of your facility."

Outside in the hallway, she laid a hand on his arm and said, "I am delighted you saw your way free to accompany me to Brazil for the orbital launch."

"I wouldn't miss it for the world." He smiled, but Mariesa did not miss the hurt in his eyes. By leaving him off the team she had as much as said she could not rely on him. Yet, the project could not have used his rough, seat-of-the-pants style of management. Perhaps that more than anything else had told "Uncle" Bennett his day was done. "Some people get too old, too soon," he said. "No, not me. Cyrus Attwood. Do you know him?"

"We have met once or twice. I have not seen him since Mother's 'New Millennium' party a year and a half ago. We had words."

Bennett pursed his lips. "Did you? That may explain some

things. I mentioned I was going down to Brazil with you when I was in New York last week. He spoke quite strongly against the project; said it would cause quite a few financial dominoes to start toppling.''

''Cyrus cannot deal with change.'' Privately, she admitted that Cyrus was correct. Change *was* threatening. It was not the ''technology'' itself, nor the market volatility that attended it. Everyone, Cyrus Attwood included, dealt with that sort of challenge evey day. But technological change implied cultural change. It raised some people up and brought others low, and that was the real root of resistance. *This may make me less important.* And so they sought to control it, to regulate it, to plan it.

''He hinted at legal actions. And at lobbying efforts in Congress.''

''Did he. Well, Champion has a majority there, though a razor-thin one.'' And he would lose that in next year's congressional election, if the economic forecasts were borne out. When would the American people realize that the economy inhaled and exhaled regardless who sat in Washington? The best the government could do was refrain from strangling the poor thing.

And conduct the occasional Heimlich maneuver.

''Yes,'' said Bennett. ''He told me that you 'ought to re-think your priorities.' ''

Mariesa barely hesitated in her stride. ''He told you that, did he?''

INTERLUDE:

The Left Hand

The problem with volunteers, thought Phil Albright, was an enthusiasm untempered by competence. Progressives often had more will than skill. The Bible had been right on that score, at least. This children of this world were wiser than the children of the light. He eyed the envelope that had been placed upon his desk. It was a Number 10 white-weave envelope, 24-pound-test paper, probably bleached in chlorine. The cheapest, most common sort. It was addressed to him and marked PERSONAL. He asked again, "You didn't see who brought this?"

"It was just some guy. I didn't think it was important." The Crusader who had brought him the envelope was also the most common sort: a young woman, college freshman, sandal-footed, baggy-dressed, devoid of makeup, a wraith from the sixties of Albright's own fading youth. She had been stuffing mailings and knocking on doors for three months now, and Albright knew it was only a matter of time before boredom and stress extinguished the commitment she had arrived with. It always was a rude awakening for these collegians when they discovered that activism was work, and required something more from them than dressing down or spouting easy slogans. Those who persevered, though . . . their price was "far above rubies."

"Thank you, Hannah. You can go back to the phone bank." Hannah left, closing the office door behind her; and Albright sighed and rubbed his face under the eyes. His sinuses were acting up again. Maybe he ought to take a pill. Phenylpropanolamine hydrochloride. Chlorpheniramine maleate. Jesus, sometimes the more you knew . . . He didn't keep medication at the office—some of his volunteers were obsessed on the subject of pharmaceuticals and he saw no point to annoying them. A little discomfort was a small price to pay for respecting the opinions of others. If the misery did become unbearable, his sister Cookie's town house—and his "stash"—was only five blocks away.

It must be the humidity, he decided. Humidity was hell on the sinuses. Washington in March was anything but sultry; but Washington at any time of year made you feel damp and wrung out.

His office was simple and sparely furnished, in a neighborhood neither upscale nor run-down. A pair of battered vertical files, an old wooden desk, a corkboard thick with pinned-up notices and clippings. Photographs on the walls showed him at Rio and Cairo and a half dozen other progressive gatherings. Shaking hands with Rubin, Fonda, Alinksy, Nader, Gore . . . Even Clinton; but you took your allies where you found them. Of all the ones he had met, he thought Carter the most admirable. By damn, the man had taken a hammer in his hand and built houses for the poor, and never mind whether it was dignified for an ex-president. Driving a nail carried more dignity than spouting after-dinner platitudes at thousand-dollar-a-plate banquets.

Albright had bought the wooden desk years ago at a secondhand salvage sale. Still serviceable after perhaps half a century of use by who knew how many owners. No metal desks for him; wood had character and, given wise stewardship, was an infinitely renewable resource. Someone had once carved the word MARY into the left corner of the desktop with a penknife, and in his more idle moments Albright traced the worn grooves with his fingertip and wondered who had carved it and who Mary had been and how it had all turned out. He sighed, picked up the envelope at last, and opened it.

It was another check, of course. This one was also for $5,000 and was from a group calling itself Americans for Planetary Preservation. A different title than on the previous checks, but the signature was the same. So either someone was disguising his philanthropy by wearing a different hat for each donation, or the byzantine politics of activism was splintering and forming new organizations at an alarming rate.

Americans for Planetary Preservation . . . Amusing how a handful of people could make themselves suddenly important by giving themselves a grand name and holding a press conference. Albright had played that game himself, back in college. He had helped form a dozen different activist groups on campus and in the neighborhoods, and then announced an ''alliance'' joining them. There had been no shortage of causes; and each cause had attracted its own penumbra of concerned students. But the core membership had always been the same familiar faces. It had been like one of those old war movies where a handful of gallant defenders, popping up and shooting from a dozen different positions, had given the impression of a much larger cadre. Progressives had been besieged in those days, too.

The Peoples' Crusades had been his most brilliant creation, once he had been in a position to remake it from the inept, awkwardly named special-interest group it had been. No mere Gideon's Band now, but tens of thousands of paid-up, card-carrying members, coast to coast, in city and town; and behind them, hundreds of thousands of supporters with ready checkbooks. And no narrow interest focus, either. The Crusades—he had chosen the plural deliberately—lent muscle and support to every fight worthwhile: against child abuse, battering, pollution, poverty and homelessness, unfair labor practices, racism and sexism, every festering disease that pockmarked the face of this otherwise beautiful country. ''Every time the weak and the helpless are oppressed by the strong and the powerful,'' his public-service spot ran, ''the Crusaders are there. If you cannot tilt the lance yourself, help to arm the ones who do.'' Some of the membership had objected to the ''eurocentric, patriarchal, warlike subtext,'' but the message was effective and that was what mattered. Crusading for the underdog pressed a hot button in the American psyche. Checkbooks flipped open if the cause was right, and never mind the fine print.

Five thousand dollars. Albright's problem was not the amount, but the anonymity. Some of the trial lawyers sent much larger donations, but they signed their names proudly. ''Americans for Planetary Preservation—John Williams, Treasurer'' might as well be ''John Doe.'' For the right cause, Albright would accept donations from the Devil himself, but he wanted to *know* he was doing it; and how much and what part of his soul the Devil thought he was buying.

The call finally came during his weekly staff meeting. Albright had always known a call would come. No one sent checks that size without finding out what they had purchased.

The staff meeting began, as it had for seven interminable months, with wrangling over the van Huyten spaceship. Half his staff wanted to make it a Crusade; half wanted to publicly support the venture; half wanted to ignore it and concentrate on more important causes. And if that added up to three halves, well, it was that kind of topic.

''I don't care if the launches are taking place in another country,'' said Felix Lara. ''That doesn't stop us from protesting the rape of the rain forest.''

Dottie Wheeler turned on him. ''I wish you wouldn't use the word 'rape' so freely,'' she told him in an exasperated voice just shy of anger. ''You cheapen it when you do.'' Dottie had been a high-school teacher until VHI had taken over her school and ousted her, and she usually spoke out against anything van Huyten sponsored.

Felix conceded with a brief hand gesture. ''Okay, okay, but that's not my point. The point is the ozone layer gets thinner as you move south and gets thinnest at the equator. So, these launches can do more damage down there.''

"Personally," said Melanie Kaufmann, "I think we ought to *support* Mariesa. After all, it is a *woman* who is running things."

"But her attitudes are masculine," said Dottie. "There's more to being a womyn than having tits, even tiny little ones."

Let a man say something like that, Albright reflected, and he'd be sued faster than you could say "sexually intimidating atmosphere." Melanie and Dottie saw eye to eye on most issues; but when gender raised its head, they went after each other hook and nail. Feminism had splintered over the last five years, with gender feminists accusing the equity feminists of every crime in the books—from Republicanism to Christianity to "a phallocentric emphasis on rationality." And the equity feminists returned the favor with accusations of patronizing victimology and neo-Victorian prudery. Albright said nothing; it wasn't his domain, and there were times when even an activist ought to remain inactive.

"There are better reasons than feminism for supporting van Huyten," Isaac Kohl suggested. "There are Green reasons. The more industry we move into space, the better off the Earth will be. Strip mine asteroids, not Wyoming. Smelt them in orbit . . .''

"Oh, God." Felix rolled his eyes melodramatically. "Big science. Big industry. And you want us to support it?"

Albright listened to the bickering with a profound ambivalence. Asteroid mining? Orbital smelters? Even Mariesa van Huyten was not talking in those terms—yet. It *was* Big Science and Big Industry, and on a scale that reduced human beings to ants, everything he had grown to hate; and yet there were aspects to it that appealed to him, or appealed to the child locked tight within him who had once watched hurky-jerky television images of men leaping on the moon. Isaac had a definite point. It *was* better than strip-mining the Earth and fouling its air and water.

Better still, of course, was not to want or need so much. To live more simply. It was that insatiable, never-satisfied *wanting* that drove even well-meaning people to dream of mining the solar system. As if, by feeding that endless appetite one could lessen it. It never worked, of course. It was an appetite that waxed on its feeding. Not-wanting was the answer; but until then, one had to be practical. If the throttle of technology were cut back too sharply, it would not be the wealthy who starved or went homeless.

And he had met Mariesa van Huyten face-to-face and found her charming and dedicated. Misinformed, perhaps; remote from the realities of life; fixated on a nice but inherently flawed and unaffordable dream; yet Albright could not question her sincerity.

So, the coin was still in the air tumbling, and had not landed heads or tails.

The issue was, however, dividing his staff. He nodded imperceptibly to Simon Fell.

His chief of staff took the cue. "We have too much on our plate right now to worry about a spaceship that's doomed to failure anyway," he told the group. "The assault on rent controls in Santa Monica and New York City hurts people more directly. And our so-called President Champion plans to gut the Endangered Species Act *and* the Wetlands Preservation Act if he can strong-arm Congress into going along. *Those* are the issues we ought to concentrate on. If we take on the spaceship as well, we can lose a lot of public goodwill for our other projects. The polls say that Joe and Jane Six-Pack support van Huyten."

"Joe Six-Pack is an ignoramus," said Felix. "He needs his consciousness raised."

"You can't take the opinions of such people seriously," Dottie agreed.

Albright kept a tight rein on his temper. His father had had the same irritating, cavalier attitude toward working people. High-school graduates. "Community college" at best. Their thoughts and ideas were uninformed, simplistic. *You just don't understand*, he used to tell workers who came to him with suggestions. And then he would brood over the lack of employee loyalty in his company. Well, the old man had been swallowed up in the recession of the early eighties, so maybe he had had a small taste of what it felt like to be discarded. Albright did not know. They had not spoken in nearly thirty years. Even at Mom's funeral, they had barely nodded to one another. "Joe Six-Pack," he reminded his staff sharply, "is a classist term intended to belittle the working people that our organization is set up to help. And 'ignoramus' is insulting."

Felix snorted. "Say 'cognitively challenged,' then."

Simon said, "Well, whether it's 'correct' of them or not, van Huyten has a lot of support among the working class. If there's any agitation, it's to bring the work into this country. I've talked to our trade-union people, and if we took any line other than that, we'd have to fight them, as well as the mon-eyed interests."

"And so the capitalist class once more coopts the worker," said Felix bitterly.

Simon shrugged. "We can only juggle so many crusades at once. It's better to pick the ones where our efforts can make a difference, and let van Huyten fail all by herself."

"That's the second time you've said that," said Melanie, with a narrow look. "How do you know she'll fail? Because she's a woman?"

"Let's say I know someone who used to work in the Office of Commercial Space Transportation, and OCST says the VHI program is in serious trouble, no matter how good a face they put on things. There is no point wasting a lance on it."

Albright wondered if that was true. Dangerous, to believe what you wanted to hear. VHI had pulled no spectacles since the St. Petersburg flight last October, and a dozen or more routine and boring test flights had driven the topic off the front page everywhere except in *The American Argus*, van Huyten's tame newspaper. Though, oddly enough, the *Argus* slant seemed to focus on the risks these days. There had been sev-eral stories of close calls, related in breathless detail; including one that had damaged a ship and injured one of the astronauts. Was a revolt stirring among the journalists in the trenches? Perhaps. Though Albright could not imagine Gene Forney run-ning so lax a ship.

Hannah the volunteer stuck her head inside the door. "Sorry to interrupt, Phil; but there's a John Williams on the phone, who wants to speak with you personally. He said you would take the call."

Albright smiled crookedly. Williams. "All right, I'll take it in here." He reached for the phone. "Excuse me for a few minutes, people. I've been expecting this call." Simon, who knew about the checks, raised an eyebrow and hustled the others out of the room. When the door closed, Albright pressed the blinking button. "This is Phil Albright."

A deep, gravelly voice answered him. "Hello, Phil. I hope you have been receiving my letters." It was a smoke-raw throat, fuzzy and liquid and hoarse. Albright imagined a large man of perhaps fifty; a comfortable man, well used to control. The checks had been hand-delivered, so Williams knew damned well Albright had received them. The inquiry was meant only to remind Albright of the amounts.

"What can I do for you?"

Albright could hear the smile in the voice, like a cat's purr; or, given the nearly liquid gurgle, like a tiger's growl. "Phil, I am concerned—as I know you are—about the long-term future of this planet; not only because of threats to the ecology, but also threats to world peace. So I feel you ought to be aware of a dreadful weapon being built in the Andes . . ."

Afterward, he filled Simon in. Simon Fell was the most valuable of his advisors. They had worked together since college days. They sketched out a plan of action. Nothing public, yet. "Williams" might or might not be reliable. Simon would quietly check things out before they resorted to press conferences or demonstrations in front of the Ecuadoran embassy. Albright had learned the hard way that the enemies of progressivism used disinformation and *agents provacateur* to make activists look foolish, or to entrap them in illegal activities. And even sincerity was no proof against rumors repeated and distorted through a long daisy chain of informants. A supercannon in the Andes? Iraq had tried to build one, before the Oil War; but it was hard to imagine who Ecuador planned to bombard with such a monstrous gun. Brazil? Gabon? It made no sense that Albright could see.

Which meant there was more going on than "Williams" had revealed. Albright was certain that the caller could have passed on far more than the few names and places he had mentioned. Given the concern, why keep mum? To protect his own anonymity? The more revealed, the smaller the pool of possible revealers. Albright pulled the latest check from its envelope once more. It was drawn on a Bank of America branch in Los Angeles, but, like the others, it had been hand-delivered to his offices. Which meant, what? Coast-to-coast connections? A courier? Twenty-thousand dollars, in total. A lot of money to spend for nothing more than an assurance that Albright would answer the phone. That "Williams" was someone with a lot of money went without saying. None of the checks had bounced.

So, scratch the usual whistle-blower. Whoever "Williams" was, he had serious money on the table and a serious animus against Wilson Enterprises—or against whoever had hired Wilson to build the cannon. Certainly, "Williams" had his own agenda. It was obvious he planned to use the Peoples' Crusades as his weapon. Ecuadoran revolutionaries—assuming there were any—would have neither the money nor the subtlety to employ such a roundabout means of attacking Wilson. Which meant, what? A business rival? That would be a hell of a note, if the Crusades wound up as a cat's paw for some conglomerate out to undercut Wilson.

But if the target was worthy, what did it matter who used whom? There were millionaires, even billionaires, who were progressive in their politics. Look at the Senate. And a super-cannon—Jesus, what if they shot off nuclear shells?—shutting down a supercannon might provide a welcome diversion for those on his staff obsessed with van Huyten's project in Brazil.

7.

Neither Is the Race to the Swift

The warning Klaxon hooted just as Ned reached the Hangar and Support Facilities. The bellowing echoed from the flanks of the hill, and all the seagulls in creation lifted wing and swirled across the sky, screeching. Ned wondered if the birds thought they had heard the bellowing voice of some seagull god, vast, unseen, and infinitely loud. He checked his watch as he strode toward the building. They must be staging the *Santos-Dumont* for Friday's unmanned orbital test. Normally, unmanned tests did not interest Ned; but the outcome of this one might determine whether there ever would be a manned test. A deep-pitched clang reverberated from within the building, and the great sliding doors on the front yawned slowly open. Ned ducked through them. PEDESTRIANS PROHIBITED, read the sign in Portuguese, English, Spanish, and Russian; but a shortcut is a shortcut.

The bright yellow tractor tug huffed and belched an acrid cloud of diesel smoke; then, with a jerk of its tie rods, it hauled the vessel from its berth toward the launch tower. The Plank rested on a self-propelled carrier with twelve sets of supporting tracks, but the tug provided guidance. Ned waved to Arturo, the driver, and stepped behind the towering vehicle and into the now-empty maintenance bay.

He was in the pit. Lubricants and bits of metal and cloth littered the floor. Technicians were just clearing from the catwalks up above, their jobs complete for the moment. Tomorrow, *Bessie Coleman* would be brought in for prep. Portuguese voices echoed in the hollow confines of the building. Footsteps clanged on stairways. The air was thick with the smell of hot oil and metal. Ned located a ladder and climbed it to the second landing. He took the stairs the rest of the way.

The others were already waiting in the meeting room when he arrived. Mendoza had the chair, flanked by two of his technicians and the composites specialist from Dow. They had a four-by-five piece of shredded aeroshell on the table and a segment of cryogenic piping. Forrest, looking uncharacteristically solemn, sat at the foot of the long table beside Valery Volkov.

Volkov had a bandage around his head and his right arm in a sling. A bruise discolored his forehead and blackened his right eye. At that, he had come off better than *Calbraith Rogers*. The Plank had lost ten percent of its aeroshell in the accident and it was not clear yet whether it could be repaired. Volkov would not meet Ned's eye when Ned pulled out the chair opposite him and sat down.

So, it wasn't as if the "*Jolly Rogers*" was Ned's personal rocket. Bonny de Magalhães had set up the pilot rotations so that you didn't always pull the same ship; but Ned had been the first to fly SSTO-X4 after delivery from Fortaleza Works and he had named her, and it had hurt to see that explosion tear away her skin.

And if Volkov wasn't one of the eight hottest pilots ever to touch the sky, *Calbraith Rogers* would be keeping company with the *Paquistão* and the *Ana Maria*. Just one more artificial reef for the abalone population of St. Anthony's Bay to sport in. Mendoza thought *maybe* she would fly again. Most of the internal systems were still good, except for the fuel line that had ruptured and spewed volatile, cryogenic oxygen across hot valves.

Some combination of pressure and vibration and performance had pierced the outside of the envelope. A manufacturing problem, of course. It had to be a manufacturing problem. *Please, dear God, don't let it be a design flaw. They'll ground the fleet if the design is bad.*

Mendoza quizzed them again over what they had seen and heard. Ned had been working Comm; Forrest had been Downrange. Val, of course, was the one with the firsthand view; but there were gaps in his memory. . . . They had gone over their stories countless times already, with Mendoza and de Magalhães and Carneiro, with the people from Dow and Pratt-Whitney and VHI headquarters; but Mendoza insisted on hearing it all once again. Perhaps he thought that the next telling would be different and he would not lose one of his precious machines.

Ned had been the first to hear the warning. . . .

Fernando, I have problem. Number Two oxy pressure dropping fast.

Then the voice of Forrest Calhoun in the downrange observation tower breaking in. *Jesus-H-fucking-Christ! The bird just blew!* Ned freezing, then repeating in a stone cold monotone, *Come in, Rogers. Come in, Rogers. Val, do you hear me?* And Yekaterina's scream, quickly stifled with a fist shoved to her mouth. She breaks for the widow's walk. She has to *see*, do you understand; but Bobbi drops her earphones—who gives a fuck about weather reports at this point?—and grabs her before she can reach the gangway, because there are, by damn, some things you ought not to see. *There has been explosion on board.* Val's voice, clear and steady—God, what a relief to hear him. The bird was still flying!—but you can hear the fear underneath, waiting to rip him apart. Katya turns and sits on the bottom rung of the gangway and buries her face in her hands. She sings something in Russian, or in something older than Russian. *Number Three and Number Five engines are dark,* Val reports. *Shutting down oxy-two. Switching to backup.* Oh, he is cool. He is cryogenically cool. A regular flying machine.

Forrest, Forrest. Can you see him?

I have visual contact. There is a hole in the fuselage, estimate four-foot diameter. Lower quad. Reference . . . A moment's hesitation while he calls the sumbitch schematics up on his board. *Reference Romeo-Fiver-Seven.*

Rogers, *this is Flight.* Krasnarov, the Iron Mike, holding down the command chair that day. Just another routine altitude-and-maneuver test. Nothing special.

Valushka! Valushka!

Zamolchát', Katya! Rogers, *this is Flight. Abort to field. Manual. I say again, manual piloting.* Yeah. Fly it by your ass, comrade. Auto-abort would use the damaged oxy-two system, or worse, try to compensate. *Udacha, tovarishch.*

Katya stands by the railing, gripping it with both hands. *Eject! Mishka, tell him to eject!*

Iron Mike's face never breaks. *We must save the ship, if we can.*

You are a monster! she shouts.

Mike says nothing. He knows.

Forrest again, from Downrange. *Gear deployed. He's vertical.* Then . . . *Shit! Two legs short. I say again: Only three legs are fully extended. Number Two is deployed halfway. No joy on Number Three.*

Easy enough to envision the layout. No support on the windward side. The Plank can land on any four legs; and probably even on three, if only they weren't neighbors. If Val manages to set down at all, he topples.

Three hundred; down at twenty.

How much propellant is left? There is a tank of hydrogen on his nose. If the Plank topples . . . If the hydrogen ignites . . . A sword of Damocles thousands of degrees hot. It melts steel.

Two hundred; down at ten.

It melts iron. *Eject, tovarishch!* Mike finally calls.

Nyet, p'zhalst'. I can save it.

No one sees it, except Forrest. *Fifty feet; small negative,* he calls out from the Downrange tower. Not even Val sees any-thing except his dials, or feels anything but the rack in his hands and the ship shaking apart around him. But he lands it. He lands it! He uses the engines at full where there is no gear extended. *Throttle up. Two and Three.* The ship dances—it's all on tape, every moment—it dances on three legs and two stalks of flame; and then—

Engine shut down.

The flames die and, ever so slowly, SSTO-X4 *Calbraith Rogers* teeters—there is a short, heart-rending moment when it appears it might actually balance—and then it topples, falls upon its windward side, and dies.

The aeroshell is tough. It is carbon-silicon carbide over ti-tanium honeycomb. It crumples; the honeycomb collapses, ab-sorbs the impact. The fuel tanks hold. The fuel tanks hold. There is no explosion; and they find out later that Valery Vol-kov had vented his hydrogen all the way down, keeping just enough to land. An awful chance. Suppose he had vented too much? Though under the circumstances, what was one more risk?

They bring out the crane. Arturo does not know the hydro-gen has been purged; he does not ask. He hooks his rig to the crew module of the now horizontal ship—a stroke of luck that it was Two and Three legs that stayed tucked in rather than Five and One. Valery might have wound up underneath. Ar-turo blows the escape bolt from the outside and his crane lifts the module free of the body and backs away from the ship as fast as its treads can take. When medals are given out, if med-als are ever given out, there ought to be one for Arturo Gus-mão.

Mendoza sat back in his chair and entwined his short, stubby fingers together. He looked at the technician on his left and the man from Dow, who shook his head and threw his pencil down to the table and turned away in disgust. That was when Ned knew something bad was in the air. The bird won't fly again. Not just *Calbraith Rogers;* none of them, ever again.

They found a design flaw and now, "it's back to the old drawing board."

But it wasn't that bad; it was worse.

Mendoza locked eyes with Ned and studied him for a long time. Indian eyes. Steady, cold, and emotionless. After a minute had gone by and the only thing he could see was Mendoza's eyes and the only thing he could hear was Forrest's harsh breathing beside him, Ned began to squirm in his seat. He opened his mouth, but Mendoza held a hand up, palm out, and gave Forrest the same treatment. The Dow man looked puzzled; the two technicians, frightened.

When Mendoza was satisfied with whatever it was that satisfied him, he said the one word that Ned had never thought to hear.

"Sabotage."

The fuel technicians flinched. The Dow man grimaced. They were only hearing a conclusion they had already drawn. Forrest began to curse under his breath, a slow, monotonous litany of bodily functions. Ned felt only an icy emptiness within himself, as if this were something he had always known; he studied his two hands, curled up into rock-hard fists.

"Who?" he whispered. Then he looked at Mendoza and said again, "Who?"

Mendoza's face was flat and his eyes empty and expressionless. "Men are flying here from the North who will discover this thing. They are clever men, Norteamericanos, who know how to read clues and find their quarry. I will find him first. I will find this man who has damaged my machine; and when I do, I will eat him for breakfast."

The Dow man laughed nervously at Mendoza's black humor, but Ned saw the second technician, a man from Roraima State, go pale, and so he knew Mendoza had meant nothing more than God's honest truth.

Ned met Betsy at Pinto Martins airport in Fortaleza. She and Lizzie came off the plane looking ragged and tired and Ned did his best to give them a cheerful welcome, despite what

Mendoza had told him last week. When little Lizzie saw him, she stopped cold, causing a man behind her to stop in his tracks and detour around. Lizzie couldn't take her eyes off Ned, and her right hand groped blindly for Betsy's skirt, to give her something for her tiny fingers to hold on to. Her left hand played with her mouth.

After what seemed an eternity, she said "Daddy?" in a voice steeped in uncertainty.

Ned broke down and cried, right there in the Fortaleza airport; and wasn't that a hell of a thing?

The flight across the Atlantic was filled with long awkward silences. Minamoto's shuttle carried fifty, but the plane was only half full, mostly with maintenance and administrative workers returning from R&R; yet Ned found himself sitting alone across the aisle from Betsy and Liz. Little Lizzie kept her face plastered to the window sucking in the sight of clouds and waves. Betsy kept hers focused straight ahead.

"Look at the positive side," Ned said at one point, after hollow observations of the weather, the smoothness of the flight, and the remarkable growth of Lizzie had played themselves into silence. "I'm only named to the backup crew. It'll be Forrest and Mike who take the ship into orbit and back. Levkin and I are training with them, but that's just a formality."

Ned kept the same cheerful, shit-eating grin plastered to his face that he had worn ever since the announcement had been made. Betsy did not answer him. She had closed her eyes, pretending to sleep. Ned turned away and stared out his own window. *Look at the positive side.* Yeah. Second choice, again. Always a bridesmaid, never a bride. It seemed as if he would spend his life as Forrest's backup. He knew Betsy was pleased by that. Pleased for his own safety, but maybe pleased at his humiliation, too. Not that Betsy cared one way or the other. There was a lot of rubble on the ground between them, and they had only begun to pick at it.

How many times can I say I'm sorry? He had asked her at Pinto Martins airport.

It's not something you say, she had responded.

Okay, but she hadn't had to use those tickets. She could have just trash-canned them and forgotten that he had ever been in her life. It needed more than just her innate frugality to explain why she hadn't simply torn them in two.

"You'll like the island," he said, aware that he had said the same thing more than once already. Betsy opened her eyes and gave him a fleeting smile.

Yeah, she wasn't hostile, just uncertain. Both of them, uncertain. Both of them, feeling that underneath the rubble there might be something worth saving. If only it was for each of them the same something.

Betsy smiled for Forrest. She always smiled for Forrest. He had charmed her first at Edwards, and they had crossed paths later at Peterson and Ames. Now he met them at the landing field on Fernando de Noronha. When Betsy reached the bottom of the stairs, he picked her up by the waist and set her down on the tarmac. "Forrest Calhoun," she said with a dimple she hadn't shared with Ned. "You haven't changed at all."

Forrest sniffed his clothing. "Gee, I was hoping you wouldn't notice," he said. Jorje handed him two suitcases from the plane's belly. "Follow me," he said. He hefted Betsy's suitcases and led them toward the main building.

Ned followed with Lizzie in tow. Her hold on his hand even now was tentative. Half-familiar, but half a stranger. A phantom of her dreams. He had been gone for a quarter of her life.

Levkin had not been the first choice for the backup crew. He was on only because Valery Volkov, with his broken arm, was off. Ned knew that because Forrest had told him, in strictest confidence. Perhaps Levkin knew it, too. He seemed to work the simulations with greater energy than usual, and with fewer jokes; as if he sensed that this might be his one last chance to shine.

Floating in the buoyancy tank they called "the Abyss," Ned watched Levkin try to couple a fueling hose to a mock-up of one of Wilson's fuel pods. The Abyss was built into a sheltered cove of St. Anthony's Bay, shielded by breakwaters from the motion of the waves. Beyond the Plexiglas and composite barriers, fish darted and arced. An octopus, hugging a rock on the floor of the bay, stared at them with an uncanny intentness, blinking its oddly human eyes at the unaccustomed brightness. The suits they wore in the Tank gave them neutral buoyancy. Not the same as "free fall" but as close as they could get on Earth's surface.

From Ned's perspective, Levkin floated sideways. The Russian carefully maneuvered the simulated hose into the fixture on the simulated fuel tank while Ned sat in the simulated Plank and simulated watching him. *And what did you do in the Plank Program, Daddy? I reached simulated orbit, Lizzie.*

A careless move sent Levkin twisting slowly counterclockwise, and a few well-chosen Russian curses filled Ned's earphones. It wasn't nice to mess with Mother Newton. He touched his mike. "Slow and careful, Gregor," he said. "Think before you act." Working in free fall had come to seem routine after so may Shuttle flights, but it was important to remember how truly different—and difficult—it was. It had very nearly cost Gene Cernan his life on Gemini 9; but those had been pioneer days, when everything was an unknown— and Buzz Aldrin had finally developed the techniques. *We're so much smarter now.*

As Forrest was so fond of saying, *it will be something completely different that kills us.*

Levkin fired a spurt from his jets to stop his slow spin. They were water jets, not rockets, and Ned rocked slightly in the mild wave they sent through the water, another reminder that buoyancy was not free fall. "I will be attempting coupling again," Levkin announced.

"Roger." *Don't strain yourself.* It wasn't as though they were practicing for the real thing. Ned felt a curious detachment, almost as if his mind were floating along with his body. He wondered if Levkin felt the same way.

Gregor made the simulated coupling on the second attempt and simulated fuel was pumped into the simulated ship.

* * *

In the shower afterward, Levkin grinned at Ned. "Is always a wonder," he said, "why we shower after being in water." The joke hadn't been funny the first five times, either, and Ned barely grunted acknowledgment.

"Your wife, beautiful woman," Levkin said over the hiss of the shower. Ned rinsed the soap from his face and looked at his companion. Levkin was a rug. Hirsute, that was the word. Great whorls of black hair ran down his torso from chest to groin and covered his thighs and lower arms. Even his back was hairy. The smooth-shaven moon face set atop this shaggy splendor seemed almost babylike in comparison.

"Sure is."

"Faithful wife?"

The question was so blandly asked that Ned had to think twice to be sure he had hard correctly. Was Levkin asking for a loan? "I believe so," he replied carefully. *More than I've been a faithful husband, at any rate. And if she had sampled a few men in the last few years . . . well, what did faithfulness mean under the circumstances?*

But Levkin's interest was apparently more philosophical. "Are two sorts husband. Those whose wife cheats; and those who have not yet found out."

"Come off it, Levkin."

"When I am coming home to Sverdlovsk from Afghanistan, I hold meeting for wives of my comrades. I think, This will comfort them to know how their husbands fare; but I leave the meeting and find three telephone numbers stuffed in my jacket pocket."

Ned laughed. If housewives were stuffing phone numbers into Levkin's pockets, they were hard-up horny, for sure.

Levkin turned the shower head to pulse. The water bursts beat a tatoo on his back, almost like a Gatling gun. "Is sometimes not so funny, my friend. Another man is coming home and his wife's new boyfriend is jealous. So they meet the man at the airbase, thinking to take him into the *taiga* and kill him. Only they have forgotten that the man is trained a *spetznatz*, so he returns from the *taiga* and they do not."

Spetznatz, the Russian Special Forces. "Jesus," Ned said.

"That's pretty brutal. I don't think Betsy's taken out a contract on me, though." *With her own hands, maybe, she'd like to strangle me; but that's different. That's a normal, healthy man-woman relationship.*

"Is good thing that orbital flight will be short," Levkin said, turning in to the shower like a man facing the firing squad. "No time to grow horns."

Ned grunted. "Yeah. Real short, in our case, since we'll be watching Forrest and Mike."

"Do not give up hope, my friend. Perhaps by lucky accident we see reversal to our fortunes."

Ned yanked his own shower handle off and gave Levkin a hard stare. But Levkin stood with his eyes closed allowing the water to hammer on his head, his face, his chest, and run with the suds down his shaggy legs into the tiled drain.

8.

Nor the Battle to the Valiant

Barry Fast found Harriet in the stables near the rear of the grounds at Silverpond. The path was not marked and he lost his way twice; but eventually, topping a small rise about a quarter of a mile behind the main building, he found a low wooden shed set in a small dale. Beyond the stables, Runamuck Creek wound its way through a meadow dotted with fences, hedgerows, and other steeplechase obstacles. He located Harriet in one of the stalls, rubbing down a chestnut mare.

The stable smelled of straw and dung and horse. Leather tackle draped over hooks gleamed in the soft, muted sunlight that filtered into the building. Harriet stood with her back to him, dressed in a tan silk blouse and contrasting jodhpurs, stained here and there with dark patches of perspiration. The polish of her black, calf-length riding boots was scuffed from use. He knew that Harriet had heard him enter, because she paused for a moment before resuming the long, slow strokes. The horse rolled its eyes and shook it head back and forth.

"I got your message," he said. "Sykes said you were back

here.'' Harriet did not respond and Barry shrugged. ''Maybe you wanted me to wait in the big house?''

''No. It is better out here.'' Harriet favored him with the briefest of looks while she continued to brush down the horse. ''But I must see to Estrella while we talk. You understand how it is with horses.''

Oh, sure, I keep a stable of Thoroughbreds over in the Lakeview subdivision. . . . ''Certainly.''

After a few more strokes, she said. ''Do you love my daughter?''

And wasn't that a hell of a question to come out of nowhere on a Saturday morning? Nor was it a question easily answered. He took hold of a bridle hanging beside the stall and rubbed the leather strap between his thumb and forefinger while he considered his response. Yes. No. Maybe. What sort of answer did she want to hear? ''I think I am coming to,'' he answered at last. ''We've become good friends over the last two years. We share thoughts and dreams—and I find her fascinating. Maybe that will become love. Maybe it *is* love.''

Harriet turned and regarded him. ''Thank you,'' she said finally.

''For what?''

''For the pause before you answered.'' Harriet petted the horse on the neck, and the horse whinnied and nuzzled against her. She dug into her pockets and removed a cored apple. Estrella took it from her hand in one bite. ''A woman of Riesey's wealth . . . Most men would have answered far more quickly, and with far more certainty.'' She gave Estrella a parting embrace and then stepped from the stall, closing the gate behind her. She brushed her hands against one another.

''You think I was after her money?''

''It seemed a likely possibility. People in our position—''

''You could have gotten to know me before you judged me.''

She folded her arms and searched his face. ''Are you certain you want me to know you?''

''What does that mean?''

Harriet shook her head. ''Mariesa is not an easy person to

love. Not even an easy person to know. I have known her all her life and even I do not understand her. This crusade of hers, this business of space stations, is all beyond me. Even if it is a good business decision—Chris seems to think so, and Chris has a level head—the *intensity* of her commitment sometimes frightens me. Its wellspring is hidden deep inside her, underneath the facile cost-benefit analyses, underneath the utopian visions. At times, she can be like a stranger."

Barry stuffed his hands into the pockets of his slacks. What was Harriet getting at? Why had she had Sykes summon him to Silverpond for this meeting? "I think," he said, "she is only looking for someone who will listen."

"And I do not?" Harriet looked away, down the line of stalls. Horses huffed, and their tails, visible through the stall gates, flicked at opportune flies. She brushed a hand across her hair and a strand came loose and dangled alongside her neck. "She used to give me books and articles to read; but they were distressingly technical and, somehow, I never found the time for them. After a while . . . she no longer gave them to me."

Instead, she gave them to me. And to every new acquaintance who showed an interest? In an odd way, Mariesa Gorley van Huyten might have jumped into his lap as deliberately as had Shannon Morgenthaler. "*Take* an interest," he told Harriet. "Ask to see the booklets; ask her to explain."

She shook her head. "It would be false, and she would know it. There is a wall between us, Mr. Fast. It is not a wall that either of us intended building, but it is no less solid for that."

"Tear it down," Barry suggested. "It worked in Berlin."

She shook her head. "The mortar has had too long to set. There were decisions deliberately made, things done or not done which can never be undone, so long ago that they have become landscape, as much a part of our lives as Skunktown Mountain or Runamuck Creek."

Barry kicked a stone away from the stables. It skipped down the straw-laden area fronting the stalls and banged gently against the barn wood wall. What had happened between Mariesa and her mother was another world, another life, and none of his business, except that he had somehow become a weapon in their mutual war. "Why am I here?" he asked bluntly. Harriet was not the sort for pointless revelations, and Barry could not escape the notion that this entire encounter thus far had been carefully orchestrated.

"May I be frank?"

No. Smile and lie like hell. "Of course."

"I do not believe that you are the right sort of man for my daughter. You have not the right background or schooling or interests; and I am not at all sure of the inner man. Yet . . . it may be that Mariesa simply needs a man in her life at this point—any man, provided he be neither thoughtless nor cruel. I have seen no cruelty in you, Mr. Fast; and I believe you give matters a great deal of thought—perhaps even too much thought." She unfolded her arms at last and gave him an intent, hard-eyed gaze. "Tell me. Have you and she been intimate?"

Barry grunted. "Would that be any of your business?"

"No, I thought not." She stepped to the stable door, outside into the late-morning sunshine. Barry followed her. The meadow grasses and the white haze of Queen Anne's lace rippled in the April breezes, giving the swells of the land the appearance of an undulating, frothy green sea. Like Puget Sound in the springtime . . . The weedy smell of sap was in the air. In the distance, a man worked at repairing the fence on the obstacle course, the sound of his hammer coming half a beat past the swing of his arm. The stableboy, a young black man wearing jeans and a straw cowboy hat, sat tilted back on a stool against the stable wall. Harriet gave him a nod and he rocked upright and, fetching a pail that sat in the dust beside him, hustled inside to resume his duties. Harriet stood with her legs akimbo and her fists on her hips and surveyed the scene.

"Did you know, Mr. Fast, that I once threatened to thwart Mariesa's program if she did not give you up?"

"She told me."

She turned and appraised him. "And she chose you." There was curiosity in her voice, and bafflement, and distress. "Oh, she dressed it up with hairsplitting punctilio, but I knew, and—more importantly—she knew. Chris eventually dissuaded me from my threat—I would have hurt far too many other people who had done me no harm—but I had already decided that her audacity deserved a reward. Come, walk with me toward the house.'' She turned and set a brisk pace along the path leading up to the side of the rill.

"You're an athletic woman,'' Barry commented, matching her stride.

"Yes. I'm in 'good shape for an old broad,' am I not? I ride every morning and try to walk at least three miles every few days. I golf weekly with my niece, Brittany. Mariesa ought to get from behind her desk more often. Too sedentary a life cannot be healthy.''

"And what 'reward' do you plan to give Mariesa?''

"You, Mr. Fast. You.''

Barry stopped dead, but Harriet kept walking and, after a moment, he ran after her. "Me?'' he asked when he had drawn abreast.

"Yes, you. I asked earlier if you and she had been intimate. I believe Riesey is looking for intimacy, that she needs it. I do not believe . . .'' She paused a moment, then continued. "I do not believe she has kissed a man other than socially for several years.''

Talk about major horny. Major horny; or major frigid. "If that's so, what makes you think she's looking in my direction?''

They paused a fork in the path. Harriet said, "My walking route takes me down to the creek side and around to the front of the house; but if you continue in this direction to the atrium entrance, you may tell Sykes that I said he ought to show you the B1 level.'' With that she turned away and her brisk strides soon put distance between them.

The first sublevel underneath Silverpond consisted of a number of storage rooms and all-purpose rooms of no interest to Barry, and he wondered what possible motive Harriet had had in sending him here. There was a game room set up with an inlaid chessboard table and a large-screen computer. A bookcase filled with boxed games and racks of disks stood against one wall, though it did not look to Barry as if the room had been used recently. Sykes patiently conducted him from room to room, apparently as mystified as Barry as to the purpose.

It was only when he opened the doors at the west end of the building that Barry understood Harriet's intention and burst out laughing.

It was a bowling alley.

Comfortable chairs, a wet bar, and tables clustered around a single hardwood lane. A rack held half a dozen balls of various sizes. At the far end, duckpins were arranged in a nine-pin diamond. Another rack held a set of larger ten-pins. There was no pinsetting equipment, but a bench on the side suggested that pinboys arranged pins manually between frames.

"How long has this been here?" he asked Sykes. *She couldn't have had this installed just because I took her to a bowling alley that time. . . .*

"I am not certain, sir," the butler answered. "I understand it was her grandfather who had the lane built, during the thirties. He used to entertain business associates down here. He was much taken with Dutch customs, old Willem was. Family traditions."

"Ah." *But, then, if the lane has been here all those years . . .* "Does Mariesa bowl often, Sykes?"

"A few times a month, sir," the butler answered. "Her grandfather taught her, of course. She is much like him."

"She must be pretty good at it, then."

"I am no expert in the game," Sykes admitted, "but I should imagine so, yes."

Barry laughed and shook his head, and understood what Harriet had wanted him to learn. "It's not the only game she's good at."

With every visit Barry seemed to penetrate deeper into the van Huyten estate and with that, deeper into the family itself; so much so that, at times, he dared to think of himself as a member of it, in the same way that Keith McReynolds, Belinda

Karr, and some of the others seemed a part. At the far south end, the property ran up the sudden slope of Skunktown Mountain. To Barry, who had grown up with Mount Ranier framed in his window, it was little more than a ridge. Even compared to the Watchungs, it was not much to speak of. Anything you could reach the top of in a pair of ordinary walking shoes did not rate as a "mountain" in Barry's book. Still, when Mariesa suggested a bit of "mountain climbing" after dinner, he had accepted readily.

The hike to the top was an easy one, though Barry did feel himself panting before they had reached it. *I'm getting out of shape,* he thought. An oak forest thick with underbrush nestled at the base of the ridge. Mariesa led him up a dirt path that wound through tangled dogwoods and spicebush and witch hazel and ground colored by pinxter flower. Leave the path and you'd be lost in the thickets. The top of the ridge, however, was a more open canopy of chestnut oak, sprinkled with sweet birch and sassafras. The summit was grassy, but barren, with only a few scattered clusters of snakeroot and wild ginger. A gazebo sat in a clearing, sheltering a bench built of oak boards and distressed brick. At the far end of the clearing, a course of brick poked from the grass and dirt: the ruins of some long-forgotten building, and probably the source of the bench. The village of Skunktown Furnace lay on the south side of the ridge, and Barry wondered if this might have been the site of the forge itself.

Mariesa took a seat on the bench. A light flush colored her cheeks and the base of her throat, and small, dark circles stained her blouse at the armpits and at the small of her back. She seemed pensive to Barry, her mind a thousand miles away; or two hundred miles up. Barry joined her and they sat together for a silent while enjoying the view. It gave him a chance to catch his breath.

The woods below encircled Silverpond on the east and west like protective arms. Farther on, the horse meadow was tinted yellow and white with coltsfoot and bloodroot. Past that, the "House of the Mound People" itself and the broad, impossibly kempt lawn in front. The entire scene had a miniature, distanced look to it, although nothing was very far below, or very far away.

Nearby, just below a crest of the hill, a springhouse of dark wood and mortared gray stone protected the source of one of the "cricks" that fed Runamuck Creek. From it, Barry could hear the faint plinking sound of water dripping into water. In colonial days, springhouses had served as refrigerators. He wondered what the name of the spring was. In this part of the country, wellsprings all had names.

"Nice view," he said after a while. The late-afternoon sunlight was beginning to linger at this time of year. Not quite summertime, but the course was definitely set. You could have an early dinner and still see the sights before dark.

"Yes. It's a bit of a walk from the house, but sometimes one needs the solitude."

Solitude. Was that why she had brought him here? Harriet had suggested that she was only waiting for him to make a move. "You're leaving in the morning?" He knew she was—it was the reason for the early dinner—but the time and place demanded idle chatter.

"To witness the orbital flight. Yes. I wish you could come along and see our facilities down there. But the gallery has limited space for observers, and a number of others have first claim to them."

"Maybe a later flight," Barry said. "Besides, I can't cut school. The kids come first."

A smile. "You sound like Belinda."

"I think Belinda and I have the same goals; just different ways of approaching them. With her, it's all process and technique. With me, it's more of a passion."

"Oh, Belinda can be quite passionate." The sudden color that highlighted her throat deepened and climbed behind the ear. She looked away. "You know what I mean."

"Hmm, I suppose so." Belinda, passionate? Usually with a woman Barry could sense *something*, but with Dr. Karr it was all business. "You're nervous." She nodded her head. "About the space flight?"

She brushed a hand through her short-cropped hair. "There is always a risk," she said.

"Still, you've got how many test flights under your belt already? Not to mention the suborbital . . . And didn't you tell me the unmanned orbital went smoothly?"

"This is rather a more complex mission," she said. "They will be deploying a resource-monitoring satelite and . . . practicing . . . a refueling procedure."

"You've done all you could do. The pilots and crew have been rehearsing. You've tested the ship inside and out, right? You wouldn't send it up if there were any real doubt."

A brief, haunted look passed across her features, gone before Barry could fully note it. "The purpose of test flight is to resolve doubts."

"Well, at this stage, what sort of doubts could—?"

"Barry, let it be!"

Barry fell silent. He had never heard her yell before. The lady was so tense she practically vibrated just sitting there. A bright red cardinal darted across the clearing and perched on the branch of a white oak on the right side of the clearing. It cocked its head side to side before taking flight. The leaves shook and rustled from its departure. "I'm sorry," he said.

"No, I should not have snapped at you. It is only that there is so much that can go wrong, and so much depends upon everything going right." Her hands were clenched into fists on her lap. "One failure can ruin the venture."

"Yeah, one 'awshit' cancels out a thousand 'attaboys.' "

A smile forced itself across her lips. "We shall require a great deal of luck, this time out."

Barry took a breath, and a chance, and placed a comforting arm around her shoulder. She did not resist. "Well, then, how about a kiss for good luck?" They had kissed casually at parties; and Harriet had dropped a few hints; and there had been that stunt Mariesa had pulled at the bowling alley. It all seemed to add up right. And what the heck? Nothing ventured; nothing gained.

The smile was weak, but she said—"Very well. I can use all the luck I can get"—and lifted her face.

Their lips brushed, softly and delicately. Improbably, for so tentative a contact, his pulse raced at the touch, and he pulled her closer to him. But when he pressed the kiss, she stiffened and shoved him hard, so that he nearly slid off the bench.

"What are you doing?" she cried, standing up ramrod straight.

He sat dumbstruck for a moment before the bitterness overwhelmed him. Then he hunched his shoulders. He had been a fool. He could not believe Harriet had suckered him so neatly. He could not believe that he had let her do that to him. "God damn it!" he said. "She set me up. That—that *woman*—set me up!"

And maybe of all the reactions he might have had, that was just the right one, because Mariesa hesitated in the archway of the gazebo and turned and said, "What?"

He smacked a fist onto the bench, hardly feeling the pain. "Your mother," he said. "She set me up."

Mariesa stepped back inside the gazebo. "Harriet. How?"

"She—" He bit his lip, but saw no way to salvage the situation except to plow ahead. "She told me you were 'looking for intimacy.' And I—I guess it was just wishful thinking on my part."

"Am I?" The color was in her cheeks again.

"She said you needed a man in your life."

The look on Mariesa's features was enigmatic, mixed parts anger and stony impassivity. "Is that so?" The voice was iron and ice.

Desperately, he said, "She said it, not me."

"I hardly need to look for men, because Mummy constantly throws them in my path."

"And now she's thrown me."

She regarded him curiously. "Yes. I wonder why? With Harriet, one must always search behind the arras." She crossed her arms and stepped out of the gazebo, where she stood staring down toward the mansion. "Perhaps," she said slowly, "we ought to give Harriet what she wants. It would be shameful to disappoint her when she has planned everything so carefully."

An odd light-headedness overcame him. He seemed to be floating on the benchtop. His own voice, and Mariesa's, came to him from far away. "I don't understand."

Mariesa turned, which framed her in the archway against the indigo northern sky. Her face seemed to shine in the deepening dusk. "I have rejected every man she has picked for me. Perhaps she thought that, by picking you, it would drive me to reject you, as well."

"And . . . does it?"

She stepped back under the roof of the gazebo, closer to him, directly in front of him. He stood up slowly. She tilted her head and looked him in the eye. "Wishful thinking?" she asked, as if she had just heard his earlier comment.

This time, it was his turn to blush. "Well, yes."

She put her arms around his neck. "Sometimes, wishes come true."

She was awkward. None of it came naturally to her. Not the kissing, not the caressing. It was not, Barry thought later, on her regular agenda. But Barry knew what to do—Lord knew, he had had enough practice. He knew how to kiss and how to touch and how to unfasten whatever begged unfastening. If the need arose, he even knew what words to say. Perhaps, at first, Mariesa had had no other intention than to defy her mother. She had come to it coldly, as a calculation, with Barry ending up as the numerator. It was the heat of anger, not of passion; but if heat is there, the passion follows. When the blood-tide rises it carries you off, whether you had intended it or not. And, if the motives were all askew with the clothing, it climaxed well enough, because, as Barry had often thought on barren nights, even when it's bad, it's good.

The kitchen sink was piled high with dishes. Glasses and flatware choked the drainer on the sideboard. A pot, caked with hardened spaghetti strands and dried sauce, sat soaking. The advantage of the solitary bachelor, Barry thought. You could put a lot of things off for a long while.

Some things, not all.

The kitchen phone was wall-mounted, and he really ought to have gotten a longer cord for it. Long enough so he could at least reach the chairs around the kitchen table. He shifted his stance, leaned against the wall by the phone, and tightened his grip on the handset. "All I said, Shannon," his voice even and reasonable, "was that I thought we ought to cool things off between us."

"Why?" The word was hard and sharp, like a dagger, or a shard of broken glass. It hung in the void in the wires that connected and distanced them at the same time. He hadn't been able to bring himself to do this face-to-face.

"I just think it's time for us to move on," he said.

Icy silence, paradoxically loud; then: "I see. You finally managed to stick it to her. You bastard."

"Look, I'm sorry you feel that way; but, even if that were true, it's not the reason." *Liar!* "I need a life of my own, Shannon. I can't spend it waiting for you to find an opening for me in your schedule."

"Barry, Barry, I don't care who else you screw. I only care about you and me."

"I'm not rejecting you. You're a great person. We had some wonderful times together. . . ."

"We can still have wonderful times together. . . ."

Shannon begging distressed him more than Shannon angry. He wanted to say, Get a grip on yourself. Have some pride. You have a husband and two kids; and I have nothing. What the hell were you getting out of me that you need so desperately? Or with a more cruel twist: I'm sure you can find someone else, Shannon. Just hop on his lap and let him know. If they had been face-to-face, what would she have done to try to keep him? He thought that Shannon was less distressed by the ending of their relationship than by the fact that he had taken the initiative to end it.

It was a long phone call, made longer because there was not that much to say.

INTERLUDE:

Voices (II)

Phil won't squat or get off the pot. He still insists that it's not worth our resources."

"Yeah, but if van Huyten *does* succeed, we'll see such a wave of mindless, technophiliac yahooism in this country that half the gains we've made in the last fifty years will go out the window."

"Well then, maybe it's time for direct action. Phil doesn't have to know everything."

"Space ought to belong to everyone, Jim."

"Well, Bob, the way I see it, no one's stopping you from going."

"To hell with spaceships. What about that supercannon that Wilson is building down in Ecuador? That's what the Crusades ought to focus on!"

"The unmanned orbital launch that they made such a ballyhoo about last month . . . ?" Well, I hear that they took a Bell Labs satellite along 'on consignment.' No fee if VHI couldn't insert it. They figured since they were going up anyway, why not do something useful while they were up there. Now *that's* frugal . . .''

"Keith? This is Jacqueline in International Sales. How are you feeling? Glad to hear it. The reason I called is I've got the *weirdest* Request For Quote I've ever seen, and I need to run it past you for the costings. No, none of the regular accountants are up to it. Remember the RFQ from the Air Force last month, asking for a price-and-delivery on a dozen of Daedalus's suborbital Planks: yes, I know they were just fishing; Congress would never appropriate for a foreign purchase. Well, we've got another one; only this one is from Federal Express. . . .''

"Okay. First, they can't reach geosynchronous orbit, so what's the point of . . . ?''
    "You mean because they can't do *every*thing, they shouldn't do *any*thing?''

"And if she succeeds—I've said 'if,' mind you—you can kiss the values of your holdings good-bye. No, I don't know what the fallout will be; that's exactly my point. Certainly I have taken measures to protect myself. I could not look my nephews' children in the eye otherwise. What? Two measures, which I would rather not discuss.''

"We are quite excited by the whole prospect, naturally. Our communication and navigation satellites are quite expensive, so any prospect of reasonably inexpensive repair or retrieval strikes us as worth investigating. We shall be watching the results of the manned orbital launch with great interest.''

"You realize whenever conservatives want to put a good face on things, they put a few token women or minorities up front. So the fact that her pilot corps includes . . .''
    "Umm, I don't think you'd want to call Forrest Calhoun a

'token' to his face. And to tell you the truth, I don't much care what motives whites have for giving us a slice of the pie, as long as we get a slice.''

''I think we see eye to eye on this one. You can arrange for the, ah, necessary supplies, can you not? Of course. I and my friends would be more than happy to donate to causes we believe in.'' He broke the connection. That took care of number one.

''And second . . . the unmanned orbital launch that they made such a ballyhoo about last month . . . ? Well, I hear that they didn't have much of a safety margin. Is it right to risk human lives when there's still a risk involved?''

''The problem with you kids today is you want to jump right into something just because it's new and exciting. In my day, we asked what the social value was. . . .''
    ''Oh, Dad . . .''
    ''And don't you roll your eyes at me, young man!''

''Yes. The funds have been deposited to your account at the Banco de Fortaleza. Half now; the other half, upon successful completion of your task. No, I do not want to know. I'm sure you will think of something.'' He hung up the phone and stared at it a moment. That took care of number two.

''Phil? This is Simon. What do you plan for Friday?''
    ''I guess I'll be watching the TV, like everyone else.''

9.

Moses Before the Promised Land

Infirmaries smelled like illness. Ned wasn't sure why—whether it was the gauze or the linens or the alcohol disinfectant or something else entirely—but you could be blind and deaf and dumb and still know it when you woke up in a hospital bed.

Forrest must feel like hell, Ned thought as he took a seat beside the man's bed. Sweat beaded his forehead and a glucose drip was attached to his arm. Forrest didn't have the right sort of complexion for it, but if he could have looked pale, he would have. "Jesus, Forrest," Ned said. "You look like shit."

Forrest rolled his eyes. "Thank you for sharing that with me, son. You should see how things look from this end."

Betsy pulled a chair away from the window and sat on the opposite side of the bed. She said, "I hope you're feeling better, Forrest."

"To feel any worse, I'd have to be dead."

"If it's any consolation," Ned told him, "Mike is just as bad off."

Forrest sighed. "Ordinarily, that would cheer me some, but

I would not even wish the Iron Mike to feel like this.''

"They said it was food poisoning," Betsy said, taking one of Forrest's hands and patting it.

Calhoun twisted his mouth. "I guess the puking and the runs clued the docs in. Who else got it?"

"Just you and Mike and Bonny. Plus a half dozen or so of the locals who were in the cantina that night. The governor has ordered Claudio to shut down for health inspection."

"Damn luck. Ned, how many times have you and I eaten Claudio's *feijoada?*"

"Yeah," said Ned, "bad luck."

Forrest squirmed in his bed. "You're never quite comfortable in these hospital beds, you know? They raise your head up and then you spend the rest of the day sliding down to the foot." He tugged at the sheet and tried to smooth it out. Betsy reached over and helped him. "Then at the end of the day, they come in and raise the foot and let you slide back up during the night. And the gowns? If it weren't that the gals enjoyed the show, I wouldn't wear 'em at all. I—"

Ned saw how Forrest's hand trembled where it clenched the sheets. "Stomach cramps?" he asked. Forrest shook his head.

"No." The man fell silent, scowling at some inner hurt and Ned waited him out. "João was here this morning," Forrest said finally.

"Oh?"

"They're going ahead with the launch."

"Oh."

Betsy relinquished her hold on Forrest and stood up. She turned away from the bed and stared out the window. Looking past her, Ned could see the distant Hangar and Support Building like a monument against the sky. The great doors were shut tight. Inside, *Bessie Coleman* was being prepped for orbit. Under armed guard and, perhaps as important, under Mendoza's careful eye. Betsy, framed in the light, seemed like a shadow against the glare.

"Damn it, Ned. I wanted it to be me."

"I know, Forrest. You and me, together." Betsy turned

away from the window and looked at him and he quickly dropped his gaze to his friend.

"No, son. Politics. It had to be a Russian and an American. That meant me and Mike, or you and Valery—before his accident, or even Bobbi and Katya, though I don't think João's gender sensitivity was quite up to that one. Ned . . ." He faltered. "God damn it, Ned, I wanted to be *remembered*."

The anguish on the man's face was almost more than Ned could bear. He turned away a little bit. To have your life's goal snatched from you at the last moment, not by any merit or lack of it on your own part, but only because a damned bug had set up housekeeping in your intestines . . . "Hell, Forrest," he said, "you want to be remembered? They made a damned *song* about your St. Petersburg flight. Some high-school girl wrote it. Haven't you heard it on the radio? '*The Cowboy and the Iron Mike went off to space together . . .*'" And how on earth had that girl learned of the nicknames the pilots used? He sang the tag line from the chorus. '. . . *And they set it down in St. Petersburg a half an hour later.*'"

Forrest chuckled. "Don't give up your day job; the recording studios aren't ready yet." The smile faded quickly and he gazed off into nowhere. "You do good, Ned. Make me proud."

"Jesus Christ, Forrest. You're not dying. It's just food poisoning. If João Pessoa wasn't such a tight-ass for keeping schedule, he'd have postponed the flight awhile so you could take her up. I mean, Bonny's down with the bugs, too; which means Heitor is Flight this time around. . . ."

But Forrest was not listening. "Claudio, he sure made a damn fine *feijoada*. Now he's shut down."

"Yeah, it's a damn shame, all right."

"Ned, you are Numero Uno, now. You and Levkin. And Ned, if I was you, I'd be mighty picky what I ate."

Ned and Betsy took a picnic basket to Mirante do Sancho and spread a blanket under the bright May sunshine while Lizzie stalked flowers and butterflies across the meadow. You had to hike in—no vehicles were allowed inside the reserve; and Ned had to sign a pledge that he would leave no trash on the ground, in the sea, or on the beach and that he would not molest any of the marine creatures. The trail was a rugged one, but the view of Sancho Beach was worth the bramble and the brush and the clambering over sharp rocks.

There were no seasons in the tropics. Some months it rained and some months it didn't—but there were no seasons as Ned knew them. No turning of the leaves into crisp auburn and gold; no ozone-sharp air freezing your breath into clouds of vapor; no springing of sweet and musky-scented color; no hazy chorus of dog-day katydids chittering through the long afternoon. Here, every day was the same day. The endless breakers from the shrugging ocean; the steady breezes from the south. Time could slide away unnoticed when nothing marked its passage.

They sat side by side on the blanket without touching. There was a space—a no-fly zone—between them. Only a few inches, but maybe uncrossable. Space and time. A few inches, and a few years. Betsy was dressed in jeans and a blue checked blouse. A Brazilian-style straw cowboy hat shaded her eyes so that Ned could not read them. Betsy had been on the island for three weeks now and they had yet to touch, save in the most perfunctory fashion. Ned wondered if they ever would touch again.

He watched Betsy set out the plates of *peixe a delícia* and roasted *paçoca*. Cearnese dishes. Strange foods under strange skies. Perfect dishes for strangers to eat. The Brazilians did not dress their meats with the same cuts as Northerners. The *bife de panela* was an anonymous grilled slab, neither rump nor flank. The *vatapá* tasted of coconut and *dendê* oil.

His belly felt the way it always did before a test flight: a hard, insoluble lump just below his breastbone. If Betsy had not come to the island, he would still have been here atop the Mirante—atop Gisela or ·Bobbi or one of the nameless office clerks with the ready smiles and the readier legs, stroking that hardness away. With any other woman, he would have had his arms around her, would have her spread upon the rock-hard soil. Any other woman would have had no other reason for coming with him. Any other woman would have had no other thought but for that sweet moment.

But this was not any other woman. This was the one he saw when his eyes were closed.

Betsy drew her knees up and wrapped her arms around them and stared toward the restless ocean. "What do I see in you, Ned? You fuck my next-door neighbor and then run off for two years; and still when you show up in my doorway, God, I feel the old ache come right back."

Ned replied slowly. "We had some good times together. It wasn't all bad."

A faint smile played across her lips. "Oh, Jesus, yes. Remember that first night in Wichita Falls? I lost count."

"I think the motel owner was shocked. He wasn't used to folks spending the whole night."

"So then tell me, Ned. If the fucking was so fucking good, why'd you have to go looking in other places?" The smile was gone now. The mouth settled into a hard, thin line.

I didn't have to go looking. It came looking for me. That was one answer, the oldest one in the Book: The woman tempted me, and I did eat. "It was my fault," he said.

"I didn't ask for the blame. There's plenty enough for that. I asked for the why. Because that is what I don't understand."

I went looking because it got harder and harder to find it at home. But that was just another way of saying, It wasn't me. It just happened. Though, in a way, it did "just happen." If you had something, if you had *it*, the women hunted you down, cornered you in honky-tonks, touched your hand making change at store counters. And it made you feel important. It stroked the old ego the way it stroked everything else, making you swell up at both ends; and it was a blast either way, because it meant you were the biggest, highest, fastest sumbitch who ever rode sky. "Sometimes—"

His hesitations drew her eyes to him at last. Brown eyes, both sad and angry—and muddied with other passions, too. "Sometimes, what?"

"Sometimes, it's nothing but habit. Because it's there; because I'm bored, or lazy, or flattered. But other times, it's a

. . . need. Like there's a hunger inside me. But never because it was love, except with you. Oh, hell. I'm no good at words.''

She turned away and cupped her chin in her hands. ''No, you never relied on eloquence.''

''But there's been a hole in my life now for two years that I can't fill. It's a certain size and a certain shape; and only you and Lizzie can fit.''

Lizzie had tired of exploring the meadow and had settled down upon the picnic blanket to read a book. She was a thoughtful child, given to books and odd, left-field questions couched in older children's terms. In the third grade now. It seemed the blink of an eye since she had started school. *A two years' absence. He had missed all the in-betweens.* She was much taken with flowers and grasses and bugs and squirmy creatures, but her interests had not gotten down the evolutionary ladder to boys yet. She was making a field guide to Fernando de Noronha for a class project. Specimens collected and pressed between the pages of books; snapshots taken of insects and animals and environments. *Ned had said, Why don't you press the insects in your books? And Lizzie had given him that high-pitched warbling laugh of hers. Silly, because it'd make the pages sticky.* She logged everything carefully in a notebook; and what names and other minutiae Ned could not supply, Arturo or Heitor or Dolores or even Bonifácio himself could. The wardens for the reserve had helped, and had given her photographs of those specimens she was not allowed to touch. Lizzie was attending a different school this year, Betsy had told him. A scholarship had come out of the blue from a new private school in south Houston. They had not only given her the month away from class but had helped her plan the project and the other lessons she would have to complete upon returning.

''You are really going to fly that thing, aren't you?'' Betsy's voice was calm, fatalistic.

''There's no backup for the backup crew,'' he explained. ''Too many people are depending on me.''

She shook her head. ''That's not why you'll go.''

Ned breathed deeply and exhaled. ''No.''

"Because you never let other people depending on you get in your way before. You'll do it because it's what you want to do. The ultimate risk." She turned and challenged him. "You say you have a hole in you that only Lizzie and I can fill? What if you had to choose between us? Between *that* woman—" And she gestured toward the north end of the island. "—And me."

That rocked him and he looked over into eyes as hard as salt flats. "Why should I have to?"

"Because maybe I don't want to have to tell Lizzie that I buried her father in a five-gallon pail. Christ, every day you went off to the flight line to test one of those contraptions, I died a little. I wondered, *Is this going to be the day he doesn't come back?*"

"I always did come back," he pointed out.

She didn't hear him. "And now you've found a spectacular, brand-new way to kill yourself, and you brought me down here to watch."

"Test pilots aren't stupid. Forrest, Valery, Mike, and the rest. The flight-test program is laid out in careful steps. We practice simulations; we study the engineering. I won't deny that there's a risk; but it's a *calculated* risk. Life is full of risk. Police, firefighters, high-tension linesmen . . . There are a lot of wives—and husbands, too—who watch their spouse go off to a dangerous job."

"Oh. Well. I guess that makes it a whole lot easier to bear."

"Look, I'll resign after this mission, if that's what you want. But just once, just this once . . ."

Betsy laughed. "Not you, Not Ned DuBois. You might have resigned if you *hadn't* gotten the flight. But once you've gone, no one's ever going to bring you back."

Which might be literally true, if the refueling did not go off as planned. He wondered if Betsy knew about that; or knew that someone had sabotaged Valery Volkov's flight.

He could see the whole thing now, clear as a schematic. Fear feeding need feeding fear feeding need. And so on, spinning around and around, flying apart from the centrifigal forces. Relationships were exothermic; you had to put energy into them to hold them together.

"I guess we're not the only hole in your life, Ned. You've got another one, shaped like a rocket ship, only it's in your head, not your heart."

Ned said, "Maybe I do. It's something I've always wanted. Even when I was a kid and they landed on the moon."

"I just can't help thinking about what can go wrong."

"Jesus, you think I don't?" *But you've got to use the fear, for planning. You can't let it use you.* "It's dangerous just to cross the street. I could have been swept away in the current fly-fishing on the Susquehanna. Or got my brains knocked out playing baseball in college. I could get killed . . . a man could get killed . . . having sex."

Round eyes, wary and solemn, turned on him. "Is this one of the times?" Betsy asked.

"One of what times?"

"When you *need* it; when it's not just a habit. When it's not even lust."

He could hear the distant whine of the oxygen compressor above the whispering surf. He blew his breath out in a gust. "Yes," he said in a soft, hoarse voice.

"Then, come closer." She unfastened the top two buttons of her blouse, giving him a glimpse of a small, flat breast. Ned felt the blood rush in his ears. He looked in Betsy's eyes.

"Are you sure?"

"No," she said, "but it's been a long two years. And you did say folks are depending on you."

Oh, that was a cold reason, but it was reason enough. His left hand slid inside the blouse and cupped her. The familiar touch roused him, roused the ache. "What about Lizzie?" he whispered.

"Later . . . For now, just . . . hold me."

His right arm encircled her and drew her to him. Her body had the softness of aluminum, yielding slowly and gradually under stress. Their lips met, awkwardly at first, then finding their accustomed posture. Ned's pulse hammered. He heard Lizzie's singsong laugh. "Daddy's kissing Mommy! Daddy's kissing Mommy!'' Later, tonight, they would make love. Then in the morning, João would announce the new flight assignments and Ned and Levkin would begin the final preparations. And Wednesday would be the dry run. And Friday . . .

Friday, he would touch the stars at last.

If only Betsy was still waiting when he touched down again.

There were tears in his eyes. He didn't know why. Whether it was the joy of anticipation, or of finding something he had thought forever lost. But it struck him suddenly that the very thing that drew him so eagerly into the embrace of women was precisely what drove Betsy away and, if neither of them could change, the future would only be the past, over and over again.

Valery Volkov had an arm in a sling and a broken collarbone, but there was nothing wrong with his voice; and it was his wife, Yekaterina, who played the balalaika, anyway. And if the day-before-the-launch party that the pilots held in the common room was a little dampened from the lack of Forrest's bass and Krasnarov's baritone, well, hell, they could all sing a little louder, couldn't they?

> *"Pomnyu, pomnyu, pomnyu ya*
> *Kak menya mat' lyubila!*
> *I nye ras! I nye dva!*
> *Ana mnye tak gavarila."*

The Russians carried the singing. Katya was an accomplished player and the tune a cheerful, lively one. Ned asked Levkin what the song was about, and Gregor explained that it was a mother warning her son not to go to the ''other side of town'' or he would fall in among thieves and be sent to Siberia in chains. Ned reflected that Russian cheerfulness was a very peculiar thing, indeed.

Betsy huddled on the other side of the room with Bat da Silva, Assistant Director Heitor Carneiro, and some of the ground crew. Betsy got along fine with the other pilots and with the staff. Betsy got along fine with everyone. She even got along with Ned, and that could be a real stretch. But Ned noticed that, whichever way she turned, whomever she talked with, she never directly faced the windows that looked out over the landing field and through which the waiting vessel was framed and centered.

And that was the one view that captivated Ned. He had tested and flown a flock of airchines in his time: the *Nighthawk*, the *Lightning II*, the X-33 and others. The SR-71 *Blackbird* had been the sweetest, sailing high and kissing the edge of space. But there had never been anything to match the Plank. He drifted to the edge of the room, toward the windows, away from the chatter and the music, and contemplated the ship alone in silence. *Bessie Coleman* was Forrest's ship, as truly as *Santos-Dumont* was Bat's or *Calbraith Rogers* had been his. A part of Forrest would go up with her. Ownership was in the heart and in the doing. What it said on paper didn't mean squat, except to the lawyers. The shriek of the compressors, the song of the oxygen, hummed indistinctly through the double-paned glass. When he touched his finger to the glass he could feel the faint vibration.

He was relaxed now; the knot in his stomach, all unraveled. Zen had nothing on sex when it came to finding your center. He felt balanced, like a shortstop waiting for the pitch, ready to go with the moment. It felt odd, that calm and balance; abnormal—as if he spent most of his life staggering off-centered. He had Betsy back and little Lizzie, if not forever, at least for the moment; and for the moment, at least, that was enough.

And he had his dream, too; the flight he had ached for since that smoky night in Galveston harbor when João Pessoa sat down across the table from him at Joe Nancy's and dangled his heart's hope in front of his bourbon-dimmed eyes.

He hadn't *won* the prize, not exactly—Forrest had—but the real winner had been scratched. Maybe that should have made the victory less satisfying, but Ned would take his fortunes any way they fell.

Levkin took the balalaika from Katya Volkov and started into another song.

"... *Vykhadila na byereg Katyushka*
Na vysoki byereg na krutoy."

Gregor was not so practiced at the instrument—he strummed rather than picked—but Katya grinned at the song he had chosen and snuggled closer with Valery. Volkov had grown more thoughtful and introspective over the last few weeks, no more the cocky "Johnny Danger." Ned wondered if the crash-landing changed him. He hadn't been up since then, of course, not with the broken bones to mend; but you had to believe in your luck—your wampum, your mojo, your wyrd—to flight-test an airchine, and sometimes all it took was one little incident to change your outlook. Katya had nearly broken down in Mission Control when *Calbraith Rogers* was coming in. Did she feel the same numbing dread now that Betsy did?

Ned turned away from the window and the waiting vessel and watched Levkin play. The Russian's smiling moon face was beaded with perspiration, his face narrowed in concentration as he gamely kept the tune and rhythm.

There were two ways to win a prize. One way was, you could be the best damn sumbitch in the running; the other, you could take down anyone who stood between you and the goal. And if you were the sort of man who—maybe! maybe!—could kill your wife and her lover, would you, for the chance of a lifetime, hesitate to grease a step or two, or slip a mickey into a pot of *feijoada*, or even file partway through a fuel line under the awful cloak of night?

Just before dawn on the morning of the flight, Ned visited Forrest in the clinic. The room was dim; thick curtains screened the window. Forrest lay in bed with an open book upon his lap spotlighted by the reading lamp on the wall behind him. He was, as Ned had known he would be, already awake.

"Sun's about up," Ned announced. "We'll be riding out to the flight line in a bit."

Forrest nodded and turned a page in the book. "I sorta

figured. You treat 'Queen Bessie' good, son. I set store by that ship.''

"Do you want me to open the curtain for you?"

Forrest put a finger in the book and closed it. "No. Don't bother."

"But you won't be able to see the launch."

Forrest shook his head. "The angle's all wrong, anyway."

"No, it isn't. You have a clear view of the—"

"Ned. The angle's all wrong."

"Oh." *From the outside instead of the inside . . .*

"Don't look so long in the face, son. This is your big day."

"It should have been yours."

"I know."

Hearing the bitterness, Ned gave his friend a sharp look. "Do you resent it?"

"Hell, yes, I resent it!" Anger swelled Forrest's voice, made it roll like thunder. "Wouldn't you? Alls they had to do was wait one lousy week and I'd be all rehydrated—buffed, polished, lubed, and ready to go. But their God-Almighty schedule came first. Now here I am like Moses before the Promised Land." He fell silent, studied the book cover for a moment. Then he sighed and hurled the book aside. It fluttered and banged against the night table and fell to the floor on its open pages. "Oh, what the hell. Open the damned curtains, Ned. It ain't your fault I'm lying here. Least I can do is wave to you."

Ned shoved the curtain aside with a single swipe. The landing field was a black ocean in the dying night. Hidden shapes blocked the field of stars: buildings, gantries, equipment not yet emerged from the gloom. In the center of it, SSTO *Bessie Coleman* was an oasis of spotlights. Behind her, a band of red like a distant fire striped the horizon. "The big hats flew in yesterday afternoon."

"Yeah, I saw the jump jet land. She sure is a purty sight. Was Benny Ortega at the conn?" Ned nodded and Forrest said, "Benedito's a good man. A good pilot. How are things between you and Betsy?"

"They're good, Forrest. They're good. Better than they deserve to be. I want to thank you, Forrest. Weren't for you—"

"Weren't for me, nothing. It was just self-interest, was all."

Ned gave him a curious look. "Self-interest?"

"Shit, Ned, you were using too many gals for yourself. Weren't leaving enough for the rest of us."

Ned flipped him the bird.

"You two going to stay together?" Forrest asked.

A good question, but one that meant thinking beyond the next forty-eight hours. "I don't know. Maybe. We've got a lot of shit to get clear of, first."

"Yeah, I hear you. . . ."

"Well . . ." Ned glanced at his watch. "It's about that time."

"Yeah. Good luck." Forrest reached a hand out and Ned grabbed it. Forrest squeezed hard and, with his other hand, gripped Ned by the wrist. "You watch your fuel level, you hear? Come back safe. It'd be no kind of poker game at all without you and Levkin to lose me money."

"Hell, Forrest. Heitor loses enough to make up for any two of us. And the fuel margin's thin, but it's there. We'll have enough to come back down, long as we don't waste it. The pod that Wilson's putting up, that's just insurance. Only . . . I wouldn't mention it to Betsy, you know? She worries when I fly."

"Hell, son, so does everyone else in the air."

Ned snorted. "Up yours." He turned to go.

"Just one thing more."

Ned waited. "What?"

Forrest's grin faded and his eyes avoided Ned's. "I'm Mr. Chief Pilot now. . . ."

"Okay. What, 'sir'?"

Forrest sucked his lower lip. "Look. There's no policy, you know. But, what Levkin's going to do . . . refueling in orbit. It's gotta be done if the Planks are ever going to be profitable. But it's dangerous. Never been done before. And what you said about the fuel margin, well, it's true. You can't do a whole lot of maneuvering, and, well . . . This is damned hard to say, but . . ."

"Will you get to the point, Forrest? I've got a flight to catch."

Forrest looked him straight in the eye. Distant eyes. Hard and worried at the same time. "If Levkin is out there and he gets in trouble—his tether breaks or his jet pack fails or whatever—and he can't get back in . . . João and Bonny and me, we've talked about it. Ned, you don't have fuel to mess around. You've got to leave him."

Ned felt ice all over. "Leave him . . ."

Forrest avoided his eyes now. They were looking inward. "That's not policy, understand. Just facts. The cold equations."

It took Ned a moment or two to find his voice. "Hell, Forrest." His throat was dry, clenched tight. "That's a hell of a note."

"It's a hell of a world."

Ned walked to the door, but stood with it half opened. He turned back. "Forrest, you know how to tell someone's a *real* test pilot?"

"No. How?"

"If they think Neil Armstrong's greatest flight wasn't Apollo 11, but Gemini 8." The Gemini/Agena had been tumbling so fast the crew was close to losing consciousness, but Neil had fought that sumbitch back into control because he had what it took. So, Ned didn't care what the equations said. A good test pilot wrote his own equations.

10.

"The Best Things . . ."

The inside of the building was polished black and silver, just the sort of high-tech image projection Barry had expected. A horseshoe-shaped black marble counter faced the entrance. A lithe woman in a light blue shirt and wearing a Sam Browne belt sat behind a bank of TV monitors and watched Barry approach.

"Hi," he said when he reached the counter, "my name's Barry Fast. I'm here for the reception."

"The space thing?" The woman hit a few buttons and studied a list that scrolled up on one of her screens. "Employer?"

"Mentor Academies, Witherspoon High School."

She nodded. "Checks out. Look over here, please. Thank you." A few more buttons, then she handed him a two-by-three-inch card with his bemused picture on it and his name and date in large-point Helvetica type. Underneath, it read, THIS DATE ONLY.

Barry clipped it to his jacket pocket. "The picture's awful," he said.

"They all are," she replied in a voice devoid of sympathy.

"Wait over there and someone will escort you to the auditorium."

"There" was a waiting area, sunk a few feet below floor level, edged with vine-infested planters and black leather benches. Tables in the center of the "pit" contained reasonably current issues of magazines like *Machine Design* and *I.E.E.E. Transactions*. Passing the time with reading material like that must make the waiting go by in the blink of a geological eon.

Barry preferred pacing. He made a slow circuit of the area. Telephone bank, cloakroom, mysterious unmarked doors leading God knew where. The security guard did not watch him, but Barry figured he was the star of the show on one of her monitors. A few strides past the waiting pit, the entrance hall opened up into a large open area three stories high centered around an elaborate fountain. He saw that he was on the short axis of a cross. On the other side, past the fountain, was a restaurant, complete with ferns and white tablecloths. Ranks of offices lined the long axis; three stories' worth, pierced by hallways leading to other offices farther back. Balconies and catwalks provided access all around.

The whole building resembled a mall, except for the dreadful uniformity of the facades. Barry tried to imagine what the place would look like if the different departments were to put up marquees and neon signs announcing themselves. Designs R Us. Human Resources—You Got the Humans, We Got the Resources. Maybe window posters proclaiming half-price sales on engineering drawings, or Purchase Orders While-U-Wait.

A rhythmic pounding drew his attention upward in time for him to spot a jogger on the third-floor walkway. The man nodded to him as he made the turn into the short axis. Barry was so astonished at the sight that he did not notice his escort until the woman touched him on the elbow.

"Oh, I'm sorry," he said. "I was just . . ." He pointed upward.

She gave him a pleasant, professional smile. "You should see this place during the lunch hour." A slender woman, she would have been tall standing next to anyone but Barry. She wore her dark hair in a pageboy cut. Barry returned the smile. Bread upon the waters.

"Barry Fast," he said.

"Yes. I know. I'm 'Windy' Gale. If you will follow me . . . ?"

Barry matched her brisk pace down the right hand branch of the long axis. "Windy Gale?" he said. "Your parents did that to you?"

"Actually, I rather like it," she said. "It's not a name that people forget five minutes after they've met you."

"Oh, I expect people remember meeting you for more than your name."

She blushed well, and her glance settled on Barry's hands. "Here is the auditorium, Mr. Fast." She opened a tall, dark-stained wooden door for him.

"Thank you, ah . . ." he snapped his fingers. "What did you say your name was?" His small joke was rewarded with a smile and Barry was reasonably sure that she would not forget his name, either.

The large, wood-paneled hall was decorated with chrome, glass, and leather in a style that reminded Barry of the twenties. Open, but with clusters of chairs and low tables. At the far end, it opened onto a flagstoned verandah. Other doors led into an auditorium, where a large projection screen had been set up. The crowd was a mix of people that Barry knew—mostly Mentor teachers—and others, presumably VHI headquarters staff, that he did not. He waved to Gwen Glendower, who was chatting with an older, gray-haired woman with a pinched face. Maria DePardo and Bernie Paulson from Molly Pitcher were present, as was Grant deYoung, Witherspoon's building manager, who was talking earnestly with Egbo and Wu. Bob and Vivian Boucher were standing next to a curious dwarf tree. First things first, though. Barry located the bar and ordered a bourbon, rocks.

A slim, pleasant-looking man with slick hair and wearing wide suspenders and a modishly cut suit wound through the crowd shaking hands. When he reached Barry, he said, "Hi, I'm Steve Matthias. John Redman—he's the goateed fellow with the long hair out there on the verandah—he and I are hosting this get-together." Matthias's hand was moist and soft. The name badge clipped to his suit coat declared him CEO of Thor Machine Tools, so Barry guessed he ought to be impressed or something.

"Mentor Academies, eh?" Matthias was reading Barry's own tag. "That's one of our smaller divisions. Hardly breaks even. Though I see you're wearing the logo." A flick of the finger indicated the hand and fireball tie tack that Barry wore.

"There are a few of us around in Mentor."

Matthias smiled. "Naturally. I see a lot of Mentor folks are here this afternoon; though not all of them. . . ." A tap of the thumb on his own discreet lapel pin.

Barry suppressed a spasm of annoyance. "Yeah, well, North Orange is just down the Grey Horse Pike."

"North Orange . . . Oh, yes. The public schools that Belinda operates. How is it going there?"

"We're making progress."

"Really? I read something in the *Times* that your SATs and HSPTs haven't changed much from when the county ran the schools."

Barry wondered if Matthias was trying to put him down or was genuinely interested in knowing the score. "It's a complicated issue," he said. "And I started on the other side of it. Most of that *Times* 'article' consisted of press releases from the NJEA. All it boiled down to is that they haven't seen an instant, spectacular change."

Matthias raised his eyebrows. "Why would they have expected to?" he said. "It takes three years to institutionalize a culture change in any organization. That's common knowledge. Thor has been pursuing the Baldrige Award for at least that long."

Whatever a Baldrige Award was; but at least the man seemed aware of the inertia Mentor faced. "The class we're graduating this month we've schooled for two years out of twelve, hardly long enough to have an impact."

Matthias clapped him on the arm. "Well, keep up the good work, Barry. Prometheus is counting on you."

Barry gave him a polite smile as the man moved on to harrass other guests. Barry did not care much for the glad-hand types. It seemed too much a put-on, the overt friendliness and personal contact concealing something haughty and solitary within. Barry took a long, sweet sip of the bourbon, filling his mouth with the smoky taste and cooling his throat on the way down.

And why on earth was Prometheus "counting on" Mentor?

"It's like everything else Mariesa does," Bob Boucher said, waving a hand at the bonsai. "Bigger and grander than it ought to be." Barry looked left and right for rescue. It was almost time for them to file into the auditorium for the live broadcast, and he might get trapped sitting next to Bob. He did not think that Boucher knew all that much about bonsai and how big they ought to be, nor that he was close enough to refer to Mariesa so familiarly. *Not as close as I've been*, he thought. He could feel her hands searching him; he could taste her breath.

"Excuse me, but are you Barry Fast?"

Barry recognized the lawyer from Matthias's earlier introduction. "Yes. John Redman, right?"

"Folks call me 'John E.' Not 'Johnnie,' mind you," he said. "John E." He handed Barry a note and, in a more serious tone, said, "Security took this call a few minutes ago."

Barry looked at Redman and at the note. When he unfolded it, he saw ordinary while-you-were-out message paper. *Barry Fast*, scrawled across the top. *John Morgenthaler. Frelinghuysen. Urgent.*

"What is it, Barry?" asked Vivian Boucher. For a moment, Barry didn't get it. Why was it urgent for him to know that John Morgenthaler was in the hospital? Then it clicked. Not John. Shannon. John had sent the message.

He wadded the paper and stuffed it in his jacket pocket. "I've got to go," he muttered, turning away from Boucher and the others.

"Do you need a cab?" asked Redman.

"No . . ." He pushed past them and hurried to the door, hardly aware of the curious glances that followed him, ice already forming in his heart.

Intensive Care was on the third floor of Frelinghuysen Hospital. Barry found John Morgenthaler in the waiting room across the hallway from the big, double-wide swinging doors. John was sitting on a worn Naugahyde sofa, staring at an unopened can of root beer in his hands. His shoes were untied and the buttons on his shirt had been fastened in the wrong holes. He looked up when Barry entered and Barry saw that his eyes were rimmed in red.

"Barry," he said. "Glad you could come." His voice was barely audible. He made no move to stand. He just sat there twisting the soda can in his hands.

"What happened?" Barry asked. "How is she?"

The aluminum can flexed in John's grip. "She took some pills, Barry . . ." His throat clenched as tight as his hands. "A whole bottle."

"Jesus." Barry's knees felt weak and he lowered himself slowly into a chair catercorner to the sofa. He found himself staring at a soda vending machine. One panel of the machine portrayed cheerful young men and women enjoying the company's product on a sunny beach. Laughing, smiling faces with lots of teeth. A helluva thing, Barry thought, to put in the Intensive Care waiting room.

He had not seen Shannon in two months. Now he might never see her again. It was an odd thought, a distancing thought, the notion that you had already seen someone for the last time. But that was the way it always happened, wasn't it? No one dies on schedule. No one pencils it in on their calendar. No one parts knowing they'll never meet again.

Intensive Care, Barry; not the morgue. Shannon wasn't dead. It was hard to imagine Shannon anything but alive. "How did it happen?"

"She's been having trouble sleeping the last few days, so . . . she probably took a few pills and then . . . You know how flaky she can get, Barry. She probably forgot that she had already taken them and took some more and . . . The stuff makes you groggy, you know. You can't think straight . . . So she took a couple more, and . . .'' His voice wound down to silence. Barry did not point out that it was the middle of the day.

Suddenly, wildly, he thought of that first time, in Philadelphia. How hungry Shannon had been for him. The intensity of her loving and the single-minded abandon with which they had coupled. She hadn't meant anything to him then. Just a body; just some good times away from home. And he didn't suppose he could have meant much more than that to her. "Where are the girls?" he asked.

"They're staying with my sister. I won't bring them here until I know . . . Until I know . . .'' He could not continue. Barry went to him and squeezed his shoulder, but Shannon's husband did not respond. A nurse appeared in the doorway.

"I/C is open for visitors, again, Mr. Morganthaler."

John looked up and blinked. He said, "You go in, Barry. She asked for you earlier. It's all right, nurse. He's a friend of the family."

Yeah. A real, God-damned good friend he had turned out to be. *Hi, I'm his wife's lover; except I dumped her for a rich woman, and that's why she swallowed a bottle of pills.* Barry followed the nurse through the double doors. Inside Intensive Care, a circle of six rooms opened off of a central monitoring station. Shannon was in Room C. A small room, barely enough space for a bed, a chair, and some monitoring equipment. The view from the window was lousy: the brick facade of another wing of the hospital.

"No more than two people at a time," the nurse said. "And no more than fifteen minutes at a time."

Barry nodded and stepped inside the room. Shannon lay in the center of a mass of tubes and wires. Her hair was badly brushed, her makeup smeared and running under the eyes. He could imagine her that morning at her dresser, assaulting her hair with angry swipes; attacking her face with cosmetics. Barry had seen that anger a time or two, had seen her lash out at the closest person. This morning the closest person had been herself. A steady, muted beep-beep played in the background. A monitor ran graphs with incomprehensible labels. Yellow, white, and red bands wriggled and spiked their way across the screen.

She was asleep or unconscious. The sheets rose and fell with the steady rhythm of her breathing. Barry found a wooden chair in the corner and sat on it. He should say something to the nurses about Shannon's looks; but cosmetics had probably been low on the priority list when she had been brought in. Still, the woman ought to be made presentable.

How many times over the last three years had they met at that shabby hotel on the other side of town? Fifty? A hundred? Afternoons of passionate, intense single-mindedness. The probing tongues and fingers. The sweet curves of her breasts and hips and rear hugged to him. The iron intensity of her arms and legs encircling him. It could make him sweat, even sitting here. Yet, what came to his mind just now was lying on a yellow blanket in the Watchung Reserve while she named each of the flowers and trees and explained to him how they all fit together into a vast mosaic. And another time, when she had crouched nude on the bed with her knees tucked up under her chin and had dreamed aloud of the lives her daughters would someday lead. And a third time, just sitting side by side in companionable silence, parked on the scenic overlook on I-80, holding hands and gazing at the stars until . . .

"Barry. You came."

He saw that her eyes had opened. "Yes. As soon as I heard."

"What happened? I don't remember. I was getting dressed this morning and . . . It was this morning?"

Barry nodded. Shannon's voice was weak and raw. They had forced a tube down her throat to pump out her stomach. "I don't know," he said.

"I remember I got sleepy all of a sudden."

"Yes." He reached out and covered her hand with his. She squeezed him briefly.

"Promise you'll never leave me."

"I—" What could he say about that, given what had happened between Mariesa and himself? The bench atop Skunktown Mountain had been as different from those wild afternoons at the motel as . . . well, as different as Mariesa was from Shannon. Awkward, rather than practiced; tender, rather than intense. And an element of cold calculation, in place of the hot spontaneity.

"Never leave me," she said again. This time it sounded like an order, or a threat.

"No," he said. "I won't."

"You can still have your rich girl, if that's what you want. I know the price must be right, and I have John, after all. He's not as rich, but his dealerships do well enough. You can have your Mariesa, but you can still have me. Nothing has to be different, does it?"

"Sure." Anything that meant he would not have to come back to a room like this, or to a colder one four stories down.

"I'm sorry we argued," she said. "It was such a silly thing. Let's not talk about it again."

It wasn't silly, he thought, *but we won't*. We'll drive a stake through its heart and bury it deep at a crossroads. And hope it will never rise back up to haunt us. "Me, too," he said.

Outside, he encountered John. He had drunk his rootbeer or he had set the can aside somewhere. He grabbed Barry by the arm when he came out. "Barry, how is she?"

He could feel the shakes beginning. "She's fine. I think she'll make it through all right."

"Did she tell you . . . ?"

Barry shook his head.

"It must have been an accident."

"Sure, John. These things happen." If John could lie to himself and Shannon could not remember, life could go on almost as if it were normal.

"I mean, she's got it all, right?" John was talking to himself, but Barry listened because John had to talk it out. "I take good care of her. A Plain Jane like Shannon, how could she do better? I don't mind it she's not glamorous. I've told her that a thousand times. I never had eyes for any other woman. You know that, Barry? Never. Well, eyes, maybe; but never a hand. She's got two beautiful girls who adore her. . . ."

He wound down at last. Barry said, "Her folks coming up?"

John nodded. "They left Miami about noon. Look, Barry, it was good of you to come. I think of all the other teachers, Shannon has the highest regard for you."

They exchanged a few more trivialities and Barry escaped at last to the parking garage that abutted Frelinghuysen. There, he sat in his car for a few minutes—the car that Mariesa had helped him buy. How could John call Shannon plain? Was the man blind? Had he never looked inside the woman he had married?

As he started the car, he glanced at his wristwatch and saw that he had missed the launch. But the reception was scheduled to last the entire afternoon, so there was still time for him to drive back to VHI. He could mingle and chat and fend off curious questions and find out how much bourbon one man could drink if it were free for the asking.

11.

"...Are Lost in Victory"

The flight to the island was quiet enough that Mariesa could hear herself think, and that was not particularly a good thing—because what occupied her thoughts was Barry and what she had done to him. The last time she had ridden *Elijah*, the DACX-102 had buzzed like a session of Congress, noisy enough even inside the fuselage to inhibit thought. Now, eighteen months later, the hum was nearly abated. McDonnell-Douglas's piezoelectric "smart flaps" on the rotor tips continually adjusted the blade angles in response to the air vortices stirred up by the spinning blades. If they did not quite create a silence, they at least imposed a hush. A hush in which she could stew in her own thoughts.

The plane carried a half dozen Steering Committee members, plus Governor Gomes and his staff, come to watch the launch. Keith, of course, sat by her side, as always. Dear Keith, looking strained and weary, but ever willing to listen to her doubts. And Correy and Wallace, too. The Inner Circle—though they never called themselves that.

"Harriet has always known which buttons to press," she

said to Keith. "I feel that my motives were all wrong. They were all a muddle. Shock and anger and, God help me, vengeance . . ." She had been troubled all day by the events on Skunktown Mountain. It was a tangle within her, a Gordian knot to the heart of which she hoped Keith could slice.

He gave her a serious look. He had listened patiently to her pain and doubts over the incident. Keith always listened patiently. "And was love anywhere in that mix?" he asked.

Was it? There was something there when she thought of Barry. It might be love. It might be what would do for love when love was not to be found. "Barry is an attractive man. Kind. Attentive. I enjoy his company. But I have had so little time for love for so many years, that I'm not sure I would recognize it anymore."

"You never do, when it comes."

"Keith, what is *your* impression of Barry?"

"My impression?" He pursed his lips and pondered her question silently. But that was Keith. He seldom answered straight off. He always gave her questions the compliment of thought. He weighed the debits and credits, the assets and liabilities. "I think," he said at last, "that he listens well. You need someone in your life who listens."

Mariesa laid a hand on his arm. "But, Keith, dear, I have you."

A fleeting smile. "Ah, well, but there are other services Barry can provide that I cannot." Mariesa felt herself blush, but Keith affected not to notice. Instead, he asked, "Did you enjoy yourself?"

From anyone else, the question would have been impertinent and offensive; but Keith had always had the knack for asking her the questions she ought to have asked of herself. His interest was personal, not prurient.

When she closed her eyes, she could see the gazebo and its bench and the darkening sky beyond. She could smell the pinxter flower in the air, and Barry's aftershave; and feel his hands upon her. Gentle hands, deft hands; and the bench, hard and unyielding beneath her. She could feel . . . a fire blossoming within her, a yearning that she had not felt in years. She had almost forgotten what it was like to lose yourself for a few moments of eternity. "Yes. Yes, I did." And she would enjoy it again, she decided, for its own sake, and for hers . . . and for Barry's. She owed him that much. Such liaisons ought to be entered into for better reasons than pique.

The delicious irony was that the sweet, crushing moment between Barry and herself might never have come had Harriet not set things in motion. So, in a way, her mother's machinations had brought about their own frustration.

Or had they? It was hard to know with Harriet. She was a perpetual amazement.

"Your Barry has one remarkable accomplishment, at least," Keith remarked. "He has gotten you talking of something other than Prometheus."

Mariesa glanced out the window of the jump jet at the restless waves below. There were other doubts that assailed her, about goals and methods and motives; and Barry was as fine a way as any to avoid them.

Mariesa noticed the lean, tanned woman lined up along the railing with the other spectators and made a point of speaking to her. "Hello, you must be Mrs. DuBois."

The woman turned and favored her with a steely look. The breeze that blew constantly across the balcony whipped the woman's long, brown hair into streamers. She pulled it aside and into place with an impatient gesture. "I must be. No one else wants the damn job."

"I am Mariesa van Huyten."

Betsy DuBois touched the proferred hand only briefly. "Van Huyten. Yeah. You're responsible for all this." Her gesture took in the landing field, the spaceship, perhaps the world.

"Say, rather, that I mobilized the desires of a great many, diverse people."

DuBois snorted. "Yeah, you sure as hell mobilized me."

"I beg your pardon?"

Betsy DuBois turned away and leaned on the railing. "The airplane tickets? The leave of absence from Odysseus Travel? The scholarship for Lizzie at that new Mentor Academy place?

You think I'm stupid, I don't know a bribe when I see it?'' She was silent for a moment, her eyes unfocused. ''Makes me feel like a Goddamned prostitute.''

''Mrs. DuBois,'' Mariesa said flatly, ''all anyone did was to make it easier for you to be here. That you came at all was your own choice. What you did after you arrived was likewise your own choice. And, for what it is worth, giving you those tickets was Ned's idea.''

Betsy DuBois shook her head and looked across the field at the spaceship. ''You ever make love to someone you weren't really sure you loved?''

And that was a question that hit much too close to home. Mariesa had no response, but Betsy did not look for one. She nodded toward the Plank, enveloped now in a plume of white vapor wafting on the Atlantic breeze. ''You know, I almost hope that thing does blow up.''

''What a cruel thing to say!''

Betsy grimaced and shook her head. ''Yeah. I didn't mean it. But my life would be a whole lot simpler if Hot Pilot Ned DuBois wasn't around.''

''All our lives would be simpler if other people were not in them.''

DuBois turned and regarded her. ''Yeah,'' she said. ''They would. Simple and dull.''

''He does want you back. Mr. Calhoun has said so, and I trust his judgment.''

''More'n I'd trust Ned's. Oh, hell.'' She scowled again at the waiting ship, as if she could see the command pilot through the distant viewport. ''Ned's not really *bad*. I mean, he's not mean, like some I tied up with; and he's got a brain—just needs more exercise, is all. His problem is, he's still a little boy. He never learned to say no when someone waves candy in front of him. He doesn't mean to hurt people, but he does.''

''Then why come back, at all?''

Betsy shook her head. ''Damned if I know. Maybe just because of his goddamn smile. And he does love Lizzie. That counts for something.''

"I saw the child yesterday when I arrived. She looks much like Ned."

"'Cept she's prettier. I told her to stay in our room, just in case." Her chin pointed toward the launchpad, where *Bessie Coleman* awaited. "I wouldn't want her to see that thing explode with her daddy on board."

"The chances of a launch accident are vanishingly small."

"Yeah, that's what everybody says; but you know, I got ears, too, and I hear things. Like maybe it can't carry enough fuel to get back down, and maybe someone on the island is screwing things up. So, you will pardon me for saying this, Miss Mariesa van Huyten, but I think you are a genuine, gold-plated bastard for sending them up when you don't know if you cân get them down again."

And that was why she *felt* like a "genuine, gold-plated bastard." But that was the burden of leadership. Sometimes you had to send people into danger. There were no sure bets, not in life, not in love; and after all that, why, you simply buttoned up and took your chances. "That is why the flight involves a refueling exercise," she told the woman. "If the refueling cannot be carried out, they are to return immediately. If they do so, there will be fuel enough. The mission profile—"

"Hell . . ." Betsy DuBois laughed in a voice that was half bitterness and half pride. "The mission can have a profile like Rudolph-fucking-Valentino, but you forgot one thing. That is Ned DuBois in that can, and he'll do what he goddamn pleases."

The thin air blew cold on the altiplano. Rick ten Boom zipped up his sheepskin jacket and stepped outside the administration building. The Ecuadoran sun burned brightly but futilely overhead. Jesus Paniagua, his segundo, was waiting on the *portico* smoking an evil, black cigar. Somewhere back in his ancestry, Jesus claimed a prince of Quito, from the time before the Incas had marched up from the south and burned the kingdom down. He blew a cloud of acrid blue smoke and said, "Did they go up?"

Ten Boom nodded. "Right on schedule." Jesus had spoken

in Quechua, the Inca language imposed on his forebearers. He could also speak Spanish, the language of a later conqueror. Ten Boom sometimes wondered if any remnant of the ancient tongue of Quito survived. "Is the Boomer fired up?"

"The counting down is on schedule." Oddly, the Incas had a word for "schedule," or something close enough to it. You wouldn't have thought it of the Indios in the land of *mañana*, but their ancestors had been bears for planning and organization. And they had done it without inventing paperwork. . . .

Ten Boom checked his watch. The Fernando site was three hours ahead of the Boomer. In another half an hour—the exact time was in the computer—the altiplano would rotate under the same launch window, and he could insert the fuel tank into the same orbit the Plank was on—with luck, just as the Plank completed its orbit. DuBois should come up just behind his target, with no need to shift orbits and use up priceless fuel. It had worked reasonably well last month. The unmanned Plank had chased and closed with a dummy tank. Close enough that a human pilot could have docked-and-locked.

He looked up toward the clear, azure sky and wondered if he would have had the guts to ride that thing up there not knowing if there would be enough fuel to come down again.

There would be enough, if barely. Van Huyten was no fool, to gamble everything on such a chancy rendezvous. Yet, without the margin Wilson's fuel tanks represented, her ships would be unable to maneuver freely, so what would be the point? If the ship went up only to come back down again, it would be a success only to the newspapers.

A sharp crack of thunder drew his eyes back to the cloudless sky. *What the hell . . . ?*

A fountain of dirt erupted on the hillside north of the ram pipeline. Ten Boom saw a crew of workers duck for cover. Jesus Paniagua threw his cigar to the dirt. "*Banditos*! We are attacked!" He drew a whistle from his shirt pocket and blew three short blasts as he ran down the steps to the nearest jeep. Five men armed with AK-47s burst from the building and joined Paniagua in the jeep. They roared off in a shower of stones and gravel toward the mountainside overlooking the site from the south. Ten Boom lifted his binoculars to his eyes and scanned the slopes there.

Bare slopes. No trees, no cover except boulders and crevices. There! A band of seven . . . no, eight. Two whites; the others, Indios, but with the swarthy skin and thick chopped haircuts that marked the Indios of the Oriente. *Aucas*, he thought. One of the white men held a shoulder launcher, while the second fit another missile into it. Stingers? Ten Boom flipped open his radio with one hand and shouted his observations to Jesus.

The second missile—he could actually see it approach—struck a supply shed south of the pipeline. *They're bracketing the pipe,* he thought. Then his heart drained, and he ran back inside the admin building.

"Get five more men," he told Francisco, "and follow Jesus. There are eight attackers. They have a missile launcher, but they probably have sidearms, as well." To his secretary, Apolonia, he said, "Get me Control."

Francisco gathered his men and ten Boom slid into the console seat. He pulled the headset into place and flipped the switch for the control room at the Muzzle, a mile away. "Süleyman? Süleyman, are you there? Is everything ready for launch?"

Süleyman Ogrut's voice sounded puzzled. "What is happening down there, *bayim?*"

"There's been an attack on the Boomer. Go to manual. Launch now! Do you hear me? Launch now, before they blow the pipe!" If a missile hit the pipeline while it was filled with jet fuel . . .

"*Evet*! Right away!" A moment later, Klaxons all along the line blared and men ran for cover. The receptionist and the clerical staff looked at ten Boom with blood-drained faces. Apolonia crossed herself. Admin was at the Breech end, where the tanks were loaded and the fuel ignited. Ten Boom sagged back in his chair, feeling helpless. It was out of his hands now.

The chatter of small-arms fire drew him back onto the porch. His binoculars showed that Jesus and his men had the attackers under fire, but the man with the shoulder launcher already had another missile in the rack.

The ground shook with the sudden jolt that told him Ogrut had fired the ram. Instinctively, ten Boom turned his glasses on the distant Muzzle end and counted. *One hippopotamus, two hippopotamus . . .*

It was hard to tell which came first. The belch of flame from the Muzzle or the shriek of twisted metal and hissing gas where the Number Eight sector took the third hit and ruptured. A geyser of flame a thousand feet high climbed into the sky, roaring like a jet airplane. A thousand feet downslope from the flaming wound, ten Boom could feel the heat on his face and arms. *The valves, Ogrut. Shut down the feeds before the whole tube goes.*

But either Ogrut was on the stick, or the automatics had survived the explosion, because the pillar of flame abruptly snuffed out. The echoes of the explosion and of the flame's monstrous hiss reverberated from the surrounding peaks for a few seconds more before subsiding gradually into silence. A cloud of blackened smoke drifted like a loose balloon on the wind.

Ten Boom scanned the damaged section with his glasses and saw ruptured, twisted steel, broken hydraulic lines; metal and glass burnt and melted and fused. Flames rippled through the shriveled grasses and the ruins of a nearby line shed. He knew the damage inside the tube might run another section or two up the line. It would be a long, long while before the Boomer boomed again.

A pair of coveralled legs protruded from behind the line shed a few dozen meters past the crater.

Ten Boom pulled the binoculars away from his face. Then he hurled them to the ground, where they smashed and shattered lenses sparkled like diamonds in the sun.

When Jesus and his party returned—but minus two who lay tarp-covered in the second jeep—they found him weeping on the top step of the portico. Jesus yanked a captive by the arm and sent him spinning in front of ten Boom.

Her. Ten Boom saw with astonishment that the captive was a slim, youngish woman in—of all things—Banana Republic garb. She wore frameless glasses, and stringy, dirt-blond hair straggled from beneath her boonie hat. Ten Boom stared at her.

"Why?" was all he could think to say.

"You bastards!" she shouted. "You killed Henry!"

The last thing ten Boom had expected was a verbal assault. He looked at Jesus.

"The man with the Stinger launcher," his segundo explained.

Ten Boom nodded. "I see." Looking at the woman once more, he said, "A murderer has been slain in the course of his apprehension. Your outrage is hollow."

She brushed her hair from her eyes with an impatient gesture. "We just wanted to wreck your weapon. We didn't mean to hurt anybody."

"And because you didn't 'mean it,' you're excused? Marcos's wife is no less a widow for that." Ten Boom felt weary. He put his hands to his knees and pushed himself upright. He did not understand people like this, people who lived for causes. They frightened him. He paused before turning away and asked Jesus, "The Aucas?"

"Aucas do not surrender." Jesus's voice was a mixture of contempt and respect. Ten Boom noticed that the woman had said nothing about their deaths.

At least they had gotten the fuel tank lofted in time, though God alone knew what its orbit was now. Would DuBois be able to make rendezvous? What if it was out of reach? He would have to get Ogrut working on the calculations. The computer must have recorded the exact time of launch, and Jameson back at Corporate should be able to get tracking data from the satellite net. It would be a terrible waste if, after all their planning, there was too much delta-V between the two orbits.

It was champagne and caviar on the flight going back.

Mariesa and her party changed to the big corporate jetliner

at Daedalus's test field in Fortaleza, and Wallace's stewards and stewardesses circulated among them serving refreshments. The interior of the executive jetliner was dressed in burgundy and silver, with comfortable but durable carpeting. Swivel seats faced one another around "tables" built into the deck. Bulkheads divided the space into several cabins. Bennett Longworth napped with a smile of satisfaction on his face; but the others continued to chatter excitedly.

Mariesa remained cautiously optimistic as she circulated. The launch had been successful, the orbital insertion "on the beam"; but, as João Pessoa himself had reminded them before their departure, the most difficult elements of the mission lay ahead.

Too true. Too true. Yet Mariesa did permit herself a small taste of victory. There was something about putting men into orbit that was a benchmark. No successful design review; no successful engine test burn; not even a successful flight within the atmosphere had quite the same savor.

It was a long flight back to New Jersey and, after a while, Mariesa retired to her private cabin. Zhou Hui sat alone on the other side of the cabin, deeply immersed in a thick paperback. She nodded to Mariesa before returning to her reading. A short while later, Keith McReynolds entered. He took his usual seat beside Mariesa and settled into it with a sigh, fastening the seat belt as always. "An exciting day," he said. "I'm glad I lived to see it."

Mariesa laid a hand on his arm. "Keith, you helped bring it about. The 'bootstrap' financing idea alone . . ."

"John E. had a hand in that, too."

"It's all right, Keith, to accept some of the praise."

McReynolds looked surprised. "Do I do that?" A moment's reflection was followed by a wry chuckle. "Though, I don't suppose they ever name the ships after the accountants."

"No. I think the pilots have the right idea."

Keith said, "Wilson should be launching the fuel pod shortly."

Mariesa checked her watch. "If everything goes as scheduled."

"Wilson has put three test tanks into orbit," Keith pointed out, "and the last one was a near perfect orbital match with our own ship. If we had had a pilot aboard *Santos-Dumont*, we could have run the refueling exercise then."

A steward wearing Odysseus Travel livery knocked and entered the cabin with a tray of champagne glasses. Mariesa waited until he had gone and the door was closed before she lifted the glass. "The Goal."

They touched glasses. "One step closer," Keith reminded her. "There are a lot more to go before we're safe." They sipped the sparkling wine. Then Keith set his glass on the table and leaned back in his seat. "I am suddenly very tired," he said. Mariesa nursed her champagne and contemplated the sky outside. A bright, bleached, stratospheric sky.

She remembered a sky much like this one, seen over mountains steep and stony. She had been on a boat with her boyfriend—what was his name? Wayne? Too long ago, a lifetime ago; he was not even a face in her memory. Over his muscled shoulders she had seen that awful, fireball pinprick scratch the heavens. When she closed her eyes, she could see it still.

What if it had hit us?

A slim risk, the logical, left half of her brain argued; but it was a prospect she hardly dared dwell upon, even in the privacy of her own mind.

The pinprick of light in the sky growing ever brighter ionizing the air until violet flame stretched from horizon to horizon. Megatons of energy unleashed, boiling the seas, tossing continents of earth into the sky. And afterward, for those who lived, if anyone lived, the endless rain and dark in which no plant would ever grow nor any fire warm. Huddling, shivering, groping in the night for another human hand, the warmth slowly leaching from the bones, until . . .

Until she woke, still shivering, in the night, the dream sending her running to the observatory just to check that everything was still in place.

Sometimes, watching the night sky could terrorize her.

"I do not know what I would have done, Keith," she said aloud, "if you and the others had not joined me." Fallen into helpless despair. Sequestered the terror into some psychiatric dungeon, where it could foul the very roots of her thinking. But Keith and Wallace and Correy had shown her a way out. They had shown her that she could *act*. Otherwise, she might have spent a lifetime drawing circles on globes, wounds where the Earth had once been struck. "It was the feeling of helplessness, as much as anything, that incapacitated me. Prometheus may have saved my sanity."

"Which may prove as important as saving the world." Keith spoke without opening his eyes. "At least to some of us."

"It cannot be as important. No one person, not even I, is as important as the entire human race."

Keith did open his eyes and the look he gave her was pained. "That is a dreadful and seductive way of thinking, Mariesa. A human being is an end, never a means. What is the point to saving humanity if in the process we lose our humanity. I am afraid that your . . . concern may draw you to *use* people in the name of saving them. Remember what Chesterton wrote: 'The best things are often lost in victory.' I have seen the way you have scratched through the names of Promethean students on your list, as if you were discarding them because they were no longer useful to the Goal. And sending Levkin and DuBois on this mission . . . There ought to have been more dress rehearsals, unmanned dockings, manned orbitals without refueling, just to test reentry procedures . . ."

And the way she had maneuvered Betsy DuBois into rejoining her husband; or the OCST man, Michaelson, into losing his job; or Wilson and Lockheed and the Artemis Project into starting their own ventures. Yet, where did you draw the line between manipulating and leading? Sooner or later, someone had to crawl out of the hole and shout, "Come on! Follow me!" And when you did, what did you do about those who would not stir, or those who tugged at passing pants legs wheedling, "Don't go. Everything is fine here in our hole."

"There is no time, Keith. There are things we must accomplish before the markets collapse in August. And we are not a government, with unlimited access to our investors' pockets.

We need a demonstrably *profitable* flight, one that will excite investors and keep them excited, even during the bad times ahead.'' Champion would be out of office in the next election, a sacrificial lamb on the altar of the Kondratieff cycle; and the next administration would not be a friendly one. Success *now* was a vital shield against the attacks that would come after the '04 elections.

Keith was worried about her ''concern.'' Her ''obsession,'' he had meant to say. Perhaps she *was* obsessed on the subject. The bouts of terror came on her suddenly and unpredictably, and she had opened herself completely only to Keith. Wallace only thought the idea was ''neat.'' It was all sci-fi abstractions to him. To Correy, it was mere common-sense contingency planning—a remote contingency, granted, but with an infinite payoff, either way. For none of them was it *personal* fear. Except for Keith . . . and perhaps he feared for Mariesa van Huyten more than he feared the sky.

Keith was smiling in his sleep. Mariesa whispered. ''You are my conscience, Keith. My 'rod and staff.' I need someone to worry over me, because I have no time for it myself.''

She reclined her own seat and closed her eyes, but restlessness forced them open again. She located her briefcase and sorted through the orderly rank of folders until she found the one dealing with the Plank flight. She read through the checklist, even though there was absolutely nothing she could do to affect the outcome. It was all in the hands of Ned DuBois and Rick ten Boom . . . and Newton.

And God.

Mariesa found prayer awkward. She had never learned to pray spontaneously—it seemed self-conscious and contrived to her—and none of the formulaic prayers seemed appropriate. It could be that reading the flight checklist and worrying over it was itself a form of prayer.

Ranks of precise times marched down the pages: day, hour, minute, second *this* would happen. The Antisana Ram would launch. The fuel tank would reach orbital insertion. The Plank would chase and close, using precious fuel. They would match orbits. That was the danger point. That was when the fuel would reach critical levels. Then Levkin would go EVA and make the attachments for the oxygen and hydrogen transfer. And after that, fuel would be no problem.

She had not been happy with the choice of Levkin. A good man, a good pilot, or he would not have been on the team; but not the best among the Russians. Yet, with Krasnarov laid up with food poisoning and Volkov still not recovered from his injuries—and Volkovna refusing to leave her husband for a flight—Levkin had been the choice by default.

Poor Volkov . . . She wondered if Chisolm's people had made any further progress in locating the saboteur. There had been some questions about the telemetry problem with the initial test; and the other accidents could have been just that. She had never been too impressed with the sanitation at Claudio's cantina. But the failure analysis of the oxygen line from *Calbraith Rogers* had been sabotage, clear and definite; so the only question was whether it was part of a larger pattern.

A light touch on her shoulder drew her attention and she looked up to see the radio operator from the cockpit. He held a message slip in his hands. "This just came through for you, ma'am," he said, touching his cap.

"Thank you." A glance at the writing showed that it was encrypted with John E. Redman's personal code to her public key. "I will let you know if there is a reply."

After the man had left, she eased out of her seat so she would not awaken Keith and crossed the cabin to Zhou Hui, who sat with earphones on reading her novel. "Hui," she said, "would you decrypt this for me, please?"

Setting her things aside, Zhou Hui pulled her portable from its stowage and inserted the private key disk. Her fingers danced across the keys, entering the message. The screen blinked and characters whirled through strange arrangements and settled into a message in clear. Zhou turned the screen to Mariesa without reading herself.

ANTISANA RAM ATTACKED BY TERRORISTS. OUT OF COMMISSION FOR IMMEDIATE FUTURE. FUEL POD LAUNCHED SUCCESSFULLY, BUT AHEAD OF SCHEDULE. NOT INSERTED

INTO PLANNED ORBIT. MORE WHEN KNOWN.

—REDMAN

It was herself, not the plane, that dipped and swayed. "Keith!" she called. "We have a problem!" She turned. "Keith!"

He had not moved. Mariesa went to him and shook him hard by the shoulder; but the only thing that happened was that his left arm slipped off the seat's arm rest and dangled by his side.

It was only for a moment that the arm swung pendulum-like before she found her voice, but it seemed to go on forever and ever. "Keith?" she shouted. "Keith! Get a doctor in here!"

The copilot knew CPR and Wallace Coyle was a certified First Aid Technician, but it was too late by far. It was Correy Wilcox who finally grabbed Mariesa by the wrists to stop her pounding on Keith's chest; and she would have started hitting him, too, except he held her too tightly. She remembered shouting, "How could you leave without telling me!"

After that, it was a confusion of faces and voices. Belinda hugging her long and hard; and Werewolf saying sadly, "He was the wisest of all of us, I think." And Bennett Longworth shaking his head, an outsider to the group and feeling it, saying, "So young to go," which from his point of view was no less than the truth. And the captain pointing out one awful truth.

The plane was in flight over the ocean, and there was no place to put the body; so the best thing would be to leave Keith strapped into his seat until they had landed.

Correy asked her to join the others in the outer cabin, but she shook her head. She could not bear the thought of Keith completing the flight alone, and the others eventually acceded to her wishes.

The remainder of the flight she spent telling Keith all her fears and hopes and begging him to understand when she did things that she had to do; and Keith listened in silence as he so often did, even when she shouted and cried. It was a long, long flight back home, and at the end of it, Keith was still dead.

INTERLUDE:

The Measure of Our Torment (I)

Jenny Ribbon could not shower thoroughly enough to feel clean. There was not enough soap in all the supermarkets in all of Wessex County for that. When she had scrubbed herself almost raw, she turned off the steaming hot water and stood for a moment with her forehead pressed against the tiles. There was only a short while longer to be endured. The big assembly where they'd watch the spaceship take off. The exams. The convocation. Graduation. Only a few more weeks, then she could go away, far enough away to never be found. But she did not know if she could endure those weeks.

She was going to be the valedictorian. She had beaten Karen Chong and Tani Pandya and she was going to get up in front of everyone and make a speech about how sorry they were to leave dear old Witherspoon and what great opportunities lay ahead, and everyone would know what horrible lies they'd be. Unemployment over ten percent. College graduates driving cabs. What was the point?

And Mom and Daddy would be in the bleachers watching her. And afterward they would point out all the little mistakes she had made. *But, darling, we learn from our mistakes. . . .*

A slip in the tub and her problems would be over. She'd never have to lie in bed at night wondering what she had done wrong this time. She stepped carefully out of the shower onto the bathroom floor.

After she dried, she stepped back into her bedroom and tiptoed to the wall that separated her room from her parents and pressed her ear against it, using a water glass as a stethoscope. Low murmurings, the sound of the television. That meant they were still awake. In the mirror over her dresser, she saw herself, white, pale, lithe. No longer a girl, not yet a woman.

She could not endure another month; she could not endure another night.

She dressed quietly, not in the long flannel nightgown that Mother had laid out beside Mr. Rumples, but in a sturdy pair of loose-fit jeans and a warm, baggy shirt. Thick socks. Hiking boots, too; though she did not pull them on quite yet. Schoolbooks pulled from her knapsack made a neat stack on her desk atop the draft of her valedictorian speech. The were quickly replaced by underwear, blouses, extra pants. The knapsack bulged tight as she zipped it closed.

She felt as if someone else were doing it; that she was standing beside another Jenny, observing her. Everything was planned, automatic. A mental checklist as thorough as any she had prepared for her classes. In the closet, there were lovely shoes; gorgeous, some of them; and they went so well with her dresses. But only the sneakers had gone into the pack, and none of the dresses. Mr. Rumples watched with a teddy bear's soulful eyes. She knew she could never take everything; but what could she leave behind? The ballet trophy from sixth grade? The swimming awards? The photograph of her and the governor of New Jersey at the Olympics of the Mind? The Girl Scout sash with the merit badges sewn carefully in rows? The ribbons carefully saved since grade school? They were all part of who she was; or who she had been. If she left them behind, she would be leaving behind a part of herself, too.

When everything was in readiness, she threw herself on her

bed and hugged Mr. Rumples. "I'm sorry, Rumpy," she told the tattered old stuffed bear. "I really am. And maybe it really is partly my fault; but I have to get away because if I don't I may never get away at all." Mr. Rumples was her own age to the day. Daddy had bought him the same day she was born and she could not remember a time when she had not shared her bed with him. He had been through the wringer—literally—but carried his years well. His faded eyes were at once stoic and sympathetic.

She turned off the light and sat huddled on her bed with her knees drawn up until the mutter of the television in the next room stopped and she heard the sound of rustling bodies turning over. She kept her eyes fixed on the glowing dial of the clock on her dresser. Give them one hour. One hour and they'd be fast asleep. She huddled with Mr. Rumples and told him again all the things that had happened to her. He had heard them all before, of course, but he always listened with a sympathetic ear.

Finally, it was time.

Jenny tied the laces of the hiking boots together and hung them around her neck. Then she shrugged into the knapsack and tiptoed to the window. The windowpane lifted easily and silently. She had oiled the runners only the day before, just to be sure. She climbed out on the sill and stood poised, ten feet above the ground. With one hand grasping the window sash, one foot braced against the outside wall, groping for the tree branch that sometimes scratched the window, scaring her to death. The branch waved around now, just out of reach. A fall and a broken neck, that would take care of things, too.

Then her groping hand found the branch and she let her weight lean onto it, slipped, swung, hooked a leg around and hung like a possum for a few moments while she collected her breath. She pulled herself around—and vowed someday to thank Mr. Snyder for all those awful gym classes. In moments, she had reached the trunk. A long hike ahead of her now, to where Chase had said he would meet her with a car. Chase had his own problems, but Chase knew about getting away.

The house behind her was dark, except for the front and backyard lights. Dark and silent, full of abandoned awards and trophies, schoolbooks and term papers, her baby shoes in bronze, the valedictorian speech, the snapshots of her and her friends stuck into the mirror frame . . .

When she looked back for a moment, she saw Mr. Rumples watching her sadly from the bed. *Good-bye, Rumpy.* How could you explain to a toy that toys were for children and, whatever it was that lay before her now, it was not childhood.

12.

Walking the Plank

The launch went off like every other launch, except that the shaking seemed to go on forever. For Ned, the initial ascent was always the worst, because it was the one part of the profile when he was not *flying*. Just lie on your back and enjoy the ride. The rest of it—attitude control, orbital transfer, deorbiting, the Swoop of Death, touchdown—was, computer-assisted or not, something the pilot controlled. His fingers twitched against the padded armrests. *Lemme at them controls....*

The control console formed a heads-up array of brightly lit gauges and digital readouts. "Coming up on rollover," Ned remarked over the ground link. "The ride's a little bumpy, though." Air turbulence battered the ship, shaking it the way the wolf shook the second pig's cabin. The walls banged. "Sounds like someone wants in." Levkin, buckled into the copilot's couch on the right, chuckled nervously at the joke.

The console clock blinked the seconds away. "Mach one," Ned announced. "Aerospike configuration holding stable." Mach one was the critical point for aerospikes, when airstream turbulence could disrupt the focus. "Coming up on max Q. I sure hope they used a good brand of glue to hold this sucker together.''

''Roger,'' Heitor Carneiro's voice in Flight. ''Be advised: Scotch Brand cellophane tape.''

Ned grinned. Heitor was a good man to have in Flight Operations. He knew the banter the pilots needed to hear.

And then, magically, they were through the turbulence to the other side. The buffeting subsided and they hurled outward at supersonic speeds. Ned thought he ought to say something memorable, just as blasé and aw-shucks as all get out, like Yeager had done in *Glamorous Glennis,* back when they thought there was nothing on the other side but a distinte-grating airchine. ''Holy shit,'' Ned said, ''that was one hell of a ride.''

So, memorable lines were not his bag. They didn't pay him to be a speechwriter.

Levkin recited a series of numbers. Fuel level, altitude, airspeed . . . Ned listened with half his attention, the other half focused on the feel of the ride. The vibrations, the hiss of air over the aeroshell, the pressure of acceleration against his face. Everything nominal. Everything right down the old groove. Just like a training sim . . . except you couldn't step outside and reboot if things went sour.

The aerospike engines reconfigured automatically to vacuum-flight mode, rotating outward to spread the exhaust footprint. The sky outside the viewports deepened from cerulean to Prussian blue, shading into violet, finally into black. Stars emerged, twinkling at first, but settling into a steady gleam even as the hiss of the air across the ship's fuselage faded into silence. Ned swallowed the lump in his throat. He had made it. He had made it, at last. Not just peeking through the window in a ship pushed beyond its envelope. He had come through the front door, this time. He was where God meant him to be.

''Coming up on engine shutdown,'' Levkin said. ''Three, two, one. Mark.''

The background roar and vibration cut off and the ship was coasting, arcing upward into its orbital slot. The abrupt cessation of thrust gave Ned a queasy feeling, one of not quite staying put. He was falling up and around the world with his ship. It was a deliciously giddy sensation. *Watch that first step. It's a doozy.* . . . Through the viewport he could see the limb of the world, bright white and blue. A ballpoint pen hung suspended, falling along with him. He and Levkin exchanged a grin, and Levkin gave him the thumbs-up sign. Then, almost reluctantly, Ned snagged the pen from the air and turned his attention to the mission checklist.

They blew the checklist on the second orbit. According to the mission profile, Wilson's backup fuel tanker should have been entering the orbital plane eight miles ahead and slightly below; but, instead of a transponder signal, they received an encrypted message from Fernando, relayed across the Atlantic GEO satellite. Even before he ran the decryption, Ned knew that something had gone badly wrong. Becoming a test pilot flying hot machines was easy. Becoming an old, retired test pilot telling stories to your grandkids . . . that was something else again. Like he had told Betsy countless time, *we take risks, but they are* calculated *risks.* Ned did not like it when the calculations didn't work out.

DELAY SCHEDULE CHECKLIST SERIES TWO-POINT-ZERO. PROCEED DIRECTLY TO THREE-POINT-ZERO SERIES.
                                                    —FLIGHT OPS

"What is it?" Levkin asked.

"I'll tell you what it is," Ned said as he stabbed the FILE & SAVE button with his thumb. "I'll tell you what it is. The goddam fuel pod didn't get off and now they have to wait for the phase and planar windows to open up again." Or maybe it was up, but in the wrong orbit. Or the transponder wasn't working. And wouldn't *that* be a bitch. . . .

They ran through the rest of the checklist with few problems. Life support. Instrumentation. Controls. They tested the attitude-control jets with short bursts. They deployed the Earth-resource monitoring satellite they had brought along.

(Sure, it was a test flight; but the client got a price break on the freight, and the Word from On High was: *Never Fly Empty*.)

Levkin suited up for the satellite deployment. He sealed his helmet and gauntlets and tested the seals just in case he had to go EVA. Afterward, he had to take everything off again, but you never knew. The bay doors might have stuck, or the sling fail to operate properly. *It's supposed to be automatic,* the old engineers' joke ran, *but actually you have to press this button. . . .*

After nearly a day in space and the checklist seventy-five percent complete, they still had not heard word one from Flight about the refueling exercise. The badness of the news, Ned reflected, is directly proportional to how long they wait to tell you. John Glenn had waited a long, long time before anyone would tell him his heat shield had come loose.

"I don't understand," Mariesa said when they came and told her. "The tanker is right behind them, in the same orbit. Why can't they just slow down?"

Of all of them on the plane, only Werewolf was qualified to answer. She could tell that he was uncomfortable being in the cabin with Keith, but Mariesa would not leave Keith, and she had to know the answers. Werewolf and she sat across the aisle, and Werewolf would not turn and look.

"Navigating in a vacuum," he said, "is not like navigating in air. You can't bank or turn. To change from one orbit to another requires energy. Fuel must be spent . . . maybe too much. If the ram had launched at the proper moment, the tanker would be in the same orbit, just ahead of the Plank. Only a bit of close maneuvering would have been needed. Even if they had launched earlier than they did . . . But now . . ." He spread his right hand and waggled it back and forth, palm down.

"But now it's not so simple," she said.

"Not so simple," he agreed sadly. "The target and chaser are in the same plane—but the tanker is a quarter revolution behind and twenty miles higher. Launching manually and on short notice, ten Boom was forced to . . . Ah, hell . . . Every revolution, the tanker will fall two hundred miles farther behind.''

"So, if they slow down . . ."

"To slow down, they must accelerate."

She frowned and shook her head. " 'To slow down . . .' I don't understand."

"Speed and altitude are inseparable," Werewolf said. "Deceleration would lower the ship to a *faster* orbit and the gap between the two craft would widen. Acceleration would lift the ship to a higher but slower orbit. The eccentricity of the orbit may also change, depending upon whether the burn occurs at apogee or perigee or somewhere in between."

"So, they should 'step on the gas' until the tanker catches up. . . ." She paused and thought it through. "Oh. I see. They have to go *higher* than the tanker, let the tanker catch up, then 'slow down faster' so they drop in just behind it." She lifted her hand to her lips. "And that means using even more fuel."

Werewolf nodded. "Twice what was originally planned, since two orbital shifts are required, plus still more fuel for the final closing-in maneuvers. If the tanker had been above-and-ahead, or even below-and-behind, matters would be less critical. They would need only to coast, and the distance would close. To rendezvous above-and-behind is not impossible; but . . ."

Mariesa insisted on knowing. "But . . ."

Werewolf made a noncommittal gesture. "It may deplete their fuel, and, if *then* they cannot refuel successfully, they may . . ." His voice trailed off.

"They will not have enough left to land," she finished for him. She saw the truth in his eyes.

"What else can I tell you, Mariesa. It's a coin toss. DuBois can close with the fuel tank. The orbital shift is doable. Pessoa's people found a fuzzy boundary transfer orbit, a Belbruno orbit, and Dolores concurs. The problem is, he can reach the fuel tank; but if he can't refuel after he gets there, there is no reserve left for landing."

"So," said Mariesa, finishing his thought, "if the fuel pod

was damaged in the attack . . . the valves or the fittings or the hosing . . .''

"End the mission now," Will said. "Bring them down while they still have the fuel."

Mariesa looked across Werewolf's broad body to the sheeted figure. Twelve hours, she thought. Twelve hours before they could land. Whatever was going to happen, it was going to happen while they were in the air. She would have to decide before they touched down. *Keith, oh, Keith, what would you do?*

Ned watched the message roll up on his screen. "Roger, FlightComm. New orbital parameters are uploading now." He knew it was going to be bad news, or they would have told him in clear instead of sending it by dark-code. Levkin leaned forward in his couch, and his lips moved as he read the accompanying message. Ned watched Levkin through hooded eyes. "How long before you need a decision, Flight?"
"Four orbits, DAX-27," Heitor told them. "After that, divergence is too great." Through the port viewport, Ned watched the coast of Thailand approach from the east. It was easy to imagine that the Plank stood still in the void and that the Earth spun beneath it. He wondered how many relays the message had bounced across, and how many intercepting parties were trying doggedly to decrypt it.

"Acknowledged." He cut the transmission and floated a while in silence. The terminator rolled across the Adaman Sea. Bangkok glowed like a pearl on velvet. Seen from above, sunset was a gradual thing, something dark that crawled across the land; but dawn came up like a nova, exploding across the lens of the horizon. *Bessie Coleman* made a complete circuit every hundred minutes, and sunrise and sunset, however stunning, grew to be commonplace. "Well," he said to no one in particular. "They left the decision up to us." He could imagine Pessoa down below, wringing his hands like Pilate over this latest foul-up. Though this time it hadn't been his fault, who keeps count of such things?

Levkin spoke at last. "I say we go down." Ned turned and

regarded him but made no immediate reply. "We have accomplished most of our checklist," Levkin went on. "We have proven that the ship can carry crew and cargo. Deploy satellite. There is no need to chase tanker . . . and perhaps fail."

Ned shook his head. "We haven't proven anything, Gregor. Nothing an unmanned Plank could not have done. DAX-26 did most of it, already."

"Then, let next flight chase tanker. DAX-28 can be launched to proper intercept orbit. Mishka and Forrest can test refueling procedures."

Yeah, that would be the easiest way to do it. The safest way. Though, if he could read between the lines, the ram would not be ready to launch another pod for a long time; and this one would have leached out before the next flight. Ned unfastened his harness and, free of the seat, kicked himself aft toward what they had dubbed the rec room, a small cabin behind the acceleration couches where you could relax, eat a meal, sleep attached to the bulkhead by Velcro fasteners. The crew module was bigger than the cab of a long-haul truck, but it was not what Ned would ever call spacious. Two couches, side by side, with twin consoles and steering yokes. Between the two couches, and below the consoles, was the opening to the crawl tunnel that led to the airlock in the nose. Ned stared out the upper port at the foreshortened view of the forward fuselage.

He grabbed a stanchion to steady himself. It was a glorious feeling, an ecstatic feeling, floating free above the world. If there never was another flight, at least there had been this one. He had touched the sky and gone to the other side. He could still go home with that. It wouldn't be *failure* to go back now. Not exactly.

He remembered Mariesa van Huyten standing on the walkway outside her rooftop observatory and dreaming of all that waited to be done up here. But that was her dream, not his. Hauling in satellites and putting them back? He was a test pilot, not a towtruck driver. Yet . . . someone had to show that it *could* be done. Someone had to be first. He sighed and struck the bulkhead with his fist . . . and began to rotate slowly backward, head over heels. Levkin came into view.

"We have to prove robustness, Gregor." Levkin did not answer; and Ned pressed on. He wondered just who he was trying to convince. "Anybody can go up and down. We have to demonstrate that the ship can handle the unexpected."

Levkin turned around in his seat. "Do we?" He wagged a warning finger. "We try to prove too much, too quickly." The Russian was now upside down from Ned's point of view. It was hard to take seriously the opinion of an upside-down man.

Still, Ned had to grant that Levkin had a point. On the original schedule, this mission had been DAX-34, the end of a graduated series of test flights. Orbital performance testing. Reentry capabilities. Rendezvous and docking. Ned feared that they were pushing the envelope out in too many directions all at once. Yet, Mariesa van Huyten was no fool. There had to be a reason for the schedule crunch. Money running out? Investors demanding results? That signal wasn't on his frequency. It was too far away, on the Planet of Boardrooms. He only knew there was a sense of urgency coming down from on high.

"The payload ratio is the critical parameter," he reminded Levkin. His slow spin brought him once more "upright," and he grabbed hold of the stanchion again. His feet floated out from under him and came to rest on the bulkhead. "If we can't prove out the refueling capabilities early on in flight test, it doesn't matter what else we prove. The key mission—satellite retrieval and replacement—needs refueling to work."

Levkin shrugged. "Is no concern of mine." A stubborn look settled on the Russian's face. Ned cocked his head and studied his companion.

"Levkin, why the hell are you here?"

The Russian frowned puzzlement. "*Shto?*"

"We all have our reasons for signing on. I wanted to touch the stars; Forrest wants to be a role model. For Mike, it's the ultimate test of man versus machine. Valery is in love with danger; and Katya's in love with Valery. Bobbi is out to prove that girls can be as tough as boys. But what about you, Gregor?'' Ned floated forward until he was hovering over the back of Levkin's acceleration couch. He gripped the headrest. "How many hands of poker have we played, how many BS sessions in the common room? And you've never said beans about what drives you. What's the itch, Gregor, that wants to be scratched?''

Levkin unsnapped his harness and twisted in his seat, the better to face him. Since Ned was now oriented fore-and-aft, Levkin's face appeared sideways. "Is simple,'' he said. "I wanted I should be remembered. That my name be written in the books, and schoolchildren would speak of me.''

For a moment, Ned could not speak. "Jesus, Levkin, is that all?''

"You want dreams? Or duty? Pfaugh!'' He pantomimed spitting. "I care not a kopeck for poetry, or for challenge. For me, fame and honor.''

"And endorsements?'' Ned could not keep contempt from his voice. "Cashing in?''

"You think I become test pilot for *money*?'' Levkin smiled broadly. "Because I am not 'space cadet,' I am less worthy than you or mighty Mishka Alexandrovitch? I think you were making no secret you were wanting to be yourself on first orbital flight.''

Ned put his face close to Levkin's. "At least I didn't poison anyone to get on board.''

"*Ya nye ponimayu.*''

Ned said one word. "*Feijoada.*'' Levkin blinked and looked away, and Ned pressed his lips together. "Yeah, I thought so. You bastard.''

Levkin turned a bland face on him. "I know nothing, comrade. Mishka and Forrest were unfortunate that the food was spoiled, but they were not hurt.''

"Yeah? *They* weren't; but what about Valery?''

"Volkov?'' Ned saw genuine puzzlement in Levkin's features.

"Valery could have been killed—*would* have been, if he weren't such a damned good pilot—and who had better motive to knock Volkov off the backup crew . . . or the *spetznatz* training to pull it off?''

''No!''

''And now, when push comes to shove, you don't have what it takes to see it through.''

Levkin snarled and his hand struck like a snake. Ned pushed away from the seat and coasted aft, toward the rec room. Levkin kicked himself free of his seat.

There was no room to duck. Levkin bounded into Ned and grabbed him by the front of his pressure suit. They began to tumble. Ned banged his temple against the bulkhead and saw stars. He broke Levkin's grip and followed up with a double-heel punch to the Russian's face. Levkin howled as they spun in opposite directions. Every turn brought him up against something hard. Levkin collided with the back of the acceleration couches. *Zero-g is hell on close-in fighting*, Ned thought. Wrestling and judo moves threw both ways. He grabbed Levkin's suit fabric as he spun around again and went into a clinch. Since they had been turning in opposite directions, that stopped the tumbling.

Levkin pulled his face up close to Ned's. ''I did nothing to *Calbraith Rogers*. Nothing!'' His breath came long and slow and rank. His bear hug felt like iron bands. Hugging Levkin like a lover, Ned found himself staring into a pool of fear and anger. He breathed heavily, once, twice, three times. Slowly, Ned relaxed his grip. ''I believe you,'' he said, with some surprise.

Levkin waited a moment longer, then broke his own hold. ''I did nothing to *Calbraith Rogers*,'' he said again.

''I said I believed you.'' Ned rubbed the back of his head where he had struck it, and winced. In training they had been drilled repeatedly on the difference between weight and mass. Now the difference had been pounded into his head at last. ''You're bleeding,'' he told Levkin.

The Russian touched himself on the left cheek. ''Nothing.''

Ned pulled himself into his seat. Levkin watched him buckle the harness. Ned flexed his hands, feeling the pain in the wrists. ''Tell you what, Gregor. Next time you want to fight, let's find ourselves a closet. We'll have more room." Levkin grunted, but made no reply, and slowly resumed his own seat.

"Tell me about the *feijoada*," Ned said.

Levkin hesitated a moment, then shoved the harness buckle home. It made a sharp click in the silence. "Was nothing. Was prank. Like when your Forrest was dumping trash on simulator with Mishka being inside. When did you suspect?"

Ned thought the question sounded like *what was the flaw in my plan, so the next one will be better?* but he shrugged. *Some prank.* Levkin didn't fool him. The moon-faced Russian, the ever-smiling *clown* of the group, had seen one man between himself and a history-making flight and had seized the opportunity to put himself on board. For the fame. And that grease spot on the simulator stairs . . . If Krasnarov had slipped instead of Bat, Levkin would have been the one to fly the suborbital. There was a coldly calculating determination beneath that grinning exterior. Not a man you ought to turn your back on.

"A few weeks ago," he said. "In the shower."

Levkin looked up sharply. "And you said nothing to anyone?"

"Without proof . . ."

Levkin shook his head and laughed. "No," he said. "You, too, wanted this flight, *tovarishch*. No one else was practiced for this mission, so if you were denouncing me to the authorities, the flight is being scrubbed until primary crew recovers." Levkin cast him an amused look. "Difference between us, *tovarishch*, is I *act*, but you accept fruits of action."

Ned wanted very much to punch the smirking face beside him, to wipe out the smug smile with a righteous fist; but the hell of it was there was too much truth in the accusation. No Levkin, no flight, and Mama DuBois's little boy would miss his own chance of a lifetime. That knowledge hurt more than the lump on his head. He sighed and reached for the communicator switch. "You win. We'll go down."

"No."

Ned looked at him. "Are we going to have another fight?"

"We will complete our mission." Ned waited, and Levkin continued. "You think I do not know what you and the others are saying? Poor Gregor Samoilovich, he cannot keep up. In every contest, he is *vtoroy*... he is number two. He walks always in Krasnarov's shadow. So, perhaps now we do not say that Levkin backed down when the task proved too difficult."

Ned did not toggle the switch quite yet. "You aren't saying this because we—"

"Levkin does what Levkin does."

Ned shrugged. "All right. Have it your way. Contact Flight and tell them what we decided. I'll start setting things up." He unlocked the keyboard and swung it out toward him and began to enter the commands.

Levkin spoke with the ground. When he was finished, he said only, "They wish us luck." Levkin looked like a man who had just agreed to gargle razor blades. Ned didn't care how Levkin felt. He thought fleetingly of Betsy. *A brand-new way to kill yourself.* There was one chance in three the rendezvous maneuver would leave them with insufficient fuel to land. Which meant the odds were with them, really. One in three was not as good as the one in a hundred they usually insisted on. Yet, the odds meant nothing if the refueling was successful. You had to trust your wyrd. "Yeah," he said. "Luck."

He set up a series of computer macros to execute the new burn sequences according to the uploaded parameters. Levkin was a strange one. The business with the food. Mike and Forrest had suffered indignity and disappointment, but no great physical harm. Claudio's business had been hurt; but that would be only temporary. And the grease spot, too ... Ned suspected earlier pranks: the paper clip that had caused Forrest to blow a sim. And the drunken fight he had had that one night outside the training center. Levkin had done what he could to bogie everyone's proficiency rating; but he had not tampered with *Calbraith Rogers*. He had not put anyone in deadly danger. He had sabotaged the competition, not the program.

The one thing Ned had been sure of was that Levkin would not sabotage his own flight. That was why he had said nothing. Like the old joke about smuggling your own bomb on board an aircraft to reduce the odds . . . But if Levkin had not sabotaged *Calbraith Rogers,* who had?

Some nobody, Ned realized. *Somebody whose name I do not even know, who walks around the island with a hammer or a soldering gun or . . .* Fortunately, Queen Bessie had been too well guarded to . . .

A sudden, cold certainty enveloped him and he canceled the sequence he had been setting up. His pulse rushed in his ears. The symbols dancing on the screen froze in their antics and vanished. Quickly, he hit other keys, recalling the orbital transfer program that Heitor had just downloaded into their computer. Then he reencrypted the program using Forrest Calhoun's public key and added a single message. Is THIS CORRECT? ASK MENDOZA. Then he flagged the message urgent and hit the Send button.

Levkin had watched in silence. Now he said with an edge of worry in his voice, "What is it, comrade?"

Ned gave him a brief and lifeless grin. "Paranoia, probably; but I'll feel a whole lot safer if I know we were sent the right course settings." Forrest would check it out. Forrest—and the brooding Luis Mendoza—those two Ned felt he could trust.

Mendoza's face grew steadily darker as he studied the code comparison on his laptop. Any darker, Forrest reflected, and the man sitting beside his clinic bed could be a soul brother. The file comparison program rolled through the code that Ned had beamed down from *Bessie* and matched it, line by line, instruction by instruction, against the master copy on Mendoza's sealed disk. Finally, jaguar eyes lifted from the screen and said flatly, "The orbital data has been altered."

Forrest Calhoun had not thought it was possible to feel any worse than he already did. "Jesus fucking Christ."

João Pessoa, standing in the doorway of the clinic room, struck the doorframe with his fist. Heitor Carneiro grimaced. Kirby Welles, the investigator down from Cerberus Security, scribbled a note on his pad. Forrest thought his goddamned clinic room was turning into a goddamned convention center. "No mistake?" the security man said. Mendoza turned to him.

"Big mistake."

Welles blinked. "No, I meant . . ."

"*I* make no mistake. The alteration is real. The alteration is no mistake. It was done with purpose. But this man—" He flicked a blunt forefinger at the laptop screen. "This man has made a mistake."

"How do you know the alteration was not accidental?" Carneiro asked. "A keystroke error . . ." But Mendoza shook his head.

"Not random error. Purpose makes pattern. *I smell his footprints!*"

Silence fell. It was not, Forrest reflected, a statement on which much commentary could follow. There were two Mendozas: one, lab-coated, analytical, precise, painstaking—a product of the universities and the cities of the coast; the other, a patient creature from the jungle riverbanks, though perhaps no less precise and painstaking for all that. Forrest was just as happy Mendoza was not stalking him. "What if Ned had executed the program?" Forrest asked.

Mendoza shrugged and his eyes danced over the lines of code. "Wrong orbit. No tanker. No fuel. Orbit decays."

Forrest shook his head. "Thank god for Ned's twisted little suspicious mind."

Heitor Carneiro said, "We ought to abort. Who knows what other problems exist we do not yet know of?"

João Pessoa nibbled on his lip and he brushed his thin mustache absently with the back of his hand. "Perhaps we should think upon it more. Ask Bonifácio for his . . ."

"If you will not speak up to the *senhora*, Seu João, I will."

Forrest pushed himself semierect in the bed. "God damn it," he said, and the others turned and looked at him. "You gave Ned and Gregor the choice. It's still their call. Give 'em the information they need to make it. Because, I tell you, you dick around too much longer and it'll be too late to make the transfer anyway, and whoever it was that tried to screw us over will have won.''

Sunlight in space was an absolute sort of thing. There was searing brightness and there was invisible darkness. Let a thing once fall in shadow and it was lost to the eye, except as it might occlude the stars. Blinking lights? To be noticed against a tapestry as varied as the starry ocean? It was a strange thought, but here, trapped in unrelenting orbits, constrained to lap endlessly along the same paths until the persistent friction of a tenuous atmosphere dragged you down, you could become lost with all the familiar landmarks of Earth clearly visible beneath you.

Somewhere a hundred and fifty miles behind them coasted the fuel tanker they sought. It fell, so FlightOps assured them, in a coelliptical orbit ten miles below their own.

''The hurrieder I go, the behinder I get,'' Ned muttered to himself.

Levkin said, ''Excuse?''

Ned grunted. ''Just an old Pennsylvania Dutch proverb. My mother's family *war Pennsylvaanish*. It's appropriate, though, don't you think?''

Levkin grunted. ''Fuel at forty-seven,'' he said.

Ragged edge. Most of the fuel they needed for landing had gone into raising their altitude above that of the tanker, but there was still some left. There was *maybe* enough fuel left, they could still abort and land even now; but coasting cost nothing—the attitude-control jets had their own, separate little tanks, enough to keep the ship dead nuts on without using the thrusters. So, the gas tank would still read forty-seven when the time came for apogee burn to bring them down to the target orbit. Ned wondered what Levkin would do when the point of no return was finally reached. But, hell, if you started out doubting that you could pull it off, you were half defeated coming out of the box.

That was Levkin's problem, Ned decided. He was like Nixon and Watergate. The man didn't believe in his own mojo. He was always looking for an edge, always looking for an angle. He'd shove you aside and *steal* the prize because he didn't really think he could win it on his own. A helluva man to be paired with. Bonny should have cut him early in the program; but it wasn't as if Daedalus had pilots to spare, and as long as everything was nominal, Levkin did all right.

The tanker, circling now below them, would slowly catch up. So there was nothing to do for the next couple of hours. Ned relaxed into a light, floating semi-sleep, content to let Newton and Kepler do the piloting. He wondered if they would be able to see the tanker when it passed them, at last.

Idly, he wondered what sex would be like in free fall. Now would be the time for it, arcing along at a lazy-but-ungodly speed, waiting to catch your target. With a ten-mile altitude difference, they would close on the target by a hundred miles every orbit. You couldn't hurry things along. You had to take things at their natural pace. Orbits, he meant; but sex, too, come to think of it. Another sort of stern chase . . . He sighed and crossed his arms over his chest, trying not to think about what lay ahead. Trying not to think about what lay behind.

> *"Simon, I want to know what the hell is going on! What were Henry and Cynthia doing down in Ecuador with a missile launcher, for God's sake? Who financed it? If the money came out of Crusades funds, there will be hell to pay! . . . Yes, I know we were Crusading against the cannon, but they killed a man, Simon . . . I know it was an accident, but we lose the moral high ground when we stoop to violence. I want answers, Simon; and I want them fast!"*

"DAX-27, this is FlightOps. Prepare for apogee burn."

Ned's eyes flipped open at the voice over his earphones. "Roj." He glanced at Levkin, who sat rigidly in his seat. He wondered if Levkin had gotten any sleep at all. The console clock showed a bright 30 SEC that blinked slowly toward zero.

"Last chance, Gregor. Yea or nay?"

Levkin snorted.

Ned had only a few seconds to reflect that since Levkin had

trained to do the refueling, Ned was putting his life in the hands of a man whose abilities he did not respect, and wasn't that a helluva note? "Six. Five. Initiate burn . . . Ready . . . Mark!" The computer kicked off the thrusters even as Ned hit the manual backup. The familiar roar of the engines shook the craft and acceleration pressed him into the seat.

"Six-meters-per-second burn," Levkin announced. Ned acknowledged. Twenty feet per second. A wasteful burn, not the subtle, economic approach originally planned, but there was no help for it now. A miserly burn would still leave them short, and it didn't much matter when you ran out of fuel whether you were two miles up or two hundred.

According to the Global Positioning network, the target was now somewhere ahead and below. A retrograde thrust at apogee would put them in a lower, faster, and more eccentric orbit. By the time they made a half revolution, they would have dropped to the target orbit—one mile down for every two feet per second burn. They would find themselves just below and slightly ahead of the tanker, just as they reached perigee and began to slow for what Forrest liked to call "the far turn." Another sharp thrust at perigee and the orbits would be matched.

After that, closing in was all in how good the pilot was.

"What is your take on VHI's effort, Mr. Attwood?"

"I will be frank, Mr. Koppel. I hear rumors that the whole program is on the edge of disaster. Corners have been cut and risks taken that a properly regulated government program would never attempt."

"Do you have any response to that, Mr. Redman?"

"Only that the 'properly regulated government program' does not exist, and enormous amounts of taxpayer money were thrown into endless studies with no demonstrable outcome."

"Of course, Mr. Redman does have a financial stake in VHI's venture."

"Which means that my lifestyle will suffer if it fails, not the taxpayers'. It might also tickle the fancy of an

*investigative reporter to ask where Mr. Attwood's finan-
cial interests lie, and how a successful VHI program
would impact them. It is not only the advocates on the
one side of a controversy who have something to gain or
to lose."*

The transponder beep brought a satisfied smile to Ned's lips.
At least *something* was working according to plan. The fuel-
tanker beacon was responding on the proper frequency. Forward radar had it bracketed, sending out pulses and hearing
that beautiful, beautiful beep coming back. The tanker was a
lover waiting in the dark, whispering, "Here I am. Here I
am." Ned and Levkin scanned the sector indicated by their
instruments. *Show yourself, baby. Come to Papa.* Why
couldn't they have painted the damn thing so it'd be visible?
Sure, regular paint would have burned off from the heat of
passing through the atmosphere at ram velocities; but there
had been a special ablative coating developed for the old
X-15 that turned the bird bright pink. *Of course, when ol' Pete
Knight saw that, he said he wasn't going to fly any damned,
pink airplane . . .*

They were coming up on orbital dawn, so both the ship and
the tanker were still in shadow. The rendezvous had been
timed so that they would have maximum daylight to carry out
the refueling, but that also meant their initial approach was in
darkness. It would be a hell of a note if they actually rammed
into the damned thing. Radar said they were okay, but Ned
would feel a whole lot better when they made visual.

"There!" said Levkin, pointing.

Ned squinted in the direction indicated—which took in
about twenty percent of the known universe. "Where?"

"A small cluster of lights. One o'clock, slightly high."

Five red lights in a perfect pentangle. "Yeah . . . I see it."

And just then, the approaching dawn sprayed the tanker
with daylight and threw it into sharp relief. Being a few dozen
feet higher, it caught the sun first. The tanker was a bright
orange, bullet-shaped cylinder, seared with black streaks and
surrounded by a glittering cloud of particles. Paint? Surface

ablation? Condensation? Ned had no idea. An off-colored band around the middle showed where the pumping and delivery connections were installed, between the bulkheads that separated the hydrogen and the oxygen compartments.

Ned began setting up the navigational computer. "All right, Levkin. Let's pull over to the rest stop and gas up." Levkin was working his hands, rubbing the fingertips against the thumbs. A brief smile chased itself across his lips, and he took his gauntlets from their compartment.

Ned engaged the computer, so it could lock on the guide stars. Immediately, an attitude-control jet fired and the craft began to yaw. Ned slapped the red Cutoff button without thinking. That had not been right. Levkin said, "*Shto eto?*"

Ned studied their target, so tantalizingly close. He reengaged the navcomp and shut it off when it again fired the attitude jets. For the next several minutes he played with the yaw and pitch controls on computer-assisted manual to damp out the rotation that the misfires had imparted. A part of his mind marveled at how controlled he was. *Just like a training sim.*

When he had the craft stabilized and had reengaged the gyros, he sat and pulled his lower lip while he studied his quarry. The gyro controls worked fine, so the problem was in the navcomp. "I think," he said slowly, "we have a problem."

Correy, his cell phone in his hand, stuck his head inside the cabin. "There's a problem," he said. "DuBois is in trouble. A cloud of reflective particles—perhaps fragments of the ablative coating, perhaps condensate from a leak in the tank—is confusing his navigational computer with 'extra' stars."

Mariesa nodded. "Keep me informed," she whispered without turning her head. Keith had been part of Prometheus and Prometheus part of him. There was nothing she could do for him now but continue to dream his dreams—and her nightmares. There was nothing she could do for Ned but wait and pray. She had not felt so helpless in a great many years.

Ned brought the ship in by hand. It wasn't impossible. It wasn't even improbable—they had simmed contingency plans in case of sensor breakdowns—and what with the burn charts from the computer library, and Levkin calling off the tanker's elevation angle and angular rate across the sky, it was just a matter of goosing the engines a little bit at a time. He was hardly aware of the passage of time, only of the feel of the rack in his hands or the engine keys under his fingertips, only the monotonous chant of Levkin's voice singing out angles as he peered through the cross-haired Close Approach viewfinder. The forward radar gave him heads-up closing velocities and distances. Fifty meters. Twenty. Ten.

Only when he had matched velocities at last, and the Plank was hanging in space a scant six meters below the dully gleaming tanker, did Ned release his hold on the controls and find that he could barely unflex his fingers. He played with the attitude jets until the tanker was directly "overhead," visible through the upper viewports. Then he shouted, "Thar she blows!" and Levkin engaged the "harpoon."

The magnetic grapple shot from its port, and closed on the tanker, unreeling the tether behind it. It struck and held. Carefully, Ned took up the slack. The last thing he wanted to do was give a sharp tug and yank the fuel pod toward the ship. No friction to stop it from drifting into them . . .

Finally, he relaxed, letting his arms float and his head loll back. Chaser and target raced ahead into nighttime.

"We did it," Levkin said. He didn't sound like he believed it.

"I'm good," Ned told him. "Damn good." And he felt good, too. He felt like he did after sex. It would be something to tell his grandchildren about.

Assuming he ever got back down. "How's the fuel, Gregor?"

The long pause before the Russian answered told him all he needed to know. There had been maybe two chances in three according to the computer sims that they would end the maneuvering with enough fuel to land anyway. But the sims were based on deterministic models, and real life was too damn fuzzy. A little variation here, a little variation there. The velocity a little higher, nozzle efficiency a little lower, the angle a few seconds off the beam . . . it all added up. It put you on the wrong side of the line.

Ned smiled. "Well, we were planning on refueling anyway. That was the whole point of coming here." He tried to convince himself Levkin could pull it off. He had done it in the water-tank simulations, again and again. Levkin had practiced with greater intensity because Levkin had *known* the backup crew would fly. But space was not water. There was no resistance to play against. No waves. No goddamned octopus staring you in the face, waiting for you to fail.

And now that all their options had run out and they were irrevocably committed, Levkin became a different man. Focused. Deliberate. He pulled on his helmet and methodically fastened the seals one by one. His lips moved, as if he were reciting the procedure to himself. Or a prayer. Then he pulled his gauntlets on and fastened those, as well. Ned imagined him a knight preparing for battle. When he was finished, he went through the checklist again. Ned didn't begrudge him the double check. Hell of a thing to wait until you were Outside to find out your shoelace was untied.

Finally, Levkin took a long breath and let it out. He looked at Ned through his gleaming faceplate. "Ready," he said with a curt nod. Ned clapped him on the shoulder.

"Let's make it happen."

Levkin unbuckled and floated free of his seat into the space between the two pilot couches. Feet first, he pushed himself into the tunnel that led to the airlock in the nose. Birth canal, Ned thought. Breech baby.

When Levkin's head had disappeared, Ned levered the safety plug into place. It was a truncated cone, small end facing forward, that pulled from a recess in the side of the tunnel. If for some reason the airlock doors in the nose failed to engage properly, and the hydrogen storage bay went to vacuum, the cabin air pressure would push the plug firmly into place, giving Ned a chance to don his own helmet and gloves. He felt as if he were sealing Levkin into a tomb. Rolling the stone across the entrance . . . and he had the strangest feeling in the pit of his stomach that he would never see the man again.

He keyed his mike. "Levkin, do you read me?"

No answer. What was wrong? Dammit. The radios had checked out no more than five minutes ago. "Levkin! Do you read me?"

"No."

Jesus Christ, another screwup. He started to say "Check out your . . ." before he heard Levkin's low chuckle and realized he'd been sucked in harder than the safety plug. "Very funny, Gregor. Very funny." It was a relief, in a way. It announced the departure of the cold-eyed, ruthless *spetznatz* and the return of the poker-playing jokester.

"I do not 'read' you, Ned; but I do 'hear' you." A pause. "I am past the hydrogen storage bay, entering airlock."

"Good luck. I'll be with you all the way."

Another chuckle, this one rueful. "I will be more alone than any man, Ned."

Styx was helping Beth fold the laundry when, to Beth's annoyance, the rerun episode of "Cagney and Lacey" on Lifetime suddenly broke off for a special announcement. The astronauts in "the corporate spaceship" had just begun their previously postponed refueling. One of the two men had just gone out into space to hook up the fuel lines and pumps. Beth snorted and said it was a waste of money, but Styx thought it was kool beans. The old cop show resumed and Beth gave her attention back to the screen while she folded with mechanical precision; but every now and then, for no damn reason at all, she looked up at the ceiling.

Levkin slid along the grappling line with short bursts from his jet pack, clipped to the line with a chock and a tether. Ned watched him through the viewport, offering occasional observations and encouragements as he kept the Plank oriented and on-station. Levkin looked like a hulking monster with the jet pack strapped to his back and the tool kit around his waist.

The equipment had been stowed in a locker just aft of the airlock, but accessible from the Outside. *No point trying to climb in and out of the ship wearing that monstrosity . . .* Levkin had had a bad moment trying to open the storage door with the turnkey, spinning counterclockwise when he tried to turn the handle the other way. Then he remembered to insert his feet into the recessed braces to give himself some leverage.

"I have made contact with the target," Levkin announced. Ned whooped, but Levkin when on. "I can gain no purchase on hull. Will use jet pack to reach pumping station. Release grapple so I can reposition it."

"Squeeze gently," Ned reminded him, as he turned off the electromagnet. "No water resistance, remember."

A small flare spurted briefly from Levkin's back and he drifted along the side of the tanker. Ned tracked him with the ship's outside floodlights. They were close enough for the lights to illuminate the shadowed portion of the hull.

When Levkin reached the central band, he found the pumping station and fuel connections. He repositioned the grapple, and Ned turned the magnetism back on. Now Levkin could jet back and forth freely between the two craft, riding the grapple while he attached hoses.

"Ned?"

"What is it?"

"There is some damage to the pod. I see surface cracks near the valve headers."

"Any evidence of leakage?"

A pause. "None. May be slow leak elsewhere, is why the cloud of particles around vessel."

Ned frowned and rubbed his face. The beard was starting to come in. They'd been in orbit now for a day and a half, most of that coasting during the "catchup" maneuver. "Yeah. Could be." There wasn't anything they could do about it if there was structural damage. At least the bastard had held together and not ruptured. "Let's get rolling."

"Is placard welded to pumping station."

Ned had a weird flash of the sign that had been welded to *Voyager* with a drawing of a man and woman—just in case any aliens happened across it in the next couple billion years. "What does it say?" he asked.

"It says, 'Self-Service Only.' "

Ned laughed. Rick ten Boom had a sense of humor, all right. He began to think this whole thing would come off right, after all.

Chase sat hunched over in the sofa watching MTV. He figured if anything went wrong, there would be a special bulletin or something. So far, nothing; so that had to be good news, right? He ran his thumb over the buttons on the remote, feeling the little lumps, but not pressing any. As long as there were no special bulletins . . .

Levkin was beginning to pant. Ned could hear it over the radio, and he supposed Flight could hear it, too, since everything was downlinked. Zero-g work looked easy. The ant lifting a boulder. But objects still had mass, and action had reaction with a vengeance, and you could wear yourself out doing the simplest kinds of motions, because you didn't just have to get things going; you had to get them stopped, too. Ned thought about calling his copilot inside for a rest, but it made him nervous to have his ship tethered to another craft, not only by the grapple, but now by two long, flexible, ceramic-polymer hoses. So he figured the best thing was to push forward and get it over with. Levkin agreed.

One of Ned's nightmares had been that the fittings on the hoses stowed in the tanker midsection would not match those on the fuel intakes, despite Daedalus having downloaded CAD copies of the drawings and specs to Wilson's engineering people. There had been design reviews and fabrication-site inspections during the months leading up to the flight, but that was just the sort of silly-ass screwup that sometimes happened.

Levkin torqued down the fasteners holding the hydrogen line in the orifice. (Getting the lines switched had been another Ned DuBois Thought Experiment. Oxygen pumping into the depleted hydrogen tank . . .) Ned toggled his mike. "Hey, Gregor."

The figure outside the viewpoint kept working. "What?"

"While you're out there, could you do the windshields and check the oil?"

Levkin made a gesture, and Ned heard suppressed laughter over his ground link. It was important to keep spirits up. I was too easy to dwell on the fact that you floated over an abyss a trillion miles deep.

The setting sun always got in the eyes of the westbound truckers on I-80, so long about suppertime the big rigs would begin pulling off the Interstate and into the parking lot of the Black Diamond Café. It got real busy that time of day, so Carol Wlodarcyk was glad to have a little waitressing help. The local business was steady, but slow. Interstate 80 brought in most of her trade and made the difference between just scraping by and boarding up the windows and walking away.

The girl, Jenny, had been a breath of fresh air from the world beyond the mountains. Carol's daddy had been a coal miner, and her granddaddy before him, and her husband Wasil would have been, except no one was digging hard coal anymore and if he had found any work wherever it was he had gone, Carol didn't expect she would ever know about it. Her whole life, she had never been out of the coal country, and Jenny had so many stories about exotic places like New York and Atlantic City and Wildwood.

The TV above the lunch counter broke into another special bulletin, and the background clatter of knives and forks on chipped Buffalo china paused as everyone watched and listened.

It reminded Carol of her childhood, when everyone had stopped with their hearts in their mouths whenever the rockets went up, when they had cheered and celebrated and the future seemed like an endless shout. Maybe it could be that way again. Lord knew, the world could use a dose of hope.

Even groundside, fueling up was no five-minute routine, and it took an hour and a half to top off *Bessie Coleman's* fuel tanks. Ned did not let out his breath until the control-panel readouts told him there was enough on board to take them safely back to Earth. When the readings crept above the red line, he and Levkin exchanged handshakes, and Levkin might have given him the old one-two Russian kiss on the cheeks except that sitting side by side as they were, it would have been too awkward. Thank God for ergonomics.

Levkin had rested aboard during the refueling. He ate a tasty meal of high-protein toothpaste (and a smuggled corned-beef sandwich) while his life-support oxygen tanks were recharged. When Ned judged that they had plenty of margin, he offered to go out and shut down the pumps on the tanker himself, but Levkin pointed out that he had not trained for it, and that Levkin would finish what Levkin began.

Outside once more, Levkin clipped his chock to the grapple line between the ship and the tanker and jetted across. Ned divided his attention between the fuel-tank readouts—volume, pressure, uniformity—and Levkin.

There was no warning. There never was.

13.

The Human Moon

One glance, Levkin was working the pump controls on the tanker; the next, and he was cartwheeling across the void. A glittering, white cloud of cryogenic fuel plumed from the tanker and both fuel lines and the grapple was snaking loose. Even while Ned watched, Levkin's chock reached the grapple's free end and the man went careening into the void.

Ned opened the general frequency. "Levkin! Levkin! Use your jets! You've got to stop your spin. Use your jets like you did in the water tank." There was no friction to stop you in space. Levkin would continue spinning until he lost consciousness; he would continue spinning forever. Clumsy fingers searched the alternate frequency, looking for Levkin's suit transponder.

Bobbi's voice: "DAX-27! This is FlightComm. What is happening?"

"No time. Tanker blew or something. Levkin's flying loose. I've got to catch him." *There!* The steady *ping-ping* echoed from the speaker. He let the navigation computer look at it. "Keep the heading, baby. Keep the heading." To Bobbi, he said. "I'm going after him. I need some burns."

Ned's eyes danced across the controls. Buttoned up. Buttoned up. Jesus! Fuel pressure dropping? The cabin wall clanged and, from the corner of his eye, Ned glimpsed the free end of the oxygen hose through the side viewport. Levkin wasn't the only thing the blowout had hurtled across the void . . . The free end—he could see a clamping ring still attached to it—whiplashed from spewed vapor.

Instinct guided his stabbing finger to the fuel intake valve shutoffs, because he never even had time to frame the thought that his hard-won, precious fuel was spurting into space. When he withdrew his hand and held it before his eyes, he saw it was shaking.

Calm down, Ned. This was no time for panic. Levkin had just replenished his suit, so he had plenty of power and oxygen. He would be okay for a couple of hours, provided his suit wasn't breached; and, if it was, it was already too late. Ned reeled in the magnetic grapple. The hoses he could do nothing about for the moment. He keyed his mike to Levkin's suit frequency.

"Gregor? Do you hear me? I have you locked in." He unshipped the gyros and brought *Bessie* to bear on the transponder heading. Levkin had picked up velocity from the blowout, north-by-Earthward from the fuel pod. Ned read the elevation angle and the angular rate of change from his console screen. There was no answer from Levkin.

"DAX-27, this is Flight. Secure and return."

Ned called up the burn tables on his onboard computer. "What's that, Heitor? We have static. I can't hear you."

"*Diablo*! You can hear me, Ned. Follow instructions."

"There is something wrong with my uplink, Fernando Base. I am receiving signals, but they don't make any sense. Here are the burn schedules I'm getting from my onboard. Run them through your sims and feed me options."

"We receive nothing groundside from Levkin's suit monitors. He is most likely dead. DuBois, you must leave him." A very long pause. "It is the burial he would have wanted."

Like hell. Levkin wanted a burial on Earth, with a fucking big heroic monument on top of it. Something schoolkids could visit. Ned set up his own simulation on a spreadsheet, using the Newtonian formulas in the library plus the ship's performance characteristics from previous test flights. Delta-V required gave you pounds of thrust required. Factor in the specific impulse of the fuel and engine—pounds of thrust per pound of fuel burned per second . . . Turn the crank and, voilá!—fuel consumption. That was the big one; because what would it matter if he could close on Levkin if it only meant the man would die Inside rather than Outside?

Well, it did matter; if not to Levkin, then to Mama DuBois's only child. He didn't want to know if he was the sort of person who could leave a friend to die. Even Levkin.

Mendoza's voice, ominous. "DuBois, this is Ships. Calculate you cannot close orbit without depletion. Repeat. Closest approach five meters after one orbit. Afterward, divergence."

"Five meters? Hell, I can go EVA and grab him as I go past."

"Negative. Do not leave ship unattended. . . ."

"Why, you afraid someone will carjack it?"

"DuBois, bring my ship back."

"Fuck you, Mendoza. I'll have to go EVA to detach the fuel hoses and secure the intake-valve hatch covers, anyway."

Heitor's voice, dry: "I see communications have been restored."

"You want to help out, Mendoza. You find out who fucked with the parameters you uploaded for the orbital transfer."

A moment of silence, followed by flat, implacable syllables. "I know."

A graphic flashed on the computer screen as his spreadsheet worked out the orbits. The curve of the Earth, encircled by two arcs. Blinking lights showed the locations of the Plank and the fuel pod, courtesy of the GPS system. A third arc and dot was Levkin, his orbit calculated from the transponder signals. Ned studied the projections. Mendoza was right. The closest he could get to Levkin, even with a big burn, was close enough to wave at him as he coasted by. That would be . . . He checked the console clock. In another ninety minutes. The ship had more computing power onboard than the whole world had had just thirty years ago, and what the hell good did it do? If only their closest approach were at their respective perigees. Orbital mechanics would slow them both down and he would have some slack for close maneuvering.

If wishes were horses. Betsy used to say, *beggars would ride.*

Hi-yo, cowboy.

The thought was so sudden, and so stunning, that Ned held his breath for fear that breathing would knock it loose. Jesus, it was a slim chance, but it could work; and the difference between slim and none was all the difference in the world.

An announcer interrupted the neurotic "New York Boomer" sitcom on the TV to report rumors of something gone "tragically wrong on the corporate space flight." Chase sucked in his breath and wondered if Captain DuBois was all right. He leaned toward the screen, wanting more. What had gone wrong? Could it be made right? But, of course, the announcer did not know, and left Chase sitting on the living-room rug to watch the oh-so-important whinings of the actors.

Cyrus Attwood swirled the brandy in his snifter and looked around the other faces in the club room. "I say, it serves them right," he said. "Hubris."

Young Bullock, his nephew and heir, shrugged and said, "Events seem to have spun out of control."

Cyrus pursed his lips and stared into his amber liquid. Yes. They had.

The worst part of the orbit was that he never lost contact with Levkin's transponder. Its steady ping-ping stayed with him for the full ninety minutes. Tantalizingly close; teasingly far. If Levkin had been eclipsed by the curve of the Earth, Ned might have convinced himself that the man was lost and that the rescue was useless. He might have reasoned out that, having risked all to replenish his fuel, he would be foolish to squander the margin now in a quixotic attempt at retrieval. But he could not turn his back while he could still hear the man's suit.

He watched the burn with one eye, the control console with the other; and with his third eye, the one that could see in imagination, he watched Levkin spinning along in the void. Unconscious, perhaps. At least, Ned hoped so. If Levkin was doomed, it was best if he never knew it. *I'd unseal my helmet, if it were me,* Ned thought; and then wondered if he could. It was a gesture of surrender, an abandonment of hope.

The transponder echoes came closer together, now. The ship was closing in. Ned had braked the Plank into a faster orbit—a bargain he had made with Fate—consuming precious fuel as his part of the bargain. He was flying the ship from the co-pilot's seat, using the crosshaired Close Approach viewfinder, searching the sky for the pebble that was Levkin. He had elevation and azimuth; he just didn't have visual. The outside floodlights probed the region where mathematics claimed Levkin sailed. If he could not locate the man before they passed . . .

And, suddenly, there he was, a flare in the heavens. Levkin had fired his jet pack. A signal. Here I am! Doppler showed a slight change in the closing rate. Hell, Levkin might be able to bring himself in! Ned flashed the outside floods three times, to let his copilot know he had been spotted.

The jet-pack flare died. Levkin must have been husbanding the last of his fuel for this moment. He must have used most of it up stopping his spin. Ned saw that the man still had a slight forward tumble. Jesus, the man must have an iron ear to endure that steady rotation for most of an orbit, saving the remaining fuel for a flare on the off chance that someone would come by and pick him up.

Ned switched over to telephoto and pulled the viewscope goggles to his eyes. Levkin stood out big against the endless backdrop. The left side of his suit was frosted white, probably from being caught in the cryogenic spray when the cracked valve had let go. His right hand, thumb protruding from a balled fist, waved slowly back and forth. Ned grinned at the crazy Russian.

"DuBois's First Rule of Space Travel," he said aloud. "Always pick up hitch-hikers."

He already knew that the two orbits would not close on this revolution; but this was as close as they would get any time before Levkin's suit failed him.

"I have visual on Gregor," he told the ground. "Tell Seu Heitor I am about to execute Plan A."

"Um, I am sitting Flight, now, DAX-27," Bobbi said. "Will explain later. Forrest and Mike have crawled over from the clinic. They're pulling for you, too."

Ned hesitated a moment, then asked, "Is Betsy there?"

"Affirmative. She is sitting with Forrest. She says to tell you that if you make it back, she is going to slap you silly for taking stupid chances."

"Tell her, no slap will ever feel better. Out."

Ned took a deep breath and began teasing the attitude jets. There was no time to waste. Time, tide, and Newton waited for no man. He turned *Bessie Coleman* until Levkin was centered in the upper-viewport bull's-eye. Levkin slowly inched across the scope. Relative angular velocity was not quite zero. Distance closed from ten to eight to six meters. Ned wondered what was going through Levkin's mind. Gregor knew enough orbital mechanics to know that if they no more than passed in the night, there would never be another meeting.

"Here goes nothing," Ned muttered, and he triggered the magnetic grapple.

The line shot from the Plank's midsection, straight and true. He could feel the reel spinning through the vibration of the deck plates.

A body in motion tends to remain in motion in a straight line at a constant speed, unless acted upon by an outside force. The "harpoon" headed for a point just ahead of Levkin. Ned cranked up the power to the electromagnet. *Come on, baby, Gregor's a small target, but he's wearing a lot of metal, and not all of it is aluminum.*

If he missed, he might have time to reel the harpoon back in and try a second shot; but he did not want to count on it.

And in his youth, along the banks of the upper Susquehanna, he had been no mean fly fisherman.

Magically, the harpoon came close enough. Either there was enough metal in Levkin's suit and jet pack to attract the electromagnet, or Levkin himself managed to reach out and grab it. It was too close to call, and Ned didn't care which way it had been. Ned stopped the reel, reversed it, and took up the slack; then, carefully, began to pull Levkin in. "Fernando Base," he said. "Gone fishing; and you would not believe the big one I hooked."

Then he disconnected the microphone and put his face in his hands and cried.

DRAMATIC RESCUE IN SPACE

News crews are racing to Brazil by fastest jets available to film the touchdown of the first ever privately financed, manned space mission. The heroic rescue of . . .

Chase made a fist and shook it. "Yes!" he said. "Yes!"

"Roberta, dear, why are you crying?"

Azim stopped in front of the electronics store on Queen Anne Boulevard where a dozen TV screens carried the story. Fatima tugged at his jacket and said, "Come on, we'll be late." Azim grunted and said, "Just a sec, babe. Something here I want to check out."

Jimmy Poole logged on to the Internet. <I knew DuBois would pull it off. I knew it.>

Everyone in the Black Diamond Café shouted at the same time. Jake from the kitchen, greasy and smelly as he was, hugged Carol and kissed her; and Jenny "Smythe" did, too.

*Tani Pandya danced with Meat Tucker in the stock-
room of Pandya's In-and-Out while the old radio continued to hiss and crackle the good news.*

A crack of thunder in a cloudless, tropical sky. Forrest Calhoun scanned the heavens, holding himself steady with his left
hand gripped on the rail of the "widow's walk." Beside him
stood Betsy DuBois, ramrod stiff. There was no point in telling
her the pilots' unofficial name for the balcony, or that Ned
had been the one to name it. She acted as if she knew, anyway.

Forrest pointed southwest, toward the sky over Ponta de
Sapata, at the far end of the island. "Here he comes."

Betsy bent down and lifted Lizzie so she could see. "Here
comes Daddy," she said. Then she gave a hard stare at the
growing speck. "You better not screw this up for her, Ned;
or I'll never forgive you."

"He screws up," Forrest reminded her quietly, "and he
won't even know."

Betsy lowered Lizzie to the balcony floor and crossed her
arms. "You're a bastard, Forrest. Do you know that?"

Forrest shrugged. "Yeah. I know it." He could not tear his
gaze away from the approaching spacecraft. That should have
been him up there. It *would* have been, if Levkin hadn't tampered with the stew. He wondered if Ned knew that the man
he had saved was responsible. He had told Ned to leave Levkin behind if an emergency developed; but Ned never did
know how to listen. Not even back at Edwards during the old
days, when they had both been bucking for slots on *Black
Horse.*

"He's coming in nose down," Betsy commented in a
tightly controlled voice. "I thought he was supposed to land
on his tail."

"He's going to execute the cross-range maneuver. We call
it the . . ." he hesitated. *The Swoop of Death.* Test pilots sure
as shit had a macabre sense of humor. They had to. "The
Flash Gordon Maneuver," he said. Betsy looked grim, and
Forrest wondered if Bat or one of the others had already used
the Phorbidden Phrase. "There he goes."

The approaching Plank arced down and then up, soaring back into the sky whence it had just come. Without thinking, Forrest made the cross over his body. "Hover," he whispered aloud. "Low throttle." Betsy looked at him, but said nothing.

From below, he could see the flames blossom on the base of the craft. The nozzles were canted inward for atmospheric flight, so there was a single, bright spike of flame supporting it. *Bessie Coleman* dropped from the sky. Landing, you didn't need as much power as taking off, since most of the fuel mass was gone. "Twelve hundred; down at forty," Forrest said. He had run the exercise so often that he could imagine himself behind the controls. "Ten hundred. Down at thirty." Betsy laid a hand on his arm.

"You can't fly it from here," she said gently. "If it fails, it won't be your fault."

Forrest shook his head. "It's my best friend up there. I can't not worry."

Betsy grimaced. "I know how you feel." Forrest looked at her.

"Yeah. I guess you do. And it won't be your fault, either."

"We made love," she said. "The night before he went up. We hadn't been with each other for near two years." Forrest put his arm around her. Her body felt small and hard against him. Lizzie stuck her face between the two lower rails on the balcony, peering between them. *Christ, Ned, do you have any idea what you walked out on? I'd give anything to have this waiting for me when I came back.*

"It's a long time," he said, "to go without."

Betsy laughed. "Don't tell me Ned 'went without,' because I'll know you for a liar if you do."

Forrest shook his head again. He still felt a little woozy from the dehydration, and he would probably have to put another day on the IV after this; but damn-all if he was going to miss the touchdown.

Queen Bessie fell to two hundred and the flames beneath brightened. "Hover," Forrest said. "High throttle." The ship paused in midair, as if resting on an invisible pillow. She gleamed like gold in the midafternoon sunlight.

"Damn. He's over Ilha Rasa." The little island off the northern point. "Bonifácio will have to send a boat over to take them off." The ship hovered for a few moments over the smaller island; then it canted to one side as the attitude jets began to fire. Forrest gripped the top rail with both hands. "Don't try it, son! Set her down now. You're almost home." He banged the rail with a fist. "Shit!"

"What's that sumbitch doing now?" Betsy asked in a weary voice.

"He's in translation mode. He's maneuvering sideways, trying to bring the ship over to the main island."

"Can he do that?"

"It was the first capability we tested, back when Mike snuck aboard *Nesterov*. Only Ned can't have all that much fuel left."

The ship danced across the waves of the narrow straits and up the narrow, rocky tip of the island, rising slightly and falling on its pillar of flame. Steam and spray leapt from the waters of the straits. Not until she was over the landing apron—not until Showboat Ned brought his craft to dead-fucking-center over the landing apron—did the legs pop out of their sheaths and the ship settle down into a pillar of white smoke. It bounced once on the landing gear and the roar of the engines cut off.

Betsy began to cry. "He did it. That sumbitch did it."

"Yeah," said Forrest. "You got to admit, the boy has style."

Bobbi McFeeley stepped through the doorway from the observation gallery. Her headset cord dangled over her shoulder. "I just wanted to see it with my own eyes," she said. "I just wanted to see it myself." She shook her head in disbelief.

Forrest said, "What?"

"Count to ten, Forrest. Go ahead. One-one thousand, two-one thousand . . ."

Puzzled, Forrest complied. When he reached ten, Bobbi punched him on the arm and pointed toward the spaceship. "That's all the goddamn fuel he had left. Ten seconds' worth."

*   *   *

They brought a cherry picker up to the side of the ship, and Ned helped ease Levkin out the main hatchway on the leeward side of the ship. Then he sat in the opening with his legs dangling over the side and breathed in the salty air. Off to his right, waves cascaded into the breakwaters of St. Anthony's Bay. He felt odd, as if he were rushing upward. Two days of weightlessness and gravity already seemed a foreign thing. He wondered if he could keep his balance if he tried to walk. He had to get his "land legs" back again before he tried climbing down the ladder on the side of the ship. Let them bring the cherry picker back for him. He had earned it; and it'd be a hell of a note if, after everything that had gone down, he fell off the ladder climbing down and broke his fool neck.

A humvee raced toward him from Admin. Forrest driving a pasty-faced Bonifácio—what was *he* doing out of the clinic?—and in the backseat: Betsy and Lizzie. Before he had to make a decision, Arturo raised the cherry picker back up and Ned climbed aboard. Below, the first humvee raced Levkin off toward the clinic. The cryogenic spray had "burned" Levkin severely even through the suit; and the uncontrolled gyrations had caused him to spew up the meal he had eaten earlier, filling his helmet with globules of . . . Ned did not even want to think about that. Harrowing enough to be the first man to orbit the planet without benefit of spacecraft; to do it with vomit in your face . . .

Ned hoped Levkin would make it through. Time enough later to smack him around for what he had done.

On the ground once more—solid ground, not moving or floating—Ned faced his welcoming committee. Bonifácio looked solemn. Maybe that was the food poisoning, or maybe it was that Ned had gone against Heitor's orders—or maybe it was simply an awareness of how close to the edge of disaster the mission had skirted.

Forrest clapped Ned on the arm and squeezed. "Mighty glad to have you back, son. You are one hell of a pilot."

"Shit, Forrest, it took you this long to figure that out? Where the hell is Heitor? I wanted to see his face, because he didn't think I could pull it off. . . . The odd look that Forrest and Bonifácio exchanged caused Ned's comment to **dry up.** "What happened?"

Forrest spat onto the ground. "Damn right, he didn't think you could pull it off."

Bonifácio explained. "It was Heitor who tampered with the orbit transfer program. Mendoza accused him in the control room. Now he has vanished."

"Heitor?"

Forrest said, "No one else had access to Mendoza's data. With Bonny in the clinic, Heitor had Flight. Seems he improvised, and Mendoza realized no one else could have made the alterations."

"Heitor," Ned said again. "Why?"

De Magalhães shrugged. "Who can say. The man was a gambler. He was deeply in debt. Perhaps someone offered to buy him out of it. . . ."

Forrest leaned close to Ned's ear. "And it's a damn small island to vanish on." Ned decided that, if he caught Mendoza picking his teeth, he would keep his own counsel.

Forrest guided him around to the humvee, where Betsy and Lizzie sat. Betsy had not gotten out. Lizzie jumped up and down in her seat, clapping her hands. "I saw you land the spaceship, Daddy! I saw you land!" Ned reached out his arms and Lizzie jumped into them. Ned spun her around.

"Did you like the show?"

"It was fun!"

Betsy climbed out of the humvee and Ned lowered Lizzie to the ground. He waited. Betsy faced him for a moment; then, she sent a stinging slap across his left cheek. "That's for doing what you did," she said. A moment later, she had wrapped both her arms around his neck. "And so is this." She pressed her face into his and kissed him, long and hard.

Ned knew finally that she did love him. The slap had proven it, not the kiss. Only someone you love can make you so angry and afraid.

Even before John E. Put down his cellular phone, Mariesa knew from his broad smile that the news was going to be good. When he told her, she closed her eyes and said, "We did it, Keith. Oh, we did it."

The brandy had made him a bit tipsy, Cyrus Attwood decided. Which meant he ought to be damned careful what he said, and to whom. He sat in a deep, leather-upholstered chair and watched young Bullock with half-lidded eyes. I'm doing it all for you, he thought. You deserve a future that is stable and predictable. Not the chaos; not the dog-eat-dog world that *she* would introduce.

"She really managed to pull it off," his nephew said, shaking his head. "Lady Luck sure smiled on her today, wouldn't you say, Uncle Cyrus?"

Cyrus placed his snifter on the end table for Stepan to collect and the club steward, ever vigilant, had swooped past and taken it almost before Cyrus had relinquished his grip. "Luck, indeed," he replied. "But luck runs out, sooner or later. For everyone."

The Measure of Our Torment (II)

The rusted old car was a bastard. Literally. The front end was a Caddy and the back end was a Chrysler. The welds where the two bodies were joined stood out lumpy against the surface. The paint had not taken uniformly, so front and back were different shades of tan. A little of this and a little of that, scrounged from the junkyards, salvaged from wrecks, stolen from parts stores; bolted, welded, epoxied, and wired together. But it worked. The engine ran ragged and it shifted like a bitch; but it worked.

Too bad Stork couldn't have put some shocks in while he was at it, Azim thought as he and Jo-jo and Zipper jounced through another of the potholes that last winter had given the city streets. Not patched yet, not even here on the good side of town. Wessex Avenue was two lanes east and two lanes west with a lane in the middle for turning. The neighborhood looked wrong to Azim, sinister. The houses lurked behind rows of trees and set back from the roads by broad green lawns. No sidewalks! It was like an alien planet in those stories they had read in school. It was like he wasn't even in a city, at all.

Sun goes down, charlie goes in. Not many people outside walking. Those who were turned and stared at the car as it drove past. White faces. Asian faces. A black man jogging along the roadside in an expensive-looking green and gold track suit. *Hey, black boys, what you be doing here?*

A good question, Azim thought, but not one Zipper had answered.

In Eastport, people out on stoops, people out hanging. Were no gangs here on the west side, just amateur, talk-tough, wear-the-hat backward, spoiled white kids; but people huddled indoors anyways.

They pulled up to the red light where Wessex Avenue crossed Maple Grove. Zipper swatted Jo-jo on the arm and pointed. "See those stores other side? Pull in there."

Jo-jo nodded and waited for the light to change. Azim leaned forward between the two in the front seats. "Why are we stopping here?" he asked. The strip mall featured a deli, a bakery, a chink takeout, a wop takeout, a franchise chicken takeout. . . . Didn't whitey do nothing but eat out?

" 'Cause I be thirsty," Zipper said.

Shit, thought Azim, we try lifting here, it's a long drive back to Eastport. Cops answered calls on the west side. Especially white calls on black kids. And he had promised Fatima he would take her to the party tonight at the white woman's mansion, where the spacemen would be. That Doobwah. And maybe Calhoun. Azim wouldn't mind meeting Calhoun.

The light changed and Jo-jo took them across the intersection and parked against the blank brick wall that made one side of the In-and-Out convenience store. The bricks were spray-painted and the handset on the public telephone was ripped off, leaving the armored cable dangling loose, so some things were just like back in the 'hood.

The stores were just beginning to light up. The streetlamp bleached the color from everything: clothes, car, even skin, leaving everything a pale, pasty gray. Car doors slammed, one-two-three. Zipper led them inside the In-and-Out and down the side aisle to the soda case in the rear. He pulled out three cans of Coke and tossed one to Jo-jo and one to Azim. Jo-jo grinned. "Thanks, Zip."

They popped the tops and poured the soda down their throats as they walked toward the counter in the front, where a pudgy-faced Indo waited with a scowl. Azim dug in his jeans for a dollar. Zipper said, "This be my treat."

At the counter, the Indo looked them over like he did not have a chocolate face himself. Damned Indo-Paks looked down their noses at blacks when they were people of color, too. It made no sense to Azim. No sense, at all.

"Three dollars, boys," said the man.

Zipper banged his soda can on the counter. "Who you calling 'boys'?"

The Indian looked surprised and blinked his eyes. Then he shrugged. "Just pay and leave. I want no trouble here."

"We not good enough for you?" Zipper demanded. "You dissin' us?" Zipper reached inside his jacket and pulled out Stork's nine. He pointed the automatic pistol straight-armed into the Indian's face. "How about you give us what you got in that cash register, man?"

The manager held both his hands up. "Do not make trouble," he singsonged.

"Then give us your money!"

Jo-jo sucked in his breath. "Dude!"

"Zipper," said Azim, laying a hand on Zipper's shoulder, "this ain't smart."

Zipper supported the gun with both hands. He shrugged off Azim's hand. "So maybe I not so smart as you," he said with a kind of bark. "You gots to decide who you be, Azim. You be sucking up to that Egbo like a good house nigger. You buy into that white-ass spaceman shit, I don't know who you are anymore."

The manager piled money on the counter. Zipper told Jo-jo to stuff it in his pockets. Azim looked out the window, down the aisles of the store, but there was no one else there. Then he saw the telephone in back of the counter. It had a row of buttons, and one of the buttons was lit up, which meant that someone in the back of the store was on the phone right now calling the cops.

"Zipper, let's get the hell out. Now!"

"What, you scared? The high and mighty Azim scared? Hey, he showing us respect now. Look at him."

"Zipper, the telephone!"

Zipper and the store manager both looked and the smile on Zipper's face grew wider. When turned to Azim, his eyes were wide and glassy and his grin was fixed. "So what?" he said. Then he looked over the counter and, without a moment's pause, shot the manager twice. The nine danced in his fist.

The sound hammered in Azim's ears. He saw how Zipper's arms jerked up and to the right. He saw the bright red blood fountain on the man's chest. It spattered Azim on the face and shirt and he jumped away. The manager, with a dazed look, slumped against the stool, his white apron turning crimson.

"You crazy, man?" Azim practically shouted.

Zipper took aim and Azim grabbed his arm just as he fired a third time. The third bullet shattered the man's jaw in a spray of blood and bone. Zipper tugged his arm from Azim's grip. "Now you got no choice."

"Baba! Baba!"

The three of them turned at the shriek and saw the girl at the stockroom door with her hands raised to her face. "Baba!" she screamed. Azim recognized her from the white school. Shit, oh shit . . .

And Zipper saw it, too. "She knows us, man." He raised the gun again. The girl—Tanu? Pandy? Azim did not even know her name—had eyes only for the counter and the blood. She didn't even notice the gun. Azim grabbed Zipper by the arm and pushed it up so the fourth shot buried itself in the ceiling. A light shattered and broken glass rained down. Another kid, with long black hair tied into a ponytail, reached out of the stockroom and yanked the screaming girl back in. The door slammed, and even from across the room Azim could hear the bolt clack into place. Zipper sent a fifth shot into the refrigerated cabinets. Maybe it went all the way through, into the stockroom behind. Maybe it hit the girl.

The whoop-whoop of sirens in the distance, coming closer. Azim shouted, "Let's go!" He had to drag Zipper and Jo-jo both stumbling out the door into the parking lot. The noise had drawn curious people from the other stores. They saw Azim. They saw the nine. Screams, and people running, dragging kids. Cars chirping as remote locks were triggered. Scrambling. Scrambling. Get away! Get the hell away from here! Two cars backed out and crunched each other's rear fenders. A Toronado and a Volvo. Zipper laughed. He trotted behind Azim and Jo-jo as they ran for their own car.

"Get in," said Azim.

"No," said Zipper.

"Get in! You stay here, you dead!"

"Yeah, well, so what? Then it's over."

"You crazy, man?" But in a sudden vision of icy clarity, Azim saw that he was. Zip's eyes had the forever look and his grin might as well have been painted on. Foam speckled the corners of his mouth. Zipper wanted a woman; the woman's name was Death.

Azim pushed Jo-jo into the passenger seat and then ran around to the driver's door. The sirens sounded like swooping eagles. As Azim slammed the door, he saw the creature that had been his homey shove another clip into the nine. Stork was going to be really pissed when he didn't get his gun back.

"There's no turning white, Azim," Zipper told him. "They got you on videotape now. You and me, robbing the store, wasting the Indo. Now you got to be who you got to be." He laughed again and gave a shout. "So, I see you in hell, Azim. . . ." He turned away and faced down Maple Grove, toward the sirens, holding the gun double-handed at his crotch.

Azim pushed the car into gear and laid rubber onto Wessex. His mind was ice, cold and clear. The pigs would radio for help, and while there would be some initial confusion—was it a Caddy or a Chrysler, ma'am?—they would have this car made.

Jo-jo was pulling money out of his jacket and fanning it.

"Look at this, Azim. Look at this."

Mostly singles and fives, Azim saw. Some tens and twenties. Hardly enough to bother for. Hardly worth a life, even an Indo's life. Zipper had gone into the store wanting what had happened. It had been his plan all along, to bring them here, to bring Azim to this. Damn him. Damn him! There had been sunlight. Azim had seen it. Egbo had shown him. Now the shades were drawn for good.

"Throw that shit out the window," he shouted. Jo-jo jerked and looked astonished.

"Throw it out?"

"Toss it!"

Looking confused, Jo-jo threw a handful of bills out the window, but he stuffed the rest back in his pocket. Azim said nothing. It wan't much; but it was more money than the boy had ever seen in one lump. Azim cut right at the next corner and went north three blocks, then took Northern Avenue back the way they had come. Let the cops find the cash. It would point them west, for a while. Maybe long enough to ditch the car and disappear.

Disappear for good. Could never go back. They had him on the store cameras. The girl knew him. He thought the white boy with the ponytail was from Witherspoon, too. The cops would be waiting for him at home. They'd tell Mama what he done, and Mama lose her last boy, now, too.

He'd never see Mama again. He knew that. Never see Fatima again, either; but women you find everywhere. You only got one mama.

"Are we going back to pick up Zipper?" Jo-jo asked.

Azim looked at him. Jo-jo didn't get it. Jo-jo never thought five minutes ahead of what was going down. Tomorrow might as well be another country. And where had he ever gotten thoughts like that? So, damn Egbo, too, for waking whatever it was that had been asleep in his brain. Never miss what you never had.

"You crying, Azim?"

Yes, there were tears there. His cheeks grew hot and he snapped at Jo-jo. "Zipper dead." Then, more gently, because

Jo-jo was Jo-jo, "He stay back and wait for the pigs so we get away." *If he lasted that long.* The gook coming out of his restaurant just as they peeled away . . . Had that been a shotgun in his hands?

"Oh, man . . ." Was that regret or envy in Jo-jo's voice? Or both. "Just like that poem we read. Hooray-shush."

"No. Not like that poem! Those Romans, they protecting their 'hood from . . ." Azim's hands were fists wrapped around the steering wheel. ". . . from people coming to rob them."

Jo-jo said nothing for a while. Azim spotted an A&P parking lot. Find a car there where the people just went in the store. Hotwire it, be gone. Ditch the Storkmobile somewheres else . . . Azim's mind was racing like an engine. Forming plans, searching out chances. He knew a guy did phony IDs. . . .

"We gots to hide, don't we, Azim?"

Azim looked at him, surprised the boy had reasoned that out. He nodded.

"How long?"

Azim shook his head. "I take care of you. Just you and me now, Jo-jo. Just you and me."

14.

What If the Bird Does Not Sing?

The reception at Silverpond was a bittersweet affair, and Mariesa detected a somber and reflective undertone beneath the upbeat chatter. It was not only that the orbital test flight had been a near-disaster—her fault; oh, her fault, for having pushed too hard and too fast; and João's, for being pushable. Ned had brought it off, against the odds; had saved, whether he knew it or not, the program itself, and with it, perhaps, the world. It was not only that some were missing from the ranks. Keith looked on from wherever he had gone (and he had gone somewhere, she was sure, even if she was no longer sure where that somewhere lay). It was not even that powerful forces were marshaling against her. The sabotage on the island; the sniping from diehards in NASA and elsewhere; the naysayers seizing on fashionable causes as excuses for obstruction. Cyrus Attwood and his allies lurking in the markets . . .

(Could Cyrus really have sent the man with the knife, or suborned the debt-ridden Heitor Carneiro; or—perhaps—even have financed the attack on the ram? Crusty, old, comfortable

Cyrus? It hardly seemed possible. Was the man mad?)

No, there was something else besides all that, and she wasn't quite sure she could name it. A sense that among the gains there had been losses. Hidden losses. Things she had sacrificed precisely to make those gains. Had that been what Keith had meant when he had warned her—very nearly his last words—that "the best things are lost in victory"?

But it was not victory; not yet. It was only not defeat.

Perhaps that was the reason for the underlying sadness that she felt; that only a handful of those present knew how much more lay ahead, and that the most desperate battles were yet to be joined.

Ned DuBois was the center of attention, which was only as it should be. He smiled his way through the press of well-wishers crowding the mansion at Silverpond, stopping every few feet when yet another round-eyed guest asked breathlessly for a recounting of those harrowing hours in space. Betsy, entwined tightly to his arm, keeping him firmly anchored to the Earth, and little Lizzie, skipping back and forth between the refreshment tables and blinking back the threat of sleep, effectively warded him from the women who would otherwise have asked for more private narratives.

And perhaps that was as it should be, too.

The guest list was an odd mix, Ned thought as he mingled. Jeweled glitterati and socialites fraternizing with middle-class business managers and rough-edged test pilots and engineers, and with a curious seasoning of teenagers and younger children, apparently flown in from Mentor Academy schools nationwide. Some sort of lottery, Mariesa had told him, based on an essay contest. Some of the guests, young and old alike, were at Silverpond because it was the place to be; some were there to be seen. Some had come to renew old acquaintances, or to celebrate the flight. But a surprising number, Ned learned, had come for no other reason than to lay eyes on Ned DuBois and touch the hem of his garment.

"Hey, Captain DuBois, 'sir.' "

Ned turned at the ironic greeting and saw the gangly,

shaven-headed young man he had met at Thor Machining and later, at the high school. And what were the odds that *this* kid would show up once again in his life? ''Chase,'' he said, slapping the kid's hand in the approved style. *Lottery, my ass.* The fix was in. But what made this kid so special? Or were all the kids invited here special in some sort of way?

He introduced Chase to Betsy and Lizzie. Lizzie stared shyly at the pewter earrings dangling from Chase's earlobes. Chase grinned at her and she ducked her face behind Betsy. Chase laughed.

''You know, Mrs. D,'' he told Betsy, wagging a thumb at Ned, ''this guy is Jenuine Beans.''

Past Chase's shoulder, Ned spied a tall, blond woman in a red evening dress whose low-cut neckline exposed bright, milky-white skin. She was advertising, Ned thought, and had her product positioned for the marketplace. She noticed Ned's regard and paused a moment in her conversation with a black-tuxedoed old gent to wet her cherry lips and trace a matching-hued fingernail idly down the track of her cleavage. Ned gave her a friendly smile. No harm. After all, he would probably never see her again. It never hurt to be friendly.

''I guess being a test pilot is, like, the phattest,'' Chase said, pulling Ned's attention away from the woman.

''Yeah,'' he said. ''It is. There's nothing else like it. But I'll be honest with you. You have to learn to live with fear. Because Death is your copilot and the day you forget it is the day he takes the controls from you.''

Chase stuck a chin out. ''Yeah, well, I'm not afraid.''

Ned put a hand on his shoulder. ''Learn to be. It can save your life.''

At Chase's urging, Ned escorted him around the ballroom and introduced him to the other test pilots. ''Iron Mike'' Krasnarov, ''Senhor Machine,'' who had flown the bird when no one knew shit and had salvaged the very first test flight, after Carneiro had sabotaged the telemetry. Katya Volkovna, the ''Ice Angel,'' first to test the Swoop of Death. ''Batman'' da Silva, who had probed the limits of cross-range maneuverability in a wingless craft. Valery Volkov, "Johnny Danger," who had made an impossible landing in a crippled ship. "Columbine" McFeeley, first woman to fly solo to the edge of space and see the sky turn black with stars. "Cowboy" Calhoun, who had made the incredible half-hour flight to St. Petersburg. Only the hospitalized Levkin, the Human Moon, was absent.

Forrest was the center of a small crowd of his own. "Well, hey," he said when he spied Ned. "If it isn't the man of the hour." He wrapped the arm around Ned's neck. "Second best test pilot in the US of A."

"You're entitled to your opinions, Forrest, however wrong they may be. Forrest, this here is Chase Coughlin. He thinks he may want to be a pilot someday."

Forrest cocked his head. "Test pilot?"

Chase shrugged. "Maybe. I dunno."

"Son, you don't *look* brain-damaged. Maybe you've been hanging around this character too much."

Chase grinned. "Maybe that, too." Forrest squeezed Ned's shoulder once before releasing him.

"Son, if you want to grow up like Ned, you're making a big mistake."

Chase's eyes narrowed, and he said, a little stiffly, "And why's that?"

" 'Cause Ned, here, he never did grow up."

Everyone in the group laughed. Ned said, "Sure, let's pretend I'm not here." *Jesus, this kid really does think I'm a hero. Even if it wouldn't be cool to show it. Great. Now I've got to be some kind of role model.* Betsy touched his arm.

"Lizzie is about dead on her feet," she said. "The butler is going to take us to our room. I'll be back in a few minutes. Try not to get in any trouble in the meantime."

Forrest made a show of studying his watch. "Better hurry then, Bet. This man can get in trouble faster than anyone I know."

When Betsy had left, Ned murmured to Forrest, "Has Kirby Welles tracked down Carneiro yet?"

Forrest shook his head. "Not last I heard. When Mendoza challenged him in Mission Control, Carneiro bolted from the pit with Luis on his heels. According to Bobbi, that Luis moves *fast*."

"Chasing that tanker was a damn-fool thing to do," Ned said. "But I was pissed off . . ." He glanced at Chase and the other kids gathered around and decided they'd heard worse language from each other. ". . . at Levkin because . . ." This time he looked at Forrest.

"Because he's a lousy cook," Forrest said. "Yeah, I know. Go on."

"Well, when he said no, I felt contrary." He shrugged. "João should never have left the choice up to us."

"It was the right choice, Captain DuBois."

Ned turned and found himself face-to-face with Mariesa van Huyten. The curly haired schoolteacher, Fast, was with her, cradling her hand in the crook of his arm in a proprietary fashion. Ned cocked an eyebrow and put on his best crooked grin.

"Why is that, Mariesa? Because it worked out in the end and made us all heroes?"

She shook her head. "No. Because the world needs to learn how to take chances again. The road to success lies between foolhardiness and a timid demand for certainty. But . . . as you say, success does justify many a decision. We have demonstrated feasibility. Investments are beginning to trickle in. McDonnell-Douglas, Lockheed, and a host of smaller firms are setting up competitive ventures. NASA may revive the X-program. For the first time in a very long time, the future looks to be an interesting one." She extended a hand and took his solemnly between both of hers. "Accept the thanks of a grateful company—VHI as well as Daedalus—and, whether they will admit it yet or not, that of the country and of the world."

Effusive praise made him uncomfortable. "I was just doing my job."

Mariesa leaned forward and kissed him on the cheek, and Ned felt himself blush. Ned DuBois *blushing* when a woman kissed him? What was the world coming to? Barry Fast scowled and Ned wondered what the man would do if he were to sweep Mariesa off her feet and plant a big wet one on her lips. Come to think of it, he wondered what Mariesa would do. It was . . . an interesting thought. Something about Mariesa van Huyten's reserve excited him as much as the matter-of-fact sauciness of that waitress in Fortaleza. Not that it mattered. He might not know what Mariesa or Barry Fast would do, but he had a pretty good idea what Betsy would do.

"If it's all the same to you, Mariesa, I'd just as soon have next week off."

"Oh, sure," Forrest said. "Make the rest of us do all the work."

Ned DuBois was a little too good to be true, Barry thought. A little too much of the aw-shucks, gee-whiz, just-doing-my-job manner to him. It had to be a put-on, right? Somehow, Barry thought he would like the man a whole lot more if he bragged openly. And he hadn't missed the way DuBois had given Mariesa the five-second ocular undressing. What was it about men like that that appealed to women? Was it the panache? The style? Certainly not the dependability. Men like that leapt from bed to bed without a second thought.

"Mariesa is on cloud nine tonight," he commented to Brittany van Huyten-Armitage while he waited at the bar in the loggia. Loggia. Barry would have said sun porch, but that wouldn't have been classy. "She's in orbit, and she didn't even need a ship to do it."

Brittany tossed her shoulder-length brunette hair and took a good swallow of a colorful, fruit-infested drink. A Singapore Sling, Barry thought. He preferred his own drinks unadorned with irrelevancies. Whatever it was, Brittany drank like a trooper and liked to flirt. She would have been real popular on the singles-bar circuit, if that had been her scene.

"She always was a little high on space," Tracy Bellingham said. "Back when we were in college together." Tracy was blond, and short where Brittany was tall. The two women were opposite ends of the physical spectrum; though they shared a tan in common. Probably from the same tropical beaches. Barry remembered how Tracy had kissed him at the New Year's Eve party, up in the Roost. An invitation if you wanted one, but full of Plausible Deniability if you took a pass. Her red dress, cut deep in front, was a definite come-on. She wasn't hunting, but she wasn't hiding.

"Not in high school," said Brittany. "Of course, I did not know her very well. She is the oldest cousin, you know, after my brother, Chris. She was several years ahead of me in school. But I never did hear her say 'boo' about space travel until after she had gone to college. I will have to admit . . ." She paused and finished half her Sling in the time it took Barry to accept his own drink from the bartender's outstretched hand. "I will have to admit that her space scheme seems to have worked. Serious investors have subscribed to her latest prospectus, now that they have seen some concrete results. Still and all, it was a terrible risk, and the family shall be keeping a closer eye on affairs from now on."

The bartender finished making Mariesa's Manhattan and passed it to Barry. "Well," said Barry, saluting with the glass, "I've got to go. It's been nice talking to you."

Brittany's lips curled in amusement. "Yes. I suspect I shall be seeing more of you."

Tracy went with him to look for Mariesa. Barry found himself a vantage point near the fireplace and scanned the throng. Tracy, with her bright red dress, stood out in a crowd. He imagined Mariesa in a similar, teasingly sultry dress.

"Brittany is always so systematic about her affairs," Tracy said, running her forefinger around the lip of her glass. "She plans each one; studies the candidates carefully and thoroughly before she makes her selection. I only wish she—"

"Sounds damned cold-blooded to me."

Tracy laughed. "Oh, I much prefer Riesey's methods."

Barry gave his companion a suspicious look, but before he could say anything, she pointed toward the foyer. "There she is." A pause. "Something seems amiss."

Barry saw Onwuka Egbo buttoning his topcoat. He exchanged a few words with Mariesa and with Belinda Karr, who each gripped his hand in turn, before he ducked out the open front door. Sykes closed the door after him. The strange, beveled glass in the door caught the light of the chandelier, giving the door an odd, sparkling appearance. Mariesa and Belinda, heads close together in whispered conversation, moved swiftly to the elevator, passing out of Barry's sight.

"I wonder what that was all about?" Barry said. *Something to do with the school.* Otherwise, why Onwuka and Belinda? Egbo had seemed agitated; he had fumbled with his coat buttons. Barry wondered if he ought to follow Mariesa and Belinda. He hadn't been asked, but if it was school business . . .

But it might be other Mentor business. Egbo was "on loan" from a private practice out west. Barry leaned his back against the fireplace mantel and sipped his bourbon. If Mariesa needed him, she knew he was here. He wondered what he ought to do with her Manhattan. Follow Mariesa upstairs? He compromised by sharing it with Tracy, though the drink was a little sweet for his taste.

It was no more than fifteen minutes later that Harriet swooped by, smiled an "excuse me" at Tracy, and hooked her talons into Barry's arm, hauling him off. She took him to a secluded alcove in the passageway that connected the ballroom with the dining room and, placing herself between Barry and freedom, said flatly, "She has gone to her study with that woman."

He thought he might play cute: Who she? But there was only one "she" in Harriet's life and they both knew it. "Do you mean with Dr. Karr? I think they heard some news regarding Mentor."

Harriet's lips thinned into a bloodless line. "Then I would suggest you haul your butt up there."

Vulgarity from the always-proper Mrs. Gorley van Huyten left Barry speechless. She started to turn away, but paused and looked him directly in the eye. "I did not think highly of you, Mr. Fast; not at first."

Really? You could have fooled me. But Barry kept his face composed.

"On second thought, you seem to have your redeeming qualities. Mariesa, of course, could do far better for herself; but, then, she could also do far worse."

"If that was meant to be a compliment, Mrs. van—"

"No, Mr. Fast. I learned a long time ago the value of compliments. Simply the facts, as I see them. I could be wrong. I often have been. I hope I am now. Go upstairs . . . Barry." She turned on her heel and, in a few quick steps, had returned to the ballroom. Barry heard her calling out a deliciously friendly greeting to some dear, dear acquaintance.

Outside, below the dormer window, May color was fading into the green of June, and the busy, sensual opening up giving way to the business of growth. The setting sun, grazing the crest of Skunktown Mountain, highlighted the festive groups chattering on the lawn, spillover from the reception. There was a lawn tennis game in progress. Katya Volkov playing against Steve Matthias, while her husband cheered her on. Sykes had laid the croquet course out with the old carved-wood wickets. A gaggle of young males fluttered hopefully, if futilely, around Bobbi McFeeley while she hammered their balls off the field.

Mariesa turned away from the window. "No, Belinda, don't bother with the lights. The evening sun will do." Belinda Karr tapped the base of the desk lamp with her fingertips, then pulled out the rolling chair and fell into it. She seemed oddly insubstantial to Mariesa, composed of soft, ruddy shadows from the soft light that filtered through the window.

"What shall we do, Mariesa?" she asked plaintively. "We've lost another one."

The pain in her voice was palpable. Mariesa ran her hand down the smooth wood of the window sash. "I doubt that there is much that we can do. Armed robbery? Attempted murder? It is in the hands of the law."

"Lieutenant Burkhardt said it was one of the other youths who pulled the gun. Thomas may have tried to stop him. The videotape is not clear."

"Then why did he run?"

For a moment, Belinda seemed at a loss. Then she said, "Mariesa, that is a most foolish question."

Mariesa sighed and, turning, pulled the window shut. The cries and happy laughter from below were cut off abruptly.

"Onwuka saw great promise in the boy," Belinda said.

Mariesa faced her. "Not all promises are kept. We lose prospects every year. A junior at Singley, Goerig and Wu was killed in an automobile accident two months ago; and the Parnell School in Seattle lost a—"

"This is different. We could have saved Thomas, if we had done more."

"*Done what*, Belinda? We are not omnipotent."

"I don't know." She looked away. "Something."

"And what of the others? Jenny Ribbon vanished God knows where. The Frazetti girl and her family swallowed up by the witness-protection program. And Tanuja Pandya . . . we may lose her, too. Could we have saved all of them, if we had 'done something'?"

Belinda put on her stubborn face. "Yes, if we had known."

"We are not omniscient, either. Prometheus will survive, regardless."

Belinda struck the desktop with the flat of her hand. "Oh, dear Lord, Riesey. I don't cry over Prometheus. It's the children that matter."

"Everything matters. The children, yes; but Prometheus, too. It was because of Prometheus that we set out to—"

Belinda stood and the chair rolled from beneath her. "No. It. Was. Not." She emphasized each word with a stab of her finger against the desk. "Or have you forgotten that I started Karr Academies long before I ever heard of Prometheus, or you. Sometimes—" She stopped and turned away. "Sometimes I wish I never had."

"Heard of Prometheus," Mariesa asked quietly, "or of me?" Belinda Karr shook her head and did not answer. "We each had a need, Belinda," Mariesa continued. "You needed to inspire your children with a positive future, something that would motivate them. I needed a generation of motivated youth, who would grow up and lead Prometheus to its fruition. Is it so terrible that our two needs satisfied one another so well? Or will you tell me now that you never sat in this very room and confessed your dreams to me?"

After a moment of strained silence, Belinda said, "Onwuka will contact us as soon as he learns more."

"This has hit him pretty hard."

Belinda pushed the chair back under the desk and arranged it carefully. She ran her hands back and forth across the chair back. "Yes."

"Keep me informed. Despite what you think, I do care."

"Yes. In an abstract sort of way."

Mariesa watched her go. Belinda paused once and looked back before stepping into the elevator alcove. When she was gone, Mariesa turned and stared out the window, not at the celebrating crowd that had spilled out onto the lawn, but at the cruel stars that pocked the heavens like a shotgun blast.

"I think I may hate you."

The voice was thin, reedy and high-pitched by a tightening of the throat. Mariesa recognized it before she even turned.

"Styx. I had not realized you had come up here."

The stick-thin, black-sheathed girl stepped out of the doorway that led into the darkened observatory. Her arms were held stiff at her sides; her hands were balled into fists. "I heard everything."

"You came up here seeking inspiration for a poem, no doubt. What is it you are working on?"

"I TRUSTED YOU!"

Mariesa turned away so she would not have to look into the hurt she saw in Roberta's eyes. "You did not hear anything. You do not know everything."

"Because I'm just a kid, right?"

"Because you have not lived with what I have lived with for as many years as I have." And had it made her just a little bit crazy, just a little bit monomaniacal on the subject?

"You are brainwashing us!"

She turned back to Styx and saw the tears racing down her cheeks; like comets, leaving trails behind them. "I would rather say that I have a vision to share."

"What right do you have to force that vision on us?"

"What right does anyone? Would you rather be fed visions of Hollywood and music videos and fashion statements? Or visions of apocalyptic disaster? If I've fed you hope rather than banality or despair, is that so terrible?'' She took a step forward with her arm held out, but Styx skipped a step backward.

''I thought you cared about me. I thought you were the only one who did.''

Slowly, Mariesa's hand dropped and hung limply by her side. ''I do care about you, Styx.''

''You want to use me. You want to play with my head, so I'll write *your* poems, instead of *mine*. If you want them so badly, why don't you get your old geezer friend to write them?''

It was odd. Until Styx had spoke, she had forgotten that Keith had died. ''He . . . passed away last week.''

She saw that jarred the girl, but steel whelmed up in her eyes—molten steel, shimmering and sparkling and pouring forth—and she said, ''Well, then, I guess you can't *use* him anymore.'' The words were blades. They cut.

The elevator hummed and the door slid open. Styx turned and bolted for the alcove, nearly colliding with Barry Fast as he stepped into view. Mariesa heard the cage door crash shut and the sound of a fist pounding the buttons.

Barry turned, frowning. ''What the hell happened up here? First Belinda runs me down getting off on the first floor; then the Carson girl does the same thing getting on.'' His tentative grin faded. ''It's something serious, isn't it?''

Mariesa felt a numb heaviness in her limbs. ''It is a long and complex story, Barry.''

He stepped close to her and took her hands in his. ''I have time.''

She shook her head. ''Promise that, if I tell you, you will not run off on me, too.''

''Hey . . .'' He pulled her to him and wrapped his arms around her. A comforting embrace, not a romantic one. *He knows how to listen*, Keith had said. ''Running off is not Barry's style,'' he said with an odd twist to his words.

Mariesa buried her face against his chest to smother the sob she felt welling up. ''I think I may have lost a daughter.''

"What?"

She tugged herself loose and flew to the window, cupping her hands around her eyes and peering through the glass. Below, leaving a wake in the milling guests, the young girl fled. Black, nearly invisible in the deepening evening shadows; flashes of white that were hands and face. "What if the bird does not sing?" Mariesa whispered.

"What was that?" asked Barry. "I didn't hear."

"What if the bird does not sing?" Mariesa said again, more clearly.

"The question from the Benchmark Test. One of the personality classifiers. I've never understood where that comes from."

Mariesa turned and faced him. It took every bit of strength in her to remind herself that Styx did not matter in the long-term scheme of things. That even she herself did not matter. Only the Goal. Always the Goal.

Asteroid. Comet. It was only a matter of time. Next millennium, Next century. Next year. It did not matter. *"You shall know neither the day nor the hour."* Earth had to be ready.

Don't let the Goal eat you up, Belinda had warned her.

If the Goal was to save the world, did it really matter if a few lives were ruined in the bargain, even her own?

Keith had thought so.

"There were three great warlords in medieval Japan," she said, "who vied with each other to unify the country. Nobunaga, Hideyoshi, and Ieyasu. Three very different men who all had the same vision." It occurred to her that the same could be said of any of them. Of the Prometheus team, the pilots, the teachers, Belinda's kids, everyone. "There is a poem about them, one that every Japanese schoolchild knows."

"How does it go?"

A deep breath failed to calm her.

> *"What if the bird will not sing?*
> *Nobunaga answers, 'Kill it!'*
> *Hideyoshi answers, 'Make it* want *to sing.'"*

She paused, thinking of Styx, thinking of the betrayal she had seen in the girl's eyes.

"And what does Ieyasu say?" prompted Barry.

Mariesa turned and stared out the window at the night into which Styx had vanished.

"*Wait.*"

Part 3

SHOOTING STAR
(AD 2007)

INTERLUDE:

Prodigals

The gun platform whispered five feet above ground level, if there was such a thing as "ground level" in the tangled, watery maze of Whiteoak Swamp. Gunnery Sergeant Thomas A. Monroe took it down to the deck, just above the sluggish waters. The lift rotors kicked up the spray underneath; while bald cypress and sweetgum decked with Spanish moss closed in overhead, cutting off the sunlight. Monroe clicked in the IR enhancement, and the undergrowth glowed in the virtual light on his helmet visor. The brackish water beneath him whorled from the ground effect. He floated through the swamp on a cloud of mist, through muck and water, and trees rising straight out of the water itself, as if they had gone wading into the sea.

The lift rotors were the special, quiet kind. "Hushprops," they were called. The blade surfaces were covered with millions of micron-length cantilever beams that continually adjusted the profile to counteract air turbulence. MEMS, they were called—microelectromechanical systems. Developed originally for noise suppression on helicopters and the big jump jets, the smart blades enabled Monroe to creep through the swamp without much more than a hum. A good idea, when you didn't know how near the enemy was.

Somewhere close by, that was all he knew. It was his job to find them.

He went to hover and upped the gain on his audio, listening up and down the frequencies for some sign of the enemy. He caught a snippet of music from a distant radio station. Otherwise, hissing silence. He had been quartering the swamp for several hours, searching for some sign of the enemy. The book said you grounded at this point and activated the camouflage MEMS canopy to save on the fuel cells while you e-searched; but there was damn little ground in sight, which meant the book needed another chapter. He ran his eyes along the top and bottom edges of his helmet visor, drinking in his platform's status. Fuel-cell loads, ammo levels, platform attitude and heading. Everything was there in pale, glowing graphs. Another hour before he'd have to stop and drink sunlight for a field recharge. Not much sun down here under the canopy.

"... raack i ar ayhew atta dock ..."

There! Someone sending in black code, and their ECM had faltered for a moment. Not friendly forces, or his onboard would have recognized the e-code. The computer opened a map window on his visor display, and gave him a bearing on the intercept. Ten o'clock, relative; one-twenty-seven, true. A twitch of his finger sent a black query to the 24 in GEO and the bounce-back superimposed his true position on the map.

According to the map, the bearing line from his location intersected an allegedly solid island at fifty yards. Monroe rubbed mental hands together.

Gotcha!

He black-coded a message to the other five platforms in his squad, and their responses appeared as red icons on the map. Monroe took his squad leader's wand and touched the icon for Sears's platform, then the position he wanted Sears to take up. That blocked one possible escape route, down the Trent to the enemy beachhead. Quickly, he positioned Miller,

LeVan, and the rest of the squad, bracketing the supposed enemy command post. Numbers appeared beside each icon, as his squadmates estimated the time to reach their positions.

Five minutes, max.

Monroe guided his own platform down a bayou that wandered off in the heading he needed. The visor map kept him oriented toward the enemy position. If his guess was right about the intercepted signal. Two problems with scouting in swamps, he reflected. Number one: finding things. Number two: getting found. If he ever lost contact with the 24, he didn't know how he'd ever get his platform out of the cypress thickets.

His radio search flagged another fragment of signal. This one, the high-pitched whine and "frying bacon" sound of two processors handshaking. That sort of signal was narrowcast, which meant he was probably on line-of-sight between the command post and one of its pickets.

Great. So he had to watch his rear, too. He touched his throat mike. "Red Thumb to Red Hand. Condition gladiola. End." Otherwise, he maintained radio silence. He guided his platform toward the edge of the channel to take advantage of the overgrowth there. The cameras on the platform's underbelly sent a continual signal to the MEMS array on his canopy, repro-ing a video of the ground beneath him. Not that visual concealment would hide his IR signature if a patrol picket cruised by. His hushprops ran quiet enough, but they dumped a shitload of heat into the air, so he wasn't exactly stealthed to the max.

He stole another glance at his power graph. Good thing the platform was mostly made of "smoke." You couldn't quite tuck it under your arm and walk around with it, but its weight came mostly from the Gatling on the prow and surface-surface birds racked on either side. You didn't need as much power to lift and move solid smoke as you did for more conventional materials.

Through a gap in the tapestry of moss he spied the enemy command center. Three swamp boats drawn up on an island in a side channel. Camouflage netting overhead. A half-dozen men and women bent over equipment. Three human guards watching the approaches from up-and downstream and another side channel. Three others wearing VR helmets, probably e-moting the pickets.

Monroe hovered at the edge of the main channel, until the rest of Red Hand checked in. He gave them all a peek video freeze of the camp. Horace Lee—one of his ancestors had been named Lighthorse, of all things!—had a visual fix, too, from upstream on the side channel, two o'clock from Monroe's position. The computer integrated the two views and mocked a holo for them on the screen. Monroe studied it for a moment, then made assignments with his wand. Picketers first. Then boats. Then mop-up.

Some of the comm, brief though it was, must have leaked through their ECM screen, because Monroe saw one of the VR picketers on the island shout and the enemy command center burst into sudden action. Boat handlers ran for the beached swamp boats and started their fans. One of the human guards ran forward into the stream up to his calves and scanned the farther shore, probably hunting for Jim Groff's position.

Shit, thought Monroe. "Red Hand, on my mark." He gave one of his surface-surface birds a look at the nearest swamp boat.

There it is, baby. Don't forget. The birds had brains the size of a pea, though what with the magswitches and all, that pea was smarter than a lot of Monroe's mess mates. "Three, two, one, mark!"

The platform bucked as the first missile launched. Before it had reached its target, he had given the second missile a look at the VR control center and sent it along behind.

The first salvo struck; his own and three of his squadmates'. "Bareface" Miller, down the main channel to his right, did not have line-of-sight and was sweeping for pickets. A bright billow of red smoke erupted among the boats and the communications gear. The cadre there began to cough and rub their eyes. One of the VR operators tore her helmet off and threw it to the ground. That would cost her demerits come debrief back at Lejune. Monroe grinned as he imagined the cussing that must be going on among Blue Heron squad.

An insistent finger tapping on his shoulder broke his concentration.

Monroe put the platform into autohover and unstrapped his own VR helmet. Whiteoak Swamp vanished, replaced by Red Company headquarters and Lieutenant Flynn. "Good work, Gunny," the lieutenant said. "The judges ruled it a clean sweep. Turn your platform over to Transport Squad and let them fly it out of the swamp. You and I have a date with the colonel back at Lejune, 'at our convenience,' by which he means 'at his convenience.' There's just enough time to skimmy back and clean up."

Monroe waited until the control link transferred; then he shut down his board. He exchanged high fives with Sears and the rest of his squad, and followed the lieutenant out of the tent into the bright North Carolina sun. Katydids scolded them and fled from their passing.

The humthree, a modified Gray Ghost with smoked body and hushprop lifters, seemed to float in its parking stall; but the lieutenant kept it on its rubbers and took the dirt road back to the camp. Monroe, who had spent the day coasting through the air by remote, shoved his boonie over his face and leaned back in the seat, enduring the bouncing and the jarring.

Thomas Monroe stood before the mirror in his quarters, the razor in his hand and his face still half covered with shaving lather. A mission, the lieutenant had said during the drive; but what mission, he did not know. B Company—and Red Hand, in particular—had been selected by higher-ups to rehearse tactics. Word up, Monroe had told him. Best damn squad in the Fifth Marines. Best in the Corps.

He grinned at his reflection. Commandant up there in Washington picked us out his own self. Damn, it felt good to be the best! Felt good to *belong*.

The smile faltered momentarily. Thomas Albert Monroe belonged. He had "belonged" going on seven years, now. But

Thomas Albert Monroe was a lie, and sometimes when he looked at his own reflection, Monroe saw only the face of Azim Thomas, and Azim Thomas didn't belong nowhere.

The inquiry came over the Net, as most of them did these days; but it was addressed to "Crackman," and there had not been so many of those since he had gone mostly legitimate.

S. James Poole, computer-security consultant, was in high demand and low supply, which made his price very dear, indeed. Banks sought him out; and confidential agencies. Even the government had used him several times, though he stayed shy of intelligence work. Business was good, because everyone wanted to know what everyone else knew, and everyone wanted to stop everyone else from knowing what they knew. Business was good enough that no one ever wondered if it accounted entirely for his wealth.

Partly, that was because a large chunk of his wealth sat in Switzerland and the Caymans under a variety of pseudonyms. Partly, that was because he had invested in the Aurora Corporation at a time when fractional ballistic transportation was still a topic for late-night comedians. The stock had been cheaper than a politician's vote, but it had split five times since then—the only bright spot in the long, sluggish, turn-of-the-century recession. And Jimmy had seen a step further and invested in interstate methane pipelines. Aurora, Daedalus, and the rest had to get their hydrogen from somewhere, and distilling methane was still cheaper than cracking seawater.

For now. Jimmy had heard rumors about aerogel separators . . .

And partly—and this was the part he never talked about, even to his other friends on the Net—Jimmy had seen the goldmine in the fourth decimal place. The computer programs that the banks used to calculate compound interest cycled daily, but they did not round the numbers off to the nearest cent until it was monthly statement time. So Jimmy had cracked security and hacked a knowbot and skimmed off everything after the fourth decimal place from every account.

A few hundredths of a cent a day did not sound like much.

But there were a lot of days. And a lot of accounts. And a lot of banks.

And every time a client hired him, Jimmy gained access to a new system, learned its gateways and back alleys, built himself trapdoors. Today, from his own den, he could go *virtually* anywhere in the world.

Poole grinned at his own pun while he studied the request from "Bee-bee." A typical outlaw hack. Someone wanted to splice a logic bomb into a software package. The bomb was supposed to be transparent to test software. (Difficult, but not impossible, if the test software lived in the same system as the target program. One way was to infiltrate the test software itself and poke out an eye.) The bomb was supposed to bang only when the program realized. Dormancy was a snap.

The big challenge was to comprehend the target software well enough to engineer the appropriate patch. Any damn-fool amateur could sabotage a system; it took a pro to do it to spec.

Poole slouched in his black, high-backed hammock-chair while he studied the terms and conditions. The promised fee was generous. "Crackman" was top of the line in that line of work. The stumbling block, as always, was enforcement of the contract. He could not exactly sue in court for payment. At no time did he consider the return address as genuine. He drummed his fingers on the padded mouse pad built into his chair's armrest. Arranged in a semicircle around his seat were stacks of monitors, processors, modems, scanners . . . everything the working stiff needed. Were it not for the wretched necessity to eat and sleep and evacuate, he could spend his life in this chair.

On two of the monitors, knowbots were marching to and fro like busy ants, finding and assembling information for his clients from target systems. Both were legal datassemblies—from public or user-fee dee-bees. His clients could have conducted the search themselves; but like tenderfeet edging into the wilderness, they needed a frontier guide, an electronic Hawkeye to blaze trail for them. Some people still could not program their VCRs.

A third monitor tracked a worm he was following. It was

not his worm, but it was a very good worm, and Poole very much admired it. He had—as yet—discovered neither who had written it nor for what purpose.

"Roberta," he said.

"Yes, lord and master." He had synthesized the op-system's voice himself, using a world-class mixer and his own fantasies. It was a soft voice, mellow, yet with a hard, too-wise edge. Sometimes, when he closed his eyes, he could even imagine the face to which the voice belonged. Sometimes, running a slightly different persona, he had the vox say things to him that he had long ago realized he would never hear from female lips.

Humans. Who needed them, anyway?

"List. 'Personae.' File. 'Bond.' Execute." Voxer syntax was still bogged down in a reverse Polish algebra, but no one had figured out how to make it more natural and still preserve precision. Poole had tried it once himself, using a simulated neural net, and had only succeeded in getting into a semantic debate with his own hardware. Easier for humans to learn to speak logically.

The list of personae he used for clandestine inquiries appeared on the main screen. He *never* moused the Net in his own persona, even legitimate searches, and he always inserted a phantom system between the persona and his own face. He had not become as good as he had by doing things off-the-cuff or carelessly. The methodical approach might be maddeningly slow to some, but it produced many results and few mistakes. He finally settled on "Tulio Gucci."

After he had defined the search parameters—name of search object, qualities of search object, geographical nexus, time depth, and so on down the menu—he gave the persona a kiss [Keep it Simple, Stupid.] and sent him on his way. "Tulio" would construct the knowbot, apparently on a system it would choose at random from the Net, and send the information back through a series of clones and dead drops.

After giving the matter additional thought, Poole called up "Igor" and sent him on a different search. Jimmy hated working for anonymous clients. He wanted to know who was behind "Bee-bee" and the mail-drop return address. Knowing might mean nothing; or it might mean that "Crackman" could adjust the fee schedule.

Meanwhile, Jimmy had legitimate clients to service.

"Tulio" reported back within a half hour, but Poole did not read the report until the next morning, over a stack of toaster waffles soggy with maple syrup. Poole did not waste many hours of his life on nonessentials, and meals were one of those. Zip-and-nuke and be done with it. He had been overweight since high school—and how those bastards had mocked him! [No one mocked him now, but it would be the work of an afternoon to destroy each and every one of those ~~bastards~~ creeps—finances, reputations. Humiliate them with false records, morphed photographs. Let them feel how he had felt all those times they had laughed or picked on him.]

The terminal on his breakfast table was fastened to a lazy Susan. He turned it to angle off the glare from the morning sun streaming through the kitchen window. Sunlight was a nuisance, too. . . .

"Tulio" had found several encrypted files at the address his client had given him. Black code. Be a ~~bitch~~ hassle to decrypt those. But there were clear files, as well.

Poole sucked on the tines of his fork while he studied the feedback. The maple syrup dripped on his chin and hands. The address belonged to an Aurora Transport system that suckled on the Net. A smart system, guarded with mice. "Tulio" had mousetrapped several and brought their code back for autopsy. Live and learn, thought Poole; or you don't live long. "Tulio" had also brought back an infection. It had fried the host system "Tulio" had pirated as a base of ops. Too bad, but that's why "Crackman" always used someone else's system to filter viruses.

He scrolled through the pirated files, looking for some sense of the size, shape, and purpose of his target. That was the only way to cost the job, and you had to cost the job to know if the fee was reasonable. No point spending more money hacking than the hack would earn. Unless it was a real bean hack.

The fee his anonymous client had waved at him would have seemed princely only five years ago, but it was just walking-around money now.

A picture gradually emerged from the memos and reports. A neural net/expert program. Aurora was apparently forecasting traffic control problems down the line; and Client wanted that control to fail, big time.

It would be quite a challenge just to *find* the program. No way was Aurora herbie enough to let that code anywhere near a gateway, let alone a dark alley. He would have to send out a worm that could slip into an Aurora system—any Aurora system—and hide in the shadows until it could clone itself elsewhere. Sooner or later, one of the clones would find the system where the target lived and send word back into the Net. He could use the old Beaumont Worm as his template. There were safeguards against it nowadays, but it never hurt to study the classics.

Amid all the corpo-jargon and cover-ass in the memos, he stumbled across the one additional infobit that made the whole hack just too delicious to pass up. It was the most beautiful joke on everyone involved, Aurora, Client, and Jimmy himself.

Acting through a dummy corporate front, Aurora had subcontracted Poole sEcurity Consultants to write the protection for the Target.

It was wonderful! It was delicious! Client wanted him to crack a safe for which the owner had hired him to write the combination! Already, he could see three different ways to hack it. His fingers danced over the keyboard [no hunt-n-pecker, he!] typing out an acceptance, which he threw down a rabbit hole in the E-mail. This would be the easiest hundred grand he ever made.

Well, not quite. There was a little matter of professional pride, too. He always did his best for a client, no matter what. And now two clients had, unknowingly, hired him to battle himself. The best against the best! Like playing both sides of the chessboard. He would be the irresistible force! He would be the immovable object! Sabotage the traffic control program *and* protect it from sabotage! Somehow, he would satisfy *both* contracts.

He had no idea how; but that was a detail.

"Igor" never did come back; and that worried him. A lot.

When the mist came off the Vltava, as it did most spring mornings, the Castle on the heights across the river seemed to float in the air above the clouds. Roberta Carson stirred on her bed, propped herself up on her elbows, and studied the sight through the frame of the open window. The Castle walls, pink in the morning sunshine, hovered above the fog that shrouded the flanks of the hill. A lone falcon circled in the updrafts around the great spire of St. Vitus Cathedral. A horn from the nearby riverfront echoed through the winding, close-in streets of Old Town. Below her window, traffic creaked into life on the cobblestones, three stories down.

> *I see a great city, the prophetess said,*
> *Whose glory will touch the stars . . .*

For three years, Roberta had lived among the American expatriates who infested the side streets of the Old Town of Threshold. Artist, writers, musicians, poets like herself. You got a different angle on life from the East Bank of the Vltava, a more mature and reflective one than was possible on the obsessively material streets of America. There was a greater depth of time here; a scale that put the callow postmodern world into perspective. Threshold was the only city in Europe that war had never torched, a city where a district called *New* Town could be six centuries old. Her former life, her former world, was far, far away.

Sitting up in bed had caused the sheet to drop and gather at her waist. Goose bumps from the chill spring air prickled her flesh, and she folded her arms across her breasts. A reflection of the motion drew her eye to the tall, dingy, ornately framed mirror on the opposite wall of the one-room flat, where she saw . . . *A Parody of Modesty.* She grinned at her reflection and tried a different pose, more classical, breasts exposed but with the hand draped coyly *just so* over her crotch. Then another pose, rather more saucy. Finally, one that was outright pornographic.

Beside her, Vaclav stirred and rolled onto his back, tugging most of the sheet to him. That meant the snoring would resume soon. Carefully, she lifted the sheets aside and stepped out of bed. Vaclav shifted again, as if there were some law of conservation at work compensating for her absence. *The science of sleeping lovers*, she thought. Then, before she could forget to do it, she padded across the room to the battered wooden table and opened her journal, where she wrote the thought down. She had no idea what would come of it. It might be a line, a motif, a poem, or even the title for an entire chapbook. Or it might never blossom at all. You never could tell. It had been a while since she had given her last reading, and Emmett Alexix, back in New York, was already asking about another collection.

She also wrote: *One woman, four poses.* And: *Image is what we choose to show the world.*

She studied herself again in the mirror. Not as scrawny as the waifs the fashion industry pushed, nor as aggressively mammalian as the upholstered *objets de self-abuse* that the men's magazines used for advertising lures. Just . . . ordinary. But ordinary was In these days. *Average* was a new sensation in a world grown bored with extremes. Vaclav had painted her several times, and so had a number of their friends. Realism was fashionable once again, and abstractionism already had the quaint and antique look of a bygone age: bloodless and cool, lacking in passion. "Cool" had once been a compliment.

Roberta wondered if her mother had ever seen any of those nude and seminude paintings of her daughter. Possible reactions ranged from Horrified Shame to a retro-Boomer sixties *That's my girl.* Not that Beth was the sort to haunt the galleries in Lower Manhattan; but the one Vaclav had done of her ironing clothes had graced the cover of her last collection, *Un-*

commonly Commonplace, and mother, just maybe, had glanced at her daughter's books.

Or maybe not.

There had been letters for a while, from Mother—and from the Rich Lady, too—forwarded through Emmett's office. Roberta had not read them, had never replied; and, after a while, they had stopped coming.

She dressed quickly and methodically in yesterday's clothes. She wanted to walk the streets while the morning was still soft. Spring mornings were best for inspiration. Time enough later for a shower, after Vaclav had awakened and they could shower together. He wasn't the best lover she had ever had, but was far from the worst; and certainly better than any of the gawky, gropy American expats she had allowed into her bed. He was her own age, twenty-four; but European men seemed to mature earlier. With Emmett, just after she had run off to the Village, she had been too young to know better and living with him had seemed finer then than it did now. Roberta tucked her journal under her arm and slipped out the door, closing it silently behind her.

The streets were just shrugging into life. Night-shift workers on their way home; housekeepers headed for the market. The metro rumbled beneath her feet. Old Town was closed to traffic, so she picked up a tram when she came to Old Town Square and rode it past the old Jewish cemetery, where Rabbi Löw, who had built the golem, lay buried. When she reached the river, she hopped off and strolled along the bank on Dvor-řaák Street, watching the barges and the river traffic. In the little sidewalk café across the street, Karel Janácek was already enthroned with his easel and his absinthe, trying to capture the vision of the Castle before the mists burned off. Each day, he made a little more progress before the light could turn and the shadows shift. Roberta wondered if he would finish the painting before the absinthe finished him.

He saw her and waved. "*Kde je* Vaclav?" he called. Roberta made a pantomime of sleeping and Karel laughed. "Morning is best for painting," he said in clipped Slavic consonants. "You are moving in with me, I paint you in morning light. I always rise in morning for you," he added.

Roberta pretended she didn't know what he meant about "rising" for her and waved good-bye. "*Sbohem*, Karel!"

She turned right at the intersection and walked out onto the Charles Bridge. It was her favorite spot to sit and think. The emperor Charles had commissioned the bridge in 1345 when he established his court in Threshold, but in the early 1700s, in a maniacal burst of Baroque creativity, the Czechs had decked the six-hundred-meter span with thirty statues and statuary groups. They lined both sides of the bridge, making it one of the most beautiful in Europe. She had thought once of writing a series of cantos, each one based on a Charles Bridge statue, but, not being Czech, had thought herself unable to do the themes justice.

Although it was early yet, a few people had already gathered on the bridge, sketching, talking, arguing. A woodwind trio had set up by the Lesser Town end of the bridge; and a puppetmaster was arranging his shadow box. Young men and women, Czech and expat, bohemians all. Just living here in Threshold was a deliciously postmodern pun. Roberta greeted those she knew and they asked her if she was going to read at the *pivnice* tonight. The Czechs loved their Pilsner and their *Budvar*, and the avant-garde here gathered in taverns, not in coffeehouses. The New Art was mellow, not jittery.

A lone woman stood with an oddly impatient stillness contemplating the statue of St. Luigarda across the street. Something about the woman seemed familiar, and Roberta gave her a second look as she passed her. But, no. She knew nobody as old as that.

Roberta perched herself on the guard rail opposite "St. John, Felix and Ivan with the Turk," nearly over Kampa Island and the Devil's Brook on the Lesser Town end. The St. John group was the statue best loved by the people of Threshold, and watching those who came to view it provided her with a wealth of observations. Unlike the painters with their easels and the photographers with their cameras and the pixies with their laptops, Roberta came to the Charles Bridge to capture the people, not the statuary.

The elderly woman moved on to study the next statue in line and then, a few minutes later, moved on to St. John of Mathy, blocking Roberta's view. The woman walked with a cane, but it seemed more a concession than a need. She was old, white-haired; face taut with expensive lifts, and dressed in the tawdry of wealth. A dead animal was draped around her neck. Roberta wondered if she was checking out each statue in sequence, allocating a set amount of time to each, like a Catholic doing the Stations of the Cross. She seemed more the sort who would try to buy the statue than to study it. Roberta's hand twitched in the special shorthand she used to note character sketches in her journal.

After a moment or two, the woman turned and saw Roberta looking at her with the journal open upon her lap. "Oh," she said. "Were you sketching? Was I blocking your view?" She spoke American English slowly and distinctly. Apparently, that was the magic key. All those wogs would understand if only you spoke clearly and slowly enough.

Roberta smiled innocently and said, *"Ne. Mluvíte česky?"*

The woman looked nonplussed and fumbled in her purse, pulling forth a traveler's phrase book. "My daughter has convinced me I ought to carry one of these on my travels," she explained. She began to page through it earnestly.

Roberta sighed and gave up the charade. "Never mind. I wasn't sketching."

"You're American." The voice was less surprised than curious.

"I'm a poet."

"Ah, yes, I understand Prague has become quite the place for the avant-garde to gather. In my day, it was Greenwich Village. The Beatniks, you know. Years before that, it was the Left Bank of Paris."

The patronizing tone was all the more offensive for its offhandedness. "You can't dismiss the New Art so easily," Roberta said with some heat.

"I beg your pardon?"

"By sticking us in a slot and slapping a label on us. We're

not the Beatniks. We're not the Lost Generation. We're doing something new here.''

''Yes, it is always something 'new.' '' She gestured toward the double row of statuary that lined the bridge. ''Myself, I prefer the old.''

''You know what? You looked like a schoolkid with a homework assignment.''

The woman raised an eyebrow, refusing to take offense. ''Really?''

''You were working your way down the line so . . . systematically.''

The woman smiled ruefully. ''My daughter told me I ought to see the Charles Bridge statuary. I mean, I have *seen* them before—I am no stranger to Prague—but I have never *looked* at them. It is not easy to take instruction from your own daughter; but I have learned in a small way to appreciate this city—and the others where I summer. At one time, I would stay only in the Intercontinental. . . .'' A nod of the head toward the American luxury hotel on the Old Town riverside. ''I would come *to* Prague, but I would not be *in* Prague, if you understand me.''

Let's give the old gal credit for that, at least. She was trying, in an earnest, fumbling fashion. She would never reach where she needed to be, but at least she knew she needed to be there. Roberta said, ''Your daughter sounds like a smart person.''

''Oh, quite. Far too smart for me; perhaps far too smart for herself. In any event, before I left home, I changed my rooms to U Tri Pštrosů. It is not so expensive, but it does have more local atmosphere.''

Not so expensive . . . The Three Ostriches, in Lesser Town, rented a grand total of eighteen rooms and suites and, with its seventeenth-century ambience, was one of the most sought-after hotels on the continent; and here was a woman who could have a suite there on a whim. A bit richer than some doctor's wife from Long Island . . .

A silver limousine with tinted windows coasted to the edge of the street and pulled up beside the old woman. *And vehicles are not allowed on the bridge.* . . . Not only rich, but connected. "Oh, dear. My driver is here to take me back to the hotel. It has been nice chatting with you, miss." She turned to the limo, and the curved, tinted glass of the half-open door sent back a reflection. A younger, thinner face; one that Roberta knew.

One that *Styx* had known.

"Van Huyten!"

The woman turned and looked at her with a frown. "Do I know you?"

"But you can't be. You're too old!"

The woman's lips thinned into a tight smile. "Old? I have always favored a straightforward honesty, myself; so I cannot complain when I hear it. Perhaps you know my daughter, Mariesa."

Bitterness rose up in Roberta's throat from a long-forgotten pool. "Yes, I knew her."

"I am so sorry, but I do not recognize you."

Odd, that the woman would actually sound so distressed. The simulation of truth by manners. "Take seven years off," Roberta said. "I was just a kid when I used to come to your mansion."

And now surprise did display itself. "Oh? Oh! You were one of *them!* Which one . . . ? A poet, you said. Then, you must be Carson. Mariesa often speaks of you. She was so distressed when you left, you know."

Straightforward honesty, indeed . . . "I'm sure she's gotten over it by now."

"Perhaps. My daughter was always rather a cold fish, but there was something about you that brought her out of herself; and now she has retreated again." A silence, as if the woman regretted having said so much. Then, "She collects your books, you know."

Oddly, that made Roberta angry. "I don't need her patronage! My books sell. How many poets can say that?" Some of the old, diehard postmoderns criticized her for that; as if the fact that the commoners bought her poetry somehow damned it. But there had always been a strong strain of contempt for working people running through the intelligentsia.

"I believe it upsets her that so many of your poems attack what she does. Oh, she is still quite involved with her stars and planets," van Huyten's mother went on. "I'm sure you know of the Aurora transportation system, though you would certainly never get *me* aboard one of those things! I fly the safe-and-sane way, by jetliner. I understand there is even talk of placing a spaceport here in Prague. Something about an ancient prophecy."

"Oh, great," Roberta said. "Ruin the country."

"I suppose it could be preserved as it is," van Huyten responded with amused sarcasm, "for the enjoyment of artists and wealthy American tourists; but that is for the Czechs to decide, is it not?" She pulled a cell phone from her purse. "I could call Mariesa, if you like. I am sure she would be delighted to hear from you. She is married now; and expecting a child in a few months."

From the set of Mrs. van Huyten's lips, she was not so thrilled with those two facts; but . . . the Rich Lady, married? "*She's* in Threshold?" Why their paths might have crossed entirely by accident. And what would she say to her if they were to meet after all this time? All the words that she had wanted to say to her in those first few months after the reception jumbled up in her throat.

"Oh, goodness, no. We . . ." A clouded look, and Mrs. van Huyten glanced away. "We never travel together. Mariesa is surely at home, or more likely at work, but I can reach her through her telephone wherever she is."

Roberta slid off her perch. "No, thanks," she said. "I got places to be, and people to see." She started away, then checked herself. "Tell the Rich Lady," she said, "that when you start pushing things around, they might not end up where you planned." Then she turned and walked back toward Old Town. Anywhere in the world, no more distant than a dozen touches on a keypad. Her old world was not so far away, after all.

-1.

Bumboat

There. Do you see it?'' Ned DuBois pointed through the viewport. From the vantage point of Mir station, the approaching Plank was a spot of light trailing behind and below—high enough to catch the sunlight around the edge of Earth. ''That's the bumboat coming up. They'll make rendezvous in half an orbit.''

''I don't understand,'' the young postdoc floating beside him said.

Ned reached out and gripped a stanchion to keep himself from drifting. ''Well, they're below us, which means they're catching up with us; but they're on an elliptical orbit, so when they reach apogee they'll touch our orbit. They'll slow as they come into apogee, rise into a slot right behind us, and then close for docking.''

The postdoc made a face. ''I know *that*. I meant, what's a bumboat?''

''Oh.'' The postdoc was a scientist on board doing some sort of research. Of course, he would know basic orbital mechanics. ''Just some waterfront slang I picked up years ago.

A bumboat is one that comes out from the port with supplies to service the ships at anchor.''

Ned pushed away from the viewport and floated back to his work center. Working surfaces and cabinets were bolted to every bulkhead, so that none of them cried out "floor" or "ceiling." It was an odd and, at first, disorienting perspective. Now, Ned wondered if he could get used to "up" and "down" again when his stint was over. A long string of computer paper was taped to one bulkhead. Big, printer-generated letters read, MOTHER VAN HUYTEN'S HIGH WAY SERVICE STATION & GARAGE. LAST CHANCE FOR GAS, NEXT 387,000,000 MILES.

Vlad Sugachev, the station commander, looked up from his computer screen and grunted. ''But it does not bring our relief crew yet.''

"Oh, you love it up here, Vlad." Ned settled into the space before his own terminal and planted his stick-fabric boot soles on one of the anchor pads. "Besides," he said, "it'll be good to have company for a change."

Vlad made a face. "Excellent. I shall have the guest bedroom prepared." The postdoc, listening, chuckled low in his throat.

"Yeah, it will be a little tight in here," Ned admitted. Mir was not exactly spacious—four meters in diameter and a shade over thirteen end to end, divided into four modules. About the size of a small, one-story ranch home. The place smelled like a locker room, too. There must be sweat molecules here dating back to the original Soviet crew.

Ned turned his attention to the job list. Two more Motorola repeaters were due in for repair; and one NAVSTAR needed an upgrade. Wilson was banging up two more fuel pods next week from the Nairobi Ram. Business was low, but steady, and beginning to pick up now that the recession was finally ending.

The computer had flagged the optimum launch windows for the retrievals, which meant he ought to be going through the preflight checklist on *Glenn Curtis*, which orbited tethered to the station. He pushed the intercom button for the "garage."

"Hey, Geoff. What's the status on Motorola 47?"

"Almost done. I'm running the diagnostics now," the payload specialist replied. "Why, what's up?"

"Company coming. We have to be presentable."

"Roj. How soon?"

Ned looked at Vlad, who studied his screen and said, "Forty-five minutes."

"Sounds about right," said the postdoc. Ned looked at him. "In your head?"

The postdoc looked suddenly embarrassed and muttered something about getting back to his ceramics. He kicked off against a bulkhead and coasted to the access lock to "Kristal," the old metallurgical lab that Argonaut Labs had converted.

"You should not tease Dr. Hobart," Vlad said. "He is very bright, or he would not be here; but he is very young and inexperienced, or he would not be here."

Ned grinned at him. "You know, Vlad. That almost makes sense." He hadn't been teasing the kid, not really. Just banter. The kid probably *could* do the math in his head. Ned scrolled to the next screen on his terminal: the Squawk List from *Glenn Curtis's* previous flight.

The Russian shrugged. "You would not send distinguished elder scientist up here to do zero-g experiment. Experiment would be if distinguished elder scientist survives. But, Hobart must work without direct supervision, so he must be himself a skilled researcher."

Ned looked over his shoulder at the manlock to Kristal. "In ceramics. What's he doing, throwing pots?"

Vlad laughed. "Whatever it is, is business of Argonaut, and not of Energia Space Transportation, nor of Leprechaun Satellite Repair."

"Yeah." Ned started to read the maintenance downloads; then he sighed, blanked his screen, and floated in space staring at nothing in particular. Just another routine fetch-and-carry. No wonder the Volkovs had called it quits. Ned wasn't sure how long he could stick it himself. The glory days of flight-testing on Fernando de Noronha were long past. A cadre remained on the archipelago to pilot design changes; but flying the Plank was an everyday thing now, even the Mark IVs. Besides, flight test was a young man's game, and Ned was looking at the wrong side of forty. Good enough to fly within the envelope; no longer good enough to lick its edge.

Damn, but those had been great times. Forrest, Bobbi, Mike. Flying the Swoop of Death when no one knew shit . . . Even Levkin had had his good points. So where were they now? Forrest, he knew, was at Pegasus Space Flight Academy at Ames Field. He was chief nose-wiper for a bunch of young wannabe space cadets, and probably twice as bored as Ned was. And Iron Mike was head pilot for Energia, and Vlad's immediate boss. He and Ned chatted from time to time, chewed over old times and remember-whens. The others he had lost track of, despite all the sincere promises to stay in touch after the wind-down. But hell, what's done is done. It would be awhile before there was a new frontier to tackle; enough of a while to pass beyond the horizon of his own personal interest.

The picture of Betsy and not-so-little Lizzie stuck to his note board was beginning to curl at the edges. *Another month and I'll be home again.* He had a regular job now. One that took him into space (the way he wanted); but *not* out on the edge (the way she wanted). Three months up; six months down. Routine enough that even Betsy had internalized the risk. It was like the old Elton John song. *It's just a job . . .* With a stab of his finger, Ned woke his screen and began setting up the flight plan for the NAVSTAR retrieval. Just like a hundred other flight plans to retrieve a hundred other satellites and Boomer pods.

Some days Ned thought the boredom was more likely to kill him than reentry, vacuum, or absolute zero combined.

"Pegasus Spaceline SSTO *Louis Blériot,* calling Energia Station Mir. Permission to dock?"

It was a young voice, Ned thought, one with a touch of nervous inexperience. Probably a cadet flying "under instruction." One of the new crop of pilots from Ames, for whom the Plank meant reading the manuals, not writing them.

Vlad Sugachev said, "Acknowledged, *Blériot*. Permission granted." Ned wondered what would happen if Vlad said no. Would *Blériot* deorbit and go home? And how could Vlad stop them from docking, anyhow? It wasn't as if Mir could dodge or run away with her little attitude-control engines. Hell, the Plank was *bigger* than Mir, though most of that was fuel tank. Still, the courtesies were important. Enough courtesies and quasi-naval etiquette and you could forget how grubby and elbow-to-earlobe everyone was after two months in space.

He and Vlad watched the docking through the outside fiberops that VHI had installed during the upgrade. *Blériot* gleamed, her fuselage relatively unscorched. Either she was a new hull, or Pegasus was fussier than Daedalus had been. (Not that Daedalus had been sloppy, but spit and polish were less important in Test than in Operations.) The docking probes telescoped from the rim of the Plank's nose collar and Vlad coached the pilot until the prongs were in the proper orientation.

The Plank coughed an engine, and the prongs engaged. Gently, they retracted and pulled the two craft together. The station reverberated from the contact. The docking collars locked and Vlad's board turned green. Still, the station chief methodically touched off each checklist item on the computer screen while Ned watched and confirmed over his shoulder. Some rituals were for more than politeness's sake. When Vlad was satisfied, he announced, "All systems are go, *Blériot*."

"Joined like lovers kissing!" declared a familiar basso over the radio link, and Ned had the sudden, twisting feeling in his gut his life was about to change.

It was Forrest Calhoun, all right; big and black and in your face. Ned could not help grinning when the man emerged from the airlock into the docking sphere. They hadn't seen each other since the final ceremony, when Pessoa had officially shifted the Plank from development testing to production. Forrest was dressed in a bright red Pegasus coverall, with the rearing stallion logo over his right breast and a ship captain's four white bands circling each wrist. Ned snapped him a fancy salute, the effect being spoiled by the fact that they were up-side down with respect to one another. Forrest laughed.

"Well, toss me out in vacuum if it isn't the . . ."

"Second-best space pilot in the world," Ned finished for him.

"Show a little humility, Ned," Forrest admonished him. "You are only the second-best in orbit. Leastwise, now that I'm here . . ."

It was a game they had played with each other since their days together at Edwards on the old X-33. Ned introduced him to the station crew floating at random orientations around the module. Vlad, Geoff Landis, the payload specialist who did most of the satellite repair work, and Dr. Leland Hobart, the researcher from Argonaut, who was renting space.

"Hobie?" A younger man had crawled through the airlock behind Forrest and now floated in the air beside him. He, too, wore Pegasus red, but with only a single sleeve stripe. His hair was cropped short on the top and shaved on the sides.

Dr. Hobart blinked. "Do I know you?" he asked uncertainly.

Ned laughed. "Chase Coughlin," he said, grabbing a stanchion and sticking out a hand at the youngster. "Don't tell me you've fallen under Forrest's evil influence."

Chase pumped his hand. "Captain DuBois Sir." A startled look crossed his face as he began to tumble slowly. Forrest reached out and snagged him.

"First rule of zero-g, son. Don't make any sudden moves 'less you're holding on to something more reliable than Ned." To Ned, he added, "This is Chase's final exam. He had to do an orbit and a rendezvous to get his certificate, so I figured, hell, why not drop in on my old buddy and see how he's getting on?" He gave Ned another look. "Son, with that bright green Leprechaun outfit you're wearing, we better not stand too close together or these folks'll think it's Christmastime."

"I'm still officially with Daedalus," Ned told him. "Just 'on loan' to Leprechaun."

Forrest squinted at the patch on Ned's coveralls. "Hmm. Cute little guy . . . What's his name? Murphy?"

Ned tapped a finger on Forrest's own patch. "At least I'm not working for Mr. Ed."

"What the hell," Forrest said. "It's all VHI . . . I think all these separate companies are the corporate equivalent of watertight compartments in an ocean vessel."

Hobart suddenly pointed a finger at Chase. "High school, right? I'm sorry I didn't recognize you right off."

Chase shrugged. "It's been a lot of years. You were a big-time football jock; I was nobody special to remember."

"I remember you now. You got in a big fight with that metalhead—what was his name?"

"Meat Tucker."

"Yeah, and he pulled a screwdriver on you. And 'Igor' had to bust it up." The two of them began to laugh. Ned and Forrest exchanged glances.

"Dear old golden-rule days," Forrest suggested.

"We have aboard genuine Stolichnaya," Vlad announced, "to celebrate your visit. We have set up in the maintenance module a party." He indicated the lock-tunnel that led to the next module.

"Oh, good. A party," Forrest deadpanned. "With girls jumping out of cakes?"

"No," Ned told him, "though we were planning to have Geoff here hop out of a Motorola relay satellite."

Landis grinned and tugged at his beard. Alone of the station's four crew members, he had had a beard to begin with. "Almost true," he said. "I did have to climb halfway inside the last job to locate the fault."

Forrest nodded. "I like a man who throws himself into his work."

"When I came on board," Dr. Hobart told Chase, "Ned pulled the same handshake stunt on me. Only he pulled me out into the center of the docking module and left me hanging out of reach of any of the walls."

"Yeah?" Chase thought that over. "So what'd you do?"

Hobart shrugged. "Newton's third law. I used my lips as a jet nozzle and blew my breath out as hard as I could."

Ned laughed. "And gave himself enough velocity that he

might have reached the nearest bulkhead sometime around March. Theory was sound, though . . ."

Forrest put a hand around Ned's neck and gave him a gentle push toward the lock. "Son, not everyone is as big a blowhard as some I could mention."

"Why, Forrest," Ned said as he checked himself at the mouth of the tunnel, "that's uncharacteristically modest of you."

The maintenance bay was the largest module on the station since Mir's reconfiguration. It had its own bay door to admit satellites for repair and was connected to the living quarters and the command module by a second manlock. About half the cubic was occupied by a Motorola signal repeater, held in place by three-axis guy wires. Forrest whistled. "Why, this here module is big enough we could all dance the bugaloo, if only half of us breathed at the same time."

"Pressurized volume is at a premium," Ned told him. "And this is still the high-rent district."

"Energia," Vlad said, "is planning to orbit additional volume next year." He began passing drinking bulbs around from a pouch he had brought with him. "Mir was designed from outset to be modular."

"I would have moved Number 47 outside," Geoff said apologetically. "Job's all done, except for the paperwork; but there wasn't enough time."

Forrest contemplated the "garage." "You surely could use more elbow room, and that's a fact."

"Well, Forrest, if you want to help us throw up a patio deck out back, you'd be more than welcome."

Forrest grinned. "I might do that."

Vlad held his bulb out. "*Gospodá*, the stars!"

The others echoed him and sucked from their drinking bulbs. Ned suppressed a chuckle. *Drinking from baby bottles* . . . Can't exactly toss the vodka back in the traditional, stiff-wristed Russian style. He noticed that Dr. Hobart had passed on the vodka for a fruit-juice squeegee.

"Whatever happened to that Meat?" Hobart asked Chase.

The two younger men floated together on the edge of the group.

The cadet pilot shrugged. ''Meat? Jeez, I dunno. He dropped out after that robbery at the In-and-Out where he worked.''

''Yeah, the shooting.'' Hobart was silent for a while. Then he said, ''They ever find Azim?''

''Not that I ever heard.''

Hobart scowled. ''Matchstick always scared me. The boy was going tick-tick-tick inside. But I can't help thinking that if he'd only come to Silverpond that day, 'stead o' hanging with his homeys, he'd be okay now.''

Ned looked around sharply. ''Silverpond? Are you talking about that party after my orbital flight?'' Hobart nodded. ''You never mentioned you were there.'' Hobart shrugged.

''If you didn't remember, what would have been the point?''

Ned shook his head. ''Seems I keep bumping into the same bunch of kids, over and over.''

Chase laughed. ''Well, you know what Styx says.''

''Who is this 'Styx'?'' asked Vlad.

''Styx,'' said Chase. ''Girl we went to school with. You knew her, Hobie. Always dressed in black? More serious than a math test. Kids called her Morticia . . . ?'' Hobie nodded slowly.

''Saw her round. Didn't know her.''

Oddly, Ned recalled her, too—from that visit he had made to Chase's high school. A quiet girl with solemn eyes. She had asked him about Jerry Godlaw. He wondered if he had met the others they had mentioned. Meat and Azim. Shit . . . Azim? Hadn't he been one of the three black kids who had blocked the doorway on him?

''Styx ran off just before graduation,'' Chase told the group. ''Then she begins grinding out these poems attacking VHI— and Ms. Van Huyten.''

''Attacking my bread and butter,'' Forrest said with a grunt.

''Wait a minute,'' said Ned. ''Do you mean that Roberta

Carson gal the media is so gaga over is your friend Styx? What's she got against Mariesa, anyway?''

Chase pursed his lips and looked at Hobart. ''She says Mentor brainwashed us into supporting VHI's space program.''

Forrest chuckled. ''Hell, that could be true. Half the applicants at the Academy come out of Mentor schools.''

Hobart sucked his bulb dry and stuffed it down the trash trap. ''So what? Mentor showed us opportunities and encouraged us to take them. That's not brainwashing.''

Chase shrugged. ''She says it goes deeper than that. Subtle propaganda in the teaching materials. Secret plans for selected students. All kinds of conspiracy shit.''

Hobart looked angry. ''She could be right and still so what? Where would I be today, wasn't for Mentor? Still stammering, 'cause where would I ever hear about that Demosthenes dude? And no way I'd be in superconductor research. Four years in college playing football and not getting taught shit, then— maybe!—a couple years in the pros butting myself silly and breaking bones so beer-swilling white guys could yell at their TVs. It's 'cause of Mentor I'm up here with you guys, instead.''

Forrest nodded. ''Sounds like you got the short end on that one, son; but I won't complain, if you won't.''

Hobart laughed. ''Word up,'' he said. ''But it could've been a lot worse for me without people like Mr. Egbo and Ms. Glendower. And you know what the worst part would have been?''

Forrest cocked his head with interest. ''No, what?''

Hobart looked momentarily grim. ''I would have thought I was on top of the world.''

Chase grinned. ''And now you are, for real.''

Geoff Landis said, ''So what's the buzz groundside, these days?''

Forrest wagged his hand back and forth. ''Same-o, same-o,'' he said. ''Recession finally seems to be bottoming out . . . again. Tampa Bay's going to be hard to beat this year—I guess because they don't have Doc, here, on their line. Wilson says he's putting up a new Skylab next year, if enough research bodies pool the cost of ramming and assembling the modules.''

Ned grunted, ''There goes the neighborhood.''

Forrest crumpled his bulb. ''Serbia is making more booga-booga at Macedonia. Things could go shit there real fast. . . .'' He launched the bulb toward the trash trap, but it sailed off at a tangent. Landis snagged it as it passed him and before it could lose itself in the guts of the relay satellite. Forrest looked abashed.

''Forgot. No parabola. Low Earth Orbit is hell on basketball. Hey, what's wrong, Doc?''

Hobart's face was knotted in a frown. ''Macedonia,'' he said. ''My dad's with the UN peacekeepers at Skopje.''

''Hey, he'll be okay,'' Chase said with a wave of the hand. ''Even the Serbies aren't crazy enough to mess with the U.S. Marines.''

''Yeah, but he be wearing UN baby blue, and he's not allowed to shoot back.''

''Peacekeepers,'' said Forrest. ''More like hostages.''

Vlad said, ''Serbia has legitimate claim. This Macedonia was once part of Yugoslavia.''

''You mean Xugoslavia,'' said Forrest. ''And before that it was part of Turkey, and before that it was part of Greece. And the Crusaders ran it for a while. I think everybody but the Rotary Club has taken a shot at running the Balkans.''

Vlad looked grim. ''Confederation would be best for all.''

''Hell, son,'' said Forrest. ''Considering the tribal baggage everyone is hauling, that would be a shotgun wedding. I say, if they don't want to live together, the Serbs should let them go.''

Vlad gave him a sharp look. ''Like your Abraham Lincoln?''

Forrest made no reply, but his lips pulled in. Even Geoff looked upset.

This tin can is too damned small for a political argument, Ned thought. He and Vlad had worked together long enough that it was easy to forget that the fellow owed his allegiance to a different country with different strategic interests. Aloud, he said, "Peace talks are still going on, right? Maybe everything will turn out okay." It was the Balkans, and precedent was against it, but hope was still possible. Vlad tensed for a moment, as if he intended to say something; then changed his mind.

"Yes. Peaceful solution is always best." Geoff and Dr. Hobart nodded in agreement. Chase and Forrest looked skeptical, but said nothing. After a moment longer, Geoff said abruptly, "Well, back to work." He tugged himself by guy wire to the side of the Motorola, where he picked up a compupad. Vlad excused himself, pleading duties, and squeezed into the airlock to the crew quarters. Ned began collecting everyone's remaining bulbs and stuffing them into the trash trap. They had achieved agreement, of sorts; but the party was definitely over.

Forrest helped Ned stock the supplies that *Blériot* had brought up. They suited up and sealed off the crew quarters and control module; then depressurized the "garage" and cracked the module's space door. It was faster to move the stock in this way than through the narrower manlock connecting the Plank's nose with the docking module. Ned felt the small puff of residual air blowing off into vacuum. The water vapor froze out into a gentle, improbable snow that coated the work surfaces in a thin sheen of frost.

Chase and Geoff off-loaded the Plank and passed the crates through the bay door to Forrest. Ned checked each item against the bill of lading and told Forrest where it should be stowed.

"You've waited a lot of years," Forrest said philosophically, "to tell me where to shove it."

During a lull, Forrest switched off his suit radio and leaned close to Ned, touching helmets. Ned took the hint and switched off his own transmitter, leaving the receiver on, just in case Landis hollered.

"What is it?" He'd had the feeling ever since Forrest's arrival that his friend had more reasons than he had admitted to for proctoring Chase's maiden flight.

"Daedalus make any requests for readiness reports the last couple weeks?"

An unexpected and obscure question; but it was Forrest's hand to play. "Yeah, sure," he said. "They asked for the quarterly proficiencies a little early. So?"

Forrest was silent a moment, considering. "So this. Pegasus did the same thing. And Valery Volkov told me that Aurora's rating her ballistic pilots ahead of schedule, too. Scuttlebutt has it that MacDac, NASA, and the others are quietly checking out their own flight crews."

Ned's pulse began to hammer. "Any idea why?" he asked casually. Something big, and something quiet; or more would have been said than "hand in your performance ratings early."

Forrest fell silent again, long enough that Ned knew he did have a notion. "Nothing that would explain so much activity in so many different quarters."

"Try me."

Forrest switched on his transmitter. "Yo, Chase, my man, what is the holdup on the electromagnet?"

"Damn stowage bolt is froze," Chase's voice responded. "Put me into a counterclock."

"Need help?"

"Nah, we'll have it."

Forrest switched his transmitter off again. "What do you know about asteroids, Ned?"

"Little rocks between Mars and Jupiter. No nightlife. What about them?"

"Ever hear of 1991JW?"

"Oh, sure. Mars, Jupiter, 1991JW, I know all the biggies."

"Don't get snooty with me, son. I'm doing you a favor against my best judgment."

The fist in Ned's belly clenched up tighter. "Forrest, you don't have a best judgment."

"Yeah, look who I pick as friends. All right, here's the whisper. Not all the asteroids are out past Mars. Seems there are a flock of them that crisscross the Earth's orbit."

"Like 1991JW," Ned guessed.

"Yeah, like that. Seems your old pal, Mariesa van Huyten,

is real interested, and wants to send a probe out to rendezvous with it.''

"A probe . . .'' He felt like he was floating. Dammit, he *was* floating! He grasped for a handhold at the same time Forrest grabbed him by the arm.

"Steady there, son.''

"What sort of probe?'' He anchored himself to a stickfabric patch against Geoff's storage locker.

"Manned probe. Pilot, co-, and a geologist.''

"Jesus.''

"Amen, brother. One-year round trip, with forty-one days of that spent at the rock. Supposed to leave Earth orbit in two years. Five-point-nine delta-V.''

"Not much prep time . . .'' Ned said doubtfully. A deep-space flight! Five-point-nine was farther than the moon! For once, there'd be no footsteps in the dust ahead of him. The blood in his ears murmured like the Atlantic surf.

"The little birdie told me its been growing under very deep wrap for at least five years, with prelims going back even farther—for a similar mission that got scrubbed. That's all I know; and I don't even *know* that.''

Ned could feel the sweat on his palms and wiped them against his thighs, a futile gesture in a spacesuit. "Whose show is it?''

"Pegasus.''

Ned studied the company patch on Forrest's suit shoulder. He grunted. "Looks like you backed the right horse.''

"Damn it, Ned.'' Forrest pulled his helmet away from contact, checked a turn, and pushed it back into Ned's face. "Damn it, Ned, why do you think I'm clueing you in; and why do you think I didn't want to?''

Forrest didn't have to say any more. Ned turned his radio back on. Chase and Geoff were guiding a large bin with Argonaut's "Greek galley'' logo stenciled on the side. More equipment for—what had Chase called him?—Hobie. Ned watched Forrest kick off and coast to intercept the others. He flew gracefully and effortlessly straight toward his target.

Once before, Forrest Calhoun had watched the chance of a

lifetime slide away from him and into the hands of Ned DuBois.

Geoff Landis shook his head and tugged his beard. His Leprechaun coverall was sweat-stained, now that he had taken his EVA suit off. "We didn't finish unloading the cargo," he said.

"What do you mean?" Ned shut down his compupad and stowed it in its locker. You learned early on always to put things away. Otherwise they tended to drift with the air circulation into unexpected places. Ned had awakened once with a pair of Vlad's undershorts settling into his face. Vlad was now a more careful housekeeper.

"I mean there's still cargo aboard *Blériot*."

"We stocked everything on the bill of lading," Ned said. He was still thinking about the asteroid mission Forrest had mentioned. Would Daedalus pilots be eligible for the flight roster? Nobody had more continuous time in space than Mama DuBois's favorite son. But you didn't have to attend board meetings to know there was a deep-seated rivalry between Pegasus and Daedalus that went all the way back to the original Plank development. He wondered if he could transfer companies without losing his seniority.

Hell, who cared about seniority? He sure wouldn't lose his education and experience. And chances were, they would want either the pilot or the copilot to be an engineer. His gaze fell on the photograph of Betsy and Liz. A yearlong flight out to an asteroid and back . . .

He rubbed his hands against his face. Jesus, look at the time! "I'm going to hit the sack," he said.

Geoff followed him to the crew module airlock. "What I mean is, why would *Blériot* lift excess cargo? It's not like there are more stops on his delivery route . . ."

Ned paused before crawling through. "Maybe they're hauling a satellite."

"Couple dozen crates about two meters long?" Geoff held his hands apart.

Ned frowned. "Cost per pound isn't like it used to be; but you're right. It doesn't make sense. Nobody lifts deadhead.

I'll ask Forrest about it.'' He pushed himself through the lock.

As he emerged into the crew module, Forrest and Chase turned to look in his direction. He had the feeling they had just fallen silent a moment before. ''What's up?'' he asked.

Forrest showed white teeth. ''We all are, son. About two hundred miles. But Chase and me, we were wondering where to toss our sleeping bags.''

''Hmm. No sleeping bags, but you can pull up a handy volume of empty space, as long as you tether yourself, so you don't drift into my bed during station night.''

''Don't flatter yourself, Ned; you ain't that pretty.'' Forrest looked around the crew module. It was about as big as a front parlor, with four bunk niches set into four of the bulkheads. ''I keep forgetting you don't need surfaces for some things.'' A bland smile. ''Handy to remember if I go on any real long trips.''

Ned let that pass. ''Geoff is curious about the crates you left on board *Blériot*.''

Forrest made a negligent wave of the hand. ''Just some Pegasus stuff.'' Chase glanced at him and kept quiet, but Ned noticed the reaction. ''Say,'' said Forrest in a suddenly jovial tone, ''you know your sign—'Mother' van Huyten? Well, she's about to be one. A mother.''

Which change of subject meant Forrest wasn't about to explain the cargo. Well, could be it was a top-secret, closed-box experiment, and Ned didn't have need-to-know. Still, it seemed curious and, damn it, Forrest looked smug enough to burst.

''I hadn't heard.'' He'd gone to the wedding, like everyone else on the project. Mariesa had looked—well, all brides looked radiant—but she had looked . . . What? Satisfied? Triumphant? Ned hadn't understood that look. Barry Fast wasn't much of a catch (though it was admittedly hard to measure up to the DuBois standard), so how had she triumphed? Marrying Fast was like fighting a war and in the end all you had was Macedonia. You had to wonder, Why bother?

''Mr. Fast was one of my teachers,'' Chase volunteered.

Ned grunted. Why should he care who she married? He had

his own marriage to think about, one he had salvaged from the scrap pile, and the only cost had been letting go of everything he had ever held dear.

Well, nearly everything. There was Betsy and there was Liz, and age would have loosened his grip on the envelope before long. He had been faithful to Betsy now for seven years. Ninety percent faithful, and you couldn't ask for much more than that.

In the "morning," Forrest wanted to chew the fat, so Geoff volunteered to check Chase out on the refueling procedures and Vlad suited up as the safety man to keep watch while they hooked *Blériot* up to one of Wilson's fuel pods that flocked along on *Mir*'s orbit. Ever since that cracked valve had blown while Levkin was refueling, regulations required a safety man. Nine hundred and ninety-nine times you didn't need him; the thousandth time you wanted to kiss him. Ned and Forrest repaired to the command module, where Ned studied his checklists for *Glenn Curtis* with one eye while watching the fiberop monitor tuned to the pod farm with the other. Both Geoff and Vlad had refueled Planks countless times; and Chase had rehearsed it in the sims, in the tank, and on short field trips using dummy pods. It was funny. The cost of Earth-to-orbit had dropped enough that flight plans could be filed for training cruises; and Daedalus could keep Planks like *Glenn Curtis* in permanent orbit.

"Yeah, it's funny how things turn out," Forrest said when Ned mentioned the thought. "Here we are, intrepid test pilots with muscle cars parked in our driveways and wristwatches like the Crown Jewels, and what are we doing now? Laying our hides on the line? Hell, no. Headmaster at a school for hotshots. Tow-truck driver. You know Bobbi and the Volkovs are senior pilots for Aurora? Yeah, they're hauling routine passenger and special-freight traffic from Recife to St. Petersburg to Woomera and points in between. Kind of makes you wish for something new and exciting to come along."

Ned stabbed a sequence of buttons and his flight plan for the next retrieval downloaded to Leprechaun headquarters at

Shannon Spaceport. "And about when do you expect that to be, Forrest?"

"Eh?"

"I checked the ephemeris in the computer. There have been three launch windows back to Ames Field since the time we finished unloading your cargo."

Forrest gave him a wide-eyed look. "A man needs his beauty sleep. Besides, I had that vodka. 'Drink and fly, if you want to die.' "

"And you keep looking at that watch of yours that's too big not to notice."

Forrest held up his wrist, and gold and chrome flashed in the cabin's fluorescent lighting. "You like it? I got it from a very sincere man on Forty-second Street in New York City. He swore it was a genuine whatever it is. It gives me my pulse rate and skin temperature, does simple arithmetic, and shows True North with uncanny accuracy." He looked at the dial and scowled. "Haven't figured out how to tell time, yet; but what the hell?"

"Forrest, quit the—" The communicator beeped, distracting him. Forrest smiled blandly.

"You going to answer your phone, son?"

Ned looked at him suspiciously and punched the Response button, hard. Some days, Forrest was too cute to live. The comm screen went to fuzz, then cleared into the face of Khan Gagrat. Shiny, bald head; ferocious, Central Asian mustache; gold hoop earring flaunted in his left ear; he was the most unlikely looking accountant that Ned had ever met—and a bizarre contrast to his predecessor, the gentle, unassuming Keith McReynolds.

"DuBois? Good. Listen. VHI has taken on a rush order from NASA. Considering our assets in place, corporate has awarded the contract jointly to Pegasus and Leprechaun. Are you ready to download?"

Khan was not big on small talk and came to the point with a directness that bordered on rude. He was, Ned was sure, the despair of corporate cocktail parties. Ned pressed a sequence of buttons on his console and entered Khan's public key. "Ready."

"Good," Khan said after a moment. The milliseconds' delay always made Earth-to-orbit conversation seem to be conducted by people not paying complete attention. "Here is your verbal briefing. Calhoun is there? Yes. Background: A programming error affected this morning's shuttle launch by the U.S. NASA. *Endeavor* made orbit safely, but External Tank jettison was delayed by twelve seconds. The ET itself is now in coelliptical orbit with the shuttle. Space Traffic Control has determined that it is a traffic hazard, due to heavy use of that orbit by satellites. Furthermore, the orbit crisscrosses those used by VHI Space Industries, as well as those used by our competitors. Do you understand the background?"

"Acknowledged," said Ned. Forrest said, "That's a big ten-four, good buddy."

"Good. Scope of Work. NASA has contracted with VHI to match orbits with the rogue tank, attach strap-on rocket motors, and boost it out of orbit. The download provides the orbital parameters and a selection of possible launch windows, including windows for deorbiting the ET without hazard to Earth-surface ocean traffic. NASA suggests the southern Indian Ocean as the best drop zone. Do you understand the scope?"

"Acknowledged. It's never been done before, Khan. Do you at least have some protocols prepared?"

He heard Forrest chuckle behind him. "Remember what Louis Blériot once said about flying . . . ? 'It's really very simple. You just have to know how to do it.' "

Ned gave him a sour look, but Forrest was unquenchable. "When do you expect to send up the strap-ons?" Ned asked Khan.

In the dead interval before Khan could hear and reply, Forrest said casually, "I may have a couple dozen back in the ship. Do you want me to check?"

Ned turned his head so sharply that his torso twisted the other way to conserve angular momentum and he came unstuck from the stickfabric. "Why, you son of a bitch!"

After he had floundered back to an anchorage, explained to Khan that he hadn't meant the CFO's parentage, and had logged off the comm, he faced Forrest squarely.

"Do you mind explaining just how you happened to have the boosters on board, seeing as how NASA didn't discover the problem until after this morning's launch?"

"Foresight?" Forrest suggested.

"Bull-sight. Somebody in VHI pulled a hack on NASA . . ." And it had to be authorized by somebody pretty high up the food chain, too. Mariesa, herself? But why? Ned shook his head. "It doesn't make sense, Forrest. I mean, why game NASA's system and put an ET into orbit just to get the contract to drop it back down into the ocean? That's gotta be nickels and dimes in VHI's cash flow."

Forrest pursed his lips and looked innocent. "Who said anything about dropping it in the ocean?"

"But Khan said . . ."

"Nah . . ." Forrest waved both hands, palms out. "*NASA* said that would be the easiest thing to do; but since when has 'easy' ever been in VHI specs? Khan's download includes a couple other burn schedules—for boosting the tank up higher."

Ned just stared at him.

"Hell, Ned," Forrest said, spreading his hands in appeal and giving Ned the most innocent stare imaginable. "Didn't I tell you yesterday I'd help you put a patio deck out back?"

2.

Prices Paid

The darkroom reminded Mariesa van Huyten of a grotto: silent, dark, with a dull red light shimmering on pools. She pulled the print from the stopper bath and the chemicals dribbled into the tray with the sounds of a seeping spring running off a cave wall into a lagoon. She held the photograph up and studied it in the ruddy illumination. Not that the eye could discern much in the mad spray of stars it portrayed, but having developed the print, she could not *not* study it.

She regarded the small, white smear of light in the center of the field with the quiet pride of proprietorship. Of course, until its orbit was analyzed, she could not be sure it was a new discovery; but she knew her patch of the sky as well as she knew the estate grounds. This was something that moved; and nothing had moved there before.

She knew the interval between exposures and a few moments with a calipers would give her the displacement; and seconds of arc per day could be converted to velocity; and that in turn would yield the distance from the sun. The astronomer's version of Kentucky windage. It was really more complex than that. One had to take the Earth's motion into account as well, so it would fall to others more talented than she to determine where this object lay, and where it had come from.

And more important, where it was headed. She shivered slightly, wondering if this might be the One. The odds were vanishingly small, but . . .

The darkroom door opened, sending a spear of light through the shadows. She whirled and saw Barry framed in the doorway.

"I have told you countless times," she snapped, "never come in here when the red light is on!"

He froze and stammered, his hand still gripping the knob. "But . . ." Then, more crisply: "Sykes says that dinner is—"

"Get out!"

Barry's face hardened and he gave her a curt nod. "As you wish." He did not slam the door shut behind him.

Mariesa turned back to her tray table. She had finished the development, fixed the image. The light would have damaged nothing. There had been no need to snap at Barry as she had. Yet, it was an ironclad rule that no one enter when the red light was on. She swallowed a sob—sobs came too easily to her these days—and laid a hand across her womb, where it swelled under the rubber apron she wore.

Anger and sorrow, and the feeling that her body had swollen to grotesque proportions. She knew it was nothing but the hormone storm that accompanied pregnancy. Intellectually, she could stand aside and watch herself rail and lash out and collapse in helpless tears and know that it was all chemical imbalance; but nothing in that knowledge gave her *control*. She was no longer master of her own body. She watched, but it was through a wall of glass. She was a vessel, now; a life-support system for someone else.

Her hand searched under the apron, under the blouse, to the drum-tight skin, and lay there waiting. But there were no kicks forthcoming and, losing patience, she turned her attention back to the photograph she had just printed.

Later, when she left the darkroom, she forgot to turn the

warning light off. With a sigh of exasperation for her growing absentmindedness, she turned about and noticed that the bulb above the doorway was not lit. Had she turned it off, after all? No. She checked the switch and it was on. After a moment's hesitation, she shoved the switch down. She would have to remember to change the bulb.

Chris van Huyten stopped at Silverpond later that day, and Mariesa welcomed her cousin with a fierce hug. "It has been *too* long, Chris," she said greeting him in the foyer. "Sykes, we will repair to the sitting room. Please tell Barry and mother that Chris is here. Sykes inclined his head as he closed the door. He took Chris's long spring coat and folded it over his arm.

"Your usual, sir?" he said.

"On the rocks, Sykes. Yes." Chris had a package tucked under his arm. A plain brown wrapper tied up in cord. With his long legs, he kept pace easily with Mariesa as he followed her down the hall. "How is my new nephew?" he asked.

"Oh . . ." She stroked her swollen belly with both hands. "I thought he wanted out last week, but it turned out to be false labor. He's been quiet since then."

"Maybe he changed his mind," said Chris with a grin.

"A decade ago, I would not have blamed him, considering the Christmas Recession and its aftermath; but things have been looking better these last few years. He ought to be eager to come out."

"And you are just as eager to have him out." Chris laughed and stood aside at the entrance to the sitting room. "I remember Marianne's pregnancies. The last month is the worst."

The sitting room was broad and open, with a bay window facing the meadow behind the house. The room was sparingly furnished, almost Quaker in its simplicity, with its emphasis on chairs and conversation. A fireplace, little used, graced one wall and, above it, the wedding photographs of three generations of van Huytens. Willem, Father, and herself.

Willem and Mathilde had pride of place. Gramper was young and "snappy" in his morning coat, with slicked-down hair and a cocky smile for the camera. His bride, engulfed in a cloud of lace, with a flapper curl pasted against her forehead, looked willing, but bewildered, not quite sure what had happened to her.

The odd thing about the grouping, Mariesa had noticed when she had arranged the pictures after her wedding five years ago, was the nearly identical look in the eyes of her father and herself, a knowing look separated by three decades, as if they shared some common secret.

Chris handed her the package he had brought, and she tore the wrapper off. "Have you brought me a shower present, Chris?"

It was a book, handsomely bound. On its cover: a color photograph of a Plank lifting off. Which ship, she was not sure, though it had the look of the early Mark IIs tested on Fernando de Noronha. The title, in boldly cursive capitals, was PROMETHEANS: A PASSION TO BREAK THE SKY. And under that, *Commercial space travel in the early years, 1996-2006.* A sticker on the cover read, "Prepublication proof copy."

"I thought you might like to see it," Chris said. "After all, VHI provided most of the material."

"Thank you, Chris." Mariesa flipped through the lavishly illustrated volume. What did they call them? Coffee-table books? There was a picture of Luis Mendoza standing with his fists on his hips on the assembly floor of Daedalus's Recife plant as the first Mark I took shape around him. Another showed João and Luis and three anonymous technicians hunched over a drawing. She paused a moment when she came to a full-page portrait photo of Edward "Ned" DuBois in his Daedalus coveralls. Three-quarters face, looking at something beyond the photographer's shoulder; eyes, distant and slightly unfocused. Just the sort of heroic pose Ned would want, with its hint of the little boy in the suppressed grin. No wonder women found him attractive.

She looked up as her mother and her husband entered. "Mother, Barry, look what Chris brought." She handed the book to Barry. Harriet could not handle such a large volume and her cane at the same time. Her mother looked at the cover, sniffed, and hobbled toward the low-slung barrel chair she favored.

"It looks very nice," she offered. Harriet was not disparaging the book, but had never learned to conceal her disinterest. Mariesa joined Barry on the sofa, looking over his shoulder while he paged through the book.

Barry grinned. He had, by some instinct, opened it to a full-page photograph of Mariesa. She leaned toward him and studied it. Had she really looked so strained and worried back then? Barry put his arm around her waist. "How does it feel to be history?" He closed the book and laid it on the glass coffee table. "You know you're past the hump when they put out books like this."

"Oh, that's only volume one," she said. Chris barked a laugh.

"God, yes. Wait until Zeus becomes operational."

"Have the modifications been finished," Mariesa asked, "on the *Gene Bullard*?"

"Everything is ready for next month's test," Chris said. "João's report ought to be in your E-basket."

"And Will Gregorson called here the other day," said Barry. "He says the Torch is ready, too, pending software validation." Sykes entered with a tray balanced on his hand. He passed among them, allowing each to take their own glass. Mariesa hated mineral water, but Dr. Marshall had told her to avoid alcohol during the pregnancy.

"You did not tell me he had called," Mariesa said.

"You were busy. The memo is in your E-basket, anyway." Barry downed half his bourbon in one swallow and turned to Harriet, who was pretending to leaf through the big book on the coffee table. "You haven't been checking your mail lately."

Harriet looked up. "She should not fret over company matters at this time; or—" A significant look at Mariesa. "—handle chemicals in the darkroom, or spend ungodly long hours at night up on the roof."

"Oh, Mother . . . I am not some delicate flower. American

pioneer women had their babies in the field and then went back to the plowing.''

Harriet nodded. "And then died young."

Silence followed Harriet's remark. Barry turned to Chris suddenly and said. "So, what's happening with FarTrip?"

"Oh . . ." Chris made a careless gesture with his hand. "Washington is dithering as usual. They don't see the 'value' of visiting an asteroid. Say what you will about Champion, but at least the man made decisions. Donaldson won't say aye, yea, or no. None of the agencies feel they have a clear direction, so they put off choices. But Russia, Singapore, and Kenya are lined up. And Brazil, of course. President Gomes owes us.''

Barry ran a finger lightly along Mariesa's shoulder. "I wish I could go out for the test. I feel I ought to contribute more.'' He spoke idly, but Mariesa could hear the wistfulness in his voice.

She settled against Barry's comforting arm and listened to the two men. A sneaky way to brief her right under Harriet's nose. Barry was attentive to her wants and clever at such misdirection.

Prometheus had grown too big for her. There was something sad about that. It was hard to keep up with all the threads. Zeus. FarTrip. The ET diversion. The contingency planning with the Pentagon. She tried to keep current on the major policy decisions. But Aurora and Pegasus and Daedalus were cultivating a dozen projects apiece. Sometimes she missed the old days, when the Steering Committee could meet, by face or by interface, and discuss every item on Prometheus's menu. But it was as impossible to imagine the inner circle gathering to discuss Aurora's Woomera-to-Phoenix schedules as it was to go through Belinda's crop of new students every year. She felt like a mother whose son had grown and left home.

And met new friends. Wilson and MacDac and the others were busy, too. Wilson had two rams in operation, Antisana and Kilimanjaro, both carefully monitored by UN commissions. Now that the economy seemed to be picking up again, other players were coming on board. The Artemis Corporation had announced plans to launch an automated mining factory to the moon, and was selling entertainment rights to finance it; and not even the Securities and Exchange Commission had objected. Economies of scale had already brought Plank production below 27 kilotroy apiece. Federal Express and the Santa Fe Railroad had purchased two ships apiece; as had Northwest Orient Airlines. Mariesa doubted Aurora's de facto semiballistic monopoly would last much longer.

A sharp pain sliced through her and she winced. Barry, with his arm around her, noticed and gave her an inquiring look. Mariesa counted off the way she had been instructed, but . . . There was no second contraction. Relief fought with disappointment as she shook her head ever so slightly. Barry gave her a gentle squeeze.

She stiffened ever so slightly under his embrace. What did he have to be condescending about? The man's contribution to birth lasted a few seconds at the most; the woman's lasted nine months, and longer.

Mrs. Pontavecchio had prepared a vitello francese for dinner, elegantly presented in a bed of cappellini and accompanied by green beans almondine. Mariesa was sure it was another of the old woman's triumphs and that she would miss these meals dearly when the cook finally retired in August. But the odor made her unaccountably queasy, and she barely nibbled at it.

She sat at the head of the table, with Barry to her right and Chris to her left. The three of them discussed Zeus. Harriet, seated at the far end of the table, facing Mariesa and engaged with her own thoughts, seemed on a different world. Mariesa thought about drawing her into the conversation. Perhaps she ought to change the topic to roses, or babies.

But, before she could say anything, Sykes appeared in the doorway and caught Mariesa's eye. She nodded, and Sykes approached her.

"Miss, I have Mr. Redman on the line. He says it is urgent. Do you wish to speak to him?"

Harriet put her fork down on her plate, a sharp clack. "Certainly not! We are eating. Tell him you will call him back."

"Did you tell John E. we were eating?" Mariesa asked the butler.

A bob of the head. "He still insists."

"Very well. Bring my phone."

Harriet fumed and bent over her vitello, pointedly ignoring the others. Barry asked her what John E. wanted, but she only shrugged. John E. came of good family. He would not interrupt dinner save for the most compelling reasons.

Sykes brought her phone and she unfolded it. "Yes, John E., what is it?"

"I thought you would want to know," the lawyer's Virginia drawl told her, "but Cyrus Attwood plans to go into Federal court Friday in Phoenix to get an injunction against next week's test of Torch."

"An injunction?" She noticed Barry and Chris start; and Harriet's studied disinterest. "On what grounds?"

"The usual. Public safety. The environment. Anything that will sound good and mask his real motives."

"I never thought I would say such a thing, but I long to read his obituary. He is like some frantic lapdog, yapping and snipping." She covered the mouthpiece and said "Attwood" to the others. Chris nodded and Barry shook his head. Harriet said, "A boorish man, though of good stock."

"It wouldn't do any good, Mariesa," John E. said with lawyerly seriousness. "There are others who are with him, and for the same reasons. Change threatens their position."

She told Chris about the injunction. Her cousin frowned and reached into his pocket, pulling out his own phone. Mariesa ignored Harriet's petulant *tsk.*

Perhaps it was time to take the white gloves off. An economic war wasted resources urgently needed elsewhere; but a sharp attack where he least expected it might teach Cyrus and his allies to restrain themselves. Cyrus owned coal mines. Oil tankers. It shouldn't be too difficult to instigate Phil Albright or someone into action. She might even be able to use the government. There were seventy thousand pages published in the Federal Register last year alone. It was inconceivable that Cyrus's businesses were in compliance with every single regulation; inconceivable that they even knew what each regulation was. So find a noncompliance, and throw him to the bureaucrats. That would take his mind off VHI.

Champion's predecessor had done that to her, she remembered, to extort campaign support. Well, it was not the weapon but the motive that mattered.

"Very well, John E. You are on the case, I presume?"

"Certainly. If your cousin is visiting—I called his office first—tell him that the Werewolf is anxious to speak with him about the test."

Mariesa thanked Redman and disconnected. She folded the telephone and laid it on the table and sat for a long moment wrapped in thought. Harriet sighed.

"I have always said that such calls do little to aid the digestion."

"Quiet, Mother. Let me think." She leaned back in her chair and drummed fingertips against the table. "Chris, you told me that the *Bullard* is ready? And the Torch?"

"Do you think Attwood'll get his injunction?" Barry asked.

"Pick the right judge and you can get anything."

"I'm talking to Will right now," Chris announced. "He wants to know what you want to do; but he'd rather pull the test off and present the courts with a fait accompli than try to get the injunction overturned."

Mariesa nodded. "Very well. I am inclined that way, also. What does Dolores say?"

"Pegasus will go along. They're simply lending us facilities. It's our call, Will's and mine."

"Do it, then."

Chris spoke into his phone. "Will? I'll leave tonight. Expect me at Sky Harbor in the morning."

Barry said, "Good luck." Mariesa turned to him.

"Barry, why don't you go with Chris. I cannot be there to witness the test. I want you to be my eyes and ears." Chris paused with his phone tucked back into his pocket and looked from one to the other. Mariesa thought he wanted to say something, but he held his peace. Harriet's long, slow exhale was more audible.

Barry frowned. "I don't think I should leave you at this point. You're due in a week."

"Nonsense. You will be back by Friday night, and nothing will happen before then. Chris, you can brief Barry on the flight out. Barry, when you return, I will want to hear every detail."

She thought it was such a brilliant solution to the problem—her inability to be present, Barry's desire to be more useful—that she could not understand the three frowns of various intensity that greeted her. No one dissented, though; and that was the important thing.

After dinner, while Barry and Chris made plans, and Harriet repaired to the solarium to rest, Mariesa took the elevator upstairs to the second floor. Even Barry frowned when she took the stairs these days. Even *Sykes* looked concerned. It was so irritating to be "looked after."

The nursery had been put into an extra room adjacent to the master suite. And a room on the other side had been prepared for the nanny. The dislocations at Silverpond that had started with Barry's advent had spread like ripples throughout the house. Furniture rearranged here; a room put to new use there. In a hundred small ways life at Silverpond had altered and adjusted, trying to accommodate the alien particle in it. And the nursery was only one more ripple. Ripple? No, more like high tide in the Bay of Fundy. She still could not sort out the emotion she had felt when she first learned she was pregnant. Joy? Dismay? Hope? Trepidation? Later, she would pick one and retrofit it. She suspected it was that way in most cases. Hindsight named the emotions.

She had had the room done in blue, of course. Harriet was a traditionalist and Mariesa had not thought the issue worth fighting over. She had, however, insisted on a "space" motif. The wallpaper and other accessories featured spaceships and spacesuited figures in childish proportions. The ceiling she had had done as the night sky, black with small luminescent points. She had conducted a dozen interviews before finding a nanny attuned to the same outlook.

The crib was an anachronism: white wood sawn and joined in an old-fashioned design—no nails or metal fasteners—and decorated with flowers and infantilized animals. On this item, Harriet had insisted. It had been Mariesa's own crib; and Harriet's before that. Mariesa had conceded. It was a connection with the past amid the images of the future. Some things ought to be done for no other reason than that.

She ran her hand along the crib rail and felt the tears rise in her throat. She set her jaw and her lips and would not let them through. What was it about joy and sorrow that they bordered so close upon one another? Both brought tears in their wake.

She turned and sucked in her breath at the sudden figure in the doorway. "Don't sneak up behind me that way!" she said.

Barry stepped toward her and held her in his arms. "Chris is leaving," he said. "We'll be flying to Phoenix to meet with Dolores Pitchlynn. I came to say good-bye."

"I just want everything to be done with," she said. He did not ask her what she meant. The test. The pregnancy. Even she did not know. With his right hand, he stroked her short-cropped hair.

It wasn't true, anyway. She did not want things done; she wanted the new things to start, to replace all the old things that had ended. She wanted the new life in her life. She wanted the fire of Zeus to pierce the nighttime sky. She wanted to watch a spot of light in orbit depart for deep space. She even wanted the mad scheme hatched by the Pentagon to bloom. Anything to break the spell of confinement and marking time that had entangled her the last few months.

She wondered if Barry felt the same way. The day he had given up his classroom position he had shut himself in the dayroom and consumed an entire decanter of sherry. Every loss left a void and every void wanted filling.

Since then, he had thrown himself into Prometheus. If he did not have the talent for technical work, he at least showed an ability to coordinate the many interlocking activities. It came from handling fifteen-year-olds, he had joked with her once.

She began to laugh and pressed her face against his chest to stifle it.

It was a hysterically funny thought; but, considering his growing enthusiasm for Prometheus, she had put as much of herself into him as he had put himself into her.

Mariesa could never remember having seen a look of pure joy on her mother's face. The occasional dry humor, a few surprised laughs; sometimes a sort of quiet contentment. But never joy. As far back as her childhood recollections went, Mariesa could conjure up a visage that had seemed worried at best, disapproving at worst. In dusty photograph albums, even the young Harriet Gorley sported that wary frown, as if anticipating all the cares of her future.

As she had matured, Mariesa began to understand some of what underlay her mother's behavior: a core of sadness that had curdled to sour over the years. Of loyalty to Piet that never quite bent into submission. The efforts of a devoted lifeguard whose charge had drowned regardless. Endurance had replaced enthusiasm in her life.

The prospect of a grandson had stirred her, much as a poker might stir an old fire. But Harriet, her empathy, withered from long disuse, responded the only way she knew. With sparks.

With control.

"I do not know why you let that man go off to Arizona with Chris," Harriet said with the sigh of a reasonable woman surrounded by fools. *That man* was Harriet's term for Barry.

They were sitting in the library. It was not quite late enough to retire and Mariesa had a stack of executive summary reports to digest. Reading hardcopy struck her as distressingly wasteful. She could not link or cross-reference documents or call up supporting files. She felt, in fact, as if she were informationally one-eyed. But the light from her monitor had begun to bother her vision lately. She hoped her tolerance would return to normal after the birth.

"Werewolf Electronics will be testing Zeus tomorrow evening," she said without looking up. "Since I cannot be there myself, I thought it best that Barry go in my place."

"His *place* is by your side. The child could come at any time."

Mariesa removed her reading glasses—on the monitor, she simply upped the point size of the text—and regarded Harriet, who sat in the tall wing-back by the alcove across the room. It would be difficult for two people to sit farther apart and still be in the same room. Harriet had a book of flowers on her lap, another campaign to be fought in her search for the perfect rose; but she sat with her place marked by a finger.

"He will only be gone two days, Mother. The probability of the birth—"

"Such talk! What do probabilities matter? Piet was with me when you were born because, drunk or sober, he knew his duty. Willem . . ." she snorted. "Your grandfather had progress reports phoned in to him."

"Duty—"

"—means standing watch even if the enemy is nowhere in sight."

"Zeus is important."

"My grandson is important."

"One does not exclude the other." Mariesa set the report she had been reading aside. Feasibility studies for the Pentagon contingency. There would be a meeting next month among the major players. She meant to attend, assuming the birth went well; but if not, she had to select a deputy. Khan, as her CFO, and John E., as her CLO, would be the best selection, though Khan's appearance and John E.'s demeanor might press a few hot buttons among the "blue suits." She squared the pile of reports and stood, cradling them in her arms. "I'm growing tired. I think I shall retire."

"Why don't you admit the real reason you want that man out of town?"

Mariesa looked at Harriet without emotion. "And what reason would that be?"

Harriet reopened her book of floriculture. "Do you truly believe he is deceived when you throw him these scraps of assignments?"

"It is touching of you to be so concerned for him."

Harriet snorted. "I never have understood what you have seen in that man. He has his charms, I admit. He is entertaining, though perhaps too glib; but he is not our sort at all. But he also has his pride. He was a teacher, and you have taken that away from him."

"It was his decision to resign his practice. There was the . . . appearance of special treatment, given his new circumstances."

"You mean, how could the other teachers and principals engage him as an equal when he was sleeping with their boss's boss?"

Mariesa pursed her lips. "Baldly phrased, but essentially correct."

Harriet shook her head. "A teacher deprived of the classroom is like a sailor barred from the sea. And that is one quality I have granted him. He is a teacher. He was a good teacher and he knew it."

Mariesa began to walk toward the door. "Sometimes, to gain one thing you want, you must give up something else you have. There are always prices paid."

"Do you remember that child who used to come here, the one who always dressed in black?"

The non sequitur turned her around at the doorway. "Styx."

"Yes, that was what she called herself, wasn't it? Did I ever tell you that I ran into her when I was in Prague last summer?"

"No." *You've been waiting for just the right time to tell me.* "How did she look to you? Is she well?"

Harriet's lips curled in amusement. "*Now* you sound like a mother. Yes, she seemed to be getting on. Very worldly, in a slatternly sort of way. Bohemian; but then, she *was* in Bohemia."

"Mother. Humor?"

"We spoke for quite a while on the Karluv Most."

"Did you? Did she say anything about . . . me?"

Harriet cocked her head as if in thought, but Mariesa was reasonably sure she remembered quite clearly. "She said, 'Tell the Rich Lady that when you start pushing things around, they might not end up where you planned.' It made no sense to me, but I assume you know what she meant.''

Mariesa nodded dumbly. The child in her belly seemed like a weight, infinitely heavy. She remembered the nights she and Styx had spent together in the Roost, when she had thought to guide the young girl's thoughts toward the stars. She remembered the dinner they had had in Princeton with dear Keith McReynolds, and the way her eyes had lit up at the thought of freedom. And now, thinking herself free, her own thoughts had become her prison. ''I cared very much for that girl,'' she said, ''and it has only turned her against me.''

''Yes. Well,'' said Harriet, ''it is a talent some of us possess.''

Dolores Pitchlynn called on Friday. Mariesa took the call in the Roost, knowing it would be a difficult conversation. She smiled her best Chairman of the Board smile for the fibercam and waited for some similar courtesy from Dolores.

But the president of Pegasus was not given to the social amenities. A ranch woman from an old southwestern family, her skin was dark and hard with the look of old leather and did not fold easily into the creases of a smile. Her sun-bleached hair was a starkly contrasting white-blond. A careful, penurious money manager, she believed in the future because, like Chris, she had studied the balance statements and the state of technology. She did not believe in it the way Keith had, or Correy or Werewolf. She had dollar signs in her eyes, not stars.

''João is butting his nose in again,'' she said by way of greeting.

Mariesa's chair was a slung-back, contoured chair with mouse controls built into the armrests. She tapped her right index finger against the pad. ''In what way.''

''He sent me a list of names for pilot-candidates for Far-Trip.''

She meant the asteroid rendezvous mission. ''I do not see how that—''

"Doesn't he think I have the personnel to staff this project?".

"Dolores, I am sure he had no ulterior motive. Daedalus has some very good pilots. Ned DuBois is one of the best. For that matter, Aurora has good pilots also; and I do not recall objections when Wallace submitted his candidates."

"Wallace Coyle did not submit a draft critique of operational plans, either. João sent me a twenty-five-page report that his chief engineer had written. I don't like being second-guessed by backseat drivers." Dolores's face set, if that was possible, into even harder lines. Mariesa pursed her lips. If Luis Mendoza had something to say about FarTrip's profile, it would probably be something worth listening to.

"Perhaps we ought to meet over this," she said. "Have your chief project engineer review Mendoza's comments, first; then contact Zhou Hui. I will have her set something up at corporate HQ after the Zeus trials. You, João, and Wallace. And Werewolf and Chris, too, since the Zeus-Torch project ties in with FarTrip. I do not want competition among my own companies."

Dolores nodded, a bare bobbing of the head that might have been measured in millimeters. "I quite understand why you gave the original project to an offshore company. The political situation at the time was unfriendly and the government could have used Chapter 35 against us. But things have loosened up. If Donaldson isn't quite the friend that Champion was, at least he's neutral. So there's no reason to favor Daedalus any further."

"May I remind you that another election swing could easily bring the old guard back into power. I do not expect it, given our projections for the economy; but we must be aware of the possibility. Donaldson may feel pressure from the left to regulate our new industries into oblivion 'in the public interest,' and Attwood and the other dinosaurs on the right may instigate just such a move in *their* own interest. So I shall not place all of our eggs in one company's basket."

"Brazilian eggs are hardly secure," Dolores pointed out.

"Though they are on the equator. Dolores, this is a fruitless discussion. Daedalus builds the Planks and operates Leprechaun through its Irish subsidiary. Pegasus operates Earth-to-orbit freight and transport. Aurora operates Earth-to-Earth. Both Pegasus and Aurora fly Daedalus-built Planks. The Steering Committee made that partition years ago. We are a family. We ought to behave as one."

For the first time, Mariesa saw genuine amusement on Pitchlynn's face. "Have you ever met my family? Never mind, Mariesa. You'll get what you want. You always do." The screen went blank.

Mariesa sighed and rose unsteadily from her chair. João and Dolores never had gotten on with one another. The older woman had always regarded the Daedalus arrangement as an affront to Pegasus, political situation or no. Mariesa checked the clock on the wall and corrected for Phoenix time. She would have to call Chris and Will at the Argonaut mountain test facility and warn them what was going on. And Wallace, too. Aurora was neutral. With luck, the four of them should be able to referee any unpleasantness between João and Dolores; or, if not, to sit on them.

The pain came in the small hours of the morning, when the false dawn had lightened the eastern sky. It felt like a knife slashing her belly. Mariesa curled on her side and whimpered, unable to draw the breath for a scream. With her right hand she searched the bedclothes for Barry and found nothing. Where could he have gone? "Barry?" But her voice was tightened to a whisper; she could barely hear it herself.

Then she remembered that Barry had gone with Chris to witness the Zeus trials. He was out on some mountaintop in the Arizona desert. Probably even now, since the trials had been set for midnight. A second wave of pain followed before the first had quite subsided, and she sucked in her breath, holding her arms tight against her womb with her hands clenched into fists. She realized she had forgotten to count the seconds between the contractions. You were supposed to do that. But all she could think of was that Harriet had been right about her time coming the one day Barry was absent, and now she would never hear the end of it.

A third contraction, and she felt hot and wet between her legs. The pain eased and she was able to draw a breath at last. She moaned softly. "Computer," she said, as loudly as she could.

Not quite loud enough. There was no response from the voice-recognition algorithm. "Computer," she said again, more hopelessly, her head sagging into her pillow. What a cruel irony. Alone and in the dark, she might give birth right here in her own bed, just like her grandmother had. Except that Tildy had been surrounded by the best medical skills of the day.

"Mother . . ."

A shadow stirred in the easy chair by the window. Large and black, it loomed against the pattern of stars beyond. Another wave of pain passed through her like fire, but she could not take her eyes off the apparition. Great, black wings spread like the embrace of death.

"Is it the baby?" Harriet's voice. Mariesa saw her mother's face floating above her in the darkness of the room. Harriet, wrapped in a bulky blanket against the evening. Mariesa nodded without speaking. Her lip was caught tight between her teeth. She could taste blood where she had bitten through. "Soon, I think," she gasped out.

Harriet nodded and strode to the intercom on the wall, where she turned on the overhead lights. "Sykes! Miss Whitmore! It's time!" She turned back to Mariesa. "Miss Whitmore will bring your bags. Sykes will drive. Can you walk or shall I have Armando and Roy assist you?"

Mariesa inched to the edge of the mattress. The sheet beneath her was sopping. "I can walk," she said, but collapsed, unable to swing her legs over the side.

"The hell you can," said Harriet. Then: "Your sheets!"

Mariesa smiled feebly. "I think my water broke."

Harriet's eyes softened. "Wait there. I'll fetch your robe."

Miss Whitmore, a blouse and a hasty pair of jeans drawn on and looking like Mariesa's kid sister, stopped in the doorway. "I set the suitcases by the door, ma'am," she said to Harriet. Then she looked at Mariesa and stopped. Her face, always pale, seemed to fade away.

Harriet spun her around by main force and gave her a little shove in the small of the back. "Send Armando and the stableboy upstairs. And have Sykes call Jim Folkes and tell him to come immediately."

"Oh, Mother . . ." Another cramp, worse than the others tied her into a knot of pain. When it had passed, she gasped, ". . . don't . . . need . . . copter . . ."

Harriet was sitting beside her on the bed, stroking her hair gently. "Well," she said, "it is a bit close, and Mr. Folkes can be here in five minutes. The car may take too long." She chuckled, though it sounded strained to Mariesa's ears. "You wouldn't want to force poor Laurence Sprague to deliver a baby in his limousine, would you?"

Mariesa blew her breath out in little puffs. It did not seem to help. "No," she said between gasps. "Poor. Sprague."

She could already hear the whap-whap of the helicopter blades when Armando and Roy came upstairs and plucked her gently from the bed. They carried her past Harriet, who huddled whispering with Miss Whitmore on the balustraded walkway overlooking the atrium outside her bedroom door. "Just strip the bed and destroy the sheets," she heard her mother say. "Perhaps the mattress, as well."

She wanted to tell Harriet that it was a mad extravagance, even for one of the Gorleys, who were known for their spendthrift ways; but the best she could manage was to turn her head to look at the damaged sheets.

It was funny. She couldn't remember having had red sheets put on.

3.

Search Light

Arizona had a lot in common with the moon. Or maybe with Mars. Not quite so barren, perhaps; but life was sparse and odd and strange. Twisting Joshua trees. Sly-eyed, languid lizards reclusive in the late-afternoon sun. Barrel-chested saguaro cacti scattered in surrender across a landscape baked and shimmering in the heat. The land had a dry, metallic smell, like a teakettle left on the stove after all the water had boiled off. Barry, who had spent his entire life in the rain forest of the Pacific Northwest, and the moist, loamy oak and hemlock of the New Jersey uplands, found the landscape disturbingly alien.

Test Site Zeus was situated in a remote corner of the Luke Air Force Base testing range in the southwestern part of the state, about as far from civilization as you could get and still be on the same planet. The sun was just touching the peaks behind them, when Will Gregorson turned the Land Rover off the county road onto a rutted dirt track. A sign by the turnoff read RESTRICTED AREA, but there were no sentries or gates in view. The road climbed sharply into the Sand Tank Mountains, past knife-edge, sandpaper outcroppings, edging against red-rocked cliffsides. In places the track was nothing more than a worn spot in smooth, exposed stone. The boundary between "road" and "landscape" became progressively more arbitrary.

Jetliner into Phoenix Sky Harbor, company shuttle jet to Yuma. Air Force chopper to the staging area at the base of the mountains; finally a four-wheel into the ragged hills. Any farther, Barry thought, and they'd mount a mule train. But treacherous downdrafts raked the hillsides and canyons by night. There was no flying this last leg.

Barry tugged the baseball hat Werewolf had given him back down over his face and settled more comfortably in the Land Rover's backseat. Why was he out here in this godforsaken country when he should have been at Silverpond awaiting the birth of his son? Because the test was important to Mariesa, and she could not come herself? Her observer, she had said. Very well. If that was what she wanted, he would observe. Five years of practice had taught him how to please her. Yet, if she could have come, would he have been invited along? Why on earth had he been so pathetically pleased to be asked?

It was only a two-day trip, he reminded himself. He touched his jacket pocket; felt the hard lump there. He was no farther away from her than a phone call.

The test was scheduled for midnight, and preparations were well under way when Gregorson parked the Land Rover beside a row of trailers parked atop the mountain. A ring of bright halogen floodlights encircled the site. The metal-ceramic Torch gleamed in the desert night, and one assembly jutted toward the heavens like a high tech antiaircraft gun. Barry shivered and hugged himself within his jacket as he and Chris circled the giant laser. No one had told him that the desert became a freezer when the sun went down.

Barry had sat through the afternoon briefing at Pegasus, back in Phoenix; but the talk about "in-view angles" and "thin-film CdTe photovoltaic arrays" and "electrodeless pulsed inductive thrusters" was all geek to him. He was in

Nerd City, by damn; and the natives (in their colorful folk costumes of lab coats, pocket protectors, and belt calculators) saw no need to translate for the *touristas*. He had taken notes anyway, because he knew Mariesa would ask later. Detailed notes, because he did not know what was important and what was not.

As Mariesa's husband, he was, ipso facto, a member of the inner circle; so he knew the purpose and scope of Zeus, if not the gory details. The laser—and its targeting software—would attempt to hit a panel of solar cells installed on a modified Plank, the *Gene Bullard*. The *Bullard* was fitted with a new sort of engine, an electrically powered thruster running off the solar cells. If the laser could hit the target, hold the target, and put enough energy into the small area of the array, it could power the spacecraft's engines from the ground. The Torch would never lift a craft from Earth to orbit, but it could take a craft already in orbit and goose it into a higher one. Say from LEO to GEO.

If it worked. There seemed to be plenty of people who hoped it would not, or who dismissed its importance. They were not all manufacturers of transfer-stage rockets, either. Curiously, it seemed to him, the biggest vote of confidence had come from Cyrus Attwood. If he hadn't thought it would succeed, he would never have gone to court to stop it.

Barry looked at his watch. *Would go* to stop it. They still had almost twelve hours. Unless Attwood's attorney was the sort to wake federal judges in the middle of the night.

"This is a one-megawatt free electron laser," Werewolf explained with a father's pride. "The focusing mirror is a ten-meter, segmented optic design. Each segment is MEMS-coordinated with its neighbors so that the whole array acts like a single mirror." Barry and the Air Force man nodded; the "blue suit" in understanding, Barry simply in acknowledgment. "The MEMS units," Gregorson went on, "are one hundred square microns each, so that the mirror resembles a membrane more than a solid structure. The receiver array is similar . . ."

Chris van Huyten tilted his head back, one hand clapped to

keep his hard hat in place. "You *have* conducted the usual validation tests, haven't you?" He didn't look at Gregorson when he said that, so he didn't see the look of annoyance that Barry caught.

"We conducted design verification testing at conceptual, alpha, beta, and configuration," Gregorson growled. "All the calculations were verified using alternative formulas before we bent tin. The fabrication processes were qualified through capability studies during pilot and startup; and the production runs were closely monitored and the results analyzed statistically to detect anomalies. The software ran—and—wrecked—ten generations of digital sims before we ever loaded it to hardware. . . ."

Chris turned around and looked at him. "That wasn't what I asked."

Gregorson snorted. "I know what you asked. You asked, did we make sure the damned contraption works when we plug it in? Hell, yes. We only had forty-eight hours' notice, but we tested all the systems. I throw that switch there and all the lights light up. I enter the right commands and the beacon sensor responds. I run the tracking program and the damned mirror follows the sky from fifteen degrees above the rising horizon to fifteen degrees above setting, and we'll get the damned test run before any injunction can reach us. Anything else?"

Chris stiffened. With his height, he could not help looking down his nose, at least a little. "It would be rather a sour note if the equipment failed to function, wouldn't you say?"

"Now, look here, Chris—"

"He's asking for my sake," Barry said on impulse. Chris turned and gave him a puzzled look, but said nothing. Barry said, "I need to learn more about project management if I'm to become effective. Validation. Verification. Failure Modes and Effects Analysis. Fault trees. It's all new to me. I don't even know what questions to ask, so I asked Chris to help me." Gregorson scowled and grunted something unintelligible.

Barry didn't know why he had put himself between the two

men. Only that he'd had the sudden sense that the tension everyone felt could easily snap back like a rubber band, and the nervous questions and impatient answers could grow into a genuine argument. Chris had asked only from the strain of the approaching deadline; and Gregorson had reacted defensively for the same reason. Only Barry remained cool and objective—because, of the three of them, he alone had no personal stake in how the test worked out.

Well, aside from the effect on Mariesa; but that was a personal stake of a different sort.

The Air Force observer, a General Beason, checked his watch. "First pass in twenty minutes," he said conversationally. Gregorson looked at him, and wiped his hands together. "Yeah."

"We'll post ourselves over here," Chris said to Gregorson, indicating an open area near the equipment trailers. "Stay out of your hair."

Gregorson rumbled. "And I've got a lot hair to stay out of." He ran a hand through his bushy mane. "Hell, I'm a spare wheel here, too. You don't think any of my engineers would let the damned *president* touch the equipment, do you?" He shook his head and shoved his hands in his pants pockets. "Sometimes I miss the old days, back in the garage in Cleveland. I haven't burned my hand with a soldering gun in a good long while."

"I know how you feel," Barry said. Werewolf looked at him quizzically, but Barry did not elaborate. If he got started on *that* subject, he might be the one who needed reining in.

Chris said, "I understand Dolores runs a cattle ranch out by Yuma, Will. She might have a branding iron you could borrow, if burning your hide is what you miss."

Gregorson screwed up his face. "Yeah, I don't see old Prunella up here freezing her tits off."

Barry tucked his hands under his armpits. "Just shows she's smarter than us."

Gregorson turned away. "Well, there's some of us, when the new world rises over the horizon, we like to be there to see it."

A light beam probed the sky briefly and a Werewolf technician called out, "Sodium illumination positive," and another answered, "We have turbulence sampling." And a moment later: "Compensating." Barry watched the engineers and technicians run through their checklists. In his own gruff style, Werewolf was a dreamer; but he had a point. If the day ever came when this night mattered, the artists would paint this oasis of light in the cold desert night, not the offices or boardrooms where high officials awaited reports. They would paint Marianne Dyson, the Pegasus engineer, hunched over her equipment, coordinating the test with the crew aboard *Gene Bullard*, two hundred miles above. In the foreground, they would put Werewolf Gregorson, whose expertise had created the great laser, leaning intently forward like a bear ready to spring; and Chris van Huyten, whose researchers had made it possible, tall and thin, his aristocratic features frozen in anticipation. And the Air Force general calmly waiting in the background swaddled in his wool-collared flight jacket and with his arms folded across his chest, only the rapid puffs of vapor steaming from his lips betraying his excitement. The techs and the riggers—one wore his hard hat backward, like a baseball cap—they would be painted in, too.

And himself. Barry Fast, onetime high-school teacher; now husband-consort and soon-to-be father. The spare-wheel observer. They'd paint him in the scene, too; though he had brought nothing to the mesa, himself. The creators, the builders, the operators, and . . . the observers. Barry shivered, suddenly and uncontrollably, as the desert wind pierced his suit coat.

The general leaned close to Chris. "How much of the megawatt do you expect *Bullard* to harvest?"

Chris rose up and down on the balls of his feet—from impatience, the cold, or both. "Using our new Argonaut cells, we expect conversion efficiency to be in the low sixties."

The general nodded. "Not bad."

"Not bad? Damn good for thin-film. Eighty percent of the beam energy is within the spot diameter, and we'll get maybe seventy percent of that. The real trick is whether Will's contraption can acquire the target and hold the spot small enough to fit within the array perimeter. The receiver is big, because we made it light—two microns of film over twenty-five microns of substrate, that's tissue paper—but it is not the broad side of a barn, by any means . . ."

Barry walked away from the others, out of the circle of light. No one would be looking for him to answer questions. Nothing would remain undone if he failed to do it. There was no reason to paint him into the scene with the others.

He walked around to the right. It was darker outside the immediate site, almost as if a curtain had been drawn between it and him. The scene seemed, by some trick of lighting, to become small and distant. Barry's shoe caught a rock and sent it skittering into the base of a short, spike-leaved plant. The leaves rustled and something unseen leapt fleeing into the night, making Barry jump.

One of the riggers had taken a seat on a stack of structural members left over from the construction. He wore a heavy flannel workshirt in red and black checks and scarred, metal-tipped palomino boots that made his feet seem twice as big. He saw Barry and made a seating motion to the space beside him. Barry shrugged and accepted the invitation.

The steel was cold; he'd freeze his butt off. Now he knew why Arizonans tolerated the daytime heat. *On the average, you're comfortable.* The rigger was a young man, mid-twenties with a fringe beard that looked almost Amish and a death-skull earring that did not. Even in the bleached lighting of the halogen poles, his skin looked dusky. His eyes were folded at the corners, but he did not look Oriental. He grinned at Barry. "Ready for the show?"

"I don't know that there'll be much to see," Barry said. "They told me that 850, uh . . . nanometers? Nanometers . . . was near the edge of visible light. We may see nothing but the 'tracer' beam that lets them know the thing's working."

"Yeah?" The rigger seemed to consider that. "Too bad. There ought to be a show." He frowned some more and scratched his beard. "The tracer's for air turbulence, right?"

Barry blinked. "That's what they tell me. You've got to

keep the beam tight, so the spot fits inside the target array. Air turbulence can spread it too wide to be useful.''

That was the second purpose of the test. The ''stealth'' purpose. The Consortium designing the demonstration solar power satellite was still hung up in environmental-impact studies. Zeus was a backdoor way to test the beam control software. Solar power satellites—''power-sats''—would face the same sort of targeting and turbulence problems aiming down toward the Earth. For some reason, Phil Albright's crowd did not seem to regard a beam from Earth to space with quite the same dread fascination as they did one from space to Earth. To the software, though, it was just a matter of plus or minus.

The rigger grunted. ''Wider the beam, the thinner the soup. That's what my buddy says. Like, you gotta concentrate those watts onto those screens.''

Jesus, even the riggers knew as much about the project as he did. ''The tracer laser lights up the sodium at the edge of space,'' Barry said. ''The instruments down here read that light and figure out how the air in between is disturbed. Then that computer tells the computer running the mirror, which adjusts the big laser to compensate.''

The rigger tugged on his beard. ''Yeah, but what I don't get is, if the air is *really* turbulent, it'll change every second, won't it?''

''And the laser passes through it in a nanosecond.'' Barry snapped his fingers. ''No matter how turbulent the air is, it can't change faster than the beam adjusts.''

''*Ai, que pendejo*! I already told you that, Chino,'' said a new voice behind Barry's shoulder. ''You don't believe me or what?''

Barry turned and saw the rigger with the ponytail and the reversed hard hat. He wore a big grin and a ragged goatee and a T-shirt that featured a desiccated skeleton in a lawn chair. The lawn chair was set in a typical Arizona desert scene, and the skeleton clutched an empty water glass. The legend read, ''. . . but it's a *dry* heat.'' The rigger glanced at Barry. ''Just because a guy wears a suit you—'' He looked back and gave

Barry an astonished stare. Then he laughed. "Mr. Fast? Is that you?"

Barry cocked his head. It was a naggingly familiar face, longer and fuller than he remembered, but . . . "You were a student . . ." The name would not come. Not one of his star pupils, then. The rigger took his hard hat off and played a few chords of air guitar. Barry slapped his knee and pointed. "Morris Tucker! Class of Ought-One." He stuck out his hand.

Chino said, "*Morris*?" and Tucker rolled his eyes as he clasped Barry's hand.

"You've blown my cover, Mr. Fast. Name's *Meat*. Thought you knew that." He didn't seem too upset, though. He perched himself on the steel between Barry and his friend, and clapped Chino on the shoulder. "This guy here," he told Chino, wagging a thumb at Barry, "was one of my teachers back in high school. A beany one, too." And he looked at Barry. "But I guess you knew that, Mr. Fast."

Barry looked away. "You don't know until your students come back and tell you." And what a feeling it was. What a goddamn, flaming-A rush when you heard it. Barry paused a moment, until he was sure he could speak. "Call me Barry," he managed.

Tucker shook his head. "Nah. I gotta stand up straight, say 'sir' or 'ma'am,' and call you 'Mr. Fast.' "

Chino said, "What kind of high school you go to, man?"

"And in return," Barry recited, "I will address you as 'Mr. Tucker.' "

They looked at each other for a moment before they both burst out laughing and Tucker said, "Yeah, those days were rated. First time I wasn't treated like a kid." He shook his head. "Remember Ms. G?" I never really got science, you know; until this one time when she burned a bunch of stuff in class. And then she wouldn't explain anything. Told us to make our own guesses—'hypotheses.' See? I remembered— and *then* we had to come up with a new experiment that would show which guess was right. Really weirded us, you know. But when we were wrong, it was because we were wrong and not shut-up-and-listen, stupid. You know?"

Barry said, "I know." He remembered how proud Gwen had been of that particular lesson; and he knew why, but he was curious if Meat knew why, too. "Seems like a roundabout way to learn about oxidation," he offered, and Chino grunted his puzzled agreement.

"Me, too. I go, why can't she just *tell* us. So one day, I'm crossing Thicket Street from the parking lot to the school, you know; and I'm thinking about that old heap I used to drive. You ever see it? A Camaro, mostly. What a wreck! I coulda left it on a Newark street corner and the homeboys'd put parts *into* it. So I'm thinking about how the bottom's near rusted out that if I stepped too hard on the brake my foot'd go through and stop the car with shoe leather . . . and I think about that experiment, and it hits me. Whack!" A fist to the side of his head. "*Rust is the flame of iron.* Oh, man, there's a metal song in that, I know it. And I realized that Ms. G wasn't trying to teach us the answers. She was teaching us how to ask the questions."

Barry saw Chris van Huyten waving to him. "Looks like they're ready to start the test." Meat looked at his watch.

"Yeah. It's that time."

Barry stood and shook his trousers, and Meat stood with him. He was surprised to notice how tall the boy had gotten. He was taller than Barry now, with lean, hardened muscles. "So, how'd you wind up here, Meat? What did you do with yourself after graduation?"

The young man momentarily lost his grin and his eyes looked inward. "You know about what happened at Pandya's, don't you?"

Barry nodded. "According to the store cameras, Tani Pandya would be dead if you hadn't pulled her into the stockroom with you."

Tucker shrugged. "Yeah, well, I don't know if I did her any favors. She was still wailing over her old man when the police let me go home. Couldn't deal with that shit, man; not then. So, I hit the road." He walked with Barry back toward the equipment trailers. Chino tagged along. "After that, I hitched to Seattle, but, man, the town was stiff, and everyone went how all the action was in Milwaukee. But I don't play goofball, so . . .'' A careless shrug, but one that hurt, and hurt bad, as Barry could see in the shrouded eyes. "Played a few gigs here and there," Meat went on, "but every herbie with an amp was booking goof, so nobody would cheese me. Metal was rusted out. I finally wound up in construction. Then I heard how the van Huytens want to build like these power satellites, you know? Me, I'm no scientist like Cheng-I Yeh, or a hotdog pilot like I heard Chase wanted to be; but . . . hell, I figure they'll need riggers up there as much as they need pilots and scientists. So, I put in an app to Ossa and Pelion when they started hiring for this, and they took me."

Barry looked at him. "Why so interested in space construction?"

"He's nuts," said Chino.

Meat did not look at his friend. Another shrug, more elaborate, more affected, more concealing. He looked at the ground while he kicked at a stone with his construction boots. He hunched his arms close to his body. "Dunno. Maybe, just once, I just want to feel I was part of something important."

Score another one for Belinda and Mariesa, Barry thought. Belinda believed that to inspire the students you needed a dream that was bigger than life. Maybe so; though it sometimes seemed that it was less inspiration than self-promotion, a betrayal of the students' trust. *Barry,* Belinda had said, *we cannot help but mold the young minds in our care to* something. *And if that something is "nothing in particular,"* that *may be the cruelest betrayal of all.*

Barry had sniffed around that excuse now for seven years, unable to refute it, yet unable entirely to embrace it. "Don't make value judgments" had been one of the watchwords of his youth; and he still believed it, or he told himself he did. Yet, it had given rise to a world without values, and with very little judgment. For dealing with diversity, value neutrality had proven a weak substitute for the search for common values.

Even the rebels would be cheated, Belinda had told him, *for without values what could they rebel against?*

Barry looked sideways at Meat and wondered where the boy

would be today if Belinda had not quietly and methodically stuffed dreams into his head. Maybe a warehouse stock handler, or a plumber. Making good money and doing valuable, if unsung, work. Or maybe snorting coke and shooting twofers in biker bars, bouncing from gig to busted gig, singing songs like a hundred other metal club bands and maybe swallowing the wrong end of a shotgun one fine winter's night. Maybe he would have wound up in the Arizona desert, anyway, dreaming about rigging the Big One. You couldn't possibly know.

Or maybe, just maybe, had he pursued them, this young man's songs would have filled some hole in the world's heart. They might even have been the songs that Mariesa had intended Styx to sing, before her poetry had drifted into screed and polemic. Was it right that Belinda had deprived the world of that possibility?

Yes. It was right. If the price of priceless song is suicide.

No, if you only dreamed another's dream.

The first pass was a qualified success. The technicians at their panels cheered and Chris van Huyten and Will Gergorson traded solemn handshakes with each other and with General Beason. Meat waved his hard hat in the air.

Barry removed his protective goggles and let them dangle from his neck. A lot of celebration, he thought, for something they had not even seen with their own eyes. The beam was invisible and the target was two hundred miles away. But all the dials and meters said A-OK. Personally, he thought that just hitting solar panels on an orbiting Plank was an achievement; like getting a kiss on your first date. To snare half a megawatt from the beam and use it to power the thrusters was—like getting some tongue back on that first kiss. (That had sure powered *his* thrusters, Barry remembered. . . .)

There was a lot of singsong back and forth among the techs about thrust, and specific impulse, and conversion efficiencies. Fifty percent was a little less than what Werewolf had been hoping for, so, after the target had passed outside the viewing angle, he and Chris put their heads together and announced that they would use a lower frequency on the Plank's next orbit, and trade some power for a tighter beam. Even if Attwood had gotten his injunction by now, no way could notice be served much before midmorning. The decision was relayed up and around the satellite communication network and an acknowledgment came back from *Bullard* within a few minutes.

Werewolf clapped his hands. "Okay, gang. *Bullard* will be back in view in about ninety minutes. Take an hour break, but don't go anywhere."

Meat shook his head. "Damn. There goes the side trip to Vegas." He reached into his shirt pocket and slipped out a deck of cards, which he riffled with the tip of his thumb. "You want to play a few hands with Chino and the boys? Or do you have something to do?" He tossed his head at the trailer, where Werewolf and the others were huddled.

"No," he told Meat. "I'm just here to take notes." He followed Meat back to where the construction workers had collected. They were excited and laughing, too. Maybe they hadn't understood the science, but, by God, they had built the fucking equipment! A guy takes pride, Meat told him, in making something work. Someone tossed around a couple six-packs of Keystone. Barry caught one can and snapped the tab. The beer was cool, but not cold, but he drank it anyway.

Meat perched at one end of a girder. Chino and a few other hard hats gathered around. One of "the boys," Barry noticed, was a young woman with a canvas tool belt and a yellow hard hat bearing the Arizona Public Service logo. Two others were Air Force tech sergeants—only fair, since this was their test range. Meat split the deck and riffled the two halves together. "Take notes, hunh? Like for school, right?" He did an accordion shuffle and gave the deck to the APS woman to cut.

Barry waited a beat before answering. He lowered the beer can from his lips. "No. Not for school." He found speech suddenly difficult. *God, I still miss teaching.* Not the pay, though teachers had been well over New Jersey's median salary even before Mentor. Not the hours. Toward the end, he'd been working like a dog. But the promise in the hopeful faces; and the challenge in the closed ones. The thought that, here and there, he had made a difference in someone's life. "I've left teaching," he said quietly. Meat twisted around in surprise.

"You shitting me? How come?"

Barry shrugged and tried to appear as if he did not care; as if it had been just one more career move. Which, in a sense, it had been. "I married my boss."

Meat's eyes widened. "Dr. Karr? But she's a —"

"No. *Her* boss."

Meat opened his mouth again, but Barry held his hand up and shook his head. Meat took the hint and did not name names. He just grinned and said, "I don't blame you. Who needs the nine-to-five, right?"

Barry scowled and tilted his head back. Yeah, who needs it? He finished the can and crumpled it.

The trailer door opened and Chris appeared in the doorway with his cell phone in his hand. "Barry!" he called.

"What is it?" But even as he spoke, his own cell phone chirped at him. He fumbled in his jacket pocket and pulled it out. At one in the morning, it could not possibly be good news. He flipped the cover open and pressed the Receive button. "Yes?"

"Mr. Fast, this is Sykes. You must return to Silverpond, immediately. There has been a . . . problem."

It was more than the night desert that chilled him. "Mariesa? The baby? What? Who?" He wasn't making sense; he couldn't put a sentence together. "What happened?"

"We will not know for several hours, sir." Probably static, but Barry thought he heard Sykes's voice crack. Almost certainly static. "A charter jet is waiting at Phoenix Sky Harbor. How soon can you and Mr. Chris be there?"

The long drive down the mountain . . . The chopper to Yuma . . . Or could they go directly to Phoenix? How long? Too long. Every minute, lost forever.

Chris had reached him, already tucking his own phone away. His face looked tight and strained. "Did Harriet call you?"

Two plus two equals . . . "Sykes." Something had happened

to Mariesa, and the first person Harriet had called was cousin Chris. She'd had the butler call the husband. Or, possibly, Sykes had called on his own initiative. Do you want the reason, Barry? Do you want to conjure up Harriet's oh-so-reasonable face and hear her say, *You and Chris were together. One phone call was sufficient.*

"Will said he'd lend us the Land Rover, but he can't spare any techs, with Bullard due back in thirty minutes." Chris struck his left palm repeatedly with his fist. He looked everywhere but in Barry's eyes.

Meat folded his hand and dropped it to the impromptu card table. "I'll drive you down," he announced. "Get lost in the dark, man, you'll go over the edge."

Barry nodded his thanks. To Chris, he said, "Did Harriet give you any details?" Chris shook his head. That was bad. If they could have said *she's out of danger* or *she's doing fine*, they would have. You could often hear the message by listening to what wasn't said.

They didn't run to the Land Rover, not exactly; but Meat had the car in gear before Barry had fastened his seat belt. Barry took his phone out and punched the speed-dial number for Dr. Marshall. Chris leaned forward from the backseat and put a hand on his shoulder. "She'll be all right," he said.

"Sure." There was no answer at Marshall's. Should he call Silverpond, or try the hospital? "Damn Cyrus Attwood!" he said. "If it wasn't for him, we wouldn't have been out here tonight."

"If it hadn't been for him," Chris answered, "the Phoenix/Allentown route would be open and Aurora could have us back East in fifteen minutes." He collapsed into his seat and looked into the darkness outside the car. "We can't afford to lose her," he said, "she's the glue that holds us together."

Barry turned away and faced forward. "There are other reasons," he said to the night beyond the windshield.

"Oh, God, yes," Chris said. But Barry hardly heard him and did not respond.

*   *   *

Charlie Jim met them at Newark Airport and ferried them by helicopter to Freylinghuysen Hospital. Red-eyed from lack of sleep, head pierced by nails of headache, mouth gummy and chin sandpaper, Barry led the way down to the third-floor critical-care unit from the rooftop helipad. He knew the way, God help him; he knew the way. They had put Shannon here after her suicide attempt.

It was even the same room. The gods of chance had a nasty streak to them.

The harridan barred the door.

"You cannot go in," Harriet announced. "She has lost a great deal of blood, and is still unconscious." They were standing in the nurses' station. Critical-care units ringed them in a horseshoe. Chris grimaced, crossed his arms tight, and turned to look through the window at Mariesa. Barry reached out and lifted Harriet by the elbows and moved her aside.

"That's my wife in there."

Four brisk strides took him to Mariesa's bedside. Her skin was pale and drawn. Her mouth hung partly open, emphasizing her undershot chin. Tubes brought her blood and nutrients from plastic, harness-hung bags, metered by small blue boxes with red numerical displays. A nurse, sitting in a straight-back chair on the other side of the bed, looked at him, then at Harriet, then back to her cliputer without speaking. She scanned certain readouts with a wand and entered other items on the keyboard.

"Mariesa?" he said, sitting slowly into another chair. "Riesey?" He never called her Riesey except in private, except when they made love. "What happened?" he asked the nurse. When she hesitated, he snapped, "I'm her husband, dammit!"

The nurse seemed to jerk, and her eyes dropped to her cliputer. "She had a miscarriage. As nearly as the midwife-doctor could determine, the fetus died three days ago, shortly after the last examination."

"Dead?" Barry remembered the nursery furniture; the wallpaper with the baby spacemen floating in it. Toys waiting to be played with; laughter and cries never to be heard. Insanely, irrelevantly, he thought, *We'll have to let the nanny go.* "His name was William."

"Excuse me?"

"The baby. We were going to call him William." *William Raymond van Huyten-Fast.* Barry had even imagined the boy's face, imagined it lighting up when he came home. "When . . . How . . ." He took a deep breath. "Dr. Marshall said everything was fine." It was a lie, a horrible lie. Manifestly, everything was not fine, could not have been fine. He said it as an accusation.

"These things happen," the nurse explained. It was no explanation at all. She might as well have said that the Fates had clipped the thread of life. For a moment, he wanted to strike her, to make her see what a cruel thing she had said; but the feeling passed. A nurse, she must have seen as bad or worse, and built her own armor over the years. "Will she make it?" he asked.

The hesitation was barely noticeable. "The chances are good."

Harriet, in the doorway, said, "The doctor needs to see her." The man behind her was a stranger, far too young to entrust a life to. But his eyes were tired, and older than his body. He had not had much sleep, either.

Barry rose and thanked the nurse. As he passed close to her on the way out, he nodded imperceptibly to the doctor and murmured, "Tired people make mistakes." The nurse's eyes widened momentarily; then she nodded.

"I'll double-check everything."

Barry smiled a weak smile and left the CCU. Harriet and Chris flanked him. He wondered if the waiting room still had that awful soda machine. At the swinging door, and before they stepped outside into the corridor, Harriet stopped and said in a low, bitter voice, "This is all your fault."

Barry had no feelings left for anger. "Mine."

Chris said, "Really, Aunt Harriet . . ."

"She was too old for a pregnancy. I tried to tell her that. I told her she ought to have it terminated, for safety's sake."

"She did it for you," Barry said, hearing cruelty in his own voice, and not much caring. "You wanted grandchildren. I never heard a word from you these last nine months."

"The blame is not mine. I'll not have it." Harriet was clenched so tight she seemed to vibrate. Her eyes were pits where hope and fear waged battle, and denial vied with misery. She slapped Barry on the cheek so hard he felt nothing.

And just as suddenly, he had wrapped her in his arms and held her tight against the storm that rent her. They both wept. It was an odd moment of oneness. They had found a ground on which they both could meet, and Barry wondered with a part of his mind if that meant there might be other grounds.

Which only meant that later, when he had returned to Silverpond to wash up and rest, and he played his voice mail and heard Shannon wishing him the prayers of John and herself and the girls, that he could really feel deep down how big a shit he was.

INTERLUDE:

A Settled Rest

The first time, Roberta missed the turn entirely. A lot had changed in seven years. Eastport was barely recognizable. The Grey Horse Pike had been widened and made restricted-access. You no longer had a stoplight every few hundred yards. You could keep going and never stop, never pause, never even know what you had passed. The little strip mall on the north side of the highway had depended on casual traffic pulling off and on the pike. It had withered and died when the road had been made a thruway. But Grey Horse Mall, a little farther down, had swollen from the traffic.

Roberta pulled off the exit ramp and turned left through the underpass, then onto the service road on the south side, and started back the way she had come. This was more like it. This was the old street! She could see in the contours of the service road a memory of the county lane she had lived on. Almost there.

The trees planted along the roadside after the pike had been widened stood in regular, equally spaced rows. "Restoration," they called it. But the old woods beside her house had been a tangle, a jungle full of monkey vines and sassafras and pinxter flower. (And poison sumac. She grinned to herself at that memory.) The woods had been smaller than an even smaller Styx had imagined, but it was a part of her childhood. Now a slice of it had been taken, and the road builder had thought that these *seedlings* could replace it.

She slowed as she took the turn and then, unbelieving, she let the car coast gradually to a stop in the gravel at the side of the road. For a minute, she sat there with her hands on the wheel of Emmett's borrowed car and stared at the ragged weeds swaying in the wind and the abutment for the traffic ramp just beyond.

The house was gone.

She turned the motor off. In the silence, the rush of cars on the highway filtered through the line of struggling trees. It had been a whisper once, through a thicker, older stand. It was a torrent now. The trees were thinner; and the traffic greater.

She stepped out of the car and into New Jersey's springtime chill. Her feet crunched on the gravel as she walked to the site. The schoolbus used to stop *here*. And the mailbox on its wobbly post had been *there*. She stepped through the space where the gate had sagged open in the weathered, unpainted wooden fence. Barnwood, Beth had called it, as if that made it trendy.

There was no sign of the house. Yes, there was. A line of half-buried cinder blocks that must have marked one side of the foundation peeked through the waving, chest-high weeds. The familiar odor of milkweed and wild onion enveloped her. The woods she remembered would return someday, and claim the spot where the house had been. A few boards with rusted nails in them, a few sheets of torn tar-paper roofing, one block of asphalt shingles the color of light shit. That had been the siding, she thought. She had always hated the color. She stooped and picked up the square. It felt moist and smooth on the back side; warm and pebbly on the face.

Underneath the shingles, sun-faded until black and white blended into one another, molded and rotted by the damp ground (though partly protected by the shingles), home to slugs and blind, pale, crawling things, lay the poster of goth-rocker Alaryk Castlemayne. She tried to pick it up, and it fell apart in her hands.

For some reason, she began to cry. She threw the shingle square as hard as she could and it sailed through the wind like an ungainly kite before banking and crashing into the weeds. She had thought about this moment for months, ever since she had encountered van Huyten's mother on the Charles Bridge. She had imagined half a dozen reactions from Beth, ranging from stony rejection to tears of joy. The one thing she had not imagined was that there would be no reaction, no reactor, not even a venue for the reacting. You could plan for every future but the one that came.

The letters had stopped coming years ago. Had it been surrender, or something more? Ought she to have opened at least the last one?

But I didn't know, then, that it was the last one.

It struck her that she was alone in a very large country. When you came right down to it, she had always counted on Beth and that old shingle-sided shack being there.

She thought again of the decayed poster rotting under the shingles and began to sob. That her mother had died and she had never even learned about it; or that her mother had left behind in an abandoned home all of Styx's childhood.

Her first thought, when she had gained control over her tears, was that she might wangle a job teaching. After all, she was a well-known poet, a leader in the New Art. Colleges ought to vie to have her *in residence*. (Not Princeton, though. The Ivies were still clasped firmly in the death grip of the post-moderns. The New Art was an abomination to the Establishment.) But New Jersey had any number of private and public colleges; and beyond that lay New York and Philadelphia. If she could not secure a post at Bryn Mawr or Chestnut Hill, she ought to turn in her credentials.

Though having lived so very far away, she wanted to stay in Wessex County for a while. So the first step was to pick up a copy of the *North Orange Register* and check out the apartments for rent. Rents were cheaper in the western half of the county, and you didn't have to drive too far to hop on the Boonton Line and ride into the city. There'd been a convenience store at the corner of Wessex and Maple Grove, she remembered, not too far from the school. It had to have a newsrack, right? And that was the side of town where she wanted to look, anyway. She'd be just as happy if she never saw Eastport, Downtown, or the Locks again.

She took the short way, straight through Downtown, or what was left of it. The old Gorton Building was gone, a profitless department store replaced by a parking lot—perfect for people who had no store to go to. Urban planning at its finest. Queen Anne Boulevard, with its boarded-up stores and sullen gang-bangers loitering on the corners. Roberta jumped the light when it changed and turned sharp left before the oncoming traffic could move. Downtown had not improved in the last seven years.

The West Side was in better shape. Middle-class and comfortable. She even saw a few signs of budding prosperity: one or two of the ranch-styles were adding second stories.

The In-and-Out was still where she remembered it. A little shabbier, perhaps. There was a rock-sized hole in the big sign above the window and a jumble of white and black spray paint on the blank wall facing Wessex. There were a half dozen people inside. Roberta pulled a copy of the *Register* from the pile in front of the ice-cream freezer and stood in line at the checkout.

A chubby Indian woman worked the register. Roberta scanned the headlines while she waited her turn. The *Register* was just as parochial and small town as she remembered. The annual Witherspoon-Pitcher basketball game had gone off without a single arrest. The Grey Horse widening project would be extended into Berwick Township. Stop the presses! Even the national news was reduced to a small-town perspective. The local office of the Peoples' Crusades announced that their organization was funding a scientific study of the effects of laser power beaming on the ozone layer. When Roberta reached the counter, she plunked down her quarter and turned away. But before she could take two steps, the woman at the counter called to her.

"Styx?"

Roberta stopped and turned. The chubby woman smiled at her expectantly. Roberta stared until the smile started to fade. "You don't remember me, do you?"

"You're Tani Pandya." The smile resurfaced. Styx couldn't believe it. Tani had been one of the brightest girls in the class, tapped for valedictorian after Jenny Ribbon had run away. What was she doing here, of all places? She should have been . . . not here.

"I read about you sometimes," Tani said. "In *The New Yorker* and the *Times*. I bought all your books."

Don't talk to me like that! Don't come on me like some herbie who has to live through someone else's accomplishments. You should have been writing your *own books,* damn *it. And we'd trade: my poems for your stories. Or your science text. Or whatever it was you were meant to do.* All she could think to say was "What are you doing here?"

Tani answered quietly, "Running Baba's store for him."

And then she remembered. "Oh. Whatever happened to your father? I left town just after the robbery."

"He died. They operated, and they repaired his jaw and replaced his blood; but he never really got well; and he died a year later."

"I'm sorry to hear that."

"It was a long time ago. It seems like another life."

"Yes, I know the feeling." She had felt that way about her childhood; and later, about her life in the States. She was a string-of-pearls person. Not one person with a continuous life, but discrete and different individuals with self-enclosed lives, each replaced at some prime moment by a successor. "But, if your father's dead, why not sell the store? Doesn't your mother have a job?"

"She sells real estate. We are quite comfortable."

"Then, why . . . ?"

"Because I promised Baba."

Styx sucked in her breath to say *that's stupid*, but Tani's eyes, when she looked into them, gazed back with the despair of a trapped animal. She didn't need another wound. Instead, Roberta said, "You have talent. Your father couldn't want you to stay here forever. Sooner or later, all debts are paid."

Tani shrugged. "Perhaps."

"Think about it, Tani."

A brief smile played around her lips. "Thank you. You are a friend."

Roberta left the store and sat for a few long minutes in the car before starting it. When she did, she pulled out on the Maple Grove side and, on sudden impulse, turned up Thicket Street and drove past Witherspoon High School.

She slowed as she passed. There was a class sitting outdoors on the flagpole oval, studying something their teacher had passed around. She didn't recognize the teacher. "Uniforms!" she shouted. "They've put the weenies in uniforms!" Like some damn Catholic school or fancy-pants academy.

All over Europe, school uniforms had been the norm. Even college students, in some places. Why should it bother her? She couldn't explain; so she settled for turning the radio on, loud. Logically, you could make a case for uniforms. The poorer students could not be teased into costly fashion competitions by those better off. And maybe it did instill a sense of community, like some people said. But she just did not like what uniforms implied about the souls that wore them. Too much order; too much obedience. The students on the flagpole oval seemed entirely too submissive, too goody-goody, wait your turn, and speak when spoken to. Styx liked a little sass in life; and Roberta hadn't changed that part of her soul. They would never have gotten a uniform on Styx! Or on Chase or Meat or Azim Thomas. Jenny Ribbon might have worn one, and Cheng-I Yeh, if those were the rules of the game; but they'd have done it with amused contempt, and found a way to show it. For that matter, most of the kids she had known . . .

. . . *the kids she had known*. It struck her, suddenly and irrelevantly, that she had been close to none of them; and five minutes ago was the first time any of them had called her a friend.

She rolled down the car's window and cranked up the volume. The radio was playing goof, of course; and she hated goof. Nothing goth was playing these days, nothing industrial, nothing house, nothing alternative. There was still rap, but it didn't have the hip-hop edge anymore. Hell, at this point she would even listen to metal, if she could find it. The kids in front of Witherspoon turned at the twangy beat and stared at the car. Styx stuck her middle finger in the air before Roberta could stop her. The boys mostly laughed; but half the girls hid their eyes.

Hid their eyes? What was the world coming to?

She peeled off and took the turn at Thicket and Wessex without stopping.

The asinine song came to an end and the local news took over. Roberta let it go. The top news story was the mayor had been convicted of something. As long as Roberta could remember, mayors of North Orange were being convicted of something. And being reelected afterward. One of them had actually run his campaign from his jail cell. And won. Why wasn't there a law like they had for child molesters, where a politician would have to have his prior convictions advertised if he wanted to run for office?

> *I'm just a poor, young lawyer*
> *I want to serve our town. . . .*

The lines began to build themselves in her mind. Styx began to grin.

The second story was that Mariesa van Huyten had been taken off the critical list and moved into private care.

A weird compression enclosed her chest while the announcer recapped the background, and for a long moment she could not breathe. Miscarriage. Hemorrhage. Intensive care. Well-wishes from around the world. Roberta sucked in her breath at last. "Oh, no, you don't," she said, swatting the radio with the flat of her hand. "You don't get off that easy! You haven't answered to me, yet."

To hell with the teaching job. She'd call the Peoples' Crusades.

May 23, 2007

2,750,000 Shares

The *LEO* Consortium

Wilson Enterprises   **Lockheed-Martin**
Pegasus Space Lines   **MacDonnell-Douglas**
Motorola, Inc.   **Energia Launch Systems**   **Ruger AG**
Ossa & Pelion Construction   **Mitsubishi Heavy Industries**

Common Stock

Price US $100 Per Share
(5.7 Dwt. Troy)

4.

Pilots of the Purple Twilight

Pegasus Aerospace had sited its South Mountain Research Center on a spur of the mountain outside the park boundaries, where a winding road off Chandler Boulevard led up through steep canyons until cactus and wind-carved rock gave way to a more peculiar forest of antennae and microwave relay towers and satellite dishes. The peak commanded a view of the Superstition Mountains to the east. An appropriate view, thought Ned DuBois, if you believed in luck.

Ned pulled his car into a parking slot close to the building's entrance, just acing out another car angling for the same spot. The red Ford Catapult inched slowly past while Ned locked his own, more prosaic rental job. When the Catty's window rolled down, Ned wondered if the other driver was going to cuss him out for "stealing" his space. Well, tough shit. Life's a bitch. You were either quick on your wheels or you went looking somewhere else.

But the other driver turned out to be Forrest, who only said mildly, "Seems you beat me out again, son." The smile looked genuine enough, but there was an edge to the words.

Forrest put the Catapult into reverse and laid rubber backing to a space farther down the row. Ned waited, jiggling the car keys in his pocket, until Forrest joined him.

"Nice car," he said, gripping hands with his friend.

"Well, I like speed," Forrest allowed. "How long's it been, old son?"

"Not since you and me highjacked NASA's external tank, two, three months ago."

"Son, we didn't hijack shit. We had a contract, remember? NASA just didn't read the fine print. Besides, abandoned property is fair game." Forrest laughed. "Why do you think captains used to go down with their ships? They had to maintain possession for the owners."

You go down with one of our ships, Ned reflected, *and there wouldn't be anything to salvage but a rain of fine ash.*

In the entrance lobby, they looked into a retinal ID box and the computer agreed that they were who they claimed to be. They entered their VHI security codes and their name appeared on the video log. Ned nudged Forrest. "Look who else is here."

Forrest raised his eyebrows. "The Flying Volkovs, eh? And good, old Bobbi. Well, well. Old home week." He ran his finger down the list of names while the guard looked uncertain whether to stop him or not. "Hmm. Guess the others aren't coming, or else we beat them here."

Two photo passes printed out and the guard put them in plastic clip-on nametag holders. Ned fastened his to the collar of his polo shirt. Forrest clipped his to his fly, thought about it for a moment, then sighed and transferred it to his shirt pocket. He took Ned by the arm. "Let's go to the show," he said. "I wonder what they're selling."

"Asteroids?" Ned wondered.

"Could be, son. Might could be."

There were about thirty pilots in the meeting room, standing in clusters, chattering and sipping from Styrofoam cups of hot coffee. Several rows of chairs had been set up facing a lectern, where a middle-aged engineering type conversed in low whispers with an Air Force general and a lieutenant in camos. Judging from the haircut, Ned figured the lieutenant for Marine Corps. Ned went to the big metal coffee urn, poured himself a cup, and studied the crowd.

It looked like all of VHI was represented. Most of the pilots were in civvies, but some had come in jumpsuits, maybe even fresh off the flight line. Pegasus red was dominant—Forrest, in a gaily colored sports shirt, was the center of a Great Red Spot—but Ned saw Valery Volkov wearing Aurora purple, and there was a sprinkling of Daedalus brown. There were at least three blue-suiters in the group, too; and a few other company colors he didn't recognize. Free hands waved through the air in universal pilot sign language, as men and women described flights to one another. An arm shot up from the center of one group and waved in the unmistakable Swoop of Death. Ned smiled to himself and made his way into the group.

Bobbi McFeeley saw him coming and put her hands on her hips. "Well, well, well," she said. "And here I thought this was an exclusive gathering."

"We've got to stop meeting like this," he told her. "How's Aurora treating you?"

"Can't complain. They won't let me." She shrugged. "What the hell . . . It's steady work, but not too exciting." She lowered her voice—a theatrical gesture, considering there were five others listening in. "Any idea what this is all about?"

Ned leaned close to her. "It's a cover so you and I could get lucky."

Bobbi snorted. "Hunh, but if you get lucky, I don't, friend. And vice versa."

Flirting with Bobbi was the safest activity he knew. Number one: there was little chance she would take him up. And number two: if she did, it would be outstanding. It wasn't being unfaithful to remember those times on old Fernando, or even to enjoy the memories. It had happened before he and Besty had gotten back together.

"Seriously, though," he said, "I'm as much in the dark as you are." He might have his guesses—the rumored asteroid mission—courtesy of Forrest, but he had learned long ago what the penalties were for spreading rumors, even true ones. *Especially* true ones. The first test everyone had to pass for project work: Can you keep a secret?

It was bad enough he had told Betsy about Forrest's conjectures. A year or more out, on the loneliest and most dangerous mission yet? She had blown hot for three days and cold for seven; and the issue still lay on the table between them. A helluva thing when he didn't know if there was a mission. Unless that was why he was here . . .

Thirty pilots invited for tryouts? They must imagine a selection process like Gideon had used.

"Are you really Ned DuBois?" asked one of the pilots with Bobbi. The way she asked, she was addressing a demigod. In the old days, that would have been the Opening Move.

"Depends," he said. "Does he owe you money?"

She laughed, though the joke hadn't been that funny. Definitely a prospect, if he were still a prospector. Not a bad looker, either. Bobbi introduced her as Alex (short for Alexandra) Feathershaft. She flew for Aurora. The others were mostly Aurora pilots, too; except for Nacho Kilbride, a Federal Express pilot, and Frank Johnson, who flew for . . .

"The Santa Fe Railroad?" Ned asked incredulously.

Johnson was rail thin and two shades lighter than Forrest. He spoke with an Oklahoma twang. "Sure enough. Long haul freight. Aunty Santy just extended her rail system, is all."

"When I was a kid," Ned admitted, "I always wanted to be a railroad engineer. Later, I wanted to be a pilot. Looks like you get to be both . . ."

"You flew the old Mark II, didn't you?" Alex asked him.

"In flight test, yeah. The Mark I was just a test bed for engine and control-system development. *Calbraith Rogers* was a Mark IIa, which incorporated some design mods that the pilots suggested. She never flew quite the same after the accident, though. All the readouts were in spec, but it never felt right."

One of the Aurora pilots shook his head. "Must have been something taking her up, knowing she'd just been repaired."

Ned nodded across the room, in Valery's direction. "Volkov had the nastier turn. He flew her coming down *before* she'd been repaired."

Forrest interrupted to tell him that Bat da Silva had arrived and led Bobbi and him over to greet the carioca pilot. The Volkovs were there, too; so it looked like class reunion time. There were handshakes and embraces all around. Bat was dressed in Daedalus browns and he gave each of them an *abbrazzo*, except Bobbi, who received a rather more passionate greeting. Forrest nudged Ned.

"See, son? I told you there was something between them . . ."

"Forrest, you couldn't get a sixteenth-inch shim between them."

"Sure do hope the man's using birth control."

Bobbi's left arm, draped around Bat's neck, flipped them the bird just before she and Bat parted. When it was Ned's turn, he said, "I'd just as soon shake hands, Bat, if it's all the same to you."

They talked over the old days, of course. That's what pilots did when the glory days were behind them.

"You would not recognize the archipelago these days, my friends," Bat told them. "I have ten test pilots working for me, now. They come from everywhere—Brazil, America, Europe, Russia—just for the opportunity to test themselves against our machines. We fly five ships as test beds for Mendoza's designs. Vila dos Remédias has doubled in size since President Gomes had a jump port built there. And always there are the big hats flying in and out."

"Old Claudio must be raking in the *reals*," Forrest said.

"Claudio has closed down," Bat admitted. "There is a hotel there, now—Executive Suites—with a much better restaurant than Claudio had."

Ned hadn't thought about Claudio—or Gisela—in years. But it was strange to think that the old ramshackle building with the wooden floor was gone. It had seemed the kind of place that would creak along forever, as much a part of the landscape as Morro de Pico or St. Anthony's Bay. He wondered where the locals went these days. A restaurant in an upscale chain hotel—white tablecloths, menus, a wine list, a bar stocked with all the fashionable liqueurs—that wasn't the sort of place Ned would hang in. Not a proper place for poker, at all. And he doubted the waitresses were as accommodating as Gisela had been.

"They needed a place for the papakhas to stay," Katya said contemptuously. She still wore her hair cut close to her scalp, still wore the tight clothing that gave her the unruffled look— inviting, but sealed off at the same time. She still wore the same equivocal smile. The pale scar tissue across her left temple was new, though. Even Aurora milk runs could have their exciting moments.

"The new restaurant is probably much cleaner," Valery said, but he didn't sound very happy, either.

Forrest shook his head sadly. "That Claudio, he sure made a damn fine *feijoada*. It's a dirty shame."

They all agreed, and the talk moved on to less bittersweet topics. The new head-to-tail flat spin that Daedalus was testing to replace the old Swoop of Death maneuver. The relative merits of the new Mark IVs coming on line versus the old, reliable Mark IIIc's that had blazed the trails from Phoenix to Woomera and Recife and St. Petersburg. When Valery complained again of being a prosaic freight hauler, Bobbi flicked a finger against his purple jumpsuit, and recited a bit of poetry for them, Tennyson's "Locksley Hall, 1842."

" 'For I dipt into the future, far as human eye could see.
Saw the Vision of the world, and all the wonders that
    would be;
Saw the heavens filled with commerce, argosies of magic
    sails;
Pilots of the purple twilight, dropping down with costly
    bails.' "

Valery said, "Hah! But Aurora is the goddess of the *dawn*. Do you think Chairman van Huyten never read that poem when she picked the name?"

"I wonder if she'd read all of it," Forrest said.

"What do you mean?" Ned asked him.

Forrest cocked his head and looked toward the Air Force pilots chatting with the lieutenant in the camouflage. He spoke:

" 'Heard the heavens filled with shouting, and there rained
  a ghastly dew
From the nations' airy navies grappling in the central
  blue.' "

There wasn't much that could be said to that and, after a moment or two of silence, the talk moved once more onto technical topics. Valery held that the new "180 swivel" was actually more dangerous than the Death Swoop. The last thing you wanted to do on close approach was put your 'chine into any kind of spin, even a controlled one.

While they talked, Ned began to notice something curious. Circulating individually through the crowd, each of them had attracted a coterie of listeners. But now, gathered together, the others in the meeting room were giving them a wide berth. The six of them formed a small knot near the center of the room. The other pilots circled them like moons—like asteroids, he thought—glancing their way from time to time.

Jesus H! Speaking of demigods . . . The Original Eight must be almost legends to the regular Plank pilots. They must feel the way the pilots of the Great War had felt about Wright and Blériot and Santos-Dumont and the other aviation pioneers. The time span was about the same. Once, it had been Big News whenever a Plank did anything at all; because whatever it was, it was the first time. Recife to St. Petersburg! Refueled in orbit! Docked with Mir! First flight to Phoenix! First flight to Woomera! First satellite fetched and returned! First one-day turnaround! Phoenix Sky Harbor Grand Reopening! Now it was all routine, and Aurora's flight schedules were posted on the Net and downloaded by all the major papers. These pilots flew something new and glamorous (and *still* a little dangerous—the *Georges Chaves* had proven that!); but in their midst were those who had dared when the whole idea was unproven.

Good thing the Iron Mike and the Human Moon *weren't* here, Ned decided, or the mojo would reach critical mass. He wondered at the absence of the other two. Then he realized that, as far as he could tell, no one from Energia was present, and he wondered even more.

The meeting was run by Aurora's chief engineer. G. H. Stine had been the guiding genius behind the Fractional Ballistic Transport System—steering site selection and infrastructure development in half a dozen countries. Johannesburg Spaceport would open next year, and Aomori the year after, once the methane pipelines were extended in northern Honshu; and there were unscheduled charter flights to Quito and Nairobi to service Wilson's ram accelerators. Only the northeast U.S. site had been stymied, thanks to a consortium of interests with a powerlock on the political machines there. Yet Stine looked like just an ordinary guy.

Half expecting a preliminary briefing on the proposed asteroid mission, Ned was surprised when the engineer gave them a pep talk on a proposed Emergency Response Plan instead. Judging by the reactions of a half dozen others in the room, a few of them had expected something else, as well.

As he addressed them, Stine ran a series of video clips across the big flatscreen on the front wall of the conference room. Mississippi floods. Japanese earthquakes. The typhoon that had wrecked Manila the year before. Shot of people living in tents or the local high-school gym. Shots of rescuers and relief workers dispensing foods and medicines.

"A common thread running through many recent disasters," he told the assembly, "is the delay in needed supplies reaching the distressed area, especially when a wide geographical district is affected. Disaster victims must often wait days before medicine and drinking water can make their way in. I'm sure you all remember Manila, and the Ankara earthquake. Kinshasa Fever is another datum. Had the vaccines reached the city even two days earlier, the death toll would have been far less."

The screen changed to a computer graphic showing a dozen

or more red lines tracing great circle routes across a globe of the Earth. The blinking lights at the head of each trajectory converged on a single site.

"Your companies, in consultation with the Office of Emergency Preparedness and the UN Relief Agency, have agreed to make available one or more Planks to a readiness pool, the Emergency Response Pool, or ERP, in case they are needed in an emergency to bring in supplies or to conduct evacuations." Stine shuffled his notes, and looked out over the ranks of pilots. The graphic was replaced by an animation showing a mix of Mark IVs and Mark IIIc's landing, or already grounded, on an anonymous landscape surrounded by mountains. "For the last five years, one Plank has always been kept on the ready line in case of an on-orbit emergency, with the responsibility rotating by informal agreement among the spacefaring companies. The time has come to do the same for on-Earth emergencies."

Someone raised a hand. "You cain't mean keeping a dozen Planks off'n the flying schedule just in case thar's an earthquake somewheres? Those doggies cost too much troy to have 'em sit in the firehouse all day."

Stine shook his head. "That's right. It may prove economical some time in the future; but for now, we'll have to rely on a volunteer fire department." A ripple of laughter crossed the room. "Pilots and vessels participating in ERP must be ready on short notice to abort their current missions, land where directed to take on supplies and fuel, and head for the emergency zone. You must be ready to land on unprepared ground—possibly at airports, but just as possibly on football fields and parking lots. There will be no refueling available; not where a hurricane or an earthquake has just done its worst. So you must be able to lift out again without the usual ground support. . . ." The earlier laughter had turned to mutters. Stine raised his voice.

"High risk, ladies and gentlemen. Make no mistake about that. With several Planks converging simultaneously on the same general locale, or shuttling back and forth along the same trajectory, the opportunities for accident will be greatly increased. Especially if the site of the emergency is outside the zones now covered by the Space Traffic Control system.''

The graphic behind him morphed as he spoke, and two of the approaching ships were shown colliding in midair. There was a stir among the assembled pilots. On a ballistic approach, God was more than your copilot. He was pilot, navigator, and bo'sun of the captain's gig.

Another smile from Stine, this time a challenging one. ''The mission profile is high-risk, but your companies have picked you as the pilots who are just dumb enough to try it—and just good enough to pull it off.'' Some of the commercial pilots sat straight in their seats and folded their arms across their chests. This wasn't in their contract. But Ned leaned forward, intrigued by the problem, and anticipating what would come next.

''Werewolf Electronics,'' Stein told them, ''Poole sEcurity Consultants, and other software-development firms are preparing an Expert Program and Knowledge Base for the STC network, so that it can instantly recalculate the traffic patterns needed to mobilize and dispatch ERP ships. In addition, they have developed an adaptive net so your onboard navigator can handle 'flocking' when ships find themselves sharing airspace. If things start happening on close approach, they will happen too fast for humans to handle. The code has been written; but after all the simulations have tested the software's wits, after all the alpha-testing is finished, someone has to take hardware into the sky and see what really happens when two ships get too close.''

Ned twined his hands together into a double fist, almost as if he were praying. Flight test. It wasn't like going into orbit, but it was damn-all on the edge, where certainty began to fray and life became real again.

Bobbi McFeeley, at the end of the row, asked the question first. ''When does flight test start?'' she asked in a lazy voice. Stine looked at his watch.

''At one o'clock, this afternoon, for those who sign on.''

Silence in the auditorium. Stine had to mean simulator runs, right? He didn't expect them to hop into a couple Planks right after lunch and play chicken . . . ? Forrest drawled, "Hell, son, that's barely enough time to chow down a burger."

Enough time for those who wanted out to leave the center. Well, they couldn't have counted on all the pilots signing up for the ERP, let alone for flight-testing the software. But it definitely sounded like a test profile that separated the true quill from the wannabes. He glanced at his friend's thoughtful face.

"What is it, Forrest?"

Forrest pulled on his jaw. "Son, do I strike you as a man who has his ear to the ground?"

"Forrest, you have your ear any closer to the ground, your head'd be buried in the sand."

A worried frown. "Well, then, if they're already up to simulator training, that software's been in prep awhile. Or they're pushing it Priority A. Or both. So how come I never heard beans?"

Ned shrugged. "Werewolf and Aurora and the Space Traffic Agency are running this show . . . why should you hear anything up there at the Academy?"

Forrest shook his head. "I hear things. Not just Pegasus things, either. I got more connections that US West. Here's another one for you. The blue suits over there . . . Why?"

"Hell, Forrest, why shouldn't Air Force be in ERP? They fly Planks, too. One of them stopped by Mir last month with an Air Force general aboard—same fellow that was talking with Stine earlier, if I'm not mistaken. Some sort of goodwill mission. A Russian Plank rendezvoused and they made courtesy calls on each other."

Forrest raised his eyebrows. "That so? Funny what doesn't make the news these days. But riddle me this, Ned, old son. I'll give you the Air Force; but what was that jarhead doing in the corner? Congress only lets USAF Space Command buy Planks. The Marines or the Navy don't have any."

And Energia isn't here at all, Ned reminded himself. Declined the invite? Or snubbed? And, either way, why?

*   *   *

They picked him for the flight tests, of course. Werewolf was looking for the cream, and they didn't come any creamier than Ned DuBois. They picked three others, as well: Bobbi Mc-Feeley, Alex Feathershaft, and a Pegasus pilot named Stan Kovacs. Forrest was passed over. He had been—in his own typically restrained words—"too Goddamned, fucking valuable running the Goddamned, fucking, son-of-a-bitch Space Academy" to spare for the "flock" program. Ned had been passed over enough times on the original Plank qualification runs that he knew exactly how his friend felt.

The flock testing would either be the smoothest milk run Ned had ever flown—baby-sitting the software that would do all the work—or it would be the single most dangerous flight in his life. It all depended on how well the net had been taught.

Neural nets were not programmed; they were trained. By trial and error. Which might be wasteful of ships—and pilots—except that the trials were run in simulations. Loads, stresses, thrusts, velocities, and other parameters were churned through a mathematical model to produce a performance profile. To make life interesting, atmospheric conditions were varied at random: air temperature, wind speed and direction. Some mighty potent testware had been challenging the flocking program for several months already, forcing it to fail, then telling it why it failed; but test software had limitations of its own; and sooner or later, you had to bring in a human teacher. The test of a system—hardware, software . . . or wetware— was how it performed under extreme conditions: at the edge; at the envelope, at the point where things fell apart and the center could not hold and only those who had it could haul it back in time.

In other words, Ned had to teach the program his own personal mojo.

He and Bobbi—older, more experienced, more careful—did most of the training. (And wasn't *that* a sure sign he was growing older—that Mama DuBois's hell-raising little boy had become the standard of mature judgment.) They flew simulated flights in a simulated control cabin—old hat to old hands—and tried this or that or the other thing to make the flocker screw up. Alex and Stan, younger and more reckless, often got themselves into situations that Ned's more mature judgment managed to avoid. Some things worked. Some things failed.

And the net would learn.

When Ned and the others finished a scenario, the testware would put the net through thousands of repeated simulations, varying the conditions at random. Each go-round, the net did a little better against the test-software bully. Failure rates dropped steadily, and Ned felt an irrational pride in his "pupil."

Cheng-I Yeh, the software test engineer, looked a little young for his post, but he sure as hell knew his ASCII from a hole in the ground. (And was probably grateful as hell that his parents hadn't named him "Oh.") He came by the simulator room periodically to post the flocker's failure rates, and to discuss the configuration and scenario simulations with the pilots. Ned appreciated an engineer who kept in touch with the wetware; he'd known too many in the past who never ventured beyond their offices or lifted their eyes from their terminals.

"It's a decaying exponential curve," Dr. Yeh commented one afternoon as he pondered the neat, mathematical beauty of the graph he had just posted. Yeh was a great believer in graphs. *Always draw a picture of the data*, he liked to say.

Ned was running through the simulator shutdown checklist with Alex Feathershaft. "I'll take your word for that, Doc." Not that he didn't know his engineering, but when it came to equations, there were three kinds: linear, polynomial, and rat-ass bastards.

"Asymptotic, of course," Yeh said absently. A sigh, and he traced the curve out with his finger, projecting it. "Too bad it never quite reaches zero."

Ned felt his heart thud. Yeh stood with his hands clasped behind his back, scowling at the graph as if it had betrayed him. "No. There's never zero risk," Ned told him. *They're getting ready to fly iron.* He could feel it in the air, feel it in Yeh's awkward stance. Good. He was tired of let's-pretend flying. Alex closed and sealed the simulator cabin door. She came over to the console and stood beside Ned and placed a hand on his shoulder.

The test engineer shrugged; then he turned and faced them. "Alpha test has reached the point of diminishing returns," he announced. "Beta test begins on Monday. You and McFeeley will fly close approach trajectories to Fernando Base. The flight director has your flight plans. See him before you leave." He would not look directly at Ned. Like any engineer, he had to believe in his equations; but it was Ned's life if he was wrong—if his team had overlooked some variable: an interaction, maybe, or a hardware-software interface.

Ned gave him a patented Ned DuBois Grin to hide the elevator sensation in his own belly. "Monday? Today's only Wednesday. That's not much time to practice the profiles. . . ." Absently, he reached up and touched Alex's hand where it rested on his shoulder.

"Management wants this program pushed."

"They do. . . . Why the big rush?" Ned did not care for programs shoved onto the fast track. Too often, "fast track" meant "shortcut."

Yeh held his hands up. "I'm just the software geek. They don't tell me anything. But you've flown enough ballistics, Ned. This is nothing new for you. You'll be sharing airspace with a second Plank, but the neural net will handle everything."

"What if it doesn't?"

A fleeting, nervous smile. "That's why you and Bobbi will be aboard. But I wouldn't worry. Worst-case scenario in the simulations is one failure in three hundred fifteen iterations, and that scenario has a dozen Planks converging from as many directions. You won't have any problems, Ned. That's word up."

Alex waited in the corridor outside the sim lab for Ned to catch up. She gave him a light punch on the arm. "First flight," she said. "You lucky bastard."

Ned rubbed his arm. "Yeah, real lucky." He wondered how

close the physical approach was planned to be. Close enough to trigger the net to avoid a collision ... assuming the net worked in hardware as well as it worked in software. After all, the sims used finite element models, a pegwork Plank of minute trapezoids. The real thing was steel and ceramic and titanium and smoke. Hell, assuming the *hardware* worked. Sensors could fail, too. Well, that was why God invented test pilots. And you knew the score when you volunteered. You'd do it again, and you know it.

Still, the whole program gave him a feeling of unseemly haste. Bonifácio had compressed the Plank schedule a time or two, but there'd been years of ground work leading up to flight test. The flocker couldn't be more than six months old, tops. Granted, clocks ran faster in the software universe, but still ... He rubbed a hand across his stomach to soothe the feathery feeling there. He wasn't coming down with an ulcer, was he?

Alex gave him another backhanded tap on the arm. "Hey ... What say you and me, we celebrate flight test and have dinner tonight?"

He collected himself. Pilots shouldn't think too much. It slowed the reflexes. "Sure," he said expansively. "Let's go see if we can round up Bobbi and Stan."

She barely hesitated. "Actually, I was thinking just you and me."

Ned gave her a speculative look. Standing hipshot in her Aurora purps, she came only to his chest. Two short, black braids bracketed her ears. The zipper that ran down the front of her coveralls was pulled a quarter of the way down. Not enough to give you a view, but enough to let you know there was one. "Were you?" he asked with a crooked smile. "Thinking you'll cook it yourself?" There were two sorts of dinner invitations. One involved dinner.

"Well, I do know my way around. A kitchen. Maybe afterward, we could have a little, you know, dessert?"

"I like my desserts sweet and sticky. Think you can manage that?"

"Does the Pope wear a funny hat?" She swatted him on the rear end with the flat of her hand.

Ned returned the compliment as she walked away. Did she wiggle her buns at him, or did she always sway that way when she walked? *Jesus H.!* What was it, some sort of pheromones he put out? There was hardly room in his pants for himself, and Alex wanted to slip in there with him. What was a man supposed to do? Baggier pants hardly seemed the answer.

She's fifteen years your junior, Ned. She's a hero-worshipper and you're a damned hero. That doesn't necessarily mean she's collecting pelts. "Dinner" could be just that, and only your ego thinks otherwise.

There was only one way to find out, though. And even an innocent dinner could morph into something else. Even without intentions, events had a way of happening. A moment comes—a look, a touch, something. You push the outside of the envelope just a little; and before you could pull it back, you lost it and found yourself spinning out of control and augering in.

But, hell, pushing the envelope . . . that's what test pilots did.

Come Friday afternoon, Ned borrowed a company jet and grabbed sky. He even asked permission from Pegasus Flight Control, and he even filed a flight plan and followed it. And when he set it down again, he was at Argonaut's hangar on the small, private airport south of Houston that serviced the high-tech hub there. That was how he managed to be waiting on the front-room sofa when Betsy came home from work.

Standing in the foyer, fumbling with her keys and purse and briefcase, she failed to notice him. Navy business suit, pleated skirt, wide-lapel jacket, red bow, all slightly rumpled. Understated gold jewelry: a brooch, earrings that caught a gleam of light. The hair done up, but coming just a bit loose after her eight-hour stint at Odysseus. He liked to see her dressed up. She looked classy. As she closed the door, Ned admired the set of her calves and the hollow behind her knees just visible under the fluttering pleats.

Turning, she saw him. She gave a start and her hand went to her chest. "Jesus, Ned," she said. "My insurance isn't paid up and you're trying to give me a heart attack." She dropped her briefcase on the chair by the window and came to him, bending close to give him a kiss on the cheek. "Welcome home."

He grabbed her wrist before she could move away and pulled her to a seat on the sofa beside him. "That wasn't much of a kiss, considering I've been away for three weeks."

"Three weeks for you, Ned, is like stepping around the corner for groceries." But she didn't pull away when Ned pressed his lips to hers. She put her hand to the back of his neck and held him.

He grinned when they parted. "Could have been three months up on Mir, right?"

She didn't grin. "Or two years in South America."

There wasn't any nastiness in the comment. She had said it the way she might have said, *The sun is out.* It was not even a major topic at *casa* DuBois anymore. A few years' worth of dirt had been shoveled onto that casket. But every now and then a reminder would casually drop into her conversation. So, was she a bitch because she never forgot; or was he a bastard because he thought she should? Or maybe both. Yet his time on Fernando de Noronha, when he had hardly written and never called and they both knew he was playing mattress Ping-Pong, was a two-year hole in both their lives; and it would be silly to pretend it wasn't there, or that they didn't know who had dug it, or why.

But there were thirteen other years between them, too; and they had been pretty good. Mostly.

With a flourish, Ned whipped the dish towel off the end table, revealing two glasses of sherry and a bottle of Harvey's Bristol Cream. He handed Betsy one of the glasses. "I thought you might want to relax after a hard day at the office."

"Did you?" She took the glass with an amused smile and waited until he had his. "Is there a toast?"

He touched her glass and the crystal tinged. "To us."

"Not very original, flyboy; but I'll drink to it."

Over the rim of his glass, he watched her throat work as she swallowed. It was always the small images that seemed to capture her the best, and they stayed in his mind like snap-shots. The way she swallowed. Her face in profile staring out a window at Pennsylvania snow. The grease on her cheek that time she had had to change a tire on her car. The curve of her leg. The sound of her laugh. The touch of her hand. The taste of her lips.

And the cut of her tongue. Let's not forget that. Too much sweetness was cloying; a proper love needed bite.

She lowered the glass and looked into it, running the tip of her finger around the rim. "Where's Lizzie?" she asked.

"I told her she could spend the night at Anne's house."

Betsy nodded slowly. "You're a helluva guy, Ned DuBois. Always thinking of other people."

He pretended to reach toward the telephone. "I could call her and tell her I changed my mind."

She took another sip of sherry. "No. Kids hate inconsistent parents. We'll just have to make the best of it." She set her glass on the end table on her side of the sofa. "You forgot the coasters, flyboy."

"What, are you going to spank me?"

"Hmm. You'd like that, wouldn't you?"

" 'Beat me,' said the masochist."

She grinned. " 'No!' said the sadist."

They both laughed and he circled her with his arm and drew her to him. They kissed again, this time more slowly. Once, twice. Her tongue played with him. They parted and she laid her head against his chest while he rubbed her back through her linen blouse. "Three weeks isn't that long," she said, running her fingers along his trouser leg. "I've had days that seemed longer. But it's long enough."

The sofa was too narrow, but the living-room floor, with a little improvisation with the throw pillows, proved more than satisfactory. And if a few things got wrinkled or tossed about in the process, well, she was planning on having that suit dry-cleaned, anyway. Afterward, Ned drifted, half asleep. Her body, where it pressed against his—firm, soft, tickly—was an anchor to reality. Her fingers played in his hair. The silence of touching seemed to last forever.

Forever ended when Betsy spoke. "They've started flying, haven't they?"

It wasn't really a question. Ned didn't open his eyes as he answered. He didn't even ask her how she knew. "Monday. I'm heading back Sunday morning."

The fingers in his hair tightened momentarily, then relaxed. "Seems crazy to me, Ned." Her voice was reasonable. He heard the strain that kept it so. "You're trying to collide on purpose."

"No problemo." He opened his eyes and looked into hers. He was close enough that he could see himself reflected there. He kissed her again, gently on softened lips. "The ships are programmed to avoid each other. The risk is minimal."

"Then take me with you."

He sat upright. "What?"

She rose too. She tucked her legs underneath her and folded her arms across her breasts. "Take me with you on the flight. You say there's no risk. Take me. And Lizzie."

"It's a test flight, for crying out loud!"

Betsy's smile was sad. "That's what I thought."

"Now, wait a—"

"I just don't understand why they at least don't try it with remote-controlled Planks."

Me, either. A couple remotes would have been prudent; but this is fast-tracked . . . "They'll go out of line-of-sight." That was the line that Madame Pitchlynn had handed them, anyway. "The remotes would have to be relayed through satellite links; or handed off from one set of ground pilots to another. Too easy to fumble; or to react too late if there *is* a problem. Those ships cost twenty-five hundred troy, apiece. It's not cheap, replacing one."

She placed one hand on his thigh. He could feel the heat, like a brand. "They could give me twenty *thousand* troy, fly-boy, and I still couldn't replace you, cheap as you are."

"Cowgirl . . ." One hand settled on her waist and he leaned toward her.

She touched his lips with her finger. "Don't say anything. Don't make excuses. Fifteen years, I have an inkling of what makes Ned DuBois tick. It's never gotten easier to live with; but if something does go wrong on Monday, at least we had this weekend. You gave me that; and I thank you for it." A quick peck; but it was the words that sent the thrill through him. Sometimes love pleased more than sex; and affection, more than love.

"You will take us back with you, Liz and me."

"Damn it, Betsy. Test-flight rules—"

"I didn't mean on the Plank. I meant, take us back to Phoenix with you. School is out for the summer; and I damn sure know I can cut a deal with Odysseus Travel to cover for the next few weeks. Hell, I could jack in my PC and do the work from your apartment out there. Tell Pegasus and tell 'em you need a bigger pad. If they won't do that much for a certified company hero, then screw 'em. And screw you, too."

"Promises, promises . . . Why so hot to come to Phoenix, cowgirl?"

She poked him on the chest, hard enough that he had to brace himself with his arm. "Three reasons, flyboy; and pay attention 'cause they're good ones. Number one: Houston in the summer ain't nothing to write home about. Number two: in fifteen years minus two of being married to a damn flyboy, I've never been in a plane with you at the controls, and I'd like to see if you're as good as you say you are."

"I'm as good in a plane as I am in a bed. Either way, I stay up a long time."

"Hunh. But, Number three, Ned; that's the killer. When Flyboy Ned flies test, he grabs for the nearest woman, and I'd just as soon that woman was me than the gal you left to fly out here to poke me on my own damn front-room carpet."

For a moment, Ned could not find his voice. When he did, he said, "Betsy, there isn't any—"

She pushed him hard on the chest, so that he toppled on his back, even as she straddled him like a horse. "Ned, what we were doing here a half hour ago, that was Truth; so don't you go spoil it with any lies. Of course there's a gal back there in Phoenix, probably has her tongue hanging halfway to the ground and her heels kicked halfway to the sky. And you wanted her so bad that you hopped in a jet plane and flew to me like a bat out of hell." She slid down and lay atop him. "And Ned," she said with her lips an inch from his, "*that* is the most beautiful thing you've ever done."

The test flight to Fernando was anticlimactic. *Louis Paulhan* approached *Vasily Kamensky* three times on the profile—once on the orbital fraction, once on descent trajectory, once on landing approach—and the neural net worked perfectly each time, maintaining the spacing between them. Ned felt almost like a passenger in his own craft—and didn't like it one bit. He almost wished something would go wrong, just so he could pull it out himself. Almost. He was no fool. He and Bobbi touched down on the old, familiar landing apron by St. Anthony's Bay at nearly the same time, and a scant dozen meters apart.

A camera crew from *The American Argus* caught the whole thing on tape. There were a few firsts still left, after all. The first near-simultaneous landing. It must have been a spectacular sight, Ned thought. Almost as spectacular as if the ships had collided. He wondered if the news crew was disappointed; but, hell, you can't have everything.

They wanted shots of Bobbi and Ned congratulating each other; so Ned took Bobbi's hand and said, "My computer congratulates your computer on a splendid flight."

Bobbi was all teeth for the camera. "Screw you," she said without moving her lips.

The base threw a party for them in the cafeteria. It was half a celebration of the successful test flight, half a "welcome home." Most of the ground crew were old hands from the qualification test days, when the base had been a closely held secret and no one had known for sure if the bird would fly at all. Arturo Gusmão was there, and Dolores, and even the laconic chief engineer, Luis Mendoza, who had flown out from Fortaleza. Bonny de Magalhães seemed older. His dapper mustache and slicked-down hair were shot through with grey, and crow's-feet decorated the corners of his eyes. Of the old hands, only João Pessoa, the president, was missing. He was in New Jersey for a top-level VHI meeting and couldn't be present.

Bat da Silva roasted them, dragging up old, embarrassing stories from flight-test days. The poker games at Claudio's, the humvee races through the Vila, the Walking Corpses Club, how Cowboy Calhoun had dumped a load of trash on the simulator cabin, or Iron Mike Krasnarov had highjacked the Plank's maidenhood. He even managed to intimate, without ever actually saying so, that the long radio silence when he and Bobbi had docked two Planks for the first time had been due to an amorous interlude in zero-g.

Ned didn't remember it all quite so jolly. Bat could have told other stories. The tension and the rivalry. How Bat himself had been shunned at first. How Forrest and Mike had squabbled like roosters. How Levkin had poisoned the food at Claudio's and greased the step in the simulator room. How Ned had very nearly drunk himself out of the program.

He could have mentioned the sabotage, too; and Valery's near-fatal crash. Or Heitor Carneiro's disappearance and Mendoza's rumored dining habits. He could have mentioned the long, lonely hour waiting to catch up with Levkin in orbit. It hadn't been all laughs, not by a long shot.

But it was hard to have fun at parties if you dwelt on the downside. If Bat chose to accentuate the positive, Ned for one would be the last to call him on it; because the good times had been just as real.

The high point was a picturephone call from Mariesa van Huyten herself. That *that* was the high point of the party showed how far down the evolutionary ladder he had fallen as a party animal. Time was, the high point would have come later, with Dolores or Floriana. They were older now, but women were like wine in that respect; and a few moments of eye contact established that the vintage was still available. But he was still feeling virtuous as all hell because of Alex Feathershaft and he hated to ruin things what with Betsy waiting zfor the return flight back in Phoenix.

* * *

Mariesa looked drawn and tired on the picturephone. Pale. She had lost a lot of weight—and had never had too much to begin with. It could have been the picture quality, or it could have been a slow recovery from her ordeal. She thanked them for their good work and the "vital and timely test flight." Ned and Bobbi responded with the usual platitudes. Ned wanted desperately to ask after her. How was her health? Was she taking things easier? (That was hard to imagine!) Was Barry Fast treating her right? But it was too public a venue. Too many others were listening. And he didn't really have the standing to ask such personal questions. He and Mariesa had never shared anything except a single night of stargazing on her observatory catwalk.

Instead, Ned expressed conventional regrets about the shortness of the flocker testing program.

"It shall prove useful, I am sure," she said. "And perhaps there will be other programs upcoming that are more to your taste."

Ned tried to act nonchalant. "I always did like long trips," he replied. "And rock collecting was a hobby of mine when I was a kid."

Mariesa raised an eyebrow. "Really?"

"Sure. Quartz. Feldspar. Agate. You name it. Geology was a hobby of mine. Like stamp collecting; although it was damn hard pasting those rocks in my scrapbook."

She laughed and took him at his word. "Have you ever collected carbonaceous chondrite?" she asked with a small, mocking smile.

"No," he said, returning the gesture, "but there's a first time for everything."

"Indeed there is, Captain DuBois. Indeed there is."

When the connection was broken, Ned turned away from the phone and found himself face-to-face with Bobbi Mc-Feeley, who had a crooked grin across her own face.

"So, Ned," she said. "Heard any good rumors lately?"

5.

Oh, You Can't Always Get What You Want. . . .

The elevator door parted and Mariesa stepped out into the reception area and almost into the arms of her assistant, Zhou Hui, who welcomed her back and guided her by the arm toward her office. Mariesa suffered the solicitude. There were worse crimes that people visited upon one another. "I shall want executive summaries," she told Hui. "Status reports on each company, on each major initiative, with a separate listing for Prometheus." When Ms. Zhou hesitated, Mariesa asked, "What is it, Hui?"

"We thought you would want to relax on your first day back."

Mariesa shook her head. "Relax? I have been doing that for the last two months. No, I need to return to the swim of things."

"I never thought I would hear a stay in intensive care equated with relaxation," drawled a soft voice from the hallway to Executive Row. Mariesa saw John E. Redman, her chief legal officer, striding toward her.

"John E.! How delightful to see you. I was not looking my

best when we last met.'' She held out her hand and he made a show of kissing it.

Still holding her hand, he said in more serious tones, ''We were worried about you.''

She matched his mood. ''It was not a pleasant experience. I do not recommend it.''

''No. I would think not. Are you certain you're fit to return?''

''I am not made of china, John E. I do not break so easily.'' No, she was not broken, but emptied out . . . that was a different feeling entirely. She felt as if she had been drained— of energy, of life. Perhaps it was the ennui of convalescence; perhaps it was that she *had* been emptied out, and a life *had* been taken from her.

The three of them entered her office together, but Mariesa halted in the doorway when she saw what awaited her. Bouquets and arrangements were everywhere: on the tables, on her desk, on the bookcase shelves. A wild variety of blooms, from prosaic roses to the most outré tropicals. The smell was a sweet and pungent amalgam of every fragrance known—the olfactory equivalent of black. Stepping into the room was like entering a jungle. She supposed it was too much to expect that her return to work would have gone unremarked.

She picked a card from an arrangement of yellow and orange daffodils. *Congratulations on your recovery. Harry and Laura.* Who the devil were Harry and Laura? Society friends from her family circles? Business acquaintances? Employees here at VHI? ''Have you kept a list of the gifts, Ms. Zhou? I shall have to send acknowledgments for each one.''

''Yes, ma'am. And ma'am? The staff wants to tell you we are happy to see you back. It was not the same without you.''

Mariesa favored her with a wry smile. ''No, I fancy it was something of a vacation. Or is John E. such a taskmaster?'' she studied her desk once more. The smell was too thick, too cloying. It reminded her of funeral homes. ''Have Buildings send someone up to remove these. We shall place some in the cafeterias and other offices, and some downstairs in the vestibule. Brighten things up for everyone.''

"All of them?" asked Zhou Hui.

"Leave Barry's and Harriet's, and a few others." For appearance's sake, if nothing else. But every arrangement was a reminder; every blossom, a pain. And she wanted them out of her office. . . .

John E. offered her his arm. "Why don't you come over to my offices until Ms. Zhou gets this place straightened up." He surveyed the forest of plants and shook his head. "You have more admirers than you think."

"Flowers are easy, John E. Even Cyrus Attwood sent flowers."

"A man who observes the conventions." John E.'s face darkened. "His injunction against Zeus is still in force."

"Judges are easy, too."

As they walked down Executive Row, officers, assistants, and secretaries alike emerged from their offices to greet her, some offering kisses or hugs, some only handshakes and murmured condolences, all offering happiness and relief that she had come through all right.

If one more person insists on giving me sympathy, I shall scream. No one really understood; no one else could possibly understand. Half of them mentioned friends or relatives who had had near-fatal encounters, and Peggy, in Data Processing, told of being herself in a terrible automobile accident. Did that establish a bond? Mariesa felt no ties. Joy created bonds; tragedy built only a terrible isolation.

It was Khan, whose comfort was the cruelest of them all, who touched closest to her heart.

"You are terribly lucky," he said patting her hands with his, "that the child was never born. There was no time to grow attached to it."

The words sliced straight through to her core, and she felt her muscles contract in sympathy, as if probing the void within her. Gone. Empty. Never to be. She parted her lips to rebuke her CFO, but caught herself when she saw wintry pain deep within the man's eyes. Instead, she thanked him meaninglessly and turned away to follow John E. If Khan's comfort came from the knowledge of the greater sorrow, she did not want to know it yet.

William, oh, William . . . Only later did she realize how precisely Khan had spoken.

On Saturday, she had gone to the nursery to direct its dismantling; but at the sight of the crib and the playthings, she had broken down and cried, right there in front of the workmen, heedless of all appearances, and Sykes had had to lead her away. Barry would not even enter the room, but had gone instead to the library, where Mariesa had later found the bourbon decanter quite empty. In the end, arrangements had fallen to Harriet, who had managed with her usual dispatch. The crib she had taken herself down to the storage room in the subbasement. But it was a long, long time before she had come back up.

"Is something wrong, Mariesa?" John E. asked.

Mariesa pulled a handkerchief from her sleeve and dabbed at her face. "No. Nothing. I picked up a slight cold while I was recuperating."

"Are you sure you are ready to return to work?"

She shoved the handkerchief back in place and stepped down the hall to the legal office. "Quite certain," she told him. "Work is the best therapy."

Even with most of the flowers removed, her office still smelled like a mortuary, but she endured it, as she would need to endure so much else. Mariesa kept the briefing small: Khan, John E., Steve Matthias, and herself. Steve had coptered over from his Manhattan offices just to give the Prometheus update in person. He liked to do that; he liked to "face" with the CEO. They sat around the low glass coffee table by the windows facing Watchung Mountain. Mariesa had tea and frosted wafers brought in and managed to survive the social chitchat before they settled down to business.

Khan Gagrat conducted the briefing. John E., long-haired and laid-back, took Khan's Indo-Afghan ferociousness in stride; but Mariesa knew that the shaven head, gold hoop earring, and drooping mustaches bothered Steve—though

Steve was far too polite, and far too circumspect, ever to mention it. It had made a striking cover photograph on *Forbes*, however. The chief financial officer was practical, organized, objective to the point of rudeness, and less disposed to splitting ethical hairs than Keith McReynolds had been. The only thing he shared with his predecessor was a fierce belief in the future.

Khan presented the current status of each of VHI's companies with meticulous precision—Asklepios, Daedalus, Demeter, Mentor, Pegasus, Thor, Werewolf, and the rest. The balance sheets were mainly favorable, which was no surprise. The economy had been picking up steadily since 2006 and most of the boats were rising with the tide. Aurora promised to break even again this year, and the deficits on Pegasus and Leprechaun were closing at very nearly the forecast rate.

"We always expected that the Fractional Ballistic Transportation System would be the main moneymaker for the first decade," Steve commented. "But cost-to-orbit is low enough now that even speculative ventures have become feasible."

Khan added, "And the markets have become sufficiently attuned to the new cost regime that such ventures can also be financed."

"Feasible *and* fundable," John E. said with slow humor. "A rare combination. Easy enough to have one without the other."

"Steel does not look good, however," Khan continued. "Vulcan has reported losses for the last five quarters."

"It has never run well since Bennett retired," Mariesa said.

Khan pursed his lips, considering the primacy of personality over economic forces. "Even the legendary Bennett Longworth would have trouble in today's market," he said. "The problem is systemic. Most of steel's applications have been usurped—by aluminum and light metals in some instances; by composites and ceramics in others; and, more recently, by 'smoke.' You may want to give some thought to liquidating the entire business," he added flatly.

"Vulcan? Why, that was one of VHI's original holdings," Mariesa pointed out. It had been Hudson Forge, once; and Van Huyten Iron Works, after that.

Khan held a forefinger erect. "You need more reason for keeping it than that it is a family heirloom." He did not quite wag the finger at her. Keith would have chided her, too; though not quite so bluntly. That's what CFOs were for. To make sure that dreams did not outrun their balance sheets.

Mariesa folded her hands under her chin and leaned back in her chair. It was good to have a problem like this. An old-fashioned, business-oriented, MBA-casebook sort of problem. One that she could consider dispassionately; one that did not pierce her so sharply. "I need more information before I can consider selling off Vulcan. What are the projections for steel? Is there a specialty niche we can exploit? Or other ventures to which Vulcan's assets can be deployed?"

"Hard to see," said Steve Matthias, "what else you can do with a blast furnace."

The others chuckled, but Mariesa pointed out that Vulcan ran electric arc furnaces, fed by scrap steel. "There must be value in the recycling, at least. John E., I would like one of your staff to lead the analysis. Khan, you will supply the necessary input. And speak to Jaleen, in Human Relations. You will need to consider the impact on the workforce, too." Gramper would not have cared about that aspect. Gramper had been of the old school, where the workers were faceless, interchangeable, and disposable; but Mariesa was a child of another era.

John E. was taking notes. He looked up at her. "One month?"

"I shall mark my calendar. Now, gentlemen. Prometheus." She leaned forward in her seat, as if she were about to take a deadfall in full leap. Everything else was for making money; Prometheus was for saving the world.

"The Goal," said Steve Matthias with a salute just shy of mockery.

John E. shook his head. "How long has it been since we drank *that* toast?"

"The enthusiasm of beginnings," said Khan, "succumbs to the doggedness of pressing on."

It had the sound of a proverb, but Mariesa suspected that

Khan could make up proverbs to suit his purpose. He hadn't been there at the beginning. He couldn't know the conspiratorial delight, the careful soundings out, the heady days of planning, the dizziness of the first few landmark steps. Launching the Plank design team; chartering the North Orange school district; selecting the test pilots . . . But at some point, every breakthrough project crossed over to the ordinary business side of things and became routine.

Yet, the Goal—the ultimate goal—was still unrealized. It would be all too easy for others to rise from the table with their winnings and not play the game to its conclusion. "Perhaps we ought to revive it," she said. "It was a bonding ritual. Steve? Your report?"

Steve threw an arm across the back of his chair. "Hasn't your husband been keeping you up to date?"

It was a challenge of some sort, but Mariesa was not quite sure what it meant, nor where Steve meant to take it. She studied his carefully neutral face. A man as cautious as Steve Matthias would not hurl a challenge lightly. "Barry is not program coordinator," she explained. "He is more of a . . . personal ambassador."

"Then why not put him inside?" Steve said with a casual wave of the hand. "I could use an assistant. Running Thor *and* being Prometheus program coordinator is pretty much two full-time jobs."

Mariesa traded a brief glance with Redman, who made a barely perceptible shrug. "We could split the two assignments," she said, "if that is what is bothering you. . . ."

Steve backpedaled. "That's not what I meant. Each project manager within Prometheus has a full-time staff to support his work. I thought the program coordinator ought to have similar resources."

"The coordinator is not to micromanage each project, Steve."

The man's face colored slightly. "I didn't mean that, either."

Khan interrupted, "I will investigate the staffing needs. As the program grows more projects, it may need more staff—or it may only need better cybernetics. It may even be reasonable to make it a full-time, independent presidency. The job has grown since the early days.''

''I don't see that last option, at all,'' Steve insisted. ''Prometheus is more of a confederation than a company. Some of our technology partners are not even part of VHI. The job really wants a coordinator, not a president.''

''Very well,'' Mariesa said, fairly sure now she knew where Steve was ''coming from.'' ''I will take the issue under advisement. Let's move on. Capsule descriptions for each project; one sentence each. Then we can expand upon them. FarTrip?''

''That would be the asteroid mission.'' Steve opened a small notebook and flipped over a tab. Mariesa thought with amusement that John E. or Werewolf would have flipped open a laptop and accessed a file. There *was* a generational borderland, and it had a very sharp slope. Steve was not much older than the others—of the Steering Committee, only Correy was older—but there were certain ingrained behaviors that he could not shake. He probably did have all the information on a disk somewhere; but he probably had everything hard copied in metal file cabinets, too.

''On track,'' he said. ''Supplemental, Earth-based propulsion system proved out in trials last—'' He stopped and looked at her with sudden concern.

''Yes. I know what day that was. Go on.''

He ducked his head. ''Astronaut selection will open in another two months. The flight-control programs are being written, behind track by three months.''

''That was more than one sentence,'' she pointed out, ''but never mind. Flocker?''

''Aurora is holding a meeting this week in Phoenix for the pilots who have been nominated for the ERP. We expect half a dozen volunteers for beta-testing the software.''

John E. said, ''Five bucks on DuBois and Calhoun.''

Mariesa said, ''Ten 'bucks' says Dolores will not release Calhoun from his Academy duties.''

Khan said, "I was disappointed that the Russians will not attend."

"It was their way of showing displeasure over the Balkan situation," said John E. "Their sympathies lie with Serbia and Greece, so they have been snubbing international ventures lately."

Steve frowned. "They won't kick us off Mir, will they?"

"There is no telling what a government will do. I'll be happy when we have our own station in place."

"Speaking of which . . ." Mariesa hinted.

Steve glanced at his notes. "The LEO Consortium projects five years to first operation. Until then, we're vulnerable to Russian politics." He consulted his notebook again. "FarTrip, flocker, LEO. Mmm. Zeus proved out the impulse engines. And Torch, of course, showed we can beam electrical power up to ships and orbital stations. Power losses were close to theory. The rest is up to the courts. John E.?"

"Werewolf has begun dismantling the Arizona laser for shipment to Wilson's site in Ecuador. Attwood is threatening that move, too, on national-security grounds."

Steve snorted. "Yeah. Like Ecuador is going to attack by beaming electrical power at us."

Khan interrupted. "Wilson has offered to lease space at both of his ram sites. But most other sites along the equator have better uses for a megawatt of electrical power than powering satellites."

So shelve the ground-based power grid for the time being. Maybe two or three to boost FarTrip. "What about the plan to put a power satellite into sun-synchronous polar orbit?" Mariesa asked. "That would seem to be the path of least resistance for now. Surely, no one can object to microwave beaming in outer space."

Steve cocked an eye. "You'd be surprised what people can object to," he said. "But . . . Let's see." More page flipping. "The Helios Consortium plans to put one up late this year. They'll run it as an electrical utility for satellites and space stations, and as a test bed for power beam transmission."

"Meanwhile," John E. drawled, "your old friend, Phil Albright, is putting the Peoples' Crusades behind a ground-based solar array outside Albuquerque. He says it would eliminate the need for 'power beams slicing through the air.' That might undermine investment in our SPS program."

Mariesa pursed her lips. "Yes, I saw him on television last week. EarthSafe Solar. We will certainly need to evaluate our strategic plans." She smiled to herself as she considered various options, layering them like a wall between herself and the pain inside her.

Sykes brought her apéritif to the Roost and set it quietly on the desk beside the computer. It was a violet liqueur in a small, thumb-sized glass. Mariesa looked up from her screen. The Roost appeared dim, a room of shadows; she had been staring into the screen too long. "Is it ten o'clock already, Sykes? I have been buried in these reports all evening." She tilted back in the chair as she swiveled away from the desk—an ergonomic design, the chair supported her body perfectly. She rubbed the bridge of her nose. "I am playing catch-up with the project details."

"I doubt," Sykes volunteered, "that anyone could hope to master all of the details anymore."

She looked into his face, expressionless as always. "Meaning, you think I spend too much time on this. Well, perhaps you are right. Once the Helios Power Plant is operational and FarTrip is on its way, the crunch will be over and I can relax, a little." She could never relax entirely, and there was always another project waiting in the wings. She reached for the apéritif. "Ask Barry if he would join me up here. Tell him it is a night for stargazing." Under the stars, on the catwalk outside the observatory, was one of Barry's favorite places for intimacy; and she had been neglecting him since her hospitalization.

"I'm afraid Mr. Fast went out earlier this evening. He had arranged a dinner party with some of the teachers he used to work with."

"I see." Sykes made no comment. "Very well, Sykes. Inform me when he returns. I shall probably still be up here catching up on my personal correspondence.''

Sykes inclined his head and retreated to the elevator. Mariesa sat awhile in contemplation. She ought not begrudge Barry his evenings out. It was only once or twice a month. Only, she felt the need for him, too; and the night outside was balmy. She remembered the liqueur in her hand and drank it down. Closing her eyes, she could imagine Barry's hands touching her gently, his fingers exploring her, bringing her slowly to ecstasy. The sweet liquid warmed her, and she felt it spread from her throat to her abdomen. She set the glass aside.

She could never have a child now. It was no longer possible.

She turned to the mass of correspondence that had accumulated during her hospitalization and began sorting it into piles. Personal. Family. Business. She tried to do a little each day and the stack was yielding slowly to her persistence.

One parcel was a padded manila envelope with a return address from the Jet Propulasion Lab in Pasadena. Business or personal? She opened it and inside she found a disk cassette and a letter from Dr. Helin.

This will confirm the asteroid sighting you sent us on 14 February. . . .

The past had a way of welling up in unexpected ways. She had forgotten this, forgotten the tingle in her limbs when she had found the dim little smear on the photograph. Events in between had shoved that aside. Developing the photographs for this find, she had chased Barry from the darkroom. It must have been about that time that the child had . . . that the child had . . . She had wondered even then at the lack of activity within her.

Deliberately, she turned her mind from those thoughts.

She was alone in the Roost, and there was no one to share the news with. Well, time enough tomorrow. *What shall I name it? Prometheus?* Perhaps *Barry,* a way of apologizing. She read the remainder of the letter. *Perihelion . . . Major and minor axes . . . Complete orbital data on diskette . . . Apollo-class asteroid . . .*

Apollo? The chill that enveloped her expunged the earlier warmth and she reached again for her drink before remembering that she had already consumed it. Apollo asteroids crisscrossed the Earth's orbit. Sometimes they struck. In high school, she had seen one graze the Earth's biosphere, barely missing her. The moon was a shield—one glance at its backside was proof enough of that—but a poor one. Earth had scars, too; not so obvious as the moon's, scoured by centuries or millennia of wind and rain, but still there for those with the wit to see them. *Something* had made all those circular lakes and seas that she had marked on her globe. They had even found Nemesis, the Dinosaur Killer, in the seabed off the coast of Yucatán. When would another such monster strike? No one knew. Not for a million more years. Tomorrow. She picked up the disk and held it before her eyes.

She had found one of the bullets in the gun held to Earth's head.

Prometheus? Barry? Not fit names for something that might threaten the Earth. *Harriet?* A sly humor to that name, but one likely to be lost on everyone, including Harriet.

No close approaches projected, the letter said. That fit Harriet, too.

Her relief was sudden, but wary. Chaos theory meant orbits could not be forecast too far ahead; certainly not for rocks subject to the whims of Jupiter and close encounters with Earth or Venus. Even little Mars might put in a random nudge or two.

She started to insert the disk in her computer but it trembled and she could not place it in the slot. She paused, took a breath, and tried again, with more steady hands. She closed the project-management program and called up Skyrock, which digested the new information. Within moments, the monitor displayed a top-down view of the inner system showing the locations of all the asteroids she had been tracking. Each appeared as a blinking dot trailing a short, hairline "comet trail" behind it, a plotting convention to indicate its path. Her two original discoveries, Gramper and . . . Yes, call it Harriet, were flagged in red. Mariesa ran the program forward and the dots whirled in an intricate ballet, their tails blurred into ellipses.

"Glo" had been right, of course. Harriet would come nowhere near the Earth; at least in the foreseeable future. A reprieve, at least from this particular bullet.

But perhaps it had made a close approach in the past? The letter from JPL did not say. Any number of asteroids passed through near space and only since the eighties had Skywatch and other volunteer groups been looking for them. Some had been seen only after they had passed, especially if they had come "out of the sun." Who knew how many had never been seen at all? Harriet might have been one of them. Almost, she wanted it to have happened. She wanted to know that there had been a close call. Years ago, her high-school beau had not even turned his head to look. Not looking was the greatest sin of all.

Mariesa returned the display to zero time, then told Skyrock to run backward.

The odd thing about celestial mechanics was that it had no sense of direction. The equations worked the same way backward as forward. The blinking dots on the screen danced just as happily in reverse, predicting—no, *post*dicting where they had been. Occasionally dots brightened to indicate a position confirmed by actual sighting.

When the display reached 2001, a queer thing happened. Two of the dots passed through each other: Harriet and another. An illusion caused by a two-dimensional graphic? She stepped the display back to that point and froze it. When she rotated the picture, she saw that both asteroids were on the same plane, too. So she pointed to each to obtain its coordinate position.

Not quite the same, she saw when the numbers were displayed beside each dot. Just an illusion caused by scale, then. She magnified the sector where the two asteroids had had their close encounter. A *very* close encounter, she saw at once. Was there any chance they actually had collided? That would be a marvelous discovery in itself. The positions, after all, were only projections and, hence approximate.

She clicked up another window to examine her log for the second asteroid. Gidget. Not her own discovery, of course; and who on Earth would name an asteroid Gidget? Eighteen confirmed observations between 1992, when she had picked it up, and 2001. After that, nothing.

She had lost track of it. She remembered now. A frustrating night. Rerunning the computer calculations. Realigning the telescope. Styx had been in the Roost with her. And that shabby little creature—what had been his name? Michaelson—had been using the reg agencies to extort money for the president's campaign. And somehow or other, she had fumbled the calculations for the asteroid's position. She had never found it since that time, and had eventually given up looking for it.

And here might be the reason. If the two *had* collided, both would have gone off in different directions thereafter, like billiard balls. What a delicious coincidence! She opened her E-mail and tapped out a quick note to J. P. Henry, at the University of Hawaii. *J. P. Any chance these two orbits meet? Mariesa v H.* Then she downloaded the relevant data, attached it to the E-mail cover letter, and sent it to the Net gateway.

It was a painstaking task and it absorbed her completely, and that, of course, was half the reason for it.

The kitchen at Silverpond was a large one with a tiled floor and drains, bright with polished pans and cookware hanging from hooks like so many dead game birds. A butcher block occupied the center of the room, along with a number of preparation tables. Stoves and lockers and a stone oven lined the walls. The smell of freshly baked bread permeated the air. Everything gleamed. Mrs. Pontavecchio permitted no dirt or disorder in her domain. Mariesa often imagined that, even while preparing a meal, she was cleaning up behind herself with the other hand. On the north wall, double doors gave access to the outside. The kitchen was on the first basement level, but faced a slope in the mound that allowed deliveries to be made directly.

Mrs. Pontavecchio hovered over the workmen installing the new refrigerator, not giving them directions, but watching with suspicion everything they did. The cook herself was a large, matronly woman with saucy, Italian eyes. Mariesa and Barry watched from beside the butcher block. Mariesa wondered how the Argonaut workmen felt working under such scrutiny.

Barry stood beside her with his arms crossed. One hand held a glass of bourbon nestled in the elbow of the other arm. "It doesn't *look* like a refrigerator," he said. "What's that thing?"

"The electromagnet," she said. She was only guessing, but the tall cylinder *looked* like what she imagined an electromagnet would look like.

"An electromagnet on a refrigerator . . ." Barry shook his head.

"According to Chris, when you magnetize a material, it warms up—because its molecules align themselves and something called 'entropy' decreases. When you turn off the magnetism, the material cools." Chris had explained the system to her several times. Active magnetic regeneration. Curie points. Ames metal. Magnetic hysteresis. She did not understand even a quarter of it; only that it kept things cold.

Barry unfolded his arms and took a drink. "How much does that puppy cost?"

Kept things cold at great expense. "Fifty-seven troy ounces. About twenty thousand American dollars."

He whistled. "Well, I guess Sears won't be stocking them."

She wondered if his sarcasm was meant seriously or as humor. "The high cost," she told him, "stems from the cryogenic superconductors and a rare earth compound of—I believe Chris said 'dysprosium' and 'erbium' with common aluminum."

Barry laughed. "It says so right on the label." Sometimes Barry could be a bit inscrutable, as if the universe were a private joke crafted for his own amusement. "What it all adds up to, though, is that rich people can afford them, and poor people can't."

"Barry, all innovations start as novelties for the rich. Automobiles, televisions, passive solar heating . . . Someone has to be the guinea pig for new technology. Experience brings the cost down eventually. In ten years, most well-to-do house-holds will have magfridges. In twenty years, everyone will. But it is not as if it were a necessity that others are being denied. I can buy a refrigerator today for far less than fifty-seven ounces that will do a great deal more than this contraption.''

He took a long swallow of his drink. ''Then why bother?''

''The device needs no HCFCs or HFCs to operate,'' she pointed out.

Barry looked at her. ''I thought you didn't buy that line.''

''I do not; but a market is a market.''

''Yeah. Money. It always comes down to money.'' He shrugged and would not quite look at her while he finished off his drink. Mariesa wondered what he was thinking. He had become indrawn in the two months since . . . since her stay in the hospital. Of course, he had been looking forward to fatherhood as much as she had been toward motherhood; still, one did pull oneself together and move on. Barry had always found it easy to lift a drink. These days, he found it harder to put one down. Ought she say something? Or should she let him grieve in his own way, as she did with the immersion of her work?

''How was your dinner last week?'' she asked, breaking the silence that threatened.

He started slightly, glanced at her momentarily, casually set his now-empty glass on the butcher block, and stuffed his hands into his pants pockets. ''All right, I guess.''

''Were Gwen and Bob there? I have not seen them in some time. Perhaps at your next affair I could accompany you.''

His sudden laugh puzzled her. ''That would be something to see.'' To her inquiring look, he said, ''Never mind. It doesn't matter. I had dinner with some middle school teacher . . . s. Bob and Gwen won't talk to me. With Bob, that's a plus; but Gwen and I always got along before.'' He fell silent and resumed his study of the refrigerator.

Mariesa didn't ask him before what. ''Would you like to return to teaching?''

He shook his head. ''It would be a little silly, wouldn't it?

I couldn't go back to Witherspoon; and my name was mud in the government schools even before you and I . . ." His voice trailed off.

"What if the Van Huyten Trust endowed you with a fund to open your own school, independent of Mentor? It would not need to turn a profit."

"There still wouldn't be a point to it, would there?" He turned and faced her at last. The workmen continued their assembly, pretending nothing was happening. "I would still have my allowance." And, oh, how his voice grated on that word! "There wouldn't be any challenge. It would be a . . . a toy school that you gave me to play with while you did your important things."

"Is there something more important," she asked quietly, "than educating children?"

He was silent for a moment. "Do you see what money does?" he said at last. "I've even lost sight of who I used to be."

"You could assemble a team of teachers and organize the school as you saw fit. You may take on partners, if you wish."

"Dammit, are you listening? I said I need a challenge."

"It would be in North Orange, of course. Sufficiently nearby our home. Perhaps in Eastport, or Downtown."

He was silent. She said, "Is that a sufficient challenge?"

"Jesus, you don't make things easy, do you?"

"Easy things are seldom worth doing."

After Mariesa had broken the connection to Fernando, she relaxed in her chair and swiveled to face the others sitting around the board table. Inevitably, that included facing old Henryk hanging above the doorway, and a half dozen or so telepresence screens. This time, only Henryk was scowling. Though to be fair, it was more a thoughtful look than a scowl, as if he were weighing (if not quite celebrating) the successful flocker test flight. The standards of facial expression had changed over the centuries. No one back then ever said, "Smile for the painter." Even La Gioconda had managed only a faint grin.

"Well," said Barry, who was sitting directly to Mariesa's right, "old Ned is as cocky as ever."

"The flight was successful," Mariesa replied. "That's what counts."

"What I want to know," Dolores Pitchlynn countered, "is how he got wind of FarTrip. It seemed pretty clear to me what he was talking about. 'Collecting rocks,' indeed."

Mariesa faced the Pegasus monitor, not the camera. It always bothered her when the telepresent looked off in odd directions instead of directly out from the screen; but she liked to see the faces of the people she was talking to. "I would guess that about half the pilots have some inkling of the project, by now."

"It was supposed to be confidential," Dolores insisted.

Steve Matthias, sitting on Mariesa's left, just past John E. Redman, made an off-camera face that Mariesa interpreted as *Give it a rest, Dotty*. João Pessoa, who had come to New Jersey for a meeting of VHI's International Division, maintained a blank look. Heinz Ruger, also present for the international meeting, ran his stubby fingers through short, graying blond hair, and said, "We are today discussing the configuration of the FarTrip vessel, no?" Always business, Heinz. His broad, Alpine face hardly ever broke a smile, and the word was that he *dreamed* about resource allocation and planning; but he wrote science-fiction novels in Germany under a pseudonym. A puckish secret life. Of all the steering group, Mariesa thought he was the most likely to understand about the asteroid threat; but she did not know him well enough as a person to approach him on that subject.

"The hydroponics are ready," Correy Wilcox volunteered. He spoke from a Gaia executive jump jet en route to Minneapolis. "The test facility aboard Mir has been operational for three months with no problem, except a tendency for the plants to grow wispy. Vasily says the tomatoes taste fine and oxygen efficiency is up about six percent."

"Will we do the six-month test with the actual flight crew?" Wallace Coyle asked from the Aurora/Odysseus screen. "It might be best not to put the flight crew through that with a year's journey following right after.''

Mariesa held up a hand. ''Let's hear what Dolores has to say, first. Then each of you can report on your subprojects.''

Dolores Pitchlynn unfolded a pair of reading glasses and placed them on her nose. ''Thank you.'' She picked up a single sheet of paper and looked out from the screen. ''I have the status report of the vessel, people. The details have been black-coded and E-mailed to each of your confidential workcenters. In brief, it is as follows. One cargo module is being refitted by our Daedalus subsidiary with life-support equipment for the one-year flight, including the hydroponic tanks that Correy is to deliver within the next month. We plan to rely on proven fuel-cell technology for oxygen generation and on packaged food stores; but the hydroponics will provide a wider margin for error. In addition, Wilson Enterprises will loft a series of supply canisters with additional fuel and support gear. These will be outfitted in orbit with electrodeless pulsed inductive thrusters and launched on rendezvous trajectories, allowing the Plank to replenish supplies en route. These loads are not mission-essential, but are intended to increase our margins. Without them, the supply budget is tight and the PERT has very little slack. The mission will be bare-bones, but still doable. With them . . .'' She raised her eyes from the paper. ''With them, the mission may be fattened with additional options.''

Pitchlynn adjusted her glasses and resumed reading. ''Refitting of a Plank will begin shortly, as soon as one is designated. I suggest the *Gene Bullard*, as it already has had EPI thrusters installed for the Zeus/Torch test. We can detach the solar panel array and leave it at the station while the vessel is in ground dock. During Phase 2, scheduled for late 2008, we will reorbit *Bullard* to skydock and gut it of all systems dedicated to ground-landing, attach the couplings for the booster stage, and perform the final readiness check.''

''The first permanent deep-space vessel,'' said Werewolf Gregorson on the Cleveland monitor. He folded his hands across his stomach and smiled a contented smile.

''Provided,'' Dolores said sternly, ''that Helios and your

ground-based laser array will be operational. The mass reduction ground-basing the power plant allows in the booster stage makes the difference between 'doable' and 'really neat idea.' The Helios utility alone will be insufficient for our purposes.''

''The second laser is under construction in Kenya,'' said Werewolf. ''We're still looking for a third site. The main hurdle is access to a power grid. When the Kilimanjaro Laser fires up, Nairobi goes dark.'' He chuckled at the joke.

''And what do the Kenyans get out of it?'' Barry asked quietly. ''Besides sitting in the dark for a couple hours a day.''

Gregorson pursed his lips and his shaggy eyebrows came together. ''I exaggerate. But if you want to know, they get a nice chunk of hard currency tied to infrastructure development; and when the first deep-space vessel leaves cislunar space for another worldlet, it will be, by God, the Kenyans who helped push it there.''

''Which means,'' said John E. with a lawyer's summing-up air, ''politics. Mariesa and I are heading for Washington next week to see if we can convince Albright to temper his criticisms of the laser system, and to check on how many senators Cyrus Attwood has rented.''

''One hell of an effort,'' Barry commented, ''for a nonprofit venture.''

''It's a world project, Barry,'' Mariesa reminded him. ''VHI is only the prime contractor.''

Chris van Huyten sat at the far end of the table with his fingers peaked. His position directly under Henryk's portrait accentuated both his resemblance and differences. Lighter, thinner, taller than old Henryk, Chris nevertheless possessed the same high cheekbones, the same snake-lazy eyes. ''It's a scientific research venture, Barry. It's funded by several governments and agencies. Gene Forney and Heimdall plan to auction the live broadcasts from the vessel and at the asteroid as a weekly television show, which will recover some of the cost, but no one expects the venture to make money.'' Mariesa could read in his face that Chris was not thrilled with the idea, but he was a trouper. He'd go along with the gag, as long as someone covered the nut.

Khan coughed gently into his hand. "*Bullard* will bring back a cargo. One of Wilson's canisters will contain mining equipment; and another, perhaps, strap-on boosters and an EPI thruster." He smiled like a cat.

Mariesa put her hands flat on the table and pressed until the knuckles turned white. "What are you talking about, Khan? Are you proposing we *move* the asteroid?"

"Well," said Werewolf with a grin, "it *is* a little far away, so we thought we'd see if we could bring it home for a closer look." Most of those around the table chuckled. So did the telepresent.

"*Why wasn't I told?*" Her voice trembled. She pushed against the table. Did they know what they were doing? To send an asteroid hurtling toward the Earth? Her worst nightmare, and they were planning to realize it?

"You were in intensive care, Mariesa," Steve Matthias pointed out. "We thought it best not to bother you."

"I absolutely forbid it." She pitched her voice calm, but absolute. She was rewarded by puzzled gazes, except from Barry who looked concerned and placed a hand on her forearm, and from Correy and Wallace, who understood her fear.

"Riesey," said Belinda on the Spokane monitor. "What is the problem?" Mariesa did not answer. Their relationship had never been the same since the night Styx ran away, and she and Belinda had grown further apart in the years following her marriage. Mentor's president seldom stopped at Silverpond for social visits anymore.

Correy's voice rose over the background hum of hushprops. "Wallace and I voted in favor," he said.

Mariesa tensed for a moment, then forced herself to relax. "I . . . see." Puzzlement rippled around the table at the interplay, and Steve Matthias turned to the Gaia monitor with his brow knotted in thought. Correy and Wallace, along with the late Keith McReynolds, were the only members of the steering group who took the threat of asteroid impact as seriously—if not quite as urgently—as she did. Correy was trying to tell her that they considered the plan safe.

Mariesa took a deep breath and gently pulled her arm away

from Barry's hand. Of course, that did not mean that they were correct in their belief. "I shall want to see the complete plans, including contingency plans, by end of business today. I will review them and give you my thoughts. Whom did you choose as prime?"

Heinz Ruger raised his hand. "Me. We estimate there is enough iron in the rock to build a dozen space stations, once orbital smelters are set up." He shrugged, flipping the upraised hand palm up. "Perhaps that takes decades before we have the facilities, but the ore will wait. Never will we have a better opportunity to bring so much material into orbit for as little cost. We are going there anyway; and if it does not work, we are no worse off."

No, we could be much worse off....

"Why wait?" asked Barry. "Just dig tunnels, or build domes, or whatever, and use the rock as your space station. I think you'd have something a lot sooner, a lot bigger, and a lot cheaper than if you boiled it with space mirrors, recovered the metals, and fabricated the structures."

Heinz looked at him dumbly. Werewolf slapped his forehead so hard Mariesa heard it through the speakers. "I will be dipped. Barry, if you ever come to Cleveland, I'll buy you a steak dinner. I hadn't even thought past schlepping it back."

"Out of the mouths of babes," said Steve Matthias with a smile. Barry smiled back, but Mariesa saw more watts in his eyes than there were in the Kilimanjaro Laser.

After the meeting, John E. fiddled with his briefcase while the others trickled out of the room and the video monitors went blank, one by one. Steve Matthias tried to outwait him, but when the lawyer unfolded his personal phone to call his office, Steve conceded the contest. He stuck his hand out to Mariesa and said he would call the next day. Then it was only herself and Barry and John E. in the room.

Redman folded the phone and put it away. "And I'll bet I know what Steve wants to talk to you about, too." He glanced briefly at Barry before giving Mariesa his attention. "Correy and Wallace seem to have some sort of special status here.

It's hardly ever evident. In fact, most of the time, they're just corporate wallpaper. But every now and then something comes up, like today, and there they are. Keith had special status, too; but we all figured it was because he was a family friend as well as CFO. Steve is supposed to be program coordinator, and he doesn't like the idea that you may have some sort of secret oversight committee second-guessing him.''

"If you ask me," said Barry, "Steve needs a little oversight.''

John E. raised his eyebrows and regarded Barry. "No offense, Barry, but he has a worse hangup with you. The others are VHI officials. Corporate staff, like Khan or me; or divisional presidents and CEOs. But you have no official standing.''

Mariesa spoke sharply before Barry could answer. "He is my special assistant.''

Redman nodded. "The chairman's spouse.''

"And don't I know it," Barry said. Mariesa saw the flush creep along his neck.

John E. spread his hands. "Understand, I have no problem. You've thrown more than one good idea into the pot, like today. But to Steve it looks as if you are Mariesa's personal agent. What'd they used to call them? The Queen's Eyes and Ears.''

"That is absurd, John E. I have set Barry to reviewing progress reports and summarizing them, and he has conducted procedure audits for me, but—''

"Oh, that must set Steve's mind at ease.''

"Why should he be uneasy," Barry wondered, "that Mariesa might be looking over his shoulder?'' He looked at Mariesa, then at the lawyer. "Does he have something to hide?''

Redman smiled broadly. "I would think so. Everyone does. That's why lawyers made discovery into fishing expeditions. But no one likes another watching over his shoulder when he's trying to get a job done.''

There was a light tap on the door and Redman's confidential assistant entered with a manila envelope, which she handed to the CLO. "Thank you, Pamela," he said. He slit open the seal with a pocketknife and pulled out another, smaller envelope. He held it by the edges and stared at it for a moment, his eyes growing sad. Then he sighed and extended the envelope to Mariesa. "Keith left this with me for safekeeping. I have no idea what's in it. His instructions were to turn it over to you if the subject of moving an asteroid into Earth orbit ever came up."

It was the most unlikely announcement. Mariesa stared at the envelope in John E.'s hand before taking it. A five-by-eight standard tan envelope, a message from the past. Though it was light enough, it felt as if it weighed a ton. She saw her name—*Riesey*—in broad curls across the front. Keith had had the finest handwriting of any man she had ever known. The last generation to master that art. Mariesa started to break the seal with her fingernail, but John E. handed her his penknife and she used that instead.

Inside was a single sheet of Keith's stationery—his personal stationery with the embossed sun and planet. It read, *Fear is fine for motivating thoughts, but not so fine for thinking them.*

Almost, she could hear his voice, see his bow tie, feel his cheerful smile on her. Barry tapped her on the shoulder and a handkerchief appeared. She took it and held it against her cheek. "I'm sorry," she said. "I still miss him." When she thought she had mastered herself, she said, "John. Do you have many more envelopes like this?"

John E. could not take his eyes off the stationery. He shook his head. "I can only hope that when I am dead seven years, there will be someone who still treasures my advice." Then, in a more severe tone, he added, "Do you care to tell me what this is all about, Mariesa? Keith knew about his heart condition for several months before the end. He knew it could come at any time and he put all of his affairs systematically in order. Yet, he thought it was important to take the time to give you advice on a contingency that was nowhere near anybody's planning horizon then and to entrust that advice to my safekeeping. I think Steve is right. There is something going on, and only you and Correy and Wallace—and Keith—are in on it." His glance at Barry was uncertain. "It is something you are concealing from the rest of us and it has something to do with asteroids."

She unfolded Keith's memo and folded it again.

"John E.," Barry said suddenly, "have you ever seen Mariesa's special globe?"

She looked at her husband with astonishment. He said, "Riesey, I may not be a math teacher, but I learned enough arithmetic to add two and two." His eyes said more—that he had not been trusted—and Mariesa, having no answer to that, dropped her gaze.

Mariesa arranged to meet Phil Albright at the Crystal Gateway Marriott in Arlington, Virginia. It was only a short distance from National Airport and connected to Washington by the Metro. Mariesa had other business to conduct in the capital, and the venue was a handy compromise between meeting him in the Peoples' Crusades offices in the District or inviting him to VHI in New Jersey.

She bought Zhou Hui with her, and John E. Redman. Werewolf flew commercial from Cleveland and they met him at the airport terminal. "In case Phil has any technical questions," Mariesa had said when inviting him.

"Technical issues are not where he's at," Werewolf had replied, but he came anyway.

Mariesa and her people waited, as arranged, at the foot of the escalator to Tuscany's, the mezzanine restaurant. The lobby was white tile; the paneling, light woods. Green plants and an open ceiling gave it an "atrium" look. Businessmen dragging suit bags, with laptop satchels dangling from their shoulders, stood patiently in line at the registration desk. The bell captain, wearing an ankle-length red coat and a white British India helmet, positioned a cart of baggage near the desk.

"There he is," said Ms. Zhou.

Mariesa saw Albright emerging from the concourse walkway on the far side of the lobby. True to his principles, he had taken the Metro Yellow Line to get here. The slender young woman who accompanied him topped him by half a head. Not that she was especially tall, but Phil Albright was himself a short man.

"Looks like he brought his secretary," Gregorson commented.

"Didn't know he had one," said John E. "I thought personal assistants went against his philosophy."

Gregorson snorted. "Like most sensible arrangements . . . That egalitarian 'we're all coequal' line he likes to hand out about the Crusades is so much horse hockey. There's Phil Albright, and there's Simon Fell and 'the Cadre,' and after that comes everyone else."

"Hush," said Mariesa. "We are here to reach a meeting of minds." *And why assume the woman is a secretary? Or that secretaries are unimportant?*

The woman wore a plain red blouse and navy skirt. No jewelry; no makeup. Black, shoulder-length hair. "Dear Lord," she said suddenly. "It's Styx!" She hadn't recognized the girl in the woman, not without the black garments and makeup she had once affected.

"Surprised to see me?" Styx said when they were close enough for speech. She did not offer her hand.

"I had heard through your publisher that you were back home."

"Hey, aintcha heard? Home isn't there anymore." Her voice was sassy, challenging . . . and defensive. Mariesa did not understand the comment, and did not pursue it. She turned to the short, dark, intense man she had come to meet.

"Phil, it was good of you to meet me like this." Albright, at least, understood manners. He shook hands with Mariesa and the others.

"I see you brought reinforcements," he said with a grin. "I'm flattered."

Implying that two of them were worth four of us. This man liked to play head games. "Shall we proceed upstairs? I have reserved a table."

Albright shrugged. "Why not?"

The restaurant had an Italian theme. Styx and Albright ordered pasta primavera. Werewolf ordered veal. Albright grimaced at the choice, but made no comment. John E. chose the wine. Being the lone Virginian, he was in some sense the host.

Once the meals were ordered, Mariesa raised the subject of the booster lasers. She laid the case out systematically, pointing out that, by supplying power to ships and facilities in orbit, they would reduce the number of launches needed.

"That's a false benefit," Albright pointed out. "Your orbital economy is projected to grow quite rapidly, so the number of launches will increase, regardless." He picked up his wineglass and studied the play of light off the golden liquid. "I don't know if our atmosphere can take it."

Werewolf huffed and Mariesa tapped him on the shin to keep him quiet. "There is no scientific evidence to support that position," she pointed out.

"There have been studies . . ."

"By scientists with an axe to grind; or funded by those who sell axes."

Albright smiled at the clever turn of phrase; but Styx leaned over the table. "I see. When the science disagrees with you, it's bad science."

"Assume honesty," said Werewolf. Styx turned her head and squinted at him.

"What?"

Mariesa raised a hand to stop him, but caught John E.'s signal and waited to hear what Will had to say.

"Assume that all the scientists are honest," Gregorson went on. "That's a stretch, because scientists are human, like everybody else. They have passions, beliefs; and sometimes those passions intersect their scientific work and . . . they see what they want to see, like Margaret Mead on Samoa. But let's assume honesty all around. The problem with data is that it's fuzzy. No measurement is ever precise. Every sample is an estimate. When a scientist says how much carbon dioxide was in the air during the Ice Age, what he really means is that that is what he got when he tested a sample of ice using a certain test method. Other samples, other methods . . . other results. As much as double, in the case of Ice Age CO_2. So with all that fuzziness, it's possible to 'find' "—he made quote marks with his fingers—"a relationship even when there is no relationship. It's called the alpha risk. If the alpha risk for a certain design of study—let's say, a study of Plank launches versus atmospheric ozone—if that alpha risk is ten percent, and you conduct ten studies, chances are about one in three that at least one of them will show a positive result. Too bad that's the one that gets on TV."

Albright shrugged. Styx said, "Why did you single out Margaret Mead?"

Werewolf's face tightened and he leaned back in his chair. He downed his wine with a single gulp. "Why bother. You didn't even hear my point."

Albright set his own wineglass on the white linen tablecloth and ran his finger across the base. "I understand your point quite well, Mr. Gregorson—may I call you Will?—but I see things from a different perspective. Call it the beta risk." He smiled. "Didn't think I knew that? I'm not mindless Luddite, you know. Not like . . . Well, we all do business with people we'd rather not, eh, Mariesa? But, Will, you want proof that there is a harm; I want proof that there is not. If you wait for proof positive, it may be too late when you get it."

"So we should act before we have proof?" asked Mariesa.

Styx grinned maliciously. "When the consequences are severe, yes."

Mariesa turned her attention to the girl. "Is that not what motivates vigilantes and lynch mobs?"

Roberta hesitated and pulled back from the table. "That's a false analogy," she said after a moment.

But the hesitation was tribute of Mentor's training. Roberta was too intellectually honest to take refuge in such casual dismissal. Mariesa could almost hear Onwuka's rolling bass: *Set up the analogies and prove that!* "Furthermore," Mariesa pressed the point, "it is impossible to prove a negative. So your insistence on such a standard," she turned her attention again to Phil Albright, "amounts to an assumption of guilt, which the accused must disprove."

"Which is bad law," John E. reminded them, "and bad science."

"You only think so," Roberta said, "because Anglos have had a privileged position in our culture and concepts from Anglo culture, like innocent until proven guilty, have been imposed on the science story."

A glance from Mariesa silenced Werewolf before his words were more than a rumble in his throat. Roberta's eyes were black and unblinking. *Shotgun barrels*, Mariesa thought with a weird sense of déjà vu. *Have I hurt her so very much?* Yet, what could she have done differently? The future puts demands on us, will we or not, and sometimes there were casualties.

"This isn't the place," John E. said, "to debate philosophy. We're meeting with y'all to discuss one particular issue. Ground-based lasers. Our meals will be here soon and I, for one, dislike talking business while I'm eating. And afterwards, it spoils the digestion."

Albright leaned back and laid one arm on his chair arm. "All right. Convince me why I should let you play with my home planet's atmosphere."

Provocatively phrased, thought Mariesa. She nodded to John E. that he should carry the ball.

John E. held up his fingers and ticked them off. "First of all, there is no evidence to support your position. Secondly— we've been over item one already, let me finish—secondly, the operations we plan to support will actually provide the data to decide the issue. Thirdly, there is considerable support for the asteroid mission, especially in the Third World—"

"Yes," interjected Albright. "Clever of you to site the lasers there."

"And fourthly, as more industry is located in orbit, the less pollution there will be on Earth."

"Hmm." Albright smiled cat-quick. "Though I find it hard to believe that any useful fraction of industry will ever move up there. And what happens to all the workers? But . . ." He held a palm out. "I'll think about it."

Roberta sucked in her breath. "Phil!" she said.

"Maybe we can set up a scientific commission to study the

effects. That is . . ." And he gave them an ironic smile. ". . . if we can find any objective scientists."

Mariesa nodded. "Something can undoubtedly be arranged. I'm sure you have limited resources, which you would rather spend on immediate and clearly hurtful problems. Too many children go to bed hungry or fail to receive proper medical care; too many women are beaten and murdered by jealous men; too many factories dump waste into watersheds and air . . ."

"Touching of you to care," said Roberta.

Mariesa turned to her and spoke sharply. "Do not assume that because I work through different means I do not care about the same ends. Many of the same ends," she admitted with an ironic nod to Albright. "After all, Holy Rollers and Episcopalians both worship the same God."

"As do Jews and Muslims," Albright pointed out. Mariesa acknowledged the point.

"My point is that neither you nor I can do everything at once, so we must do something first. Every donated dollar you spend on one crusade is a dollar you cannot spend on another crusade."

"So why waste money fighting you, when I can spend it fighting someone else?"

"There is no shortage of legitimate targets."

Albright nodded, as if to himself, and looked off with a thoughtful expression. Mariesa wondered what was going through his head.

"Understand, I'm sympathetic to some of your goals," Albright said. "But I'm wary of how you plan to get there. I don't think it's wrong, or even hostile, to insist on being careful, and testing each step before taking it and seeing where it leads. These ground-based lasers of yours sound harmless enough, but we both know they're only the first step to solar power satellites beaming power at the Earth; and that has already been decided against."

"Right," said Werewolf. "We can't have all that cheap power available to people."

Albright gave him a hard look. "It won't be all that cheap,

and you know it. And there are lots of other problems. Not just atmospheric heating or ozone depletion. But there are consequences to cheap power—to lifestyle, to other cultures, to population growth. Life is a web, don't you see?'' And Mariesa thought she could almost hear pleading in his voice. Paul preaching to the Athenians.

''I know,'' said Werewolf. ''You would rather preserve other cultures in quaintly picturesque squalor than see them become Westernized and wealthy. You do know that wealth is the only known antidote for population growth?''

''That's only a correlation; not cause and effect,'' Albright said.

''I'll remind you of those words the next time your people release a study.''

John E. reached for the wine bottle, placing himself between Gregorson and Albright, both of whom fell silent. Redman made a good referee, Mariesa thought. He knew how to intervene without appearing to. Bringing Werewolf had been a mistake, she decided. The man was too argumentative; he wore his contempt on his sleeve. Will was an outstanding entrepreneur, but a lousy politician. Which was why he had nearly lost control of his own company, before Mariesa had stepped in and bought it.

''We can agree to disagree,'' the lawyer said. ''I might point out, however, that obtaining a driver's license could be the first step on the path to a bank robbery; yet, that is no reason to forbid the license. You may oppose the SPS project without opposing the ground-to-orbit power system. In any event, no SPS construction is projected for some time to come; and there are, as mentioned earlier, more urgent projects that need your attention.''

Mariesa let it set at that point. No hearts and minds would be won around this table today, and she did not want to back Albright into too tight a corner. Who knew how much of Albright's hard-line position was conviction and how much was concession. Albright had factions to deal with, just as she did, and had to juggle them with all the same dexterity.

During the meal, conversation drifted into more casual matters. The rain in the Midwest. The Serbian ultimatum to Macedonia. The Washington Metro—the one thing in Washington, Mariesa conceded, that seemed to work well, possibly because it was only quasi-governmental and was required to turn a profit. The new Caribbean Baseball League. (The Havana Gulls were battling the San Juan Conquistadores for first place. The Mexico City Toltecs were in firm possession of the cellar.) Albright wondered what the effect would be on the American and National Leagues, with so much prime talent now staying home to play. Mariesa was delighted to find in Albright another aficionado of the graceful and patient nineteenth-century sport. It opened another window on how the man's mind worked. He did not think from week to week, like a football fan, but in longer terms. She thought that, under other circumstances, she could like this man.

She tried to draw Styx out more than once and received only sarcasm or hostility in return. Finally, she gave up the effort, but felt unaccountably depressed during the remainder of the meal. It made no rational sense, but she wanted Roberta Carson to *like* her, if for no other reason than that she once had.

You can't always get what you want, the poet had said. Yet, what could she give up that would regain the look that had once been in young Styx's eyes? If she conceded every point to Albright, if she gave up on the Goal and turned her back on the dangerous skies—even assuming the Steering Committee would let her—Mariesa suspected that even that would not be enough. It was not as simple as weighing assets against liabilities and achieving a positive balance. She had once won a trust and then lost it, and had no idea how it might be won back again.

When Albright and Roberta had gone, Mariesa and her people lingered. John E. opened his briefcase and passed out the briefing papers for the morning meetings. Profiles of senators and congressmen; their voting records; their public finances; their primary backers. "You might as well forget Bowman," Redman said. "What money he doesn't get from Attwood's fronts, he gets from the Trial Lawyers, which means courtesy of our *quondam* dinner guest.''

''We will meet with him,'' Mariesa said, ''to let him know that *we* know he is taking money from both sides. He will be *shocked,* of course, to learn that Planetary Preservation is a paper shell for Attwood's Klondike-American Oil. What about Phil?''

The lawyer shrugged. ''Odds are Albright will try to block our ground-based laser system; but it's not a priority with him. It's the orbital SPS system that he plans to kill.''

''Let him try,'' Gregorson said.

''Well, John,'' Mariesa said quietly. ''You know what needs doing.''

6.

Promises Kept (I)

Barry studied his reflection in the dresser mirror and tried to decide just what it was he had become. There was a wide range of choices. It started with reptile and went down from there. The motel mirror was old and spotted where the silvering had begun to show through, and there was a spiderweb crack in the upper right corner, as if something had been thrown against it years ago. In the clouded glass, Barry appeared cloudy himself—he had no edge, no definition, and, where his image intersected the mosaic of cracks, he was fragmented.

He ran a finger under his eyes where the skin had begun to sag. The hair on his temples was now a decided gray. A step back and he could see that his body had begun to lose its tone. *You're passing the midpoint, Barry. Soon, you'll be spending more time looking back than looking forward.* And what did he have to look backward to? By now, he had thought to have some accomplishment to point to. "I don't get any respect," he said aloud. Even that sounded pitiful. Rodney Dangerfield had done it better.

In the mirror, the figure on the bed stirred and sat up. "I've always respected you," Shannon said. "Even after you married that woman. I knew it wasn't for real."

But it was. There was *something* that formed between him and Mariesa, something born of mutual respect, possibly of loneliness, too; or a sense of fragility and the desire to protect; almost certainly with a *soupçon* of defiance shaken like Toabasco into the stew. There had been that hazy, late-summer afternoon atop Skunktown Mountain when Mariesa had first opened herself to him. And the beach in Rio Grande do Sul; and the ski lodge in British Columbia, places where Prometheus and VHI could be remote, if not entirely forgotten. There had been nights of sharing hopes and dreams and a vision of the future. Nights never exactly of passion, but of an affection that often transcended passion; when, afterward, they had lain side by side and built castles higher than the air.

And those delicious, giddy months when they thought that between them they had created a new life. His hand shook and he laid it on the dresser top.

"They don't take me seriously," he said, "but I'm the boss's husband—who knows what pillow talk goes on—so they humor me. Matthias is outright hostile. And Gregorson usually makes a point of mentioning how he built up his fortune by hard work. Meaning, he didn't 'marry money.'" Barry ran a hand through his hair. Was it thinner? "Even Mariesa can be so wrapped up in her projects, she forgets to come home or forgets I'm there. She sends me out on silly, meaningless errands. Procedure audits." He was going out again in two weeks, after Mariesa returned from the management retreat. "Hell, the only one who treats me like a person is Harriet. Unfortunately . . ." He twisted his mouth. ". . . .it's a person she doesn't like."

Shannon pulled the sheets aside so he could see her. "Come back over here, Barry, and I'll treat you like a person."

He wondered if that was actually true. What did she see when she looked at him? Barry Fast, with all his hopes and dreams? Or a handy dalliance? Age was working on Shannon, too. Her delicious roundness had softened, and the laugh lines around her eyes and mouth had become permanent. Yet, flesh responds to flesh, and the old familiar expectations coursed through him. She saw, and smiled. "We'll always have each other; won't we, Barry?"

At least until the quarterly management meetings are over and Mariesa returns to Silverpond. He looked into the mirror again and despised what he saw. Just how had he come to this? What had once been beguiling and—face it—ego gratifying had become "sneaking around." Did Shannon, who had always faced this dilemma of spouse-and-lover, feel the same conflict tearing at her? He studied the reflection of her eyes. Expectation mixed with . . . what? Hunger? No, he decided. Guilt was not one of the shakers in Shannon's personal spice rack. It was her complete lack of guilt that at once attracted and repelled him—and so held him firmly in place, unable to move. And yet, without Shannon, he had no tie at all into the life he used to live. A simpler life, in a smaller pond, when he had been a bigger frog. It could be that he held to Shannon because that was all that was left to hold on to.

"Of course we will." The words came easily, from long practice. Shannon had asked for that assurance often enough; and now that her girls had left home, it seemed to him as if she sought it more often than before. Was it easier for her to get away now, or only more important to her?

"Mariesa offered to set me up with my own school," he said, turning from the mirror.

Shannon pressed her hands together and said with exaggerated pleasure, "Oh, how *cute!* Your *very* own school. What else has she bought you?"

The words were slaps. His hands closed tight around the knobs on the dresser drawer. There was nothing to pick up and throw. He looked again at the spiderweb cracks in the mirror and wondered what other couples had pressed each other's buttons in this room.

"It's not funny," he said.

Was it his voice? His tone? Shannon dropped the mocking pose. She pushed herself upright and sat with her back against the headboard and braced her arms along the top. "No, I guess it's not. I wouldn't like being kept, either. '. . . *only a bird in a gilded cage . . .*' Only you're a cock, not a hen.''

"Thank you for making me feel better," he said with heavy irony.

"I can make you feel better."

"I meant here." He tapped his head.

"That, too."

He crossed the room and stood over the bed. "How would you like to come in with me?"

"Only if you come in with me."

He had meant in the new school Mariesa had proposed. "I'm serious."

Shannon slid back down against the pillows. "So am I."

Sometimes, when she was in this mode, it was hard to keep her serious. Feeling helpless, Barry climbed into the bed and lowered himself onto her. When their flesh touched, he trembled. She felt hot pressed against him, still moist from their first encounter. She put her hands on the back of his head and pulled his face to her. He kissed her, and their tongues parried, caressing each other.

Afterward, he laid his head on her abdomen while she twirled his hair with her fingers. The delightful odor of sweat and musk filled his breath. Soon enough, showers and the false scents of perfume and lotion. For now, he drank her in. The soft curve of her belly and thighs; the sound of her tuneless humming. The smell and the touch and . . . he kissed her belly once, twice . . . the taste of her—salty and tangy. Even—as his head rose and fell with her breathing—even his kinesthetic sense was filled with her.

It was a soap-bubble world. Touch it and it would burst.

"We never talk," he said. The words came out before he knew what the words would be.

"Hmmm?" She was still drowsy with the lovemaking. "Of course we do. We talked all afternoon. In between," she added with a meaningful loft of the eyebrow. "And I agreed to join your new school, didn't I? That was smart, Barry. Now you and I have an excuse to get together."

"That wasn't all I had in mind." And it could make things more complicated, not less. "If I do decide to open this school, it's not going to be a . . . cover-up." He realized suddenly how deftly she had turned his earlier comment aside, how she had been doing so for years. "And when I said we never talk," he went on, "I didn't mean about the latest book, or the latest movie. Or how the world is going crazy, or rising from its deathbed, or both at once. I meant we never talk about *us*."

He could almost feel the way she froze. Her belly stopped its even rise and fall, and her fingers stiffened in his hair. "What is there to talk about?" she asked, in a voice at once authoritative and wary.

Oh, God . . . "I'm not saying we shouldn't see each other . . . I just wonder sometimes where this is going."

"Does it have to go somewhere? Can't it just be?"

Let it be . . . Barry placed a train of kisses up her body, pausing on the breasts, ending on the lips. "Of course. It's just . . ."

"Just what, lover?" She held his face tight between her hands and kissed him hard. He saw the flush grow in her neck and spread across her chest. With his free hand, he fondled her.

"Just . . . Why?" he insisted. "What have I got that John hasn't?"

She pushed him away from her and gave him an appraising glance, top to bottom. "Start with good looks and tight buns and go on from there."

He ignored her attempt to divert him again and pressed the question. "I've never questioned good luck when it came my way. I just took it and was glad. When you came my way, I took you, too; and I've been glad . . ." *More or less.* ". . . ever since. But . . ."

Now she did push him away, and sat up hard in the bed. "Growing introspective in your old age, are you? You want to know? You want to know why? I'll tell you. Because you can string enough sentences together to make an actual paragraph when you talk. Because even when we argue you have interesting things to say. God, when I'm with you I feel like

I'm allowed to *think*. And Barry, never once in all these years have you told me how lucky a plain-looking girl is to have you."

"You've . . . never looked plain to me." *Liar.* But free sex more than balanced looks—and he suspected that Shannon knew that just as much as he did—because what the hell did she know about his mind before she slid into that booth beside him in Philadelphia?

The unexamined life, Plato had said, is not worth living. Sometimes, Barry thought, the examined one is not much better.

Mariesa threw a small dinner party at Silverpond. Harriet, always more the social creature than her daughter, threw herself into the arrangements and managed to be pleasant to everyone, including Barry. Chris van Huyten was there, and his wife Marianne. Gwen Glendower from Witherspoon came with Belinda Karr, and both greeted Barry with cool civility. Aaron Venable, director emeritus of Argonaut's New Jersey lab near Red Bank, brought the guest of honor.

"Hobie," said Barry, greeting the young man in the foyer with Mariesa. "Welcome to Silverpond." Just as if Silverpond were his to give welcomes to. He transferred his grip on his bourbon and pumped Hobies's outstretched hand. "Can I get you a drink?" Ever the genial host, and besides, his own glass was nearly empty.

"A fruit juice, if you have it, Mr. Fast," the young man replied. He was as solidly built as Barry remembered from school, with broad features and a thick torso that seemed wider than it was tall, and the strong arms that always looked as if they were about to grab something. Only his eyes were different—deeper and more thoughtful. Unless it was the world that looked at him differently.

"The man of the hour," said Chris van Huyten. "Mr. Superconductor, himself." Barry turned to fetch the drink and Dr. Venable tugged at his sleeve.

"A little white wine, please? We must toast our young Einstein."

Hobie lowered his head and muttered. "Ain't no Einstein," Barry heard him say, with just a hint of the stammer that had pigeonholed him in high school. Barry had taught many a student over the years and was always gratified when the bright ones succeeded; but there was something almost transcendent when one transformed. If both Meat and Cheng-I had met their respective destinies, Hobie had created his from whole cloth. Barry drew Hobie a little to the side as he was leaving the foyer and whispered.

"Don't have to be Einstein. Just be Hobie." The man flashed him a grateful smile as he allowed Chris to drag him into the parlor with the others.

In the library, Barry found Sykes already pouring drinks at the sideboard. He looked up when Barry entered. "There was no need to trouble, Mr. Fast." He placed a glass of orange juice, liberally iced, on the serving tray.

Barry picked up the bourbon decanter and replenished his own glass. "It's no trouble, Sykes." He eyed the fruit juice. "Do you know what *everyone* drinks?"

"All of the family's special guests."

Barry tossed his head back and downed half the bourbon. A sweet, pungent taste, the bite dampened by its numbing predecessors. "I could have done it."

"There was no need for you to bother, sir."

"Yeah." Barry looked into his glass, twirled it so the liquor danced and spun. "That's the problem, isn't it? There's no *need* for me to do anything."

"Sir?"

Barry lifted the glass to his lips, inhaled the aroma; but then he set it down on the sideboard. "Tell me, Ed. What do you think I should do?"

The butler lifted the serving tray. "It's not my place to say."

"Suppose it was. Suppose you and me were down at the corner tavern hoisting a few. Better yet, suppose you *were* me."

Sykes paused and regarded him. The serving tray was perfectly horizontal; the liquid in the glasses hardly stirred from the movement. He said, in the carefully neutral tones he always use, "For one thing—if I *were* in your situation—I might reduce my consumption of alcohol."

Barry laughed. Sykes waited him out. Barry picked up the remainder of his drink. "You know," he said, "it's a common misconception that drunks don't know how much they drink." He finished the glass; filled it once more. "I could tell you to the dram."

"But you think you can handle it." For once, through the flat neutrality, Barry thought he heard emotion.

Barry snorted. "Hell, no."

"It would be rather a poor show to spoil young Dr. Hobart's dinner."

The disapproval was plain, now; and somehow, coming from Sykes, it stung more. From Harriet, disapproval was so continuous that one grew numb to it. Barry set his glass on the table with the deliberate care of the man who is tipsy and knows it. "You're right, Ed. You're damn, fucking right. I'm a shit; but I'm not *that* big a shit."

"Would you like some coffee before you rejoin the others?"

"Yeah." Barry walked to the bay window that faced the meadow behind the mansion. "Make it a 'Hobie.' Black and strong." Caffeine did not really counteract alcohol. That was a folk myth; but maybe if you believe strongly enough it would work . . . The shadow of the "Mound" stretched across the restless grasses toward the sunlit flank of Skunktown Mountain. How long had it been since he and Mariesa had lain together up there? Some days it seemed a memory of a different life.

"And, sir?" Barry turned and gave Sykes an inquiring look. The butler was all imperturbability again. The perfect, unobtrusive presence. A gentleman's gentleman in a house of women. "There is a message, should you ever encounter the gentleman that Ms. Mariesa once married. He was a charming fellow, and I rather miss him."

Barry smiled without humor. "You and me both, Sykes. You and me both."

* * *

During the dinner, Dr. Venable made a gaffe.

Chris and Hobie had taken turns trying to explain the significance of Very High Temperature Superconducters to Harriet, who had trouble understanding how anything below zero Fahrenheit could be considered a high temperature at all. If sparring with Harriet over the years had taught Barry anything, it was that she was not stupid; but certain matters were simply not in her mental world. Years ago, she had decided—or she had been taught—that science was not for ladies, and now the concepts had no point of entry to her thinking.

"It was the time in Kristal that led to the breakthough," Hobie said. "It took three trips up on Mir before I got it right, but the microgravity let me line up the thallium and other stuff near perfect, without any of the crystalline obstructions you get in a macrogravity field. It's like . . . You ever see fans at a game make the Wave in the stands?"

Barry, at least, knew the words. Superconductor, maglev, and all the rest. BSCCO, TBCCO, and a host of compounds that most people had never heard of. And Hobie's three-dimensional "periodic table of superconductors," which he had used to predict the properties of his new compound. Barry noticed how raptly Mariesa listened while Hobie talked. As host and hostess, he and Mariesa sat at opposite ends of the long table. Seen through the faintly surreal buzz of the liquor, Mariesa seemed vastly distant, as if the far end of the table receded from him at a steady rate. The coffee and the bourbon did battle down below. He had hardly touched his pasta. *I hope I'm not going to be sick. . . .* His head felt like someone had used it for a nail. Or a hammer.

"Well, Chris . . ." Mariesa said. "Shall we begin planning a maglev rail line?"

Chris held up a hand. "First things first, coz. We need to get 'Hobartium' out of the lab and into production; and that is no small problem. Then we have to figure out how to wire-draw it without destroying its properties. . . ."

"Yeah," said Hobie. "That'll be important. Make hoops."

"Hoops?" Mariesa raised an eyebrow. "Why?"

Shoot baskets, thought Barry. But that was wrong. Hobie was a football player.

"Uh . . ." Hobie scowled ferociously, a look that had once sent defensive linesmen into shivers, but which now looked only thoughtful and intense. "Send a current through a hoop, get a magnetic field." Chris nodded yes, so Barry nodded yes along with him. "Okay. So the Earth has a magnetic field, too. I figure, you play the hoops right, the resultant vector is . . . well . . . straight up." The gesture he made with his hand was small, but they all looked toward the ceiling. Chris whistled.

Dr. Venable chuckled. "You would need a very powerful field for that."

"Word," Hobie said simply. "Four thousand kiloamps at north magnetic. Accelerate at three-point-three g's. Get eleven or twelve klicks per second, final velocity."

"Sounds fast," Barry said.

"Mars in a hundred and fifty days, straight from Earth surface."

There was dead silence around the table.

"Mariesa," said Chris with a sudden laugh. "I give Hobie's magships twenty-five years and they'll be carrying most of the orbital transfer traffic."

"Do you, Dr. van Huyten?" Hobie said. He bent over his plate. "I give them fifteen." He shook his head as he twisted his linguine on his fork. "And to think," he added, "in high school, I couldn't even spell superconductors."

"Now they'll name them after you," said Chris.

"I owe it all to you, Mr. Fast and Ms. Glendower, and the others."

Gwen preened, and Belinda said—with what Barry thought a self-congratulatory air, "Mentor tries to stimulate thinking in its students."

Dr. Venable chuckled. "Mariesa even enlisted me!" he said.

Gwen frowned and adjusted her glasses. "I don't remember you visiting the school. . . ."

"No, no, no." The old man waved his hand peremptorily.

"It was years ago. Hobie worked at the labs one summer and we made it so he could fix a problem for us." He shook with suppressed laughter as he remembered.

Mariesa had stiffened and gave Dr. Venable a distressed look. "Aaron!"

Gwen said, "I don't understand."

Barry laughed, suddenly understanding. "He means it was a setup job. Right, Doc?" If the glance Mariesa had given Dr. Venable was distressed, the one she sent his way was pure anger. The truth will set you free, but it will also piss people off. But didn't Hobie have a right to know how he'd been manipulated?

In the awkward silence that formed, Hobie said, "So, then Styx was right all along."

Belinda said, "Hobie, not all learning takes place in the classroom. Mentor's charge to educate its student-customers does not end at the schoolhouse door."

"Which must mean you're still pulling the same stunts."

Belinda looked at Mariesa helplessly. Mariesa said, defiantly, "Of course."

Hobie lifted his fork. He looked up. "Is this the part where I'm supposed to run away across the field?" No one answered him and he snorted. "One thing you learn in football, you don't win games running away from the goal."

"Then, you have no ill feelings?" Mariesa asked after a slight hesitation.

"Well, I always did wonder about it, later on; 'cause I never saw anything else run that sloppy in the lab. So what if the situation was rigged? It was still up to me to solve it. That wasn't fake. I really did solve it. I scored a touchdown, me." He struck his chest with his thumb. "All you did was make sure I was handed the ball. And the way I felt afterward . . . ? If you manipulate a hundred other kids into feeling that way about themselves, I say more power to you. How would I ever have gotten up the nerve to tackle superconductors? I told Chase Coughlin so, the time he was up making deliveries. So, no, I don't feel bad about what you did." He slipped the linguine into his mouth and chewed. He put the fork down, took a drink and swallowed. "How *you* feel about it," he said without looking at anyone, "well, that's your problem."

On the road. The Queen's agent . . . Managers welcomed him with a wide range of sincerity as he made his rounds. On the road, with time to think.

The measured thud of the giant Niagara press made the floor shiver. The steel strip indexed into the feeder and four hundred tons dropped on it, closing to a precise distance. The trim scrap dropped out a chute into the red hopper, and the part slid into a drop-bottom metal tub filled with similar parts. Barry craned his neck, looking toward the top of the machine, where a cam translated the spinning wheel into up-and-down motion. The sharp odor of hot machine oil tickled his nose and he shifted his safety glasses to a more comfortable position. The forty-ton Blisses at the end of the line seemed puny in comparison with the Niagara.

"Impressive," he said. "When it comes to raw power, nineteenth-century tech wins, hands down."

Steve Matthias leaned close to Barry's ear. "The technology's even older than that." His voice sounded faint through the foam earplugs required in the press room. "Wooden cams ran iron forges in the High Middle Ages. The water in the raceway would spin the water wheel and the cam would raise and lower giant hammers." He looked down the row of presses with a proprietary air. "It wasn't for nothing that she named this division Thor."

Barry didn't ask who "she" was. He tilted his clipboard and made a notation. Matthias very deliberately did not look at what he wrote. "I have to point out," Barry said, "that the output tub doesn't have an identification placard giving the part number and other traceability information."

Matthias said, "Are you getting a kick out of this, Barry?"

"Do you agree that that's a violation of Thor operating procedures?" Barry insisted. He found these procedure audits tiresome, and suspected Matthias was right that much of it was nitpicking, but he'd be damned if he'd let the man get the better of him.

"Oh, absolutely," Matthias said expansively. "Except the tub's only half full and the operator doesn't put the tracer tag on it until it's full and he's ready to move it out to the staging area. Until then, hell, he *knows* what part he's running." Matthias cupped his hands and hollered. The operator looked over and Matthias beckoned him.

"You don't have to . . ." Barry started to say.

"Spud, isn't it?" Matthias shook hands with the operator, a brawny man with enormous shoulders showing through a sleeveless T-shirt. Spud wore a shoulder-to-knee apron with a union pin on one strap. When Barry shook his hand he noticed that the man's right pinky was missing, and thought again of the four-hundred-ton press coming down. Matthias shouted to be heard through the press noise and the earplugs. "Spud, what part are you running?"

The operator reached into the parts bin and pulled out the flattened metal shape. "That's a P/N387-22010-BV." The bin clanged when he tossed the part back. "A right-side fuel tank spar for Daedalus Aerospace. Job order's hanging at the work station."

"Thanks." Matthias clapped him on the back. The man gave Barry a scowl and returned to work. Matthias turned on Barry and displayed teeth. "See? He doesn't need a bin placard until the bin leaves the press. It's the *next* operation that needs to pick this part out from a hundred others."

Barry suppressed a sigh. "Then you need to rewrite the procedure that requires the placard."

Matthias made a note on his own clipboard. "Well, I'll be sure to get someone on the grammar and punctuation right away."

Look, this isn't my idea of a good time, either. "I'll call it a minor nonconformance, since it's only procedural."

"Fine by me," said Matthias cheerfully. Together, they left the press area and entered a warren of corridors, where men and women bent over desks and conference tables and squinted into multicolored computer screens with wire-body diagrams. It was quieter here. The thumping of the Niagara was a muted tramp, like an army of giants come marching to Armageddon. Barry pulled the foam plugs from his ears.

"Where to next?" asked Matthias. "Precision grinding? The plant manager told me he's making some valve bodies for the Plank's hydraulics."

"How about the cafeteria, and I buy you a cup of coffee? There're a few questions we need to get straight."

"You mean, like where a comma goes in a work instruction? You were an English teacher, right? So this must be right up your alley."

Barry kept a tight rein on his temper. "No. I mean, like, what your main problem is."

Matthias regarded him a moment, then shrugged. "Sure. You want the nitty gritty? I don't like working with amateurs. That clear enough for you?"

"Crystal."

"You've never dealt much with executive management, have you?"

"No, but I worked with teenaged discipline problems."

"Ouch." Matthias scratched his cheek; then he suddenly grinned. "I guess I deserved that. And come to think of it, you should have been at last month's management retreat. . . . Come on. The cafeteria's this way." He turned right and led Barry down another corridor of anonymous gray partitions. "But let me tell you where I'm coming from. I run the best damn division in the corporation, by any measure you care to name. P and L, labor relations, return on equity. Maybe it's not as glamorous or as sexy as Will's electronics or Dotty's aerospace; but show me how to build a Plank or a megawatt laser without machine tools or fabricated parts. That may be the nineteen-thirties out there . . ." A jerk of his thumb over his shoulder. ". . . but the twenty-oughts stand on our shoulders. When I joined Prometheus Group seven years ago, they had made fantastic progress, all right; but they were tangled up in all sorts of procedural inefficiencies. The schedule was slipping every week. I cleaned things up. Tightened procedures. (Yes, I do know the benefit of well-crafted procedures.

I'm just not anal-retentive about it.) We brought administrative rework down to ten percent, and shortened the critical path on the PERT by twenty-five percent." They had come to a door. Matthias stopped and opened it. "So you see, I might be feeling a tad underappreciated."

"The way I heard it," Barry said levelly, "you more or less forced your way onto the committee for our own personal advancement."

Matthias laughed and ushered Barry through the door. The cafeteria was an open area laid out in gray and burgundy tile and decked in chrome. The walls were lined with counters, one for entrees, another for sandwiches, still another for dessert and bottled beverages. Neon signs adorned the walls above the counters. It looked like a food court at the mall. A few workers occupied the tables. "I see you've been talking to Will and Correy," Matthias said. "Correy Wilcox is a fine one to talk about personal ambition, though. He got his own company out of the deal. Tell me, Barry, what do you know about Pickett's Charge?"

Barry picked a Styrofoam cup from the stack and poured himself a cup of coffee at the hot-beverage island. "Gettysburg," he said, wondering at the non sequitur. "South lost. Lee's dumbest move. What's your point?"

"Well, there were a whole lot of generals led those troops. Some of them went up there for their homes; some because they hated Yankees. Some went because they'd do anything Marse Robert asked them to; and some went for the glory. One brigadier went because he planned to run for the Confederate Congress after the war and needed a top military record. But you know what, Barry? *They all went.* And not any of them came back."

Matthias poured a cup for himself and added cream and sugar. Barry followed him to a table near the wall. "To extend the analogy," Barry said, "is Prometheus 'Marse' Mariesa's dumbest move?"

Matthias tested the coffee as he sat down. He looked at Barry. "That all depends on how it comes out, doesn't it?"

He grimaced briefly, took another sip. "Me, I just want to see it done as well as possible."

"A mercenary," Barry suggested.

"That's not an insult in my book. The Lafayette Escadrille and the Flying Tigers were mercenaries, too. Tell me, Barry, where do you fit in? Which of the generals are you?"

Barry moved his cup on the table. The coffee was still too hot to drink. "General?" he said. "You've got an awfully inflated idea of who I am."

Matthias shrugged. "Adjutant, then. Why did *you* sign on for the charge up the steepest goddamn hill in history?"

Barry avoided his eyes. "My reasons are . . . personal."

"Ah." There was a long silence and Barry finally looked up. "I'll be damned. My apologies, Barry," Matthias said. "That's the one reason I hadn't expected. I never did peg you as a True Believer. And you sure aren't with Chris and the rest of the cost/benefit crowd." His smile, which had always been a professional one, turned personal. "No wonder she's sending you into every nook and cranny of the program."

"I don't understand."

Matthias waved a hand at the clipboard Barry had set on the table. "We do process audits every month. Each one of my plants. We ask all the same questions you do. So where's the value-added, I wondered? What does VHI get out of all this?"

My question exactly. Barry shook his head. "I give up. What?"

Matthias folded his arms and settled back in his chair. "A better-informed Barry Fast."

Oddly enough, of all the reasons Barry had conjured up to explain his otherwise pointless missions, that had not been one of them. Get him out of her hair. Give him some busywork so he'll feel useful. Those reasons had occurred to him all too easily. Did that tell him something about Mariesa, or about himself?

"It's your turn, Steve," he said. His own coffee was finally cool enough to drink. "Which of the generals are you?"

Matthias grinned broadly. "Me, I'm Longstreet. 'Lee's

Workhorse.' He was the only one who saw the attack could never work and tried like the devil to convince the boss; but when he had it to do, he did the best damn job he could.''

Barry's hotel room looked out over the lake, over choppy blue waters with wind-whipped whitecaps. One line of freighters steamed east toward Buffalo; another, west to Cleveland. Ship and harbor flags stood out stiff in the breeze. On the far horizon was a smudge of Canada. This region was where America's heart had once beat, the whole rim from Buffalo to Milwaukee. They called it the Rust Belt now, in faintly condescending tones; but, if all the go-go was in the Pacific Northwest these days, there were still big men with names full of consonants who kept watch over furnaces and forges and presses around the rim of the lakes.

A sound at the door pulled Barry's attention away from the window, and he saw a manila envelope slide through the space between door and carpet. Another fax from Mariesa? Usually hotels just lit the message light on the phone, but some delivered them to the rooms. Barry crossed and picked it up. It was a thick one. Standard eight-and-a-half by eleven, with a sheaf of heavy-stock papers inside.

Photographs, he saw when he had sat on the edge of the bed and opened the envelope. He pulled them out and studied them, one by one, and his stomach turned slowly to stone. Shannon parking her car at the Pole-Kat Motor Lodge in Skunktown Furnace. Another, of Barry parking elsewhere on the same lot. Shots of each of them entering the same cabin, cleverly framed to assure the viewer that they had been taken on the same day. The stone in his stomach grew heavier with each print.

The fifth photograph proved that whoever had taken them had placed a camera inside the cabin. Which had to mean that the smarmy room clerk was in on it.

There were fifteen photographs in all. It was not pornography, not exactly. Pornography was art; consciously posed and framed. Candid shots like these were groping, clutching, squirming bodies. Two rutting animals and not two human lovers. It hadn't been that way at all, he remembered. There had been tenderness; there had been care.

There had also, evidently, been carelessness.

Damn Harriet to hell! He would never have believed the woman would stoop this low. Barry's supper churned in his stomach and he pressed his hand against his shirt.

The last one was the worst. It was a shot of Shannon alone, facing the camera. *The lens must have been fixed into the mirror frame somehow.* It looked slightly down toward her from a point just above her head, encompassing face, breasts, waist, and thighs. Shannon never used much makeup, and what little lipstick she'd worn had been kissed away. Her hair was tousled. The camera had caught her in a private moment.

He had never seen her from the outside like this. Naked, rather than nude. Never seen Shannon save through the filter of his own eyes.

The picture, more than any of the others, made him ashamed. He hated them, whoever they were. He wanted to close his hands around their throats.

Instead, he closed them around the sheaf of photographs and tore them in two and flung them across the room. They fluttered like leaves in a storm.

It was eight o'clock and the sun was just a memory. Barry had gathered the torn photographs. He wanted to burn them, but that would have set off the smoke detectors and the sprinklers, and how did you explain *that*? The last photograph, the one of Shannon alone, he kept for a moment, holding the two halves together. Then he stuffed that, too, back into the envelope.

After that he went for a walk in the night. He stood for a while in the parking lot with his hands jammed in his pockets. It was a sultry night, the heat of the day combined with the moist breeze off the lake. It was the sort of night when you could not sweat.

The air-conditioning in his room struck him like a dash of cold water. He found his way to the bed and sat on its edge.

The telephone jarred him from his reverie. He stared at the

instrument while it rang. Three times, then nothing. It must have gone to the hotel's voice mail. A moment later, it rang again. Someone didn't like voice mail, or wanted to speak to him in person. This time, he crossed to the writing table and picked up the handset.

"Yes?"

"Did you have a nice walk?"

A question with a message: we have you under observation. It was a man's voice, whiskey-raw and liquidy. An older man. Sometime or other he had heard that voice, but no face rose up in his mind to speak it. "Who is this?"

"A friend."

"Really."

"Friends try to protect each other from their silly mistakes. Did you receive the materials my man dropped off at your room?" Barry said nothing, and after a slight pause, the voice continued. "I'm certain you did. They were quite . . . informative, wouldn't you say?"

Barry squeezed the handle of the phone, imagining it was his caller's neck. "You are a pile of shit," he said.

A pause. "I am only looking after your own interests. You would not want those pictures to get into the wrong hands. People who might use them against you and force you out of your cozy new life. Or even submit them for, ah, professional publication." A wheezy intake of breath.

"What do you want?" Barry asked.

"A man who gets right down to business. I saw that on the photographs, too." His laugh gurgled in his throat. A smoker and a drinker, Barry thought. And old. *May you drop dead, schmuck.* "I want only what you want, that those photographs never see the light of day."

"You could destroy them, and the negatives, if that's what concerns you."

More chuckles. "I'm afraid there are no simple answers. Archimedes once said that if he had a place to stand and a place to put his lever, he could move the world. I have a lever."

"Get to the point." *This is a man who is clever and wants you to know he is clever.*

"Your wife has a private space program," he said.

"So do a lot of people, these days."

"Ah, but your wife is the center. If she drops out, the others will fade, or perhaps regroup and rethink their priorities. The . . . frenzy that has possessed them will be lifted once its source is muted."

Barry didn't believe that, and he wondered if his caller did. "And you want me to tell her to stop?" Now Barry laughed. His caller did not know as much as he thought. "She wouldn't listen, not on that subject, not even to me."

"Good heavens, no," said the voice. "I want you to encourage her. Some of her advisors are too—shall we say, too conventional in their thinking? They try to dissuade her from her more daring plans. I want you to support her in those ventures. Urge her to fund them as they deserve."

Of all the demands he had expected, that was the least likely . . . This man had compromising pictures of the husband of the richest woman in North America. Shouldn't he at least ask for money? "Encourage her? You don't need to blackmail me into that."

"Blackmail is such an ugly word, Mr. Fast."

"Not so ugly as the deed."

"Nor so ugly as a married man shacking up with his whore mistress in a two-bit motel. . . . Come, now. Let us not bandy pointless insults. It is impossible to blackmail an honest man. And you know as well as I what I want you to do."

"You want her to spread herself too thin, to waste resources on marginal projects."

"Hubris is a weapon, Mr. Fast. As a student of literature, you should appreciate that. Your wife's schemes are madness. They can lead nowhere but to financial ruin—for her, for me, for everyone—and I am determined that they not ruin any more innocent bystanders like Doyle Kinnon. She brings death and must be stopped—by any means. I have done—things I never thought I could do. . . ."

The guy is bonkers. "What if I said no? What if I became the Voice of Caution?"

"It would be a poor sword that had but one edge."

By now, Barry's rage had turned to ice. If his caller saw no way to use the photographs to force Barry to do his bidding, he would use them to destroy Mariesa's marriage. And Shannon's. If he said yes, at least he could buy time. *He could put the moment off.* Given time, who knew what countermove he could come up with? "I'll think about it."

"Think carefully. Lives and reputations are riding upon your choice. But, tell me . . ." And now Barry heard honest curiosity in the voice. "This woman that you fuck. She is not so attractive as your wife; and certainly not so wealthy. So . . ."

"So, why?"

"Yes. Exactly. Why?"

You couldn't explain anything true to a man whose values were all external. What did he know of enthusiasm, either Shannon's or Mariesa's? What did he know of the inner life, of hopes or dreams or fears. Barry said, "I made a promise once, and I've kept it. Leave it go at that."

An obscene chuckle rumbled in his ear. "You are a curious man, Mr. Fast. A curious man. I have never heard faithfulness used to excuse adultery."

Barry hung up first and it was an act of will to not throw the phone across the room. Yet, he had to strike out at something, so he pummeled the pillows on the bed. He hammered the mattress with his fists.

How had he ever gotten tangled up like this? Looking back, he could see a thousand forks in his life when there had been better choices; but looking back, he could not see how he could have taken them. Leave Shannon in the hospital, so she could try again, and maybe succeed? Her suicide would have been his fault. He did not want that on his soul, either.

On his return trip, Barry stopped off in Manhattan and visited the public library on Fifth Avenue, where he spent the afternoon reading through periodical indices until he finally found a reference to Doyle Kinnon. It led him to an article in the *Wall Street Journal. Plant Closing Ends in Tragedy.* The Peoples' Crusades had shut down a Klondike-American Oil depot in Alaska over seepage into the groundwater. Two hundred people had lost their jobs, including fifty Athapaskan Indians, and one foreman, Doyle Kinnon, had gone home and swallowed his revolver.

Tough breaks all around, but Barry could not see what it had to do with Mariesa, unless some convoluted daisy chain of cause and effect that led from the Plank flights to the refinery.

One other solid bit of information did come out, though. Among those who had lost, not lives or jobs, but investments was Cyrus Attwood, majority stockholder in Klondike-American. At least he knew why his blackmailer had not asked for money.

Barry wasn't sure how the information helped him, but knowing your enemy's name was supposed to give you power.

7.

Lost Lamb

The summer management meeting was held in Phoenix, partly because Mariesa liked to rotate the meetings around the country, partly to give Pegasus and Aurora a chance to show off for the rest of the divisions. VHI had taken over the Phoenician Resort for the week and filled it with presidents and vice-presidents, and even a few van Huytens. Chris was present, of course; but Brittany had come, also—the golf course at the resort was reputedly splendid—and so had Norbert, who hardly ever left New England and then never for anyplace so vulgar as the Southwest. Even Aunt Wilhemina had come, "just to see how affairs are getting on." It was Mariesa's own fault, really. She had awakened a few of her relatives.

The reception was held in the grand ballroom, and the corporate and divisional officers mingled with the family trustees. The drinks helped loosen tongues, which was not all bad. Nor all good. If in vino there was veritas, who knew what lurked in martinis?

"All I am saying," said Piper Cosgrove with just a touch

of lèse majesté and endangering his drink with the wave of his hand, "is that we should focus our resources on the sub-orbital trade. That is a proven market, less speculative than the orbital businesses."

Mariesa smiled politely. Piper was head of Hermes Retail and ran chains of both discount and upscale stores across the country. He had never been invited into Prometheus—Mariesa doubted he dreamed, even in his sleep—and he never missed a chance to downplay the program's importance. "Piper, I can remember when you thought the suborbital venture was a non-starter."

"And he was right," said the tall, rail-thin man at Piper's side. "It *was* a gamble. We were damned lucky it paid off." Jimmy Undershot was old, almost cadaverous, with thoughts that ran as slow as his speech. He ran Morpheus Plastics through a system of brilliant hiring coupled with benign neglect. It was even money among the corporate staff that his retirement in two years would go utterly unnoticed. "That doesn't mean we should leap on every speculative venture that comes our way."

If Piper was miffed because he had never been asked on board, Jimmy—like Brad Hardaway at Demeter—smoldered because some of his underlings had been. Several Morphean vice-presidents and middle managers had been up to their elbows in Promethean projects. Jimmy nursed a pique seven years long. "Uncle" Bennett, also excluded, had behaved far more graciously and with more understanding.

"Take this Helios business." Piper jabbed with his index finger when he talked, a habit that Mariesa found boorish, although she doubted the man was aware that he did it. "A power utility in outer space? Who's out there to buy the power?"

"Mir, for one," Mariesa pointed out.

Piper rolled his eyes. "Great. And they'll pay us in genuine rubles."

"One customer will hardly support the business," Jimmy pointed out.

"Comsat is interested, and Motorola. If satellites no longer need heavy and expensive internal power plants, their costs will drop considerably.''

''And of course,'' said a familiar voice by her elbow, ''the LEO Consortium will need power, too. One Helios may not be enough, in the long run.''

It was Belinda Karr. She nodded to Mariesa and traded perfunctory handshakes with her two colleagues. The senior principal of Mentor was dressed in a broad-shouldered blue suit with wide lapels. She made no attempt to cover the gray spreading in her hair, but wore it like a badge of honor.

''The LEO Consortium,'' Jimmy said, ''is another bad example. Half the members are VHI companies. How can we make money selling to one another?''

''It reminds me of the old retailers' joke,'' said Piper. ''Two merchants were marooned on a desert isle and all they had was a derby hat between them. When they were rescued two weeks later, they were both rich from selling the hat back and forth.''

Mariesa gave the joke the thin laugh it deserved and Piper and Jimmy moved on, leaving her with Belinda. How did men so devoid of imagination ever come to run a business? Granted, imagination often counted for less than thoroughness; but at the margin, it was audacity that mattered. You could not cross a chasm in short, careful steps. ''Those two are certainly cautious.''

Belinda drank from her white wine. ''Caution? I'd call it obstruction. João was complaining to me earlier tonight that orders from Morpheus are chronically late. Jimmy says that interdivisional sales don't generate real income, so Daedalus— and Pegasus, too—tend to drop down his production queue.''

''It's the bell curve,'' Mariesa said watching Jimmy circulate and glad-hand other presidents and officers. Slow, but methodical. A man of careful procedures. ''The innovators are at one end; and the diehards are at the other.''

Belinda cocked her head. ''And who's in the middle?''

''Missourians. 'Show me.' If they see it works, they'll go along.''

Belinda smiled without humor. ''The great, silent majority," she said. "Silent, because they have nothing to say."

"Don't be catty, 'Linda. They are also the ones jerked back and forth in the tug-of-war between the two extremes." Mariesa wondered if Belinda was right and Jimmy was hamstringing the Plank schedules deliberately. While Jimmy did have a point about interdivisional sales, in the long term the creation of new wealth always paid off, and it did not matter how the tokens were traded among merchants. "Perhaps," she told Belinda, "I ought to speak to João."

She turned to leave, and Belinda said, "We found Jenny Ribbon."

Mariesa stopped and gave her a puzzled stare. "Who?"

Belinda had always had a short, broad build, but with a pleasant, open expression. When she closed up, she looked like a brick wall. "I see you've forgotten her. She didn't pan out, so you've crossed her off your list."

"Oh!" Mariesa laid a hand on Belinda's forearm. "No. It was the change of subject. I apologize." Jenny Ribbon . . . Jenny Ribbon . . . She *had* forgotten. One of the original roster, that first year at Witherspoon. Did Belinda honestly expect her to remember someone from seven years ago? Mariesa tried to conjure up an image of the girl, but failed. Uptight, she remembered. Strung out. *Some kids we push too hard; some we don't push enough.* But how was one to know, until, pushing, something broke? "Where did you find her?" Not "how," but "where."

Belinda set her wineglass aside half-finished. A passing waiter snatched it up without asking. "At our boarding school in Pittsburgh, under an assumed name. Hope Schools take in children of single mothers in exchange for volunteer staff work, but the Commonwealth obliges us to take in a certain percentage of Orphans Court cases. They found Jenny on the street in Pittsburgh and placed her with us. We put her through community college and, after she graduated, she stayed on at Pittsburgh's Hope to help out. Jenny Smythe, she calls herself now. She helped create the dragoon system for welfare moms. That's what finally brought her to my attention."

Mariesa took a sip of her Manhattan, uncomfortably aware

of Belinda's act of setting her wine aside unfinished. "What is the 'dragoon system'?" she asked. "It sounds like eighteenth-century military police."

Belinda smiled fleetingly. "Dragoons were mounted infantry. When they reached the battle, they dismounted and one dragoon in every four held the horses while the other three fought. What Jenny did was translate that. Four single mothers form a—squad, I suppose you could call it—three of them work and pay the fourth pro rata for day care. Conservatives hate it because the arrangements are 'communal' and there's no stigma attached. Liberals hate it because the money doesn't come from the government, so the recipients have no incentive to vote for liberals."

"You are not being fair, Belinda, to either camp."

The short woman shrugged. "I stopped being fair years ago, when I decided being effective was more important. Do you realize, Mariesa, that the next generation of children may be educated by welfare mothers?"

"How so?"

"Because about half our volunteer mothers volunteer for classroom work."

"Are they . . . qualified?"

"Considering that schools of education already get the bottom cut of the students . . . ? We don't even have to screen out the drug addicts or the hopeless. Mostly, those don't volunteer; and the ones who do . . . Well, that tells me they have promise, and we put them into the state rehab program and tell them to come back clean. Riesey, elementary education was ruined when intelligent women found other outlets than teaching for their talents. We went to Wall Street. We became lawyers, doctors, engineers . . . All well and good, and I wouldn't turn the clock back a minute; but it created a 'brain drain' in our schools. Well, now we have a class of women who are largely unemployable elsewhere; but by and large they are *not* stupid. A few years at Mentor's Normal Schools can bring them up to specs. After all, they don't have to teach nuclear physics, just the four Rs: reading, 'riting, 'ritmetic, and rhetoric. Jenny calls it our 'barefoot teacher' program."

"Echoes of Red China."

"Another reason our conservative donors don't like it. Our liberal donors don't like it because it's 'no frills.' Mariesa, if the choice were between a basic, no-frills education with standard-grade teachers . . . or an excellent one with fascinating options and brilliant teachers . . . Why, there'd be no choice, at all. But, Riesey, *that's not the choice.*"

"No, I don't suppose it is. You've been doing yeoman's work, 'Linda, and on a shoestring budget." Everyone needed strokes now and then, even Belinda. If Mentor had never turned a profit, it had never needed a subsidy, either. No one bought Mentor shares expecting a dividend; unless one remembered that not all profits came as money.

"Riesey . . ." Belinda hesitated, then said, "No, I've bent your ear long enough. I better give João his turn."

"Belinda . . ." The senior principal paused, half turned, and Mariesa searched her eyes for the woman she had once known. The woman who had spent so many evenings at Silverpond, plotting until the early morning how they could grow the children the future needed. If that woman were anywhere, she was somewhere in those hazel pools.

"Do you have an up-to-date list for our original class at Witherspoon? I would like to see how they are getting on."

"Planning to move Jenny Ribbon from the 'loser' column to the 'winner' column?" Belinda's question was sharp. It stung, like a wasp.

It took a hand on the arm to keep Belinda from leaving. Mariesa wanted her to understand. She desperately needed her to understand. "No. Nothing like that. God, what do you think of me? I only thought I . . . should keep *some* direct contact with that thread."

Belinda gave her a stern and worried look. "Yes, you should. Too many megawatt lasers or impulse engines . . . or asteroids . . . can distract you from the important things. . . ."

Nodding agreement, Mariesa froze at the mention of asteroids. "Asteroids," she said, choosing her words carefully, "can be important, too."

Dryly: "So, I've surmised."

"Belinda, I have been thinking. How many children are on your list this year?"

"Nationwide? About three thousand. Why?"

A far cry from the first few years, when they numbered only a few score. "That is far too many for me to review personally," Mariesa said. "But what if I reviewed just the North Orange students? What if you left off the ordinarily bright, the Cheng-I Yehs or the Jacob Ullmans or the Tommy Schwoerins, and just gave me the others?"

"Like Roberta Carson?"

"Yes, like her. The . . . odd ducklings. That list may be short enough that I can manage it."

"I will have you a list by Monday of next week."

"Good. Thank you." Mariesa reached out suddenly and gripped the other woman by both arms. "Belinda, come to Silverpond, like you used to do? Please? There are so many things we need to talk about."

"Shoes and ships and sealing wax . . . All right, Riesey, I'll come. Tell me, has Harriet mellowed?"

"Like a fine vintage."

Belinda laughed. "I'll bet. And Barry? I haven't seen him here."

"He is at home, holding down the fort. After I get home, I'm sending him out on another management audit." She hesitated a moment and toyed with her glass. That was why you walked about a reception with a glass in your hand. It gave you something to do while you thought. "You have never cared much for Barry, have you?"

Now it was Belinda's turn to hesitate. "He was an excellent teacher," she said.

"I meant personally."

Belinda was silent. She fussed with some lint on her jacket sleeve and would not look at Mariesa. "You married him." She spoke so low that Mariesa scarcely heard her.

"You can still speak your mind."

She raised her head. "I didn't mean—Oh, never mind. You want me to criticize a woman's husband to her face? All right, I'll take you up on that; and then we'll see if that invitation to Silverpond still holds. And if it doesn't, well, I'd rather find out now.'' She breathed once. ''I never did understand why you married him.''

Mariesa looked around the room and saw that no one was listening; but she took Belinda by the elbow and guided her toward an empty nook. Cozy chairs clustered around an open space facing each other. Neither of them took a seat. ''He is a charming and thoughtful man,'' Mariesa told Belinda. ''He listens to me when I run on; and when we talk he does not simply tell me what I want to hear.''

''Hunh. Then why didn't you marry Keith while he was still with us? Never mind. What *do* you want to hear, Riesey?''

Mariesa tilted her chin up. ''The truth. I want genuine opinions. I want engagement, not agreement.''

''Then Barry *does* tell you what you want to hear, doesn't he? I'll tell you something, dear. Either Barry is exceptionally forthright and honest or he has found the most novel way I ever heard of for kissing up.''

''Do you think he is a social climber, then? Believe me when I say I recognize the type.''

''No, I think he is terribly sincere. And I mean that he is sincere in a terrible way. He goes with the flow, every time; but . . . sincerely. The man cannot make a decision—''

''Oh, come now, Belinda. He chose to join Prometheus. He chose . . . me.''

''Did he, Mariesa? Or did he just hang around until that was the way the flow took him? Oh, I don't know. I don't think he knows, either. But I would hate to see him standing halfway between two equally desirable options.''

When Belinda left, Mariesa elected to stay alone in the nook for a while. A company officer would find her sooner or later and pour out his wails and moans or his pet ideas. For the moment, she enjoyed the solitude. Belinda did not know Barry, not like she did. Belinda had never seen Barry weeping alone for hours over a baby never born.

The test pilots arrived at Silverpond by ones and twos. Ned DuBois and Forrest Calhoun came together, roaring up the access road almost before the call from the security gate reached the house. They rode in a low-slung red sports car as bold and brassy as themselves, Calhoun at the wheel. Speeding over the hump in the road near the edge of the broad front meadow, they nearly took flight.

"Rocket pilots," said Harriet, shaking her head as she and Mariesa watched from the window.

Mariesa wondered how a woman like Harriet could be so entirely unaffected by the new age. Harriet would have fit just as comfortably on the grand liners of the Atlantic or the "jet set" of the sixties. Someday, she might well travel into orbit— if her circle went, she would go—but she would never do so with the sense of adventure that people like Ned brought, or the vision of the future that people like Will and Chris had. For her, it would just be another Grand Tour, to be endured for the sake of its social utility.

At least those silly names, "astronaut" and "cosmonaut," were falling into disuse. The new decade inclined toward plain language, and young men and women were likely to cough and roll their eyes when their elders rolled out the circumlocutions and neologisms of the past.

Mikhail Krasnarov stepped up beside them in time to see the red sports car disappear onto the parking apron behind the swell of the Great Mound. He brushed his drooping mustache with the knuckle of his index finger. "I see Calhoun has not changed," he said dryly.

Mariesa turned away from the window and nodded to Sykes, who was waiting by the front door. "These are the last," she told Harriet. "Shall we join Dolores and the others on the verandah?"

She took the lead across the empty ballroom toward the white-marble arcade, that opened onto the rose garden in the rear. Krasnarov trailed behind. "It will be good to see Calhoun again," he said. Mariesa looked over her shoulder.

"I thought you and he did not get along."

Krasnarov heaved his massive shoulders in a very Russian shrug. "We have done great deeds together. That makes a bond." Unexpectedly, his eyes twinkled and he smiled. "We have also suffered food poisoning and 'heaved our guts' together. That makes a greater bond.'' Mariesa laughed, but Harriet only sucked her breath in. *Rocket pilots,* Mariesa could hear her think.

The afternoon was warm and her guests gradually filtered outdoors onto the patio overlooking Harriet's ornamental shrubs. The roses were still in bloom, a shattering variety of shades that nature and craft had created. One of them Harriet herself had created, a hybrid of a white floribunda and a stunning black tea rose she had found in a west Irish village. Its blossom, a startling silver, was called Harriet's Sterling.

Mariesa doubted any of the rocket pilots appreciated the fine points of rose culture, although Harriet managed to trap one of the geologists, Ignacio Mendes, into a seemingly interminable lesson. He stood with hands in pockets, nodding while Harriet pointed and explained.

Calhoun stood at the edge of the flagstone steps that led down to the garden and the fountain of Hyacinth. Tall, vase-shaped planters, each bearing an ornamental hedge, flanked the stairs and marked the end of the marble patio balustrade. Calhoun gripped a mug of beer and sipped from it from time to time as he watched the others. Mariesa approached him and he lifted his mug in salute.

''Black Sapphire Malt,'' he said. ''My favorite. Tell me you keep a cellar full just in case I drop by.''

''Sykes is a marvel, isn't he? I don't know how he does it.''

Calhoun grunted and took a long swallow. He leaned an arm against the planter. ''I count nine,'' he said. ''Six pilots and three geologists. So, unless this asteroid rendezvous expedition is bigger than we've heard, there are going to be a lot of disappointed faces come next year.''

When it came to intrigue and digging for information, pilots were amateurs. They wore their questions on their lapels, like ribbons. ''That will all be covered later, when Dolores briefs you.''

"For now, it's drinks and hors d'oeuvres, right?" Calhoun tried hard to mask his disappointment.

"This is a social affair," she agreed. "I had become too distant from the project; so I asked Dolores if she would hold her meeting here."

"Sure. Uh ..." Calhoun looked uncomfortable and stared into his now empty mug. "I, uh, heard about your baby. That was tough. I felt bad for you."

The sudden upwelling took her by surprise. She felt herself float, as if lifted on a wave, and for a moment everything grew distant. It was only for a moment, though, and she maintained rigid control until the feelings subsided. "I have tried to put that behind me," she said. "Life goes on."

Calhoun said, "Yeah. I really felt sorry about that."

Mariesa thanked him and fled his presence. She sought out the verandah, away from the bright sunlight, and stood there alone in the shadows while she regained her composure. *William* . . . But there was no face for that name. No laughing smile; no tears to wipe away.

"Are you all right?"

She turned, and it was Ned DuBois in an open-necked polo shirt and the sun behind him. He held a tall glass, frosty with iced tea, and wore an uncertain smile.

"Yes," she said. "Yes. I'm all right. It was just ... too much sun."

"Yeah. You've got the wrong complexion for it. That's for sure." He looked left, and right. "Where's my main man, Barry?"

Mariesa had never seen anything pass between Barry and Ned but wary looks and sly cuts, and the question had been couched in mocking tones. Why was it that Belinda and Ned . . . and Harriet . . . were so unenthused about her husband? Granted, there might have been an element of analysis in her choice of Barry—or in his choice of her, damn Belinda—but still, was she the only one who saw anything in him?

"He is in Erie, Pennsylvania, visiting one of our facilities."

Ned shook his head in faux admiration. "That Barry. Always on the move."

"Are you enjoying the reception, Captain?"

He paused at the deliberate change in topic, and his voice lost its bantering tone. "Sure," he said. "But I'll enjoy it a lot more when you tell the others you've selected me."

"That will be for Dolores and the FarTrip Steering Committee to decide."

Ned was all agreeability. "And you are just an innocent bystander."

"Do not presume too far, Ned."

"I'm—sorry. But it cost me a lot to come here to this meeting, and I needed to know if it was worth it."

Mariesa frowned and cocked her eyebrows. "Pegasus paid your airfares and lodging. . . ."

His eyes grew somber and he looked away. "It cost me a lot," he repeated. "But to walk on another world . . . To land on another planet, even a small one . . . Well, you understand how I feel."

Actually, she did not. She did not understand people like Ned at all. Adventurers. Risk-seekers. They sought the high frontier along with the dreamers and the entrepreneurs, and someone had to break trail; but Mariesa could not hear the. sirens that called them. "We each have our own drives," was all she said.

"Why three crews?" he asked. "I'm not asking which one I'm on," he added quickly. "But one flight crew and one backup and one . . . what?"

She shrugged. There was no reason to withhold that information. They would hear it all at the briefing later today. "It will be a one-year flight out and back," she reminded him. "Pegasus plans to test the onboard life-support systems for six months prior to departure."

"So, the third crew gets to sit in the ship and circle the Earth for a while. Make sure the air and water regen and the hydroponics and all can hold up?"

"Think of it as another sort of test flight."

He smiled crookedly. "Think of it as a booby prize. That crew will be too fatigued afterward to act as backup or prime. All right, I see where you're coming from; but you don't need primo meat for a test like that. Any three bods will do.''

"Captain DuBois, we will have only one departure window for this expedition. I *will* have three competent crews in training for it.''

"Sure. Just don't serve them *feijoada* before the flight.'' He laughed. "I guess I don't have to ask why the cadre on this is all stag.''

"It will be a yearlong flight,'' Mariesa said dryly, "in rather close quarters. We would rather not jeopardize the mission with potential, ah, hormonal conflicts. Two men and one woman could prove . . . sticky.''

Ned scratched his cheek. "Two women, one man, though . . . I might give that a shot. But, why not an all-girl crew?''

"Dolores and I,'' she stressed the name, "gave that possibility serious thought. Studies have shown that women—'' She stressed that word, too. "—are better suited for tasks that require patience and painstaking attention to detail, and a yearlong flight to an asteroid surely meets that requirement. But, despite advances in equipment and ergonomics, upper-body strength will be too important to the mission's success.'' Not to mention, liberated thinking to the contrary notwithstanding, that if an all-female expedition went bad it could prove a public-relations disaster. Not because certain quarters—like Cyrus—would try to make it appear as if an unqualified crew had been selected for political correctness's sake, but because society still regarded men as the disposable gender.

"Well . . .'' Ned rubbed his left hand on his pants, an unconscious gesture that drew her attention to his flat stomach and tight jeans. "Well,'' he said, "don't be too sure about those hormones. After a year in close confinement, even Mike Krasnarov might start to look awful pretty.'' He shifted his glass to his left hand and held out his right. "Come on back outside. Too much shadow is as bad as too much sun.''

Almost, she told him to start practicing. That he and Krasnarov—and Mendes, the geologist—had already been chosen for the flight crew; with Calhoun, Kravchenko, and Steuben as backup. It would be quite an ego boost; but the one thing

Ned DuBois had never needed in his entire life was an ego boost.

The radio whispered softly in the background while Mariesa worked on her scrapbook. *"According to many scientists, the asteroid trip is only a publicity stunt whose motives are to score political points with third-world countries. Cosmologist Daryll Blessing . . . [A different voice speaks.] 'There are so many better ways to . . .'"*

Mariesa tried not to listen. Dr. Blessing had never approved any space venture except when he received the funding. She hunkered over the black scrapbook pages. She had started the book after the management meeting in Phoenix, and there were a number of years to catch up on. Although she had downloaded photographs and newspaper articles and other material from Netbases, she had elected to prepare the book itself the old-fashioned way, with mucilage paste and acetate on acid-free, heavy-stock black paper.

"According to official sources in Athens the relocation of a Greek motorized regiment to Thessalonika is a routine rotation—"

"Computer," Mariesa said aloud. "Radio. Off." The background murmur fell silent and Mariesa heaved a sigh. The earlier concert music had been pleasant, but voices were distracting.

She looked up briefly when Harriet entered the library tugging off her gardening gloves and homing in on the liquor rack, where she poured herself a sherry. Mariesa leaned again over her work, arranging the photograph on the page. "Mrs. Pontavecchio wants to know if she should lay out a late board," she heard Harriet say. "She says you have not eaten all afternoon, and the sun is now down."

Mariesa looked up. "Is it? My, the time flies."

Harriet clucked. "A cliché, from you? Usually, you avoid those like the plague."

Her mother's face did not even twitch, and Mariesa searched it for evidence that the humor had been intended. It was difficult to imagine Harriet making a joke. Though it did seem to her that her mother had grown less distant since the hospitalization; and there was a vague memory, possibly from childhood, of her mother rising from a rocking chair and rushing to her bedside when she had cried. She gave her mother a tender look.

Encouraged, Harriet crossed the room and stood behind her, studying the scrapbook over her shoulder. She had an earthy smell from leaning into the dirt of her flower beds, and the hand she laid on her shoulder had a gentle touch. *Don't speak*, she thought. *Let's not quarrel.* The moment was too precious to spoil with a quarrel; but if Harriet spoke, a quarrel would grow, as surely as weeds sprouted from the wind.

"A fine-looking young man," said Harriet. "Who is he?"

Mariesa had centered the photograph on the page, the only item on that page. Scrapbooks were supposed to be disorderly, but Mariesa could not fight her own penchant for organizing. "That is Chase Coughlin, the day he graduated from the Space Academy." Self-conscious in his red coverall uniform, standing against a photographer's background of stars and planets, flanked by American and Pegasus flags. The ensign's pips sparkled on his shoulders. He still shaved the sides of his head; but the earring that dangled from his right ear was Prometheus's hand-and-fireball. Mariesa grunted softly.

"What is it?" Harriet asked.

"Nothing. I was just remembering the day he and I met. I would never have said he showed such promise."

Harriet said, "Oh?" Then she said, "Oh." A moment later, she asked, "Was he one of the students you had to our house that first year?"

"Yes. Yes, he was."

Harriet sniffed. "I thought he looked familiar. I saw him grope that poor young girl, the one that became a poet? He was waiting on the verandah when she came up from the garden. He grabbed her and tried to kiss her, so she slapped him on the face. And let me tell you, he deserved it."

I refuse to quarrel. I refuse to quarrel. Mariesa turned a few pages, to one that contained the cover of Styx's last book of poems. There was also a photograph clipped from a news story. It showed her standing with Phil Albright in front of an array of solar panels in the New Mexico desert. They were holding a giant check between them. Two hundred thousand dollars made out to EarthSafe Solar. The check, from Japan-America Friends of Solar, was endorsed by Arthur Kondo. Mariesa touched Styx's image briefly.

Harriet tsked. "I do not know why you are wasting your time on such things." She turned away and walked to the bookshelves against the back wall, where she appeared to study the titles.

I refuse to quarrel. I refuse to quarrel.

But they both understood the quarrel had been there, defined by its very absence.

The next day, Laurence Sprague dropped off a haggard and rumpled Barry. Mariesa welcomed him with a glass of fruited iced tea, but he added a splash of white wine to it before he drank. Mariesa said nothing. He seemed distracted to her. When she touched him on the thigh that night, as she often did to express her willingness, he turned aside and was soon asleep.

In the morning, he still seemed edgy and preoccupied but, when she asked him about it over breakfast, he only said, "Three cities in ten days? How would you feel?"

"Did you visit Morpheus, as I asked?"

Barry shook his head. "Yeah. Beats me why you just don't fire that guy, Riesey. Matthias, at least, is a go-getter; but Undershot . . . Jesus. He came back from the management retreat while I was still doing the audit, and he hit the ceiling."

"I've explained about VHI's peculiar structure. . . ."

"Yes, it's a federal union." Barry jabbed at the omelette on his plate. "I know. I know. Partnerships. Subsidiaries. Minority ownerships. The Trust owns some things; you own others personally; and some of them are public. It sounds like the Holy Roman Empire."

"That might be a good analogy," she said dryly, "if only . . ."

Barry looked up and grinned at her. "If only the HRE

hadn't been so ineffective.'' He turned his attention back to his omelette. ''I talked to Williams, Undershot's production VP, about the delays you mentioned on the phone. He told me privately he'd see what he could do to work around the old man.''

''Thank you, Barry. I knew I could depend on you.''

His grin wavered. He looked at his plate. ''Yeah. Thanks.''

Sykes brought the morning mail on a silver tray. He stopped first at Mariesa's seat, then at Barry's, before carrying the remaining letters off to Harriet's rooms. One of the letters was from J.P. at the University of Hawaii, and she opened that first, only to sigh in exasperation.

''A bit of miscommunication, I'm afraid,'' she said in response to Barry's question. ''I had asked a friend whether it was possible that two asteroids I am tracking had once collided. But J.P. thought I was asking about orbital transfers for a Plank mission, and he calculated the burn that would be sufficient to shift from the first orbit to the second. Bother!''

''No chance that really was a single track?''

''Oh, quite impossible, I assure you. Granted, an asteroid may shift orbits; but only when it is deflected by a planet's gravity well. Even if Mars or Jupiter had been nearby, a transfer this great would have been like . . . Oh, like making a sharp left at the corner.''

Barry began to open his own mail. It may have been the morning sun streaming through the French windows behind him, but it seemed to Mariesa as if Barry went pale when he looked inside a large manila envelope.

''What is it?'' she asked him.

''Nothing,'' he said with an angry growl. ''Someone doesn't trust my memory.'' He slapped the envelope on the table and resumed his attack on his omelette. The egg fell off his fork as he lifted it and he laid the fork down, too. He snatched up his napkin and wiped his hands.

That night, she and Barry were intimate. He caressed her with more tenderness and kissed her with greater hunger than he had in many months. ''I do love you,'' he told her more than once. Mariesa, allowing the waves of pleasure to pulse through her, replied, "I know. I know."

She was not the sort to abandon herself to ecstasy. She was no "moaner and groaner," though sometimes when the moment came she would laugh. Sometimes, she thought she was a cold fish, that she had never learned to express her feelings because Father had, and Mother did, and Gramper hadn't any to express. She had kept them in so long that they stayed in now by habit, like dogs behind invisible fences. She thought that might be a defect in her character; that other concerns—and the great fear—had grown so large they consumed her life and left no room for anything more personal. If so, the realization gained her nothing. It was a fact, like any other fact. Like the moon circled the Earth. You could know it, but what could you do about it?

She was not simply passive. Her hands and tongue knew which places to explore. And yet, the one reason she most treasured Barry was that he knew, as her earlier, occasional liaisons had not, that sometimes a man best expressed his love by restraint. An encircling arm, a brief squeeze of the hand, could mean more than a few minutes of grunting and pushing. The best love lay in giving pleasure, not in getting it.

Which meant that on some nights, as tonight, when Barry seemed in frantic need, it was her own duty to give that pleasure back.

INTERLUDE:

Roadkill on the Infobahn

Sometimes the answers just dropped out of nowhere. Jimmy Poole did not believe in God, unless Destiny was a god; but sometimes the coincidences in life gave the appearance of meaning and pattern. He could estimate the probabilities; calculate the permutations and combinations. He could show you—if you'd only sit still and LISTEN—that a significant concatenation was not only possible but likely.

He swiveled side to side in his chair as he typed. <<DO YOU KNOW WHERE THE FILES ARE KEPT?>>

The cursor blinked once, twice, three times. It had taken a long time tracking down Igor's killer through the electronic demimonde. Identifying "Bee-bee" was proving much harder. Mighty Mouse, on the other end of the link, had hinted of secret knowledge. Jimmy didn't much like the Mouse, but neither Lightning Wizard or Doctor Daemon had been able to help. Professor Bean he had been unable to locate, which might mean he [she?] had gone legit, like Jimmy sort of had. Or the Feds had him. Or the phone company.

<<YES>>, the screen told him.

Jimmy licked his lips. Now, all he had to do was find the system where the files were. *That* was the problem. Finding grubs under rocks was a no-brainer. Finding the right rock was not.

<<CAN YOU GIVE ME ACCESS? >>

<<I CAN GIVE YOU A NAME. >>

Jimmy rubbed his fingers on the touch pad/arm rest. He swung back and forth in his chair and kicked his feet. His fingers danced on the keyboard. <<NAMES ARE GOOD. PASSWORDS ARE BETTER, BUT NAMES ARE GOOD.>>

<<CYRUS ATTWOOD. >>

That name! Jimmy jerked and brought his two forefingers up in a cross. Jimmy's hate was a cold thing, a freezing in his gut. It was hate, but it interfaced with fear, as well. <<HE KILLED IGOR! >>

<<???>>

<<ONE OF MY KNOWBOTS TRESPASSED—ACCIDENTALLY!—ON ATTWOOD'S SYSTEMS, *AND HE KILLED IT.*>>

A moment or two passed before the response came from . . . wherever it came from. Mighty Mouse could be half a world away or over on the next block. The Net could, paradoxically, shrink the world and widen it at the same time, so that you could 'face with people and share your thoughts and never know where they were. The Mouse was a good hacker, one of the best. Not as good as "Crackman" in his outlaw days, but sometimes other people knew things.

<<ROADKILL ON THE INFORMATION SUPERHIGHWAY, EH? >> posted the Mouse.

That wasn't funny. Igor had been special. But he could not expect anyone, not even another surfer like the Mouse, to understand his loss. Some people had children. Igor was a child of his brain, springing like Venus from his own brow. Jimmy typed furiously. <<"INFORMATION SUPERHIGHWAY" IS SO SECOND WAVE! IT'S NOT A HIGHWAY. HIGHWAYS ARE CONCRETE; FIXED CONFIGURATION. THE NET IS ORGANIC. IT GROWS AND CHANGES.>>

When Mighty Mouse had logged off and the link was broken, Jimmy disassembled the phantom node he had been working from and covered his electronic tracks. Always pick up after yourself, his mother used to tell him. Good advice, especially when hacking the Net.

Afterwards he popped himself a can of Jolt, dropped onto his sofa, and sucked on Jolt while he considered what the new information meant to him. Attwood was Bee-bee. Or Bee-bee was Attwood's creature, which amounted to the same thing. And Bee-bee had hired Crackman to sabotage Aurora's traffic control program, *flocker*.

Which Crackman had duly done.

Bee-bee had been satisfied with the work and the money had accordingly changed hands, slithering from one nexus to another across the Net, ducking into "phone booth" accounts to change identities, slipping down back alleyways, through a keyhole, and ultimately into the bank account of S. James Poole, computer security consultant, complete with a phony invoice on a dummy corporation and all taxes apparently paid.

Life was good.

He looked around his home. The Tadjik rug. The inlaid wood chess table, where he regularly played with himself— the best against the best! The silver cappuccino maker with the gold American eagle atop it. He lived comfortably, no doubt about it; but his creature needs were few. Most of what he spent went into more equipment; and there was money in some of his accounts that he would never spend in his lifetime.

And it was all chump change to Attwood.

The thought that he had done the dirty work for Igor's killer bothered him.

The logic bomb Crackman had planted in *flocker* was fiendishly clever, yet ultimately simple. *Flocker* was modelled on the flocking patterns of birds. Birds never collided because there was a four-rule algorithm with an emergent structure, and one rule was "veer off if you get too close to another bird." Crackman's bomb reset that trigger distance to a negative number. It was a beautiful piece of work, really.

Well, as long as people weren't killed.

But that was the beauty of it. Crackman had a contract with Attwood, but world-renowned S. James Poole had one with

Aurora: *Keep the code secure.* So Crackman's fuse wouldn't light until *five* or more Planks were sharing airspace, and Aurora's traffic projections didn't show anything like that kind of traffic density until the middle Teens. And by then, the software rewrites would be several revs up.

A hell of a bomb that never goes off; but it fulfilled both contracts. Bee-bee had been satisfied. He paid to the penny. Couldn't beef because the bomb met all his specs.

But he hadn't known then that Bee-bee was "Attwood Igorkiller." Attwood didn't play word games.

Jimmy rubbed his cheek with the soda can. "Attwood," he muttered. "Every time I roll a rock over, Attwood comes crawling out."

The buzz from the Jolt was beginning to hit. He bounced a little on the sofa, squirming to a more comfortable position. If Attwood was smart enough to trap Igor, he was smart enough to know the bomb was bogied. And waiting five years or more before it pops . . . ? Jimmy didn't think he was into delayed gratification, either. Old as the weasel was he couldn't afford delays. But the bomb, even with the bogie, made happy smiles for him.

Which had to mean that Attwood was playing another game. The problem was, what game? And did Jimmy want to play? The more involved he got, the more likely that Attwood would trace Crackman to Poole; and that would interest far too many people. And some of them wore badges.

8.

Code Dancing on the Crypt

The call came in the middle of the night, at an hour when the stars had taken on a look of cold distance and the dawn seemed a lifetime away. But for every midnight there is a dawn somewhere else on the planet, in a different land, speaking different tongues. The sun comes up as red as blood, and the clank of treads and the tramp of booted feet striking ground scatters the songbirds with the cry of feeding ravens.

Mariesa awoke disoriented in the darkness, lying nude beneath the white, silken sheet. Barry's body, turned upon its side, heaved slowly with the tide of his breathing. She stared into the night, where a gap in the curtains revealed a slice of sky. Lights gleamed out there like distant balefires. Before she could wonder what had awakened her, the intercom buzzed—again, she supposed. Barry stirred and rolled over and his eyes blinked open. Mariesa raised her voice. "Computer. Intercom. Accept."

It was Sykes, his voice hesitant with apology. "I am dreadfully sorry to bother you at this unfortunate hour, miss; but the caller insisted." Mariesa stifled a yawn and wondered, weirdly, if Sykes had put on his long coat to buzz her. She could not imagine talking to the man in his pajamas. Or . . . Surely, Sykes did not sleep in the nude! She suppressed a giggle. It was a manic hour.

"What is it?" asked Barry. Mariesa made a wait-and-see gesture.

"Who is calling, Sykes?"

"The caller claimed to represent the Pentagon." Sykes could put a dram of skepticism in an ounce of speech.

Electricity ran through her and her arms tingled. Suddenly, she was fully awake. "Did he give you a name?"

"He said to say, 'Eagles,' " said Sykes, his skepticism fading.

Imagine, if eagles were to flock . . .

"I will take the call, Sykes." She sat up on the edge of the bed and groped for the telephone on the nightstand beside the bed. The mattress sagged as Barry sat upright beside her. She could feel the heat of him close behind her, hear the tension in his breathing. He turned on a bed lamp on the headboard and she blinked in the sudden light.

"Yes. This is Mariesa van Huyten."

It was General Beason, as she had suspected. After he had given her the news, she hung up the telephone and sat quietly on the bedside. Then, suddenly aware of her nakedness, she began to shiver. Barry's arms enveloped her from behind.

"What's wrong?" he asked.

"They've crossed the border."

Her pulse was a drumbeat in her ears. She twisted and pressed herself against him, against his flesh, and clenched him tight within the circle of her arms.

Dr. Leland Hobart whistled as he knotted his tie in front of his apartment mirror while the TV chattered the morning news. Normally, he hated morning staff meetings. Real science was action, not talk. But they were meeting to discuss *his* discovery. Argonaut Labs, one of the world's premier research labs, was holding a special meeting to discuss further experiments and the papers that would be written. Hobart's Law, Dr.

van Huyten had suggested with a sly wink, and Hobie hadn't argued too hard. He didn't look for honors, but he didn't turn them down, either.

His discovery. Not hobartium (and the world, it seemed, was to be stuck with that name, too) but the "periodic table" he had contructed to predict it. Hobartium, after all, was only a fact, a *discovery*; the evidence that confirmed the table. It was no different from a dozen other superconductors discovered over the last generation. But the table, that was something new in the world, an *invention*, a creation of his mind. The table imposed order on the facts, predicting the superconducting properties of a compound from the elements and their proportions.

His grin grew wider as he recalled his high-school nickname. As an all-conference offensive lineman, he had been called the Doorman.

In a way, Hobart's Law would open doors, too.

". . . Macedonia . . ."

The word caught his attention. Hobie turned his head to look at the television in the corner. He liked to run the news channel while he dressed in the morning. Usually, it was mental Muzak, but . . . Today, as he listened, his heart grew cold and his tie dangled, half knotted, from his neck.

"Greek and Serbian forces entered Macedonia along the Vardar valley this morning in a two-pronged invasion that cut the country virtually in half. Fighting continues at this hour on both fronts as invading forces close in on the capital, Skopje. A UN demand for an immediate cease-fire was vetoed by Russia in a Security Council vote. President Donaldson has called an emergency meeting of the National Security Council and of top congressional leaders to discuss the crisis. Meanwhile, concern grows for the UN peacekeepers stationed in the country.

Hobie leaned into the TV screen and shouted, "What about the peacekeepers? What about my dad?" But the newsreader did not say.

The phone rang ten minutes later and it was Mom. He spent

the next half hour telling her lies and giving her assurances about things he did not know.

He missed the meeting.

Phoenix in the summer was a convection oven. Scorching winds blew down the desiccated bed of the Salt River, replacing warm air with warmer, turning sweat to basting. The Valley of the Sun, they called it? It might as well be a valley *on* the sun. The smart folk ventured out in cutoffs and tank tops; the smarter, robed like Arabs. The smartest of all stayed indoors with their air conditioners maxed out.

Of course, like everyone said, it was a *dry* heat.

One thing Phoenix had over Houston, Ned reflected as he drove Betsy and Liz up winding Pima Canyon Road into the city park on South Mountain: at least the mosquitoes didn't eat you alive and leave your blood-drained corpse by the roadside. Atop South Mountain, the air was noticeably cooler, which might be a good thing mentally as well as physically. Tempers rose with temperatures; and the old "reptile brain" might take a hint from the reduced ambient and chill out.

The inscription was carved into the rock near the summit, and Ned had no trouble finding the spot. There was even a picnic area for the occasional *tourista*. He pulled the car to the side of the road and put it in park. "All out," he announced.

Lizzie ejected from the rear seat in an instant. Ned watched her skip over to the historical marker. "Hard to believe she'll be Sweet Sixteen in a few months," Ned commented.

Betsy had been silent the whole way up. "She's grown up faster than I like," she admitted. "I swore that no daughter of mine would grow up as streetwise as I was, as early as I was."

"You've done a good job."

"So have you, when you've been around."

And there it was. The wriggling little serpent that crawled between them. "I'm not running out on you," he insisted. *This time* was unspoken. "I'll only be gone a year. Whaling ships out of New England were gone for two years."

"And didn't always come back with a full crew."

He touched her on the shoulder. "There are three crews. Two chances out of three, I get to stay home and watch on TV, like you."

Her arms were folded and she stared out the side window at Lizzie. "What, the Great Ned DuBois? Where's your confidence?"

"Betsy," he said, willing her desperately to understand, "I *had* to bid. This is the only chance I'll ever have to set foot on another world."

"Ned, you don't even have both feet on this one." She laughed to herself. "And maybe that's why. One of them's always searching for a toehold somewhere else. Damn it, *I know what it feels like*. When I was growing up on the X-Bar-R, I wanted another world, too: Wichita Falls." She laughed again. "Not too exotic, considering. Not an asteroid floating out there in the sky. But excitement is all in where you are when you're wishing. When I reached the Falls, all I wanted was to see Dallas someday, and the art museums and the symphonies, and other things I'd only dreamed about. So don't think I don't know what that hunger feels like, flyboy. I can remember when all you wanted was to fly; and then, when all you wanted was to reach orbit *just once*. And after you get to this pissant little rock with even less nightlife than Wichita Falls, assuming you can find it and not go sailing forever into space, what is it that will be all you ever wanted to do?"

Ned remained deadpan. "They say Mars is nice this time of year."

Betsy cried, something between laughter and tears. "God damn you, Ned! It's not the going. It's not even the absence. It's the coming back. It's the thought that I might never see you again. Or taste you; or feel you inside me. Or see that stupid, shit-eating grin of yours plastered over your dim-witted face." She swiped her eye with the sleeve of her blouse. Then she reached out and took hold of his chin. She shook him once, and pulled him to her and kissed his lips. "There's only two ways to avoid losing something you love," she said when they parted. "And one of them is *you don't lose it*."

Ned didn't ask what the other one was. He pointed through the side window. "Lizzie wants us," he said. Betsy looked at him a moment longer, then yanked the door handle and stepped outside.

Ned followed Betsy to the rock, where Lizzie pointed out an inscription she had found. "This is the stupy bean, units. We booked this dwem first semester, and here he is hard-driven in silicon."

"What does it say?" Betsy asked. *What did she say?* Ned wondered. He studied the Spanish incised in the living rock. Less of a foreign language than what teenagers talked.

"It says, 'Kilroy was here,' " Ned told her. Lizzie laughed. "No, it's *Español* and it goes . . ." She followed the wording with her finger. "Coronado: where he passed from Mexico to Aycos, in the Year of Our Lord 1539."

Ned grinned. "See? I was right." It was an old, old hunger, to see new places. A man had stood on this spot more than four and a half centuries ago and felt it. The ancient Greeks had left such messages scratched on the walls of the pyramids, themselves already ancient before the Greeks had come. Ashoka had dotted India with inscriptions; da Gama, the coast of Africa. There was something in human nature, he thought, that compelled them to say, *Hey! I was here. I once passed this way. Don't forget.* He vowed that, if he was selected for the asteroid mission, he would leave his name scratched indelibly into the rock.

We come in peace for all mankind . . . Bullshit. That was PR platitude. You went because you couldn't not go. You went for yourself.

So sudden and unexpected was the high-pitched beep that Ned's heart skipped. Betsy looked at him with wary eyes as Lizzie, oblivious, prattled on. "That herb, Tommy Schwoerin, he thinks that dump that was newsed during kid-dom is the bean word and you could *calculate* all this. He's so far over the top, he's under the bottom." Ned hardly heard her as he fumbled at his belt for his phone.

He flipped the phone open. They had given him one on joining the ERP and it had never chirped at him until now.

And it was too soon. The flocker had only been through a few test flights, never with more than three birds. They hadn't found the envelope yet. "DuBois," he said.

"This is Stine. Rendezvous. Pegasus Field. Soonest."

"Roger. Half hour, tops." He folded the telephone closed and shoved it back in its holster. He looked at Betsy. "I've got to leave."

She looked at his belt. "I've hated that thing ever since you brought it home. I always knew that, someday, it would take you away from me."

Gunnery Sergeant Thomas A. Monroe didn't ask too many questions when his skillets were in trouble, and the Marines were his homeys, no doubt about it. So, when Lieutenant Flynn called out the platoon just before reveille and told them that fellow Marines were in deep shit, it was a foregone conclusion that the Red Hand would go in and bring them out.

How was another question.

The briefing officer showed them satellite photos of the terrain (which was mostly pretty rugged) and computer sims of the topography from skimmer level. It was no surprise to Thomas that the sims looked just like the ones he and his men had been training with for the last couple months. The commandant was paid to think up contingencies and somewhere in the Corps, Thomas was certain, other platoons had been training with other sims.

"The situation in Macedonia is politically and ethnically complex," the briefing officer said. He was a tall, balding man with a prominent nose and a bushy beard. Captain Dove, and wasn't that one hell of a name for a military man? "The original Greeks were displaced by Slavs centuries ago. The land has been at times part of the Greek Byzantine Empire, the Bulgarian Empire, the Ottoman Turkish Empire, Serbia and the Yugoslav Federation. The majority of Macedonians speak a language that is essentially a dialect of Bulgarian, but twenty-one percent of the population is Albanian. So . . . If any neighboring nation does *not* have a claim to at least part of Macedonia, I haven't heard of it. Throw in a religious mix of

Muslims and Orthodox Christians, and you have an idea what Macedonia is like.''

Thomas chuckled to himself. *Be like old North Orange.* NO-men and Nation and Lords fighting over their 'hoods. Only these white gangs were whole countries and some of the dissing went down centuries ago. If that's what it meant to have a history, Thomas would just as soon take things one day at a time.

Captain Dove looked at his watch. ''As of oh-eight-hundred this morning, Turkey has warned Greece to withdraw from Macedonia or face the consequences. Bulgaria has also sent severe notes to Belgrade and Athens. There have been military movements in Croatia and Albania, as well. In short, ladies and gentlemen, a great big gob of Balkan shit is about to hit the fan, and a reinforced company of the Second Marines is smack-dab in the center, occupying the Skopje airport, along with a contingent of Swedish marines and Nigerian MPs. Our mission is to extract them from the situation. After that, the peckerheads can shoot each other to extinction and I won't give a rat's ass.''

Sears raised his hand. ''We go in shooting?''

The captain said, ''You will be taking your skimmers, fully armed.''

''Good. 'Cause I don't wear no baby-blue helmet and I won't tote a gun I can't shoot.''

The other men in the squad made fists in the air and said, ''Woof, woof.'' Sears had quoted from a rap that was making the rounds in the Corps in the last few weeks, but expressing a sentiment some two hundred years old.

''Although Greece withdrew from NATO following the colonel's coup in 2005,'' the captain continued, ''we do *not* believe that Greek troops will fire on the rescue mission from their positions south of the city. You can make no such assumption about the Serbs, who cover the airport from the north. Your platoon will land first and secure the airport perimeter, as you have been practicing, and provide cover for the evacuation of the UN peacekeepers.''

''How many Serbs are there?'' asked Bareface Miller.

"Too damn many," said Jo-jo. The rest of the platoon laughed. Years ago, when Thomas Monroe had been Azim Thomas, he had promised Jo-jo that he would take care of him, and he had kept that pledge. Azim did not know if Jo-jo's mama had smoked or snorted or what, but the boy had never been too quick. The structure of life in the Corps had proved good for Jo-jo. He did a good job on maintenance, as long as nothing was too out of the ordinary; and he knew enough to call on his gunny if they were.

"We estimate," said Captain Dove, "regular Serb troops amounting to two divisions plus a reinforced armor brigade behind them making its way south from Niš."

"Versus one platoon of Marines?" asked Le Van.

"Seems fair," said Thomas. "One country; one platoon." More laughter greeted his remark. "Question, Captain?" When he received a nod from the briefing officer, he said, "Those maps you showed us. This Macedonia don't have no coastline. So, how we gonna get there? Through Greece?"

Captain Dove shook his head. "This mission depends on speed and surprise to work. You will go in by air. Special transportation will arrive from Phoenix in about . . ." He checked his watch again. "Two minutes."

There must have been a storm coming, because a short while later Thomas thought he heard thunder rumble across the sky.

Jimmy was surfing when the balloon went up. He was lurking in restricted areas, too; but how else could you learn anything useful? Public knowledge was worthless when it came to finding the edge; otherwise, the public would be rich.

He knew something big was going down when a dozen or so knowbots and datassemblers that he kept out in the Net rummaging through trash cans came lurching back to base gorged with info and regurgitated right on his screen. Documents. Abstracts. Summaries. Tiled and layered on his screen. An autovirus skimmed the documents and highlighted key words.

And the word was war.

Jimmy whistled and called up *Mr. Stockmart*, his securities trading spider, and sent him out with instructions to identify anyone with prior knowledge of the romp and to match any stock trades they made. If you're going to piggyback, piggyback on the insiders.

As he settled back in his chair with a satisfied smile, his screen scrolled up a list of Planks.

And what did that have to do with a war in the Balkans? He debriefed the knowbot that had brought the info in and threw the backtrack onto an auxiliary screen. He spun in his chair and studied the code on the other screen, tracing the 'bot's path from node to node all the way back to . . .

The Pentagon.

His lips pursed, but this time no whistle emerged. Quickly, letting his fingers do his thinking, he broke all military connections. Pentagon was heavy beans; he didn't want to mess with that.

Yet, his curiosity was up. There were a dozen Planks on the list, and some of them had civilian registry numbers. What were they doing on a Pentagon list? He moused into the databases for the civilian owners. Aurora, Pegasus, Leprechaun . . . Their chastity belts yielded to his coaxing fingers. Aurora first, because his work for them had let him plant trap doors in their system. And once inside Aurora, he could locate keys and gateways into the other VHI nodes. . . .

In five minutes he had a composite list of Planks, crews, and flight plans.

They were all headed for Macedonia.

In Jimmy's line of work, adding two and two could come in real handy. There were UN peacekeepers at the airport in Skopje. A dozen Planks were heading that way. And that added up to . . . Two of the civilian ships were stopping at a Marine base along the way. Rescue mission or reinforcements? It didn't matter.

A dozen was more than five.

That was a different sort of arithmetic, and it added up to a lot of subtractions.

A part of Jimmy's mind untensed. He hated unsolved puzzles. At least now he knew why Attwood hadn't fussed over the bogied logic bomb.

But what kind of lunatic pranks the Pentagon? Jimmy could see now that *flocker* had always had a military subtext. Who would ever need to handle more than three or four Planks, unless you were going for massive surprise? That was why he had picked five Planks as a trigger. AeroSpace Force would come down on Attwood like a California mudslide; didn't matter how rich or powerful he was. He must be crazy to risk that. Or, like they said, be "strongly motivated."

But so far as Attwood knew, he was safe behind the facade of "Bee-bee," who was safe behind the facade of "Crackman." And if the boys in blue asked anyone any hard questions, it would be the security consultant. Yet, Jimmy was in the clear, too; because the bomb had been installed by Crackman *before* Jimmy had completed the security code. Embarrassing, maybe, but not actionable.

It might not matter anyway. No guarantee any Planks would arrive on collision course. Granted, it was hard to project close approach trajectories, because there would be all that last-minute maneuvering. Still, *possibility* did not equal *probability,* and if he did nothing, things could still work out. Try to warn Aurora, and there might be questions raised.

Idly, he scanned the list of Planks on his auxiliary screen and a name caught his eye. He sat upright in his command chair. Chase Coughlin? Ensign/co-pilot on *Calbraith Rogers II.* He had heard something or other about Chase becoming a space cadet. He'd hero-worshipped that astronaut, DuBois, so it wasn't too surprising to find them teamed up.

Chase had made high school a living hell for Jimmy. That time in the locker room, when he had watched Jimmy undress and caught him . . . The world would not be worse off if Chase weren't in it anymore.

Jimmy relaxed in his chair. Everything would be bean, one way or the other, if he just relaxed.

Chase Coughlin supervised the loading of *Calbraith Rogers II* while Captain DuBois handled the refueling. The compressors shrieked as they sucked the oxygen from the air and liquefied it. It sounded to Chase like the banshee's wail. They'd wait to top off the hydrogen. No sense risking a spark while they loaded cargo. Where they were going there weren't any gas stations, and the trip had to be both ways.

The Marines loaded their skimmers using a crane and tackle. Chase used hand signals to the crane operator to guide the vehicles to the cargo-bay door, where he could attach the drogue and winch them inside. The bay could hold three of the machines with their squads. A hundred yards north on the parade ground, *Bessie Coleman II* was loading the other three. It would be an uncomfortable trip for the Marines—three g's without contour seats, just hammocks—but Chase assumed they were prepped for a lot worse than that.

How much you pay me to go chasing after crazy guys with guns? No way, José. Except that he and Ned were taking old *Cal* right smack in the middle of a war, and probably the Macedonians wouldn't shoot and *maybe* the Greeks wouldn't shoot, but the Serbies sure as shit would make up for both of them.

The Marines fussed over the loading of their skimmers like they were family pets and checked all the stays after Chase had tied the craft down with cables. Chase didn't know how that worked, but he gathered that a platoon ran six platforms and the platform jockeys were specially trained with virtch helmets and all and, hell, maybe while they were slaved into the system they felt as if they *were* their platforms.

"All right, gunny," he said into his headset when he was ready for the last one, "we're bringing yours up now. . . . No, don't try that. . . . Oh, shit." Chase tugged his headset off and looked over the lip of the cargo door.

The whine of the oxygen compressor took on a funny note, like it was singing in harmony. The second voice was a shush, like a blowing wind. The third skimmer platform rose from the ground in a billow of dust and debris. Chase backed away from the opening and the skimmer bobbed into sight, framed in the bay door. He shoved the headset to his face. "Hey," he said, "what's the ceiling on those things?"

"Not sure," the gunnery sergeant's voice answered. "Down there, somewhere. Why'n'cha have the cargo doors down at dock level, fool?"

"Because, asshole, that's where the engines and half the fuel tanks are."

The skimmer inched forward into the bay. Chase shrugged and began guiding the pilot in with hand signals. The idiot was flying it in person, Chase saw, not by remote. Balls. The platform bucked as it entered the bay. Then the computer, or the pilot, compensated for the fact that the forward fans were inches from the surface while the aft fans were about a hundred feet in the air. The cargo bay was filled with the angry hum of the propellers. They might be smart hushprops, but the cargo bay was an echo chamber and Chase's teeth rattled from the buzz.

The pilot settled into the spot Chase had indicated and grounded. The roar of the lifters slowly faded, though Chase's ears continued to ring afterward. The pilot, who had flown in a prone position, rose to his knees and unsnapped his helmet. He was a skinny black man. "Fly 'em on, we load 'em faster," he said.

"No shit, Sergeant," Chase said. It was bad enough the man had risked the whole loading operation, but he might have damaged *Calbraith Rogers* in the process. "Most places I load and unload, up and down don't matter."

"Yeah." The sergeant hopped off the platform. "You be right. But someday, maybe we gots to get on and off this landing boat damn fast. So I just wanted to see if . . ." His voice trailed off and he stared at Chase. "Oh, shit," he said.

Chase pointed a finger at the gunnery sergeant. "Oh, shit."

There were few things Ned did not like about flying Planks. One of them was the fact that, once committed to a trajectory, there wasn't much he could do but go along for the ride. Not until landing approach would he have control again, and even then flocker and the autopilot had their fingers in the pot.

Another thing he did not like was when code was uploaded into his flight computer while he was in flight. The last time that had happened was on the orbirtal test flight with Levkin, and then there had been deliberate sabotage in the code.

"What the hell is it?" he asked Chase, but his copilot only shrugged. Computers were not his gig. Ned toggled the ship to ship. "Eagle I to Eagle II."

"Go, Eagle I." The voice was Alex Feathershaft's, Forrest's copilot.

"Put on the Cowboy. Over."

"What's up, son. You getting talk-talk on your black box, too?"

So, Forrest was getting an upload, too. "That's affirmative. Black codes check out. . . ." Otherwise, the upload couldn't access, so it had to be legit, right? "But, I better check with ground."

"You do that, good buddy."

Ned switched over to Air Force STC. "Falconer, this is One."

"Go, One."

"We are receiving upload to our navcomp. Is that you? And why? Over."

A pause and Ned heard excited voices over the comm link. Then a firm voice said, "That's a negative, One. No upload. Backtracking commenced. We will inform."

"Shall I abort?"

Another pause, longer. "Negative. The flock is flying. No friendly aborts on your trajectory. Out."

"No friendly aborts," Ned muttered. "Hell, the target isn't all that friendly, either."

"It's only a twenty-seven-minute flight," Chase said. "I hope they make their minds up, real soon."

"There," said Ned, pointing to the screen. "They're putting up a screen."

He watched the lines of code chase each other back and forth across the terminal screen as encryption schemes flip-flopped. Dueling transmitters, he thought. But who was the intruder; and could Falconer stop him before the eagles converged on close approach?

"What the hell?" said Chase.

A single line of code spelled out <c:Chase Coughlin> followed by a transmission code. He looked at Ned, and now it was Ned's turn to shrug. "Looks like someone's calling collect."

Chase set up the channel and referenced the coordinates on the comm screen. "It's directed to a telephone channel on Atlantic Twenty-Four," he said. Ned sent ID XMIT and a voice answered immediately.

"Chase? Chase? That you? Tell them to stop code dancing. I can't keep up with encryption changes in real time."

"Why the hell should you?" Chase shouted. "Who the hell are you and why are you messing with our flocker?"

An impatient cough. "Poole Security. I'm your guard dog, fool."

"Jimmy? Jimmy Poole?"

"There's a bomb in your flocker. I'm trying to defuse it, but someone is dancing on the crypt and I can't get through to them. Military, my guess. Tell them I'm legit. Damn it, I *wrote* part of it. That's why I've got all the keys. I'm trying to save your butt, butt-head."

Chase and Ned exchanged a glance. Ned mouthed, "Can you trust him?"

Chase said, "We went to school together; but we weren't what you would call skillets." He thumbed the transmitter. "Uh, I will tell them, Security. And, uh, thanks."

"Don't thank me, crudball. I'll get you back one day for all the times you dumped on me; but this is the wrong time and the wrong way and it benefits the wrong person. Now bug off so I can finish."

Chase cut the channel and Ned said dryly., "Nice friends you've got."

"Yeah," said Chase. "And they seem to be popping up everywhere."

"How do you know a big-name computer whiz like Poole?"

Chase thumbed the transmitter. "I went to school with him. He's el geeko herbie, but computer code gives him a hard-on.

If he says he's defusing a bomb, he is. Falconer, this is Eagle One. . . ."

Ned let Chase handle the call. The kid could vouch for this Poole character, Ned couldn't. And if Poole was debugging a program while it was executing in real time on a twenty-seven-minute flight, he must be passing good at it. Ned laughed and shook his head. Outside the viewport, the sky had darkened and stars were beginning to appear. They were nearing apogee. Whatever it was that Chase's friend was up to, he'd better hurry.

9.

A Pillar of Iron; A Wall of Brass

The ship fell like an elevator; and Azim fell along with it, braced in his hammock against the thunder beneath their feet. The hover platforms jiggled in their restraints, as if eager to dash out and perform.

"Here's the latest from satellite recon," Lieutenant Flynn announced from his sling. He'd been plugged into the comm net all during the flight; even while, for a few brief minutes, they had floated weightlessly about the cabin and Azim had known—without a porthole in sight—that they were really and truly in outer space. "The Serb mortars and the big artillery up in the Crna Gora overlooking Skopje are more interested in the remnants of the Macedonian northern army than in unarmed UN peacekeepers. But there are a few units staged on Kumanova and along the Pčinja River east of the city taking occasional potshots at the terminal building. Estimate one hour before Serbie can redeploy anything heavy against the landing zone. Our job is to clear the ridges and make that *two* hours or more."

Young punks, thought Azim. Sitting around bored with guns

in their hands. He'd known their type back in North Orange. Deadly, but without the discipline of a real fighting man; and dangerous precisely because they acted at random. Their officers—if they deserved the name—didn't lead so much as run with the pack. He had known street gangs that were better organized.

Though maybe not quite so well armed.

The ship had barely touched down—was not even done rocking on its hydraulic supports—when Jo-jo and the other handlers sprang into action, unshipping the platforms from their restraints. Azim donned his helmet and gloves and flexed his fingers. The helmet was black. The blinking red light in the corner of his vision turned amber, then green; and suddenly he was seeing through the platform's sensors. His breath came slow and shallow. He would be floating again, soon.

"Bay door opening," he heard Chase's voice over the intercom. The wall "in front" of him pulled aside with a hiss. The breeze slowly tore the cover of smoke away and the bright sunlight poured in. His visor went white, then recovered as the circuits compensated for the light. The airport terminal was dead ahead. He could see the faces of the trapped marines staring through the shattered windows. To the right, he could see the other spaceship, the *Bessie Coleman*, like a pillar of iron no more than fifty feet away, hissing and pinging as she cooled. Distant thunder boomed as another artillery barrage rained down on Skopje.

"Okay!" shouted the lieutenant. "We've got fifteen minutes to reach station. Go! Go!"

The skimmer platforms leaped out of both vessels, dropping toward the ground in a shriek of compressor fans, until they bounced on their ground-effect cushion. It was a maneuver they had practiced over and over, using the jump tower at the Army's parachute school. Bareface's skimmer hit the tarmac and struck sparks before righting itself. He and Le Van (who had been in the *Bessie Coleman*) sped off in opposite directions. Before they cleared the apron, two more skimmers had disgorged, and then two more, skittering off in all directions.

* * *

Gunnery Sergeant Thomas Monroe flew his skimmer through the brush along the hillside. He banked and swerved like a leaf under power, swooping up and diving. He *was* his fighting top. He danced on feet of swirling air. The platform's cameras were his eyes and its pickup mike his ears. Its computer was his brain, thinking long, cold thoughts. Its twin automatics were his fists; its six ground-to-ground laser-guided missiles were his kicks; and the centerline-mounted Gatling was his dick.

The weird thing was that Azim was still inside the *Calbraith Rogers*. Yet he saw and heard everything from skimmer level.

Azim heard the distant burp of a Gatling gun, and saw from his map display that Le Van had already reached his position.

"Okay, gunny," said the lieutenant over the command circuit, "I've reached the terminal. Here's how things stand. All the officers in the Second are down—dead or wounded. Senior man is Sergeant Major Mike Hobart. He says that the Greeks are holding their fire, and are mostly still strung out on the road from Titov Veles. Execute deployment B. Repeat. Deployment B-as-in-Bozo . . ." Azim acknowledged and relayed the message to Le Van and Bareface.

Satellite recon downloaded right on time. Azim had never known an op to go off without a fuckup, but this one was hip-hop so far, timed down almost to the heartbeat, so that they'd get this sky-eye update just as they reached the Serbie sniper positions.

The map display lit up and showed him the other five platforms. ECM gave radio locations for the Serb positions. Either COINTEL had broken the Serb codes or Serbie was too macho to use any stinking codes. "Go on, Annie. Find the bossman." Annie was Radio Group Traffic Intelligence and Analysis, or RGTIAN. Raggedy Anne to her friends; Raggedy Anal when she didn't work right . . . Annie was an AI-construct from Werewolf Electronics that identified command positions by analyzing message frequency and integrating transmissions with subsequent troop movements. Basic reasoning was that anyone who sent and received a lot of traffic was giving orders and hearing reports.

Raggedy Anne highlighted four locations. Company and platoon HQs? Azim didn't know what the Serb disposition was, or how it was organized. Hell, he didn't even know if it *was* organized. He took his wand from his belt and made assignments. Sears was closest to the brightest spot. Azim told Groff to back him. He gave two of the others to Bareface and Le Van and took the last one himself. Horace Lee was watching their backs in case the Greeks got curious. Satellite recon and the up-and-down said his own target was on the other side of this ridge.

The top surface of the skimmer and its pull-up canopy was covered ninety percent with MEMS, Micro-Electro-Mechanical Systems. In training school at Lejune, they had talked about microscopic cantilever beams erecting or flattening on signal and displaying different colors as a consequence. Azim had always thought of them as tiny little pricks, coming erect or flaccid. Using inputs from three sensor arrays on the bottom of the platform, the MEMS reproduced a grainy image of the ground on the skimmer's upper surface. It didn't make the platform invisible—hell, its rotors kicked up too much dust for that!—but it did make it damn hard to draw a bead on. . . .

Azim took his platform to the head of the gully before he went up and over the crest of the ridge. That brought him out behind and to the left of a cluster of soldiers. They were huddled around a field table under camouflage netting, and one was holding down a flapping map and pointing.

He gave them a cough of the Gatling and they flew apart and flopped like rag dolls shaken by a tiger. It didn't bother Azim. He had seen the cluster of bodies in the UN humvee on his way to his position. That humvee had had a truce flag on its radio mast. Probably the UN commander going out to "negotiate." No one who shot unarmed opponents was a real soldier, anyway, in Azim's opinion.

Not that Azim gave a rat for Macedonians, either. Switch the shoes and the macks would be uptown in the Serbian 'hood, happily shelling civvies in Belgrade. But "maybe cut no never mind," as his mama used to say. The Serbies had made a career out of popping civilians: in Croatia, in Bosnia, in Kosovo, in Vojvodina—and even in their own precious Serbia, when the military dog pack had finally turned and bitten the hand holding its leash. In the process, they had made enemies of Croats, Muslims, Albanians, Hungarians, and each other. Though the way Captain Dove had explained it, those gangs had been dissing each other a long time, anyway.

A whole country full of poor white trash was the way Azim figured it.

He cruised along the ridge line flushing out snipers. Several of them threw their rifles down and ran; a few raised their rifles and fired; one dropped to his knees and made the sign of the cross backward. None of it helped. Working methodically along the crest, he cleared the ridgeline.

"Position Apple, clear," he reported when he reached the end. He saw from the map projection that Sears and Bareface Miller had also cleared their sectors. "Red Hand, report."

"Position Grape, clear."

"Position Peach, clear, gunny."

The reports came in from each of the "fingers." All the positions had been cleared, except poor Horace Lee, who had to report Position Pineapple as "no activity."

Azim touched the command circuit. "Fruit salad," he said.

"Tasty," said Flynn. "The flock is perching. Bugout in fifteen."

"Retreat, hell," said Sears. "We just got here." Laughter among the panel techs and skimmer crew. He heard it with his ears, not over the comm link, which reminded him that he was in fact sitting at a console set up in the cargo bay of a jump ship.

"Put a lid on it," Azim growled. Distractions broke the illusion of skimming. That could disorient you at just the wrong moment.

And the heavens erupted like a string of firecrackers.

It was a sight that Azim never forgot. He saw it from the skimmer in the hills and he heard and felt it at his console inside the ship. Sparks blossomed from horizon to horizon.

They fell in from the north and from the west. Two came up from the south. All converging on the landing apron at the Skopje airport until the sky was filled with ships. He saw the Air Force star on three of them. He saw the red stallion and the winged sun. And a green leprechaun hammering on a satellite. One of the ships wore the insignia of Northwest Orient Airlines; and one of them was the goddam Atchison, Topeka & Santa Fe! And if there was one thing that Azim regretted as the sky flamed and thundered and the ships swooped and touched down on every vacant spot of tarmac, it was that not one of them bore the globe-and-anchor.

It cost him a moment to reorient himself after the distraction of the mass landing; and that almost cost too much. His skimmer broke out of the brush and hit a paved road running left to right. To the right, it led down to the airport. To the left . . .

A column of armored vehicles coming up at the double quick.

"Shee-it!" Azim slapped the controls, and the skimmer rose and banked in the air as a burst of heavy machine gun fire tracked him. He let the command circuit see the action. "Permission to take out a big, motherfucking self-propelled howitzer! Sir!" The Serbies must have started rushing some heavies over from Skopje town as soon as the first jump ship landed. If they got those guns in place, they could start shelling the field. Azim didn't know how tough those Planks were, but he thought a direct hit with a seventy-three would be pushing things.

"Permission granted," Lieutenant Flynn said dryly.

Azim hadn't waited. He brought his skimmer around in a loop, coming at the lead gun from the forward quarter. The driver's head stuck out of the cabin hatch. He wore road goggles and stared at Azim like some kind of insect. Azim locked on with his laser and let one of his birds see the target. Then he kissed it good-bye and did a bugout.

The blast turbulence caught his skimmer and tossed it like a Frisbee. He canted to thirty-three degrees and the attitude board lit red. Skimmers had to play level, or nearly so, or they lost the ground effect. Azim fought the controls, bringing the starboard fans to max. Breakfast fought against vertigo as the signals from his eyes [canted!] fought the signals from his inner ear [sitting down and level!] The "fighting top" wig-wagged and settled into a wide bank as the computers controlled the verniers on the thrusters.

As he came around, he saw that the gun was immobilized, its treads blown and a red and black cloud of greasy smoke enveloping it. Of the driver whose head had been sticking out, there was no sign.

His second pass took out the troop carrier that was next in line. The deuce-and-a-half bucked like John Henry had kicked its ass and its gas tank whumped into flame. Serbs leapt shrieking from the back end.

That ought to block the road—for a while, at least. Bring a couple more fingers in from the Red Hand and grab that column round the neck. Azim touched his wand to the two nearest skimmers on his console and gave orders. Tighten up the defensive perimeter in this sector. The icons for Groff and Sears moved toward his quadrant.

On the third pass, some Serbie herbie got lucky and Azim's skimmer took a spray of automatic weapon fire right across the forward sensor panel. Azim's visuals shattered into static, then went black.

Shit and double shit! He hit the auto-abort without thinking and the skimmer went into random evasion and come-home mode. Azim yanked his helmet and gloves off and threw them to the floor of the cabin. "Lost contact," he said. He stood from his console seat and strode to the cargo-bay door. In the distance, he could see a mushroom cloud of black smoke rising behind the hills to the northwest.

That's where I was, he thought. Serbies coming in that way. While he watched, another smoke column climbed skyward, so Sears must have reached the position. All along the tarmac, UN troops were clambering up rope netting into the waiting Planks. Third squad was deployed as traffic cops, waving the evacuees to available space. The Swedes were actually waiting in line at the base of one jump ship. Crazy squareheads . . .

Azim checked his watch. Slippage. The loading was going slower than planned. The Serbies were bringing in artillery faster. *No plan survives contact with the enemy.* "Eyes, when do we get another sky peek?" He asked Tech Sergeant Shwartz.

"Satellite's coming into position 'bout now, gunny," the woman assured him. "Minus thirty."

Jo-jo came to his side and touched him on the sleeve. "You okay, man?"

Azim kicked at the door frame. "Yeah. Damn." Jo-jo pointed.

"Skimmer coming."

His fighting top had appeared at the edge of the landing apron, darting this way and that like a pinball. "Sergeant Moon," he said. "See if Red Thumb answers. She's in line of sight. Give her a bearing and bring her straight in."

The hatch in the center of the cargo bay ceiling opened and the jump ship pilot stuck his head down in. "We wrapping up already?" he asked. "One of your platform's coming in."

Like I didn't know that... Azim sent a glare in his direction, then he did a double take because even upside down...

"Don't I know you?" the pilot asked him. Azim turned away.

"Don't see how," he muttered. Jo-jo leaned close to him and whispered.

"Hey, he be the spaceman come to school that time."

"I know," Azim said between clenched teeth. Figures. Doo-Bwah was Chase's big hero back then; so now they hooked up. Which meant pilot and copilot could both make him, if Doo-Bwah remembered.

Jo-jo's eyes grew slowly wide as the implications sank in on him, too. "'Zim," he said. "I don't want to leave the Corps. Don't want to run no more."

Azim clapped him on the shoulder. "Ain't gonna run no more."

"Damn!" Azim turned at the shout and saw the sky tech,

Shwartz, at her console. "Gunny! Second Serb column coming in due west along the main road."

Azim strode briskly to the console and looked over her shoulder. "You sure?"

Shwartz pointed to a line of "ants" on the image. "Computer matched this against the last peek and highlighted everything different. Those suckers weren't there before."

"Damn. Sears?"

His number two looked up from his skimmer console briefly. "No can, gunny. Hands full."

Azim's skimmer had come to the base of the jump ship and hovered there, its autobrain not up to the strain of any more precise approach. It knew it was near home base, but there was a big, honking jump ship in the way. "Status on Red Thumb?"

"All go, but the visual remotes," said Moon from the maintenance panel. "She can fight and fly, but she's blind."

Jo-jo said, "I can fix it. Take twenty."

Azim stooped and picked up his headset and helmet. "Ain't got twenty." Grabbing his rifle, he vaulted the lip of the cargo door and climbed down the netting. Jo-jo leaned out and yelled at him.

"Where you going, man?"

"Gots a job to do." He leaped the last ten feet onto the back of the fighting top, which bucked and swayed from the impact. The sky tech, Shwartz, leaned over the lip and shouted.

"You're crazy, gunny! There are a hundred Serbs in that column. What are you going to do?"

Azim grinned like a skull and held up a pair of "bananas." "Use two clips."

He clapped his headset in place and his bucket over that. The goggles were useless and he didn't need the gloves. Lying prone, he gripped the hand controls in both fists. This was the way it ought to be flown, anyway. Real, not virtched. His feet found the stirrups and he kicked the riser and the skimmer rose on its feet of air. Floating, floating. Azim felt gloriously free. A leaf carried on the wind, except he controlled the wind.

For once, eye and ear did not battle each other as he slewed and sped across the airport like a stone skipped across the waters at the old canal lock.

Funny that he should think of that. He hadn't seen Eastport in seven years; hadn't thought about it much. But all of a sudden he remembered playing by the green, scummy water with Jo-jo and Zipper while bugs chattered in the weeds. He wondered if anything had changed; if, rolling downhill like it had been, the old 'hood had finally hit bottom.

He took the skimmer down the highway at full throttle. *Have to take them as far off as possible.* Get too close, they sit back and play potshot. As many Planks as on the field, they bound to hit some. On his display screen, a blinking red light showed his location. But without a twenty-four to eyeball the killing ground steady, he had only what he got from the eye before it dropped below the horizon. You could project positions, based on last observed location; but . . .

Nitwit computer says they be just around that bend in the road. Ice formed in Azim's brain, like that time the Nation had cruised by the old playground; or later, after Zipper had nined the old Indo at the In-and-Out. Ice—glittering crystal and coldly clear. He knew exactly what he had to do. He could see every move laid out ahead of him. Right out to the end.

He turned sharp left onto the scrubby field beside the highway and settled down into the brush a few hundred yards off. Twigs and branches snapped under the platform's weight and the wind tore the dust from the air above him. Wait here. They come to you.

He toggled the comm. "Red Palm—" And, Jesus, he always got a kick out of that code name. . . . "Red Palm, this is Red Thumb. In position."

Lieutenant Flynn was a few seconds in answering. "We have you located, Red Thumb. You are too f—"

"Going to radio silence, now. Don't want no one homing on this homeboy."

"Gunny—"

Silence enveloped him, and he felt acutely alone, far away from everything he ever knew or loved. He remembered that dumb-ass poem they'd memorized in school "Horatius at the Bridge." Shit. Here he was playing out that same scam, and it wasn't even his own 'hood he was sticking up for.

Well, yes it was. The Marines were his skillets, now. He'd die for them like he would have died for the Lords.

And he knew he would die here. . . .

He knew that, and Flynn knew that; which was why he'd had to cut the lieutenant off—before he could order Azim back. The map display told him all he needed to know. Sears and Groff were still tied up with the first column, and the other three were too far off, guarding their own sectors. And no way could he take out this whole column himself. He had four birdies left in their launchers. The Gatling and the automatics could make shredded wheat out of infantry, but once the birdies were gone all he could do about armor was wave bye-bye as they rolled past.

He pushed the toggle switch that brought the clamshell up to enclose him. Blind, now, with the outside visuals fried like they were, but he could still hear. The audio pickups were still good. He would hear when traffic passed his position.

"Then up spoke brave Horatius, the Captain of the Gate . . ." He whispered the words aloud in his enclosure. Damn, how could he still remember them?

Hope those Serbies stick to the road. Be a hell of a thing, a tank rolled over him. "To every man upon this earth death cometh soon or late . . ." He'd rather it was later, though. Shit. He activated the MEMS system. In theory, now, the clamshell cover looked just like the ground underneath him. Be just another bump in the ground. [What he'd be when they buried him, too.] Assuming the undercarriage microcameras still worked. Assuming the MEMS array on the canopy hadn't been damaged in the earlier fight. Assuming that the ground underneath him didn't look interesting and draw the eye of some Serbie nature-lover . . .

"But how can man die better than fighting fearful odds . . ." he whispered hoarsely.

Speaking of which, here came the fearful odds now. The

clatter of treads, the hum of tires. The coughing of engines, the tramp of feet.

Let some get by. Hit the middle, the snake turns to bite.

He knew he would have to think fast, once he popped the canopy and rose into the air. He'd have to scan the column, pick his targets, and kiss his birds one-two-three-four. Then play peekaboo with the infantry until he ran out of ammo. Or his guns jammed. Or some damn pencil-neck Serb geek finally popped him.

One last weapon. Big red switch under the deck. Flip it open, arm it. Kiss a Serb platoon good-bye. Kiss Azim good-bye, too; but by then he probably wouldn't care.

Not like Zipper at the In-and-Out, though. Zipper never did care.

Fuck Zipper. *Because of him, I be here, getting my ass shot off.* Except, where'd he be, if he'd stayed in Eastport? Get his ass shot off there, too.

Just do it. Those Serbies could probably hear his heart pounding anyway. He triggered the turbines and the canopy pulled away as the platform shot into the air amid a cloud of dirt and leaves and broken branches. Vehicles were lined up like ducks. Sitting ducks, except they could shoot back. . . . Infantry trudging along both sides of the road, some riding on the backs of personnel carriers and self-propelleds.

Three self-propelled guns, he saw in an instant. One old Soviet tank. Four, five troop carriers mixed in between. First gun was an old SU-100; behind it, a BMP-1, which mounted a 73mm gun. Behind the tank was an old Czech 152mm self-propelled howitzer.

He swung the Gatling gun along the column, front to back, scything down the infantry before they had even reacted to his sudden presence. Then he eyeballed the laser sight and pinned each target. First gun; *launch.* Second gun; *launch.* Howitzer; *launch.* Tank; *launch.* The platform bucked each time from the recoil. No more birdies. He grabbed the hammer for the Gat again.

Let's move! Only dead folks stayed put for long. With his foot controls, Azim kicked the skimmer sideways along the column, going for the driver's cabs on the trucks.

The Serb line erupted in flames as the birdies nested. The howitzer's barrel flew end-over-end into the air and came down on the back of a troop truck. The tank slewed sideways, the treads on one side shredded, and presented its rear. Damn, for one more bird . . . *Send it up yo' ass.*

He hammered at the infantry with the Gatling, swooping down on them like a hawk. With his foot controls and his left hand, he made the skimmer duck and jump and weave. *Felt* different fighting from the skimmer, too. Not like glove-n-goggles. Azim could hear the shriek of the missiles. Feel the heat of their exhaust. Smell the stink of the powder and the casings spewing from the Gatling like a wall of brass. As the Gatling's barrel spun, the skimmer tried to twist the other way; but the onboards kept a tight leash on the fans and compensated for the . . . Turk? No, torque. Azim laughed. It was a screech, a howl.

Return fire now from the dazed infantry. Bullets pinged and ricocheted off the Kevlar prow, slanted to slough off bullets to the side. He'd damn well caught them with their pants down diddling each other. Looked like more artillery down the line, but they couldn't get past the burning hulks in front of them without leaving the paved road. "Not used to someone shoots back, are you?" he shouted. No way they understood him; no way they could even hear him; but he wasn't shouting for them to hear. "Your mama!"

Thunder rolled across the Macedonian countryside. From the corner of his eye, Azim saw a Plank rise from behind the airport terminal. You couldn't see the flames from its engines except now and then when they flicked in tongues. Up fast. A second jump ship followed close behind. Then a third. It was a beautiful sight and Azim's heart rose with them.

Must've finished loading. Bugout time. Timetable called for Red Hand to fall back on the *Coleman* and the *Rogers* and scramble aboard. Azim checked the map display. Just a glance, because he had to keep hopping. Up, down, left, right. Never still for very long; Gatling never silent for long. Sears and the other skimmers were already on the apron loading. No way could he make it back in time. He hoped Jo-jo would let his mama know what had happened to him. Maybe Chase would. Shit, wouldn't that be a kick in the head?

Might as well finish it here. Even if he did not make it back, so what? Chase blabs, the cops come and haul him off. So he might as well be dead.

A gun began barking down the line of Serb vehicles and the sky was pockmarked with bursts of black smoke. An AA gun, Azim realized. If they got the range, they could pop the Planks as they launched and all this was for nothing. He worked the thrusters with his feet and sped along the ragged Serb column a foot above the undulating ground. He saw it—a self-propelled ZSU, with a pair of 57mm AA guns on a T-54 chassis. Azim swooped across its flank and saw the gunner furiously cranking down the barrel toward Azim. *The ZSU-57-2 can also be used against ground targets,* he heard the briefing officer's calm tones as he pointed to the photograph.

No missiles left . . . He raked the gun with the Gatling. The barrel spun and the individual shots blurred into a single, hacking cough. The Serb gunner was tossed from his seat. Another man ran to service the gun and Azim blew him away, too. The other gunners scattered.

His left arm went numb and an instant later Azim heard the bumblebee hum of the bullet that got him. His tracking board told him which direction it had come from. *Real nice to know* . . . He turned the port-side pop gun on that bearing and let loose. Two, three Serbs grabbed sky; the others kissed dirt.

But one-armed, he couldn't maneuver and shoot at the same time. He let go of the gun controls and grabbed the stick. Time to move the franchise.

From the corner of his eye, he had kept count of the Planks rising from behind the terminal. The eleventh was a bigger boom, a larger ship. That was SSTO *Bessie Colemen*, a LEO orbiter like the *Rogers*, with more fuel and cargo capacity than the smaller FBTS jump ships. And damn if her pilot wasn't that same Forrest Calhoun he'd wondered about all those years ago. He'd met the man briefly at Lejune, just before they jumped for Yugoslavia. Shook his hand.

Eleven down, one to go.

No. That was *eleven up, one to go.* . . .

The Serbies must have realized that, too; because the forward units pushing toward the airport gave up, which was good, and turned their attention to Azim, which was not so good. Toward the rear of the column, he saw a couple three humvees—or maybe they *were* old patch-up jeeps—coming around off-road through the brush, so someone in back must have looked up "deployment" in his handbook. The heavy-caliber machine guns bouncing on their backs looked like serious weenie.

Two mags left for the Gat. And his right arm was getting tired from the strain of working both controls. *Oughta complain,* he thought, *motherfucking platform's not handicapped-friendly.* There was no pain in his left arm; not yet. Probably never would be.

The *Rogers* lifted off then, and Azim was well and truly alone, except for a hundred or so Serbies. The front end of the column was a shambles. Burning trucks and guns, twitching bodies. But the back end was coming up now, and the advance parties were turning back, and he couldn't keep his skimmer hopping too much longer. Maybe it was time to think about that switch behind the little door. . . .

There was something wrong with the *Rogers.* It was rising too slowly and, even from here, Azim could see that the cargo-bay door was still open. Damn! Had one of those Serb shots hit lucky? Jo-jo was aboard that jump ship—and Chase—and if the *Rogers* went down, there be nobody tell his mama whatever happened to her boy.

He yanked hard on the control stick and kicked the pedals and his skimmer darted across the road, between two of the burning guns. The flames roared and blossomed from the backwash of his lifter fans. Bullets spanged against his armor from both sides, but this time, thankfully, nothing came through the gun ports. Instead, as he passed between the two squads, they shot at each other. Azim howled laughter.

There was a hummock in the ground on the other side of the road. Not much, but . . . *Seize the high ground.* He brought the skimmer around and settled it atop the mound. When he let go the yoke, his right arm felt like a sausage. He punched the cutoff with his fist and the rotors whined into silence.

A squad of Serb infantry must have thought the skimmer was disabled, because they shouted and charged up the slope to where he had grounded it. Azim gave them a convincing counterargument, which left half of them flopping in the grass. The others went to ground and began firing from cover. His armor rang like a roof in a hailstorm. A bullet found the forward gunport and glanced off his helmet. It was like being hit with a hammer. Azim saw double.

One of the jeeps was coming into position now. The other two, coming up the other side of the road, were probing for a path through the line of burning wreckage. Some other Serbies must have figured Americans were too stupid to mount a tailgun on a skimmer and worked their way to the side. With the videos out, he couldn't see behind, so he told the tailgun's pea-brain to shoot anything that moved.

Another bullet found something. The control board spat sparks and the map display went dead. Well, he didn't need the map no more, anyway. He knew where he was. Up shit creek. Nothing here to shoot at but bogies. Be a damn shame if they nined the fire control brain, though. He could only aim and shoot one gun at a time.

The machine gun mounted on the jeep began to chatter and the hailstorm on his armor turned into some jazz drummer on weed. Azim returned fire, but the range was extreme and the jeep driver drove his charge in an evasive maneuver. Which ruined the gunner's aim, but which kept Azim busy enough for the others to dash forward and dive into new positions.

Azim's Last Stand.

A Serb rifleman came suddenly erect, pointing toward the sky, the last gesture he ever made. Then others were turning and firing into the air.

What the hell? Azim risked a glance and saw the most bizarre sight he had ever seen. The *Calbraith Rogers*, a fucking spaceship, was sliding sideways across the sky. *I didn't know they could do that....* In the open mouth of the cargo bay, a squad of Marines poured fire into the Serbs surrounding Azim. He could see Jo-jo, hanging to a lanyard with one arm and firing his machine gun with the other. There was Flynn and Sears and the rest of Red Hand. There was the sergeant major who had been in charge of the UN troops. And Chase, who was a fucking *civilian*, and couldn't know anything except which end the bullets came out.

Which, under the circumstances, was enough.

The high ground was always the best position; and it looked like the lieutenant had invented his own high ground. The Serbs began to scatter under the rain of lead and the *Rogers* drifted after them, walking on feet of flame. The few who were left around Azim's position fired wildly at the spaceship or at the skimmer. Azim let the computer note the vector of each slug and sent a stream of fire along the return path. One by one, the guns fell silent.

The *Rogers* had reached the roadway and began to follow the line of vehicles, scorching them with her exhaust. Fabric caught fire. Flames erupted from gasoline tanks, enveloping trucks and cars in steel-melting heat. A caisson blew up. Serb regulars scattered in all directions, away from the enormous flying torch that swooped down on their equipment. Azim watched it for a while, then he closed his eyes and rested his cheek on the handle of the forward gun.

Thunder, roaring wind, and searing heat brought him round again. Looking through the forward gunport, he saw the *Rogers,* gear extended, settle to the ground a little ways in front of him. Painfully, Azim pushed himself erect with his good arm. The left one, throbbing and with pain just beginning to soak in, dangled limply by his side. Chase was sitting in the open cargo-bay door with a stupid grin on his face.

"Need a lift?" he asked.

Skopje
by roberta carson
from: *Styx Up*

Were you at Thermopylae when Persia crossed the sea?
Did you lay your bones between your homes and the
  spears of the enemy?
Or did you stand before Chalons with old foes at your
  side
And with sword and shield refuse to yield, and stemmed
  the Hunnish tide?

Did you ply a boat to Dunkirk? Did you drive a taxicab
To the Marne's grim banks and never charge a fare?
Did you roll down rocks at Moorgarten? Or die at
  Manzikert?
Did you shout back "Nuts!" in the frigid Christmas air?

If you were no strutting conqueror; but fought for hearth
  and home . . .
If you warded the defenseless and shielded them from
  harm . . .
If you swooped in for the rescue, if you ground a tyrant
  down,
Accept the thanks from the world's poor ranks;
You've *earned* your plot of ground.

10.

Promises Kept (II)

Mariesa was watching the television coverage from the day couch in the sunroom when Barry came up behind her and began to massage her shoulders. Mariesa reached up and held his hand. "It was Azim Thomas," she told him. "The Marine that held off the Serb artillery until the Planks were off. He was going by the name Thomas Monroe. His picture has been all over the networks."

"I heard. What will happen to him now?" Barry asked.

She sighed. "Two things, I suppose. He gets the Congressional Medal of Honor; and he gets brought in for questioning by the North Orange police."

"It doesn't seem fair." His hands caressed the curve of her neck. "I remember the store videotapes, and it looked to me like he tried to stop Tyler . . . Uh, Zipper." He shook his head. "Onwuka always did have a bad feeling about Zipper. He told me once that there was gold inside Azim, but as deep as he could dig into Zipper, there was nothing there."

As far as Mariesa knew, the North Orange police had not even been searching for Azim, but publicity did funny things to prosecutors' minds. Who could resist the temptation to strut for a high-profile case? "If I have any influence over matters," she said, "the charge on accessory and on interstate flight will be dropped." She could not allow them to take the boy. What could it possibly mean now but vindictiveness? "I am certain that the tapes can be computer-enhanced to show more clearly what happened."

Barry stopped rubbing. "I'm sure they can be." He fell silent and Mariesa craned her neck to look at him. Barry's face was a mixture of conflicting emotions. His mouth hooked down and his eyes were troubled.

"What's wrong?" she asked.

"Nothing." He came from behind the couch and nodded toward the television. "They said on the news that more than two hundred Serbs were killed in the fighting, and only three Marines."

"You forgot the twenty-seven Marines, four Nigerians, and two Swedes killed before the rescue. Or don't they count?"

"Of course they do; but that fellow . . ." He indicated the newsreader. ". . . has been saying it was not a fair fight."

Mariesa said dryly, "It was not supposed to be. Besides, 'that fellow' only reads what Cyrus Attwood gives him to read, and Cyrus is determined to 'spin' any news story that involves my ships. Most of his media employees have different agendas than he has, but Cyrus can play his own tune regardless of the instrument."

"What is it, a war between you two?"

Cyrus and her. The old man in the shadows, sitting back and pulling strings because the future terrified him. And herself, dirtied by the struggle because . . . (And it struck her suddenly.) Because she, too, was terrified of the future. "Yes." And her laugh sounded odd, even to herself. "It is a war; only we don't use bullets."

"Except one."

"What . . . ?"

Barry turned away and walked to the window, where he stood with arms folded, staring into the draperies. He pulled them aside. "When the Peoples' Crusades shut down that

Klondike-American Oil depot in Alaska, Doyle Kinnon, one of the foremen, shot himself.''

''And is that supposed to be *my* fault?''

Barry turned at last, but his arms remained resolutely folded. ''Albright undertook the Crusade because a big money donor named Arthur Kondo suggested it. Kondo had given EarthSafe Solar two hundred thousand dollars in the name of Japan-America Friends of Solar, and you don't ignore a 'friend' like that.''

''I thought crusaders were not influenced by such matters; but never mind. What is your point?''

''Just this. Arthur Kondo is actually a Tokyo-based trade negotiator for Van Huyten Industries. You have to peel back two or three layers of the onion to find that, but it's true.''

And who taught you to peel onions? she wondered. ''What of it? I do not dictate how my employees spend their free time.''

''Don't play games, Mariesa,'' Barry snapped. ''Remember who I am? I'm your husband. *I'm on your side.* No way Kondo can scrape together two hundred grand. Japan-America is a front, a shell. It has a donor list, but you add up all those nickels and dimes and it's still peanuts—except for the two hundred 'Special Friends' who gave a thousand apiece. And— Don't interrupt, please. And each of those two hundred donations can be traced through a maze of transactions back to VHI. So tell me, Mariesa. Why did you launder so much money into EarthSafe? Just so Albright would listen to Kondo and go after Klondike-American?''

''No, that was simply a handy coincidence when I needed to strike Attwood.''

''And so Doyle Kinnon kills himself. . . .''

She rose from the sofa, with her arms held stiff at her sides. ''I am not responsible for that!''

''*You* set the events in motion.''

''Or Cyrus did, when he sent a man with a knife to threaten me. Or Albright, when he decided that even barely detectable amounts of a discharge were Earth-threatening. Or Klondike, by overreacting—there were accommodations short of closure.

Or maybe even that supervisor himself, if he was the one responsible for authorizing the discharge. How far back do you go to find the Prime Mover? Don't tell me *I* set events in motion!''

She stepped away from the day couch toward him. Through the window louvers, in the distance, she could see Harriet atop Estrella trotting toward the stables, and past that, the meadow undulating toward Skunktown Mountain. She and Barry stood regarding each other, for a long moment; then Barry flapped his arms, once.

"Look, I'm sorry I brought it up."

"Get out!"

"Riesey . . ."

"I said get out!"

"All right." He held his hands up, palms out: a gesture of surrender. Or of helplessness. "All right. We can talk again after you've calmed down." He took a step backward and turned and circled the couch so he wouldn't come near her. At the doorway that led into the ballroom, he paused with one hand on the doorpost, and turned again. Mariesa felt as if she were vibrating. A turning fork, humming on some unheard frequency.

"One last question, Riesey; and you don't have to answer. But I wonder . . . what would Keith McReynolds have said?"

It was a long time after he left that she stood there by the window, and not once did she hear the answer.

She settled on a small affair—an open house and reception—to honor the Witherspoon graduates who, by an odd concatenation of chance, had assured the success of the Skopje rescue.

Michael Hobart brought his wife, Philippine Flavie Leland, as well as his son. He was dressed in his blues, as was Azim Thomas and Azim's friend, "Jo-jo" Kirby. Azim's mother, a plump woman with work-worn hands, watched her prodigal with eyes that brimmed with tears, as if she expected him to leap out of the window and vanish from her life once more. A blue, star-speckled ribbon hung around Azim's neck. Every now and then his left hand, bound in a sling, would reach out and touch the medallion that dangled from the ribbon, as if to assure him that it was still there.

During the reception, Chase, Azim, and Jimmy Poole gathered in the library alcove where her special globe had once been, and stood there with their backs turned, as if they had built a wall between themselves and the rest of the party. It seemed strange to think of them as young men in their mid-twenties, and not as children. Mariesa did not disturb them as she passed by, but she could overhear Jimmy Poole's braying voice.

"... can't prove it legal, but it was Cyrus Attwood. Used an outlaw hacker named Crackman to bogie the code and plant the logic bomb. That Crackman is one bean dude, let me tell you; and I'm trying to wangle the angle for almost a year. Then I find out how the flock is going up, you know? Talk PRESsure? Man ..."

Ned DuBois in a dinner jacket looked as unlikely a specimen as Mariesa had ever seen, like a fish wearing fur. He seemed to be in a constant struggle with his tie, and the tie was winning. He had brought his wife, Betsy, who spent most of the open house inspecting the paintings that hung about, surprising Mariesa by identifying several of the artists. Mariesa found Ned talking with Hobie, Jo-jo, and Hobie's father. Mariesa apologized for interrupting and laid her hand on Ned's forearm. "I wanted to commend you, Ned, on the control of the Plank that you demonstrated in a crisis."

Ned chuckled. "Does that mean you think I'm a hell of a pilot?"

"Man," said Jo-jo, "you should've seen it. He really toasted them Serbies."

Ned's smile faded. "I'm not too happy about that."

Michael Hobart rumbled. "I won't waste my tears. They came looking for trouble and they found what they were looking for. They were picking my men off one by one—unarmed UN peacekeepers—just for sport!" Hobart-*père* was large and broad-shouldered, like his son. Angry, he presented an awesome sight. "An hour earlier, that column you helped destroy was shelling equally unarmed civilians in Skopje town. So I can't say I'm too sorry they got back some of what they'd been giving."

"Besides," said Hobie, "Azim helped get Dad out of a tight spot. You couldn't just go off and leave him."

"No way," said Jo-jo, bobbing his head vigorously.

"The answer to your question, Ned," Mariesa said, "is that I do think you are 'one hell of a pilot.' " Then, with a slight gesture, she led him apart from the others. "I have spoken to Dolores and the others on the FarTrip Steering Committee," she told him in a low voice. "They agreed that the ability to think coolly in an emergency is just the quality they want in the command pilot."

Ned had a tall pilsner glass of beer. He lowered it now.

"The FarTrip assignment is yours."

Ned seemed a little dazed. He shook his head, as if to clear it. He swallowed, once; and perhaps only Mariesa could see how the pilsner glass shook ever so slightly. "Another world," he whispered. "To set foot on another world . . ."

"Do I take that for a yes?"

Ned straightened. "Who's number two?"

"For the command chair, Commander Calhoun."

"No. I meant, copilot; but . . ."

"The copilot will be Russian."

"Mike Krasnarov."

"Very likely, but that has not been decided. Kravchenko is very competent."

Ned grinned suddenly. "But if Nikolai snores in his sleep, it could be a *real* long flight."

Sykes announced dinner then, and they all moved slowly toward the dining room. Mariesa saw Ned catch up with Betsy and take her arm. He leaned close to her and whispered, and Mariesa supposed he was giving her the good news.

Armando was serving dessert when the gatehouse called to say that there was a woman who wanted urgently to see Azim Thomas. Mariesa, puzzled, gave permission to admit her. A few minutes later, Sykes came to the table to explain that the woman had come to the front door, but would not enter Silverpond. She wanted Azim to come to the door, instead. Rather than create a scene, Mariesa dabbed at her lips with her napkin and rose from the table. "Excuse me," she told the others, and left the dining room.

It was Styx, as she had half suspected. The list of those who would not set foot in Silverpond was not a very long one.

Mariesa could see Roberta through the mosaic of beveled glass. She could see a score of Robertas, large and small, upright and inverted; but when she opened the door there was only one. "Roberta," she said, in as welcoming a voice as she could muster.

"Where's Azim?" was all she received in response.

"Sykes is bringing him. Would you care to step inside?"

"Nah. I'd be crashing a real important party, and besides, I'm particular about what houses I walk into."

"You were not always so particular," Mariesa said.

"Yeah. Well. Live and learn, or you don't live long."

Sykes returned with Azim Thomas in tow. "What is it?" the gunnery sergeant wanted to know. He peered at Roberta with uncertain recognition. "You want to see me, girl?"

"No," said Roberta. She reached to the left, out of sight of the doorway, and tugged another young woman into view. A short woman, with dusky skin and a wide, round nose. Hair chopped short in bangs across her forehead. "But here's someone," Roberta continued, "you need to talk to."

A silence formed that seemed to stretch on and on. *Who is it?* Mariesa wondered. One of Azim's old girlfriends? It was Azim who broke the silence first.

"Shit," he said. "You that Indo girl from school." *Tanuja Pandya,* Mariesa suddenly remembered, the one whose father had been killed by Azim's friend. Azim took a step forward, onto the porch, and Tanuja moved back, away from him. "I aint't going to hurt you none, girl," Azim snapped. His right hand, half raised, made a gesture of helplessness. He turned and glared at Mariesa and Roberta. "Leave us be awhile, okay? Don't want no—"

"Witnesses?" asked Roberta.

"Fuck you, Styx. I'm going down the bottom of those stairs." He turned to Tanuja. "You want, you come down there, too. Maybe we gots something to say, we say it." He bounced down the flagstoned staircase, balancing himself with his good hand on the rail. Tanuja Pandya hesitated and looked first at Roberta, then at Mariesa.

"Go on," Mariesa said. "If that is what you want." Tanuja pulled her lip between her teeth and nodded slowly.

"It's hard," she said, "to be reminded." Then she followed Azim down the stairs, leaving Mariesa and Roberta on the porch standing in front of the open door.

"Are you certain you will not step inside?" Mariesa asked again. Roberta shook her head and Mariesa came out onto the porch herself. "As you wish." It was still light out—July days were long and the evenings short and soft. The sky was overcast and seemed to be lit by indirect lighting. Everything was bright in the waning daylight, yet nothing cast a shadow. "Why did you bring her here?" she asked.

Roberta raised her head. "People have a right to know. People have to face up to their own lives." She shook her head to throw a curl of black hair off her brow.

"Do they?" Mariesa asked. "Azim broke with his old life. He learned. He is not the same person you knew in school."

"Didn't know him then," Styx replied. "But what the hell makes you think it was Azim needed closure?"

Mariesa looked at the girl. "You did this for Tanuja."

Styx looked away, into the bushes that robed the crest of the Great Mound. "I didn't want her to die of the wounds she got in the robbery."

"I . . . see. You wouldn't be manipulating her life, then?"

Roberta gave her an angry glance. "I'm doing this for *her*, not for me. That makes a difference."

Mariesa stepped back inside the house and saw Sykes waiting patiently for instructions. She sent him up to the Roost and told him where to find the envelope he was to bring back with him; then she returned to the porch. Roberta was staring down the gently curving stairs, as if trying to see beyond the bend to the parking apron below.

"My mother died, you know," Styx said quietly.

"Oh," said Mariesa. "I hadn't known. I'm sorry."

"No, you're not. What did you know about her to be sorry about? She hated you, because you were rich. Because she thought you bought me away from her."

"I never had such an intention. . . ."

"We argued all the time. She kept me in a cage. No fooling. Bars on the window and everything. She died while I was in Prague and I never knew about it until I came back. And all those things we said to each other, they were still there. And all those things we never said to each other, they never got said."

"And so you brought Tani to meet Azim. So they could say things to each other."

Styx turned and looked at her with coal-black eyes. "Don't psychoanalyze me," she said. "You don't have the right."

The breezes of twilight started, a rush of air across the Mound that stirred the grass into restless motion. Like waves on the sea, Mariesa had always thought. She looked down the stairs. "I wonder what they are saying to each other," Mariesa said.

"That's between the two of them," Roberta responded. "It's none of our business."

"What if . . . one of them says the wrong thing?"

"Then, that's what they said." Styx turned her pale gaze on her. "You still don't get it, do you, Rich Lady? People own title to their own lives. They can muck things up, if that's what they want, and you or I get no say in it."

"That cannot stop me from caring."

Roberta looked away again. "When have you ever cared?"

"Sometimes," Mariesa admitted. "Perhaps not often enough." Sykes reappeared in the doorway with a thick manila envelope in his hand. Mariesa took it and thanked him, and Sykes bowed gracefully and retreated. "I read your poem. The one about Skopje that appeared in the *Atlantic Monthly*." Roberta turned around with her arms folded. "I thought it was very good."

"Did you?" The young woman would not accept the compliment. "It was nothing. A piece of doggerel I threw off and transmitted before I could think better of it." She made a face. "That's the problem with electronic submissions. You can send things before they're really ready."

"Nevertheless, I thought it was good."

Roberta shrugged. "Maybe the world needs more heroes. Maybe the world is ready for heroes again."

Yes. Mariesa thought. *That's why we tried to grow some.* Mariesa looked at the envelope she held. Seven years of painstaking research by Luanda Chisolm. Evidences carefully tracked down, documented, copied, pieced together. Bank records, taped conversations, depositions. It wasn't all legal—it would *never* make it into court, and it had never been intended that it should—but it was all true. The evidence showed how money from Cyrus Attwood funneled through the Peoples' Crusades financed an armed attack on the Antisana Ram. Used the right way, this information would bring down Cyrus Attwood. It would bring down the Peoples' Crusades with it.

"Tell me, Roberta. Is Phil Albright one of those heroes?"

"You damn betcha!" Roberta said. "There's nobody who cares about as many things as deeply as he does. He's the only one in the country who sees the future the way it ought to be."

"Perhaps not the only one," Mariesa said wryly. "And perhaps you are right that the country needs heroes. Perhaps it needs a dozen different sorts of heroes. In the sky and on the earth, and in the schools and on the battlefield. Heroes who care and heroes who think. Even heroes who might struggle against each other." She held the envelope out to Roberta. "Take this. I had intended only to show you its contents; but you may take it and decide for yourself what to do about it."

Roberta accepted the envelope with a suspicious squint. "What is this?" she asked. She opened it and pulled out a sheet at random.

"I will tell you one other thing. As far as we could determine, Phil Albright himself knew nothing at all about the matters described.''

Styx had always cultivated a pale complexion only one shade up from a sickly pallor. Now, she seemed to blanch almost into transparency. Her eyes darted across the bank statement she had pulled, then lighted on Mariesa's face. "Why are you giving me this?"

"As you said, Roberta. People have a right to know."

"You're trying to destroy the Crusades!"

"I am trying to destroy Cyrus Attwood and his nephews. He has been using the Crusades as a cat's-paw. I thought you were the one who was shocked by manipulation."

Roberta shook the envelope. "What if I destroy this?"

"Do you want my advice?"

"No."

"Still, you shall have it; if only so you can ignore it. Make a copy of what I have given you and put the originals in a safe place. A bank deposit box, perhaps. Then take the evidence and show it to Phil. However much we disagree on some issues, he is an honest man. Between the two of you, you may yet save the Crusades from the rot within it."

"You never give up, do you?" Styx said bitterly. She shoved the bank statement back into the envelope.

"What do you mean?"

"You're still trying to direct my life!" She waved the envelope under Mariesa's face. "Damn you. Damn you. I don't need you. I don't need anyone!"

"Then I feel very sorry for you."

Styx raised her arm as if to throw the envelope to the ground; but instead, turning, she tucked it under her arm and fled down the stairs. Mariesa listened to the footsteps fade. Shortly, she heard a car engine start, and a few minutes later Azim Thomas walked slowly into view.

His uniform was disheveled and the ribbon around his neck was askew. He looked somber and unusually thoughtful. When he saw Mariesa waiting on the porch he hesitated.

"Sykes can direct you to a washroom where you can

straighten up,'' she told him. Azim nodded silently. "Is everything all right?" she asked.

He nodded again, and added, "Sometimes, you just gots to stand there and take it. Sometimes, people, they just gots to unload, you know?"

She stepped aside so he could pass her. "Yes," looking down the silent, darkening steps. "I know."

Entire days could go by when she did not think of William. She considered that both as a hopeful sign that the pain would someday fade and as a distressing one that she could ever forget the loss. There were other days, when she could think of little else besides the son who had never been. Flashbacks, as those on drugs might experience, but to times that had never happened. Holding a baby in her arms . . .

On days like that she welcomed distractions. Some of them.

Barry took her up to the top of Skunktown Mountain in the early morning, when the dew was still fresh on the meadow and the birds sang the sun into rising. They sat side by side on the bench in the gazebo overlooking Silverpond, and she thought wistfully of that soft summer's day seven years ago when they had made love for the first time. She thought how she had used him then as a way to score off Harriet, and how she had been neglecting him ever since the miscarriage. Was that why he had brought her up here?

"Barry," she said, but he answered with a hush. He took her hand in his, gently, but she could feel that he was anything but relaxed. He sat stiffly and, with his left hand, he fussed with the manila envelope he had brought with him.

"You know I love you, Riesey," he said at last.

"It has come to my attention," she said. But her dry response did not elicit the grin it usually did. His smile could light up his whole face, but she had seen little of it lately. He had been moody and irritable ever since his last trip. Sometimes they quarrelled over inconsequential matters.

"I'm serious. I love you. I would do anything not to hurt you. And I believe in what you are trying to accomplish."

Something in the way he said that—*I would do anything not to hurt you*—told her that hurt was coming. Unwillingly, she clenched up. "What is it?" Half a plea, half a command.

He sighed. "There's no easy way." Without another word, he gave her the manila folder. His face did not flicker. It was impossible to discern his thoughts.

Mariesa opened the folder and extracted the contents.

They were photographs. . . .

Of Barry and a woman . . .

And the two of them were . . .

She slapped the pictures facedown on the bench and looked away. Barry shifted and sat straighter, but still his face did not betray his thoughts. Mariesa fought for breath against a sudden pain in her stomach. "What," she said. She had to take a deep breath. "What is this?" She waved a hand at the photographs. She found that she could not bear to touch them.

"Riesey . . ."

"No!" She pulled away from him. The pictures, dislodged, scattered to the ground. One flipped over, revealing intertwined arms and legs. She would not look at it. She stared through the gap in the trees. Below, like a toy building, Silverpond sat atop its mound, bathed in a clean morning sunlight that seemed almost sourceless.

"Why?" she asked after a very long time, measured in heartbeats.

"Ask Cyrus. You hit him; he hits you back. This was payback for Klondike-American. He wanted me to sabotage our space program."

She turned and looked at him. "That was the wrong 'why,' Barry."

He wouldn't meet her eyes. "I know what kind of person I am. Jesus. Ever since I saw those pictures, I've known all too well. I'm not proud; but if I tried to hide them, if I tried to keep them a secret, Attwood would own me. I'd give in to him, sooner or later, and do what he wanted. This was the only way I could stop him."

"By showing me the pictures yourself."

"Yes." He looked up at her, improbably eager-eyed.

"Don't you see? What you and I have built is too important to let Cyrus Attwood get a lever on me."

"What *you and I* have built? What part of it did *you* build?"

He flushed. "I kept you alive when the work would have killed you!"

"Well, thank you very much!" She stepped on the photographs scattered on the dirt and ground her heel into them. "And it's still the wrong 'why'! I don't care why Attwood took the pictures. I don't care why you showed them to me. I want to know why you were there for the pictures to be taken at all!"

He froze for a moment and Mariesa could feel, even at the far end of the bench where she had placed herself, everything run out of him. But when he spoke, he did not address her question. He closed his two hands into a ball, which he shoved into his lap, and stared at the worn and trodden ground. "It's funny, you know. All my life I just took things as they came. Never once did I stand up for a principle. And now because I wouldn't play Cyrus Attwood's game, I've screwed things up worse than ever."

"You are not trying to tell me that this was all out of loyalty to me?"

He grunted a laugh. "Funny thing, but it's true." He did look at her now. "What do *you* do when you've taken on obligations that conflict? What if your whole goddamned life is one big jigsaw puzzle, and none of the pieces fit each other? When you've made too many promises and you've got to keep them all."

She stood up, straight and stiff. "I don't do that, Barry. I don't drift with the tide. I chart my own course."

"No matter who you leave behind?"

"I'm not the one with my photograph taken."

"Then maybe you ought to be. Jesus, our whole life together has been a deception—from the day we first met. Or don't you remember your little dress-down act at the hotel? You like to keep little secrets. Schemes within schemes. Prometheus within VHI, and the inner circle within Prometheus. And you, within the inner circle. When half of Prometheus thought the goal was cheap space transportation, others knew there were space stations behind it, and still others knew there was solar power behind that. Tell me, Riesey, have you ever told anybody everything? You kept things from Belinda, and she resents it. You manipulated the school curriculum, and Styx resents it. You used staff people from Morpheus and Demeter, and Jimmy Undershot and Brad Hardaway resent it. You always have something going on behind the scenes. How long have you and I been married . . . how much have we shared in pillow talk over the last five years . . . and not once did you ever talk to me about that . . . fear of yours? Sometimes," Barry said, "I think you can't *not* keep things to yourself. Sometimes I think you can't open yourself to anybody. Not to me, not to Harriet. I wonder: not even to Keith?"

She dropped her eyes to the envelope in the dirt. No. Not even to Keith. "Everyone keeps secrets," she said bitterly. "Not everyone betrays." She turned her back on him and walked toward the path that led down from the hill. His voice chased after her, followed her down.

"Maybe you ought to shack up with someone besides Prometheus. Did you ever think of that?"

It was always the guilty that had the most excuses, who hurled the most countercharges. She began to walk more swiftly down the trail off Skunktown Mountain, pushing blindly past the shrubs and low hanging branches, not quite breaking into a run. Her feet stamped the hardened dirt of the path, tripped once on a protruding root—but she caught herself and did not fall. She left him behind, atop the mountain, and never looked back.

Distance is the healer. Distance and solitude. Mariesa did not stop running until she had reached the old family lodge high above Jackson Lake. Of all their houses, this one had always been Father's favorite; but they had stopped coming here after Father's death. An occasional ski outing in college; a few of the early management retreats. More often she had leased it out.

There was no one staying there now. The lodge was dark

and silent; the furniture, shrouded in white sheets. It smelled of age and disuse. Dust lined everything. She had not called the caretaker before flying out, so nothing had been turned on. Nor had, she thought wryly, the neglect been corrected. She had packed a bag and abandoned Silverpond before Harriet had returned from the city. Not even Sykes knew where she had gone, though he knew Laurence Sprague had driven her to the airport. And Barry, as far as she knew, was still sitting on that bench atop Skunktown Mountain. Only Charlie Jim, who had flown her here on the company jet, knew; and he was sworn to silence.

They would track her down, eventually. She was too important to disappear for long. Until then, she had only herself for company; and how long had it been since that? She dropped her overnight bag into her old bedroom—somehow, it did not seem right to take her parents' room—and hoped that during the angry stuffing of it some more coherent part of her mind had included all the things she would need.

She walked from room to room, touching things. Her tour brought her to the back deck, which stood on stilts on the edge of a broad cirque, where God himself had taken a bite from the mountainside. Through the evergreens that clothed the sharp, stone-littered slope she could glimpse the waters of Jackson Lake winking in the moonlight. She stood there for a while, hypnotized by the blinking. Finally, she returned to the bedroom and pulled the protective cover off the bed.

There was a mattress pad, but no linens, but she did not particularly care. She stripped and then rummaged in the overnight bag for pajamas. The subconscious, or whoever had packed, had fallen down on the job. There were underwear, toiletries, a change of clothing—even a swimsuit! But no pajamas.

It didn't matter. It was high summer, August, and, though the Rockies were always cool, they were not excessively so at this time of year. She searched in the closets until she found an old flannel blanket woven in a faux-Indian design and brought it back to the bedroom with her. She stopped before the full-length mirror on the bedroom closet door, but it was too dark in the room to see herself.

She went to the French doors that led to the deck and pulled the curtains wide. In the moonlight, her body glowed like a pearl. Across the cirque, a man sitting feet-on-rail on his own deck saw her framed in the doorway and nearly tumbled off his seat. Mariesa pretended not to notice him. Instead, she returned to the mirror and studied herself in the silver light.

Why that other woman, and not her? Was she too thin? Her breasts too small? Her hair cut too boyishly? Or was she too reserved when the moment called for abandon? Or was it not physical at all? On some subjects, she knew, others did not share her intensity. Could it be only a search for a change of subject?

She could flog herself all night over imagined shortcomings. It was a disservice to Barry to treat him so. He was an actor, too, with intellect and will. And so, too, was the woman. And it could be that each of the three of them had built a piece of the final product, each for his or her own reasons, with never any need that those reasons correspond.

Is it the bell that rings, ran the old Japanese riddle, *or the clapper? Or is it the meeting of the two?*

She and Chris and Belinda and Steve and Correy and Ned and all of them had different reasons for traveling the road they did, and if they found themselves together for a time, it was because those needs converged. If she feared the asteroids, and Belinda wanted to inspire the children, and Wallace got all misty-eyed just thinking about space, and Steve wanted to advance his career, and Luis Mendoza thought only about building his engines, and Dolores and João wanted only to score off of each other, and Ned DuBois wanted to touch another world, what did it matter in the end?

She shivered and goose bumps formed on her body. She wrapped her arms around herself and padded softly to where she had thrown the flannel blanket. She whirled it around herself like a cape. *Show's over*, she thought to the man across the cirque. She wondered if he had had time to get a camera. Only fair to have pictures of herself as well.

She wriggled into the bed and rolled the blanket up like a cocoon. Sleep was a long time coming and she wished, but only for a moment, for the bottle that Barry had used so long for comfort.

In the morning, after she had brushed her hair and teeth, she decided on a swim in the pool. Water was a cleanser, too. The bathing suit her brainstem had packed was a two-piece, of an Italian design that had been quite fashionable the year she'd had it made. Doubtless no one wore the style anymore. It fit, though snugly; a reminder of the years that lay between her and a frolic in the water.

She was being foolish, of course. She saw that immediately when she stepped out the side door and discovered the pool empty. A tarpaulin had been stretched across it and a season's worth of pine needles had accumulated in its lap. A faint, turpentine-like odor permeated the air. Mariesa sighed and she sat down on the steps that led to the pool. She didn't know what she wanted to do now; or if she wanted to do anything.

"Going for a swim?"

She looked up at the question and saw the man from the lodge across the cirque. He was blond-turning-gray, broad-shouldered, and with a smile that was a credit to his orthodontist. His arms and legs, where they protruded from swim shorts and pool shirt, were covered with light, golden curls that glistened with beads of water. "You're welcome to use my pool, if you wish. And you can use my phone to get your caretaker on the stick."

He had seen her last night standing naked on the balcony deck. He had more in mind, she was sure, than neighborly generosity. "If your wife doesn't mind," she said.

He laughed. "She already has her half. What I've got left is all mine."

She stood and held a hand out to him. "I am Mariesa van Huyten. What is your name?"

His smile faltered a little, then returned. "Wayne." He turned and led her off and she followed, her sandals slapping against the paving stones. He moved with grace, legs and arms in perfect balance. She judged him to be about her own age and, if he kept a lodge on this part of the mountain, of her own class.

Pausing at the gate to his own grounds, he opened it and bowed her through.

"I appreciate the loan of your swimming pool, Wayne. I—" It hit her suddenly, leaving her speechless. She stopped, half through the gate. He turned and gave her an inquiring look. "Wayne," she said. "Wayne Coper?"

"I didn't think you recognized me."

"I didn't. I mean I hadn't. I mean . . . Wayne. It's been a long time."

"Not since prep school," he agreed.

"What are you doing here?"

He shrugged. "It's August tenth," he said, as if that explained everything. It didn't, but everyone had their own private world of reasons.

His was a lovely pool, with gently curving sides, filled with clear, blue-green water heated to a comfortable temperature. Steam curled off the surface and made a sort of mist above the pool. Diving into it was a rebirth. She moved through the water with slow strokes, arching her back, floating. She broke surface and shook the water from her face. Wayne was sitting by the poolside with two glasses of iced tea in hand. "How do you like it?" he asked.

Mariesa kicked off the side of the pool and coasted across. She gripped the edge and floated there. "It's refreshing," she said. "Better than sitting in an unopened house feeling sorry and bitter."

Wayne looked momentarily serious. "Tell me about it."

For a moment she thought he was prying, but then she saw he was making a comment, not a request. "When did you build this lodge?" she asked. "Your family always kept a house down by the lake."

Another careless shrug. "My first wife got that in the settlement."

"I'm sorry to hear that."

"Yeah, it was a great house. But . . . lawyers like me, we

keep long hours, and come home at unexpected times.''

Mariesa pushed herself out of the water and sat on the edge of the pool. It was done up in Mexican tile, an eye-twisting riot of color. The water ran off her and pooled where she sat. The dry, high-altitude air sucked it off her skin. She could feel the sun beating down on her. Wayne handed her a pool towel and she patted her face dry. ''It's good to have someone to talk to,'' she said. ''I don't know what I was thinking when I flew out here, but sitting alone in that house . . .''

''Are you ready to talk about it?''

She turned and looked at him, ran her fingers through her hair. Maybe she ought to let it grow out again. Her hair had always been one of her best features. Harriet had always marveled while combing it out when Mariesa had been a child. ''No,'' she said. ''Not yet.'' He handed her one of the iced teas. She tasted it and could detect no liquor. He wasn't trying to get her drunk. He had always done that in prep school. ''You've changed.''

''We all do. It's called growing up. Back when we were going together, I was a real asshole.''

''Tosh. You were a teenaged boy.''

''That's what I just said.''

She laughed. She hadn't laughed since Barry had shown her the pictures. She couldn't imagine telling Wayne about the pictures. She couldn't imagine admitting they existed. They documented Barry's failing, not her own; yet she could not help but feel ashamed. ''Why is August tenth special?'' she asked. ''Is that an anniversary, or something?''

His face darkened under his tan and he looked down between his feet. ''You're going to think I'm an idiot.''

''No. Tell me.''

''Well, I promised one time that I would meet you at Jackson Lake every August tenth.''

''What?'' She turned so sharply she nearly slid off the slick tiles and into the pool. Wayne reached out and grabbed her arm to steady her.

''Careful.''

''I don't remember that,'' she said.

"I do. It was the last summer before college. We were on the boat out on the lake."

And suddenly, she did remember. That had been the very day she had seen the firestar, the day she had seen what the future might become. And here was her past, come to remind her of it. Funny, that they both remembered that day, but for such different reasons. "Do you mean to say you've been coming here every year on August tenth, just in case I might show up?" It was an astonishing thought. It was, in a way, frightening.

"Well . . . no," he admitted. "I did for a while—at first— but after your dad died, you never came out here anymore." He laughed softly. "Then, a few years ago, I figured that if you finally did show up, you would really need for someone to be here."

She stared at him for a long time; then, with a sudden, convulsive movement, she rolled over, face down on the cold, wet tiles. "Rub some oil on my back, would you, Wayne? I want to work on my tan." She pulled the straps of her bathing suit off her shoulders and waited.

Wayne said, "Are you sure you want to do this?" They both knew what he meant; they both knew it was not a suntan.

"Yes," she said.

"He hurt you, didn't he?" he said tentatively. "But you still think you may love him. Otherwise, why try to even the score?"

"Psychoanalyze me later, Wayne. And save your guesses. I know what I want."

"Then you're luckier than most of us." Cold, oily drops hit her in the small of the back and she shivered at their touch. "I think I've always been sort of halfway in love with you," he said while his hands stroked her, spreading the oil. "Or with my memory of you, anyway. That's why my second wife got the Maserati."

"Wayne, how many wives have you had?"

"Only two. I'm a slow learner; but I'm not stupid."

"I won't be the third."

"I know that."

She tried to look back over her shoulder, but she couldn't see him. "You don't mind being used this way."

He laughed. "To make love to a beautiful woman on my pool deck? It's not exactly a fate worse than death."

She had to laugh with him. It looked like the old hormone-driven Wayne was still there, too. She twisted around and lay on her back.

"Are you ready to do the front?"

When Mariesa returned to Silverpond a week later, Barry was already gone. His closets were empty; as if he had never lived there. Too much remained unresolved. If they were to break over this affair, she ought to at least understand what the affair meant. Harriet did not yet know exactly what had happened—only that Barry had moved out—but she walked the halls of Silverpond with a curious mix of sorrow and satisfaction.

There was a week's worth of decision-making and correspondence to catch up on. HELIOS was building up to a launch time early the following year. The Antisana Ram was down for annual maintenance and Wilson wanted to rearrange scheduled supply shoots around the Kilimanjaro Ram. FarTrip had settled on the *Gene Bullard*, as expected, and it would come down to land dock next month. All things considered, Steve Matthias had done good work, making those decisions required, while deferring those needing Mariesa's agreement. If he was more a mercenary than a true believer, he at least gave good measure for his pay.

It was hot and humid in the Roost. The observatory dome was open and the late-August night descended through the slit, carrying with it the odors of wood lily and foxglove and the sweet smell of mown hay. Crickets chirped in the woods around the estate, their sound muffled by walls and the distance. It would have been a good night to lie outdoors, a good night to spend with Barry on a blanket thrown among the wildflowers . . .

Mariesa sighed and bent over her writing desk. On the main desk, the computer sparkled as multicolored icons flickered and jaunted across the screen. The laser printer hummed to itself, waiting for the datassembler to swoop back from the Net and download its file. She picked up the letter she had written and read it over, adjusting the half-lens reading glasses on her nose.

> *Dear Jenny,*
> *I am writing you as chairman of VHI, the parent company of Mentor Academies and the Hope Schools, to tell you how proud I am of the work you have done. Dr. Karr has told me of the many projects you have carried out and the ideas you have suggested for caring for our charges. I am sure you have read of the recent rescue mission at Skopje, in Macedonia.*

Should she mention that her classmates, Chase Coughlin and Azim Thomas, had taken part? But that would reveal that Mariesa knew that Jenny Smythe was Jenny Ribbon. Mariesa decided to respect the young woman's wish to remain anonymous. She took her fountain pen in hand again and continued to write.

> *Rest assured that you, and your coworkers, have been conducting rescues no less important. I know that the compensation and recognition are meager compared to many other occupations; but some payments are incalculable. I hope that someday, when you are older, some of those you have rescued look you up for no other reason than to thank you. This is, Dr. Karr has assured me, a payment far beyond rubies.*
> *With my very best wishes,*
>
> > *I remain yours,*
> > *Mariesa Gorley van Huyten*

She signed it with a flourish. She had written by hand in blue ink. No form letter. No impersonal company boilerplate. The stationery was embossed in silver, with a Harriet's Sterling rose curled in the upper left corner.

The printer began to run and Mariesa set the letter aside to be addressed later. She took the color photograph from the discharge tray and opened her scrapbook. It was the formal portrait the Marine Corps had taken of Azim Thomas when he finished basic training a few years ago. Thomas stood decked in dress blues beside an American flag. He looked pleased, but wary; and perhaps a little cocky—and entitled to all three.

Harriet entered the Roost. Harriet *never* came to the Roost. She stepped carefully, like an explorer entering uncharted ground. "What are you doing now, Mariesa?" her mother worried. "We are meeting the Vogts for dinner tonight, or have you forgotten?"

"I haven't forgotten. This won't take long." She hadn't forgotten what a "herbie" Ernie Vogt was, either; but Harriet had her own rules. She flipped through the scrapbook, past the group photograph of the men and women around the Arizona Laser (Morris Tucker was third from the left), until she found a blank page. She placed Azim's photograph on it to see how it would look. Not many pages left. She would have to get a new volume soon. "I need to catch up on how my children have been doing."

"Your children?" Harriet's voice was disembodied, floating in the air somewhere behind Mariesa's left shoulder. "What are you talking about? You have no children."

She took a moment to thumb back a few pages. Azim, her troubled, angry boy. Styx, the rebellious one. Chase, so proud in his spacer's uniform. Jimmy, the smart one; too smart, maybe. And serious, earnest Tani . . . she had sold her father's store at last and entered college. Mariesa would start a page for her, soon. "Oh, yes, I do," she said in a whisper. To herself, not to Harriet. She did not care if Harriet understood at all. "Oh, yes, I do."

The future was a complex thing, built of many components. There were futures you could plan and build. Futures of metal and fire, bright shining as the sun. And there were futures you could grow on hope. Belinda—and Keith—had been right all along. These children, her children, mattered as much as—no, more than—the satellites and the ships. Because what purpose would it be to save the world if there were no world worth saving?

She applied the mucilage paste to the back side of the print-out photograph and set it firmly in the center, holding it until the glue set. Then she closed the book carefully and sat for a while listening to the sounds of the night.

EPILOGUE:

May 16, 2009, On the Shore of the Endless Ocean

Bat da Silva wriggled through the manlock into Mir Station and Ned DuBois shook hands with him when he was finally inside. "You old son of a gun," he said.

"Hello, Ned." Bat rubbed his mustache flat with the knuckle of his forefinger. "I am not too late. I saw *Bullard* as we made our final approach. She is—how do you say it?—awful?"

"Awesome would be better," Ned told him. Gorgeous might be better still. *Bullard*, grappled to Mir by magnetic tethers, was a flower of bright solar panels that gleamed like gold and silver in the sun. "Did you bring it?"

Da Silva grinned. "Of course. It was not easy finding him, but as you said, it was right. Excuse me." He grabbed a handhold and reached over to grip the hand emerging from the manlock. He pulled Bobbi McFeeley into the module, where she floated at odd angles to both Ned and Bat. It was something Ned had gotten used to on his various shifts on the station.

"Hey, Ned," she said. "How're they hanging?"

"This is orbitsville, Dona Bobbie. They don't hang; they float." He kicked off the wall toward the manlock that led into the External Tank. "Come on, I'll show you how the upscale half lives."

"What was that contraption I saw in parking orbit as we closed?" Bobbi asked, following him.

"*Glen Curtis*," he told her. "Being retired this month. Chase and I—you meet Chase Coughlin, yet?—we're taking her down after FarTrip leaves. She's all tanked up and ready." He touched down on the bulkhead next to the manlock and punched his code into the keypad. The hatch opened with a hiss.

"I was talking about that other bird. It looks like a goddam F-16 fighter plane!"

"Oh!" Ned laughed; and Bat said, "That is a Lock-Mar cruiser. Thought you knew."

"Bat, honey, I been reading nothing but baby books for the last year."

"Yeah. How's the kid doing?" Ned asked them. Bat's grin was wider than his skull. *Lookee what I did!* Ned remembered that feeling.

"I brought pictures," he said.

"Just like his daddy," Bobbi said, poking Bat in the ribs with her elbow. "Always crying for more. But what do we need another kind of orbiter for, anyway? I like the Planks just fine."

Bat said, "Have you ever seen photographs of early airplanes? No two were alike."

Ned shrugged. "Makes me no never mind." Lock-Mar's cruiser took off horizontal, just like a plane. Using jet fuel, too. When it reached 43,000 feet it took on another 150,000 pounds of oxidizer from a tanker. And from there . . .

Bobbi shook her head. "Sure, but . . . hydrogen peroxide? That stuff's awful. They'll chew up those NK-31G engines of theirs like potato chips."

Ned was expansive. "Let a thousand flowers bloom and a hundred different designs contend. They'll probably find one kind of ship's good for some things and another's good for other things." Bat bent over and pulled himself through the lock. Bobby gripped the sides of the lock.

"Levkin flew the cruiser up, you know," Ned told her.

"Levkin? No fooling? I thought he quit."

"Quit VHI, anyway. A good career move, all things considered. He is back in the game now. Signed on at Lock-Mar." He helped Bobbi through the lock with a firm shove on her center of gravity. Then he followed her through.

The "back porch," as everyone called the External Tank addition, was spacious, the size of a 747 aircraft with partitions and equipment set up in odd positions and orientations. In microgravity, you could use all the volume, not just the walls. But for the party, most of the furniture had been belayed against the bulkheads.

Forrest Calhoun floated in the middle, the center of attention, just where he figured he always belonged. Mike Krasnarov floated beside him—also with a probable opinion on where the center of the gathering lay. Mendes, the geologist, by contrast, was content to float on the sidelines, deep in conversation with Dr. Hobart and the other scientists working on board the station. When Forrest saw Ned returning with Bat and Bobbi, he boomed, "Hail, hail, the gang's all here!" Levkin and the Volkovs were already floating nearby.

It was a noisy party, but subdued at the same time. Everyone had one eye on the clock. FarTrip would be leaving soon, and the crew would have to get buttoned in. The news people, looking faintly seasick and totally ridiculous with the camera bands strapped to their foreheads, drifted, quite literally, among the pilots and technicians, interviewing whoever would talk to them. Drinks were fruit juices. No sense risking impairment; but Ned knew there was a bottle of champagne hidden aboard Mir for later.

Forrest wrapped an arm around Ned's neck. "Son, I'm going to miss your sorry ass. I really am. We ought to be going together, you and me."

"After that comment about you missing my ass, I'm not so sure I'd want to be locked in a can with you for very long."

Forrest guffawed. "You were always the one to beat, Ned.

You know that. The others—Mike, Valery, Bobbi, and the rest—they were good; but it always came down to you and me in the end. We're both number one, son; but there can only be one number one.''

"Damn it, Forrest. You keep calling me 'son,' but you're three years younger than me.''

"Ah, but so much older in wisdom and experience,'' Forrest said blandly.

"Ah, the hell with it.'' He wrapped his own arm around Forest. "I'll miss you, too,'' he said.

"Maybe we can get a long-distance poker game going,'' Forrest suggested.

"Forrest,'' said Bobbi McFeeley-da Silva, "you can't play poker by mail.''

The big man sighed. "Suppose you're right,'' he admitted. "If I can't see Ned's face, I can't know what cards he's holding.''

"In your dreams. Bat? Give it to him.''

Bat anchored his feet to a stanchion and held out the package he had brought. Forrest exchanged a look with Mike Krasnarov. "What is it?'' Krasnarov asked.

"Claudio's *feijoada*,'' Bat said. "Just the thing for the going-away meal.''

Forrest threw back his head and laughed. "Claudio always did make one damn fine *feijoada*. But I think Levkin here ought to take the first spoonful.''

Gregor Levkin scowled, but Valery Volkov nudged him and said, "It's a big honor, *tovarishch*.'' Levkin thought about it, then expelled his breath.

"I break bread with you, then,'' he said.

"Long as you fix what you break,'' said Forrest.

You couldn't see anything. You ought to be able to see something. Chase said as much after Vlad Sugachev, the station chief, announced that the power beam from Helios had locked on to *Bullard*'s array and the Antisana Laser was just coming around the horizon. Bullard's impulse engines would get continuous power from the sun-synch, from the ground lasers, or from the sun itself. Only when the ship was out of efficiency range would she jettison the impulse stage and switch to onboards; but by then the vessel would have built up a respectable velocity and could conserve the rest of her fuel for closing on the asteroid.

"I hope everything works all right," Chase said. He had said it several times already.

"Don't worry," Ned told him. "I sat in that can for six months and we tested every system on board fifty percent past nominal limits."

Chase didn't quite look at him. "Too bad you're not going."

Ned sighed. "Yeah. Too bad."

Bobbi McFeeley said much the same thing an hour later, when *Bullard* was already a shrinking light in the sky, and it was time for Bat and her to resume their interrupted delivery schedule. They had some drop-offs to make at the LEO Consortium construction site.

"I wonder how many schedules VHI juggled to get us all up here," Bat wondered as he lingered at the manlock.

"And Lock-Mar," said Ned, who was seeing them off. "Levkin's test flight was no coincidence, either. I think Dona Mariesa has a good sense of theater, that's all." He shook hands with them both and they promised to see each other again, Real Soon Now. He even allowed Bat to give him a Latin kiss on the cheeks, figuring to get the same from Bobbi.

Bobbi paused in the opening before following Bat out to *Santos-Dumont II* and faced Ned. "I always figured," she said seriously, "that you had the inside track on FarTrip. Too bad."

Ned accepted her condolences. "Yeah. Well, them's the breaks."

She shook her head. "No fooling. The skinny was you had a lock on it after Skopje."

Ned wouldn't look her in the face. He stared at the bulkhead, in the direction of Earth. He could feel the tug of its mass, feel the pull in his heart. He didn't dare turn in the other direction. He could feel that pull, too. "I made a list one time of all the things that were important to me, and I ranked them. There were two things ranked higher." He tried to pass it off, as if it didn't bother him; as if his heart did not strain to race after Forrest. To go farther and faster than anyone had ever gone. To set foot where feet had never stepped.

You always knew when you had done the right thing, because it always bugged you afterward.

He rejoined Chase in the crew module after *Santos-Dumont* had cast loose. They watched through the viewport as it braked into a lower orbit and pulled ahead. "You can still see *Bullard* with the telescope," Chase told him, "but she'll pass behind the Earth soon."

"Where's LEO?" Ned asked. He didn't want to talk about FarTrip anymore. He had made his choice. He had weighed what he had in each hand and had to decide what to hold on to with both. He wondered if Mariesa had been surprised when he had told her of his decision.

"Should be coming up soon," Chase said. "It's in a slightly higher orbit, so we overtake it now and then." He was silent a moment, then added, "Guy I know's up there, helping build it."

Ned didn't know what he was supposed to say about that, so he said nothing. He watched the limb of the Earth, knowing that the construction site would be too small to see even when it did come within view. Slowly, a pale white ghost peeked around the edge of the planet. The moon. Luna was half full from this angle, craters and mountains thrown into sharp relief.

"Jeez," said Chase. "Look at that sumbitch. It looks close enough to touch."

"It's an optical illusion," Ned told him.

Chase said. "Seems a shame nobody goes to the moon anymore."

"Give it time," Ned said. "We're building an infrastructure. And you know what they teach you at the Academy? 'Once you reach orbit . . .' "

"... You're halfway to anywhere. Yeah, yeah, I know.

Half the del-V is just getting off Earth. So you tank up in orbit and . . ." His voice trailed off into silence.

Ned looked at Chase; and Chase looked at Ned.

"You're not thinking what I'm thinking, are you?" Ned said.

"We couldn't do that, could we?"

"*Glenn Curtis* is all topped off and ready to take dirtside. Might just take us a little detour. What do you say?"

"Ned, we could get into really serious shit. . . ."

"We'd need flight programming, though," said Ned, shaking his head. "Have to whump it up before our scheduled deorbit; and that's in what? Four hours? Hell." He folded his arms and scowled at the moon. It seemed to be growing smaller as it emerged from behind the Earth. Getting farther.

The silence lasted another heartbeat or two before Chase said, "I know a guy . . ."

Mariesa was meeting with John E. when Khan brought the news. They were sitting tête-à-tête at the coffee table, by the window that faced First Watchung Mountain. The tea was Darjeeling, and the tea biscuits had been flown in just that morning from a darling pastry shop in Rotterdam. About one-third of the paintings in her office had been replaced by photographs. A subtle touch, and one that some of her staff had not yet noticed. She wondered if she would live long enough to replace all of them.

She glanced at her watch as she reached for her cup. "Harriet should be touching down in Aomori soon," she said. John E. shook his head in wonder.

"I would never have believed it, if she hadn't told me herself."

"Mother is a stickler for convention. When her circle decided that three days in orbit would be such a delicious outing, well, Harriet simply had to go along."

"She'll be all right, won't she?"

"Nippon Spaceways tourist boats are all certificated. This isn't their first flight, you know."

John E. smiled gently. "I don't see how you let the tourism industry slip through your fingers."

Zhou Hui's disembodied voice interrupted them. "Ma'am? Mr. Gagrat is outside. He says it is urgent."

Mariesa sighed. "It's always urgent," she said to John E. Raising her voice: "Send him in."

It was hard to read Khan's face. He was the ultimate technocrat; to him the world was data. If there was passion there, it was a passion for numbers and abstractions. Seeing them sitting by the window, he strode briskly across the room. Mariesa held a cup out.

"Would you like some tea, Khan?"

"No," he said brusquely. "One of our Planks has been hijacked."

Mariesa and John E. exchanged looks. "What happened?" she asked.

"DuBois and Coughlin were supposed to ferry the old *Glenn Curtis* down to Earth for salvage. Instead they've taken it on orbit toward the moon."

"Have they?" Mariesa set the teacup down on the table and leaned back in her chair. "Have they?" She began to laugh. "I will say this about Ned DuBois: The man is consistent."

John E. scowled. "Are you certain of the information, Khan?"

The CFO nodded curtly. "Sugachev tracked them. They are going to the moon, all right."

John E. sighed and reached into his jacket pocket. He pulled out his wallet and extracted a hundred-dollar bill. Then he reached out and slapped it into Mariesa's waiting palm.

"I hate it when you're always right," he said.

Mariesa rubbed the bill between her fingers. "I like to win," she told him.

"As Robert A. Heinlein did and all too few have done since, Michael Flynn writes about the near future as if he'd been there and was bringing back reports of what he'd seen. A splendid piece of work."
—Harry Turtledove

It is the beginning of the twenty-first century and one woman is determined to bring America and the world back on track in the technological future. She has the strength, the intelligence, the money. It will be done. This is the story of the rebirth of innovative technological expansion on Earth and in space.

"Michael Flynn has restored heroism and romance to near future space exploration. Not to be missed."
—Nancy Kress

Firestar is a broad, sweeping saga of the near future. Michael Flynn has a lot to say, and this is the book where he says it." —Roger MacBride Allen

This is the best book ever written on the science, people, and politics needed to move us into space—to stay." —Charles Sheffield

53006>

A Tom Doherty Associates, Inc. Book

0 37145 00699 4

ISBN 0-812-53006-3

Printed in the U.S.A.